PALM

TREES

IN THE

SNOW

PALM TREES

IN THE

SNOW

LUZ GABÁS

TRANSLATED BY NOEL HUGHES

Previously published as *Palmeras en la nieve* by Planeta in Spain in 2012. Translated from Spanish by Noel Hughes. First published in English by AmazonCrossing in 2017.

Published by AmazonCrossing, Seattle

www.apub.com

Amazon, the Amazon logo, and AmazonCrossing are trademarks of Amazon.com, Inc., or its affiliates.

ISBN-13: 9781503941694
ISBN-10: 1503941698

Cover design by Shasti O'Leary Soudant

Printed in the United States of America

For my father, Paco,
for the infectious passion with which he lived his life;
and for José Español,
for being the passion in mine.
Thanks to both, this novel exists.

For my mother, María Luz, and my sisters,
Gemma and Mar,
for their unconditional support, always.

And for José and Rebeca,
who have grown up with these pages.

Tonight you both will love with desperation because you know it is going to be the last night you spend together. Never again will you see each other.

Never.

It will not be possible.

You will caress and kiss with the intensity of two anguished souls filling themselves with each other's taste and touch.

The tropical rain falls furiously on the green railing of the outdoor passageway that leads to the bedroom, drowning out your rabid moans. Lightning flashes, momentarily gaining victory over darkness.

"Let me see you, touch you, feel you for just a few more minutes."

In a corner of the room, two worn leather suitcases. Resting on the back of a chair, a raincoat. An empty wardrobe with the doors ajar. A hat and a photograph on the table. Beige clothes on the floor. A bed converted into a love nest by the mosquito curtain surrounding it. Two bodies tossing together in the dark.

That will be it after eighteen years.

You could have defied the danger and decided to stay.

Or you could never have gone. You would have avoided the rain, the damned rain. It insists on punctuating the saddest moments of your life.

You would not have suffered such a dark night.

The drops rebound on the windowpanes.

And she . . .

She could not have set her eyes on you when she knew it was better not to.

She would not have suffered this cruel clarity.

The rain lashes, infusing the scene with melancholy. It belongs to no one.

You have enjoyed many nights of calm, tender, mystical love. You have enjoyed the forbidden pleasure. You have been free to love each other in plain sight.

But you have not had enough.

Pull off your skin with your nails! Bite! Lick! Steep yourselves in each other's scent!

Take her soul and give her your seed, though you know it will not germinate.

"I'm going."

"You're going."

"You will remain in my heart."

Forever.

Two sharp, quick knocks on the door, a pause, and then two more. It is the agreed-on signal. José is on time. You have to hurry or you will miss the plane.

You cannot hurry. You cannot separate yourselves from each other. You only want to cry. Close your eyes and remain in this state of unreality.

The time destined for you has elapsed. It will not return. You have already talked. There will not be tears; things are the way they are. Perhaps in another time, in another place . . . But you did not decide where to be born, to whom or to what to belong. You only decided to love each other, knowing that sooner or later this day would come.

You get out of bed and begin to dress. She remains sitting with her back against the wall, hugging her legs, her chin resting on her knees. She studies your movements and closes her eyes to imprint in her memory each detail of your body, your hair. When you finish dressing, she gets up and walks toward you, wearing only a necklace made from a fine leather cord and two shells. She has always worn that necklace. One of the shells is a cowrie, a shiny kiss-curl the size of an almond. The other is a fossilized *Achatina* shell. She takes off the collar and puts it round your neck.

"They will bring you good luck and prosperity on your journey."

You circle her waist with your strong arms and draw her toward you, inhaling the smell of her hair and skin.

"My luck ends here and now."

"Don't despair. Wherever you are, you will be part of me." Her big eyes, though filled with sadness, convey great certainty. She wants to believe that not even death will separate you, that there is a place where you will be together again, with no time, no pressure, no restraints.

You place your fingers on the necklace's shells. The cowrie is as smooth as her skin and sparkles like her teeth. The opening evokes a perfect vulva, life's entrance and exit.

"Will this *Achatina* also deliver me from the cloven-hooved demons?"

She smiles, remembering your first time together.

"You're as strong as a ceiba and as flexible as a royal palm. You will withstand gusts of wind without cracking, roots firmly planted in the soil and leaves reaching to the sky."

Again two sharp, quick knocks on the door, a short pause, and another two knocks. A voice rises above the storm.

"I beg you. It's very late. We must be going."

"I'm coming, Ösé. One minute."

One minute and good-bye. One minute that asks for another, and then another.

She goes to dress. You tighten your hold.

"Stay like that, naked. Let me see you, please."

Now she does not even have the necklace to protect her. And you have nothing to give her?

On the table, the hat that you will never need again and the only photo you have of the two of you together.

You take one of the bags, place it on the table, and take out a pair of scissors. You fold the photograph, separating your image from hers, and you cut it.

You hand her the fragment with you leaning against a yard truck.

"Here. Remember me just as I am now, in the same way that I'll remember you."

You look at the other half, where she is smiling, before putting it in the pocket of your shirt.

"It kills me not to be able to . . . !" A sob prevents you from continuing.

"Everything will be fine," she lies.

She lies because she knows that she will suffer each time she crosses the yard, or enters the dining room, or places her hand on the white banister of the elegant stairs. She will suffer each time she hears the sound of an airplane overhead.

She will ache each time it rains like tonight.

"Everything will be fine . . ."

You hold her tightly in your arms, thinking nothing will be fine from now on.

In a few seconds, you will take your bags and your raincoat. You will passionately kiss her. You will walk toward the door. You will hear her voice, and you will stop.

"Wait! You forgot your hat."

"I won't be needing it."

"But you will remember who you were for many years."

"You take care of it. Remember what I have been to you."

You will return to her and kiss her with the warm, impenetrable, and languid tenderness of a final kiss. You will look in her eyes and grit your teeth to avoid crying. You will softly stroke each other's cheek. You will open the door, and it will close behind you with a slight sound that to you will seem like a gun going off. She will rest her head on the door and cry bitterly.

You will go out into the night and melt into the storm, which refuses to abate for even a second.

"Thanks, Ösé. Thank you for your company all these years."

They are the first words you speak after leaving the bedroom on the way to the airport. They seem strange, as if it were not you pronouncing them. Everything seems strange: the road, the buildings, the metal terminal, the men who pass by.

Nothing is real.

"There is no need," José replies, desolate, putting a hand on your shoulder.

Tears shine in his wrinkled eyes. He has been like a father to you in this initially strange land. The passing of time is evident in his teeth. When your father wrote about José in his letters or told stories in front of the fire on winter evenings, he always said that he had never seen teeth so perfect and white. That was an eternity ago.

Hardly anything is left.

You will not see José again.

The intoxicating smell of nature's greenery, the solemn sounds of the deep songs, the racket of the celebrations, the nobility of friends like José, and the constant heat on the skin will eventually feel distant. You will no longer be part of all this. The moment you get on the plane, you will go back to being an *öpottò*, a foreigner.

"My dear friend José . . . I want to ask you one last favor."

"Name it."

"When it suits you, sometime, if you could, I would like you to take some flowers to my father's grave. He is all alone in this land."

How sad it is to think that your remains may rest in a forgotten place, where there will be nobody to spend a few minutes in front of your grave.

"Antón will have fresh flowers on his grave as long as I live."

"Tenki, mi fren."

Thank you, my friend. For getting me out of trouble. For helping me to understand a world so different from mine. For teaching me to love it. For being able to see further than the money that first brought me here. For not judging me.

"Mi hat no gud, Ösé."

"Yu hat e stron, mi fren."

My heart is not good. Your heart is strong, my friend. Your heart is not well, but your heart is strong.

It will survive all that comes.

You will survive, yes. But you will never forget that for many years, you spoke in four languages that are all unable to describe how you now feel: *Tu hat no gud.*

The plane is waiting on the runway.

Good-bye, *vitémá*, bighearted man. Look after yourself. *Tek kea, mi fren. Shek mi jan.*

Take care. Shake my hand.

You will let the clouds drag you for thousands of kilometers until you land in Madrid, where you take the train to Zaragoza. Later, you will get on a coach and, in a short time, be with your own again. All the hours of the journey will seem too few to distance yourself from these years, the best years of your life.

And this, recognizing that the best years of your existence were spent in distant lands, will be a secret that you will keep in the deepest recesses of your heart.

You cannot know that your secret will see the light of day over thirty years from now. You cannot know that one day, the two halves of the photo so cruelly separated will be joined together again.

Clarence does not exist yet.

Nor your other Daniela.

As the plane gains height, you will watch the island grow smaller and smaller. The place that once invaded your very being will turn into a slight speck on the horizon and then disappear completely. Other people will travel on the plane with you. Each of you will remain silent. Each of you will carry your stories with you.

You can only whisper a few words, surrendering to the tightness in your chest: *"Ö má we è, etúlá."*

Good-bye, your beloved island in the sea.

1

The Cruelest Month

Pasolobino, 2003

Clarence held a small piece of paper in her hands. It had been stuck to one of the many almost-transparent blue-and-red-bordered envelopes particular to a past era. The writing paper was wafer thin, so that it would weigh less and be cheaper to send. As a result, portraits of lives were squeezed within impossible margins.

Clarence read the bit of paper for the umpteenth time. At first, she had been curious. But now, she felt an increasing sense of disquiet. It was written in a different hand than the one used on the letters strewn on the sitting room table:

> . . . *I will not be returning to Fernando Po, so, if you don't mind, I will rely on Ureca friends so that you can continue sending your money. She is fine, she is very strong. She's had to be, now that she is missing her good father, who, I'm sorry to tell you as I know how*

it will affect you, died a few months ago. Don't worry,
her children are also fine—the eldest, working, and the
other making use of his studies. If you could see how
different everything is compared to when you worked on
the cocoa . . .

That was it. No dates. Not even a name.

Whom was this letter addressed to?

The addressee could not be from her grandfather's generation. The texture of the paper, the ink, the style, and the handwriting were all more modern. Furthermore, as was made clear from the last phrase, the letter was addressed to a man. This limited the circle to her father, Jacobo, and her uncle Kilian. Last, the paper had appeared beside one of the few letters written by her father. It was strange. Why had not all the letters been kept? She imagined Jacobo saving the note, then deciding to take it out again without noticing that a piece of it had been torn off in the process. Why had her father done this? Was the information contained in the letter that compromising?

Clarence tore her gaze from the letter with a stunned look, placing it on the big walnut table behind the black leather chesterfield sofa as she rubbed her sore eyes. She had been reading for over five hours without a break. She sighed and got up to throw another log on the fire. The ash logs began to spit as the fire took hold. The spring had been wetter than normal, and she was cold after sitting for so long. She stretched her palms toward the fire, then rubbed her forearms and leaned against the mantelpiece, over which hung a rectangular wooden trumeau topped with a carved wreath. In the mirror, she saw a tired young woman with circles under her green eyes and rebellious strands of chestnut-colored hair escaping from her thick plait. She brushed them away from her round face and examined the fine lines on her forehead. Why was she so alarmed after reading those lines? She shook her head as if a shiver had run through her body, went back to the table, and sat down.

She had classified the letters by author and date, starting with those from 1953, when Kilian had written every fortnight. The contents matched her uncle's personality to perfection; the letters were extremely detailed in their descriptions of his day-to-day life. He told his mother and sister about everything. There were fewer letters from her father, often just three or four lines added to his brother's missives. Lastly, her grandfather Antón's notes were short and sparse and full of the formal phrases typical of the 1930s and 1940s. He mostly reported that thanks be to God, he was well and wished that all there were well also. Sometimes he thanked those—relations or neighbors—who were helping maintain the House of Rabaltué for their generosity.

Clarence was happy that nobody was at home. Her cousin Daniela and her uncle Kilian had gone down to the city for his checkup, and her parents would not be coming up for another fortnight. She could not help but feel a little guilty about reading the intimate confessions of those still living. It was very strange to see what her father and uncle had written decades ago. This was normally done while putting a deceased person's papers in order. It felt much more appropriate to read her grandfather's letters, someone she hadn't even known. She already knew many of these anecdotes. But narrated in the first person, with the slanted and trembling hand of someone not used to writing and laced with bottled-up nostalgia, the letters brought out a mixture of strong feelings in her. Her eyes had filled with tears on more than one occasion.

She remembered opening the dark wardrobe at the bottom of the sitting room when she was younger and brushing the letters with her hands as she formed an image of what the House of Rabaltué had been like a century ago: press cuttings yellowed with age; travel brochures and work contracts; old livestock bills of sale and land leases; lists of shorn sheep and live and dead lambs; christening and memorial cards; Christmas greetings in uncertain strokes and faded ink; wedding invitations and menus; photos of great-grandparents, grandparents, great-aunts and great-uncles, cousins and parents; land deeds from the seventeenth century; and the land exchanges between the ski resort and the heirs of the house.

It had not occurred to her to give any attention to the personal letters. Back then, the stories of Kilian and Jacobo were more than enough. But after attending a conference of African speakers, some foreign and upsetting sensations had begun to nest in her heart. She was, after all, the daughter, granddaughter, and niece of colonists. From that moment on, a curiosity had risen inside her for everything to do with the lives of the men of her house. She remembered the sudden urgency she felt to go up to the village and open the wardrobe, the impatience that gripped her when her commitments at the university delayed her. Fortunately, she had been able to free herself of everything in record time to take advantage of the empty house—a rarity. She was able to read all the correspondence in complete and utter peace.

She wondered if anyone else had opened the wardrobe in the last few years; if her mother, Carmen, or her cousin Daniela had rummaged through the past; or if her father or uncle had ever felt the need to see themselves once more as the youth who had penned these lines.

She quickly dismissed the idea. While Daniela liked the old stone-and-slate house with its dark furniture, she never took her interest further. Carmen was not born in the house or the area and had never felt that it was hers. Her only mission, especially since the death of Daniela's mother, was to make sure the house was kept clean and tidy and the larder was kept full and to find any excuse to throw a party. She loved spending long breaks there, but was grateful to have her own home that was completely hers.

Jacobo and Kilian were like all the other men from the mountains; they were reserved to an unnerving degree and very strict about their privacy. It was surprising that neither of the two had decided to destroy the letters, as she had done with her teenage diaries, thinking that the act of destruction would erase everything that had happened. Clarence weighed various possibilities. Perhaps they were aware that there was nothing in the letters that would put them in the line of fire. Or perhaps they had simply forgotten about their existence.

Whatever the reasons, she would have to find out if something had really happened—precisely because of what was not written, and the questions raised by this piece of paper lying in her hands. It was a fragment that could change the peaceful life of that house in Pasolobino.

Without getting out of the chair, Clarence stretched her arm toward a small chest on the coffee table, opening one of its little drawers and taking out a magnifying glass to look more closely at the edges of the paper. In the bottom right-hand corner, a small outline could be seen where a number appeared: a straight line crossed by a hyphen.

Then . . . the number could very well be a seven.

A seven.

She drummed her fingers on the table.

A page number was unlikely. A date perhaps: 1947, 1957, 1967. From what she had gathered, none of the three fit the description of colonial life for a few Spaniards on a cocoa plantation.

In fact, nothing had caught her attention except those lines where the anonymous writer said that he or she would not be going back as often, that someone sent money from the House of Rabaltué, that three people whom the recipient of the letter—Jacobo?—knew were well, and that a loved one had died.

Whom would her father be sending money to? Why would he have to worry that this person was fine and, more specifically, that they were doing well at work or studies? Who was this person whose death was felt so deeply? Ureca friends, the note said . . . She had never heard of this place before, if it was a place . . . A person maybe? And the most important of all: Who was *she*?

Clarence had listened to hundreds of stories about the lives of the men from the House of Rabaltué in distant lands. She knew them by heart because Jacobo and Kilian needed no excuse to talk about their lost paradise. What she had thought was the official story always took the form of a tale that began decades before in a small Pyrenean village, continued on a small African island, and ended once again in the mountains. Until now, it had never crossed Clarence's mind that it could be another way: the story starting on a small African island, continuing in a small village in the Pyrenees, and ending again on the sea.

But they had seemingly forgotten to tell her some important pieces. Clarence let her novelist's mind wander and frowned while she mentally sorted through the people Jacobo and Kilian talked about in their stories. Nearly all of them belonged to her own inner circle. Not strange, considering that the instigator of this exotic adventure was an adventurous young man from the valley of Pasolobino who weighed anchor in an unknown land at the end of the nineteenth century, around the time her grandparents, Antón and Mariana, had been born. The man had awakened on an island in the Atlantic Ocean located in what was then called the Bight of Biafra. In a few years, he had amassed a small fortune and became owner of a fertile plantation. Far from there, in the Pyrenees, single men and young couples decided to go and work either on the plantation of their old neighbor or in the city close to it.

They swapped green pastures for palm trees.

Clarence smiled as she imagined those brusque and reserved men from the mountains, tight-lipped and serious, accustomed to the white of the snow, the green of the fields, and the gray of the stones, discovering the bright colors of the tropics, the dark skin of half-naked bodies, the flimsy buildings, and the caress of the sea breeze. It still surprised her to imagine Jacobo and Kilian as the main characters in one of the many books or films in which the colonies are seen from a European viewpoint. Theirs was the only version she knew.

Clear and unquestionable.

The daily life on the cocoa plantations; the relations with the natives; the food; the flying squirrels; the snakes; the monkeys; the great multicolored lizards; the Guinea sand fly, the *jején*; the Sunday parties; the tom-tom of the *tumba* and *droma* drums . . .

This was what they had told them. The same as what appeared in Uncle Kilian's first letters.

How hard they worked! How difficult life was there! Indisputable.

. . . *her children are also fine* . . .

The date had to be 1977, or 1987, or 1997 . . .

Who could explain the meaning of those lines? She thought of asking Kilian and Jacobo, but quickly admitted that she would be very embarrassed to confess to having read all the letters. Occasionally curiosity had led her to ask daring questions during family dinners when the subject of the colonial past had come up, but both men had developed an uncanny ability to divert the conversation toward more innocent topics. Coming out with a question directly related to those lines and expecting a clear and honest answer was a lot to hope for.

Clarence lit a cigarette, got up, and went toward the window. She opened it a little so the smoke could escape and breathed in the fresh air of the rainy day that had slightly dampened the dark slate roofs of the stone houses that squeezed together below her. The elongated old quarter of Pasolobino still retained an appearance similar to that in the black-and-white photos from the beginning of the twentieth century, even though the majority of the houses had been refurbished and the streets were now paved instead of cobbled. Beyond the village, whose origins could be traced back to the eleventh century, extended the estates of tourist apartment blocks and hotels that had come with the ski resort.

She directed her gaze toward the snowy peaks, where the spruces ended and the rocks began, still hidden under a white blanket. The dancing mist on the summits was an astonishing sight. How did the men of her family withstand being so far from these mountains for so long, so far from the morning smell of the damp earth and the peaceful silence of the night? There must be some attraction in the splendor unfolded in front of her eyes when nearly *all* those who had traveled to the island had ended up returning home sooner or later.

Just then, the person she should ask came to mind. Why had she not thought of it before?

Julia!

No one better than Julia to answer her questions! She had lived on the island through the family's history and shared her longing for the exotic stories of Jacobo and Kilian, and she was always willing to have long conversations with Clarence, whom she had treated with warmth since she was small, possibly because Julia only had boys of her own.

Clarence quickly put out her cigarette in an ashtray and went from the sitting room into her office to call Julia. As she crossed through the large foyer, she could not help but stop in front of the huge painting that hung over an exquisite wooden arch handcrafted by seventeenth-century artisans. It was one of the few treasures that had survived to attest to the lost nobility of the house.

The painting showed her father's family tree. The first name she could read in the lower corner, which dated from 1395, Kilian of Rabaltué, continued to intrigue Clarence. No one could explain how an Irish saint who had traveled through France and ended up in Germany shared a name with the founder of her house. This Kilian probably crossed from France to Pasolobino through the Pyrenees, and his traveling gene, plus his hair's copper streaks, set up house there. From his name, a large trunk rose straight up with reaching branches, on whose leaves the names of brothers and sisters were written along with their husbands and wives and the following generations' descendants.

Clarence stopped at her grandfather's generation, the pioneers of far-off lands, and went over the dates with her eyes. In 1898, Antón of Rabaltué, her grandfather, was born. He married Mariana of Malta, born in 1899, in 1926. In 1927, her father was born. In 1929, her uncle Kilian arrived, and in 1933, her aunt Catalina.

Family trees were very reliable in the area. Everyone knew where everyone else came from. In the appropriate box, she saw her own date of birth, name and surname, and the house where she was born. Sometimes the surnames were replaced by the name of the house and the village of origin, as many of the newcomers came from neighboring villages. The trunk drew one's eyes from the first Kilian to the last heirs in direct line. It was normal for names to repeat themselves generation after generation, evoking past ages of counts and ladies—the old names on old papers had the strange ability to fuel her imagination: Mariana, Mariano, Jacoba, Jacobo, a Kilian or two, Juan, Juana, José, Josefa, more than one Catalina, Antón, Antonia . . . Through reading family trees, one of her great passions, Clarence was able to imagine how life flowed without major changes: being born, growing up, having offspring, and dying. The same earth and the same sky.

The last names that appeared on the tree, though, showed a clear break with a petrified past. The names of Daniela and Clarence broke the monotony. It was as if at the time of their birth, something was already changing, as if their parents were marking them in some way with new meaning. As adults, they learned that Kilian had chosen the name Daniela without his wife, Pilar, being able to stop him. It was a name that he had always liked, and that was it. But Clarence was named by her mother, a great reader of romance novels, who had foraged through her husband's traveling past until she came up with a name grand enough to satisfy her: Clarence of Rabaltué. Jacobo had not offered any objections, perhaps because the name, coming from an old African city, reminded him every day of that idyllic past so often recalled by both him and Kilian.

Standing before the tree for a moment, Clarence let her mind open new boxes on the lines immediately above those of herself and her cousin. What names would future generations have, if there would be any? She smiled. At the speed she was going, years would pass before another line was filled, which was a shame, as she understood life as a long chain where all the links with names and surnames formed a solid and extensive whole. She could not understand how anyone could not know of the generations before that of their grandparents. But of course, not everyone had the good fortune of growing up in the same familiar environment. In her case, her understandable, if slightly oversized, attachment to her birthplace, her valley and her mountains, went above and beyond mere genetics. It was something deeper and more spiritual that calmed her existential fear of nothingness. Perhaps because of this wish to be part of an intimate link between the past and the future, Clarence had succeeded in focusing her linguistics research on the study of Pasolobinese. The recent defense of her doctoral thesis, which had left her exhausted and saturated with the academic world, had made her not only the world's foremost theoretical expert on the nearly extinct language, but also the guardian of her cultural inheritance. It brought her great pride.

Nevertheless, she had to admit that on occasion, she regretted the amount of time this study had taken away from her life. Especially with relationships. Her love life was a disaster. For one reason or another, her boyfriends never managed to stick around longer than twelve months. She had this in common with Daniela, only it did not seem to affect her cousin as much, maybe because she was six years younger or simply because she was more patient. Clarence smiled again, thinking about how lucky both of them, as only children, had been to grow up together. What would she have done without the girl who replaced all her childhood dolls? Despite being so different, they felt like sisters, sharing thousands of experiences and adventures. She remembered the honor code that they agreed on when Daniela was old enough to go to parties with her: If they felt the same way about a boy, the one who met him first got a clear run. Luckily, because of their personalities— Daniela was shyer, more practical, and perhaps less passionate—and because of their tastes—Clarence was attracted to solitary, mysterious men with muscular bodies and her cousin to average ones—their loyalty had never been put to the test.

Clarence sighed and let her imagination fly for a few seconds, envisioning the names of her invisible descendants on the chart.

Suddenly, a shiver went up her body, as if someone had blown on the back of her neck or tickled her with a small feather. She made a face and turned quickly, frightened, before immediately feeling ridiculous. She knew that no one would be back for a few days and all the doors were well shut—she was not overly skittish, though perhaps more than she would like to be.

She shook her head and focused on what she had to do: call Julia. She passed through one of the diamond-paneled doors into the room underneath the large wooden staircase. Her office was dominated by a wide American-oak table where her cell phone was sitting.

She looked at the clock and calculated that Julia, a fairly methodical woman, would have gotten home from church by now. When she was in Pasolobino, she and a friend went to five o'clock mass, took a walk around the village, and had a hot chocolate before driving home.

Strangely, Julia did not answer at the house. Clarence called her cell phone and learned that she was now playing a card game with another friend. She was so focused that they hardly talked. Just enough to agree to meet the following day. She felt a little disappointed. There was nothing else to do but wait.

For *one day.*

She decided to go back to the sitting room and tidy up the papers that she had spread out. She returned the letters to their place and slipped the note into her purse.

After the excitement of the last few hours, she suddenly did not know what to do with the rest of the day. She sat on the sofa in front of the fire, lit another cigarette, and thought of how much had changed since Antón, Kilian, and Jacobo went to the island, especially time. Clarence had computer, e-mail, and telephone to instantly connect with her loved ones. These developments made her generation impatient; they could not handle uncertainty, and any slight delay became a slow torture.

Now, the only thing concerning Clarence was that Julia could explain the meaning of those few lines. In her mind, they could only mean one thing: her father might have regularly sent money to a strange woman.

The rest of her life had suddenly taken second stage.

The next day, at exactly half past five, Clarence was at the church entrance, waiting for Julia. She had been admiring the majestic silhouette of the Romanesque tower for only a few minutes when the door opened and the trickle of people attending daily mass emerged, greeting her gently. She quickly spotted Julia, small, sensibly dressed, with a short chestnut bob recently trimmed and a pretty scarf around her neck. Julia gave her a beaming smile.

"Clarence! Haven't seen you for a while!" She gave her two loud and friendly kisses and linked their arms to walk out of the church grounds and past the stone wall topped by high ironwork railings. "I'm sorry I didn't pay you much attention yesterday, but you called me in the middle of a good hand. What brought you here? Work?"

"I don't have many classes this term," answered Clarence, "so I have free time to do research. And you? Are you going to stay long this time?"

Julia's mother's family was native to the valley of Pasolobino. She still owned one of the many houses dotted around the fields a few kilometers from the village. Her mother had married a man from a neighboring valley. They traveled to Africa when she was very small, leaving her to be minded by her grandparents until her parents' hardware store began to do well and they could bring her with them. There, Julia married and gave birth to two children. After finally settling down in Madrid, she and the children enjoyed short holidays in Pasolobino, occasionally joined by her husband. After her husband's death two years ago, Julia's visits to her birthplace got longer and longer.

"Until October at least. That's the good thing about having grown-up children. They don't need me." She gave a wry smile before adding, "And this way they can't leave me with the grandchildren at all hours."

Clarence laughed. She liked Julia. Although you would not think so upon first glance, she was a strong-minded woman. She was also cultured, observant, prudent, and sensible, very open and easygoing, with a certain air of sophistication that made her stand out. Clarence was convinced this was due to her well-traveled past and her years in the capital. Yet when Julia was in Pasolobino, it was like she had never left. Her down-to-earth ways won her many friends. Though she joked about her children and grandchildren, she could not help but offer her assistance whenever needed.

"Would you like a hot chocolate?" suggested Clarence.

"The day I don't want one will be the day you should worry!"

They walked slowly through the narrow cobblestone streets, leaving the old quarter behind. They took the wide avenue that divided up the new part of the village, with high lampposts and four- and five-story buildings, to the only shop in Pasolobino, where—according to the expert, Julia—the chocolate passed her test. You could turn the cup upside down without spilling a drop. "When you grow up with pure cocoa," she always said, "it's impossible to abide substitutes."

During the walk, they talked about day-to-day things, bringing each other up to date on their families. Clarence always thought she felt a shift in Julia's tone when she asked about Kilian or Jacobo. It was very subtle, but preceded by a nervous clearing of the throat.

"It's been a while since I last saw your uncle. How is he?"

"He's doing fine, thanks. Starting to get on a bit, but nothing serious."

"And what's your father up to? Doesn't he come up?"

"He does, just not as often. He doesn't like driving much anymore."

"From the man who used to love cars!"

"I think he likes the cold less as he gets older. He usually waits for better weather."

"Well, it's the same with everyone. You have to love this area a lot to be able to put up with its savage climate . . ."

Clarence knew this was her opportunity to easily redirect the conversation.

"Of course," she agreed. "Especially if you've lived in the tropics, right?"

"Look, Clarence." Julia stopped in front of the chocolate bar. "If it weren't for certain circumstances . . . anyway, the way we had to leave, I mean . . ."

They entered the bar, Clarence guiding Julia inside, delighted she had taken the bait.

". . . I would have stayed there . . ."

They went over to the free table closest to the window; took off their jackets, bags, and scarves; and sat down.

"They were the best years of my life . . ."

Julia sighed, made a gesture with her hands to the waiter for two cups, then realized that she had not asked Clarence. She looked at her, and Clarence nodded before speaking.

"Do you know where I was recently?"

Julia arched her eyebrows inquisitively.

"At a conference in Murcia on Hispanic-African literature." Clarence noticed the astonished look on Julia's face. "Yes, it also surprised me at first. I knew something about African literature written in English, in French, even in Portuguese, but nothing in Spanish."

"I had no idea." Julia shrugged. "Well, to be honest, I never thought about it."

"It seems there is a large unknown quantity of literary work both here and there. These writers have been neglected for years."

"And why did you go?" Julia allowed the waiter to serve them their chocolate. "Has it anything to do with your research in the university?"

Clarence hesitated. "Yes and no. The truth is that after finishing the thesis, I didn't have much of an idea what to do. A colleague told me about the conference, and it made me think. How is it that none of this occurred to me after spending all my life listening to Dad's and Uncle Kilian's tales?"

She clasped the cup of cocoa in her hands. It was so hot that she had to blow on it a few times before taking a sip. Julia stayed quiet, seeing how Clarence closed her eyes to taste the mixture of bitter and sweet, just the way she had taught her.

"And did you learn anything?" she asked at last. "Did you enjoy it?"

Clarence opened her eyes and placed the cup back on the saucer.

"I enjoyed it a lot," she answered. "There were African writers living in Spain, others who live abroad in various countries, and those of us from here who were discovering a whole new world. They talked about many things, especially the need to promote their works and their culture." She stopped for a second to check that Julia was not getting bored. "In fact, it was a real discovery to find out about the existence of Africans who share our language and grammar. Surprising, isn't it? Let's just say that their topics differed a lot from the stories I heard at home."

Julia frowned. "In what way?"

"Obviously, the colonial and postcolonial eras were discussed a lot. The ideological inheritance that conditioned writers' lives; the admiration, rejection, and even rancor toward those who had made them change the course of their history; their traumas with their identity; the attempts to make up for lost time; the experiences of exile and being uprooted; and the myriad ethnic groups and languages. Nothing at all compared to what I thought I knew . . . And I doubt if there were many colonists' children at the conference! I, for one, didn't open my mouth. I was a little ashamed . . . you know? Even an American lecturer recited poetry to us in his native language, Bubi . . ."

She put her hand in her bag, produced a pen, and took a paper napkin. "Which is actually written like this: *Böóbé.*"

"Bubi, yes," Julia repeated. "A Bubi writer . . . I admit I'm surprised. I didn't think—"

"Sure, sure . . ." Clarence interrupted her. "Don't tell me! My childhood dog was called Bubi." She lowered her voice. "Dad named him . . ."

"Yes, not really very appropriate. Typical of Jacobo. Of course"— she sighed—"they were different times . . ."

"You don't have to explain, Julia. I'm telling you so you can understand that, for me, it was like suddenly seeing things from the other side of the fence. I realized that sometimes it's necessary to ask, that it's not enough to take everything they say to us as gospel."

She put her hand into her beige suede bag and took out her wallet, reaching for the paper fragment that she had found in the wardrobe.

"I was sorting out papers in the house, and I came across this among Dad's letters." She handed it over, explaining that it had been written sometime in the 1970s or 1980s. She stopped suddenly on seeing Julia's face. "Are you all right?" she asked, alarmed.

Julia was pale. Very pale. The paper shook in her hands like an autumn leaf, and a tear began to trickle down her cheek. Clarence took her friend's hand.

"What's wrong? Have I said something to offend you?" she said. "If so, I'm very sorry!"

Why had Julia reacted like this?

There was silence for a few seconds. Finally, Julia shook her head and raised her eyes. "Nothing's wrong. Relax. I'm just being a silly old woman. It's my husband's handwriting. I got emotional when I saw it."

"Your husband's . . . ?" Clarence asked, puzzled. "And do you know what it means?" Her curiosity got the better of her. "It mentions two people and their mother, and another dead person, four, there're four . . ."

"I can read, Clarence," interrupted Julia, raising a handkerchief to her eyes.

"Yes, sorry, it's just very strange. Your husband writing this letter to Dad."

"Well, they knew each other," Julia said in a careful tone.

"Yes, but as far as I knew, they didn't send letters to each other," Clarence replied, picking up the slip of paper. "They saw each other when you came up here for the holidays. I would have found other letters, I think. But no, just this one."

Julia turned her head to escape Clarence's piercing stare, gazing at the passersby on the street as her mind was transported to another time and place. For a brief moment, the stone, wood, and slate buildings turned white, and the nearby ash trees became palms and ceibas. Not a day had gone by without her thinking of her beloved piece of Africa, where she had passed the most intense years of her life. Yes, she was grateful for her wonderful children and grandchildren and their comfortable life in Madrid. But at the bottom of her heart, it was the memories of those years that came to mind when she woke up every morning. Only someone who had been in the same situation could understand, like Jacobo or Kilian.

In spite of their long lives, Julia was convinced that they had not had a single day of peace.

What should she tell Clarence? Had Jacobo or Kilian told her something? Maybe now, at their age, they could not avoid that hidden part of their consciences. What would she have done? How could she have lived all her life with such a burden?

She let out a deep sigh and turned back toward Clarence. The young woman's eyes, a deep green identical to those of Jacobo and Kilian, graced a well-rounded face encased by beautiful wavy chestnut-colored hair. Julia had known Clarence since she was little and knew how persistent she could be.

"And why don't you ask your father?"

Clarence was surprised to hear such a direct question. Julia's reaction was making her even more certain that something suspect was going on. She blinked a few times without knowing how to answer; she looked down and starting tearing the paper napkin into bits. "The truth is, Julia, I'd be embarrassed. If I show him the note, he'll know I've been rooting through his stuff. And if he has a secret, I don't think he'll tell me just like that, not after all these years." She straightened herself up in the chair and sighed. "Anyway, I don't want to put you under pressure." She sighed again. "But it would be a shame if something so important were to disappear into oblivion . . ."

Clarence hoped that Julia would firmly answer that she was wasting her time, that there was no secret to reveal, and that she was dreaming up a story. Instead, Julia remained silent, only one question running through her mind: *Why now?*

Beyond the window, the rays of weak April afternoon sunlight struggled in their annual battle to dissolve the tiny crystallized drops of intermittent rain.

"Why now?"

Julia remembered her husband complaining about how—according to him—the witch doctors had a bad influence on the natives. *"I have never seen anything as foolish,"* he used to say. *"Is it that difficult to understand cause and effect? In life and in science, a series of circumstances cause things to happen one way and not another. But no, for them there is neither cause nor effect. Only the wishes of the gods."*

Maybe the time had come, yes, but she would not be the one to betray Kilian and Jacobo. If God or the Bubi gods wished it so, Clarence would discover the truth sooner or later. And better sooner than later, as they did not have much time left.

"Listen, Clarence," Julia said at last. "My husband wrote this letter in 1987. I remember it perfectly because it was on that trip that he learned an old acquaintance had died." She paused. "If you are really interested in knowing what it means, go there and find someone named

Fernando. He's a little older than you. Only one of the sons is of interest. It's likely that they still keep records in Sampaka, because the plantation is still in operation—not doing very well, but it's still there. I don't think they destroyed everything, but I'm not completely sure. Look for Fernando. The island is no bigger than this valley . . ."

"Who is this Fernando?" asked Clarence with sparkling eyes as she pointed to one of the lines on the piece of paper. "And why do I have to look for him in Sampaka?"

"He was born there. That's all I'm going to tell you, dear Clarence," Julia answered firmly. She looked down and petted Clarence's hand in hers. "If you want to know more, it's your father you have to talk to. If Jacobo hears what I have told you, I'll deny it. Is that clear?"

Clarence reluctantly agreed, but that reluctance was quickly replaced by a growing excitement. In her head, she repeated the words over and over: *Go to Sampaka, Clarence. To Sampaka!*

"I have something very important to tell you."

Clarence waited till those still eating looked up. Her cheerful and talkative family was seated as they always were around the wooden rectangular table. At the head was Uncle Kilian, who had presided over all lunches and dinners for as long as she could remember. Although Jacobo was older, Kilian had assumed the role of head of the family, and it seemed Jacobo had been happy to accept an arrangement that allowed him to stay linked to the house of his birth without any further obligations. All who were there felt the house as theirs, but Kilian was in charge of its upkeep, renting the fields for grazing since they no longer had cows or sheep, weighing the merits of selling more parcels of land to the growing ski resort, and retaining the traditions, customs, and celebrations of a house that, like all others in the village, saw its history changing with the tourism that had saved it from ruin.

To the right of Kilian, the untiring worker, sat Jacobo. Despite being over seventy, both brothers remained big and strong—Jacobo sported a generous stomach—and both were very proud of retaining fine heads of dark hair even if streaked with gray. On Jacobo's right always sat his wife, Carmen, a good-looking and happy woman of medium build, with smooth, rosy skin and short dyed-blond hair. To Kilian's left, in front of Jacobo, sat the responsible and sensible Daniela, who had inherited her dark copper-streaked mane from her father, Kilian, and—according to the village elders—the fine and delicate traits of her mother, Pilar. Finally, at the far end of the table, opposite Kilian, sat Clarence, where she had learned to interpret the ritual gestures of her uncle at each meal. It was easy for her to know whether he was in a good mood from the way he folded his napkin, or how he stared at something on the table for a time.

After a few minutes, Clarence realized that her announcement had gone totally unnoticed. It had been days since they had all been together, and the dinner had led to a typically boisterous conversation. At that moment, her parents and her cousin continued gossiping about the neighbors and the latest happenings in Pasolobino, while her uncle remained lost in thought. Clarence took a sip from her glass of wine. She got on better with her uncle than with her own father. For her, Kilian was open and vulnerable despite appearing to be a quiet, hard, and distant man. Jacobo had a better sense of humor, yes, but it was also changeable and could become bad tempered without warning, especially when he did not get his way. Fortunately for the rest of the family, Carmen had developed an incredible ability to weather his storms, easily directing her husband to give him the impression that his opinions were neither totally rejected nor totally accepted.

How would Clarence's father react when he found out what his daughter was going to do? After another sip of wine for courage, Clarence raised her voice.

"I have some news! And it might shock you."

Everyone turned his or her head. Everyone except Kilian, who raised his gaze from his plate with the reluctance of someone who did not believe anything could shock him.

Clarence bit her bottom lip. She suddenly felt nervous. After the intensity of the last few weeks, when she had done nothing but plan—pulling photos, maps, and articles from the Internet and learning where Ureca was—what was going to be the adventure of her life, at that moment, her heart beat unsteadily.

Daniela looked at her expectantly, and when her cousin did not speak, she decided to help: "Have you met someone? Is that it, Clarence? When are we going to meet him?"

Carmen clasped her hands in front of her and smiled. "No, that's not it, Daniela. It's . . . well . . . that—"

"I can't believe it!" boomed Jacobo. "My daughter is at a loss for words! Now I am intrigued!"

Kilian looked straight at Clarence with an almost imperceptible movement of his eyebrows, trying to encourage her to tell everyone what was so important. Clarence closed her eyes, took a deep breath, and let it out.

"I'm going to Bioko on Thursday. I already have the tickets and all the paperwork."

Kilian did not even blink. Carmen and Daniela let out surprised shouts almost in unison. A metallic sound rang out as Jacobo dropped his fork to his plate.

"What are you saying?" her father asked, more surprised than annoyed.

"That I'm going to Bioko, that's to say, to Fernando Po—"

"I know perfectly well what and where Bioko is!" he interrupted her. "What I don't know is what gave you the idea to go there!"

Clarence had the answer well prepared, to outline a reasonable and safe trip and put her family and herself at ease.

"You all know that I'm part of a linguistics research team. I'm now focusing on African Spanish, and I need to do some fieldwork to collect real samples. And what better place than Bioko to do it?"

"I had no idea that you were interested in African Spanish," her mother commented.

"Well, I don't tell you everything I do at work . . ."

"Yes, but this, in particular, is something very close to our family," Daniela said.

"Actually, I've only recently steered my research in this direction. There's very little published on it." Clarence really wanted to ask them about this Fernando, but she held back. "And I've always been curious to learn about your beloved island. All my life listening to your stories and now I've got the chance to visit!"

"But isn't it dangerous there? Are you going on your own? I don't know if it's a good idea, Clarence," her mother said, shaking her head with a worried look.

"Yes, I know it's not an easy tourist destination, but I have everything planned. A university colleague has contacts with a lecturer there, and both of them have helped me sort out the visa paperwork. Normally it takes weeks to get one! There is a direct flight from Madrid, around five hours, a cakewalk . . . Now that I think about it . . . ," she added, full of double meaning, "would any of you like to come? Dad, Uncle Kilian . . . wouldn't you like to see it again? You could reconnect with old acquaintances!"

Kilian squinted his eyes and pursed his lips as Jacobo answered for the two of them.

"Who could we meet? None of the whites are left, and the blacks we knew would be dead. Anyway, the whole place must be a mess. I wouldn't go. What for?" His voice seemed to break. "To suffer?"

He turned to his brother but did not look directly at him.

"Kilian, you wouldn't want to go back at this stage in life, would you?" he asked gently, trying to keep his tone neutral.

Kilian cleared his throat and, making crumbs of a piece of bread, answered categorically, "When I left, I knew I'd never go back."

Silence reigned for a few seconds.

"And you, Daniela, what about you? Would you like to come with me?"

Daniela hesitated, still surprised that Clarence had not told her about her decision. Clarence looked at her cousin, those big brown eyes lighting up her face. She was the only one who had not inherited the green eyes shared by her father's side of the family. She often complained about it, but their intensity surpassed the prettiest-colored eyes in existence. Daniela was not conscious of this, but people often felt bewildered when they met her gaze.

"How long are you going for?" she asked.

"About three weeks."

"Three weeks!" Carmen exclaimed. "But that's a long time! And if something happens to you?"

"Nothing is going to happen to me, Mom! From what they have told me, it's a fairly safe place for foreigners, as long as you don't do anything suspicious, of course . . ."

That comment alarmed her mother even more.

"Jacobo, Kilian . . . you know the place, would you please tell her to forget this idea?"

They began speaking as if Clarence were not there.

"As if you don't know your own daughter!" exclaimed Jacobo. "In the end, she'll do what she wants herself."

"She's old enough to know what she's doing, don't you think, Carmen?" said Kilian. "We were even younger when we went—"

"Yes," Carmen interrupted him, "but it was safe then. Now, a young white girl traveling alone . . ."

"From what I've read, people still do business there, and they come and go without any problem," added Kilian. "And aid organization volunteers . . ."

"And how do you know this?" Jacobo wanted to know.

"The Internet," Kilian responded, shrugging. "I'm old, but I like to be informed. Daniela showed me. This computer thing is a lot simpler than I thought." He gave his daughter a smile. "I had a good teacher."

Daniela returned his smile.

"And is there no work colleague who could go with you?" insisted Carmen to her daughter.

"The truth is that none of them thought much of a trip to such an uncivilized country . . . But I have a *personal* interest"—she emphasized the word—"which they don't share. I will get to see the places from your stories!"

"You won't recognize anything!" Jacobo interjected. "You will only realize the pitiful state of the country. Misery and more misery."

"The exact opposite of what you have told us, isn't it?" intoned Clarence. "It tends to happen. Fact is always stranger than fiction."

Kilian frowned. He sensed a rare impertinence in his niece's voice. "Clarence," he said in a kind but firm manner, "don't talk about what you don't know. If you are that interested in going, go and make up your own mind, but don't judge us."

Clarence did not know what to say. It was as if her uncle had read her mind! To ease the slight tension, she turned to her cousin.

"Well, wouldn't you like to come with me?"

Daniela shook her head. "It's a pity you didn't tell me sooner!" she answered regretfully. "I can't take three weeks off just like that. But," she added, "if you end up falling in love with Fernando Po, I'll go with you the next time. That's a promise."

Clarence imagined that Daniela thought a few weeks would be enough for the same kind of romance that had bewitched their fathers. But the men had spent years on the island. Clarence would be traveling under different circumstances and in a different age.

"Oh, I don't know if a few weeks will be enough for me to fall in love . . . But who knows?"

The question hung in the ensuing silence. Still, it could barely hide the deafening voices repeating over and over again in the heads of the two brothers: *You knew that this day could come. You knew. It was just a question of time. The spirits have decided it. There is nothing you could have done. You knew.*

You have to know the mountains to understand that April is the cruelest month.

In the lowlands, Holy Week brings the resurrection of life in spring after winter's desolation. Mother Earth wakes up and emerges from the depths of hell, coming to the land's surface. In the mountains, she doesn't. In the mountains, she remains asleep for at least another month until she allows the pastures to sprout.

So in April, nothing grows; the land is barren and the landscape still. Nothing moves. There is a soft and shapeless calm that takes over, a calm very different from the stillness before a tornado or snowstorm. In April, you have to look up, up toward the peaks and the sky, and not down on the barren land, to find signs of life.

In the sky, there is movement; the mists grip the mountains' slopes, and it rains for days. The fog stretches down, covering the valley in a faint twilight that lasts until, one day, without any warning, a gap opens in the sky and the sun emerges to heat the earth and win the battle against winter. Victory is certain; the wait, devastating.

This month of April was especially wet, week after week of a steady and constant drizzle that did not help the already gray mood. Yet the night Clarence announced her trip, the leaves began to tremble, rocked by the emergent north wind that threatened to displace the rain. It began as a whisper that increased in volume until turning into strong currents of air that crashed against the shutters and sneaked under the doors and around the very feet of the householders.

That night, Kilian and Jacobo recalled scenes that, although not lost, had remained dormant through the murmurs of time. Yet only a few words had been necessary for the scenes of their youth to come alive again, burning with the same intensity as decades past.

Neither of them could imagine that due to innocent curiosity, Clarence would set off events in very unexpected ways. She would become the instrument of chance—that capricious rival of cause and effect—so that her every move made much fall into place.

That night, after Clarence announced her trip, when the leaves of the trees beat against their branches, the villagers closed their eyes, lying down in the solitude of their beds as, in a flash, the north wind became the harmattan.

2

Pantap Salt Water

On the Sea, 1953

"Come on, Kilian. We'll miss the coach!"

Using an old board to shift the snow that had stuck shut the front door, Jacobo tried to raise his voice above the howls of the January winds. When he finished, he pulled up the lapels of his raincoat, tugged his hat onto his head, picked up his suitcase, and placed the wooden skis on his shoulder, stamping on the ground to mark the path that they would take down to the village—and to warm up from the intense cold that had his feet frozen.

He was about to shout out his brother's name again when he heard voices in the Pasolobinese dialect coming from the stone steps that led to the patio. Just then, Kilian came out onto the street with their mother, Mariana, and their sister, Catalina. Both were wrapped up in heavy, coarse black woolen coats; their heads were covered with thick-knitted shawls, and they steadied themselves with wooden poles to stop from slipping in their old stiff leather boots, which were only a fragile barrier against the cold.

Jacobo smiled at seeing his mother carrying two parcels wrapped in newspaper. There was a hunk of bread with bacon in each of them for the journey.

"I'll go ahead with you, Jacobo," said Catalina, grabbing on to his arm.

"Fine," her brother agreed before affectionately telling her off. "But you should have stayed in the house, Miss Stubborn. This cold is no good for your cough. You're pale, and your lips are blue."

"It's because I don't know when I'll see you again!" she whined, trying to put a rebellious lock of black hair back under the shawl. "I want to make the most of the time I have with you."

"As you wish."

Jacobo turned his head to take a last look at his house before walking slowly with his sister along the frozen streets. The snowfall from the last few days came up to their knees, and when it was lifted by the wind, you could not see more than two meters ahead.

A few steps behind them, Kilian waited for their mother, a tall and robust woman, to adjust the collar of her old coat to cover her throat. He glanced at the front of the house to try and memorize everything about it: the cornerstones, the wooden windows parched by the sun and set in thick stone, the shutters anchored to rusted hinges, the lintel over the jambs that guarded the sturdy door marked with large walnut-size nails, the cross engraved on the main stone of the entrance arch . . .

His mother observed her son and felt a pang of fear. How would he fit in to a completely different world? Kilian was not like Jacobo; he was physically strong and full of energy, fine, but he did not have the overwhelming courage of his elder brother. Since he was young, Kilian had always shown a special sensitivity and thoughtfulness that, as time went by, became hidden under a cloak of curiosity and expectation that pushed him to try to copy his brother. Mariana knew how hard the tropics were. She did not want to cramp her son's desire to learn, but she could not help feeling worried.

"You still have time to change your mind," she said.

Kilian shook his head from side to side.

"I'm fine. Don't worry."

Mariana nodded, taking hold of his arm as they began to walk along the fading path marked out by Jacobo and Catalina. They had to bend their heads and shout, without looking at each other, because of the unusually fierce gale.

"This house is left with no men, Kilian," she said. There was no contempt in her voice, but some bitterness. "I hope that one day your efforts will have been worth it . . ."

Kilian could hardly speak. Times would be difficult for his mother and young sister: two women managing a property in a harsh environment where there were fewer and fewer people. For the last two or three years, many young people had decided to leave for the provincial capitals in search of work and a better life, encouraged by the news in the few papers—*El Noticiero*, *El Heraldo*, *La Nueva España*, and *ABC*—that arrived by post to some of the richer neighbors. Reading the adverts, one might think that the future was anywhere except in that land forgotten by progress. Still, he already missed it, fearing their final good-bye. It was the first time he had left home and his mother, and all the excitement of the previous days had now transformed into a knot in his stomach.

He envied Jacobo, the speed and determination with which he had packed his luggage. "Our clothes won't be of any use to you there," he had told Kilian, "so only think about what you will wear on the journey there and back, the best you have. Besides, everything is cheaper there. You can buy anything you want." Kilian had packed and unpacked the few clothes—shirts, jackets, trousers, underwear, and socks—many times to ensure that he had picked the right things. He had even made a list of all his belongings, which he then stuck to the inside of the case to remind him of what he was taking, including the packets of Palmera double-edged razor blades and his Varón Dandy aftershave. Of course, both his father and his brother had been to Africa many times and were used to traveling, but he was not, even though he had always wanted it with all his heart.

"If it weren't so far . . ." Mariana sighed, clutching her son's arm even tighter.

Six thousand kilometers and three weeks—it now seemed like an eternity—was what separated Kilian's beloved mountains from a promising future. Those who went to Africa came back with white suits and money in their pockets. The families of those who emigrated did well and did so quickly. However, that was not the only reason Kilian was leaving. After all, the income of his father and brother was more than enough. In his heart of hearts, he had always been tempted to go out and see for himself what others from the valley had seen of the world, even if it meant a long and arduous journey.

"The money is always a help," he countered again. "In these houses, something always comes up, the cost of the shepherd, the harvesters, the builders. Besides, you know that for a young man, Pasolobino is a bit limited."

Mariana understood it better than anybody. Things had not changed much since she and her husband, Antón, had left for Africa in 1926. Life in the village meant livestock and more livestock, sheds full of manure, mud, snow, and cold. There was no scarcity, but you could not aspire to much more than surviving with a little dignity. The climate of the valley was very hard. Life depended on the weather. The crops, the fields, the farms, and the animals: if the harvest was bad one year, everybody felt it. Their sons could have stayed to work in the pyrite mine or been apprentices to the smith, the builder, the slater, or the carpenter and supplemented their income from cattle and sheep. Kilian was quite good with livestock, and he felt happy and free in the fields. But he was still young, and Mariana understood that he wanted new experiences. She had also gone through this: very few valley women had the chance to travel so far. She knew that what entered the senses when one was young left its mark.

A gust of wind hit Kilian's suitcase, pushing him back. They trudged along in silence accompanied by the roar of the wind along the narrow street that led to the bottom of the village. Kilian was happy he had said good-bye to his neighbors the previous afternoon and that the snowstorm had prevented them from coming out onto the street. The doors and windows of the houses remained closed, adding to the spectral scene.

They made out the shapes of Jacobo and Catalina a few steps away, and the four of them formed an unsteady huddle at the edge of the fields.

Mariana observed her three children together, telling jokes to ease the tension of saying good-bye. Kilian and Jacobo were strong and attractive men who needed to stoop down to talk to their sister, a thin young woman who had never had much health. She knew Catalina would miss Jacobo's jovial nature and Kilian's patience. All of a sudden, Mariana missed her husband terribly. It had been two years since she had last seen Antón. And it seemed like centuries since the five of them had last been together. Now the two women would be all alone. She felt like crying but wanted to look strong, as she had been taught since childhood. Real mountain people never showed emotion in public, even if just with family.

Jacobo looked at his watch and said it was time to go. He gave his sister a hug and pinched her cheek. He went to his mother and gave her two theatrical kisses, telling her in a high voice that they would be back when she least expected it.

She whispered to him, "Look after your brother."

Kilian hugged his sister and held her by the shoulders to look at her straight; her chin began to tremble, and she burst out crying. Kilian hugged her again, and Jacobo nervously cleared his throat and repeated that they would miss the coach.

Kilian approached his mother, making a great effort not to falter. Mariana hugged him so tightly that both felt the spasms as they tried to keep from sobbing.

"Mind yourself, Son, mind yourself," she whispered in his ear. Her voice trembled. "And don't be gone too long."

Kilian nodded. He fit his skis' cable ties to the heels of his boots and tightened them with the metal levers a palm's length from the tips. He put the parcel of food in a bag, picked up his suitcase in one hand, and began to ski after Jacobo, who was already disappearing down the eight-kilometer slope that led down to Cerbeán, the biggest neighboring town, where they had to get the coach to the city. The road did not go as high as Pasolobino, built at the feet of a giant rocky mass that reigned over the valley. In winter, skis were the fastest and most comfortable way to travel over the snow.

He had barely gone a few meters when he stopped and turned to get a last look at the dark figures of his mother and sister against the gray background of tightly packed houses and smoking chimneys.

Despite the cold, the women remained there until they lost sight of the young men.

Only then did Mariana bow her head and allow the tears to roll down her cheeks. Catalina moved closer, silently took her arm, and led her slowly to the house, wrapped in gusts of wind and snow.

When the brothers got to Cerbeán, with reddened cheeks, hands stiff with cold, and bodies sweating from the exercise, the wind had died down a little. They swapped their ski boots for laced shoes and left the boots beside the skis in a tavern close to the coach stop, where one of their cousins would come to collect them and return them to the House of Rabaltué.

Jacobo clambered up the rear ladder of the coach to tie the suitcases to the roof rack. Afterward, both brothers took their seats toward the rear of the bus. The driver started the engine and announced that they would be leaving in five minutes. The coach was practically empty. It was not the time of year when the people of Pasolobino normally traveled, but it would soon fill up on the journey so that the last passengers would arrive in the city standing or squashed together on the steps located to the driver's right.

Jacobo closed his eyes to take a nap, relieved to be sheltered from the intense cold—it was not particularly warm inside, but it was tolerable—and to not have to make the first part of the journey on horseback like his father had done. Kilian entertained himself by looking through the window at the featureless countryside, which remained white for a good part of the journey until changing to gray rocks, through whose tunnels they left the mountains behind and approached the lowlands.

He knew the route. It was the only one that led to Barmón, a small provincial town seventy kilometers from Pasolobino. Barmón was the farthest Kilian, at the age of twenty-four, had traveled in his life. Some of his childhood friends had had the good fortune to get so sick that they needed specialist medical attention in the provincial or even regional capital; he had grown up as strong as an ox. Livestock marts in Barmón had been his most direct source of information of the outside world, with traveling salesmen from all parts there to sell their wares to the stockmen after they sold their animals. They bought cloth, candles, oil, salt, wine, household furniture, tools, and presents to take back to the mountain villages.

For him, this hustle and bustle of men and women proved that there was a universe beyond the narrow road hewn out of rock that led to his valley, a universe that was barely described by the words and drawings in his geography and history schoolbooks, the anecdotes of the older generation, and the news on National Radio of Spain, Radio Paris

International, or the revolutionary—according to his father's brother—Radio Pyrenees.

Jacobo woke up soon after passing Barmón. He had not heard the ruckus caused by the dozen adults and children who had boarded the coach with baskets of food, nor the cackling outcry of the hens in cardboard boxes. Kilian was still amazed by his brother, who could sleep in impossible positions, at any hour. He was even capable of waking up, chatting for a while, smoking a cigarette, and then going back to sleep. Jacobo maintained that it was a good way of saving energy. At that moment, Kilian did not mind Jacobo's silence. After saying his good-byes in Pasolobino, he even appreciated the chance to become better accustomed to the changes in scenery and his mood.

In one of these intermittent waking moments, on sensing Kilian's pensiveness, Jacobo put his arm around his brother's shoulder and drew him toward him vigorously.

"Cheer up, man!" he said in a loud voice. "A couple of drinks in the Ambos Mundos bar will cure all your ills. An appropriate name, don't you think?" He laughed. "Ambos Mundos!" *Both worlds*, Kilian thought to himself.

Hours later, they finally arrived in the big city. There was no snow in Zaragoza, but a strong north wind, almost as hard and chilling as that in the mountains, blew. Regardless of the cold, the streets were full of people: hundreds of men wrapped up in woolen coats, slightly stooped, holding their hats or caps with one hand, and women pressing their bags to their chests. Jacobo guided Kilian to the hostel, a narrow building several stories high in the Plaza de España. It was where Antón and Jacobo normally stayed when they passed through the city. They left the suitcases in their Spartan room and rushed back out again for those drinks.

First, following the custom of many who came to the city, they went through the narrow alleyways of the old quarter, popularly known as El Tubo, to go and visit the Basilica of Our Lady of the Pillar and ask the Virgin to watch over their journey. They then had a plate of fried squid in a crowded bar, where they accepted the offer of a bootblack. With their shoes shining, they milled about as the crowd diminished and the shops closed. In the middle of the paved streets, where the trams and black cars circulated and where buildings had been built up to eight stories high, the two men ambled, Kilian pausing often to take in everything.

"You're acting like a country bumpkin." His brother laughed heartily. "What are you going to do when we get to Madrid?"

Kilian asked him about everything. It was as if the nerves of the previous days had spun into an urgent curiosity. Jacobo was pleased to act as his expert guide, putting on an air of superiority. He still remembered his bewildering first trip.

"Do you see that car?" he explained as he pointed at an elegant black vehicle with a front grille, round headlights, and gleaming roof rack. "That is one of the new Peugeot 203 sedans that they are now using as taxis. That other one is an English Austin FX3, a wonderful car. And this is a Citroën 11 CV sedan, known as *the Duck* . . . Nice, isn't it?"

Kilian nodded, distracted by the elegance and monumental bearing of the classical facades of the buildings, such as Banco Hispano Americano and La Unión y el Fénix Español, with their large square and round windows, their columned entrances, their decorative attics, and their wrought-iron balconies.

Exhausted after their intense day, the two young men finally decided to go to the famous café that Jacobo had suggested. Kilian read the lighted sign in amazement, claiming the establishment was one of the biggest of its kind in all Europe. He entered through the double doors after his brother and hesitated, stunned. Just a wide staircase and a few arches with white columns separated them from an enormous two-story room full of voices, smoke, heat, and music. A thin railing ran the length of the second floor to allow upstairs customers to enjoy the view of the orchestra located downstairs in the center of the room. A scene from a film he had seen in Barmón came to mind, a scene where a young man came down a similar set of stairs with a raincoat hanging perfectly from his arm and a cigarette dangling in his hand. Kilian's heart beat wildly. He took in the myriad of tables, wooden chairs, and booths, the conversation between men and women who, at first glance, seemed distinguished and sophisticated. The women's V-necked dresses, with bows on the front, were light, gay, well fitting, and short in comparison to the thick half-length skirts and dark wool jackets of the mountain village women, and like Kilian, the men wore white shirts under their jackets, some of which sported a handkerchief, and thin black ties.

For a few seconds, he felt important. No one here knew that barely twenty-four hours earlier, he had been cleaning manure from the sheds.

Jacobo raised his hand to say hello to someone at the back of the room. Kilian turned and saw a man waving at them to come and sit at his table.

"It's not possible!" his brother exclaimed. "What a coincidence! Come, I'll introduce you."

They maneuvered between the tables, on which they could see packets of Bisonte and Camel filter-tipped cigarettes, matchboxes of all shapes and sizes, glasses of anise or brandy in front of the men and champagne or Martini Bianco in front of the women. The place was packed with people. Kilian was fascinated by the size of the room, which allowed some to talk quietly in the corners while others danced near the orchestra. There was nothing like this in the whole valley of Pasolobino, not even close. In summer, dances were held in the town square, and in winter, every now and then, there were small parties organized in sitting rooms, where the furniture had to be taken out and chairs placed in a circle against the wall to make room. The girls remained seated until the boys invited them to take a turn on the improvised dance floor or they decided to dance with one another to the pasodobles, waltzes, tangos, and cha-chas played by an accordion, a guitar, and a violin that could not, for an instant, compete with the catchy, carefree rumba now coming from the trumpets and saxophones.

Just before reaching their destination, Jacobo turned and whispered, "One thing, Kilian. From now on, when we are with other people, we must not speak in Pasolobinese. When we're alone, it's fine, but I don't want to look like a country bumpkin. Okay?"

Kilian agreed, though it would be difficult to stop thinking and speaking in his native language.

Jacobo greeted the man with a hearty handshake.

"What are you doing here? Weren't you in Madrid?"

"I'll tell you about it. Sit down with me." The man pointed at Kilian. "And this must be your brother."

Jacobo laughed.

"Kilian, this is Manuel Ruiz, a budding doctor based in Guinea for who the hell knows what reason." Manuel smiled and shrugged. "And this is my brother, Kilian. Another one who doesn't know what he's doing."

They shook hands and sat down on a semicircular leather couch. Jacobo sat on a wooden rung-backed chair. The melodious singer, dressed in a silver-trimmed gray jacket, began to sing a well-known Antonio Machín ballad, *"Angelitos Negros,"* or "Little Black Angels," and was applauded by the audience.

"You don't have anything like this in Madrid?" joked Jacobo to Manuel.

"Dozens of them! And twice as big! But I came to sign new papers to work in Sampaka. They offered me a nice contract."

"You don't know how happy that makes me! Dámaso is too old for that type of life."

"If only I was as experienced as Dámaso . . ."

"Fine, but he can't manage everything. And when are you going down?"

"I'm going back to Madrid tomorrow. They've got me a ticket for Thursday on the . . ."

"*Ciudad de Sevilla!*" both of them exclaimed before bursting into loud peals of laughter. "We're also going on that ship! Brilliant!"

Jacobo realized then that they had excluded Kilian from the conversation.

"Manuel used to work in the hospital in Santa Isabel. From now on we will have him all to ourselves." He raised his head, looking for a waiter. "This deserves a toast! Have you had dinner?"

"Not yet. If you like, we can eat here. It's *chopi*."

"*Chopi*, yes!" Jacobo let out a chuckle.

Kilian understood that this word referred to mealtime and accepted their suggestions from the menu. Just then, a silence descended as the soloist repeated the last verse of his song where he reproached the painter for never remembering to paint a black angel in a church. His performance was roundly applauded, an ovation that increased when the pianist began to play some fast-moving blues that only a few couples dared dance to.

"I love boogie-woogie!" Jacobo announced, clicking his fingers and rolling his shoulders. "It's a pity I've no one to dance with!"

He swept the room and waved to a group of girls two tables away who answered with shy giggles and whispers. He thought about going over and asking one of them, but decided not to.

"Well, I'll soon be able to sate my needs."

Kilian, who did not like dancing very much, surprised himself by following the rhythm with his foot. He did not stop until the waiter returned with their order. When he saw the plates, he realized how hungry he was. Since breakfast, he had eaten only the hunk of bread and bacon that Mariana had prepared and the fried squid. He wondered if the smoked salmon and caviar canapés and the cold chicken and beef stuffed with truffles could fill his stomach. He was accustomed to more substantial stews, but he found them delicious, and washed down with several glasses of wine, they did the trick.

When they finished dinner, Jacobo asked for a gin, whining that even here in the biggest place in Europe they did not have a whiskey to his liking. Manuel and Kilian made do with a *sol y sombra* of brandy and anise.

"And you, Kilian?" asked Manuel. "How do you feel starting this adventure? Nervous?"

Kilian had taken an instant liking to the doctor. He was a young man, around thirty, medium height, fairly thin, fair haired, and fair skinned, with intelligent blue eyes behind thick tortoiseshell glasses. His deliberate way of talking proved that he was an educated and serious man, though—like Kilian—he became open and friendly with a little alcohol.

"A little," Kilian replied. It was hard for him to admit that he was actually very frightened. He had gone from raising livestock to having drinks with a real doctor in the best nightspot in the region's capital. "But I'm very lucky to be in good company."

Jacobo gave him a loud slap on the back.

"Don't be ashamed, Kilian. You're scared out of your wits! But we have all gone through this—right, Manuel?"

Manuel agreed and took a sip of his drink. "On my first journey, I was ready to turn back when I reached Bata. But the next time, it was as if I had never done anything other than travel to Fernando Po." He paused. "It gets into your blood. The same as the damn mosquitoes. You'll see."

After three hours, many drinks, and a red tin of thin Craven A cigarettes, which Kilian found pleasantly mild compared to the strong black tobacco of home, the brothers said good-bye to Manuel and returned, unsteadily and with glazed eyes, to the hostel. On reaching the Plaza de España, they crossed the tramline, and Jacobo rushed down the stairs to the public toilets. Kilian waited for him above, leaning on an iron railing. The neon-lit signs on the surrounding roof terraces helped the stout four-armed streetlights illuminate the square and its center, a fountain with a bronze statue on a stone battlement pedestal.

Under a cross, an angel stretched one arm toward the sky and held a wounded man without the strength to clutch the fallen weapon at his feet. Kilian went over and concentrated on the inscription that a lady, also cast in bronze, held in her hands. He learned that the angel on the pedestal represented Faith and that the monument was dedicated to the martyrs of religion and the fatherland. He raised his eyes to the heavens, his view blocked by neon words—"Avecrem," "Gallina Blanca," "Iberia Radio," "Longines: The Best Watch," "Dispak Tablets," "Phillips." It was an effort to think straight. He felt a little dizzy, and the alcohol was not the only culprit. He had left home just hours earlier, but it felt like centuries. And from what he had gathered from Manuel and Jacobo's conversation, he still had a long and strange journey ahead. He returned his gaze to the statue of Faith and prayed for luck and strength.

"Well, Kilian?" Jacobo's mellow voice startled him. "What do you think of your first night away from Mom?" He put his arm around his brother's shoulder and began to walk. "A lot of new things today, weren't there? What you saw in Ambos Mundos is nothing compared to what's next . . . Isn't that what you were thinking?"

"More or less."

Jacobo put his hand on his forehead.

"I can't wait to drink the whiskey in Santa Isabel! That one doesn't give you a hangover. You'll see. Have you packed painkillers?"

Kilian nodded, and Jacobo gave him a slap on the back.

"Well, tell me, what do you most want to see?"

Kilian paused. "I think it's the sea, Jacobo," he replied. "I have never seen the sea."

Although it was his first time traveling by boat, Kilian did not get seasick. Many of the passengers wandered on deck, haggard and green faced. It seemed that seasickness was not cured by traveling more often, as his brother did not look so great, and this was his third time on the *Ciudad de Sevilla*. That something this size could float was beyond him. His relationship with free-running water had been limited to catching trout in the small streams of Pasolobino.

Kilian thought of his mother, his sister, and their life in Pasolobino. How far away it all was from the middle of this ocean. He remembered the cold that had followed them to Zaragoza and later by train to Madrid. The closer they got to Cádiz, the better the temperature became, and so did his state of mind as he received a frame-by-frame view of Spain on the durable tropical sleepers of the railway lines. When the ship left port and dozens of people waved white handkerchiefs in the air with tears in their eyes, the thought of his loved ones made him sentimental, but Jacobo, Manuel, and other companions planning to work in the colony had helped cheer him. Thus far, the voyage had been enjoyable, though he could not remember having so many days of rest in his whole life.

Always full of nervous energy, Kilian thought this much leisure was an unforgivable waste. He was already looking forward to some physical work. How different he was from Jacobo, who always looked for the chance to rest! He turned his head to look at his brother, reclining in a comfortable chair beside him, a hat covering his face. From the time they had left Cádiz, and even more so since Tenerife, Jacobo had done nothing except sleep during the day and spend the nights partying with his friends in the piano room or Veranda Bar. Between the alcohol and the seasickness, he was constantly tired.

Kilian, however, tried to get the most out of everything he did. Every afternoon, in addition to practicing his broken English with a dictionary, *Naijalingo*, he read the back issues of the magazine *La Guinea Española* to get an idea of the world he would occupy, at least for the next eighteen months of his first campaign. The full campaign added up to twenty-four months, but the last six, also paid, were a holiday. And the contract had begun the moment he left Cádiz. He had spent almost two weeks getting paid to read.

In all the issues of the magazine on board—all published the previous year, 1952—the same ads appeared in the same order. First was the advert for the Dumbo stores on Calle Sacramento de Santa Isabel, and just after it one for Transportes Reunidos on Avenida General Mola, offering repair and transport services in the one *factoría*, what they called shops and general services in the colonies. Last, the third ad showed a man who recommended the magnificent Rumbo tobaccos with a sentence in large type: "The cigarette that helps you think." Jacobo had told Kilian that there were many different and very cheap tobacco brands in the colony and that almost everyone smoked because it drove away the mosquitoes. After the ads came religious articles, various news items from Europe, and opinion pieces.

Kilian lit a cigarette and concentrated on the magazine in his hands. He was enthralled by an article on children baptized between 1864 and 1868: Pedro María Ngadi, José María Gongolo, Filomena Mapula, Mariano Ignacio Balonga, Antonio María Ebomo, Lorenzo Ebama . . . It was odd. The first names were typical, but the surnames sounded African.

Next, he read an article on the more than five million German children who lost their families in 1945. How distant the war seemed to him! He vaguely remembered letters from his father that his mother had read aloud—before folding them and devotedly putting them in the pocket of her skirt—letters in which he described a worrying social atmosphere on the island because of the nascent nationalist movements led by fears of being invaded by British and French troops. His father recounted how most everyone on the island wanted to remain neutral, though some were pro-Allies, and in the governor's circle, they were more pro-Nazi. In fact, there was a time when German newspapers with Spanish subtitles were freely available.

The Spanish Civil War and the European war were now over. But from what Kilian had read during the voyage, Africa had not escaped political conflict. One article detailed how excommunication was threatened for any Kenyan sympathizer of the Mau Mau religious movement and its leader, Jomo Kenyatta, because it defended the expulsion of European influence on Africa and a return to their pagan rites.

The column made Kilian think. Expel the Europeans from Africa? Hadn't they brought civilization to a savage land? Were Africans not better off? These questions were beyond his understanding, but that did not mean he did not mull over them. Anyway, the idea he had of the black continent came mainly from his father's generation, a generation proud of serving God and country. And from what they had told him hundreds of times, working in the colonies meant serving the Almighty and the Spanish nation. Though they returned with their pockets full, they had also accomplished a noble mission.

Nevertheless, Kilian had many questions about how to relate to people so different from him. The only black man that he had met worked in the bar on the ship. Upon first seeing him, he had stared impolitely, looking for big differences between them apart from the colors of their skin and the man's perfect white teeth. But there was nothing. As the days went by, he stopped seeing a black man and came to know Eladio the waiter.

It was most likely that the stories he had heard about blacks had little bearing on reality. When Antón and Jacobo talked to their family in Pasolobino, they referred to the coloreds doing this and the coloreds doing that. José was the exception; all the others seemed to be just an impersonal mass. Kilian remembered seeing an old postcard Antón had sent to Jacobo. It showed four naked-breasted black women. Antón had written in pen: *"Look at how peculiar the black women are. This is how they dress on the streets!"*

Kilian had studied the photo closely, finding the women pretty. They wore fabrics rolled and tied at the waist like skirts, the *clote*, which covered them down to their ankles. From the waists up, they were completely naked except for a simple necklace and some fine cords on their wrists. Each one had different breasts: high and firm, small, separated and generous. Their figures were svelte and their facial features extremely pretty, with full lips and large eyes. Their hair was gathered into what seemed like thin plaits. It was a beautiful photo. Though it was strange to find it on a postcard. The postcards he had seen were of monuments or picturesque corners of a city, country, or landscape, even people dressed elegantly, but . . . four naked women? They could not have known how it would be used. The photo made him feel strange, as if they had been treated the same way as an interesting insect.

He had the same feeling now while looking at one of the many photos from the magazine he was reading. It showed a group of blacks dressed like Europeans, with shirts and jackets, caps or hats. It was a normal photo, but for the caption: "The joy of Christmas brings about these scenes of outlandishly dressed men on farms and in villages." He was surprised, knowing from his father that on special occasions, some natives dressed up as *nañgüe*, a type of carnival clown to make people laugh, whom the missionaries called *mamarrachos*. But he had imagined them with masks and straw suits, and not dressed as Europeans . . .

Jacobo's hoarse voice interrupted his thoughts.

"I hope we'll be able to travel there by plane soon. I can't take any more of this!"

Kilian smiled.

"If you didn't drink so much at night, perhaps you wouldn't get so seasick."

"Then the days would seem longer and less bearable . . . And Manuel?"

"He's at the cinema."

Jacobo joined Kilian, took off his hat, and glanced at the magazine.

"Have you anything interesting for me today?"

Kilian began to give him the daily report. In less than two weeks, they each had developed their own routine. Manuel and Kilian read while Jacobo slept. When he woke up, they shared anything that had intrigued Kilian.

"Just now I was going to read an article about Bubi—"

"What a waste of time," Jacobo interrupted him. "You won't need Bubi there for anything. The majority of the natives speak Spanish, and you will spend your time surrounded by Nigerian farmhands on the estate. You should study the Pichinglis dictionary I gave you. You will need it all the time."

On the table, there was a small brown book with a worn cloth cover titled *Dialecto Inglés-Africano o Broke English*, written in 1919, as announced on page one, by a priest from the Missionaries, Sons of the Immaculate Heart of Mary. Kilian had tried to memorize some words and phrases, but he found it very difficult, as he had never heard it spoken. In the book, a word or phrase appeared in Spanish with the translation into African English, Pidgin English, Pichinglis or *Pichi*, as the Spanish called it, and its pronunciation.

"I don't understand why the language is written in one form and pronounced in another. It makes it double the work."

"Forget about how it is written. You won't have to write letters to the Nigerians! Concentrate on the pronunciation." Jacobo took the book and his brother's new black pen with its gold cap. "Look, the first thing you have to do is memorize the basic questions." He underlined the page. "And then you learn the expressions that you will say or hear."

Jacobo closed the book and left it on the table.

"They will tell you that they are sick, that they can't work, that they don't know how to do it, that it's very hot, that it's raining a lot . . ." He lay back in the deck chair, clasped his hands behind his head, and sighed. "The blacks always look for excuses not to work. The same as children! You'll see!"

Kilian laughed, thinking that Jacobo had just described himself.

He picked up the small dictionary to see the phrases his brother had underlined and was shocked to see the translations: "I'll teach you," "Work," "Come," "Shut up," "I'm sick," "I don't understand you," "If you break this, I'll hit you." These were the words that he would be using in the following months! He refused to believe that over the last few years, Jacobo had not had a deeper conversation with the workers. Though it should hardly surprise him. The stories his brother told normally stuck to the parties in the clubs in Santa Isabel.

Jacobo moved his hat again and prepared to continue with his never-ending siesta.

"Jacobo . . ."

"Hmmm . . . ?"

"You've spent years there. What do you know of its history?"

"The same as everyone else! It is a fruitful colony, and you can earn money . . ."

"Yes, but . . . who owned it before us?"

"The English, the Portuguese . . . How would I know?"

"Yes, but . . . before, it was theirs, the natives, wasn't it?"

Jacobo let out a snort. "You mean the savages. They are lucky to have us. Otherwise they'd still be in the jungle! Ask our father, who gave them electricity."

Kilian remained thoughtful. "Well, it wasn't too long ago that we got electricity in Pasolobino. And in many Spanish villages, the children got on thanks to powdered milk and tinned American cheese. It's not like we are the greatest example of progress. If you look at the few photos of Dad as a child, it's hard to believe they really lived as they did."

"If you're so interested in history, you're sure to find some book or other in the plantation offices. But you will be so tired that you won't even want to read, you'll see." Jacobo reclined in his deck chair and placed his hat over his face. "And now, if you don't mind, I need to get some sleep."

Kilian's gaze passed over the calm sea, as flat as a pancake. That was how he described it in a letter to Mariana and Catalina. The sun projected its last rays over the horizon. Soon it would be swallowed up.

In the mountains, the sun hid at dusk; at sea, the water seemed to engulf it.

He never tired of seeing the marvelous sunsets on the high sea, but he was anxious to walk on dry land. They had docked for a night in the port of Monrovia, capital of Liberia, to load and unload goods, but they had not been able to get off the ship. The coast there was more or less uniform. He could see forests of acacias and mangroves and an endless span of sandy beach with various villages. After that, they traveled along the Kru coast, home of a race of strong men good for work, as explained to him by his Galician companions: "The Kru are like the Asturians and Galicians in Spain, the best workers." His father had seen these men launch their canoes into the sea as European ships and boats were passing, rowing to offer their services for all kinds of jobs. He used to tell them the legend of how the men worked until they considered themselves independent and they had twenty or thirty women at their disposal. It was probably no more than that, a legend, one that brought a smile to the faces of white men as they imagined themselves satisfying so many females.

Kilian lit a cigarette.

As happened every night after dinner, groups of people chatted and walked along the deck. In the distance, he made out the nephew of the civil governor, traveling with his family from Madrid to return to Guinea after an extended stay in Spain. A few meters away, other future plantation employees played cards. As the days went by, they became more and more like the colonial experts. He smiled, remembering his clumsiness when faced with the unusual amount of cutlery that accompanied the dishes in the dining room. But his initial trepidation had relaxed during the lazy, monotonous days and nights on the gently moving ship.

Kilian closed his eyes and let the sea breeze caress his face. One more night. His mind turned to home, and he went over the names of the households, wondering what they were doing. He thought and dreamed in his mother tongue.

He spoke in Spanish and listened to English, German, and French on the ship. He studied African English. He wondered whether Bubi was for the island's natives the same as Pasolobinese was for him. He wondered if anyone would want to know the history and customs not only of the Metropolis—the name given to Spain as the colonizing country—but also of that cold and beautiful part of the Pyrenees that now seemed so small.

He was eager to know more about this world, which certainly endured under the colonization. He would like to know the history of the island, of the women and men in the photographs.

The native. The authentic.

If anything remained of it.

When Kilian spotted his father dressed in shorts, a bright shirt, and a pith helmet on the quay in the port of Bata, the capital of Río Muni, the continental part of Spanish Guinea, his soul had already been invaded by the heat and the green.

Before his eyes lay the most beautiful part of the continent, the perennially green region, covered in tropical forest. Everything else was superimposed: neither the low buildings nor the enormous lumber ships docked in the port nor the hands waving in the air, greeting people, nor the men carting goods to and fro.

It was surreal.

But here he was. At last!

"What do you think, Kilian?" his brother asked.

Jacobo and Manuel were beside him, waiting for the gangway to be extended so the passengers could disembark. From all sides, a multitude of people bustled about, carrying out different tasks. Both on board and on land, the shouts of various languages could be heard. Kilian watched the scene in amazement.

"He's dumbstruck!" Manuel said, laughing and giving Jacobo a poke.

"Do you see the number of blacks, Kilian? And all the same! You'll see. It will be the same as with the sheep. For the first two or three months, you won't be able to tell them apart."

Manuel frowned. Kilian was not listening, because he was spellbound by the sight unfolding before his eyes.

"There's Dad!" he exclaimed.

He waved and began to descend with a light step, followed by Jacobo and Manuel, equally eager to step on solid ground again.

The hug he gave Antón was brief but heartfelt. For some minutes, the greetings, introductions, stories, and impatient questions got mixed together. It had been two years since Kilian had seen Antón, and he did not look well. His sunburned face was lined by wrinkles, and his big but well-proportioned features had begun to turn flabby. He seemed tired, and his hand was constantly touching his belly.

Antón wanted to know how everyone was in the village. His brother, also called Jacobo; the close relations; and the neighbors. He saved his questions about his wife and daughter until the end. When he asked about Mariana, Kilian could make out a look of sadness in his eyes. He did not have to explain anything. The campaigns were long for any man, but longer for a married man who adored his wife.

After a moment's silence, Antón looked over Kilian, stretched out his arm, and said, "Well, Son. Welcome again to your birthplace. I hope you will be happy here."

Kilian gave a knowing smile and turned to Manuel to explain.

"Did you know Jacobo was born here? And I came two years later. After the birth, my mother got sick, so we went back home."

Manuel nodded. Many people could not take the intense heat and humidity.

"In other words, I was born here, but I don't have any memories of the place."

Jacobo leaned across to continue the explanation in a low voice. "Our mother never came back again. My father came and went, and between one cocoa campaign and another, siblings were born. Sometimes, he would see the baby when it was almost two. Then he would leave a new seed and return to the tropics. Of six children, three have survived."

Kilian gestured nervously to warn him that Antón might hear, but their father was absorbed in his own thoughts. He saw how Kilian had changed, tall as ever, thinner than Jacobo, but now a fully grown man. It seemed impossible that time had passed so quickly since he was born. Twenty-four years later, Kilian had returned to his first home. At first, Antón had not been in favor of his son's decision to follow in his brother's footsteps and come to Africa. The idea that he would leave Mariana and Catalina alone to look after the house and the land pained him. But Kilian could be very stubborn and convincing, and he was right when arguing that another injection of money would be good for the family. So Antón had decided to ask the owner of the plantation for work for Kilian, and the owner had accelerated the paperwork so the journey could be made in January, just in time to prepare for the harvest. Kilian would have enough time to adapt to the country and be ready for the most important months, especially the toasting of the cocoa, which would begin in August.

The bustle of people and suitcases around them told Antón that they should go to a different part of the quay. There was still a couple of hours' journey from Bata to the island.

"I think that the ship to Santa Isabel is ready to weigh anchor," Jacobo told them before turning to Antón. "It was very good of you to receive us in Bata and travel with us to the island. Maybe you didn't trust me to bring Kilian safe and sound?"

Antón smiled, not a common occurrence, but Jacobo knew how to coax it out of him.

"I hope you made use of the long journey to bring your brother up to speed. Although from the look of you, I'm inclined to think you spent more time in the piano room!"

Kilian intervened in a serious voice, even if his smile gave away the joke, "I couldn't have had better teachers than Jacobo and Manuel. You should have seen my brother teaching me Pichi! I'm almost fluent now!"

The four burst out laughing. Antón was happy to have them there with him. Their youth and energy would help make up for the fact that he had begun to lose steam. He looked at them proudly. In appearance, his sons were very similar to him. Both had inherited his green eyes, typical of the House of Rabaltué. From a distance, they looked green, but up close they were gray. The boys had wide foreheads, long noses thick at the base, high cheekbones, and pronounced jaws and chins, though Jacobo's was much squarer than his brother's. They also shared the same thick, dark hair, though Kilian sported copper highlights. They stood out because of their height, wide shoulders, and strong arms—Jacobo's arms were thicker, more accustomed to physical work. Antón knew the effect that Jacobo had on women, but that was because they had not met Kilian yet. The harmony of his features neared perfection. It reminded him of his wife, Mariana, when she was young.

However, their characters could not have been more different. While Jacobo liked to party with the airs of a young gentleman who had no option but to work for a living, Kilian had a high sense of responsibility, sometimes too high. It was something Antón would never admit; he preferred his son to be hardworking and upright instead of fickle like Jacobo.

In any case, it seemed the brothers understood and complemented each other well; that was important in a strange land.

On the short trip between Bata and the island, Antón was especially talkative. After they regaled him with stories about the journey and Jacobo's constant seasickness, he told them about one of the first journeys he took without Mariana, from Tenerife to Monrovia, when the ship suffered through a terrible storm.

"There was water everywhere, the suitcases floated in the cabins. One minute you were flying, and the next you were drowning. We were lost for three days with no food. Everything was destroyed. In the port of Santa Isabel, they were waiting for us as if waiting for a ghost. They thought we were dead." He stared toward the horizon, then turned to Jacobo, who was astonished. "It was the only time in my life I was ever afraid. Fear—no, terror! Fully grown men crying like children . . ."

Kilian shook his head. "I don't remember you telling us this story before. Why didn't you mention it in your letters?"

"I didn't want to worry you," his father replied, shrugging. "Do you think your mother would have let you come if she had heard this story? Anyway, I could not have done it justice. As my good friend José says, it is difficult to describe fear—once it has gotten into you, it takes a lot to get rid of it."

Jacobo put his hand to his chest.

"I promise never to complain about the journeys again and to enjoy the sight of the whales and dolphins escorting the ships."

Kilian looked at his father. There was something different about him. Normally he was a serious man, difficult and authoritarian. But from the way he had told the story of the shipwreck, Kilian had sensed a slight sadness in his father's voice. Or was it fear? And there was that movement of his hand to his side . . .

"Dad . . . are you all right?"

Antón composed himself.

"Very well, Son. The last campaign was just harder than expected." It was obvious he wanted to change the subject. "The harvest was not as good as we had hoped due to the fog. We had more work than normal."

Before Kilian could press further, Antón turned to Jacobo.

"Have you brought your birth certificate?"

"Yes."

Kilian knew that the interrogation would now begin. Jacobo had warned him.

"And the good-conduct cert and the police cert?"

"Yes."

"The military service record?"

"As well. And the antituberculosis medical certificate with the official stamp, and the certificate from the teacher saying I can read and write . . . For God's sake, Dad! You reminded me five times!"

"Fine, fine, but you wouldn't be the first one to be sent back for not meeting the entry requirements. Did they vaccinate you against yellow fever?"

"Yes, Dad. I was vaccinated on the ship, and I have the paper that proves it. Anything else?"

"Just one, and I hope you haven't forgotten . . ." His voice tried to sound hard, but his eyes shone. "Have you brought the things I asked your mother for?"

Kilian sighed, relieved.

"Yes, Dad. Jacobo's suitcase is full of clothes, ham, chorizo, hazelnuts, tins of peaches, and Mom's marvelous pastries. We have also brought a long letter from her that she closed in front of me with seven wax seals so no one else would open it."

"Good."

Jacobo and Manuel remained silent as they neared their destination. They were looking forward to arriving, but they had lost the innocence, excitement, and nervousness that now fell over Kilian on his maiden voyage.

Jacobo knew well that the novelty would soon wear off. Everything would be reduced to working on the plantation, the parties in the city, waiting to get paid, and the yearning to return home and rest. Then it would begin again. The same cycle every twenty-four months. Even knowing all this, he still felt butterflies in his stomach as the boat turned toward the port of the island's capital.

"Look, Kilian," said Jacobo, "we are entering the bay of Santa Isabel. Don't miss a second of this!" A gleam appeared in his eyes. "Whether you like your time here or not, whether you stay two or twenty years, whether you love or hate the island . . . listen well to what I'm going to say! You will never be able to erase this image from your mind. Never!"

3

Green Land

Indeed, his arrival in Fernando Po would be ingrained in Kilian's mind for the rest of his life. As the ship came closer to the island, he made out a coastline of small beaches, inlets, and bays, where the lush vegetation met the sand and turquoise-colored water. Kilian could barely take in the vibrant shades, from the pale green of the first shoots and summer apples to the deep green of the forest, passing through the intense and brilliant green of rain-watered spring pastures. A strange sensation overcame him, of softness, freshness, and peacefulness, mixed with the power, exuberance, fullness, and fertility emanating from so much growth.

The ship veered to move abreast toward the wide bay of Santa Isabel, which looked like a huge horseshoe ribbed in green and dotted with white houses surrounded by palm trees. Two natural breakwaters—one to the east, called Punta Fernanda, and the other to the west, Punta Cristina—lay at the foot of an impressive mountain awash in mist. It reminded Kilian suddenly of the peak that rose over Pasolobino.

"They'll moor the boat to that old pier," his father explained, pointing to a small concrete jetty that served as the dock. "I've heard that they are going to build a new port below Punta Cristina, where you will be able to dock parallel to it. Good thing, this one is a bit inconvenient."

Kilian realized that the ship had stopped perpendicular to the coastline and that various barges were preparing to load and unload passengers and cargo.

They went toward the stern to disembark. A subtle aroma of cocoa, coffee, gardenia, and jasmine began to mix with the smell of saltpeter. Although it was evening, a stifling heat surrounded them.

"It's very hot," muttered Kilian, patting the beaded sweat on his forehead. "And so green. It's all green!"

"Yes," Jacobo agreed. "If you stuck a post here, it would sprout roots!"

On the pier, some men carried sacks of coal, others moved drums, and others helped unload the barges. One could imagine how frantic it could be during the harvest months when hundreds of coffee- and cocoa-filled sacks left for different destinations around the globe.

"José will be waiting for us up there," Antón told them.

He signaled with his head toward a sloping path that paralleled a wall over which they could spot the first buildings. He took Kilian's suitcase and shouted at a pair of workers to come over. "Eh, you! Come here!"

The men gave each other annoyed looks.

"You hear what I said?" Antón raised his voice and began walking toward them. He gave the suitcase to one of them and pointed to Jacobo's and Manuel's luggage. "Take this! Quick! Up!"

The men obeyed; they took the bags and, trailed by the white men, walked toward a steep, narrow path that connected the pier to Avenida Alfonso XIII, beside the Plaza de España.

"Kilian, did you know that this path is known as the slope of the fevers?" asked Manuel.

"No, why's that?"

"They say it's because no one who manages to get up the path can escape the fever. You'll see."

"Now it's not that serious, thanks to the medicines," Jacobo interjected, "but a century ago, all those who came died. Everyone. Right, Manuel?" Manuel nodded. "That's why they sent one expedition after another. There wasn't a chance of resistance."

Kilian felt a shiver. He was happy to have been born in a more modern age.

"I never saw it," said Manuel, "but I've been told that years ago, a train ran up this narrow path. Is that true, Antón?"

"Oh yes. I saw it," replied Antón, stopping to catch his breath. "It was useful for moving cargo to the dock. They began building it in 1913, hoping to link Santa Isabel with San Carlos, in the southeast. But the project was abandoned twenty-five years ago because of the frequent breakdowns and the high maintenance costs in virgin rain forest."

Kilian smiled, imagining a small toy train going round such a small island. The path they were on was certainly quite steep, but the distance to their destination was fairly short, at least for someone used to high mountains. And they didn't even have to carry any luggage. Still, he noticed that his father, who he remembered as a strong and fit man, was gasping.

They soon left behind the ivy- and *egombegombe*-covered wall— small, white, delicate flowers appearing among the large carmine, yellow, and green leaves—and reached the top. Before them, a grand esplanade opened out like a balcony onto the shoreline, separated by a balustrade adorned with streetlamps every few meters. In the middle of the esplanade, interspersed with carefully tended flower beds, rose colonial buildings with lateral balconies and gabled roofs. Kilian looked up at them in awe.

"That is the Catholic mission," Jacobo explained. "And this other one is the La Catalana building. It has a bar at ground level that you'll soon get to know. And this one that has left your jaw hanging is the magnificent cathedral—" He interrupted himself. "No. Better to leave the tourist information for another day, I know you . . . Don't worry, you'll be coming to Santa Isabel plenty of times."

Kilian said nothing, admiring the delicious symbiosis of nature and harmonious, light buildings, so lively and different from the solid stone houses of Pasolobino. His gaze moved from one building to another and from one person to another, from the indistinct garb of the whites to the colorful fabrics of the natives.

"There is José," said Antón, taking Kilian by the elbow. "Oh boy! He brought the new car, very strange. Come on, let's go. We have to get to the plantation before dinner so that you can meet the manager."

The smiling man waited for them beside a shiny black Mercedes 220 sedan. Kilian's father introduced him to José, of whom he had heard so much during the holidays in the House of Rabaltué.

"José, this is my son Kilian. At last you get to meet him in person. And I don't know if you know Manuel. He is going to be our doctor from now on."

José greeted them with a wide smile that revealed his perfect white teeth surrounded by a short gray beard. He spoke in perfect Spanish— though with a peculiar accent when sometimes pronouncing the r as the French would do, or when stressing the intonation at the end of each word. It gave his way of speaking a clipped rhythm.

"Welcome to Fernando Po, Massa," he said three times, bowing his head slightly as he addressed Kilian, then Manuel, and finally Jacobo. "I hope you have had a pleasant trip. The luggage is loaded, Massa Antón. We can leave when you are ready."

"Why didn't you come in the Land Rover?" Antón asked.

"A piece fell off at the last minute and Massa Garuz gave me permission to take this one."

"Well, you are starting off on the right foot."

Jacobo, imitating a dutiful chauffeur, opened the rear door to allow Kilian and Manuel to get in.

"This jewel is only for important people," he said. The men gave a happy smile and made themselves comfortable in the beige leather seats. "Dad, you too, please. José will go in front. I'll drive today."

José and Antón exchanged looks.

"I don't know if Garuz would like that," Antón said.

"Oh, come on," replied Jacobo. "He doesn't have to find out. When am I going to get another chance to drive a car like this?"

José shrugged and went to the front of the car.

Sitting between his father and Manuel, Kilian observed José in detail. He noticed that there was a strong bond between him and Antón, even friendly, the result of having known each other for so long. He had to be a few years younger than his father. José was a Bubi, like the majority of the island's population, and he worked as foreman in the cocoa-bean dryers, something rare, as it was normally a role filled by whites. The hardest work was carried out by Nigerian laborers, the majority Calabars, coming from the Nigerian city of Calabar.

Antón told him that when he first came to the island, José was assigned as his *boy*, the name given to the young servants that whites housed to look after their clothes and residences. Each white had his own boy—Kilian would get one as well—and families could have more than one if needed to look after the children. As the years went by, thanks to his capacity for work and ability to get on with the plantation laborers, Antón had finally convinced the manager that José was perfectly capable of supervising the work of the dryers, the most delicate part of the cocoa production process. Over time, Lorenzo Garuz had to admit that there were exceptions to the commonly held Western belief that all Bubis or island natives were lazy.

They drove through the straight streets of Santa Isabel, laid out symmetrically to incorporate functional white buildings; left behind the colorfully dressed pedestrians who helped create the impression of a lively, bright, summery, and pretty city; and continued onto a dusty dirt road through the first few rows of a leafy, dense cocoa plantation.

"You will see, Massa," said José, looking at Kilian through the side mirror. "On the flat land, everything is cocoa and palm trees. Land over five hundred meters, on the hillsides, coffee trees. And at the top, banana trees and Manila hemp."

Kilian nodded to thank him. José was delighted to again describe the route in the way he had probably done long before, first with Kilian's father and later with Jacobo. At that moment, Antón and Manuel stared out in silence, the car windows open so that some air could get in.

They had traveled around five or six kilometers when Manuel urged Kilian to look through the front windshield.

Kilian gasped in surprise. For a few seconds, he thought that his eyes were playing tricks on him. In front of them, a large signpost told them they were coming into . . . Zaragoza! It did not take him long to figure out that it was the name of the village closest to the plantation.

"This village was founded by the first owner of Sampaka," announced Antón while they were passing close to a tree around twenty meters tall located in front of a building. "Mariano Mora was his name."

Kilian, who knew the story, nodded, thrilled to see with his own eyes what he had only heard in tales.

"Yes, Kilian, the one who was born near Pasolobino. And he also built the church."

Manuel did the math in his head. That was over fifty years ago.

"Did you get to meet him?" Manuel asked.

"No. When I came here for the first time, he had just died from a tropical disease. Many remember him as a hardworking, sensible, and prudent man."

"Like all those from the mountains," Jacobo bragged.

Manuel raised his eyebrows before asking, "And who took over the plantation? His children?"

"No. He didn't have any children. His nephew continued the business. It still remains in the hands of the family. Those who got your and Kilian's documents in order in Zaragoza, the real Zaragoza, are also descended from him. The only one who wanted to come here and look after the plantation was Lorenzo Garuz, who is both manager and a major shareholder."

The village, made up of little huts, was so small that they reached the territorial guard post in just a few seconds. Jacobo stopped the car beside two rifle-carrying guards who were calling good-bye to a third guard, Maximiano. He turned toward the car and frowned while the others politely greeted the new whites and thanked José for the latest delivery. Kilian did not like the look of this Maximiano, who was tall and strong with a face totally pockmarked from smallpox. The man said nothing; he just bent down to pick up a box and left.

"And who was that?" Jacobo asked, putting the car in gear again.

"I don't know," his father replied. "I suppose he's from another post. Sometimes they swap."

"First lesson, Kilian, before we enter the plantation," Jacobo explained. "You have to make sure that the guards get presents regularly, tobacco, drink, even eggs. The more you give, the faster they'll come when you need them."

Antón nodded.

"Normally, there are no problems," he added, "but you never know . . . A while ago, on other plantations, the farm laborers rioted, complaining about their contract conditions. They were lucky that the territorial guard intervened." Kilian began to get a little nervous. "But don't you worry about it, that was many years ago. Now they live fairly well. And one of the jobs of the whites is to prevent conflicts among the coloreds. You'll learn."

Jacobo slowed down as they approached the plantation.

Santa Isabel had left a deep impression on Kilian, but the entrance to the Sampaka plantation made him catch his breath.

The landscape had completely changed; what had been city buildings and kilometers of cocoa trees became a red earthen track flanked by enormous palm trees that rose into the sky and blocked out the sunlight. For each meter the car advanced through the tunnel of palms, alternately producing intermittent light and shade, his curiosity gave way to a certain anxiety. What would he find at the end of this dark, seemingly endless passage? He had the feeling of descending into a cave through a regal corridor, as if a troubling force drew him in while a voice in his head whispered that once on the other side, he would never again be the same.

He did not know it then, but years later, he would have to order new palms for that drive, which would become an emblem not only of the most majestic plantation on the island, but of his own relationship with the country. For now, it was simply the gateway to a plantation whose size totaled nine hundred hectares.

At the end of the drive, they stopped to say hello to a short, well-built man with white curly hair, sweeping the steps of the first building.

"How are you, Yeremías?" asked Jacobo from the car window. "You get plenty hen?"

"Plenty hen, Massa! A lot of hens!" answered the man with a smile. "We're never short of eggs here! Welcome back!"

"Yeremías is the handyman," explained Jacobo to Kilian and Manuel. "He is the gatekeeper, the night watchman, the one who wakes us up in the morning and brings us bread! And he is in charge of the henhouse and telling the *gardinboy* what to do!" He turned back. "Eh, *wachimán*! Remember these faces, because we will be going out a lot at night!"

Yeremías nodded and waved as the car slowly made its way through the hens and goats. Before them appeared the central yard, called Sampaka, like the plantation, where there were two swimming pools, one for the black workers and another for the white owners and staff. Kilian realized he would need to learn to swim. On the plantation, a river running through it—also called Sampaka—there were two more yards, Yakató, named after the African eggplant that looked like a tomato, and Upside, or the upper part, which was pronounced *obsay* in African English.

Altogether, the three yards contained a large number of buildings apart from the storehouses, garages, and new cocoa dryers. There were homes for over five hundred laborers' families, a carpenter's workshop, a chapel, a small school for the youngest children, a hydroelectric station that produced light and power for both the manufacturing facilities and the yards and homes, and a hospital with a surgery, two rooms with fourteen beds, and a house for the doctor. In the biggest yard, one in front of the other and beside the main stores, were the manager's house and the house for European employees, mostly Spaniards.

Kilian was stunned. No matter how much he had been told, he could not have imagined that a single property could encompass a small town with hundreds of inhabitants, surrounded by the exuberant landscape of a cocoa plantation. Wherever he looked, there was movement and action: men carrying boxes and tools, and trucks that came with supplies or workers. It was a continuous coming and going of black men, all dressed in khaki-colored shirts and ripped trousers, all barefoot or with leather-strapped sandals covered in dust.

Suddenly, he felt a knot in his stomach.

The excitement of the journey was turning into something like vertigo. He was afraid!

He was with his father and his brother—and a doctor—and he was short of breath. How was he going to fit into that vortex of green and black? And the heat, the bloody heat, it was now threatening to suffocate him.

He could not breathe. He could not think.

He felt like a coward.

He closed his eyes, and his mind filled with images of home, the fire burning in the hearth, the snow falling on the slate roofs, his mother preparing desserts, the cows stumbling on the stones in the streets.

The images came one after another, slowly calming his spirits. He had never felt so caught off guard.

He was homesick.

He would have given anything to close his eyes and appear in the House of Rabaltué. He had to overcome this . . . What would his father and brother think if they could read his mind?

He needed to breathe fresh air, but there was none to be found.

For a while, Antón watched his son. He had not noticed that the car had stopped in front of the employees' house. After such a long journey, he thought that his sons would like to get fixed up in their rooms, wash, and rest a while before meeting the manager. They would have time enough to see the main stores and the plantation the next day. They got out of the car, and Antón said to Manuel, "Until Dámaso goes, you will stay here. Afterward, you will move into the doctor's house."

He addressed the others. "Jacobo will go with you to your rooms and show you where the dining room is. I'm going to let Mr. Garuz know that you are here. We'll see each other in half an hour. Ah! Jacobo . . . it would be nice if your brother had a harmless *salto*."

Jacobo fixed not one but two glasses of water mixed with brandy, taking them to Kilian's twenty-square-meter room with a bed, a large wardrobe, a nightstand, two chairs, a table, and a washbasin with a mirror. The drink had an immediate relaxing effect on Kilian's unsettled mood. Bit by bit, he began to breathe normally, the tightness in his chest began to abate, his knees stopped shaking, and he felt prepared for his first interview with the owner and manager of the plantation.

Lorenzo Garuz received them in his office, where he had been speaking to Antón for a while. Garuz was a strong man in his forties with thick dark hair, a sharp nose, and a short mustache. He had a friendly but firm voice, and his tone was that of someone well used to giving orders. Sitting on the floor, a small boy with dark curly hair and slightly sunken eyes like the manager's amused himself by taking bits of paper out of a metal wastebasket and then putting them back in.

Garuz welcomed Kilian and Manuel—and Jacobo on his return from the holidays—and immediately checked if they had brought all the necessary papers. Kilian noticed that his father was frowning. Garuz finally put the papers away in a drawer and motioned for them to sit down in front of his desk. On the ceiling, a ventilator slowly moved some air around.

"Right, Manuel," he started to say, "you already have experience here on the island, so I don't have to explain much to you. Dámaso will be here for another fifteen days. He will bring you up to speed on everything. This is the biggest plantation, but the men are young and strong. Things won't be too complicated. Machete cuts, bumps, bruises, malaria attacks . . . nothing serious." He interrupted himself. "Can I ask you a couple of things?"

Manuel nodded.

"How come a young man like you, with a promising future, prefers the colonies to Madrid? And why have you swapped Santa Isabel for our plantation? Other than the generous salary you'll receive . . ."

Manuel did not hesitate. "I'm a doctor, but also a scientist and biologist. One of my passions is botany. I have already published some studies on the flora in Guinea. I want to make the most of my time here to increase my knowledge of the plant species and their medical applications."

The manager raised an eyebrow. "That sounds interesting. Anything that will increase our knowledge of the colony is good. I hope you'll find the time."

He turned to Kilian. "And you, young man? I hope you have come prepared to work. That's what we need here. Energetic and determined people."

"Yes, sir."

"You'll spend the next fortnight learning. Watch how things are done and follow your fellow workers. I have already told your father that you will begin above, in the Obsay yard, with Gregorio." Kilian noticed that Antón pursed his lips and Jacobo made a face. "He has been here many years, but he needs somebody strong to put things in order."

"I thought Kilian would be with me in the Yakató," Jacobo intervened. "I could also teach him—"

Garuz raised his hand to stop him. He was certain that if Kilian turned out to be a good worker like his father, keeping the brothers separate would help improve the overall performance of the plantation.

Just then the child cried out with joy. He came over to his father and handed him the treasure—an eraser—that he had found under the desk.

"Very good, Son. Here, put it in that cabinet." He looked at Jacobo and then Kilian. "It's already decided. Of the three yards, Obsay isn't working as well as it should be. It will be good to have someone new to drive things along. That's my decision."

"Yes, sir," repeated Kilian.

"And remember that the workers should be treated with authority, determination, and justice. If you do something wrong, they will criticize you. If you don't sort out the problems properly, you will lose their respect. Never show weakness. And don't allow excessive familiarity. It can be misinterpreted. Do you understand me?"

"Yes, sir." Kilian could have used another *salto*.

"One more thing. I believe you do not know how to drive, do you?"

"I don't, sir."

"Well, it's the first thing you'll have to do. Tomorrow you'll be equipped with the proper clothes, a pith helmet, and a machete. Antón, who is his boy?"

"Simón. The new one."

"Ah, yes! He seems like a good lad. Although you can never be sure. As soon as they learn your weaknesses, they come and go when they like without telling anyone. Ah, well . . . Life is tough on Fernando Po." He pointed to the other three men. "Nevertheless, if others have adapted, I don't see why you won't."

He looked at his watch and stood up.

"I assume that you are hungry for dinner. Everyone else will have finished, but I have told them that you will be over a bit later. I hope you will excuse me." He motioned toward his son. "It's getting late and I have to get back to the city. His mother is very strict about his schedule."

The other men got up and accompanied Garuz to the door, where each of them shook hands with the manager. They went out to the yard toward the building in front of them, where the dining room was located beside the living room and below the bedrooms.

On the walk to the dining room, Kilian asked, "What's wrong with this Gregorio?"

"He's a bad type," muttered Jacobo. "You'll see. Be careful."

Kilian gave his father a questioning look.

"Don't mind him, Son. You . . . just do your work and it'll be fine."

Manuel noticed a waver in Antón's voice; he looked at Kilian as he entered the dining room and sat down where his father pointed. He hoped that the young man would be able to get to experience the various pleasures of the island once he passed the initial tests of cutlass and *poto-poto*, the machetes and mud.

For the moment, Kilian opened his eyes with a childlike amazement at the food the servants had put out on the table.

"Spanish ham!" he exclaimed. "And stewed hen with potatoes!"

Jacobo laughed. "What did you think? That you'd be eating snake? The food is the same as home, even better," he added.

"We Europeans normally eat European food," said Antón. "But we are lucky enough to have a wonderful chef from Cameroon who combines the best of Spain and the best of Africa."

"And that over there, what is it?" Kilian pointed to a bowl.

Manuel bit his bottom lip with pleasure.

"Mmmm . . . That's great! *Plantín!* They have prepared fried banana with rice and palm oil as a welcome treat!" He opened his napkin and began to serve himself. "Your first exotic dish, my friend. You won't be able to live without it."

Kilian looked at it skeptically, but quickly had to admit the other men were right: the chef deserved applause. Thanks to the food and the good wine, Kilian was able to enjoy the meal, but he could not avoid fleeting images of Pasolobino, the sea voyage, and the island. Neither could he stop thinking about his first day of work with this Gregorio. His eyelids grew heavy as the wine drew out his exhaustion.

He was hardly paying attention when he heard his father get up.

"I'm going to bed, it's late."

Manuel and Jacobo decided to stay a while longer, but Kilian also got up, bleary-eyed.

"I'm going as well, or nobody will be able to wake me in the morning."

"Don't worry, you'll wake up," said Jacobo. "From half past five onward, it's impossible to sleep here."

They said good night, and Antón and Kilian left the dining room. In silence, they went up the wide staircase guarded by elegant columns and thick spindles, turning right to take the outside passageway that led to the bedrooms and was protected by a green wooden railing.

"Good night, Dad."

Antón headed to his room, a few doors farther down, but changed his mind. He turned to Kilian and looked into his eyes. He wanted to tell him so many things, to give him the strength he would need in the coming months to adapt to life on the plantation, and offer to help him in anything he needed. But he did not want to be overbearing—when it came down to it, Kilian was a fully grown man—or finish an exhausting day with a sermon. So he sighed, gave him a slap on the back, and simply said, "Don't forget to fit the mosquito net properly, Son."

A few hours later, a deep and penetrating sound, like the tapping of sticks on wood, unsuccessfully tried to bore into Kilian's head while he was still in a deep sleep. A quarter of an hour later, another hollow and fast drumroll announced the second call to get ready for work.

Someone knocked on his door as an early morning breeze rolled in.

"Massa, Massa! The *tumba* has sounded! Wake up or you will be late!"

Kilian lumbered out of bed and went to the door. A young man shot past him, carrying various packages in his arms and talking nonstop.

"I have brought you a cotton shirt and a durable pair of trousers. I'll put them here on the bed, together with the pith helmet and machete. If you hurry, you can still get coffee. And don't forget your top boots."

"You speak Spanish."

The young man tilted his head.

"Yes, of course, I'm Bubi," he said, as if that were answer enough.

Kilian nodded vaguely. "What's your name?"

"Simón, Massa. At your service."

Kilian remembered that this was his boy. He tried to remember his features, which were altogether likable. Simón had almost completely round eyes and a slightly snubbed nose, like José's. His hair, short and curly, was so dark it was impossible to see the dividing line with the skin on his forehead, which, furrowed by three horizontal lines, seemed strange on someone so young.

"And how old are you?"

"I'm not sure. Probably sixteen."

"You're not sure?" The lad shrugged. "Well, Simón. Now what am I supposed to do?"

"In ten minutes everyone has to be in formation in the yard. The whites in front."

Kilian looked through the window.

"It's still dark . . ."

"Yes, Massa. But when work begins, it will be daylight. Here the days are all the same. Twelve hours of night and twelve hours of day, year round. The shift is from six to three." He took the shirt from the bed. "I'll help dress you?"

"No, thanks." Kilian gently refused the offer. "I can do it myself."

"But . . ."

"I said no," he repeated firmly. "Wait for me outside."

In five minutes, he washed himself, got dressed, picked up the machete and the pith helmet, and left the room.

"Do I still have time for that coffee?"

The lad followed him at a quick pace along the corridor. On coming down the stairs, Kilian saw a mass of men sorting themselves into rows in the main yard. He quickly went into the dining room, drank four sips of the delicious coffee Simón handed to him, and went outside. A few meters away, he recognized the white figures taking the roll in front of hundreds of black men waiting for the beginning of the day. He took a deep breath and finished waking up on the short walk as many eyes watched him. He imagined that everyone wanted to see the new employee, and he gripped his helmet to hide his nerves.

"Just on time, Kilian," said Jacobo when he got to his side. In his hand he was holding some papers and a flexible switch. "A minute later and you wouldn't have been paid."

"What?"

"Those who aren't here on time can't get into the line and don't get paid for that day." He gave him an elbow in the ribs. "Relax, that only applies to the coloreds. Did you sleep well?" Kilian nodded. "Look, the one that's to the right of our father is Gregorio, or Massa Gregor, as they call him. He is preparing new brigades for Obsay. Good luck. We'll see each other in the afternoon."

Kilian looked closely at Gregorio, who had his back to him as he talked to Antón. He was a dark-haired man, thin and bony, almost as tall as he. Kilian greeted the two men. Gregorio turned. He had dark eyes with an icy gaze and a small mustache over thin lips. Kilian looked at his father before stretching out his hand.

"I'm Kilian, your new workmate."

Gregorio held a small leather whip whose handle he stroked methodically, sliding his fingers a couple of centimeters up and down the shaft. He stopped to accept Kilian's handshake. He observed him in detail.

"So you're Antón's other son. Soon your whole family will be here."

Kilian found Gregorio's hand cold, his smile forced, and the comment rude. He looked at his father and asked, "Where are you working today?"

"I am staying here, in the stores in the main yard. Fortunately, I no longer have to go out to the cocoa trees."

The noise from four enormous trucks with rounded hoods and wooden trailers interrupted the conversation. Gregorio went over to the rows of men and pointed at those who had to get on. Antón passed him and muttered through his teeth, "You'd better be good to the boy."

"He'll learn all he needs to know about surviving here," Gregorio replied with a smile.

Antón shot him a warning look and returned to his son.

"Go with him, Kilian."

Kilian nodded and trotted over to the trucks.

"The brigades are made up of forty men each," Gregorio told him. "One brigade per truck. You can begin counting now."

He noticed a puzzled look on the young man's face as he saw the large mass of workers.

"Look at their clothes to differentiate them. They always wear the same."

The men hopped on the trucks slowly but nimbly, speaking in a language that Kilian did not understand. He assumed it was Pichi. And to top it all, the only Spaniard he could talk to for hours was the one who was now shouting out all his sentences in the same routine tone.

"Come on, you're all asleep! *Quick! Muf, muf!*"

Only a few men were left to get onto the truck when a thin and wiry youth, a sad look about him, stopped in front of Gregorio with his head bowed and his hands crossed at his thighs.

"And what does this one want! Let's see! What thing you want?"

"I de sick, Massa."

"All time you de sick!" yelled Gregorio. "You're always sick! Every day the same story!"

"I de sick for true, Massa Gregor." He raised his hands to his chest as if to plead. "I want quinine."

"How your name?"

"Umaru, Massa."

"Right. Umaru. You want quinine?" The whip cracked against the ground. "What do you think of *this* quinine?"

Kilian opened his mouth to intervene, but the man got up onto the truck without complaint—although he shot a defiant look at the white man—followed by the last of the men, who were now quicker getting aboard. The driver of the first truck beeped the horn.

"You, stop standing about!" Gregorio shouted at Kilian, walking toward the front of the truck. "Get into the cabin!"

Kilian obeyed and sat in the right-hand seat while Gregorio climbed in behind the wheel. The convoy started out. For some minutes, neither of them said anything. Kilian looked out and saw how the barracks and the yard building gave way to cocoa trees covered by a canopy of banana trees and erythrinas, which provided shade for the delicate cocoa tree.

In some places, the branches from either side met to form a tunnel over the dusty track.

"I thought whips weren't used anymore," said Kilian.

Gregorio raised his eyebrows. "Look, lad. I've been here many years. Sometimes you have to use forceful means to get them to obey. They lie and lie. If they miss a day due to illness, they still get paid. You'll soon learn. They're excusers and superstitious. What a combination!"

Kilian said nothing.

"Regarding the whip, the day they take it from me, I'll leave. Why do you think your brother carries a *melongo* switch? The owner wants profits, and this is how you get them." He took a cigarette from his shirt pocket and lit it, exhaling smoke. "If you want us to get on well, you don't hear or see anything from now on. Clear?"

Kilian gritted his teeth. Of all possible work partners, he had to come up against this cretin. He became annoyed with his father and his brother for not warning him that men like that existed. He was not so stupid as to think that everything was going to be a bed of roses, but he had never stopped to think what "forceful means" really meant. He was itching to snap back, but knew better than to create problems on the first day.

The truck braked hard, and he hit his head against the windshield.

"What the hell!" he blurted out.

He grew silent when he saw what was happening in the truck in front. Some men had jumped from the back of the truck while it had been moving and lay twisting on the ground in pain. Others shouted and pushed their companions to try and get down. The driver had stopped the truck and came back to survey the scene, in shock. Another man ran toward them, waving his arms and shouting something that Kilian did not understand: *"Snek, snek!"*

"Damn it! I can't believe it!" Gregorio jumped to the ground, mad as hell.

Kilian was quickly by his side.

"But . . . what happened?"

"A blasted boa fell into the back of the truck, and they went crazy!"

He started walking, shouting orders to one and all, but the majority lay on the ground, injured. Those who were able to walk stayed as far away from the truck as they could. Kilian followed him without knowing quite what to do.

"Get the machete!" Gregorio shouted at him. "Now!"

Kilian ran back, got the machete from the seat, and returned a few steps away from the back of the truck.

He froze.

There in front of him slithered the biggest snake he had ever seen. It was a three-meter-long boa.

"Get up there and kill it," Gregorio ordered.

Kilian did not move. He had come upon other snakes in his life, especially while cutting the hay in the fields in the summer months, but they seemed like worms in comparison.

"Did you not hear me?"

Kilian still did not move. Gregorio sneered.

"I see that as well as being a novice you are also a coward. Give me that!"

He grabbed the machete from Kilian's hands, put one foot on the mudguard, and without thinking twice, set about slashing at the animal. Blood spurted everywhere, but it did not seem to worry him. Each time Gregorio thrust at the boa, he let out a furious bellow. When he finished, he speared a piece of the meat with the tip of the weapon and raised it above him so everybody could see.

"It's only an animal! An animal! You're afraid of this?" He pointed it at Kilian. "You're afraid of this?"

He began throwing the bits of dead snake to the ground. He jumped down, told the driver to turn around, and came over to Kilian, who was struck silent.

"You! Get those who are badly injured into the truck! They are to be taken to the hospital so the new doctor can begin to work. And the others, divide them up into the other trucks."

Kilian looked from one side to the other, deciding to begin with those men closest to him. He noticed one lying down, holding his head in his hands. Kilian knelt beside him. He did not understand what the worker was saying, but he saw that he had a cut with blood streaming from it and large tears coming from his eyes. Kilian took a handkerchief from his pocket and pressed it to the cut to stem the flow while explaining in Spanish.

"You no talk proper," the man repeated, with Kilian unable to understand him. "I no hear you."

Another man knelt down beside him and began to speak softly to the injured man. His words seemed to calm the man down. He motioned him to remain seated for a while. Grateful, Kilian tried to communicate with the impromptu helper.

"Your name?"

"My name is Waldo, Massa. I'm . . ."

"Bubi, yes. And you speak my language." Kilian raised his eyes to heaven and sighed. He immediately noticed that, like Simón—whom this man resembled, except for the absence of lines on his forehead—Waldo was dressed differently from the rest of the workers. He was wearing a white shirt, short pants, kneesocks, and strong boots. He must be older than Kilian's boy, given that he could drive. "I suppose you are one of the truck drivers."

"That's right, Massa."

"Right, Waldo. You will be my interpreter. Could you ask him if he is able to walk to the truck?"

The two men exchanged various sentences. The injured man shook his head.

"What's he saying?"

"He thinks he can walk, but he says that he won't get onto this truck full of snake's blood."

Kilian opened his mouth in surprise. He again heard shouts behind him; he turned and saw Gregorio trying to force men to get onto the blood-spattered truck.

"This man no good. Send him *na Paña*," the injured man said solemnly. Kilian looked at him and saw he was pointing at Gregorio. "I curse him."

"Waldo?"

"He says . . ." The man hesitated, but under Kilian's insistent stare decided to continue. "He says that this man is no good, that he should be sent back to Spain, and he curses him."

Before the white man had time to grasp his meaning, he hurried to explain.

"Massa, the Nigerians are very frightened of snakes. They believe that if they touch one, the evil spirits that live in it will bring bad luck and illness to them and their families as well."

Kilian looked at him in disbelief, put his arms akimbo, took a deep breath, and went over to Gregorio, who was rudely insisting that the injured men get up onto the truck.

"If we don't clean the blood, they won't get on," he said as calmly as possible.

"Don't be stupid. If one gets up, they'll all follow. Even if I have to beat them!"

"No. No, they won't." Kilian remained firm. "So we have two options. We can send Waldo in this truck to go and get a clean one from the yard or we can clean it ourselves."

Gregorio looked at him with clenched fists. He considered the options to sort out the situation before it got out of hand. Hundreds of eyes were waiting to see what would happen. There were too many blacks for two whites. If he forced them to get on, they could riot. And if he sent for another truck, they would brand him as soft for giving in to these stupid superstitions.

"Very well," he agreed. "Since you have so many ideas . . . how will we clean the truck?"

Kilian looked around him, went over to the trees that shaded the cocoa trees, and pulled off some leaves as big as his arm.

"We'll cover the floor with these leaves. That way they won't touch the blood."

In a few minutes, Kilian had piled up enough leaves to carpet a good area. With signs, he asked for help from some of the men and got them to bring the leaves in their arms. As he got onto the truck, he again heard the murmurs of disapproval when the soles of his boots came in contact with the viscous liquid, but he continued with the job. From what he could see, no one else was going to help him. Not even Gregorio. The massa just smoked a cigarette with an arrogant air.

When he finished covering the back of the truck, Waldo had already brought the injured men over so they could see how comfortable the bed was. Kilian fervently hoped that they would not complain; if they did, he would look like a complete idiot. He jumped down, took the machete, and cleaned it with a smaller leaf that he then threw to the side of the road.

"Tell them to get on, Waldo," he said, trying to make sure that his voice sounded confident even if his heart was beating hard. "Explain to them that they won't be touching any blood now."

Waldo talked to the laborers, but none of them moved. Gregorio spat out the cigarette butt, moved his head, clicking his tongue, and began walking to his truck.

"I will bring the whip," he said, "but this time, you'll use it."

Kilian heard Waldo say some phrases in Pichi. He imagined that he had translated Gregorio's words for them, because the man with the head wound stretched out his arm to grip the truck, put his foot on the ledge that sometimes served as a footrest, and got onto the back. Once up, he extended his hand toward the white man to return the bloodied handkerchief to him, but Kilian refused to take it.

"*Tenki,*" said the man, and Kilian answered with a nod.

One after another, the more than twenty injured laborers got on the truck. Waldo returned to his post as driver and started it up. As he passed Kilian, he waved. Gregorio maneuvered his truck so that the other could pass on the narrow track, then signaled to Kilian to get into the cabin so they could continue the journey to Obsay.

They did not speak a word to each other all day. For about three hours, Kilian followed in the steps of his partner between the rows of trees, clearing brush with the machete and pruning one cocoa tree after another. Nobody explained anything to him, so he just copied the laborers, who knew exactly what they had to do. Slowly but surely, they advanced to the beat of the rhythmic and slightly variable pattern of their work songs. Kilian found that the singing was a good way of keeping his mind occupied to reduce the monotony of the work. On occasion he found himself in a strange relaxed state, as if someone else were holding his machete.

They had started on the trees closest to Obsay when Gregorio gave the order to stop for lunch. They retraced their steps toward the yard, laid out in the same way as Sampaka, although much smaller.

Kilian was sweating buckets in the hot sun. The workers sat down near a wooden building built on thick white columns where various cooks prepared the meal in huge pots. Gregorio had disappeared, and Kilian did not know where to go.

"Massa!"

Kilian spotted Simón, carrying a basket on his head. He was very happy to see someone he recognized.

"What are you doing here?"

"I have brought you your food."

"Don't we all eat together?"

Simón shook his head. "The laborers are allocated their food every week, and they give it to their cooks to prepare for each day. If they are in the woods, it is brought to them, and if they are in the yard, they eat here, like today. Each white man gets his food from his boy, except when they are in the main yard. Then they eat in the dining room."

Kilian grew more and more thankful for Simón's explanations.

"And how do you know where to find me?"

"It's my job, Massa. I always know where you are."

Kilian sat down on the ground, leaning his back against a wall that offered a few meters of shade. Simón sat down beside him and pulled bread, ham, hard-boiled eggs, and drinks out of the basket. Kilian drank with gusto, but he was not hungry. He dried the sweat from his brow and cheeks with his shirtsleeve and rested his eyes for a few minutes. In the background, he could hear the murmurs coming from the workers. He sensed some voices increasing in volume and approaching steps. He opened his eyes and saw two men arguing. They stopped in front of him and between shouts seemed to be trying to explain something to him. Simón got to his feet and interrupted them so they would speak one at a time and explain what was wrong. Then he turned to Kilian.

"They are squabbling because they say the cook has changed their malanga."

Kilian furrowed his brow. When he did not respond immediately, the men resumed their argument. Kilian straightened up.

"And what does that mean?"

"The malanga, Massa. One of them had a fatter malanga, and that's why he marked it. When he went to get it, the cook had given it to someone else. He wants his malanga before the other eats it."

"And why are you telling me?" Kilian still did not understand.

"You are the judge, Massa. They will do whatever you say."

Kilian swallowed. He scratched his head and got up. Gregorio was still missing. He looked over to the workers' simple kitchen. The murmuring stopped as everyone watched. He cursed to himself and determinedly walked over to the cooks, followed by Simón.

The cook in question remained with his arms folded before two plates that contained cod, rice doused in a red sauce, and what appeared to be a boiled potato. Kilian looked at the two plates. In one, the potato was considerably larger than the other. This must be the malanga. The two men continued to gesture that they both were the owners of the bigger one. Just then, he remembered a young Jacobo and himself. They were beside the fire, waiting for their mother to take the ashes off the first baked potatoes of autumn and give one to each member of the family. When Kilian got his, he began to complain because it was much smaller than his brother's. And what did his mother do?

He signaled the cook to give him a knife. He divided both malangas into two equal parts and put one of each on either plate. He returned the knife to its owner, and without saying anything, he went back to where he was before and sat on the ground. Simón came over to him and insisted that he eat, as there were many hours still to go before dinner. Kilian nibbled, but without much appetite. The absurdness of the situation with the potato was still going around in his head.

"It was the fairest way, don't you think?" he said finally.

Simón put on a thoughtful expression, and his forehead wrinkled.

"Simón?"

"Oh, yes, yes, of course, Massa," he replied. "It was fair . . . but not for the real owner of the big malanga."

During the following days, Kilian spent his time amid the noisy trucks and dusty tracks, Nigerian work songs, shouts in Pichi, machete slashes, quarrels and arguments, and the leaves of banana, erythrina, and cocoa trees.

When he arrived at the yard in Sampaka, he was so tired he could barely eat; he attended the driving lessons given by Jacobo and Waldo, wrote a few lines of forced happiness to Mariana and Catalina, and went to bed early, itchy with sweat.

Antón and Jacobo were not oblivious to his struggles. At dinner, he barely spoke, and it was obvious that there was no friendship between him and Gregorio. They simply ignored each other, although Gregorio pestered Kilian by making comments in front of the manager, questioning his courage and strength, comments that made it difficult for Jacobo not to get involved in a fight with him.

One night when Kilian stood to go without finishing dessert, Antón decided to follow him to his room.

"Give it time, Son," he said as they left the dining room. "It's hard at first, but bit by bit, you will adapt. I know how you feel. I went through it as well."

Kilian raised his eyebrows. "Did you also have to work with someone like Gregorio?"

"I wasn't talking about that," Antón quickly interjected. "What I mean is . . ." He scratched his head and lowered his gaze. "I don't know how or when, and I hardly know anything about the rest of Africa, but the day will come when this small island will take control of you, and you'll never want to leave. It might be man's amazing ability to adapt. Or perhaps there is something mysterious about this place." He stretched out his hand to point out the landscape that extended into the distance and looked Kilian in the eye again. "But I don't know anyone who has left here without shedding tears of grief."

Years would have to pass for Kilian to understand each and every one of those words with the intensity of a curse fulfilled.

4

Fine City

The Fair City

"All right," Jacobo said, giving in, "but you're driving on the way back."

Kilian quickly got into the open-back van that everyone called a *picú*, a simplification of the English pickup, before his brother changed his mind. After fifteen days of intensive classes with Waldo and Jacobo along the roads of the plantation, he had gotten his driving license for cars and trucks. Still, to venture into the city was another story.

"As soon as I've done the route once with you, I'll be able to do it on my own," he promised.

The manager had asked them to buy tools and materials from the stores in Santa Isabel. The day was swelteringly hot and hazy, typical of the dry season, which lasted from November until the end of March. In *the dry*, trees were felled for new farmland, firewood was prepared for the dryers, the cocoa trees were pruned, and the *bikoro*, the weed that grew around it, was cleared. Additionally, the seed nurseries were tended, and the roads and tracks on the plantation were built and mended. Kilian had learned that the most important task was ground clearing, keeping the machetes in use despite the terrible heat, up and down, from one side to the other, to get rid of the weeds that mysteriously sprung up from one day to the next.

It was early in the morning, and Kilian was already sweating inside the *picú*. Soon the itching that had taken control of his body from day one would return. He would have given anything to have four hands to scratch himself. Unfortunately, the remedies passed on by Manuel had not solved the problem. He could only hope that his skin would become used to the surroundings and the stinging pains would fade.

"You have no idea how much I miss the fresh mountain air!" He sighed, thinking of Pasolobino. "This heat will be the death of me."

"Stop being dramatic!" Jacobo drove with his elbow leaning on the open car window. "At least our clothes aren't sticking to our skin at the moment. Wait and see when *the wet* comes. From April to October, you'll be terribly sticky all day."

He stretched his arm out the window so his hand could play with the breeze.

"Thank God, today we'll have the Saharan wind's apprentice, the harmattan, to relieve us."

Kilian noticed that the sky above the narrow road was covered by a fine suspended dust and had taken on a reddish-gray hue.

"I don't understand how this annoying wind that clouds everything and hurts the eyes can be a relief." He remembered the snow-clearing gales. "To me it's stifling."

"Well, wait and see when it really blows! You won't be able to see anything, not even the sun, for days. You will chew sand!"

Kilian made a face of disgust. Jacobo looked at him out of the corner of his eye. His brother's skin was sunburned, but weeks more would have to pass before it developed into a deep tan. The same would happen with his mood. He himself had gone through this process. As Kilian's arms became more muscular and his skin tougher, he would become less like an aloof teenager and grow used to the rigors of the wild land. Jacobo could imagine what was going through his brother's head. Between the suffocating heat, the exhausting work, the inane arguments of the laborers and foremen, his body being possessed by a continuous burning, and his *marvelous* relationship with the insufferable Massa Gregor, his brother surely felt incapable of encountering any of the wonders he had imagined before coming to the island. Perhaps, Jacobo thought, the time had come to introduce him to some of his native girlfriends to lift his spirits. One of the advantages of a bachelor's life in Fernando Po was that there were no limits to desire!

"So, how are things going in Obsay?" Jacobo asked nonchalantly.

Kilian took a few seconds to answer. Jacobo was the only person he could confide in, but he did not want to seem whiny. Jacobo radiated power and energy from every pore of his skin. He never went unnoticed. Kilian had never seen him sad, not even during his school days. Jacobo was sure of what he wanted out of life: to enjoy every second to the fullest without asking any deep questions. He had to work because he had no choice, but if there was a bad harvest one year, it was not his problem; he would get paid all the same. He would not suffer. Jacobo never suffered for anything.

"Has the cat caught your tongue?"

"Eh? No, no. Gregorio is still the same, making me lose face in front of the laborers. He tells them behind my back not to pay any attention to me, as I'm new, but later he sends them to me to sort out their problems. Waldo told me."

"He's jealous of you. Garuz said he needed someone to put things right in that yard. It was very intelligent on his part to send someone new who shows interest in doing things right. If you continue like this, you'll soon be in charge of the main yard."

"I don't know. Maybe I'm just not a leader. It's difficult to get the laborers to do what I tell them. I have to repeat things twenty times.

They wait until I get annoyed and shout at them, and then they look at me with a smile and do it."

"Threaten to warn the guards. Or send them to the Santa Isabel Labor Office for fines."

"I've already done that." Kilian bit his lip. "The problem is I've told them a thousand times what I'm going to do, but later I regret it and don't follow through. And then they don't believe me. They don't take a darn bit of notice."

"Then give them one or two cracks of the cane and you'll see how they obey!"

Kilian looked at him in surprise.

"But I've never hit anyone in my life!" he protested.

"You've never?" joked Jacobo. "Have you forgotten all the fights we had when we were children?"

"That was different."

"If you can't do it, order one of the foremen to do it instead. Problem solved." Jacobo's tone got a bit harder. "Look, Kilian, the sooner they respect you, the better. Many other Spaniards would like to be in your position, earning what you earn . . ."

Kilian nodded in silence. He looked out the window and saw some small monkeys who seemed to be waving to the *picú* from the cocoa trees. A thick green blanket led to the outskirts of Santa Isabel, where the track turned into a tarmac road.

"We'll first do a quick trip round the city so you can get your bearings," Jacobo said. "We have plenty of time. And stop scratching yourself! You're making me nervous."

"I can't help it!" Kilian placed his hands under his thighs.

Jacobo drove through the narrow streets, which seemed to have been drawn with a ruling pen, from the seafront to the river consul, marking the boundary with the forest. They began by visiting the high part of the city, mainly inhabited by Nigerians. Throngs of children ran about with rubber balls made from the viscous liquid of the rubber tree, or shooting dry pellets from makeshift blowpipes using the hollow branches of the papaya tree. Young men and women, the men bare chested and the women carrying bundles on their heads and children in their arms, walked along the exotic stalls filled with local produce or goods imported from around the globe. The sellers, using leaf swats, tried to shoo away the persistent flies that prowled around the sticks on which fish and monkey and *gronbif*, a field rat the size of a hare, meat were strung. The spicy smells of the prepared stews, on display beside kola nuts that the natives ate to combat tiredness, and of the fresh vegetables laid out on sheets of the *Ébano* newspaper or on banana leaves, reached the car. It was a cornucopia of noise, color, smell, and movement. A feast for the senses.

Kilian noticed that although the majority of the women were wearing blouses over the *clotes*, which the soft breeze made stick to their legs, some women had bare breasts. With a roguish smile on his face and a gleam of novel excitement in his eyes, he gazed at the dark, firm nipples of the girls. He smiled, imagining his girlfriends in Pasolobino dressed, or rather *undressed*, like so.

The houses in the upper quarter were built of sheets of zinc or calabo wood, with the roofs also of zinc or palm leaves called nipa interwoven with cords of *melongo*. As the brothers neared the area where the Europeans and wealthy businesspeople of all races lived, the buildings turned into a series of similar houses surrounded by well-kept gardens with exotic fruit trees—papayas, coconuts, mangoes, guavas, and avocados—and shrubs covered in flowers—dahlias, roses, and chrysanthemums. The lower level and the rear of many of these houses were storerooms and shops, and the upper stories were the living quarters.

Jacobo stopped the pickup in front of one of these houses, jumped out, and motioned to his brother to do the same. "I'm going to the chemist's at the corner for a minute to see if they can give me something for that *cro-cró* that's killing you." He pointed to a shop named Factoría

Ribagorza, owned by a family from the valley of Pasolobino. "Start on the list and tell them to put it all on the plantation's account."

When he went in, Kilian was surprised by the wide range of objects that were stacked on the floor and shelves. He recognized all types of tools—typical of a hardware shop—beside jars of preserves, shoes, sewing machines, perfumes, and car accessories. A pleasant little voice called from behind him:

"If you can't find what you're looking for, it can be ordered."

He turned around and discovered a girl about his own age, quite pretty, not very tall, brown haired, and with a friendly look that he found vaguely familiar. To his surprise, he saw she wore green pleated trousers and a white short-sleeved diamond-patterned sweater. A fetching red scarf adorned her neck. The girl squinted at him and exclaimed, "But you're Kilian, Jacobo's brother! You look a lot alike! Don't remember me?"

Then he remembered. He had been to her house, some three kilometers from Pasolobino, accompanying his father. Each time Antón returned from Fernando Po, he visited the grandparents and family of the girl and brought them packages from her parents, who lived on the island. While Antón talked with the adults, Kilian played with a mischievous child who told him that one day she would go to Africa.

"Julia? Forgive me, but you've changed so much . . ."

"So have you." The girl moved her hand in the air up and down. "You've grown a lot since"—she calculated in her head—"you were ten."

"Has it been that long since you've been home? I mean, Spain? And your parents? Are they well?"

Julia nodded. "Things are going well for us here, so after finishing secondary school at the Colonial Institute, I decided to help with the family business." She shrugged. "Every year I say I will go back to Pasolobino, and for one reason or another, I don't! I'm always asking Jacobo about our beloved mountains. Has he come back from his holiday yet?"

Kilian brought her up to date on the village, answering all her questions about recent christenings, weddings, and funerals. For some minutes, the conversation about their common world, Pasolobino, made him forget his itchiness.

"Sorry for the interrogation!" she suddenly exclaimed. "And what about you? How are you adapting to your new life?"

Kilian stretched out his arms so that she could see the state of his skin.

"I see." Julia played it down. "Don't worry. It goes away in the end."

"Everyone says the same thing. They say I shouldn't worry." He stooped down and lowered his voice. "I must confess something to you. I thought colonial life would be different."

Julia burst out laughing. "Within a few months, you will have changed your mind!" He scoffed as she put her hands on her hips and cocked her head. "How much do you bet?"

At that moment, the door opened and Jacobo entered. He came over and affectionately greeted the girl, giving her two kisses on the cheeks. Kilian noticed how Julia blushed slightly.

"Great to see you again. How did your holidays go?"

"I always enjoy holidays. And even more when they are paid!"

"You didn't miss *us* even the slightest bit?" Julia teased.

"You know what happens when *we cocoa men* leave the island." Jacobo retained the ironic plural. "*We* are tired of weeds and machetes . . ." Seeing the disappointment on her face, he qualified himself. "But you also know that *we* like to come back. By the way"—he quickly changed the subject—"be sure we remember to buy limes. They sure go through them!" He turned to Kilian. "Have you got everything we need?"

His brother shook his head. He took the list out of his pocket and gave it to Julia, who busied herself preparing the goods while the men looked at the shelves in case they needed anything else.

"That's nougat from last Christmas," said Julia on seeing Kilian trying to decipher the contents of a tin. "As you can see, we have everything here."

"Tinned nougat!"

"When somebody wants something, it sharpens the mind."

Soon the parcels were ready. Jacobo signed the receipt and paid for a bottle of Tullamore Dew Irish whiskey with his own coupon.

"For the old doctor's going-away party," he whispered to Kilian, giving him a wink. "It's tonight."

Julia accompanied them to the pickup. "How would you like to come to the house for lunch or dinner this week? My parents would be happy to see you." Before Jacobo had a chance to make an excuse, she added, "And it would be good for Kilian to get out of the forest."

Jacobo had a different type of party in mind for his brother. Such soirees were fine for young married couples. Single men looked for other types of entertainment. He tried to come up with a polite way of refusing the invitation, but Kilian interrupted. "Thanks, Julia. We'd be delighted. Wouldn't we, Jacobo?"

"Yes, yes, of course."

"We'll see each other this week then." Julia beamed. "I'll send you an invitation with the boy. Bye for now!"

Satisfied, she turned around and went back to work with a spring in her step.

Jacobo put his hand in his pocket, took out a small jar of cream, and threw it angrily to his brother before getting into the vehicle. "Take this!"

Kilian got into the pickup and began to spread the cream on his arms and the top half of his chest. Jacobo drove in silence.

"Do you mind telling me what's bugging you?" Kilian asked after a while.

Jacobo pursed his lips and shook his head. "She certainly got her way!"

"Are you referring to Julia? She seemed a very nice and intelligent woman. She's easy to talk to and has a great sense of humor."

"She's all yours."

Kilian frowned, then let out a roar of laughter while slapping his thighs. "So she's in love with you! You kept that very quiet . . ."

"And what's there to say? She's not the first nor the last to chase me."

"They won't all be like Julia."

"You're dead right." Jacobo nodded with a devilish smile. "In other circumstances, I would take her for a stroll down Lover's Lane at Punta Fernanda. But it's too early."

"Too early for what?"

"What do you think? For me to get engaged." When he saw that Kilian looked confused, Jacobo gave an over-the-top sigh. "Boy, sometimes you're a bit thick. Look, Kilian, here, at our age, we all have many . . . let's say . . . *girlfriends*, but no one steady. Well, some do have a steady girl, but not like Julia, I mean, not one of ours, but the steady ones cause problems because they become infatuated and want money, or they entangle you with a child . . . I try not to have anyone steady. I hope you'll also be sensible . . . I don't know if you get what I'm saying."

Kilian had gotten some idea. He looked down at his hands. "But our father as well? I mean, someone married who spends long periods alone here . . ."

Imagining Antón in the arms of a woman who was not Mariana caused a strange knot in Kilian's stomach.

"Look, I don't know what he might have done when he was younger, nor have I asked him. But since I've been here on the island, I haven't heard or seen anything untoward. And usually these things come out."

Kilian breathed out a sigh of relief.

"Anyway, I'm not surprised. You know what Dad's like on religion and morality . . ."

"And he loves Mom a lot . . . He wouldn't do that to her—be unfaithful, I mean."

"Well, yes, but other married men also love their wives back in Spain and don't hesitate to look for company to keep themselves amused during the long campaigns. Love has nothing to do with these things."

Kilian did not completely agree, but he did not comment. Far from answering his questions, the embarrassing conversation had led to many more. He decided to put an end to the serious mood.

"And where do you see your *girlfriends*? In the fortnight I've been here, I haven't seen any . . ."

Jacobo gave him a rakish grin. "You'll see, Kilian, you'll see. What's more, I think it's time that I introduce you to them soon. You're the very type who'd easily fall for someone like Julia. I'm not going to let you miss the best this island has . . ."

"Thanks for your concern," said Kilian derisively. "I hope I measure up."

He noticed that his brother was smiling. Turning his head and looking out the window, he saw that they had returned to Zaragoza. His first visit to the city had made him feel better. The itching had not stopped, but his talk with Julia had made him feel less lonely, and the drive through the tunnel of palm trees did not seem so strange. He even noticed a comforting gesture of familiarity in the *wachimán* Yeremías's greeting.

"By the way, Jacobo," he said when the pickup stopped in front of the white-columned porch of the beautiful main house.

"Yes?"

"It was my turn to drive."

After unloading the purchases, Jacobo took another vehicle and went off to Yakató. Kilian sat in the driver's seat to join in the day's work at Obsay. He moved the *picú* forward a few meters in fits and starts and stopped again to return the hello he got from Antón, who was walking at a distance toward the main stores accompanied by the ever-present

José. Kilian waited until they had gone into the building—he did not want any witnesses. Fortunately, at this time of day, there was nobody in the main yard.

He arrived at Obsay, sweating buckets but proud that he had not stalled the engine even once. He parked the pickup and started walking briskly to the cocoa trees along the main path. A little later, he heard the workers singing. A few meters farther on, he spotted a woman dressed in a colorful *clote*, carrying a large empty basket on her head. He assumed she was looking for wild fruit or wood. Suddenly, the woman stopped as if she had heard something from the undergrowth, and without hesitating, she went into the jungle. Kilian did not pay it any mind, knowing that the Calabar women were used to the forest. They often went there with food for their husbands when they were working.

He continued his journey until he heard the murmuring of the laborers, the chop, chop of pruning and slashing, and the whirring of the sprayers spitting out the Bordeaux mixture of copper sulfate and lime that stopped the young plants from getting the mildew that attacked during the rainy season.

Soon afterward, he came upon the first workers of a long row and saw Nelson, one of the foremen, at the end of it. He gave him a thumbs-up to ask if everything was going well. The man nodded. Kilian then looked at the laborer closest to him. He racked his brain for a simple question, wanting to give the workers the chance to see how his Pichi had improved.

"Whose side Massa Gregor?"

"I no know, Massa Kilian." The man shrugged, raised his hand, and waved it toward various places. "All we done come together, but he done go."

Kilian did not understand anything, but nodded. He wasn't sure what to do, so he began walking through the laborers, paying attention to what they were doing and moving his head up and down as a sign of approval, until he got up to Nelson, just where the cocoa trees ended and the jungle began. Nelson, a well-built man as tall as Kilian, with a completely round, flat face and the beginnings of a double chin, was squabbling with a man while shaking the sprayer he held in his hands. When he saw Kilian, he straightened up.

"Everything's fine, Massa," he stuttered in Spanish with a strong accent. Spanish proficiency was a prerequisite for promotion to foreman. "The mixture should be properly stirred to prevent damage to the trees."

Kilian agreed. He felt a little ridiculous pretending he was in control when there was so much he did not know. He would have preferred to help in the yards, fixing the barracks. When it came to building and construction, he could run rings around them, thanks to the many hours spent maintaining the house and the hay sheds in Pasolobino. As far as cocoa went, he was still clueless.

"I'll be back in a minute," he said to Nelson, collecting some fresh leaves from the ground.

Going into the woods to relieve oneself was a good way of ending an awkward conversation. The first meters were fairly clear, but after a few steps, Kilian had to use the machete to clear the way to get to a suitable spot. He pulled down his trousers and relaxed, observing as a yellow-and-black spider put the final touches on a thick web that stretched from one plant to another. Just as well, he thought, that he was not afraid of spiders or tarantulas. These crawlers were ten times bigger and hairier than those in Pasolobino, but none were immune to a good stomping. Snakes were a different matter. He could not stand them. Kilian was always on guard, especially after the incident with the boa.

When he finished, he cleaned himself with the leaves and stood up by grabbing on to a branch that suddenly came to life. Kilian stumbled back and stood dead still. The greenish-brown branch was slowly twisting. He squinted his eyes and made out a head and a tongue slithering in the air.

Slowly, he did up his trousers and began walking backward. He turned and hurriedly walked away, his heart beating wildly. After a few minutes, he realized he was heading in the wrong direction. He cursed under his breath and retraced his steps. Just then he heard an exclamation, only a few meters from where he stood. He listened carefully and recognized Gregorio's voice. He had probably gone into the woods for the same reason. He gave a sigh of relief. His partner knew every inch of the area. He charged through a small clearing in the undergrowth,

"Gregorio! You're not going to believe it, but I . . ."

He stopped dead.

Gregorio was lying facedown, wrapped in the intense embrace of someone between whose legs he was convulsing and moaning. A woman's hand pointed to Kilian. Gregorio turned his head and swore.

"Do you like watching or something?" he shouted as he got to his feet and tried to pull up his pants.

Kilian went red seeing the man's penis, still erect between his bony legs. The woman stayed on the ground, smiling and completely naked on the orange *clote*. Beside her was an empty basket. He recognized the woman who had gone into the forest from the cocoa trees.

"I'm sorry . . . ," he began to apologize. "I went into the forest and got lost. I didn't mean to disturb you."

"Well, you have! You've left me half done!"

He motioned to the woman to get up. She rose and fixed the cloth around her waist. She picked up the basket, placed it on her head, intending to leave, and put out her hand to the massa.

"Give me what you please," she said.

"No chance!" Gregorio replied. "This time I didn't finish, so it doesn't count." He made gestures for her to disappear.

"You no give me some *moni*." The woman gave him an annoyed look.

"Go away! I no give nothing now. Tomorrow, I go call you again."

The woman gritted her teeth and went off in a huff. Gregorio picked up his helmet from the ground, shook it, and put it on his head.

"And you," he said to Kilian sarcastically, "don't leave the path if you don't want to get lost." He passed him without a second look. "You being so brave, you wouldn't survive even a couple of hours in the jungle."

Kilian clenched his fists and followed him in silence, still embarrassed. Without warning, another wave of itches invaded his skin, and he began scratching furiously.

His brother was right. He would have to wake up.

That night, as arranged, they all ate dinner together to say farewell to Dámaso, an even-tempered man with a completely white head of hair and soft features who was returning to Spain after almost three decades of service as a doctor in the colony.

They sat around the table, grouped by years of experience. On one end sat the longest-serving employees: Lorenzo, Antón, Dámaso, Father Rafael—who was in charge of saying mass in the village of Zaragoza—Gregorio, and Santiago. At the other end sat those under thirty: Manuel, Jacobo, Kilian, Mateo, and Marcial. Except for the harvest party or some official visit, rarely was the dining room so lively. While the boys, including Simón, served the meal, the older men reminisced about their first years on the island; the young ones listened with the arrogance of inexperience.

When the meal was over, the manager honored his good friend Dámaso with a speech. Kilian did not hear much, due to the generous glasses of Azpilicueta Rioja wine that Garuz had brought, not to mention the burning sensation all over his body. There were rounds of applause, emotions, and words of thanks.

As more wine was poured, the conversation grew louder.

"Have you said your good-byes to everyone?" Mateo asked mischievously. A likable man from Madrid, he was small and wiry, his lips always ready to break into a broad smile under his sharp nose and thin mustache.

"I think so," answered the doctor.

"Everyone?" insisted Marcial, a hairy man almost two meters tall with full features and a heart as large as his hands, which were like shovels. He was Jacobo's partner in the Yakató yard.

The doctor shook his head, smiling.

"Those who really matter to me are at this table," he said, gesturing to them all.

"If Dámaso says he has, he has." Santiago, a quiet and sensible man around Antón's age with lank hair and a thin, pale face, came to his defense.

"Well, I know a person who will be very sad tonight," Jacobo chipped in.

The younger ones burst out laughing. Everyone except Kilian.

"That's enough, Jacobo!" reprimanded Antón, glancing warily at Father Rafael.

Jacobo raised his hands and shrugged innocently.

"Young man, don't be cheeky," threatened Dámaso, wagging his finger in the air. "Let he who is without sin cast the first stone. Right, Father?"

The others laughed again. Father Rafael, a friendly man with a round face, a set of full lips, a beard, and a receding hairline, went visibly red in the face. Dámaso hurried to clarify. "Of course, I wasn't referring to you, Father Rafael. I was quoting the Bible. These young people!" He shook his head. "They think we're all cut from the same cloth."

"Look where it's gotten them." The priest nodded. "I never get tired of repeating that the longer a man can go without a woman, the better off he is, health- and pocket-wise. Yet I'm afraid it's like preaching in the desert in this land of sin." He sighed and looked at Kilian. "Mind who you mix with, young man. I'm referring to these ruffians, of course," he added with a conspiring wink that brought on another bout of laughter.

"Well, I think it's time for bed, don't you think?" Dámaso put his hands on the table and pushed himself up. "I've a long journey ahead of me."

"I'm also going to bed," said Antón, yawning.

Kilian and Jacobo exchanged glances, both thinking the same thing. Lately, he was always tired. There were dark bags under his eyes. What a change from the father they remembered from their youth! They had never once seen him sick. He had been a strong man, both physically and morally. Years before, just two days after arriving in Pasolobino from Africa, he would work in the fields as if he had never left. *Perhaps he should take a holiday,* thought Kilian. *Or retire from the colonies, like Dámaso.*

The old doctor said good-bye to them one by one with a warm handshake before heading out the door with Antón, Lorenzo, Santiago, and Father Rafael. Jacobo also left, making a sign that he would be back shortly. As he got to the door, Dámaso turned and said, "By the way, Manuel, can I give you a last piece of advice?" Manuel nodded. "It has to do with Kilian's itch." He paused to ensure that all the younger ones were listening. "Salicylic iodized alcohol." Kilian's eyes widened, and Manuel fixed his glasses, smiling thankfully for the subtle manner in which Dámaso had passed the baton. "Get him to rub it all over his body, and in a fortnight the rash will have disappeared. Good night."

"Good night and a good trip," Jacobo said as he returned with the bottle of whiskey he had bought in Julia's shop. "If you don't mind, we will have a last drink to your health."

Dámaso gave him a friendly pat on the back and left with a heavy heart, thinking of the many nights he had spent in just the same manner.

Jacobo asked Simón to bring clean glasses. Between sips and laughter, Kilian learned that the person who would miss Dámaso most was Regina, his *close friend* over the last ten years.

"Ten years! But doesn't he have a wife and children in Spain?" he asked, slurring his words.

"Exactly for that reason!" Marcial gave him another shot. He was capable of taking three times the amount of alcohol as everyone else. "Spain is very far away."

"And what can we do about it? They know our weakness!"

Kilian thought of Gregorio writhing in the forest and his conversation in the pickup with Jacobo.

"There is no doubt that our girlfriends help make life on the island more bearable." Jacobo raised his glass above his head. "A toast to them!"

The others drank.

"And what will happen to this Regina now?" Kilian asked.

"What happens?" responded Marcial, fighting with the buttons of his shirt. The ceiling fan did not offer the slightest relief from the heat. "She'll be sad for a few days, and then she'll look for another. It's what they all do. Though she's getting on a bit," he added, slowly scratching one of his big ears. "Either way, she has lived very well these past years, like a lady. Dámaso was a gentleman."

Kilian, glassy-eyed, contemplated the deep amber color of the liquid in his glass. He found their notions of gentlemanly behavior peculiar. According to them, it was normal to share such intimacy with a woman for ten years and then return to the warmth of your wife's arms as if nothing had happened.

Manuel had been watching Kilian for a while. He could imagine the questions going through his mind. It was not easy for the young Spaniard, brought up in an environment where adultery was considered a crime and couples could not even show affection in public. Here, sex was enjoyed with the same lack of ceremony as meals. These were rules that most men adapted to easily, but not all. Compared to his friends, Manuel led a relatively chaste life.

"And what happens if children are born from these unions?" Kilian asked.

"There aren't that many really . . . ," Jacobo interjected.

"True, the coloreds know how to avoid it." Gregorio nodded.

"Yes, there are. I know there are," Manuel interrupted in a hard voice. "But we don't want to see them. Where do you think all the mulattos in Santa Isabel come from?"

Mateo and Marcial traded looks before hanging their heads. Jacobo took advantage of the moment to refill the glasses.

"Look, Kilian, usually the child lives with the mother and she receives financial support. I know of very few cases—I could count them on one hand—where the mulatto children were recognized or sent to study in Spain. It's very rare."

"And do you know of any case in which a white man has married a black woman?"

"To date, no. And if anyone has tried, they would be forced to go to Spain."

"Why would anyone want to marry a black woman?" scoffed Gregorio.

"There's no reason!" responded Marcial, pushing his wide shoulders against the back of the chair. "If they already give you everything you want without a visit to the altar."

Jacobo, Mateo, and Gregorio smiled knowingly. Manuel wrinkled his nose as Kilian fell silent.

Gregorio had been closely watching him. "So you are interested in the subject. Is it because you want to try them out?"

Kilian did not answer.

"Leave the guy alone, come on," said Mateo, gently nudging his arm.

Gregorio squinted and leaned forward. "Or maybe it's because you think Antón is a saint? With the years he has spent on Fernando Po, he's sure to have had a load of *miningas!*"

"Gregorio . . . ," insisted Mateo on noticing the color drain from Jacobo's face.

It was one thing to joke; it was another to lie maliciously. Everyone there knew Antón extremely well. And in any case, conversations among gentlemen had an implicit bond of discretion. Even jokes had limits. That's how things worked on the island.

"It's possible you have mulatto brothers and sisters running around out there," continued Gregorio with a nasty smile. "What would your mother think, huh?"

"That's enough," Jacobo seethed. "Be very careful about what you say! Do you hear me? That's a lie and you know it!"

"Fine, fine, relax!" Gregorio said arrogantly. "But as far as I know, he's just as much a man as everyone else . . ."

Manuel turned on him next. "Much more of a man than you."

"Don't get us started," added Mateo, stroking his mustache.

"I was only winding up the new guy!" Gregorio protested. "It was a joke. Although I wouldn't put my hand in the fire, not even for Antón."

Kilian moved the whiskey around his glass in slow circular motions, thinking clearly again. He raised his eyes and stared, hard and cold, at Gregorio. "The next time you insult me or my family," he spit out, "you'll regret it."

Gregorio let out a snort and got to his feet. "You don't have a sense of humor either?"

"That's enough, Gregorio," said Manuel sharply.

"Yes, enough." Marcial stood, towering above him.

"You are well protected"—Gregorio pointed to the others—"but one day you won't have anyone else around to defend you."

Jacobo strode toward Gregorio and gripped his arm powerfully. "Are you threatening my brother?"

Gregorio tore himself away and stormed out. Marcial and Jacobo sat down and took another shot to calm their nerves.

"Don't mind him, Kilian," said Marcial finally. "He wasn't like this before. He's grown brutish. A barking dog . . ."

"Well," answered Kilian quietly. "That's the last time he gets away with it."

On Friday night, Yeremías gave Simón a note from Julia's boy, inviting the brothers and Antón to dinner at her family's house.

Kilian waited until Saturday morning before telling Jacobo. At six, he went down to the yard, where the laborers waited for their week's wages. They stayed in rows until they were called, one by one, to get their money and put their fingerprints on the list set out on the table. The job, like doling out food on Mondays, took two hours. As the laborers waited to hear their names, they rubbed their teeth with the ever-present chock sticks, small brushes made from roots, which made their teeth the envy of all.

Kilian found Jacobo and gave him Julia's note to read.

"Very clever," he scoffed. "She sent it to you to make sure we go. Look at all the days available! But no . . . she had to pick Saturday."

"And what's the difference between one day and another?"

"Saturday nights are sacred, Kilian. For everybody. Look at the men. Aren't they happy? They get paid this morning and will spend some of it in Santa Isabel tonight."

"Shall I let her know that we are going, or not?"

"Yes, yes, sure. Now go with Gregorio or you'll never finish. Today he's as easy as pie."

When Kilian got to Gregorio's table, his partner gave him the list of brigades. Without meeting his gaze, he got up from the table and said, "Here, you continue. I'll go and prepare the material for Obsay. Nelson will help you."

Kilian sat down and continued reading the names on the list. He noted that Simón looked bored. The lad was dressed the same as every other day, in shorts and a short-sleeved shirt, both beige. His feet were covered with a pair of simple sandals made from leather straps instead of boots. Though he was mostly similar in appearance to other lads his age, Simón had enormous eyes that shone as if on continuous alert, moving from side to side to take in everything that was going on around him. Kilian waved at him to come over to the table and help Nelson in translating. As he called out another name, the man stepped up with another at his side, complaining nonstop. Kilian cursed his bad luck. The day had begun with another argument.

"What's going on, Nelson?"

"This man says that Umaru owes him money."

The name sounded familiar. Kilian looked up and recognized him from the day of the boa incident. He was the one who had begged for quinine.

"Why do you owe him money?" he asked.

Although Nelson was translating, Kilian could tell just from Umaru's gestures that he had no intention of paying anything. The other man kept interrupting, growing more and more annoyed. A silence fell over the rest of the workers as they stopped to listen to the row.

"Ekon offered him his wife. Umaru accepted her services and now doesn't want to pay."

Kilian blinked and pursed his lips to stop from laughing. He looked at the handsome man, of medium height, with very short hair, high cheekbones, and dimples in his cheeks.

"You're telling me that Ekon *lent out* his wife?"

"Yes, that's right," answered Nelson without batting an eye. "Umaru is single. Single men need women. The married ones take advantage if the woman is willing. Ekon wants his money."

"*Moni, moni*, yes, Massa!" repeated Ekon insistently, nodding.

"*Moni*, no, Massa! *Moni*, no!" repeated Umaru, shaking his head.

Kilian sighed. He hated acting as judge. At this rate they would never be finished.

"Are there any witnesses?" he asked.

Nelson translated the question loudly. A colossus almost two meters tall with arms like legs stepped forward and spoke to the foreman.

"Mosi says he saw them in the forest. Twice."

Kilian smiled. It seemed he was not the only one who stumbled onto illicit happenings in the forest. He asked the amount owed, took the quantity out of Umaru's envelope, and put it in Ekon's.

"There is nothing more to talk about." He handed over the two envelopes to the satisfaction of one and the anger of the other. Afterward, he turned to Simón. "Do you agree?"

Simón nodded, and Kilian exhaled in relief.

"*Palabra conclú*, case closed, then," Kilian said.

At seven o'clock, the day ended and darkness descended. Kilian and Jacobo got into the pickup to go to the city. At the entrance, Jacobo shouted to Yeremías, "Remember to get Waldo to do what I told him!"

"What does Waldo have to do?" Kilian asked.

"Nothing important."

On the way out of Zaragoza, Kilian saw many of the laborers laughing and joking with their shoes in their hands. They had changed out of their old and dirty clothes into long trousers and clean white shirts.

"What are they doing?" he asked his brother.

"They're waiting for the bus to go out and celebrate in Santa Isabel."

"And why are they carrying their shoes? So as not to dirty them?"

"More likely so as to not wear them out. They try and save as much as they can." He chuckled. "But tonight they'll be spending a little of their earnings on alcohol and women. By the way, I see you're scratching less."

"Manuel prepared Dámaso's remedy. It seems to be working."

"Ah!" exclaimed Jacobo. "There is nothing like experience!" Kilian agreed.

"Hey, Jacobo. Don't you think Dad should go home? Each time I see him, he's more exhausted. He didn't even want to come with us to dinner tonight."

"I agree, but he's very stubborn. I've brought it up many times, and he just tells me he knows what he's doing and that it's normal to get tired at his age. He doesn't even want Manuel to examine him. I don't know."

They parked the pickup in front of the Ribagorza store and climbed the side stairs to knock. Julia took less than two seconds to swing open the door and invite them into a large and welcoming living room, which opened onto a terrace that served as both a dining room and a sitting room. It had a large table with wooden chairs in front of a rattan sofa. Kilian's eyes wandered the walls, decorated with pictures of African themes, a red wooden spear almost two meters long, and a carey shell. The exception was a photograph of Pasolobino that brought out a nostalgic smile. On his right was an ivory tusk on a small piece of furniture, and scattered round the room were numerous ebony figurines. The most Western touch came from the Grundig record player and radio that sat on a small table beside the sofa, next to some issues of *Hola* and *Reader's Digest*.

Julia introduced Kilian to her parents, Generosa and Emilio, and offered the brothers a *contriti*, a popular island infusion, while the cook and the two boys finished preparing and serving the meal. Among the delicacies, Generosa had ordered the cook to prepare some toast with Iranian caviar and to cook a *fritambo*, an antelope stew that Kilian found delicious.

"I was hesitant to open a jar of marinated meat that my mother sent me from Pasolobino," explained Julia's mother, a stocky woman with smooth skin and shoulder-length wavy hair in a brown skirt and a knitted ochre jersey, "but I finally decided on my cook's star dish. I hope you will come again. Then I will prepare you one of my mother's recipes."

Kilian liked Generosa and Emilio. He talked for a long time with them; they wanted to hear about the goings-on in Spain, so he repeated what he had already told Julia in the shop. Generosa reminded him of his own mother, although she was more talkative than Mariana. She still had mettle from her youth in the mountains, maintaining her excellent health. It was necessary to have endured so many years on Fernando Po. Emilio was a man of medium build, with only a few wiry hairs, a short mustache, and bright eyes like his daughter's. Kilian saw that he was quiet and easygoing, well mannered with a smile never far away. Emilio asked after their father, whom he had not seen in days, and regretted that his health was not as good as it used to be.

"Do you know," he said, "how lucky we were to have each other when we arrived here for the first time? How different everything was! Now the roads are paved and have drains. We have water, electricity in the houses and streets, telephones, just like Pasolobino!"

Kilian picked up on the irony. There could not have been two worlds more different than his village and Santa Isabel. The Europeans who came from large cities would probably not notice the difference, but Kilian, a man used to livestock and villages full of mud, did. He began to understand how Emilio and Generosa had managed to adapt so well to the comforts of a place like this. They had even been able to give Julia a good education in the schools on the island, a luxury . . . Perhaps one day he would be able to love this bit of Africa as Julia's family did, but for the moment, he still sighed over the smallest details, such as the discovery, in a corner of the dining room, of a simple altar to the Virgin of Guayente—patroness of their valley—along with an image of Our Lady of the Pillar and the memory of parties in his house rekindled by the taste of the mellow wine from the small cask that Generosa had received from home to accompany the typical lard pastries from Pasolobino.

Julia laughed. During the meal, the girl had been busy trying to win Jacobo's attention with jokes and intelligent conversation. She had dressed up very prettily for the occasion, in a Vichy yellow-and-brown short-sleeved dress and her hair tied up in an elegant chignon that showed off her features. Kilian was sorry that his brother was not interested. They would have made a very good couple, even more so tonight with Jacobo looking impeccable in his linen trousers and white shirt. Julia and Jacobo were young, attractive, and fun. A good combination, thought Kilian. He felt sad for Julia, seeing the hopeful anticipation in her eyes when Jacobo responded with a smile or a laugh.

One of the boys indicated that coffee would be served on the porch that led to the garden, lit up by kerosene lamps swarming with mosquitoes. The night was so clear that the moon would have been enough, projecting its light over the great mango and the huge avocado trees—Kilian reckoned that they were between eight and ten meters tall—that reigned over the exotic trees in the garden. Julia suggested that they play a game of cards, but her parents wanted to continue the conversation.

Julia's father was afraid that the winds of independence of places like Kenya and the Belgian Congo would arrive in Guinea and put their businesses in danger. Generosa skillfully but conclusively ended the conversation when she gathered that Kilian was not going to stop asking questions. The young man felt a little frustrated, as he would have willingly shared what he had learned about the Mau Mau movement on the ship. He could not begin to imagine that this perfectly organized colonial world had any cracks. Nevertheless, he did not want to be rude and followed the new topics of conversation.

Every now and then, Jacobo glanced at his watch. He could imagine where and what Marcial and Mateo were up to at that moment, and a knot of urgency formed in his stomach.

A few minutes later, a boy came to tell them that a worker from Sampaka, Waldo, was there to fetch Massa Kilian and Massa Jacobo and bring them back to the plantation.

"Some Calabars were celebrating a party in the barracks"—Waldo talked quickly when he entered, in an agitated manner that Kilian found a little forced—"when they got involved in a big fight, with machetes and everything."

"They are like animals!" Generosa commented, blessing herself. "They are probably from that cannibal sect. Haven't you heard? In the market they said something about how they had eaten the bishop in Río Muni . . ."

"What are you saying, Mom?" Julia protested.

Jacobo asked Waldo to continue.

"Several men are injured," continued the lad, "and no white man around to restore order, not even the new doctor."

Jacobo put his hand out to Emilio, kissed Generosa and Julia on the cheeks, and dragged his brother out of the house while Kilian repeated his thanks for the pleasant evening and promised to return soon. Julia went out with them to the pickup while they loaded Waldo's bike in the back and said good-bye to them with a glint of frustration in her eyes.

Jacobo drove quickly until, after a couple of blocks, he stopped the pickup, got out, gave the bike to Waldo, and put some notes in his hand.

"Good work, lad!"

Waldo lit a portable lamp and went off, happy to have earned such easy cash.

Jacobo got back into the pickup and turned to Kilian with a wide smile.

"You rogue!" Kilian reproached him, chuckling.

"Welcome to Saturday night in Santa Isabel!" his brother said. "Here we come, Anita Guau!"

Jacobo stepped on the accelerator and drove like a lunatic. Kilian became infected by his brother's joy.

"And what *hola-holas* have we here?" Just after the brothers entered the dance hall, a well-padded woman with an ample bosom greeted them affectionately, holding out her hand to them. "It's been a long time since I last saw you, Massa Jacobo! And this must be your brother! Welcome! Come in and enjoy yourselves!"

"I see nothing has changed, eh, Anita?" Jacobo took her hand while scanning the place. He made out his friends and waved to them. "Look, Kilian. Even Manuel is here. But I don't see Dick or Pao."

"Who?"

"Some friends who work in Bata, in the logging industry. They normally turn up on Saturdays . . . Well, I'm going to have my favorite whiskey. White Horse, black label. Difficult though it is to believe, it's cheaper than beer. The advantages of a free port."

They went over to the bar, and Kilian noticed that, indeed, the majority of the drinks ordered were spirits. The waitresses served generous quantities of whiskies with names he did not recognize— they must have been Scotch or Irish—and well-known brandies such as Osborne, Fundador, 501, Veterano, or Tres Cepas. *In the houses of Pasolobino,* he thought in astonishment, *one of these bottles would last almost a year. In Anita's, a few seconds.*

Jacobo asked for two glasses of White Horse as Kilian studied the open-air dance floor. The club was an enormous closed patio divided in two: on the right, a roof protected the bar and table area against possible showers; on the left, the dance floor was uncovered and bordered by the surrounding buildings. Numerous children stationed on the adjacent balconies watched the antics down below. White and black men with black women dressed like Europeans moved to the beat of the six-piece orchestra extracting frenetic music from different-size drums, a xylophone, a pair of maracas that looked like pumpkins, and a trumpet, resulting in a curious mix of African percussion and familiar Latin rhythms. Kilian found himself swinging his shoulders; this music was contagious.

Jacobo gave his brother a drink, and they advanced toward the tables at the front, joining Manuel and Marcial, who were drinking with two pretty women. Between laughs, they pointed to the dance floor and saw Mateo trying to follow the breakneck rhythm of his partner, a woman much larger than he. Marcial got up to get two seats for the brothers. In a corner set aside for talking and drinking, dark fabrics covered the windows, which created an intimate atmosphere heated by tobacco smoke and the smell of perfume and sweat.

"I'd like to introduce you to Oba and Sade," said Marcial. "They just arrived from the continent. This is Jacobo and Kilian."

The girls offered their hands to the men. Oba, more petite than her friend, wore a wide-skirted V-necked yellow dress with a tight bodice and a bow at the front, her hair in a European-style bob. To Kilian, Sade's height and haughty pose gave her the appearance of a beautiful queen adorned by colored-seed bracelets and crystal-beaded necklaces. A pale-pink dress showed off her figure with buttons to the waist and a white cotton neckline and cuffs that matched her sandals. Her hair was gathered in tiny buns, and the gaps between them created small mosaics that made her large eyes look even bigger and her lips fuller.

"Would you like to dance?" asked Oba in perfect Spanish.

Marcial and Jacobo agreed, and the four of them went to the dance floor. Manuel went for more drinks and on his way met Mateo, who returned to the table alone. Kilian smiled when he saw Jacobo match Sade's provocative weaving and the disproportionate height difference between Oba and Marcial, who had to bend down to dance.

"I'm wrecked!" Mateo, sweating, sat down beside him. "These women have the devil in their bodies! And you . . . why aren't you dancing? You only need to ask one of them."

"The truth is I'm not very fond of dancing," Kilian confessed.

"I didn't like it either, but once you let yourself be carried along by the sounds of the dundun, djembe, and bongo drums, it gets easier." He laughed, seeing Kilian's look of surprise. "Yes, I've even managed to learn their names. In the beginning, they were all tamtams . . ." He searched for his glass while scanning the room for a new partner. "It's very lively here tonight. There are a lot of new girls."

Manuel arrived with the drinks. "You are not going to believe this! Gregorio and Regina are at the bar. Her mourning period was very short! What are you two talking about?"

"About the drums, the girls . . . ," responded Kilian. "Where are they from?"

"Coriscans, Nigerians, Fang, and Ndowé from Río Muni . . . ," listed Mateo. "A little of everything."

"And Bubis from here?"

"Bubis, no!" said Manuel. "If they lose their virginity, they are punished."

"It's amazing the different cultures in such a small place," commented Kilian, remembering Umaru. "So this is the famous spot that makes the whole week bearable."

"It's not the only one, but it is the best," explained Marcial, keeping up to the rhythm of the music with his glass. "Sometimes we go to Riakamba, behind the cathedral. And there is also the Fernandino Club, but I don't like it at all, because the girls aren't as loose as they are here." He let out a chuckle. "They act like the white women, all dainty and decent."

"It's the equivalent to the white man's casino," Manuel qualified, amused by Mateo's explanation. "That is where the elite blacks go. It's frowned upon for a white man to dance with a black woman there. Here it's different. For a few hours, we are all equal."

Marcial and Sade returned to the table without their respective partners.

"What happened to the other two?" asked Manuel.

"Oba has abandoned me for someone her own size," joked Marcial, his large frame making the seat creak as he sat down. "And Jacobo has met an old girlfriend. Kilian, he said you should go back with us." He shook his head. "That man doesn't waste any time!"

Sade sat very close to Kilian and cheekily asked for a sip of his whiskey, gently placing her hand on his thigh. The other men exchanged amused glances. Kilian got nervous as he felt a tingling in his trousers and hastily tried to distract everyone.

"I was told today that some natives on the continent have eaten a bishop. A banned sect or something?"

Mateo and Marcial shook their heads as Sade and Manuel laughed in unison.

"You whites are afraid that we will eat you!" she said in a high voice. "And that we will take your power . . ."

Kilian frowned.

"There are tribes on the continent that hunt and eat gorillas," explained Manuel. "A *bishop* is a species of gorilla with a goatee similar to that of the first missionary priests. By the way, they also eat *diplomats* . . ."

Sade nodded while looking out the corner of her eye at Kilian, who blushed and finished his drink in one gulp. Marcial butted in.

"Lads, lads! Will you look at the beauty who has just arrived!" They all looked up at the woman in the lilac dress, showing off her tremendous figure in extremely high heels. "That one is definitely my size!"

He shot off in the woman's direction, but stopped after a few meters. Another man much bigger than he had already offered her his arm to lead her onto the dance floor. Marcial turned around and went back to the table.

"Mosi *the Egyptian* is a lot of Mosi, isn't he, Marcial?" Mateo sympathized.

"I know! Nothing I could do . . . Ah well, I'll have another drink."

Sade got up and took Kilian by the hand. "Let's dance," she insisted.

Kilian allowed himself to be dragged onto the dance floor. He was happy that the orchestra was playing a beguine, similar to a slow rumba. Sade stuck her body against his, intoxicating him with her deep eyes. Kilian was surprised by her overt advances. He felt a mixture of curiosity and desire. His past experiences were limited to a house of ill repute in Barmón, where his brother had taken him, flush after a livestock fair, to make him a man, then various encounters with girls who worked in the big houses of Pasolobino and Cerbeán. He remembered Jacobo's word after Kilian's first—and disastrous—time: *Women are like whiskey. The first sip is difficult, but when you get used to it, you learn to savor it.* Over time, Kilian learned that what his brother said was partly true. But unlike Jacobo, he did not go looking for that pleasure often. He needed some type of mutual understanding, or affinity, even if fleeting.

In this situation, Sade knew exactly how to convince him. It seemed as if she really wanted to enjoy herself with him. Kilian began to feel the desire between his legs grow.

"If you like, we could step outside," she suggested sweetly.

Kilian nodded, and they left the club, heading toward the back. They walked hand in hand along a quiet and tranquil street of small cottages until reaching the end, where the buildings stopped and the green blanket began. Sade led him through leafy trees, whose moon-shadowed outlines hid other couples, until they reached a place that seemed discreet and comfortable.

Sade rubbed her skin against his, roaming his body with an expert hand and guiding his hands around her curves while uttering arousing words in her own language. When she saw that he was ready, she lay on the ground and opened herself to him. Kilian entered her with a dizzying mix of desire and confusion, as if he could not believe that his body could respond with so much hunger. Without speaking, he rocked inside her until he could not take any more and exploded. The sensation throbbed through his veins, and he remained lying down for several minutes until she gave him a pat on his shoulder for him to get up.

They fixed their clothes with clumsy movements. Kilian was in a daze. He had yet to recover from the intensity of the encounter. Sade gave him an understanding smile, took his hand, and went with him back into the club. At the bar, they parted ways.

"I'd like to see you again," she told him with a flirtatious wink.

Kilian made an ambiguous gesture with his head, leaned on the bar, and ordered a drink. Bit by bit, his breathing returned to normal. Still, he needed a few minutes before going back to his friends. They might talk about these things casually, but he could not. He did not want to be the butt of their jokes nor have to give explanations. As far as he knew, Marcial, Mateo, Jacobo, Gregorio, Dámaso, even Manuel—well, maybe not so much Manuel—understood the island's pleasures. And, in a few minutes, he had become one of them. So quickly! So easily! His head was spinning. Would he see Sade again? Would she become his steady *friend*? They had barely spoken two words! He did not know what she was like or what she expected from life or if she had brothers or sisters, parents . . . Everything had happened so quickly. What did she expect from him? She had told him that she would like to see him again. Would he end up giving her money every month in exchange for exclusive favors? Was that how things worked? He was overtaken by a slight pang of conscience. The best thing would be to not return to Anita Guau for a reasonable period. Yes. Time would tell.

He smoothed down his hair a few times, took several sips from the glass, and went back to the table at the front, posing as if everything were normal.

"Where is Sade?" asked Mateo, curiosity dancing in his eyes.

Kilian shrugged and looked over at the dance floor. "She dropped me."

"Poor lad," said Marcial, clicking his tongue and waving one of his enormous hands in the air. "Maybe next time."

Manuel studied Kilian's face. He was not telling the truth. Maybe Kilian and he were more similar than first appearances would suggest. He fervently wanted to meet the woman of his dreams, a difficult task in this paradise of temptation.

"I think I'll go back to Sampaka," Manuel said, getting to his feet. "You can come back with me if you want, Kilian."

Kilian agreed. The others decided to stay a while longer.

The journey back was mostly silent. Once lying in his bed, Kilian found it difficult to get to sleep. Later, the moans coming from his brother's room merged with his own images of Sade. He had had a good time with her, yes. A good time. That was it. That was all. He did not have to make anything more of it.

The following morning, Jacobo, yawning, came into the dining room to have his breakfast. He saw Kilian, alone, focused on the coffee in front of him, and said, "Good morning, little brother. What? Nothing in comparison with the girls in Pasolobino or Barmón, right?"

"No," admitted Kilian quietly. "Nothing at all."

Jacobo bent down and whispered in his ear, "Last night was my treat. A welcome present. You don't have to thank me. If you want to do it again, it's up to you." He poured himself a coffee, yawned loudly, and added, "Are you coming with me to eleven o'clock mass? Luckily it's not in Latin here."

5

Palabra Conclú

Case Closed

A few days later, the manager sent Kilian and Gregorio to collect some heavy pieces from Julia's parents' store. Lorenzo Garuz had learned from Antón that the relationship between the men was at best tense, and he hoped that a good long spell away from the plantation would do them some good. Garuz had known Gregorio for many years. He did not consider him dangerous, maybe a little violent, but he knew how to get people to obey him. Besides, he was the perfect filter to screen employees who had what it took. After a period in his hands, the young ones either left the colony or became magnificent workers, something Garuz expected would happen in Kilian's case.

Kilian did not open his mouth once on their way to the city. Not only because he had nothing to say, but also because Gregorio had made him drive. All of Kilian's attention was focused on carrying out a perfect performance at the wheel of the big round-cabined truck with its wooden trailer. He had no intention of giving Gregorio any reason to pick on him again. The robust Studebaker 49 advanced first along the path and then down the road as smoothly as the young driver could manage.

When they entered the store, they were greeted by a radiant Julia. Kilian did not know why, but the young woman had been happy for the last few days. The dinner had gone better than expected. It was not easy to get Jacobo to pay attention for more than five minutes in the shop. She made trips around the most popular places in Santa Isabel, went to twelve o'clock mass on Sundays in the cathedral, and had an aperitif in the Chiringuito in the Plaza de España, hoping, on the seafront, to casually bump into him, but it never happened. So the two straight hours that she had been able to enjoy Jacobo while his brother entertained her parents had felt like heaven. Seeing Kilian with another man in the entrance to the store made her heart skip a beat until she recognized Gregorio and pleasantly greeted both.

Kilian was happy to see Julia again, although deep down he was a little ashamed of the manner in which they had said good-bye to her and her family on Saturday.

"The order is out back," said Julia. "It would make more sense to move the truck there. My father is checking to make sure everything is there."

"Well, Kilian," said Gregorio, "you are the driver today."

Julia saw Kilian make a face at Gregorio's tone. She hardly knew the man, and their dealings were just on a commercial basis: Gregorio would hand her samples of screws, and she would diligently search for them in the corresponding boxes.

"Was the conflict on Saturday night sorted out in the end?" Julia asked casually.

Gregorio furrowed his brow. "Saturday night?"

"Yes. They told me there was a big fight in Sampaka, with many injured . . ."

"And who told you this?"

"A boy came looking for Jacobo and Kilian."

Gregorio shook his head and laughed. "Nothing happened on the plantation on Saturday night."

Julia blinked, perplexed.

"But . . ."

"I saw Jacobo and Kilian in Anita Guau around eleven . . ." When Julia blushed, he continued, "All the young lads from Sampaka were there. And very well accompanied."

Julia gritted her teeth, and her chin began to tremble in fury. Jacobo had tricked her. And her parents!

She had gone over their conversation a thousand times, and she was convinced that she had passed his test. They shared a common childhood in Pasolobino and an adolescence in Africa. It was absolutely impossible that their compatibility was not as clear to him as it was to her; otherwise, he would have looked for any excuse to have joined in the others' conversation. And he had not done it! He had enjoyed himself and laughed with her. Even more, long and sweet moments had passed before he took his marvelous green eyes from hers. And their hands had brushed against each other's at least three times!

She felt completely deflated.

Gregorio cunningly returned to the attack. He pretended to look with interest at the objects that were on the counter and spoke in a soft voice. "I don't know about Kilian, but Jacobo has become a complete *mininguero* . . . I suppose he won't take too long in coaching his brother on native girlfriends." He clicked his tongue. "The young don't listen. Too much alcohol and too many women takes its toll. Well"—he looked up and smiled; Julia was ready to burst into tears—"that's what happens. They are not the first, nor will they be the last."

Julia used Kilian's entrance, followed by Emilio, to turn around and bite her bottom lip.

"Gregorio!" greeted Emilio, holding out his hand. "It's been a good while since I last saw you! How are things? Don't you ever leave the jungle?"

"Not often, Emilio, not often." He shook the man's hand warmly. "There is always something to do. I only leave the plantation on Saturdays, you know . . ."

Julia brusquely turned around. She did not want her father to find out about the brothers' bad manners.

"Dad," she intervened in a calm voice, "I can't find bolts this size." She handed him one. "Could you look in the store, please?"

"Yes, of course."

Kilian noticed the change in Julia. She would not even look at him, and her hands were trembling. He looked at Gregorio, puzzled.

"I hope I haven't upset you," Gregorio whispered, frowning.

"Me?" she interrupted. "How could you upset me? You think white women don't know how you waste your time?" She shot Kilian a hard stare. "We're not fools!"

"Hey! What's going on here?" Kilian asked. "Julia?"

"I seem to have put my foot in it," confessed Gregorio, twisting his lips in false consternation. "I told her where we were last Saturday night . . . all of us. You don't know how sorry I am."

Kilian clenched his fists. If it had not been for Emilio coming back at that moment, he would gladly have hit Gregorio. He looked at Julia, feeling like a worm under her hurt gaze. She turned her head and went back into the shelves.

The men chatted for a few minutes and said their good-byes, Gregorio with a triumphant little smile on his face. Emilio went looking for Julia and asked her, "Are you all right? You don't look well."

"I'm fine, Dad."

Julia tried to smile, even though she was raging inside. She did not know how, but Jacobo would pay for his lie. The moment had arrived to change tack with him. She sighed resolutely and promised herself to be patient.

Outside, Kilian let his anger loose.

"Did you enjoy that, Gregorio?" he whispered sharply. "What do you gain from this?"

"Don't you lecture me!" He irritably clicked his tongue repeatedly. "Don't you know you will catch a liar quicker than a cripple?"

"You deserve a good thrashing!"

Gregorio squared up in front of him with his hands on his hips. Kilian was half a head taller than he, but Gregorio had more physical strength.

"Go ahead, come on." He rolled up his shirtsleeves. "Let's see if you have the guts."

Kilian exhaled.

"Shall I make it easier? Do you want me to start?" Gregorio pushed the younger man with both arms. Kilian took a step backward. "Come on!" He pushed him again. "Show me how brave the men from the mountain are!"

Kilian grabbed Gregorio's wrists with all his strength, with his muscles tensed, until he perceived in the other's dark eyes a weak flash of surprise and let go in disgust. He walked to the truck, climbed into the cabin, and started the engine.

He waited until Gregorio got in and then drove at top speed, as if he had not done anything else in his whole life.

A couple of weeks later, March arrived. It was the hottest month of the year, the precursor to the rainy season. On the plantations, the cocoa trees, with their smooth trunks and large egg-shaped leaves, began to sprout small yellow, rosy, and reddish flowers. Kilian marveled that the blooms grew directly from the trunk and the older branches. The heat and the humidity of the following months would allow the cocoa berries or pods to emerge from these flowers. On the fruit trees of Pasolobino, if there was not an unexpected or late frost, the hundreds of buds would become dozens of fruit. Jacobo had told him that the thousands of flowers springing from each cocoa tree would produce only around twenty pods.

The days passed without much happening. Work was routine and monotonous. Everyone knew what they had to do: repair houses, prepare the crops, and get the dryers and stores ready for the next harvest in August.

Kilian also seemed more relaxed in his routine. Gregorio had been more cautious since the argument in the store, which Kilian had not shared with anyone, least of all his brother. Gregorio still was not doing much instructing, but he was not picking on him either. Even so, Kilian kept alert.

Although he had gone back to Anita Guau a couple of times more, he had not required Sade's attentions, something that did not seem to faze her as she satisfied her many other admirers. Manuel and Kilian had discovered that both preferred the films in the Marfil Cinema or a good chat in any of the seafront terraces as the huge bats flapped away from the palm trees at dusk.

One morning, while Antón and José were showing Kilian the workings of the different parts of the dryers in the main yard, Manuel came over and showed them a card.

"Look, Kilian. My old friends from the hospital in Santa Isabel have sent me some invitations to a formal dance in the casino this Saturday. I hope you'll come with me. I'll tell the others as well."

"A party in the casino!" said Antón. "You can't miss it. The elite of the island will be there, Son. Plantation employees normally don't get the chance."

"I'd be delighted." Kilian's eyes lit up. "But what do you wear to a place like that? I don't know if I have the right clothes."

"A jacket and tie will be enough," Manuel explained. "The invitation says that formal wear is not required, so we don't need to rent a dinner suit."

"I'll lend you a tie if you haven't brought one," offered Antón.

Manuel said he would see them at lunchtime, and the others continued their tour around the dryers, raised roofs over enormous slate sheets where the cocoa beans would be roasted. José approached some workers as Kilian turned to Antón.

"Dad, I'd like to talk to you about something . . . ," he started in a serious voice.

Antón had a fair idea what Kilian wanted to talk to him about. "Yes?"

"Jacobo and I think you should go back to Spain. Even though you deny it, we know that you are exhausted. It's not like you. Why don't you go and visit the doctor in Zaragoza?" Antón did not protest, so he continued. "If it's the money, you know that what Jacobo and I earn is more than enough to cover all the expenses and more . . . And how long has it been since you last saw Mom?"

Antón gave him a faint smile. He turned his head and called José. "Do you hear what Kilian is saying? The same as you and Jacobo! Maybe you're all in this together?"

José widened his eyes with a feigned look of innocence. "Antón"— his friend had not allowed José to use the term *massa* for some time when talking in private—"I don't know what you are talking about."

"You know perfectly well, you rogue. It seems that you all want to be rid of me."

"It's for your own good," Kilian insisted.

"Your sons are right," José interjected. "I don't know how you will manage another harvest. I'm sure that the doctors in Spain will prescribe you something to make you better."

"Doctors, José—the farther away, the better. They cure one thing and mess up another." Kilian opened his mouth to protest, but

Antón raised his hand. "Wait, Son. I spoke to Garuz yesterday. After the harvest, I will spend Christmas at home. I didn't want to tell you until I was sure. Afterward, I'll come back here, and depending on my condition, I'll work in the office."

Kilian would have preferred it if his father would say farewell to the colony for good, but he did not push it. Maybe once he got to Spain he would change his mind. As a man accustomed to physical work, he might find it strange to take a post as massa *clak*, which was what the workers called office clerks, though they often gave all the literate whites on the plantation that title. Anyway, his father was a stubborn and private man. He would do whatever he wanted no matter what anyone else said.

"I'm relieved," Kilian admitted. "But it is still a long time until autumn."

"Once the dryers are going at full blast, time will pass so quickly that before we know it, we will be singing Christmas carols, right, José?"

"Agreed!"

"The tons we have shipped over the years, you and me!"

His friend's eyes brightened. Kilian loved to listen to Antón and José reminisce over old times that went back to the beginning of the century. It was difficult to imagine a small Santa Isabel with bamboo and calabo wood houses similar to village huts or the streets of firm red earth instead of tarmacadam or the native aristocrats having afternoon tea and remembering their English education or going to Catholic mass in the morning and Protestant service in the afternoon to practice tolerance. José laughed as he recalled his childhood, when men his father's age sweated inside their frock coats and raised their top hats slightly to greet the elegantly dressed women in their Parisian hats.

"Did you know, Massa Kilian, when I was born, there was not even one white woman in Santa Isabel?"

"How is that possible?"

"There were some in Basilé with their colonist husbands. They had a very hard life. But in the city, not one."

"And the days when the Trasmediterránea ship docked in Fernando Po—every three months, Son—they even closed all the stores!" Antón added. "Everybody came to the harbor to get news from Spain . . ."

"And did you know, Massa Kilian, when I was a boy, the whites had to go back to Spain every two years to survive tropical life. Otherwise, they died in a short time. It was rare for a man to endure many years. Now things are different."

"Yes, José," said Antón in a whisper. "We've seen a lot, you and I. Times have really changed since I first came here with Mariana!"

"And they will keep changing, Antón!" added José, shaking his head in resignation. "How they will change!"

On Saturday, Kilian put on a light-colored suit—which Simón had pressed—and a tie; he combed his hair back with brilliantine and looked in the mirror. He hardly recognized himself. The perfect gentleman! In Pasolobino, he had never had the chance to dress up like this. He had only the one dark suit for the main village festival and the weddings of some cousin or other.

At seven on the dot, Mateo, Jacobo, Marcial, Kilian, and Manuel left for the party.

On the way, Kilian joked with his brother. "I thought Saturdays were sacred. You are going without your shot of Anita Guau?"

"You have to be open to everything," responded Jacobo. "It isn't every day you get the chance to go to the casino. Besides, if it's no fun, we'll leave. The *ñanga-ñanga* way we're dressed means we will be successful tonight no matter where we go."

The others chanted the phrase, laughing. Kilian joined in when he understood that the funny word, *ñanga-ñanga*, meant elegant.

The casino was located in Punta Cristina, thirty meters above sea level. They went through the small entrance gate and into a courtyard with a tennis court and a swimming pool with two diving boards surrounded by black-and-white square tiles. From the terrace's long arched balustrade, over which leaned a solitary palm tree against the horizon, the men could make out the whole of Santa Isabel's bay, full of anchored boats and canoes.

Of the group, only Manuel had been in the casino before, so he led them directly to the music. They entered a building with laminated wood windows, then crossed a large room where people talked cheerfully and went out to a terrace circled by a softly lit white wall. In the middle of the terrace there was a dance floor surrounded by white marble tables. At that moment, the floor was empty. Men and women, whites and blacks, all looking very elegant as they greeted one another. On the stage sat an orchestra with THE NEW BLUE STAR written on the players' music stands; Kilian thought the orchestra was fairly full in comparison to what he had seen before, and they played pleasant background music.

"After dinner, they will play dance music," explained Manuel, raising his hand to greet some acquaintances. "I'm afraid tonight is going to be rather hectic. There are friends here I haven't seen in a long time."

"Don't worry about us," said Jacobo, taking a glass from a passing waiter. "For the moment, we will find a good spot and wait for them to come over and say hello to us."

His friends winced at the sarcasm. It was no secret that Mateo, Marcial, Kilian, and Jacobo felt a little self-conscious. They were not used to frequenting places like the casino, where the crème de la crème of the city gathered. Despite their impeccable appearance, they could easily be found out as plantationers not sophisticated enough to rub shoulders with this crowd.

Jacobo signaled for his companions to follow him to a table near the door to the dining room, a good vantage point to observe both the mingling inside and out on the dance floor. Soon after, Kilian and Jacobo heard familiar voices: Emilio and Generosa, accompanied by two other married couples, plus Julia and two friends.

"Julia! Look who's here!" Emilio beamed at the brothers. He turned to the girls. "Jacobo and Kilian with some friends . . . You could make a group!"

Various introductions and pleasantries were exchanged before Generosa and the other couples continued on their way. Julia and her friends sat down, and the brothers remained standing with Emilio. Out of the corner of his eye, Kilian noticed that Julia was a little tense and let her friends, Ascensión and Mercedes, lead the conversation. They wasted little time asking Marcial and Mateo about the plantation, then their childhoods in Spain. In turn, the girls shared what they did in Santa Isabel and boasted about being able to enjoy the sports facilities in the casino whenever they wanted.

Emilio, in high spirits because of the drink, stayed a while longer.

"So this is your first time at the center of the European upper class? And where do you normally go partying?" He waved his hand in the air and lowered his voice. "Don't tell me, I can imagine. I was young once too . . ." He winked. "Anyway, as you can see, everyone mixes here, whites and blacks, Spaniards and foreigners, if and when we share a common denominator. Money."

Jacobo and Kilian shot each other a telling glance: if this was the criteria, they certainly did not meet it.

One by one, Emilio pointed out various people while listing their professions—salesman, banker, civil servant, landowner, customs agent, vehicle importer, another salesman, lawyer, doctor, colonial businessman, head of the Colonial Guard . . .

"That one is the owner of a heavy machinery and car company. He has the agency for Caterpillar, Vauxhall, and Studebaker. The parents of Julia's friends work for him. And that one over there is the secretary of the governor general of Fernando Po and Río Muni. The governor wasn't able to come today. A shame. I would have introduced you to him."

Kilian had never seen so many important people in one place. If one were to come over, he would not know how to start—much less continue—an even moderately intelligent conversation. Surely these people talked about important current events. He glanced again at Jacobo, who seemed to be listening to Emilio attentively, though his eyes were scanning the place for a more enjoyable corner. Luckily, someone made a hand signal from afar.

"Boys," said Emilio, "I believe my wife requires my presence. Enjoy yourselves!"

The brothers joined the group, where Ascensión and Mercedes shared a sharp wit, despite their different appearances. Ascensión had blond, almost white hair, a turned-up nose, and blue eyes inherited from her German grandmother. She was wearing an indigo dress with a drop waist, a wide belt, and a round neckline. Mercedes was sheathed in a tight-fitting green crepe silk dress with a full skirt and had her dark hair gathered up in a high chignon, highlighting her prominent nose.

Several waiters came over to their tables with trays overflowing with delicious canapés. The group ate, smoked, drank, and chatted for a good while. Kilian appreciated the easy conversation of Mateo, Marcial, and Julia's two friends. Julia herself would not even look at them. She remained silent, her head very straight, listening with feigned interest to everyone else's comments. Kilian thought that she looked gorgeous, with her crushed-silk dress, white polka dots on light blue. A thin strand of pearls graced the neckline of the dress. The only thing missing was the smile that normally lit up her face. It was impossible for Jacobo not to pick up on her coldness, even though Kilian had not told him of Gregorio's indiscretion.

Around ten o'clock, Julia started to look at her watch persistently.

"Are you waiting for someone?" Jacobo finally asked.

"Actually, I am," she replied in a hard voice. "I suppose it won't be too long before your boy arrives to rescue you from this boring party."

Jacobo was struck dumb as Kilian hung his head. Julia looked at them triumphantly, and the others fell silent, caught by surprise.

"How did you find out?" Jacobo said, sounding more annoyed than penitent.

"And what does that matter?" She straightened herself up even more in the chair. "Do you want me to tell you where you were that night at eleven o'clock?"

"That's none of your business. As far as I know, you are not my girlfriend."

Jacobo got up and left. The others remained silent. Kilian did not know where to hide himself. He looked at Julia, her chin trembling. The orchestra picked this moment to play a pasodoble that received a large round of applause from the guests. Kilian got up and took Julia by the hand.

"Come, let's dance."

She accepted, thankful that Kilian had saved her from an embarrassing situation. They walked in silence to the dance floor. He circled her waist with his arm, and they began to move to the rhythm of the music.

"I must warn you that I am a terrible dancer. I hope you'll forgive me if I step on your toes . . . and for the other day. I am truly sorry."

Julia raised her eyes toward him, tears still glistening.

"It's obvious I picked the wrong brother . . ." She nodded, trying to smile.

"Jacobo is a good person, Julia. It's just that . . ."

"I know, he doesn't want to commit. At least not with me."

"Maybe it's too early." Kilian did not want to see her suffer.

"Oh, come on, Kilian! I'm not fifteen!" she protested. "And this is Africa. Do you think I don't know how Jacobo enjoys himself? What annoys me most is that men like him think that white women are completely stupid. What can a *mininga* give him that I can't? What would he think if I offered my body to him like they do?"

"Julia! Don't say that! It's not the same . . . You can't compare yourself to them." The song seemed endless in that moment. "Now you are angry, and with good reason, but . . ."

"I can't stand these double standards, Kilian!" she interrupted. "Everyone turns a blind eye to the looser black girlfriends, while the white women have to wait until you get tired of them before you come looking for a good and faithful wife. What would happen if it were the other way round? If I got together with a black man?"

"Julia, I . . ." Kilian swallowed. "All this is new to me. It's a difficult subject."

"You haven't answered my question."

Kilian hesitated. He was not used to talking about these things with a woman, but Julia could be really persistent.

"It's different with men . . . I don't think this is an appropriate conversation."

"Yes, right . . . for a woman," she finished, irritated.

To Kilian's relief, the pasodoble ended and the orchestra moved to a swing number.

"Too complicated . . . ," said Kilian, forcing a smile.

They walked off the dance floor, passing Mateo, Ascensión, Marcial, and Mercedes, paired off for the number. Kilian and Julia walked in silence to the table, where they met Manuel having a drink.

"I'm taking a break," he said to Kilian. "I haven't stopped talking since we got here."

"Manuel, I'd like you to meet Julia, the daughter of friends of my parents."

Manuel stood up and, very politely, greeted the young woman. He noticed how her blue hairband pushed back her brown hair and revealed a pretty face with thoughtful eyes.

"Manuel is the plantation's doctor," explained Kilian. "He worked in the hospital in Santa Isabel before that."

"Haven't we met before?" she asked, studying his dark-blond hair and the pale eyes behind his thick tortoiseshell glasses. "I'm sure you've been to the casino before."

"Yes. I used to come to swim. And on Sundays to play cards or have a drink with people from work."

"I come every Sunday, and every now and then in the afternoon. How strange that we haven't met until today!"

"Well, since I've been in Sampaka, I don't go out as often."

"If you'll excuse me, I'm going to get something to drink," Kilian said, wanting to give them some space.

He was happy to have some time to himself after swallowing Julia's bitter accusations. Inside, the voices had grown louder. He waved to Generosa and Emilio and continued until he reached the billiard table, where he spotted Jacobo enveloped in a cloud of smoke. Jacobo looked at him but did not beckon him over. When he got closer, his brother didn't look up. "Ah! There you are." Kilian wondered if he was still angry at Julia. "These are my friends Dick and Pao. They have come from Bata. We met on my first trip."

Kilian held out his hand, soon learning that Dick was an Englishman who had worked in Douala for years before working in the logging industry with Pao on the continent. From time to time, they took advantage of their friendship with the pilot of the Dragon Rapide to make the hour-long crossing from Bata to Santa Isabel. Dick was tall and strong with pale skin reddened by the sun and brilliant blue eyes. Beside him, the Portuguese Pao was a lanky mulatto with a sharp nose. They had not held back on drinks and, between laughs, insisted on telling Kilian about the last time they saw Jacobo.

"It was on an elephant hunt in Cameroon," his brother explained with glassy eyes. "The most extraordinary experience! There was a whole group of us setting out with shotguns. We followed a guide along a trail of broken leaves left by the beast. A noise like an earthquake told us that we were close, and not much farther there were more . . ."

"You were scared out of your life!" Dick chimed in with accented Spanish. "Your face was as white as a sheet . . ."

"It sneaked up on me! The guide, an expert hunter, of course, shot him in the ear, and the elephant went crazy. We started to run in the opposite direction . . ."

"We knew that since the animal was so big, it would be hard for him to turn around," continued Pao, chortling. "But that day it didn't turn at all. With blood gushing from his ear, he continued straight ahead with us close behind . . ."

Kilian took an increasing dislike to Dick and Pao. There was something about them he did not trust. Dick did not look him in the eyes, and Pao's laughs were cruel.

"Finally, the animal began to slow down. We shot him several times and"—Jacobo raised the palms of his hands—"the elephant vanished! He disappeared from sight! The hunt ended and there I was, frustrated because I didn't see him fall!"

"These devils take an age to die." Dick took a drag from his cigarette and held the smoke in his lungs before letting it out.

"This one, a couple of days!" Pao interjected. "When we returned with the guide and found the body, it was still warm."

"It took a number of men to carve it up. And they left nothing but the bones!" Jacobo raised his glass. "The tusks were as tall as that door!"

Kilian had found the story quite gruesome. He was used to hunting mountain goats in the Pyrenees, but he could not imagine a scene like the one described. Since the days of Adam, the suffering of animals could be avoided with an accurate shot. He did not know any man from home who could enjoy the prolonged torment of one. He could only shake his head and say, "It sounds very dangerous."

"It certainly is!" Dick looked at him with his cold, expressionless blue eyes. Kilian turned his head to light a cigarette. "I was on a hunt where the elephant caught one of the blacks with his trunk and flung him to the ground, trampling him into a pulp of flesh and bones."

"Not even his mother could have recognized him!" Pao laughed insipidly, showing off his crooked teeth.

Kilian had heard enough. What a night he was having! Between Julia's outburst, the extreme wealth on display, and the story of this cruel hunt, he guessed that his first night in the famous casino would be his last. The drink was going to his head, so he pulled at his tie to loosen it.

"What's wrong with you now?" Jacobo asked in a low voice.

"It turns out that I'm happiest in the forest," murmured Kilian, lighting another cigarette with the butt of the previous one.

"What did you say?"

"Nothing, nothing. Are you going to stay much longer?"

"Oh, we're going to go to somewhere a bit livelier." Jacobo paused, wondering whether to invite his brother. "You can go back to the plantation with the rest."

"Yes, of course."

If I can avoid annoying them . . ., he thought ironically.

After Jacobo, Dick, and Pao left, Kilian watched some young men playing billiards until some raised voices caught his attention. He turned and saw Emilio, all steamed up, arguing with a hefty black man in an elegant tan suit. Generosa was pulling her husband's arm, but he took no notice. The discussion got louder, and the crowd began to fall silent. Kilian went over to see what was happening.

"How can you, especially you, say that to me, Gustavo?" Emilio almost shouted. "I have been a friend of your father's for many years! Have I ever treated you badly? I dare say I have lived more years on the island than you!"

"You don't want to understand, Emilio," Gustavo hissed. A few drops of sweat beaded on his furrowed brow and slid down his temples past a pair of large square-shaped glasses. "You whites have exploited us enough. Sooner or later you will have to leave."

"Yes, of course, that is what half of you here tonight would like. That we leave so you can keep everything . . . my business as well! Well, you won't get it, Gustavo!" He pushed his finger into the man's chest. "I have worked my fingers to the bone in this land so that my family could have a better life. I won't let you or anyone else threaten me!"

Generosa, beside herself, did not know what to do. She pleaded with her husband to leave and looked relieved when she saw Julia come over with Manuel.

"Nobody is threatening you, Emilio! I thought you were more reasonable. Have you ever considered our position?" Gustavo's nose flared in agitation.

"In your position?" roared Emilio. "Nobody has ever done me any favors!"

"That's enough, Dad!" Julia took his arm and gave the two men a hard stare. "Others have been punished for less than this! Tell me what's going on. Are you going to allow damned politics to ruin your friendship? If so, you're wasting your time. Things won't change here for many years to come."

The two men fell silent, but neither apologized. Emilio finally agreed to follow Generosa toward the exit. Little by little, all those present resumed their conversations. Manuel and Kilian accompanied Julia and her parents to the door.

"Are you all right, Julia?" asked Manuel softly as she caught her breath.

"Fine, thanks, Manuel." She held out her hand affectionately. "I had a very nice time with you. In fact, it was the only nice part of the night." She saw Kilian make a face and hastened to add, "The dance with you wasn't bad either. Still, it would be best if we left. How embarrassing, my God! I won't be able to come back to the casino for weeks!"

"I'm sorry, my child," said Emilio sadly. "I couldn't help it. Generosa, he rattled me."

"Relax, Emilio," his wife comforted him, nervously adjusting her fine lace gloves. "I'm afraid that from now on, we'll have to get used to the demands of these ingrates."

"That's enough, Mom." Julia looked at Kilian and Manuel. "We'll see one another again."

"I hope so," Manuel said wistfully. "And soon. Good night, Julia."

Manuel and Kilian remained at the door of the casino for a few seconds until they were out of sight.

"A charming woman," said Manuel as he cleaned his glasses with a handkerchief.

Kilian grinned for the first time all night.

A few days later, Julia was handed a note from one of Sampaka's boys: "I am truly sorry for my behavior. I hope you will forgive me. It will not happen again. Jacobo."

These few lines swirled around in her head for several days. She could not stop thinking about the sparkling green eyes, the black hair, and the muscular body of the man she had thought she wanted. Soon, she convinced herself that this could mean *something*, that her insolence in the casino had made him realize that they could share a future together.

This lasted for two weeks, but she could not manage a third. She needed to see him and hear his voice. She thought of different ways to meet him, but each felt wrong: another dinner in her house would awaken her mother's suspicions; she was not sure if Jacobo would accept an invitation to go to the cinema or for a meal or drink, and she did not want to risk a refusal; and resorting to another group outing at the casino did not seem a good idea after her father's outburst, which was probably still being gossiped about. That was the worst thing about Santa Isabel: in a city so small, it took weeks for a little bit of news to fade.

Julia had a sudden harebrained idea: She would go and see him on the plantation one night after dinner. She had been there twice with her father and remembered the main house perfectly. She would make up some excuse and sneak into Jacobo's room, where they could talk alone and maybe . . . She bit her bottom lip, caught up in the excitement of her scheme. If anyone were to catch her entering the bedroom passage, she could always say she had a message for Antón from her father. Nobody would blink!

She chose Thursday as the perfect day to carry out her plan. On Thursdays, her parents played cards with the neighbors, so it was the day Julia used the car to go to the cinema; there was no reason why Jacobo shouldn't be in Sampaka then.

That night after dinner, Julia dressed as usual so as not to raise suspicion, although she did take some time to make sure her makeup was perfect. When she got in front of the wheel of her father's red-and-cream Vauxhall Velox, she undid the two top buttons of her pink flowery dress with elbow-length sleeves, and she also changed her pale lipstick to something more vibrant. Her heart was beating so fast that she could feel it despite the throb of the engine.

She quickly left the city lights behind and entered a dark stretch of road. The headlights barely lit up a few meters ahead. A shiver of fear went through her body. She could sense the life that flowed through the jungle's veins at night. When passing through the village of Zaragoza, the weak flames from the fires in the flimsy houses cast shadows through the unglazed windows. Julia wished she had picked a night with a full moon. Out of the corner of her eye, she could see the palm trees at the entrance to Sampaka appear and disappear like ghosts. When a white-haired man carrying a small lantern raised his hand to get her to stop, her heart skipped a beat. The man approached the window, surprised when he saw a lone white female at the wheel.

"Good evening, *mis*," greeted Yeremías. "Can I help you?"

"I have a message for Massa Antón." She had practiced the phrase so often it came out naturally. "Is it always this dark?"

"We have had a problem with the electricity. I don't know how long it will take to fix it." Yeremías pointed to a place. "You should park a little before the house. The Nigerians have filled the main yard—"

"Okay, fine." She nodded, wanting to hurry. "Thank you."

Julia drove the car on until she was suddenly surrounded by a mass of men dancing with machetes in their hands. Some of them held up kerosene lamps, making the whites of their eyes pop in the darkness when they bent down to peer at the strange driver. Julia calculated that if she left the car there, she would have to walk fifty meters through the crowd to the steps of the colonial house. Another option was to stay in the car or beep the horn like a lunatic, turn around, and leave. She took a deep breath, panicked, though the men did not appear violent. They looked at her for a second and then continued on their way. She decided to get out of the car. With trembling legs, she walked quickly, hearing comments with words she did not understand, but their tone was clear. Dozens of naked chests and muscular arms surrounded her as a cold sweat covered her body, and her vision grew cloudy. When she got to the bottom of the steps and bumped into someone she knew, she was ready to faint.

"Julia! In God's name! What are you doing here at this hour?"

She never knew that a voice could sound so comforting. She looked up. "It's not that late, Manuel. I'm here to give a message to Antón from my father."

"And couldn't you have sent one of the boys?"

"They weren't at home," she lied, and realized she was blushing, "so I came on the way to the cinema."

"That's some detour!"

Now with Manuel, Julia dared to look back at the men in the yard. "Can you tell me what's going on?"

"The laborers have organized a massive hunt for jungle rats."

"Hunting *gronbifs*? In the dark?"

"That way they will catch more. If they don't exterminate them now, the rats will reproduce too much and damage the new crop. Afterward, they hold parties and eat them."

"And the whites participate?"

"I don't, although I admit I'm curious. The other employees and foremen will do the rounds to make sure there are no problems."

Julia did not know whether to laugh or cry. Of all the possible setbacks, it had never crossed her mind that rodents would spoil her plans.

"Would you like to have a look?" asked Manuel. "The jungle is full of mysteries at night."

Before Julia could answer, she was interrupted by Jacobo's voice as he came down the stairs with Kilian, Mateo, Marcial, and Gregorio.

"What are you doing here?"

Julia bit her lip hard as she came up with another lie to get her out of this mess. She held on to Manuel's arm, and as the heat rose in her cheeks, she replied, "Manuel invited me to come and see the hunt. I was delighted to accept."

Manuel gave her a confused look, but something in her eyes led him not to say anything. They let them pass, then waited until the groups divided into areas and set off. Manuel asked her to come with him to one of the storerooms to get an oil lamp and suggested that they stay at the back of the brigade, in the cocoa trees nearest the plantation. Only whispers and the occasional sharp strike of a machete could be heard. Apart from the suffocating vegetation and the disturbing sensation that millions of insects were running under her feet, the hunt itself was not at all exciting.

"I feel like somebody is watching us," whispered Julia, rubbing her arms.

"That always happens in the jungle. If you'd like, we can go and have a coffee in the dining room and wait until they come back with their trophies."

Julia gratefully nodded. On the way, they talked happily, as if they had known each other for years.

The sound of drums brought them back to the plantation.

In front of the laborers' barracks, the women had lit several fires and started roasting some of the jungle rats that had been beheaded. Kilian had thought the hunt would never end. He was thankful for the warmth of the fire as the night chill announced the coming of the wet season. A worker came over to the white employees to offer them a bottle of *malamba*, and Simón ran to get some glasses. He returned with Antón, Santiago, and José, ready to join the party. Only the manager was missing. Garuz normally went home to his family in Santa Isabel when he finished work. He did not stay overnight on the plantation unless completely necessary.

"This is strong as hell!" Mateo puffed and waved a hand at his mouth after feeling the sugarcane moonshine burn his throat. "I don't know how they can take it."

"Surely you should be used to it by now!" joked Marcial, emptying his glass in one gulp and raising it to Simón for a refill.

Kilian tried a sip of his *malamba*. His eyes filled with tears, and he began to cough.

"Careful, lad!" Marcial slapped him on the back. "You have to drink it bit by bit at first. This weed killer doesn't go to the stomach. It goes straight to the blood!"

"It looks like we'll all have hangovers tomorrow morning," warned Antón, smiling and wetting his lips with the liquor.

Kilian, his cheeks still burning, was happy to have his father there with them. He closed his eyes, tried the liquid again, and felt a pleasant heat run through his muscles. When he opened his eyes, he saw Julia and Manuel approach.

Julia gave a start when she saw Antón and tried to turn, but Manuel took her arm and whispered, "Relax. Your secret is safe with me."

If Manuel ever figured out why Julia went to Sampaka that night, he never told.

Julia nodded, excited by the chance to join an African party.

"You're still here?" asked Jacobo, surprised.

"Julia!" Antón was also taken aback. "It's been a long time! How are Generosa and Emilio?"

"Very well, thanks. My father misses his evenings with you."

"Tell him I'll come around soon. And what brings you here at this time of night?"

Manuel came to her aid. "I promised her I'd invite her to a *gronbif* hunt."

Jacobo frowned. "The hunt has been over a while. I thought you'd have left by now."

"And miss the show?" she answered flirtatiously.

"I don't know if it's an appropriate place . . . ," began Jacobo, looking to Manuel and Antón.

"For a white woman?" she finished with a wry smile. "Come on, Jacobo. Don't be so old-fashioned."

Antón looked at his eldest son and shrugged. The sudden memory of an inquisitive Mariana pestering him to let her see one of those dances brought a small smile to his face. That was thirty years ago. A lifetime! He sighed, drank a little more *malamba*, and sat down in the chair that José had thoughtfully set out; that night he decided to be swept away by the drums and into the past.

Kilian sat on the ground next to Manuel and Julia, distancing himself from the rest of the employees. This was also his first African party, so he could understand her curiosity. He was confused by

Jacobo's reaction. All of a sudden, his brother could not stop looking at her with a furrowed brow. Was it possible that he was jealous? Kilian did not think it would be bad for his brother to get a little taste of his own medicine. Kilian accepted another glass from Simón, and a marvelous sense of well-being enveloped him. He let himself be carried away, along with Julia, by the magic of the night springing from the flames of the fire.

Many of the women had decorated their necks, waists, and ankles with collars. They wore frayed skirts that swayed with the vibrant, infectious, and repetitious music coming from the drum skins. The veins of the musicians' arms traced their glistening muscles.

The rhythm accelerated, and the dancers began to twist and writhe, moving every centimeter of their bodies at a frenetic pace. Their breasts swung in a mesmerizing pattern before the proud gazes of their men. Julia would have liked to remove her dress and become infected by the energy of their pleasure. Manuel glanced at her out of the corner of his eye, bewitched by the inquisitive sparkle in her eyes. She seemed to absorb the scene and inject it directly into the blood in her veins.

The impossible movements continued for quite a while. The women were joined by some men, even white men, in a dance that was devilishly wild and erotic. Kilian recognized Ekon, Mosi, and Nelson. He laughed to himself. If Umaru had been there, his group of *recognizable* men would have been complete. The bodies shone and drops of sweat trickled down their taut limbs. When Kilian's chest—and surely those of the rest of the white men—was about to burst, pleading for breath, the pace slowed down and the young lads practiced some steps until the music stopped. The hunks of meat and more drinks were passed around amid the shouts and songs of the Nigerians and the silence of the Spaniards, still ecstatic and shaken by the ancestral dance.

For Julia, the magic broke when she looked at her watch.

"Good heavens! It's so late. My parents!" she said in a whisper.

"If you'd like," Manuel leaned over and whispered in her ear, "I'll take another car, follow you home, and we can tell them that we met at the cinema and went to have a drink afterward."

"You'd do that?"

"I'd be delighted. But we won't tell them what film we saw." He winked.

Julia and Manuel said good-bye to the others and left. Jacobo followed them with his eyes.

"Good-bye, Julia," called Gregorio. "Regards to Emilio."

She turned around and waved vaguely.

"I didn't know you knew Julia," said Jacobo.

"Oh, yes. In fact, I saw her in the shop a couple of weeks ago. She asked me about some incident on the plantation. I explained her error. Didn't your little brother tell you?"

Jacobo looked at Kilian, who gave a resigned nod.

"Gregorio, you are a total ass," he spat out. He sprung up and stood squarely in front of him. "Get up! I'm going to smash your face!"

Antón and the others quickly gathered round. Gregorio stood, ready to confront Jacobo. Many laborers observed them with an amused gleam in their eyes. It was very unusual for two white men to fight.

"You're not going to do anything, Jacobo," said Antón firmly, grabbing his arm. "We are all tired and drank too much. In the morning, we'll see everything differently."

Jacobo stalked off, followed by Mateo and Marcial in search of more drink. Gregorio sat down, looking around for some woman to finish the night with.

Kilian decided to retire with the older men. His legs felt like rubber, and he had to make a serious effort to walk straight so that his father would not notice how drunk he felt.

The heat was still with him when he entered his bedroom. There was still no electricity, and he walked clumsily toward the window to open the wooden blinds. He stumbled against a soft object and nearly fell over. Just then, he heard a whisper that sounded like a hiss. He turned around, and all the blood rushed to his head as his muscles became paralyzed in terror. Just there, insolently upright, with a triangle head the size of a coconut, he saw a snake over one meter in length weaving back and forth.

Kilian wanted to move, but he could not. He felt bewitched by the devilish animal. It had a pointed snout and two sharp horns separated by smaller ones between its nostrils. On its head, a big black arrow-shaped mark stood out, matching the black diamonds joined in twos by yellow lines and forming a fascinating mosaic down its back.

He wanted to shout, but he could not. The snake came toward him, swelling its body and increasing the intensity of its hiss. It projected itself forward, revealing its large hooked fangs, full of deadly venom. Kilian's eyes located his machete on a chair. He only had to stretch to get it, but his arm felt as heavy as a wooden beam. His temples throbbed, and a great vacuum turned his body into a hollow trunk.

He had to do something.

He concentrated all his efforts on his throat muscles and let out a quivering bellow, increasing in volume as his hand clasped the machete and he swung it round to lop off the head of the snake. He continued shouting as he kept hitting, turning the snake into a mass of bloody meat with a fury he could not control. His own blood started to circulate through his veins, sending pulses of moonshine-fueled euphoria through him. He skewered the head with his machete and strode out of the bedroom.

On the veranda, he bumped into Simón, who had run toward the bedroom after hearing the shouts. He caught him with his free hand and shook him.

"This didn't get into my room on its own!" he howled. "You are in charge of my things! Who paid you to do it, hey? Who?"

Simón barely recognized the man who held his arm in an iron grip. "It wasn't me, Massa!" he pleaded. "I was with you all the time outside!"

Two doors opened, and Antón and Santiago appeared. They quickly released Simón as Kilian scanned the group still by the fire. Disjointed images flashed through his mind of naked bodies moving to the beat of the drums, incoherent laughs and twisted smiles, blood and more blood, an elephant collapsing in agony, headless rats, slithering snakes, machete chops, Mosi, Ekon, Nelson . . .

He fixed his gaze back on Simón.

"Have you seen anyone wandering around here?"

"No, Massa . . . well, yes, Massa." The lad bit his bottom lip.

"Which is it?" shouted Kilian, waving away Antón and Santiago.

"When I came for the glasses, I saw Umaru coming down the stairs."

"Umaru . . . Clean the room!" Simón ordered him. "Now!"

Kilian flew down the steps, crossed the yard in leaping bounds, and showed the head skewered on the machete to those who remained by the fire. The light of the kerosene lamps cast a grotesque shadow on the ground. Jacobo, Marcial, and Mateo jumped up, startled by Kilian's bloody appearance.

"He's not to move from here." He pointed at Gregorio. "Nelson! Where is Umaru?"

"I don't know, Massa." The foreman shrugged. "I haven't seen him for a while."

"Find him and bring him! You hear me? Tell him make him come. Bring him, blast you! And bring your switch as well!"

There was a deadly silence. The women gathered the children together and crept quietly away. Jacobo and the rest exchanged confused glances. Antón, Santiago, and José arrived and stood by them.

Shortly afterward, Nelson appeared, holding Umaru by the arm. He shoved him in front of Kilian.

"Who ordered you to put this"—Kilian brought the head of the snake toward Umaru's face—"in my bedroom? Hey? Who paid you?"

Umaru's teeth began to chatter as he repeated the same words over and over.

Nelson translated. "He says he knows nothing. He says he was dancing at the party the whole time."

"That is a lie." Kilian spat out the words. "You were seen in the bedroom passage." He threw the machete to the ground and held out his hand to Nelson. "Give me the switch." Nelson hesitated. "I told you to give me the switch! Umaru . . . if you no tell me true, I go hit you!"

Antón stepped forward to intervene, but Jacobo stopped him. "No, Dad, let him sort this out."

Kilian felt the thinness of the switch in his hands. Pain rose in his temples, his chest, his teeth . . . He hated this place! He was tired of the heat, the bugs, the orders, the cocoa trees, and Gregorio! God, if he could only return to Pasolobino. He could hardly breathe. Umaru continued to say nothing. Dozens of eyes waited for Kilian's next move. He raised his hand and let loose a belt on Umaru's arms. Umaru screamed in pain.

"Hold him, Nelson!" He raised the switch and asked again, "Who paid you, Umaru?"

Umaru shook his head. "I no know, Massa! I no know!"

Kilian circled and hit him again, this time on the back, once, twice, three times, four . . . The lashes opened thin furrows on the skin, and blood dripped to the ground. Kilian was out of control. He did not hear Umaru, who, on his knees, begged him to stop.

He was about to hit him again when a hand grabbed his arm and a quiet voice spoke. "That's enough, Massa Kilian. The lad has said he will tell you everything."

Kilian looked up. It was José. He felt disconcerted, once again a hollow man. Kilian was incapable of looking him in the eye. Umaru stayed kneeling. Between snivels and whimpers, he explained that they had found a nest of *bitis* in the cocoa trees, near the border with the jungle, that he had called Massa Gregor over to kill them, and that the massa had ordered him to go and find a box, where Umaru had kept them until nighttime. The lack of electricity helped give him the chance to sneak into the bedroom.

"And your fear of snakes?" Kilian asked in sudden apathy. "How much did Massa Gregor pay you to get over it?"

He did not wait for an answer, turning instead to the mastermind, who tilted his head back with a slight smile.

"Congratulations," said Gregorio with disdain. "You are now almost like me. You'll do well on the island."

Kilian held Gregorio's ratlike gaze. Then without warning, he punched him so hard in the stomach that he fell to the ground.

"Case closed." He threw the switch down in rage. *"Palabra conclú."*

He walked away, shrouded in total silence.

When Kilian went into the bedroom, he saw that Simón had cleaned everything and left a lamp lit. There was no trace of the snake. Kilian sat on the bed and buried his head in his hands. His breathing still felt unsteady. The last few minutes of his life paraded clearly across the dark screen of his mind. He saw a white man brutally beating a black man. He saw how he broke the skin until blood poured out. He saw dozens of men silent and unmoved as the blows continued. That man was him! He had allowed himself to be overcome and hit Umaru in blind rage! How could it have happened? What demon had taken over his psyche?

He was disgusted with himself.

His head went around in circles. He could barely get up. He went over to the basin, his insides wrecked with nausea, and vomited until not even bile was left. He raised his head and saw his face reflected in the mirror hanging over the basin.

He did not recognize himself.

His green eyes, sunken in two dark bowls against the pallor of his angular blood-splatted cheeks, seemed grayer than ever, and his forehead was marked by deep lines.

"I'm not like him," he said. "I'm not like him!"

His shoulders began to shake, and deep sobs rose within him.

Kilian cried bitterly until he had no tears left.

The following morning, the manager called for him. In his office, Kilian found Gregorio, Antón, and José.

"I'll get straight to the point," said Garuz gruffly. "It's evident that you can no longer work together." He spoke to Gregorio. "I will send Marcial with you to Obsay. He is the only one who can keep you under control, and he doesn't mind going."

He turned to Kilian, who had to make a real effort to keep his composure. The man's words reverberated in his head with the intensity of a drill. He had gotten up with a terrible headache and still had some blurred vision. Hopefully the *optalidones* he had taken on an empty stomach would soon take effect.

"From now on, you will work with Antón and José in the main yard. Don't take this as some kind of reward. One more incident, no matter what, and you're sacked, is that clear?" He rapped the desk with his fingers. "I'm only giving you this chance for your father, so you can thank him. That's all." Garuz picked up some papers. "You may leave."

The men stood and walked toward the door in silence. Kilian was last, his head low so as not to have to look at his father. Outside, the others broke away. Kilian decided to go to the dining room for a coffee to wake himself up. Soon after, Jacobo entered.

"I was looking for you." Jacobo's voice sounded hoarse. "Dad brought me up to date. Are you all right?"

Kilian nodded.

"I'm happy that I'm not going back to Obsay," he said, "but I'm sorry for taking your place. I suppose it was your turn to be in the main yard."

"No way!" Jacobo shook his head. "I'm perfectly fine where I am. In Yakató, nobody controls me." He winked and gave him a friendly elbow.

"Mateo and I have set it up very well. In the main yard, everything can be seen. But we wastrels, we prefer darkness."

He saw that Kilian did not laugh and grew serious.

"You did the right thing, Kilian. You showed them who's the boss. From now on, they will respect you. Gregorio as well."

Kilian pursed his lips. This newfound authority did not make him one bit proud. He sat and accepted the coffee offered by Simón. With a wave of his hand, he did not let the lad add any brandy.

"I'm off," Jacobo said as he left his brother. "We'll see each other at dinner."

When Jacobo passed through the doorway, Simón came over to Kilian as if to talk, but he restrained himself.

"I'm fine, Simón," said Kilian. "I don't need anything else. You can go."

Simón did not budge.

"Is there something wrong, lad?"

"You see, Massa . . . there is something you should know."

"What is it?" he said, slightly annoyed. The coffee had warmed his stomach, but the headache persisted. The last thing he wanted was to listen to insignificant problems. He had enough with his own.

"Last night something happened, Massa. Two friends of Umaru wanted to get you back for the beating and came after you."

Kilian, stunned, raised his head.

"Yes, Massa. After the party, José did not go to sleep like everyone else. He told me he noticed something strange. He stayed up all night for you. Yes, yes, and so did I. Using the darkness, they went up to your room, and there we were hiding. José and me and two of the guards who owe José some favors." He opened his dark, shining eyes. "They were carrying machetes to kill you! You were very lucky José was there, Massa! Very lucky!"

Kilian wanted to say something, but he could not. He lifted the cup, and Simón went for more coffee.

"What will happen to them?" Kilian finally asked when the boy returned from the kitchen.

"They will be sent back to Nigeria. Umaru as well. But don't worry, the *big massa* won't hear everything. And nobody will say anything. I don't think anyone else will try it again. There is no danger now, Massa, but it would be better to close your window and your door properly for a while."

"Thank you, Simón," murmured a pensive Kilian. "For your help and for telling me."

"Please, Massa . . . ," the lad pleaded, "don't tell José I told you. He knows my family, we're from the same village . . . He made me promise not to say anything."

"So then why did you?"

"You are good to me, Massa. And the thing with the snake was not right. No, Massa, it was not right."

"Relax, Simón." Kilian got to his feet and put a hand on his shoulder. "I'll keep the secret."

Kilian went outside, where he looked up to the sky, contemplating the low dark clouds. He could breathe the humidity. As the hours went by, the heat would be sticky, but he welcomed the chance to enjoy a new day despite his headache, the remorse that had taken hold of his heart, and the fear of what might have happened.

At a few meters' distance, he made out the unhurried walk of José, who moved from one end of the yard to the other, organizing the men for the day's tasks. He was a man of average height, strong despite his thin physique, which starkly contrasted the muscular bodies of the laborers. From time to time, he would stroke his short gray beard slowly and pensively. The workers respected him, perhaps because he looked like their fathers. He knew each one's name and talked to them firmly but without raising his voice, gesturing energetically but without violence, as if he knew how they felt at every moment.

As he looked at José, Kilian felt enormously grateful. They had tried to get revenge while he was asleep . . . He owed him his life! If José had gone to bed like everyone else, at this moment, Kilian would be . . . dead! Why had he done it? Perhaps for Antón. A shiver ran through his body. He did not know how, but he would find a way of showing this man that his noble and brave act had been worth it.

That same night, Kilian took a pickup and, without saying anything to his companions, drove to Santa Isabel.

He went into Anita Guau and went straight to the bar to order a whiskey and ask for Sade.

That night, Kilian clung tightly to the body of the woman with cold greed, enjoying her like the moss enjoys the ceiba tree: celebrating life without feeding off it.

6

Inside the Bush

1955

The last truck of cocoa sacks drove out along the royal palm drive heading for the port in Santa Isabel. Kilian saw it go with relief, pride, and satisfaction. He had successfully completed his first full campaign on the island. After twenty-four months, he considered himself an expert in the cocoa production process. Sampaka's cocoa was famous all over the world because of the meticulous way it was made to achieve maximum quality. It sold for five pesetas more per kilo, and tons of it were produced. This meant an absolute fortune. And Kilian had helped after endless hours in the dryers: day and night checking the texture of the bean by hand, making sure that it swelled without flaking and that it was roasted just enough—not a second more nor a second less—so it did not turn white. The dry and well-fermented cocoa that filled the sacks, ready for shipping, was thick, chocolate in color, brittle, fairly bitter to taste, and had a pleasant aroma.

With tired faces, Jacobo and Mateo sat down on a low wall, and each lit a cigarette. Marcial stayed standing.

"I'm wrecked," huffed Mateo. "I've even got cocoa dust in my mustache."

Jacobo took a handkerchief out of his pocket and wiped his forehead.

"Garuz will be happy with this harvest," he said. "The best in years. He'll have to give us bonuses!"

Kilian was also exhausted. More than once he had been tempted to copy the odd laborer and use the din of the Christmas parties to escape from work. He sat down beside the others and accepted the cigarette his brother offered him. He inhaled deeply. A fine chocolate-colored dust had seeped into every last pore of his skin. When the dryers ceased all their activity, the smell of roasted cocoa persisted. The sun was going down, but the terrible heat had not abated. Still the echoes of the Christmas carols and boozy parties of his second Christmas away from home seemed strange in the sticky heat. He remembered the mass on the twenty-fifth of December—short sleeves, skin tanned by the sun, and the midnight dips in the pool on the plantation. This dry season was hotter than normal, and the occasional shower in Sampaka did not give any relief from the sweltering heat.

"In the mountains of Pasolobino, I'm sure it's bitterly cold, right, lads?" said Marcial, opening the tiny buttons of his shirt with difficulty.

Kilian imagined his parents and Catalina in front of the fire while the livestock fed themselves in the sheds and the snow covered the fields in a thick blanket. He missed them, but with the passing of the months, the terrible homesickness of the first weeks on the island had faded. It was not pulling at his heartstrings as hard.

"The truth is I'm looking forward to a change of scenery," commented Kilian.

"Well, it won't be too long now. When Dad returns—because I'll bet you anything that he will be back—you'll be going to Spain on holidays. I'm jealous!"

Antón had said good-bye to his sons as if he were never returning to the plantation. Kilian was also convinced that, as last year, he would be back, rested and a little heavier.

"Hey, don't complain," Kilian reproached his brother. "You'll be going soon."

"It kills me to say it, but I have to admit that you've earned the right to go first, hasn't he, Mateo?"

Mateo agreed.

"Who would have thought? Even your appearance has changed. When you arrived, you were all skin and bone. And look at you now! You have more muscles than Mosi!"

Kilian smiled at the over-the-top comparison, but the truth was he had given his all so that his father, his brother, his work colleagues, and the manager would be proud of him, and also to make up for the incident with Umaru and Gregorio. It had not been difficult, as he was used to hard work. He remembered his first days on the island. Despite everything, he had fit into the daily routine set out by the sounds of the *tumba*, the *droma*, and the Nigerian songs. Soon work would begin again outside in the cocoa trees at the edge of the jungle, hours and hours of the machete falling implacably on the *bikoro*, the Bordeaux mixture being sprayed on the young shoots . . .

"In the end, I have to say that you were all right, Dad and you and Julia . . . Yes, I've gotten used to the island. But a good long rest at home won't do me any harm."

He noticed out of the corner of his eye that Jacobo pursed his lips when Julia's name was mentioned. The previous November, amid the festive dances, concerts, and canoe races of Santa Isabel's festival, Julia and Manuel had made their engagement official. From then on, they were inseparable, traveling the island in search of plants for Manuel's studies, having afternoon snacks in the Moka Parador, or enjoying a good film or a refreshing dip in the casino's swimming pool. Emilio and Generosa were delighted. Manuel, as well as being an educated and well-mannered man, was a doctor. *Their daughter* was engaged to a doctor. Jacobo appeared to accept the news well, although, deep down, his pride had been wounded. He was fully aware that he had lost his chance to win the heart of an extraordinary woman. So he continued dividing his existence between Sampaka and Santa Isabel, only regretting a lack of friends for his parties. Bata was not close enough for Dick and Pao to come to the island regularly, and Mateo and Marcial alternated between their dissolute flings and their dates—each time more frequent—with Julia's friends in the casino.

"The one that will miss you is that little belter . . ." Mateo maliciously half closed his eyes. "What's her name? I always forget it!"

"Which one of them? He's got all of them mad for him." Marcial scrunched his lips in a kiss. "Careful, Jacobo. Your brother is gaining ground on you."

"Well, he has plenty to do to catch up with me!" Jacobo laughed. "He looks more like a Claretian father than anything else. Do you know what the girls in the city tell me?" He looked at Kilian. "They're saying that you are going to take on the rough appearance of the plantationers who disconnect themselves from the world."

"Fine, fine. It's not that bad. And you two," Kilian jokingly counterattacked, pointing to Mateo and Marcial alternately, "you remember what you want to remember. I suppose that with Mercedes and Ascensión, you'll forget about the friends in Anita's."

"Completely," Mateo agreed with an impish look. "And the opposite as well."

The four burst out laughing.

"Yes, yes, you laugh," said Jacobo sarcastically, "but I see that like Manuel, you will make the engagement official and start having afternoon snacks in the Parador."

"Everyone's hour comes sometime, Jacobo." Marcial shrugged his broad shoulders with a resigned smile. "Sooner or later, but it comes. The years pass and a family has to be formed, says I."

"I'm going for a shower. It's dinnertime." Jacobo jumped to his feet and began walking to the dining room.

"It's bloody amazing how much that lad likes black meat!" whispered Mateo to Marcial, shaking his head. "I don't know if he could get used to the other now."

Kilian scowled. The same thing always happened: after a good laugh, there was always a bitter aftertaste. He lit a cigarette and let the others pass him. He enjoyed this moment where, almost without warning, day became night. He leaned back against a wall, waiting for the shadows, and he thought of Sade.

In his mind, he drew the svelte figure of the woman, her long legs, her smooth skin, her generous and firm breasts, her long, thin face with dark almond-shaped eyes and full lips. Like the dark dust that pervaded the atmosphere, the dizzying succession of days in the last few months had also been bittersweet, rivers of sweat compensated by an excellent harvest and by short moments with her. As Kilian's body and limbs filled out and his skin took on a permanent tan, he noticed he was as successful as Jacobo at a dance. Decked out in their white linen shirts, perfectly ironed, their baggy beige trousers and their brilliantine-doused dark hair, the brothers had no problem getting the attention of women—white and black. Kilian knew all too well that going out with Jacobo meant finishing up fairly drunk on whiskey and in the arms of a pretty woman, but he had gotten tired of this months ago. So he had decided to restrict his outings to the city to those sporadic encounters with the beautiful Sade. She never asked or reproached him for anything. He went to the club, and there was his Sade, always willing to be with him after weeks had passed. Kilian enjoyed his occasional moments with her, and he laughed at her fresh sense of humor and her worldly and affectionate attitude.

In the end, he had not been able to avoid everyone finding out about his relationship, and he had to put up with the jokes. He tried to act indifferent, and even gave witty replies, but in his heart of hearts, he felt ashamed. He was no different from the rest of them, even getting to the point of asking himself if one day he could think of Sade as a woman that he could plan a future with or start a family . . .

The answer circled his insides until it became confused with the craving for another cigarette, and that is where it stayed, crouched and cowardly like a rat in the forest.

A few days later, Jacobo approached Kilian with a telegram he had received from Bata.

"It's from Dick. He's inviting us on another elephant hunt in Cameroon, and to spend some time in Douala. Garuz is happy. I'm sure he'll give us permission. It's a pity that it coincides with the harvest party at the Fishing Club next Saturday. The whole world will be there. And I also have tickets for the evening's boxing in the Santa Isabel stadium. Slow Poison versus Bala Negra." He swore. "We go through months with nothing and then everything at once! What'll we do?"

Kilian had no intention of going to any of the events, especially after hearing about the hunt from Dick and Pao. And he did not fancy another big party. As for boxing, he got no pleasure in seeing two men beating each other till they collapsed.

"I won't go to Cameroon," he answered. "It's bound to cost a lot of money, and I'm saving it for my trip to Spain. But you should go without me."

"Yes, but . . ." Jacobo clicked his tongue. "I'll tell you what. We'll do it next time. Then, we'll go to the party . . . We can go to the boxing match afterward."

Kilian said nothing.

A few meters away, José appeared with a load of empty sacks left over from packing the cocoa. He stopped to tell a worker to sweep better and not to leave any of the husks that remained in the dryers; they would be sold to make low-quality cocoa.

Kilian smiled. José was something else! He had never met such a meticulous person. Over the last number of months, Kilian had gotten to know him better than any other employee on the plantation. Truthfully, he felt comfortable in his company. José was a quiet man—his rare outbursts lasted no more than a few seconds—blessed with an innate wisdom.

"Don't tell me you have other plans with José," said Jacobo, looking in the same direction as his brother.

"Why do you say that?"

"Come on, Kilian, I wasn't born yesterday. Do you think I don't know that you escape with him to Bissappoo whenever you get the chance? I can't understand it."

"I've only gone three or four afternoons."

"And what do you do there?"

"Why don't you come one day and see?"

"Go up to Bissappoo? For what?"

"To spend the afternoon. To talk to José's family. You know, Jacobo, it reminds me of Pasolobino. Each one does what they have to do, and later they gather to tell stories, like we do at home beside the fire. There are loads of young children laughing and playing pranks, and their mothers get annoyed. Their culture is mysterious and interesting. And they ask about our valley—"

Jacobo waved his hand in annoyance. "For God's sake, Kilian! There's no comparison!" he said with slight contempt. "How could you prefer that village to Santa Isabel?"

"I didn't say that I preferred it," retorted his brother. "There's time for everything."

"I can imagine the intelligent conversations you have there!"

"Hey, Jacobo"—Kilian sighed—"you know José as well. Is he that different?"

"Apart from being black, you mean . . ."

"Yes, of course."

"That's already enough for me, Kilian. We're different."

"To speak to them, they are different, but to sleep with them, they aren't?"

Jacobo squinted. "You know what?" He raised his voice. "I think the holidays will do you good!"

He marched off angrily. Kilian did not flinch. Jacobo was a bit short-tempered. Tonight he would be back to his normal self.

Kilian looked around again for José, who was on his way to one of the stores. He called out his name in Bubi, "Ösé! Hey, Ösé!"

José looked up and joined the young man.

"Have you any plans for the coming weekend?" Kilian asked.

"Nothing special." José shrugged, knowing that Kilian probably needed a good excuse to get out of something. "One of my daughters is getting married."

"Gosh! And that's not special?" Kilian asked. "Congratulations! Which one?"

By now, Kilian knew José's history. His mother was Bubi and his father Fernandino, the name used to refer to the descendants of the first slaves freed by the British in the previous century. The majority came from Sierra Leone and Jamaica and mixed with other freed Africans and Cubans. From what José had told him, they had once been an influential bourgeoisie family, but when the Spaniards acquired the island, they lost their status. From his father, José had learned English and Bantú English and had been sent together with his brothers and sisters to the Catholic mission school. He was one of the few natives his age who could read and write. José married a Bubi woman and had several children. Continuing his father's tradition, they also attended the Catholic school. Not all the Bubis approved of this. The more reactionary ones thought that white culture offended their spirits and traditions, though they had no option but to obey the colonists.

"The last one," responded José.

"The last one!" exclaimed Kilian, pretending to be scandalized. "Good God, Ösé! But . . . isn't she five?"

Kilian knew that the young Bubis got married at twelve or thirteen, but he also suspected that the little girl who affectionately hugged him each time he went up to the village was the smallest of the numerous other children born of polygamy. The practice was frowned upon by the Spanish Catholics, so José never talked about his other wives, if he actually had any, and especially not in front of the missionaries and priests like Father Rafael, who were still trying to free the natives from their ancient customs.

José let the comment fly over his head. He looked around him to make sure that everything was tidy before going to dinner. When they had gone some meters, he turned and asked, finally, what Kilian had been waiting to hear.

"Perhaps you would like to come to a Bubi wedding, Massa Kilian?"

Kilian's eyes lit up. "I've told you a thousand times not to address me like that! I'll accept your invitation if you promise me not to use the word *massa* again."

"Agreed, Ma—" José corrected himself with a wide smile, "Kilian. As you wish."

"And I don't want you to be so formal with me either! I'm much younger than you. Agreed?"

"I won't call you massa, but I'll still be formal. It is difficult for me not to . . ."

"Oh, come on! You've had to adapt to much more!"

José shook his head but did not answer.

Waldo took them by truck to the southeastern border of the plantation, where the track became unsuitable for road vehicles. From there, José and Kilian continued on foot along a narrow path crossed by hundreds of branches, lianas, and leaves that screened, and occasionally completely blocked out, the sunlight. The sounds of their steps were softened by the springy carpet of fallen leaves dotted with palm pips from the fruit that had rotted on the ground or been eaten by monkeys. Kilian enjoyed listening to the trills and chirping of the blackbirds, nightingales, and *filicotoys*; the chatter of the parrots and the cooing of a wild pigeon that intermittently broke the solemn calm; and the grave silence under the soft green and living canopy through which they walked with difficulty. The scenery and sounds of the island were very beautiful. It was no surprise that centuries ago, the island's discoverer, the Portuguese Fernão do Po, had called it Formosa, meaning "beautiful."

Kilian imagined other men like him journeying down this same path in centuries past. It was the same path, they said, but it always looked different because of the tenacious vegetation. How many machetes had moved the plants that kept sprouting back? On his previous trips to Bissappoo, and in answer to Kilian's many questions, José had told him about the island's history. Kilian knew the long-living ceiba trees held many stories in their wrinkled trunks, as well as multitudes of languages.

The island had been Portuguese until Portugal swapped it with Spain for other territories. Spain wanted its own source of slaves to transport to America. At this point in the story, Kilian always shuddered at the thought of José, Simón, Yeremías, or Waldo being captured to be sold in the same way as caged animals. As the Spaniards did not really take control of the island, the English war and merchant ships made use of it to collect water, yams, and live animals for their scientific, commercial, and exploratory voyages on the Niger River, on the continental part of Africa, and to control and keep in check the slave market, as England had already abolished slavery. Kilian thought of Dick, dressed in old-fashioned sailor's clothes as he freed his Bubi acquaintances. But Dick did not seem the hero type.

For many years, English was spoken on Fernando Po. England wished to buy the island, but Spain resisted, so in the middle of the nineteenth century, the English navy opted to move to Sierra Leone and sold their buildings to a Baptist mission. After that, the Spaniards tried once more to set up effective settlements with more complete expeditions, incentivizing the colonists and sending missionaries to convert the village natives, easier to convert than the city Baptists like José's paternal ancestors, until they dominated.

Kilian saw himself as one more link in this chain of men who, for one reason or another, had made the tropics their temporary home, but he was pleased to live in a more peaceful, civilized age than those previous. Still, in the middle of the wild jungle, it seemed completely the opposite.

After clearing the way with machetes and negotiating fallen trees, they decided to stop and rest in a clearing. Kilian's eyes stung from the sweat, and his arms bled slightly from small cuts from the branches. He cooled off in a stream and lay down on a cedar, close to José. He closed his eyes and inhaled the acrid smell of the dead leaves, ripe fruit, and damp earth that a barely noticeable breeze guided through the trees.

"Who is your future son-in-law?" he asked after a while.

"Mosi," José responded.

"Mosi? *The Egyptian?*" Kilian shot up. That was the colossus from the deforestation job. When he tensed his muscles, the sleeves of his shirt stretched to breaking point, and his head was shaven. It was best not to get on the wrong side of him.

"Yes, Mosi *the Egyptian.*"

"And you are happy with this?"

"Why wouldn't I be happy?" When Kilian did not answer, José said, "Does it surprise you?"

"Well, yes . . . I mean . . . I think he's a wonderful worker. But I don't know why I thought that you would prefer your daughter to marry one of your own."

"My mother was Bubi and she married a Fernandino . . ."

"I know that, but your father was also from Fernando Po. I was referring to the Nigerian laborers who come earn money and later return to Nigeria."

"Don't take offense, Kilian, but though they earn less, in this respect they are the same as the whites, yes?"

"Yes, but the whites aren't marrying your daughter. They won't take her far away."

"Mosi won't take her away." José seemed annoyed. "The Nigerian contracts force them to return to their country after a certain period. But if they marry in Guinea, they can set themselves up here, open a bar or a shop, or work a small plot of land. Above all, here they can get an education for their children and hospital services that they don't have in their own country. Don't you think those are good reasons? Many workers save up to pay the dowry and marry one of our women, which is what Mosi has done."

To Kilian, paying the dowry reminded him of the old stories from the valley. Only in his valley, it was the woman who had to supply the sum and not the other way round.

"And how much is Mosi going to give for her?" he asked out of curiosity.

José gritted his teeth. "White man no *sabi* anything about black fashion," he murmured.

"What did you say?"

"I said that the whites haven't got a clue about black customs!" He jumped up and stood before Kilian. "Look, *Massa*." He used the word harshly. "Let me tell you something. No matter how many times I explain some things, you'll never understand them. You seem to think

I don't love my daughters, or that I sell them as if they were sacks of cocoa."

"I didn't say that!" protested Kilian.

"But you believe it!" He saw the young man's look of disappointment and adopted a fatherly tone. "I think it's good for my daughter to marry Mosi because Mosi is a good laborer. They'll be able to live on the plantation for many years. When they are girls, Bubi women enjoy themselves and have fun, but once they get married, they don't do anything else but work for their husband and children. They are in charge of everything, the firewood, the fields, collecting water . . ." He counted the tasks on his fingers. "The women plant, cultivate, harvest, and store the malanga. They prepare the palm oil. They cook. They bring up the children . . ." He paused for a moment and raised a finger in the air. "While their husbands spend the day"—the finger danced in the air—"from here to there, drinking palm wine or chatting to other men in the village house."

Kilian remained silent, playing with a twig.

"Marrying Mosi is good for her," continued José, now more relaxed. "They'll live in one of the family barracks in Obsay. My daughter is a good student. She could help in the hospital and study to become a nurse. I've already spoken to Massa Manuel."

"It's a good idea, Ösé," Kilian said hesitatingly. "I'm sorry if I upset you."

José nodded as Kilian got to his feet and said, "We'd better keep walking."

Bissappoo was located on one of the highest parts of the island, so there was still a good distance to go before getting to the most difficult part of the journey, which was when the path began to slope upward. Kilian grabbed his bag and his machete, put on his pith helmet, and began walking behind José. They trekked in silence for a good distance, going farther and farther into the jungle. The tree trunks were covered in parasitic plants, ferns, and orchids, on which rested a multitude of ants, butterflies, and small birds.

Kilian felt a little awkward with the silence. They had worked together many times without exchanging a word, but this time it was different. He regretted that José had misinterpreted his comments, born out of curiosity rather than bad manners. As if he had read his mind, José stopped and, with his hands on his hips, in the same way as if he were talking about the weather, commented, "This land belonged to my great-grandfather." He gave the ground a small kick. "Just here. He exchanged it for a bottle of alcohol and a rifle."

Kilian blinked in surprise, but grinned at what he thought was a joke. "Stop it! You're pulling my leg!"

"No, sir. I'm serious. This land is good for coffee, because of its height. One day there will be a plantation here. The gods will decide if we'll get to see it." He glanced at Kilian, who still had a frown of disbelief on his face, and cheekily asked, "How do you think the colonists got the land? Have you met a rich Bubi?"

"No, but . . . Come on, I don't believe it was all like that, Ösé. Your great-grandfather's case was an exception." He tried to defend the men who with tremendous effort had transformed the island into what it now was. "Besides, doesn't every native get assigned four hectares for his own crops?"

"Yes, a few hectares that were theirs to begin with," responded José sarcastically. "Very generous of the whites! If they hadn't repealed the law a few years ago, you yourself could have opted for a thirty-hectare plot in ten years, or less if you called in a favor."

Kilian felt like an idiot. He had never thought of the natives as the owners of the island. He was still just a white colonist who thought the history of Fernando Po started with the Portuguese, the English, and especially the Spanish. He was sorry for having had so little tact with the man he owed his life to.

"Well, I . . . Actually . . . What I mean is that . . ." He let out a snort and started slashing all the plants in his path. "It's clear that I just keep putting my foot in it today!"

José followed, his face beaming. It was impossible to be annoyed with Kilian for very long. This young man, nervous and bursting with energy, wanted to learn something new every day. Although he had had a rough time at the start, seldom had a European adapted so quickly to the arduous work on the plantation. And Kilian was not one to just give orders. No. He was the first to go up a scaffolding, lift sacks, drive a truck, or take off his shirt to dig a hole or plant a palm. This attitude had shocked the laborers, used to the lash of the *melongo*. José thought that, in part, Kilian did all these things to please his father, even if he was not aware of it. He looked for Antón's approval and, by extension, the rest of the family's. He continually had to show how strong and brave he was. And even more so now with Antón showing obvious signs of being worn out.

Yes, Kilian would have been a good Bubi warrior.

"Look at the way you cut the undergrowth! With men like you, Kilian, the whole colonization would have taken two years, and not decades. Did you know that the members of the first expeditions died in a matter of weeks? Like flies! The ships were sent with two captains so that there would always be one in reserve."

"I don't understand why," Kilian scoffed. "It's not that difficult to adapt."

"Ah! But that's because things are different now. When there were no whites, the Bubis knew how to live in harmony on the island. The hard work, the work that is now done by the blacks, you did, the whites. You dug under the burning heat of the tropical sun and in the places where it was easiest to catch malaria. And there was no quinine then! In less than a hundred years, this island full of so-called cannibals has become what you see now."

"I can't imagine you eating anybody," joked Kilian.

"It would surprise you to know what I'm capable of!"

Kilian finally smiled. "And what did you live on before us? As far as I know, even the plots you tend come from our seeds."

"This land is so rich that you can live with little. The gods have blessed it with fertility. The wild fruit trees produce oranges, lemons, guavas, mangoes, tamarinds, bananas, and pineapples. Cotton grows wild. And what about the bread tree, with fruit bigger than coconuts? With some livestock, and growing our yams, we had more than enough."

"It's obvious, Ösé," said Kilian, drying the sweat with his sleeve. "You don't need us for anything!"

"Ah! And the palm trees! Do you know any other tree where everything can be used? From the palms we get *topé* or wine; oil for stews, condiments, and for lighting the home; we use the leaves to roof our houses; from the canes we make houses and hats; and the young shoots we eat as a vegetable. Tell me, has Pasolobino any tree like the sacred palm?"

He paused for breath.

"Have you noticed how they rise up to the sky?" José looked up, his voice ceremonious once again. "They look like columns holding up the world, crowned with the plumes of a warrior. The palms, Kilian, were here before us, and they will be here when we are gone. They are our symbol of resilience. Come what may."

Kilian looked to the sky, suddenly moved by José's words. The tops of the joined palms appeared to form a celestial vault where the fruit bunches twinkled like stars and constellations. In the tops, a soft breeze rocked the branches toward the sky, as if making a leafy gesture toward eternity.

He closed his eyes and allowed himself to be drowned in the moment. Everything distant seemed near. Time and space, history and countries, heavens and earth melded together in an instant of tranquility.

"We are now in the *böhabba*!"

With that, José broke the heavenly spell. A few paces away, the path opened out, and Kilian glimpsed the plain that Bissappoo villagers had allocated for growing yams. To the right, he saw the shed where they made the traditional red palm oil. On a previous trip, José had shown him how it was meticulously produced. Women pulled out the heart of the petals and made a pile that others covered with palm leaves to get it to ferment; others milled them with a big stone in a hole shaped like a mortar dug in the ground and with stones covering the bottom; and others picked out the fruit pips and put the macerated pulp to boil in a pot over a fire to extract the oil.

"You'll see what a great celebration it is!" said José, happy among his own. "For special celebrations, the women always prepare plenty of food and drink."

Kilian nodded. He was as nervous as if it were his own family's wedding. He had spent more time with José over the last two years than he had with many from his own village. He worked, talked, and shared his worries with him. In turn, José had invited him to learn about his home outside the borders of Sampaka. He was in direct contrast with most of his neighbors in Bissappoo, a place that Father Rafael described as backward and reactionary. José was able to get along with whites and blacks equally, adapting to civilization without forgetting his traditions, and allowing a foreigner like Kilian to share in such family occasions as a daughter's wedding.

Kilian scratched his head. He was embarrassed to say how he felt, but he thought that José deserved it. He had never found the right opportunity to thank him.

"Listen, Ösé," he said, looking him straight in the eye. "I didn't tell you before, but I know what you did for me that night with Umaru. Thank you very much, my friend."

José nodded.

"Tell me one thing, Ösé. What I did wasn't right. But you helped me. Did you do it for my father?"

José shook his head. "I did it for you. That night I listened. You were a grown man and you cried like a child." He shrugged and raised the palms of his hands. "You were sorry because your heart is good." He gave the young man a couple of light thumps on the arm and in a whisper confided, "The spirits know that we all make mistakes sometimes."

Kilian sincerely thanked him for his words. "I also want you to know that although I'm white and you're black, when I look at you, I don't see a black man. Rather, I see José . . . I mean, Ösé." Kilian lowered his eyes, a little embarrassed by his outburst of sincerity, and scratched his arm. "You know what I mean."

José became emotional, shaking his head as if he did not believe what he had just heard. "If I hadn't walked all the way here with you," he said, "I would think you had drunk too much *topé*. We'll see if you still feel the same way the day after tomorrow, when you've suffered the consequences of a Bubi wedding celebration." He raised a finger in friendly caution. "Ah! And I'm warning you! If you put a hand on any of my daughters or nieces, I'll release the savage inside me!"

Kilian laughed. "Wouldn't you like me for a son-in-law?"

José did not answer the question. He looked at the women making palm oil, let out a long whistle, and began walking toward them.

When they passed the jars of water from the perennial springs, with which the Bubis from Bissappoo prayed for the growth of the village, and crossed through the wooden arch, on whose sides stood two *Ikos*, or sacred trees to keep away evil spirits, Kilian remembered the first afternoon he had come to the village with José. Warned by the whistles that a white man was approaching, men, women, and children came out to see with a certain mistrust. He had observed them in turn, and in some cases, he had to admit, with revulsion, especially the older men. Some of them sported huge hernias and ulcers, and others had pockmarked faces from smallpox or deep scarification. Under José's instruction, these men greeted him with respect and formality and invited him to enter their world.

Kilian also remembered that the variety of the amulets hanging from the arch—sheep's tails, animal skulls and bones, hen and pheasant feathers, antelope horns, and snail shells—had surprised him. In Pasolobino, they used to hang goats' legs over the houses and place stones in curious designs on the roofs, on top of the chimney stacks, to ward away witches. The fear of the unknown was the same in all parts of the world: in Africa, they had their evil spirits, and in the Pyrenees, the witches. Once inside the village, however, the differences between Pasolobino and Bissappoo could not have been more striking. The Spanish village consisted of clothed white bodies and solid buildings to shield inhabitants from the cold, the African village of seminaked black bodies and flimsy houses open to a public square. The first time that Kilian went to José's village, he could never have imagined that such different worlds would converge in his heart.

Some children pounced upon his pockets, hoping to find some sweet or other. Kilian, laughing, handed out small candies and confections that he had bought in Julia's shop. Two or three women lugging baskets of clean clothes and food waved. Several men stopped their slow walk and left on the ground the arch they used to clamber up the palms, shaking his hand by holding it affectionately in their own and placing it on their hearts.

"Ösé . . . where are all the women?" Kilian asked. "It seems I won't be able to put your threat to the test!"

José laughed. "They are preparing the food and getting themselves ready for the wedding. There's only a few hours to go. All women take a long time to get made up with *ntola*."

"And what shall we do in the meantime?"

"We'll sit down in the *riösa* with the men and wait."

They went toward an open square where the children played and the village meetings were held. In the center, under the shade of the sacred trees, there were some bushes with a number of stones that were used as seats by a group of men waving to them in greeting. A few paces farther on, two small cabins had been built for praying to the spirits.

"Don't you have to change your clothes?" Kilian left his rucksack on the ground beside the other men.

"Am I not all right as I am?" José wore long trousers and a white shirt. "I'm wearing the same as you . . ."

"Yes, of course you're all right. It's just that I thought, as you are the father of the bride, you would be wearing something more . . . more . . . of your own . . ."

"Such as feathers and shells? Look, Kilian, at my age, I don't have to prove anything. Everyone knows me well. I'm the same here as down there, on the plantation. With a shirt or without one."

Kilian nodded, opened his bag, and took out tobacco and alcohol. The men gestured happily. The younger ones spoke in Spanish, and the older ones, who were around the same age as José and Antón, communicated through signs with the *öpottò*, or foreigner. When they saw that it was impossible, they turned to the translators. Kilian always showed respect, and if he had any doubt, José was there to help him. He sat down on the ground, lit a cigarette, and waited for the men to finish sifting through his presents.

He noticed that a snakeskin, whose name—*boukaroko*—he found difficult to pronounce, hung with the head facing upward from the lowest branch of one of the trees, instead of being in the high branches, as he remembered. The Bubis believed that the snake was like their guardian angel, umpire of good and evil, who could shower them with riches or inflict them with illnesses. For that reason, respect was paid once a year by bringing the babies born during the previous year to touch the tail of the skin with their hands.

No movement was seen outside the houses built around the square. They were all identical huts, all the same size and protected by a stake barrier. They were rectangular in shape, with the side wall barely two meters high and the front and back walls slightly higher for the roof. The walls were made from stakes tied together with lianas, the roofs from palm leaves tied with rattan to the rest of the structure. Kilian had entered José's hut only once, as life was mostly lived outdoors. He had to stoop down a lot—the door was too low for him—and he was surprised that there were only two rooms separated by a door made from a tree trunk, one room with a fire and the other for sleeping.

"What are you looking at so seriously?" asked José.

"I was thinking that my house in Pasolobino is as big as forty of these houses."

One of José's sons, who went by Sóbeúpo in the village and Donato in school, was about ten years old. He translated his words to Bubi, and the old men gasped in admiration.

"And why do you need such a big house?" the child asked, eyes wide.

"For everything. In one room you cook, in another you talk, in others you sleep, and in the rest you store the firewood or the food for the winter, the wine, the apples, the potatoes, the beans, the salted pork, and the beef . . . each thing in its own place. Downstairs"—he motioned to Sóbeúpo to bring him a twig to make a drawing on the ground—"and in other buildings, the hay is stored so the livestock can eat when there is snow."

When he said the word *snow*, laughter erupted. Kilian imagined that the rest of the afternoon would continue, as on previous occasions, with a bombardment of questions about snow and the freezing cold. Sure enough, a few minutes later, they asked him again about the skis that the inhabitants of Pasolobino used to go down to other villages or just to have fun through the fields. He rolled his eyes and stood up to give them another demonstration of how they worked. He put his feet together, flexed his knees, raised his hands in fists with his elbows tucked into his waist, and moved his hips from one side to the other. He was met by a chorus of laughs, gasps, and hand clapping.

"Sorry, Kilian . . ." José wiped his eyes while trying to hold back another peal of laughter. "You have to understand that we've never seen snow. There isn't even a word for it in Bubi!"

Moving their arms from the sky to the ground, the younger ones continued to improvise translation for the others—white water, frozen drops, white flakes, suds crystals, cold dust—and they all moved their heads with confused looks and furrowed brows, the corners of their mouths pointing downward, rubbing their chins with one hand while trying to understand this marvel from the spirits of nature.

This went on for a couple of hours. It was true, thought Kilian; the men had nothing better to do than talk.

At last, as evening fell, some movement was seen in the flimsy houses, and in an instant, the square filled with people.

"The ceremony is about to begin," warned José, getting to his feet. "I have to sit with my wife now, Kilian. We'll see each other later."

Several young women grouped together and went toward the bride's hut, singing and dancing. When the bride appeared at the door, a murmur of approval arose. Kilian also let out a breath. He could not make out the young woman's face, because she was wearing a wide-brimmed hat, dressed in peacock plumes fixed to her hair with a wooden pin, but her pure cocoa-colored body was full of harmony. Her torso was graced by small, firm breasts surrounded by red drawings of *ntola* and *tyíbö*, crystal beads, and shell collars that also adorned her slim hips and well-proportioned arms and legs. Everything about her seemed delicate, and yet her upright bearing and well-defined movements drew him to her with a magnetic force.

While the people cheered, the girl walked around the square a few times, singing and dancing, with the crystal beads caressing her skin, until she sat down in the square's preeminent position to await her parents and her future husband. Like Kilian, Mosi stood out as he towered over the others, but the straw hat decorated in hen feathers on his head made him look even taller. His enormous arms and legs were covered in pieces of shell and snake vertebrae, and greasy collars made from animal innards hung from his neck. He did not stop smiling. When the girl approached, he greeted her with a bow, and his smile grew broader.

A man who appeared to preside over the assembly came toward the bride and spoke to her in a tone that varied between advisory and threatening. In the last row, a familiar voice explained to Kilian that the man was urging her to always be faithful to her husband. He turned, happy to see Simón.

"I had to escape, Massa Kilian," whispered the lad with a unassuming smile. "Massa Garuz is bringing guests after the harvest party, and he wanted everyone there. But I couldn't miss the wedding, no, Massa, not this one. The bride and I have known each other since we were children. We are almost all family here."

"It's fine, Simón." Kilian put him at ease. "You've gotten here just in time."

"You won't say anything to the big massa then?"

Kilian shook his head, and the lad's face lit up.

"I followed the path you and José opened, but I didn't have time to change." He pointed to his clothes, the same as always: white shirt, short trousers, socks to the knees, and thick boots. Then he took off his shirt and freed his feet. "That's better!" He pointed toward the couple and exclaimed, "Look! It's the mother of my mother!"

An old woman went over to the couple and got them to join hands, speaking softly. Simón explained that she was giving them advice. She told the man not to abandon this wife despite the many others he could have and told the woman that she must remember her duty to look after her husband's lands, make his palm oil, and be faithful to him. When she finished speaking, some voices shouted.

"*Yéi'yébaa!*"

Then everyone, Simón included, opening his mouth wider than anyone, answered.

"*Hïëë!*"

Kilian did not need the lad to understand that these shouts of joy were the equivalent of a Spaniard's "Hip, hip, hurrah!" On the third time, infected by the jubilation, he even dared to repeat the response.

Everyone began to file past the couple one by one to congratulate them and wish the bride their best while the others continued with the cheering. She answered with a smile and a slight bow of her head.

Kilian was pushed forward and had no option but to stay in line and offer his respects to the newly married bride. He searched his head for the appropriate words to congratulate a Bubi bride in a native village on the island of Fernando Po, situated in that remote part of the world. But she was his friend's daughter. He would wish her well the same way he would the daughter of any friend. He searched for José, who smiled to him from where he was and nodded his head, giving permission.

Kilian felt butterflies in his stomach. So there he was! A white man in the middle of an African tribe in the middle of the party fanfare.

When he told his grandchildren, they probably would not believe him! A few steps from the bride, he was able to study her profile in more detail, but the hat continued to cover her face. She seemed young to him, maybe fifteen.

Too young to get married, he thought. *And especially to Mosi.*

There were three or four people to go before it was his turn. Simón, who had not left his side, translated.

"*Buë pale biuté wélä ná ötá biäm.*" Don't penetrate unknown regions.

"Ebuarí, buë púlö tyóbo, buë helépottò." Woman, don't leave the house, don't wander the streets, don't go with foreigners.

"Bué patí tyíbö yó mmèri ò." Don't break the delicate shells of your mother.

Kilian did not notice her raising her hands to remove the pin from her hat. Suddenly he was in front of her. "I . . . Congratulations! I hope you will be very happy."

She let the hat fall to one side, raised her head toward him, and looked into his eyes.

In that moment, the world stopped and the singing fell silent. A pair of big, intelligent, unusually bright eyes pierced through him. He felt like a tiny insect caught in the threads of an enormous spiderweb, waiting with the serenity of knowing that death was imminent, to be devoured in the resounding silence of the jungle.

All the features of her rounded face were in perfect harmony: her forehead, large; her nose, small and wide; her jaw and chin, perfectly finished, a set of lips beautifully glossed in carmine and blue . . . And her eyes, large, round, clearer than the most transparent liquid amber, designed to transfix the world. For one fleeting moment, she belonged to him alone within the ethereal veil that covered them.

The eyes were not those of a bride in love, missing the sparkle of a woman on the day of her wedding. Her timid smile pleased the guests, but her expression portrayed sadness, fear, and determination, resigning herself to a situation that in her heart of hearts, she did not accept.

How was it that he had not noticed her before? She had a hypnotic beauty.

"Why is it that your eyes are blurred on such a special day?" he asked in a barely audible whisper.

The girl trembled slightly.

"Would you understand it if I were to explain it to you, Massa?" she asked. Her voice was soft, a little high-pitched. "I don't think so. You're white and a man."

"I'm sorry," apologized Kilian, with the sleepy movement of someone who had woken from an enchantment. "I forgot you speak my language."

"It's the first time you've asked me anything." Kilian noticed that the girl was addressing him informally, and it felt strangely intimate.

He tried to speak, but Simón touched him on the elbow and whispered that Mosi was beginning to get impatient. Kilian looked up at the groom. He seemed taller than ever.

"Gud foyun," he said finally in Pidgin English. "Good luck."

"Tenki, massa clak," answered the colossus.

When the good wishes were finished, the new couple began to walk around the village, followed by people striking wooden bells with clappers and singing solemnly.

The nuptial procession ended, and the feast and libation of palm wine began, spilled all over the place in honor of the spirits. The milky drink washed down the wedding banquet of rice, yams, wild pigeon breasts, squirrel and antelope stews, sun-cured slices of snake, and a variety of fruit. From nine at night until dawn, the dancing did not stop, fueled by doses of alcohol to regain strength and keep spirits roused.

José made sure that Kilian's bowl was always full.

"Ösé . . . your daughter, the bride . . . how old is she?" Kilian asked, a little tipsy.

"I think she'll be sixteen soon."

"You know, Ösé? We spend so much time with the men in the *riösa* that I don't know if I've met all your children."

"Two women got married in other villages," José began to explain with some effort, "and two in the city, where their husbands work in the houses of some wealthy whites. Here in Bissappoo, I have two sons working the land."

"But . . . how many have you got?" Counting Sóbeúpo, the numbers did not add up.

"Between children and grandchildren, many of those you see today are part of my family." José let out a cackle. "For Father Rafael, I have four daughters and two sons. But I can tell you the truth." In a slurred voice, he confessed, "The bride was born before Sóbeúpo, and three more came after . . . with another woman . . ."

He pursed his lips and rocked his head. A little withdrawn, José went on.

"The Bubi gods have favored me, yes. I have many good children. And hard workers." He pointed in the direction of the newlyweds, then brought the finger round to his head and added lovingly, "She is very intelligent, Kilian. The smartest of my ten children! When she can, she picks up a book. With Massa Manuel she will learn many things. Yes, I'm happy she'll be living on the plantation."

"The truth is I never noticed her before," said Kilian in a careful tone.

How was it possible that an almost midnight-blue man like José could have a dark-caramel-colored daughter?

"The whites, you always complain that all blacks seem the same to you." José laughed in merriment. "Well, let me tell you . . . the same happens to us!"

If I had met her before, Kilian thought, *I can assure you that it would be impossible for me to mistake her for another.*

He looked to her.

Was it his imagination, or was she doing the same?

Mosi drank and drank, holding her tightly to show the world that she was his. Kilian tried in vain to erase the thought of Mosi taking her naked body.

"What are you thinking about, my friend?" José asked.

"Nothing . . ." Kilian shook his head. "You know, Ösé? Celebrations are the same everywhere. In my village we also eat, drink, and dance at weddings. Tomorrow the euphoria will have passed, and everything will be the same."

"It's never the same, Kilian," commented José dogmatically. "Two days are never the same, like two people are never the same. See this man?" He used his head to point to his right. "I'm black, yes, but this one is even blacker."

"You're right, Ösé. You're living proof of it." José tilted his head now, curious, and Kilian deliberately paused and finished off his *topé* in one gulp. "You're now addressing me informally! That wasn't so hard, was it?"

Kilian closed his eyes. He could hear the silence inside him. All the racket in the village sounded like a distant murmur. The alcohol had given him a soothing sensation of levity.

There is a brief instant, just before falling asleep, when the body seems to lean over the edge of a cliff.

It's vertigo.

It barely lasts a second. You don't know whether you will sleep or die and never wake up. Consciousness stands still.

That night, Kilian dreamed of naked bodies dancing around a bonfire to the rhythm of the drums. A woman with enormous light-colored, almost-transparent eyes asked him to dance. His hands took control of her waist and rose up to her small breasts, which vibrated incessantly to the music. The woman whispered words that he did not understand. Then she pressed herself against him. He could feel the soft pressure of her nipples against his naked chest. Suddenly, her face was that of Sade. He recognized her dark almond eyes, her high cheekbones, her slender nose, and her lips like autumn raspberries. Beside him, enormous men rode women while the songs became more high-pitched and intense. When he looked at her again, the woman was a blurred figure who would not let him leave. Her caresses became more and more intense. He resisted; she forced him to look.

"Listen. Look. Touch. Let yourself go!"

He woke drenched, his head buzzing because of the alcohol, and covered in red bites from the tiny *jején*. He had forgotten to put up the mosquito net.

Kilian seemed to hear music, but when he stuck his head out the door of the hut they had prepared for him, he saw that the village was deserted.

He remembered the long and intense night. José had explained to him that in Bubi tradition, there were two types of weddings: *ribalá rèötö*, marriage to buy a woman's virginity, and *ribalá ré ríhólè*, marriage of a couple in love. The first was the only legitimate one, even if the woman had been forced into the contract.

The buyer paid for the bride's virginity, as it was thought that a woman who had lost it lacked all value and beauty. The second, a marriage of a couple in love, was considered illegitimate. There were no celebrations, nor solemnity, nor a party.

Could she have lost her worth and her beauty?

He doubted it.

It was a splendid morning. The temperature was perfect. A light breeze cooled the sultry night air.

But Kilian's body was burning.

7

Tornado Weather

Kilian went down the slope as fast as he could. The ship bringing his father from Spain had docked a while ago, and he was late. At the bottom, three men were unloading the last barge on the pier. Out of breath and sweating, he stopped so he could look for Antón. The sun's rays glinted off the shoals of sardines in the sea. He shielded his forehead and squinted.

Against the horizon, he made out the silhouette of his father, sitting on his leather suitcase with his shoulders slightly hunched. Kilian took a few steps in his direction and opened his mouth to call him, but stopped. There was something wrong. He had expected to find his father pacing, annoyed at being the last passenger to be collected. Instead, Antón looked deep in thought, gazing at some invisible point beyond the bay and the royal palms. It made Kilian shudder as he put on a cheerful voice.

"Sorry, Dad! I couldn't get here any sooner."

Antón raised his head and, still lost in thought, greeted him with a sad smile.

Kilian was shocked to see his face. In a few months, he had aged years.

"There was a fallen tree on the road after last night's storm," he continued. "You know how these things are . . . I had to wait a good while until they cleared it."

"Don't worry, Son. It was nice to sit."

Antón rose slowly, and they hugged. Although his father's body was still that of a tall and well-built man, Kilian felt the profound weakness in his strong arms.

"Come on, let's go." Kilian scratched his head and picked up the case. "You don't know how much we are looking forward to hearing news from home. How are Mom and Catalina? Was there a lot of snow when you left? And Uncle Jacobo and his family?"

Antón smiled and raised his hand. "We'd better wait until we meet up with your brother," he said. "That way I won't have to answer everything twice!"

When they got to the end of the pier, Antón glanced up at the steep path and puffed.

"Do you know, Kilian, why they call this the *slope of the fevers*?"

"Yes, Dad. Don't you remember? Manuel told me on my first day."

Antón nodded. "And what did he tell you exactly?"

"Well, that no one escapes from . . ." He offered him his arm. "Dad, it's normal to be tired after such a long journey."

Antón accepted his arm, and they went up the path slowly. Kilian did not stop talking the whole way back to Sampaka, bringing his father up to date on happenings on the plantation, the other employees, the new laborers and the older ones, their friends in Santa Isabel, the days working in the cocoa trees . . . Antón listened and nodded, smiling from time to time, but he did not interrupt once.

He had lived long enough to know that his son's monologue was fueled by the fear of having to give, for the first time, his arm to his father, who felt tired and old.

"Massa Kilian!" an out-of-breath Simón shouted from the window of the truck. "Massa Kilian! Come quickly!"

The vehicle had raised a cloud of dust along the cocoa-tree track. Kilian was checking that the squirrel traps had been set properly. Squirrels in his country were cute. On Fernando Po, they were bigger than rabbits and ate the cocoa-tree pods. Some even had wings to glide from one tree to another. The truck approached, its horn beeping incessantly. Simón got out in a flash.

"Massa!" he shouted again. "Did you not hear me? Get into the truck."

"What's wrong?" Kilian asked.

"It's Massa Antón!" Simón panted. "He was found unconscious in the office. He's in the hospital with Massa Manuel and Massa Jacobo. José sent me to look for you. Come on!"

Even though Simón drove at a breakneck speed, to Kilian the journey felt like an eternity.

Since March, Antón's health had been getting steadily worse, though he remained composed in front of his sons. On occasion, he even joked, saying that paperwork was much harder than working among the cocoa trees. Kilian and Jacobo had finally forgone their six months of holidays and asked that they be postponed until their father was feeling better.

The only thing that had changed about Antón was that he now felt the constant need to tell his sons, in minute detail, about the finances of the House of Rabaltué. He repeated the number of livestock they should herd, the correct price at which to sell a mare, the price of lambs, a shepherd's salary, and the number of reapers they would need that summer to cut the hay and store it for the next winter. He also instructed them on maintaining the house. It needed reroofing, the shed needed a beam changed, the henhouse wall needed support, and everything had to be whitewashed. With the salaries of the two brothers, along with what was earned from the sale of livestock, he calculated, they would have enough to undertake all these tasks. If one salary failed, they would have to do things bit by bit and fix something each year. And in case they had not properly understood him, he wrote down all the calculations on dozens of sheets in duplicate using carbon paper: one copy for the brothers and another to be sent to Spain by post.

Antón had also used some of his moments alone with Kilian to tell him in greater detail about what it took to be a good master, like the relations between houses in Pasolobino and Cerbeán and the debts and favors given and owed between the family and neighbors from time immemorial. Kilian listened to him without interrupting. He did not know what to say. It made him very sad to know that his father was dictating his will to him, even if he used the pretext of letters from home, which arrived with ever more frequency. It was evident that his father felt a pressing need to leave everything in order before . . .

The truck braked abruptly at the door to the hospital. Kilian went up the steps three at a time and burst into the main hall. A nurse directed him to a room beside the doctor's office. There he saw his father lying in bed, his eyes closed. Jacobo was in a chair in the corner and rose as he saw Kilian. José stood beside the bed. A nurse gathered instruments onto a small metal tray. When she turned to leave the room, she almost bumped into Kilian.

"Excuse me!" she apologized.

That voice . . .

The young woman looked up, and their eyes met.

It was her! The bride of his dreams! Mosi's wife!

He did not even know her name.

José began to ask his daughter something, but at that very moment, Manuel entered.

"He is sedated now," he said. "We gave him a higher dose of morphine."

"What do you mean by a *higher* dose?" Kilian asked, confused.

The doctor looked at José, who shook his head.

"Can we talk in my office?"

They all went into another room. Manuel got straight to the point.

"Antón has been getting morphine for months to withstand the pain. He did not want anyone to know. He has an incurable illness, untreatable and inoperable. It's just a question of days, I'm afraid. I'm sorry."

Kilian turned to Jacobo.

"Did you know?"

"As much as you," Jacobo answered in a sad voice. "I had no idea that it was this serious."

"And you, Ösé?"

José hesitated before answering. "Antón made me promise not to say anything."

Kilian dropped his head in grief. Jacobo put an arm on his brother's shoulder. They knew that their father was sick, but not this sick. How could he have hidden the seriousness of the situation from them? Why had they not thought more of his constant tiredness, his lack of appetite? Everything was due to the heat, he had told them a thousand times . . . to the blasted heat! Did their mother know? The brothers looked at each other, their eyes filled with angst. How were they going to tell her? How do you tell a woman that her husband is going to die thousands of kilometers from home and that she will never see him again?

"Will we be able to speak to him?" Kilian managed to ask in a faint voice.

"Yes. He will be conscious for short periods. But I hope that the morphine works to ease the final agony." Manuel patted him a few times on the arm. "Kilian . . . Jacobo . . . I am so very sorry. Everyone's time comes sometime." He took off his glasses and began to clean a lens with the corner of his coat. "Medicine can't do any more. Now it's all in God's hands."

"God doesn't send sickness," José commented when they were back beside Antón, his eyes still shut. "The creator of beautiful things, the sun, the earth, the rain, the wind, and the clouds cannot be the cause of anything bad. Sickness is caused by the spirits."

"Don't talk nonsense," responded Jacobo while Kilian took his father's hand. "Things are as they are."

José's daughter watched them from the door.

"For us," she said in a soft voice, "illness is a curse from the spirits of the ancestors who have been insulted or offended by the patient or his family."

She went over to José, and Kilian noticed then that she was wearing a short-sleeved open white coat over a light-green dress with large buttons.

"That is why we show such fervor when asking for their intercession, to please them with sacrifices, drinks, and funeral rites."

José looked pleased by her explanation. Kilian remained silent.

"Well then, tell me," said Jacobo, his eyes flashing, "what are you doing in this hospital? Why don't you go and invoke your spirits?"

Kilian winced at his brother's harsh tone, but she replied in the same quiet and delicate voice.

"What can't be avoided can't be avoided. But we can ease a patient's suffering." She walked over to Antón and very carefully placed a damp cloth on his forehead. "Most pains can be calmed with simple remedies of hot or cold baths, with ointments and rubbing palm or almond oil, *ntola* cream or poultices of herbs and leaves, and with potions of palm wine mixed with spices or with seawater."

Kilian observed her delicate hands on the white cloth. She lightly pressed it against his father's forehead. Then she picked it up and put it back in the bowl, where she soaked it again, squeezed it of excess liquid, and lovingly returned it to his forehead and cheeks. He remained absorbed in this process for a good while. In the background, he heard the others' conversation, but in his mind, he could only see those hands.

He did not want to face this.

"Sometimes," José began, referring proudly to his daughter, "Massa Manuel allows her to use some of our ancestral knowledge—"

Jacobo, irritated, got to his feet. "Well, since you know so much, what cure is there for my father?"

Kilian snapped to attention. "Calm down, Jacobo!" he scolded. "This hurts José just as much as it hurts us."

Jacobo let out a snort and sat back down.

"Tell me, Ösé," Kilian said, his eyes again fixed on the young nurse. "What would you do if it were your father?"

"Kilian, I don't doubt the foreigner's medicine, and I don't mean to offend, but in his state, I . . ." He hesitated, then finally said with conviction, "I would ask a witch doctor to pray for him."

A sarcastic laugh rang out. Kilian waved at Jacobo to hush and asked José to continue.

"If it were my father," he resumed, "I would take him to the chapel of the most powerful guardian spirits of my village to free him of the affliction that is tormenting him."

"But we can't move him, Ösé," Kilian objected.

"Maybe I can get . . . ," José proposed cautiously, "our doctor to come here."

Jacobo rose in a fury. "Of course! In exchange for tobacco and alcohol."

Kilian said nothing as José's daughter looked up and stared directly at him, waiting for an answer. Her light-colored eyes seemed to tell him that it was worth trying. Would he dare ask for help from the natives? She silently challenged him.

"Fine," he agreed.

She smiled and turned to her father.

"Send Simón to Bissappoo," she said plainly.

Jacobo headed toward the door, shaking his head. "This is ridiculous!" he roared. "All this contact with the blacks has made you crazy, Kilian!"

He slammed the door. Kilian ran after him and stopped him at the entrance.

"Where did that come from, Jacobo?"

His brother could not look him in the eye. "It's obvious! For some time, you have preferred José's advice over mine."

"That's not true," Kilian protested. "Dad and José are friends, Jacobo. He only wants to help."

"You've heard Manuel. Dad is going to die. It's inevitable. Maybe you want to cling to false hopes, but I don't. He is being well looked after. That's what matters." His voice trembled. "I only want it to be over as soon as possible. At this stage, it's for the best."

He looked at Kilian, whose lips were pressed closed. Jacobo tried to remember the moment when Kilian began to distance himself from him. It had been so long since his young brother had asked him incessant questions and listened to his answers in awe. Things had changed too quickly. Kilian no longer needed him, his father was dying, and Jacobo felt more and more alone. The island was to blame for everything. It trapped its inhabitants in its invisible net, and it would finish them all off as it had done to others before.

"You've become pigheaded, Kilian. Leave Dad in peace, do you hear me?"

"I have given my consent. I've no intention of going back on it," Kilian replied firmly to his brother.

"We'll see about that."

Antón had brief moments of lucidity in which he was able to talk to José and his sons, especially Kilian, who barely moved from his side in the hours that followed. It was perhaps the first time in their lives that they spoke without shame about very private matters. The distance from home, the stormy June weather, and the certainty of a farewell allowed for endless confidences to be shared among the mountain men.

"Kilian, you needn't stay here the whole time," Antón told him again. "You can't leave your work. Go with Jacobo, go on now."

For Jacobo, the walls in the hospital were collapsing around him. He preferred to cover for Kilian at work to get away from the painful scene.

"I'm not leaving you, Dad. They can do without me. We are only waiting for the fruit to ripen for the next harvest. I don't know if it's just me imagining it, but each year the cocoa pods are bigger . . ."

"I'm fine here," Antón affirmed with as much conviction as possible. "The nurses look after me very well, above all, José's daughter. Have you noticed her eyes, Son? They are almost transparent . . ."

Kilian nodded. He knew very well. Whenever she appeared in the door, his mood lightened just a bit. Otherwise, he was very frightened. He had seen animals die, and it was horrible. He had seen relatives and neighbors in the funeral parlors of the valley. The certainty that he would be present when his father took his last breath made him sick. But he had no choice. His mother would have handled this better. At least with more affection. He thought about Mariana and Catalina. He had just sent a telegram to break the news. He had cried so much writing it that now in front of his father he had no tears left.

"Kilian?"

"What is it, Dad?"

"You will have to take charge of the house and the family. You are more responsible than Jacobo. Promise me."

Kilian agreed without realizing the weight of that promise. He would be in charge of the House of Rabaltué, like his parents and their parents before them.

"Why did you come back, Dad, if you weren't feeling well? There are good doctors in Spain. You would have been comfortable at home."

Antón paused before answering. "Well, like the elephants, I chose my place to die. I've spent so many years here that it seems right. This land has given us a lot, Son. More than we have given it."

Kilian was not convinced.

"But Dad . . . think of Mom . . ."

"I don't know if you would understand if I tried to explain."

Kilian had heard that sentence many times in his life. "Try."

Antón closed his eyes and sighed. "Kilian, I didn't want your mother to see my lifeless body. It's as simple as that."

Kilian was struck cold.

"Your mother and I," Antón continued, "have loved each other very much in spite of the distance. When we said good-bye, we both knew we wouldn't see each other again. Words weren't necessary. God has willed for me to go first. I'm thankful for it . . ."

His voice broke down. He blinked, and his gaze grew cloudy.

"I'd like to rest a little," he said in a low voice.

Kilian wished he could go back to the green fields of the mountain so his mother could cook him a rabbit stew or mountain goat with chocolate sauce and make ring-shaped pastries on feast days, for his father to bring him presents from a distant land, for his sister to complain about his pranks with her hands on her hips and his brother to dare him to walk along the highest stone walls. He wanted to taste a hunk of bread with sugar and cream from the cow, and for the snow to cover the autumn gloom.

When his father was gone, he would bear the responsibility for looking after his family. He wanted to be like Jacobo, to be able to banish grief with a few jokes and some *malamba*, whiskey, and brandy *saltos*.

But he was not like that.

He rested his head in his hands as a shiver went down his spine.

His soul yearned for the snow.

He was getting older, and he was afraid. Very afraid.

The door opened, and Kilian looked up hopefully, but it was José. He gripped Antón's hand with affection.

"Ah, José, my good José!" Antón opened his eyes. "You are also here now. And that face?" He tried to joke. "I am luckier than the natives, José. Do you know, Kilian, what the Bubis used to do when someone was very ill? They would take them to a hut in the village and leave them there. Every day they would leave a roasted banana or yam and a little drop of palm oil. That continued until death put an end to the man's suffering."

He paused from the strain of talking.

"A missionary who spent many years among the Bubis, I think his name was Father Antonio, told me that. Tell me, José, is it true?"

"The spirits are always with us, Antón, in a hut or in a hospital. We are never alone."

Antón gave a small smile and closed his eyes. José released his hand gently and went over to Kilian. They heard raised voices outside the door.

"Father Rafael is arguing with the doctor," José told him in a whisper. "Your brother has told them that you are thinking of letting one of our doctors treat Antón."

Kilian frowned and went into Manuel's office. The men fell silent. Manuel was sitting in front of his desk, faced by Jacobo and Father Rafael, who remained standing.

"Is there a problem?" Kilian asked.

"Yes, there is, Kilian," responded Father Rafael, his cheeks flush with anger. "You must know that I'm not happy with one of those witch doctors coming near your father. He is in the hands of the one and true God."

Kilian gave his brother a withering look, and argued, "My father . . . our father . . . has spent his life between Pasolobino and Fernando Po. I don't see why he can't say farewell to this world with the traditions of both."

"Because it's not right!" the priest exclaimed. "Your father has always been a good Catholic. What you want to do is absurd!"

"If Mom were here," Jacobo butted in, "she'd make you see reason."

"But she's not here, Jacobo! She's not here!" shouted Kilian. Suddenly weary, he sat down in a chair, lowered his voice, and asked, "Is there any place on the island, in the civil government, or commandments of the church where a law is written that explicitly forbids a black to pray for the salvation of a white's soul?"

"No, there isn't," replied Father Rafael sharply, taking short steps with his hands clasped over his large stomach. "But you are blowing things out of proportion, Kilian. What you want isn't for a black to pray, you want him to cure your father. You are doubting not only the work of the doctors, but God's will. That's a sin, son. You are challenging God." He turned to the doctor. "Manuel, tell him that all this is . . . totally unreasonable!"

Manuel looked at Kilian and sighed. "There is no cure, Kilian, with our medicine or that of the Bubis. Everything you do will be a waste of time. And although it's not forbidden, if Garuz hears of this, he'll be furious. He won't think it suitable for us to follow black traditions." His fingers drummed on the desk. "It's not the time for jokes, you know . . ."

"I trust José's discretion," replied Kilian obstinately. "And I hope I can also rely on yours. Anything else?"

Father Rafael pursed his lips together and shook his head. He airily went to the door, put his hand on the knob, and said, "Do what you want, but I will give him the last rites after that—" He stopped and rephrased his words before leaving. "*I* will be the only and last one to give him extreme unction."

An awkward silence fell. Jacobo, who had remained silent, began pacing from one end of the room to the other, running his fingers through his hair, and sighing. He finally sat down beside his brother.

"He's also my father, Kilian," he said. "You can't do this without my consent."

"Is it not enough that I want to do it? What does it matter to you? Manuel, you yourself have told us about the plants that you are researching . . ."

Manuel shook his head.

Kilian put his elbows on the table and rubbed his temples, fighting back tears. "He's only fifty-six years old, damn it! Do you know how many grandchildren José has? Dad will never get to know his! He's done nothing else in life but break his back to make a better life for us, for his family, for the house . . . It's not fair. No. It isn't."

"Fine, suit yourself." Jacobo exhaled, finally defeated. "But I don't want to know anything about it." He shot a sideways look at the doctor. "Manuel?"

"Look, it's nothing to do with me. I'm fond of you, Kilian . . ." He hesitated. "I'm fond of you both, Jacobo. It won't be of any use, neither good nor bad." He shrugged. "After so many years on Fernando Po, few things can surprise me at this stage."

The following morning, when the *tyiántyo*, the witch doctor, arrived, Antón was barely able to babble a few incoherent words. He named people and occasionally smiled. All of a sudden, his face was filled with pain, and it became difficult for him to breathe.

Only José and his daughter were with Kilian in the room.

Just after entering, the Bubi doctor and priest thanked the white man for the generous presents he had sent through Simón. He then prepared his intervention. He first put on a showy hat of feathers and a long straw skirt and lit a pipe. Then he began to tie various amulets on Antón's arms, waist, legs, and neck. José posed respectfully, standing with his head bowed and his hands crossed, and his daughter moved around the room, following the requests of the doctor with exquisite diligence. The amulets were of snail shells, bird feathers, locks of sheep's hair, and leaves from the sacred *Iko* tree.

Kilian observed the scene in silence. He assumed that these objects, like those at the entrance to Bissappoo, acted to ward away evil spirits. When he saw his father decorated in this manner, part of him began to regret not listening to his brother. But in some part of his heart beat a small flame of longing, fed by the stories of miracles that he remembered from his youth. He thought of the image of the Faith of Zaragoza, who held in her firm arms a broken man, and fixed his eyes on Antón, waiting for something, an open smile, that would show that it had all been a false alarm, a cold, or a deceptive bout of malaria.

The witch doctor untied a gourd filled with small shells from his waist, and the ritual began. He invoked the spirits and asked them to reveal the illness, its cause, and the most effective medicine with which to cure it. He took out two round and smooth stones from a leather bag and placed one on top of the other. The stones, José explained, were the essential tool to find out if the patient would live or die. There was no other alternative.

The witch doctor spoke, whistled, murmured, whispered. Kilian could not understand either the questions or the answers. When José translated the final diagnosis—the patient had not fulfilled his obligations with the dead and would probably die—the weak flame was extinguished in Kilian's heart. He bowed his head as José made the customary promise to the witch doctor to fulfill his own obligations with his deceased ancestors. The Bubi doctor nodded, pleased, and gathered up his things and left.

"You have done the right thing, Kilian." José, grateful for the respect the young man had shown to the Bubi traditions, put a hand on his shoulder.

Kilian did not feel comforted by José's words. He dragged over a chair and sat down beside his father. José's daughter gave him a timid smile, turned down the sheets, and left, followed by her father. For a good while, Kilian held Antón's hand tightly gripped in his own, soaking in his father's spent heat. The blades of the ceiling fan whirred in monotonous beats.

Much later, Jacobo entered the room, accompanied by Father Rafael. The two brothers respectfully observed Antón receive the holy sacraments and the apostolic benediction from the hands of the priest.

Suddenly, as if he could feel the presence of his two sons, Antón began to show a restlessness that could not be calmed, even with a fresh dose of morphine from Manuel. He held the hands of the brothers with unusual strength and moved his head from side to side, as if fighting a colossal force.

For a moment, Antón opened his eyes and said in a loud and clear voice, "The tornadoes. Life is like a tornado. Peace, fury, and peace again."

He closed his eyes, and breathed his last.

It was hoarse, and quick.

Kilian, completely devastated, saw the feared loss of expression, the rigidity of the face, and the stiffness of the flesh. Death.

When the worst tornado that the old men could remember struck the plantation, Kilian studied it in order to understand his father's final words. Till then, a tornado had simply been a combination of wind, rain, and furious electrical discharges. A suffocating heat preceded the phenomenon; during the tornado, the temperature dropped between twelve and twenty degrees; and after the rain, the intense heat returned.

But this time he could not be a mere spectator; his spirit mixed with the storm. He himself rumbled and got destroyed.

It all started with a small cloud in the zenith, a small cloud that got bigger and darker as it neared the horizon. All living things ceased activity.

Not a sound was to be heard.

Kilian remembered the intense calm just before the first snowflake, the sensation of unreality.

An absolute, deep, and solemn silence reigned. Distant echoes of thunder were heard, and the lightning grew so intense that for some minutes, it looked as if the atmosphere were on fire. And suddenly, the wind, gusts of such fury that the trees were horizontal to the ground.

The tornado lasted longer than normal and ended in a furious downpour. The wind and the rain threatened to end the world, but when they stopped, the atmosphere was filled by a delightful purity. The living beings began beating again, as if born of a regenerating fire.

They decided that Antón was to be buried in the cemetery in Santa Isabel.

The nurses swiftly cleaned and dressed his body before them. José's daughter painted little marks on his chest close to his heart.

"These signs made with *ntola* purify your body," she murmured. "Now you will be received with full honors by both your white ancestors and ours. You will be able to pass from one realm to the other without difficulty."

The coffin left the hospital and crossed the main yard of the plantation on a truck that would take it to the city. The plantation employees followed in two vans and the manager's Mercedes, driven by a sad Yeremías, who had asked Massa Garuz to be allowed to drive the two brothers in remembrance of the deceased. As the funeral cortege passed, most of the workers closed the doors and windows in their houses, and some tolled wooden bells.

The Africans believed that the soul followed the body until it was buried. And even once buried, the soul lingered around the places where the dead person had lived. The bells were meant to frighten and disorient the soul so it would not return to the village. Kilian listened to José's explanations while the royal palms of the entrance to Sampaka covered them in dappled light. He let his imagination fly to the summits of Pasolobino, wondering what the burial would have been like in the village. When someone died, the body stayed for a time in the house for the wake when the rosary was said. The murmur of the prayers and litanies in Latin served to soothe the pain of those present. While the prayers were repeated, nobody cried or lamented; in repeating the same thing over and over, their breathing became regular.

In times past, the men prepared the coffin, the grave in the cemetery, the chairs in the church, and the house to receive visitors, and the women cooked large pots of beans for the relations and neighbors of other villages who came to pay their respects. Sometimes they cried or asked if the meal needed more salt. For the children, a funeral was like a party where they got to meet distant relations, only unlike in other parties, some people cried. The following day, the strongest males in the family carried out the simple wooden coffin on their shoulders through the main door of the house, onto the street, where mourners could follow it to mass. Afterward, the priest led the procession to the cemetery. All journeys made with the body were accompanied by the slow and steady toll of the church bell.

Kilian had never asked why the bell tolled like that at funerals.

Perhaps, like the Bubis' bells, it served to disorient the soul.

Pasolobino was very far away.

Would his father's soul be able to find its way back home?

At the cemetery, they had chosen a corner under the shade of two enormous ceibas for Antón's remains to rest. Several men, hired by Garuz, placed a simple stone cross that the brothers had engraved with their father's name, that of his house, and the places and dates of his birth and death. It seemed very strange to Kilian to memorialize Pasolobino in Africa.

All the plantation's employees, including the manager and Manuel, along with Generosa, Emilio, Julia, and acquaintances from Santa Isabel, attended the burial. Of all of them, Santiago was most affected by the loss. He had come to the island at the same time as Antón, decades ago. From time to time, Marcial patted him on his shoulder, but that only made him shed more tears down his gaunt face.

When the coffin descended into the earth, the feet in the direction of the sea and the head toward the mountain, as directed by José, Jacobo gratefully clung to Julia's hand. He felt her free hand stroking his arm. When the earth had covered the hole and Manuel came over to tell his fiancée that everyone else was leaving, Jacobo resisted letting go of that soft hand. Finally, Julia went on tiptoes, gave him a kiss on the cheek, stroked his face with slight loving touches, looked at him with eyes overcome with grief, and left.

Kilian and Jacobo remained there as José went to collect some objects that he had hidden before the burial. With a spade, he dug a hole at the head of the grave and planted a small sacred tree. He then surrounded the mound with some stones and stakes.

"This will banish the souls of other dead people," he explained.

Jacobo withdrew a few paces but did not say anything.

Kilian's eyes remained on the words engraved on the stone cross.

Who will visit your grave when we are no longer here?

He knew that it would be difficult even for José to tend the grave. Yeremías had explained to him that once the dead were buried, Bubis were afraid of visiting cemeteries. They believed that doing so could cause many deaths in the village. If it were in Pasolobino, his mother would initially go every day to keep Antón company in his eternal rest, and later, every week. There would always be someone talking at his feet.

Why did you come back from Spain? he thought.

He would have to relive the last days when writing the letter to his mother. She would want to know all the details: his last words, the moment of extreme unction, the priest's sermon praising her husband and remembering the most important moments in his life, and the number of mourners and condolences received. Kilian would have to put it in writing and pretend that he was well and that she did not have to worry. Life went on, and he had a lot of work, and they wouldn't be short of money.

"What are you thinking about?" José asked.

"I wonder," Kilian answered, gesturing to Antón's grave, "where he is now."

José came closer. "He is with our ancestors. I'm sure he is happy with them."

Kilian nodded and said a simple prayer wishing his father a good journey, wherever he might be.

Jacobo walked to the gate of the cemetery so that they would not see him cry.

Antón died at the end of June 1955, the same day the celebrations began in his valley, honoring the patron saints of summer. In July, the fields began to be cut in Pasolobino; in August, the cocoa harvest in Fernando Po, which continued until January of the following year. They were the hard months of work in the dryers.

Kilian worked day and night. His whole life revolved around work. And when he rested, all he did was smoke and drink more than he should. He became withdrawn, taciturn, and short-tempered. Jacobo and José began to worry. Nobody could withstand such physical toil. At first, they thought that it was the result of Antón's death, but he did not improve as the weeks passed.

He was continuously restless, imagining problems in the dryers. He shouted at the workers, something he had never done before, and he worried about everything.

"Kilian!" his brother pleaded. "You have to rest!"

"I'll rest when I die!" Kilian answered from the roof of one of the barracks. "Somebody has to do it!"

José frowned. Sooner or later, he would collapse.

A little after Christmas, Kilian fell ill. It started with a temperature slightly above normal that in a week went up to 104 degrees Fahrenheit. It was only then he agreed to go to the hospital.

For days he was delirious. And in his delirium, the same scene repeated itself over and over again: He and his father were in a house, and it was pouring outside. One could hear the gulley in danger of overflowing and flooding everything in its path. This gulley had burst its banks before and dragged away the strongest houses. They had to leave, or they would die. Kilian insisted, but his father refused; he told him he was very tired and to go on without him. Outside, the wind and rain roared. Kilian shouted in desperation at his father, but he kept sleeping in his rocking chair. Kilian cried and shouted as he said goodbye and escaped.

A hand squeezed his to comfort him. He opened his eyes, blinking away his nightmares, and frowned at the fan moving above his head. A pair of big light-colored eyes looked down.

When she felt that Kilian was fully awake, José's daughter gently brushed aside the copper locks from his sweating forehead. "If you haven't honored your dead properly, the spirits will torment you. You don't have to offer goat and chicken sacrifices. Honor them well, in your own way, and Antón's spirit will leave you in peace. Let it go. After all, God made everything, even the spirits. Let him go. That will be enough."

Kilian pressed his lips together tightly, and his chin began to tremble. He felt tired and weak, but he appreciated the kind words. He wondered how many hours or days she had been a silent witness to his suffering. She continued to stroke him. He did not want her to stop. Her hands were slim, and her fresh breath was but a few centimeters from his parched lips. He opened his mouth to ask her name, but the door suddenly opened and Jacobo entered like a hurricane. The girl sat up, but Kilian did not allow her to let go of his hand. Jacobo reached the head of the bed in three bounds and, seeing that Kilian was conscious, exclaimed, "My God, Kilian! How are you feeling? What a fright you have given us!"

He frowned in the direction of the nurse, who, though she had pulled back her hand, did not leave Kilian's side. For a few seconds, the girl sent shivers down him.

Wow, Jacobo thought, *where did this pretty one come from?* He quickly pulled himself together.

"How long has he been awake? You didn't think to alert me?" Not waiting for an answer, he turned to Kilian. "Bloody hell! A bit more and you'd be off with Dad . . ."

Kilian rolled his eyes, and Jacobo sat on the bed.

"Seriously, Kilian. I've been very worried. You've been here for five days with a raging fever. Manuel assured me that it would break, but it took its time . . ." He shook his head. "It will take time to get your strength back. I have spoken to Garuz, and we think that you could recover your strength on the ship home . . ."

Jacobo caught his breath as Kilian spoke. "I'm happy to see you too, Jacobo. But I'm not going home."

"Why?"

"I don't want to. Not yet."

"Kilian, I have never met anyone as pigheaded as you. Look, a letter from Mom arrived a couple of days ago." He put his hand in his shirt pocket and took out the letter. "Fresh news! I was dying to tell you. Catalina is getting married! What do you think of that? To Carlos, from the House of Guari, do you remember him?"

Kilian nodded.

"It's not bad. He's not from one of the big houses, but he's a hard worker and honorable. Mom has written about the dowry, to see what we think . . . The wedding won't be until after the mourning, of course—that's why they haven't made it official—but . . ." He stopped when he realized that his brother was not showing any sign of happiness. "Lad, you've gone from one extreme to the other. You used to be interested in everything, and now you are interested in nothing. Life goes on, Kilian, with or without us . . ."

Kilian turned his head toward the window, and his eyes met those of the young nurse, who had not left his side as Jacobo was talking. She pretended to get the thermometer and his medication ready. With a slight nod that only Kilian noticed, she agreed with Jacobo's last words. *Life goes on,* he repeated to himself, absorbed in those heavenly eyes.

They heard a rap at the door.

"Perfect timing!" Jacobo stood.

Kilian turned his head and recognized Sade's statuesque figure covered by a simple knee-length white cotton dress with a printed trim of blue lobelias, like small pointed palms, held at the waist by a narrow belt. He had never seen her dressed like that, without jewelry or makeup. In fact, he had never seen her in the full light of day. She looked even more beautiful than in the club.

"I sent her a message yesterday," explained Jacobo, triumphant.

For weeks, he had been unable to convince Kilian that the troubles of the soul could be sated by desire. Now his brother had no excuses.

"I didn't want you to spend so many hours here on your own. She offered to keep you company. I have to get back to the dryers. Sade will look after you until you're yourself again, Kilian." He looked at his watch, got up, and gave him a few pats on the shoulder. "I am leaving you in good hands!"

As Jacobo left, Sade sat on the edge of the bed. She kissed the tips of her index and middle fingers and caressed Kilian's lips with them, until he turned his head away.

"This can't be right, my massa," she reproached him in a melodious voice. "You haven't been to see me for weeks." She clicked her tongue. "I'm not going to let you forget me."

She winked at the nurse and added, "You can go. I'll watch his temperature."

Kilian noticed the nurse tense. She met his gaze and gave him a tired and grateful smile. As if reading his mind, she put the palm of her hand on his cheek. Sade raised her eyebrows and whispered to him soothingly in Bubi. Kilian did not understand their immediate meaning, but he closed his eyelids, and a comforting sleep took hold of him.

Time passed on the plantation, and the wet season arrived, alternating between pouring rain, fleeting showers, and crisp breezes that succumbed to the sticky daytime heat. Even when a small tornado let loose its fury on the cocoa trees, covering them in erythrina leaves, the work did not stop for a second. The fruit of the cocoa—whose scientific name Kilian had learned was *Theobroma*, or food of the gods—kept growing and ripening on the trunks. When they turned to a reddish color, they were ready for harvesting.

From August to January, week after week, thousands of cocoa pods passed through the hands of the seasoned workers. Watched over by Jacobo, Gregorio, Mateo, and the foremen, the laborers collected the ripe and healthy berries with a small hook shaped like a scythe fixed onto a long stick. With great care and dexterity they *picked* the cocoa, letting it fall without touching the others. The chosen pods, which they piled up beside the cocoa trees so that other men could come and break them open with their machetes and extract the grain, which they filled into sacks and stacked along the track.

The main yard overflowed with activity for many days and nights. Those in charge of the trucks transported the sacks from the cocoa trees and tipped their contents into large wooden tanks, where they fermented for seventy-two hours, allowing a thick, viscous liquid to leak out. After fermentation, other men spread the beans over slate sheets in the dryers, under which flowed a current of hot air that heated them up to 160 degrees Fahrenheit.

Kilian, José, Marcial, and Santiago took turns supervising the drying process, which lasted between forty-eight and seventy hours, to make sure the workers did not stop turning the beans until the supervisors were happy. Then, they transferred the beans into large wheelbarrows with holes in their bottoms to allow the beans to cool and later put them through the cleaning machine before packing them in sacks meant for various destinations.

Finally, it was done. Thanks to the methodical workdays, Kilian's impatience in the months prior to his illness started giving way bit by bit, turning into apathy.

This permeated all aspects of his life except work, where he still stood out for his dedication and effort. He went to Santa Isabel only when it was his turn to buy material in the stores or when Sade threatened that she would come to his room if another month went by without seeing him. More than likely, the threats were Jacobo's way of forcing him out. Kilian knew she was not faithful to him. He stopped going to the cinema, he managed to get the rest of the employees to stop asking him to go with them to their many parties, and he declined invitations to dinners with Julia, Manuel, Generosa, and Emilio. He felt happy only in the solitude of the jungle, and he gladly accepted José's company only because he talked to him without lectures.

When Antón had been dead for almost two years, Jacobo went on holiday to Spain to attend Catalina's wedding. When he returned, he poured a whiskey for his brother and himself and told Kilian all the details of his stay in Pasolobino.

"Everyone missed you, Kilian," he finished. "Catalina would have liked to have had both of us to walk her down the aisle in Dad's absence . . . And Mom, well, strong as ever. You should have seen how she made sure everything went well, the menu, the dresses, the church . . ." He chuckled. "She turned the house upside down to get it looking its best!"

"Did you tell her that we can't both go at the same time?"

"Yes, Kilian, I told her. But she knows nowadays you can catch one of those new planes and be home in three or four days."

"The plane is too expensive. With the wedding and the dowry and without Dad's salary, we can't be given to excess."

"In that you are partly right." Jacobo drained his glass. "You know, when you came here four years ago, I had a bet with Marcial that you wouldn't last a full campaign."

"And you lost the bet!" His brother nodded. "I hope it wasn't too big."

The two of them laughed, as if nothing had happened and they were the same young men full of dreams, as strong as the trunks of the ash trees at the foot of the snowy peaks of Pasolobino. They both gazed into their glasses, nostalgic, until the door opened.

"It's great to find you both here!" Manuel grabbed a glass and sat down beside them. "I saw light from the window and wanted a bit of conversation. I'd come more often, but I finish up tired, and then I can't be bothered."

"That's what happens when you live in a house on your own." Jacobo filled his glass.

"I hope for not too long . . ."

Kilian raised an eyebrow. "Are you thinking of leaving?"

"No, not at all." Manuel raised his glass level with his eyes. "Here's to my wedding."

After the initial surprise, the brothers joined in the toast with him.

"Julia, her family, and I are going to Madrid in fifteen days. We'll get married there, and then we'll be away around three months. Well, Generosa and Emilio will return sooner, to run the business."

Jacobo downed his drink and put his glass on the table with a thud. "I'm happy for you, Manuel," he said in a forced cheerful tone. "Truly. You have been very lucky. Julia is a wonderful woman."

"I know."

"Yes," Kilian added. "It's great news, Manuel. And afterward, what will you do?"

"Oh, Julia agrees that we will live here, in Sampaka, in the doctor's house. It's big enough for a family. And she knows how to drive, so she can continue working in her parents' shop. For the moment, everything stays the same."

"Not quite the same, Manuel, not quite . . ." Jacobo tried to joke. "You will be under watch at all hours!"

"It's easy having Julia as the *wachiwoman*, Jacobo, very easy." Manuel smiled.

Kilian saw Jacobo make a face and said, "And have you not thought about moving to Madrid? Won't life on the plantation be boring? Julia is used to the city, isn't she?"

Manuel shrugged. "Julia is more from Fernando Po than anyone else. She doesn't want to hear a word about leaving. In any case, if she finds the adjustment difficult, we can always rent a house in Santa Isabel. We'll see . . ." He stretched his arm to reach the bottle and get another glass but looked at the clock and changed his mind. "Well, now that I've told you the latest news in my otherwise mundane existence, I'd better go. I still have to take a look at a couple of patients before going to bed."

When they were alone, Kilian looked at Jacobo and said in a neutral voice, "You took that better than I expected."

"How else should I have taken it?" Jacobo scoffed.

"Lad, you let her escape. You know that I would have liked her for a sister-in-law."

"Don't talk nonsense, Kilian. I did her a favor."

"What do you mean?" Kilian raised his eyebrows.

"Well, it's fairly obvious. Someone like Julia deserves someone like Manuel."

"I'm surprised that you are so understanding, Jacobo." He shook his head.

Jacobo stared at him with sadness, resignation, and craftiness all at once. He raised his glass and gently knocked it against his brother's.

"Life goes on, Brother."

Julia and Manuel returned from their long honeymoon at the beginning of autumn, and they moved into the doctor's house in Sampaka. Julia started to travel every day to the city to work in her parents' store.

On a rainy November morning, Jacobo went to the shop to collect an order for material. When he parked the pickup, he saw Generosa and Emilio, elegantly dressed, getting into their red-and-cream chrome-finished car. Of all the expensive cars on the island, Jacobo was especially fond of this '53 Vauxhall. He went over and said a friendly hello.

"Sorry, we can't stay, Jacobo." Generosa smoothed the collar of her damask silk cinnamon-colored jacket in the passenger seat. "But we're late for mass in honor of the patron of the city, and then invited to brunch in the general government." She pointed to her husband proudly. "Have you heard? Emilio has just been appointed to the Neighbors Council." The man waved a hand in the air. "Nothing happens for months, and then everything happens at once! We have to start preparing next year's festival already. It will be the centenary of the arrival of Governor Chacón and the Jesuits, and the diamond jubilee of the Claretian missionaries on the island."

Jacobo held back a smile on seeing Emilio's impatient scowl.

"By the way," she continued, "have you heard about the tragedy in Valencia? Almost one hundred people dead after the Turia burst its banks!" Jacobo had not heard anything. "Well, tell Lorenzo Garuz that the government of the colony has responded to the call. We collected two hundred and fifty thousand pesetas, and cocoa will also be sent. Any help is welcome."

Her husband put his foot on the accelerator without letting out the clutch.

"Yes, now, good-bye, good-bye."

"Julia will look after you, lad," said Emilio before setting off. "She's in the store. Come whenever you want. And bring your brother."

Jacobo nodded and thought with a mother like that, it was not strange that Julia had such a determined character. He went toward the back of the store, flanked by overflowing shelves, and made out Julia's figure climbing up a rickety ladder, trying on tiptoe to get at a box that was just out of her reach. Jacobo could see nearly the whole length of her tanned legs under a fiery red skirt and felt a glimmer of unexpected desire. A small voice in his head reproached him again for letting her escape. He had not forgotten her comfort at Antón's funeral. A woman like her would always be at her husband's side. You only had to look at Manuel's face to realize how happy he was with her, with his wife.

He choked on the words as he thought them.

Julia was married to another.

Another small voice appeared, reminding him that marrying her would have meant not only the loss of his coveted freedom, but also a tie to the island. Jacobo enjoyed his life on the island, for now. He would not do what his father had done. He would not sacrifice so many years for Fernando Po. Sooner or later he would return to Spain. Kilian would do the same. And Julia would stay near Santa Isabel. As sure as the sun rose each day.

Then what was he doing standing there, staring at a friend recently married to another friend? Manuel was that, a good friend. Even for Jacobo, this overstepped his bounds!

He stealthily crept closer.

"Be careful, Julia!" he said, an evil glint in his eyes.

The girl was startled. She grabbed on to some iron bars above her head to get a firm footing on the top rung of the ladder just as a pair of strong arms caught her by the waist to lower her slowly down to the ground. Jacobo saw her thighs, her waist, her chest, her neck, and her red face. When she got to the ground, her face was level with the man's torso, and for a few seconds, she did not dare raise her head to look at him.

She had never been this close to Jacobo.

She breathed in his scent.

She should get out of the embrace but did not want to. He had caught her; he should be the one to let her go. Her heart beat strongly. Jacobo moved her away a few centimeters, searching for her eyes. She lifted her chin to him and discovered something strange, different, in the man's green eyes. They were darkened by a doubt, hesitation, desire.

Julia half opened her lips as he bent down to taste them with tender abandonment, both delaying with ardent listlessness the inevitable guilt. She pressed herself to him to feel his hands covering her back, in a brief moment of possession and surrender, and caressed his black hair with the tips of her fingers.

Julia and Jacobo kissed, slowly and greedily, until they stopped for air. Then she took his hands and undid the embrace.

"Don't ever do that again," she said, her voice faltering.

"I'm sorry." Jacobo shook his head. "Actually, no, I'm not sorry."

"I meant giving someone on a ladder a fright. I almost killed myself. Well, and the other thing as well."

"It seemed to me that you were enjoying it . . ." Jacobo tried to circle her waist.

"Too late, Jacobo." Julia put the palms of her hands on his chest and pushed him gently. "Too late."

"But . . ."

"No, Jacobo. I promised before God and my family to be faithful to my husband."

"Then why did you let me . . ."

Julia would have liked to tell him that it was the prize for the many hours she spent dreaming about kissing him, about having him this close. She would have liked to have said how happy he made her by showing in his eyes that they could have had a future together. If he had wanted to . . . But it was too late now. She shrugged and answered, "It just happened. We will never mention this again. Right?"

Jacobo grudgingly agreed, though he was used to succumbing to passionate encounters without much thought. They could never deny that something special had happened. How could she regain her composure so quickly after having shared such a breathtaking moment? From his experience with white women, he would have understood tears of guilt, immediate regret, or even the complete opposite, an offer of occasional secret meetings . . . but this conscious denial of a desired pleasure left him dumbstruck.

"What do you need to get today?" Julia asked, straightening her dress.

"Eh, I'd better come back another day." Few times in his life had Jacobo felt so incapable of small talk.

"As you wish."

At that moment, a slight girl with short dark hair pulled up in a wide pink ribbon entered the store.

"How are you, Oba?" Julia inquired. Jacobo recognized Sade's friend from Anita Guau. "Jacobo, we have hired Oba to help us in the store. My parents are getting busier and busier, and I can't be here all hours of the day. I've got other commitments now . . ." She paused.

"It's a good idea," he said flatly. "Well, I'd better be going. See you soon, Julia."

"Good-bye, Jacobo."

Jacobo left the building and stood in the rain for a few minutes before slipping into the pickup. Inside the store, Oba followed Julia through the shelves as she explained where everything was kept. When she got to the stairs, Julia stopped for a few seconds and put her hands to her lips. Oba, a talkative girl, said, "That good-looking massa . . . I know him, you know? Are you friends? Well, he and I have friends in common. Sometimes we meet up . . ."

"Oba!" Julia shouted. When she saw the girl's expression, she changed her tone. "Don't get distracted, I still have a lot of things to show you."

The last thing Julia wanted at that moment, with the taste of Jacobo still on her lips, was for someone to drag her back to reality.

Toward the end of December, all the plantation employees received a written invitation to celebrate the new year at the doctor's house.

"For weeks we have been trying to celebrate our wedding with you, but we put it off for one reason or another," a radiant Julia explained to her guests. "We finally made it coincide with, you know, New Year's, new life . . ."

Kilian saw the newly married couple quite often, but that day he found Julia especially happy. She was wearing a pale-yellow silk dress that flared at the waist, and her hair was done up in a high chignon that highlighted her porcelain skin. Julia was not a beauty, but she was gorgeous when she smiled. Manuel's and Julia's parents were also in attendance and very happy.

Julia had decorated in a style similar to that of her parents' house in Santa Isabel, simple and welcoming. The dining room was not very large, but she had managed to get a table that could comfortably seat fourteen: her family, the six employees, the manager, the priest, and two close friends, Ascensión and Mercedes, who, from what they all could gather, had gotten engaged to Mateo and Marcial, respectively.

Kilian spent a few seconds looking at two peculiar pictures hanging on the wall. On a black background, with ingenious and narrow brushstrokes, the artist had represented forms that were clearly identifiable. In one, several men were steering a canoe down a river, through leafy vegetation. In the other, various feathered warriors with spears were hunting a beast. Julia passed by him on her way to the head of the table.

"They're nice, aren't they?" Julia said. Kilian nodded. "I bought them recently from a street stall. They're by someone called Nolet. I fell in love with them the minute I saw them. They are . . . How can I put it? Simple and complex, serene and violent, enigmatic and transparent . . ."

"Like this island," murmured Kilian.

"Yes. And like any one of us . . ."

Many of the guests were suffering from hangovers after the previous night in the casino, but the atmosphere there was relaxed thanks to the special menu, typical of Pasolobino, which Generosa had prepared for the occasion. They ate a smooth chickpea puree followed by hen fricassee. The tender pieces of meat dipped in flour and fried in oil before being stewed over a slow heat with wine, milk, walnuts, garlic, onion, and salt and pepper brought on memories of absent mothers. For dessert, they tasted an exquisite rum soufflé with egg-yolk pastries.

Kilian noticed that Jacobo was unusually quiet and barely looked at Julia. Their greeting too had been cold and distant. He did not make much of it. More than likely his brother had celebrated New Year's Eve too hard and was not up for small pleasantries.

At one point in the conversation, the other young men exchanged so many jokes with Manuel over his new status as a married man that in the end, he blurted out a proverb.

"When your neighbor's house"—he pointed at Mateo and Marcial—"is on fire, carry . . ."

"Water to your own!" finished Ascensión, fondly pulling Mateo's mustache.

Everyone burst out laughing.

After dessert, two boys served Johnnie Walker and Veuve Clicquot. Emilio, red faced and eyes shining, got to his feet, raised his glass, and proposed a toast to the married couple and the family that, as Manuel had confirmed that very week, would soon be increasing. The guests cheered, applauded, and made risqué comments that turned Julia red. Father Rafael shook his head. Ascensión and Mercedes ran to congratulate their friend and the future grandmother, and all the men clapped Manuel and the future grandfather on the back.

Kilian used the racket to get up and go out to smoke a cigarette. Julia, still with reddened cheeks, followed and rested against the railing that surrounded the small garden.

"Congratulations, Julia," Kilian said, offering her a cigarette, which she refused.

"Thanks. We are very happy." She clasped her hands over her stomach. "It's a strange feeling . . ." She looked at Kilian. "When are you going to go home, Kilian? How long has it been since you last saw your mother?"

"Almost five years."

"That's a long time . . ."

"I know." Kilian pursed his lips tightly.

Julia studied him. Kilian and Jacobo both gave off an overwhelming sense of strength, but they could not be more different. She knew that there was a special sensitivity in Kilian. He suffered inside. He had suffered on his arrival, in adapting to the island, in gaining the respect of his companions, when accompanying his father in his final moments, by refusing to go back to his family . . . It could not be easy to control that compassion, humanity, and even tenderness around men toughened by hard work and an extreme climate. Each brother produced different feelings in her. The attraction she felt for Jacobo was directly proportional to the fraternal love she felt for Kilian.

"I couldn't last that long without seeing my child," she insisted. "I'm sure I couldn't."

Kilian shrugged. "Things happen like that," he said.

"Sometimes, things are as we want them to be." She remembered the kiss with Jacobo and shivered. She could have avoided it but had not wanted to. "This is one example. What would it cost you to take a ship or a plane home?"

"A lot, Julia."

"I'm not referring to money."

"Neither am I." Kilian stubbed out the cigarette, leaned down, and put his forearms on the sun-heated railings. "I can't, Julia. Not yet."

He changed the subject. "I see that your new life agrees with you."

"Oh, yes, but don't think . . . At first, living together takes a lot of effort."

"Manuel is a good person."

"Yes, very good." Julia looked down at the ground. "I'll make a deal with you. I'll tell you a secret if you tell me why you don't want to go home."

Kilian smiled. She was truly tenacious.

"It's too soon."

"Too soon?" Julia frowned. "For what?

"For everything. To see the suffering on Mom's face, to bump into memories of Dad at every turn . . . For everything, Julia. Nothing will be the same as when I left. Distance keeps feelings at bay." He sighed. "Now it's your turn. What secret could you possibly have?"

Julia was quiet for a few seconds. In her case, she thought, distance cooled temptation. She decided to sidestep the question. "I've learned that your sister is also pregnant. Children are always a reason to be happy. Do you know that my father is already thinking of names for our baby? He says that if it's a girl, it can have whatever name I want, but if it's a boy, he will be named Fernando, no matter what. He has bet a thousand pesetas with his friends in the casino that there is a Fernando in every house of Spaniards who have been to Guinea. We have gone through the families, and in the end, he might be right!"

Kilian could not help smiling. "The name is nice. Very appropriate."

"I could suggest it to Catalina. Although she might prefer to call him Antón, like his grandfather, if it's a boy, of course."

"I don't know. Repeating names only invites comparisons. In the end, you don't know which is the original and which is the copy."

"Oh, come on, Kilian! What is José teaching you?"

Kilian raised an eyebrow.

"Life is a circle. It repeats itself. Like nature. Nowhere else is it easier to see the circle of life and death." Julia shrugged. "Once you learn that," she continued, "everything is much easier. Do you know what my grandmother told me time and time again, in our valley when I was young? To know how to live, you have to know how to die. And she had seen many people die. I won't even mention the civil war . . ."

Julia felt a shiver and rubbed her upper arms.

"We'd better go in," said Kilian, straightening up.

"Yes. I'll bet you anything that I know what they are talking about at the moment."

"Politics?" he wagered.

Julia smiled. Kilian looked into her eyes and gave her an affectionate kiss on the cheek.

"You deserve everything good that happens to you, Julia," he said before winking and adding, "although you don't keep your deals . . ."

She reddened. "And you too, Kilian. You'll see . . . The best of life has yet to come."

Immediately after the pair entered the dining room, Mateo, Marcial, Asunción, and Mercedes said their good-byes to go meet friends in the city. The others continued talking at the table about politics, as Julia and Kilian had guessed.

"I heard it the other day in the casino," said Emilio in a strong voice. "It seems that there has already been a warning from the UN on decolonization. Carrero Blanco has proposed forming provinces."

"And what does that mean?" Santiago asked.

"It's obvious," intervened Lorenzo Garuz. "This will all become a Spanish province."

"I'm not that stupid," said Santiago, smoothing down his sparse hair with his bony hand. "That I understand. I'm referring to how things will change as a province."

"Well, it seems reasonable to me. After so many years, what is this but an extension of Spain?" Emilio raised his glass toward the boy so he could refill it. "But of course, the coloreds don't see it that way. I can barely talk to Gustavo anymore because we always end up shouting at each other. Can you believe he had the nerve to tell me that it was just a strategy to continue our exploitation?"

"I can imagine his simple logic," commented Father Rafael. "If they are provinces, decolonizing cannot be put on the table."

"He said the same. Well, in slightly stronger terms, but that's what he meant."

"Bah, I don't think any of this will go forward," Generosa intervened. "Without Spain, there is no Guinea, and without us, they will return to the jungle where we found them." Julia winced. "In fact, the colony costs more than it makes. But they don't seem to appreciate that."

"Well, I'm not so sure about that," said Jacobo, thinking of the tons of cocoa from the last harvest. "We know better than anyone what it makes, don't we, Mr. Garuz?"

"Yes, but . . ." Garuz shook his head. "Who pays for the schools, the hospitals, the city maintenance and services, if not Spain? I don't know . . . we might just break even."

"That is even impossible," Generosa commented. "Have you seen the orphanage? Who pays for the sixty children who live there? And what about Moka? I was with Emilio a few weeks ago at the inauguration of the tap-water system for Moka, Malabo, and Bioko and the handing over of houses to cooperative members. The Board of Native Affairs has paid for half of each of the houses, which even have double-glazed wooden windows . . ."

"And that's not all," added Emilio, raising his voice. "Where do you think Gustavo went not too long ago? To Cameroon, to meet up with that gang of independence fighters. They were even talking about a possible federation with Gabon!"

"Of course," Father Rafael interrupted, "since France is about to grant independence to Cameroon and Gabon, it will become infectious. After all our work teaching them the right way! Did you notice what happened this Christmas? The streets of Santa Isabel were filled with *mamarrachos* with their masks. Before they did not leave their own areas, and now they parade about in their offensive colors, making incoherent noise. Is this what the freedom crusades want? The bishops already warned about it in a recent pastoral letter. The greatest enemy will soon be the communist ideology."

"I hope that the conflicts in Ifni aren't repeated here," said a worried Garuz.

Everyone agreed. Morocco, which had gained independence a year ago, was now reclaiming the small Spanish territory. News had reached them that the Ifni garrisons had been attacked by Moroccan nationalists supported by their king.

"If France doesn't stand firm, I don't know what will happen."

"Dad!" Julia exclaimed, worried that Emilio would get too riled up.

"Your friend is taking serious risks," Gregorio commented. "One of these days, they will arrest him and send him to Black Beach. The governor doesn't want any messing around."

"I think it's good that he guards the frontiers with Cameroon and Gabon, and that he detains anyone who rebels against Spanish authority in these lands," affirmed Generosa with conviction. "This is Spain and will remain so for a long time. There are many Spaniards fighting every day for our businesses. Spain won't abandon us."

A sudden silence followed. Manuel waved at the boys to refill the glasses.

"We can be a real pain sometimes, we old ones, isn't that so, children?" Emilio smiled at Jacobo, Kilian, Manuel, and Julia. "Ah well, I propose another toast to you, to the future . . ." He raised his glass in the air and the rest followed suit. "Happy new year. I wish you all many happy years."

Kilian clinked his glass, preoccupied. He could not properly comprehend their concerns, but of course he was only an employee on one of the many plantations on the island, not the owner of a business. If he had to leave the island, he would look for another job in Spain, and that would be it. He would not leave much behind. He drank, then shuddered, wondering how the members of José's extensive family would celebrate the new year in Bissappoo.

Months later, Julia and Manuel's son was born. In the end, they decided to name him Ismael because according to what Julia told the brothers after the christening, Emilio won the bet and realized that there were too many Fernandos all over the place. Around the same time, Catalina gave birth to a boy named Antón. He died at the age of two months from capillary bronchitis, which they found out about in a sad letter from their mother.

Kilian took the news badly, deeply saddened for his sister. She would find it difficult to get over this hard test. Catalina had never enjoyed good health. The pregnancy had not been easy—she had been on bed rest for the final months—and during delivery, they were worried about losing her. He remembered how his father's death had affected him and tried to imagine how Catalina felt after losing a child. Her pain had to be deep, cutting, and unbearable.

For the first time in a long time, Kilian decided to write a letter to Mariana and Catalina in which he promised that in a few months, at the beginning of the following year, he would come home. Perhaps, he thought as he chose the difficult words of condolence, the unexpected joy of his return would help to distract, if not lessen, her pain.

As if the land had begun to say its good-byes, that year the harvest suffered an unexpected virulent attack of *Characoma*, a caterpillar that bores into the cocoa pod husks. The plantation was a pitiful sight to behold. There was not a pod that could have been saved from the tiny pink crawlers. The scales and scabs of the necrotized skin covered almost the entire surface of all the pods. Due to the infestation, the ripening process could not be tracked. In some areas, the harvest suffered delays because the scabs had not only halted access to sunlight, but also prevented the fungicides from working properly. Though the harvest was already hard in itself, that year they had more work to do than ever. To prevent other invasive attacks from the plantations' persistent colonizers, drastic measures had to be taken. Once the pods were split, the shells were collected to be buried, burned, or covered in lime. The sucker branches also had to be burned, all fruit had to be taken from the trees, and pesticides had to be sprayed earlier and more often.

"Garuz will not be happy," said José as he picked up a handful of beans and returned them to the slate sheet in the dryer. "Between the rain and the bugs, the cocoa won't be nearly as good as other harvests."

Beside him, Kilian seemed nervous. Every once in a while, he kicked the ground with the top of his right foot.

"What's the matter? Is it time to dance?"

"For the last few days, my foot has been itchy. And today it hurts as well."

"Let me see."

Kilian sat down and took off his boot and sock. "It's just here." He pointed to under the nail of his fourth toe. "It really itches."

José knelt down and came close to confirm his suspicions. "You've caught a chigger." He chuckled. "You're the same as the cocoa trees. A bug wants to colonize you." He saw the look of disgust on Kilian's face and hurriedly explained. "Don't be frightened, it's very common. The chigger is so small you can pick it up anywhere. It gets into your fingers and toes and eats the flesh with its elongated snout while filling a pouch of young. See? The offspring are in this lump."

Kilian stretched his arm to quickly pinch it out, but José stopped him.

"Ah, no. You have to take the sac out very carefully. If it rips, the offspring will spread to the other toes. You wouldn't be the first to lose one."

"I'll go to the hospital this instant!" Nervous and disgusted, Kilian put on his sock and boot as carefully as he could.

"Ask for my daughter," José advised him. "She's an expert at removing chiggers!"

On the way to the hospital, walking on the heel of his right foot, Kilian felt suddenly excited. It had been weeks since he had seen José's daughter. He had to admit that on the few occasions he had gone with his friend to Bissappoo, he had harbored the hope of meeting up with her there, but apparently she did not go to the village very often. Her life was split between the hospital and her husband. On one occasion, José had commented to him that he found it strange that they did not have any children, after four years of marriage. Four years! Kilian could not believe it had been so long since her wedding day. He remembered the girl stroking him when he had been sick. Since then, they had not had a chance to see each other alone. Sometimes he had seen her crossing the main yard, determined and resolute, looking for José. She would approach her father, give him a friendly greeting, agree with his comments about the job, and throw her head back to laugh in the suffocating heat of the recently roasted cocoa. Kilian always waited for the moment in which she discreetly turned and looked at him with those eyes.

He had to admit it, yes. Many days, enlivened by the songs of the plantation's laborers, the fantasies of them together had entertained him for hours and hours. Of all the possible women, he had gotten his hopes up for a married woman. Fortunately, he reasoned, as he climbed the building's steps, nobody could know his thoughts or his feelings. And thanks to the disgusting bug that was trying to take over his foot, the possibility existed of enjoying a precious while alone with her.

He entered directly into the large hall where the sick laborers were seen and glanced over the beds laid out in an orderly manner on both sides of the room. A male nurse came over to him and directed him to a small room where the treatments were carried out. Kilian knocked on the door a few times and without waiting for an answer opened it.

He let out a surprised gasp, and his hopes melted away.

His brother was in a chair with his shirt stained in blood and a wooden gag between his teeth while José's daughter stitched a deep cut on his left hand. The woman paused as Kilian walked into the room.

"What happened to you?" asked a worried Kilian.

Jacobo took the gag out of his mouth. His face was covered in sweat.

"I cut myself with the machete."

"What were you thinking?" He looked at the nurse. "Manuel isn't here?"

"He's gone to the city," she answered. Seeing that he continued to look at her, she added, with a little arrogance, "But I know how to cure wounds like this."

"I'm sure you do," Kilian replied firmly. "Is it serious?"

"A couple more stitches and I'll be finished. The cut is clean but deep. It will take some days to heal."

"Just as well it's my left hand!" said Jacobo. "At least I can button my trousers by myself." He giggled nervously. "It's a joke. Come here, Kilian, talk to me while this beauty finishes. It's the first time I've had stitches, and it hurts a lot."

Kilian dragged a chair over, and the nurse continued her work.

Jacobo winced. "You are so pretty, yet you cause so much pain!"

Kilian placed the wooden gag between his brother's teeth, who pressed hard while breathing agitatedly. Kilian frowned on seeing the cut and admired the way José's daughter showed no signs of distaste. *She must be used to seeing worse things.* She soon finished the last stitch, cut the thread, disinfected the wound once again, covered it with clean gauze, and carefully bandaged the hand.

"Thank God you're finished." Jacobo passed his tongue along his dry lips and sighed. "A little more and I would have been in tears."

"Don't worry, Jacobo. Your dignity is safe." Kilian gave him a few pats on the arm.

"I hope so . . ." He winked at the nurse. "Because everything comes out here."

She did not even flicker as she collected her things and got up. "You'll have to come back in a couple of days so that the doctor can look at the wound and tell you when the stitches can come out. Try not to move the hand too much." She turned and went toward the door.

"Wait!" said Kilian. "I need you too."

She turned around. "Excuse me. I thought you came to look for your brother." She frowned. "What's the problem?"

"A chigger."

"I'll be back in a second," she said with a smile. "I need a bamboo stick."

"Did you notice, Kilian?" said Jacobo when she had left. "She's informal with you, but not with me."

His brother shrugged. "It must be because you look more serious than me," Kilian commented, and Jacobo let out a big guffaw. Kilian went on, "You know, you can go if you want. You probably want to have a coffee after having gone through that."

"No way. I'll wait until the nurse is finished with both of us."

Kilian tried to make sure his voice did not sound frustrated. "Whatever you'd like."

He could not speak to her alone, but he treasured the impression of her fingers on his ankle, on the instep of his foot, on his heel, on every centimeter that she had to touch while she was cutting the edges of the chigger egg sac with the bamboo until it came off completely. He memorized each and every one of her movements throughout the few short minutes it took, while Jacobo chatted on, as if there were nobody else in the room with them, about his brother's upcoming trip to Spain. She seemed to be concentrated on what she was doing, but there was an instant when Kilian noticed her expression cloud over and a fine wrinkle appear between her eyebrows. It was when Jacobo joked, "And what will Sade do without you? Do you want me to look after her in your place?"

Kilian pursed his lips and did not answer.

In the weeks before his trip, Kilian could not help comparing himself to the Nigerian workers on the plantation. Like them, when he had arrived, he was a wiry lad full of curiosity; now he would return to his country years later a muscular, large, and well-built man. He had also collected things that he had bought to take home and earned a generous amount of money. The only difference was that the laborers went back to Nigeria because in their contracts, skillfully written so that the capital would not only not stay in Guinea, but would return to Nigerian territory, it was stipulated that they would receive fifty percent of their salary in the colony and the other fifty percent in their country. In Kilian's case, the thousands of kilometers' distance separated two extremes of the same country, so his trip would only involve a confrontation with his past, a past that six years on a cocoa plantation in tropical climes had not erased from his heart.

However, when he arrived in his valley after a night in Zaragoza—where many women now wore trousers; where the Fiat 1400 along with the occasional SEAT 600 had displaced the Peugeot 203, the Austin FX3, and the Citroën CV; and where the café Ambos Mundos had disappeared—and made out the outskirts of Pasolobino after climbing up the stony path in the same dark-gray coat that he had not worn since leaving, behind the mare who, led by one of his cousins, had carried his bulky baggage, he felt a strange mixture of sensations. He lifted his face toward the rigid outline of the village against the clear sky of a cold March day in 1959.

Pasolobino and the House of Rabaltué were exactly as he remembered them, except for the building that was going to be the new school and the extension to the hay shed of his house. The people had not changed much either, even if time had aged them.

At first, Kilian found it hard to have a fluent conversation with Mariana, her gray hair done up in a discreet and tight bun that highlighted the new lines on her face. He could barely hold her maternal look. He used small talk as a barrier to keep his emotions under control. Still, Mariana did her utmost to catch him up. Kilian was jealous of her outward strength, with which she encouraged a gaunt and downhearted Catalina not to neglect her daily chores and to look after her husband, Carlos, because—she said—life goes very quickly and she had lost three children and a husband and continued to battle for the next ones to come, and there would be next ones; sooner or later, more always came. As far as she could remember, no house had stayed empty for long.

Kilian delivered presents all over the village. The most delicate objects, bought in the Dumbo store in Santa Isabel, were for his mother and sister: beautiful cotton and silk fabrics, two Manila blankets and bags, a gorgeous embroidered tablecloth, and new covers for the beds. For the relations and neighbors, he had brought tins of Craven A cigarettes and bottles of the best Irish and Scotch whiskies—luxuries in that part of the world—and fruits completely unknown in Pasolobino, like pineapples and coconuts. To the astonishment of everyone, he sliced a coconut in half with one blow of his machete, and then he offered those around him the chance to drink the liquid inside before tasting the crunchy coconut itself.

The girls from the neighboring houses, now women, smiled flirtatiously at him. On visits, he patiently answered the same questions while smoking his favorite cigarettes, Rumbo, and trying to adapt to Pasolobinese. They whispered between laughs when hearing the linguistic peculiarities of the plantation that had infected the good-looking young man, especially in his short and simple sentences and his strange vocabulary.

After the novelty of his return quieted down, Kilian got thrown into work in the sheds, pruning the trees and getting firewood ready, cleaning the weeds from the walls of the buildings, fertilizing the fields for the livestock, and plowing the plots for summer. He spent many hours outside in the slumbering fields, waiting for the timid greeting of the cold spring.

Nothing had changed much. The stables retained the heat of the animals restless for their impending freedom. The same smoke licked the sides of the stone chimneys crowned with the unshakable stones to frighten away the witches. Kilian had to work hard not to compare the world of Pasolobino with the island of Fernando Po. He found the streets dirty and uneven; the bodies, soft and milky white; the clothes, monochrome and boring; the sunlight, pale and weak; the green landscape, subdued; the climate, too serene; and the House of Rabaltué, cold and solid, like a rocky mountain.

However, when he admitted to himself that so many years had left a deeper mark than he thought on his body and soul, the blood pulsed in his veins, he closed his eyes, and his thoughts became a tornado of images that mercilessly threw him again at the feet of the colossal volcanic peak of Santa Isabel, permanently adorned in mists, covered in forest to near its summit and marked by the scars of its streams.

There, in the silence of his imagination, Kilian allowed himself to be possessed by the sun and the rain of a paradise where, day after day, the luxuriant growth of the thousands of plant species confirmed the absolute tenacity of the cycle of life.

Recurrent, constant.

Unstoppable.

8

The Royal Palm Tree Avenue

2003

She was finally in Santa Isabel!

She corrected herself: She was finally in Malabo!

It was not easy to refer to the city by its current name. And much more difficult to talk about the island of Bioko instead of the Fernando Po from her father's and uncle's stories.

Clarence opened her eyes and followed the ceiling-fan blades with her eyes for a few seconds. The heat was suffocating and sticky. She had not stopped sweating while unpacking her luggage, and the refreshing effects of the shower had not lasted long.

And now what? she thought.

She got out of bed and went onto the balcony, breathing in the same viscous humidity that had met her after the flight. She still felt in a daze from the rapid change of scenery. She tried to imagine her father's impressions when he first stepped ashore here, but the circumstances were completely different. He certainly did not have the feeling of arriving in a country run by a military. She huffed as she remembered the customs line at the modern airport; several times she had had to show her passport, her good-conduct certificate, her vaccine chart, and the invitation from the National University of Equatorial Guinea before going through various checkpoints where they opened her bags and nosed around everything she had with her. They had made her fill in an immigration form explaining the reasons for her trip, and they had asked her for the name of the hotel where she would be staying. And to top it all, she had to take that wad of papers with her at all hours to avoid problems in any of the many police checkpoints they had warned her would be found everywhere.

She lit a cigarette and inhaled deeply, contemplating the sun's reflection on the palms between the flaking houses, listening to the chirps of the birds mixed with the children playing soccer in the alley opposite, and trying to decipher the voices of the men and women in colorful clothes, on the street with cars of all makes and in all conditions. What a special place! On this small island, the size of her valley, people of different countries had lived and spoken at least ten languages: Portuguese, English, Bubi, African English, Fang, Ndowé, Bissau, Annobonese, French, Spanish . . . She might have left some out, but one thing had been made crystal clear in just a few hours: the Spanish influence remained strong.

The Spanish colonizers, including her own family, had definitely left a deep imprint on the country.

She thought of her strange relationship with Fernando Po–Bioko. A small piece of paper and some words from Julia had given Clarence the definitive push to fulfill one of her life dreams: to travel to the island whose stories had been rattling around her head since childhood. She had finally gotten the chance to stroll along the paths that her forebearers had walked for so many years. Breathe the same air. Enjoy the same local color. Feel happy with their music. And touch the soil where her grandfather Antón lay.

This trip was the most daring thing she had ever done in a life completely given over to study. She had had enough courage to answer a faint call that echoed in her heart.

Someone older than she born in Sampaka . . .

From the very moment that Julia had talked to her about Fernando Po, a suspicion had grown inside her that her blood could still be on the island. And if she had a brother? What other thing could Julia have been referring to? Clarence could barely think it! Much less say it out loud! She had often felt tempted to confide her anxieties to her cousin Daniela, but in the end, she decided to wait until she had definitive proof, if there was any.

But if it was true?

How could her father have lived with it? And her uncle . . . He should know! It would be impossible for him not to . . . unless she was wrong and had to look for a cousin instead. She shook her head. The letter was with her father's mail. Besides, she could not believe that Kilian could have done something like that. He was the most upright and responsible person she knew. Her uncle was a man of his word, capable of ignoring all else when the truth was at stake, be they troublesome subjects on land borders or on the relationships between neighbors or family.

For a moment Clarence was shocked at the ease in which she had excused her uncle and blamed her father, but she was not a child anymore. She did not find it at all unlikely to imagine her father escaping from an unwelcome situation, to put it mildly, and more so if it had to do with a black child. In more than one conversation, her father had made racist comments. When she grew indignant, he closed the subject with *"I've lived with them, and I know what I'm talking about,"* to which Kilian responded *"So did I, and I don't agree."* Daniela celebrated her father's reason with a smile. As if he would ever recognize a black child! And more so in the Spain of forty years ago!

Clarence slowed her thoughts; she had only a piece of paper, Julia's words, and four separate bits of information that she went over again and again.

Of the first letters written by her uncle Kilian, she had not been able to extract any information that would shed light on Julia's hints. One of the letters described how well looked after her grandfather Antón had been, especially by the native nurse, and all the people who had attended the funeral and later burial. Apart from Manuel and Julia, she had heard some of the names before. After Antón's death, her uncle wrote less frequently, and the letters were more repetitive, focusing above all on the finances of the House of Rabaltué.

Only one of the letters was a little more personal. In a short paragraph, Kilian tried to console Aunt Catalina over the death of her baby and, straight after, announced his trip to Spain, about which he would add details—on what ship he would travel, what city he would arrive in, how long it would take—in later letters. He stayed in Spain until 1960 and returned to the island, intending to work for two more campaigns, each two years in length. His plans were to return to Pasolobino for good in 1964 at the age of thirty-five. It was probable that her uncle was planning, the same as Jacobo and many others, to retire from the cocoa campaigns to start his own family at home.

However, something did not fit.

There were very few letters written after 1964, but their existence showed that his stay in Guinea had been extended longer than expected.

Something had happened in 1965, after Aunt Catalina's death.

And it coincided with a short reference to a confrontation between Kilian and Jacobo that she had found in another letter. Could that be the reason her father left his job on the plantation? An argument with his brother?

Clarence clicked her tongue. It did not make sense. Their relationship had endured the passage of time, so it could not have been that serious. What had happened?

She looked at her watch. There were still two hours to go before dinner. She decided to stroll down Avenida Libertad. It had been difficult for her to choose hotels because of the very limited selection available in the city. She had ruled out the well-known districts of Los Angeles and Ela Nguema so as not to have to depend on buses. The historic four-star Hotel Bahía, in the middle of the new port, was the one she liked most, but she had finally picked the Hotel Bantú, as it was near all the must-see places in the city and because the reviews were fairly positive.

She walked toward the city's old quarter, which, although not well looked after in comparison to the European places she was used to, she found in better condition than the dirty outskirts that she had seen in the taxi from the airport to the hotel. Apart from the children who flocked to her, two things caught her eye and brought a faint smile to her face. The first was the electricity cables that, tangled and loose like artificial lianas, had the run of the place, forming a complex aerial maze that connected one street to another. And the other was the strange combination of vehicles that drove on the irregularly paved streets. Her father had passed his love of cars down to her, so she was able to identify run-down Lada Samaras, Volkswagen Passats, Ford Sierras, Opel Mantas, Renault 21s, BMW C30s, and several Jeep Laredos, beside new Mercedes and Toyota pickups.

Malabo looked like an Antillean or Andalusian city. It was full of colonial buildings from the English and Spanish periods. It was evident that the successive presence of Portuguese, British, Spanish, and businesspeople who traded with the Antilles had left a very particular mark on the architecture. Among the low-rise dilapidated buildings would suddenly appear an old house with a balcony that reminded her of a Spanish hacienda with wrought-iron balconies.

And palm trees, loads of palm trees.

After some time, she stopped, worn out and thirsty. She heard music coming from a small blue building with a corrugated roof. She peeked in and saw it was a bar, a simple bar like those in the villages of her valley. There were three or four tables covered with oilcloths, Formica chairs, and a small counter behind which hung various calendars whose pages were intermittently fluttered by a small fan. The music did not succeed in drowning the noise of a generator situated beside the bar.

When she stepped inside, the four or five patrons fell silent and looked at her in surprise. Clarence blushed and hesitated before asking for a small bottle of water. She was served by a burly middle-aged woman with a high-pitched voice who immediately tried to wheedle information from the foreigner. Clarence preferred not to go into too many details about the reasons for her trip. Beside the door, two young men with sweaty shirts did not take their eyes off her. She decided to drink the water slowly and steadily and leave the bar casually, acting as if she knew exactly where she was.

She looked outside, and her heart missed a beat. But how . . .

She gave a friendly if quick good-bye and went out onto the street where, to her surprise, night had fallen.

She shook her head, sure she had been in the bar for only a few minutes!

She began to walk the lonely street, trying to make out the route home. Where had everyone disappeared to? Why did only some of the streetlights work?

A few drops of sweat began to bead on her forehead and neck.

Was it her imagination, or did she hear steps behind her? She quickened her pace. Maybe she was being a little paranoid, but she could swear that someone was following her. The men from the bar? She quickly turned her head without reducing her pace and made out two police uniforms. She cursed out loud. She had left all her papers in the hotel!

A voice called to her, but she ignored it and continued walking quickly, trying to hold back the urge to run, until the next corner, where she bumped into a group of teenagers who surrounded her, amused.

Clarence used these few seconds of confusion to turn right, where she began to run and take different streets to lose the police. When it felt as if her heart were going to burst in her chest, she stopped, panting and completely soaked in sweat. She leaned against a wall with her eyes closed.

A babbling sound indicated that the river was nearby. She opened her eyes and realized that she had walked northeast instead of south. A huge green wall stretched out before her eyes. But what had happened? The city had looked easy to her from the plane! As if the straight and parallel streets were drawn with a steady hand from the very shore of the sea toward the interior.

She blamed the books she had read on the plane. She felt a shiver. If she was afraid at that moment, how would she have been able to withstand a five-month journey on a ship subject to storms, knowing that the destination was an island where if you did not die at the hands of the ferocious and hostile natives who poisoned the waters and slit throats and beheaded the seafarers, you would succumb to fever? To calm herself, Clarence tried to put herself in the place of the hundreds of people who, over the centuries, had made the expeditions to take possession of these lands, long before Antón, Jacobo, and Kilian enjoyed the golden colonial period, and she felt another shiver.

She had read that they used to sleep fully clothed and with guns in their hands, gripped with fear; that sometimes the crew was not told the destination to prevent mutiny; that many were political prisoners who were promised freedom if they managed to survive two years on Fernando Po . . . She imagined the pioneers who were given grants of land, the prisoners dreaming of freedom, the missionaries—first Jesuits and then Claretians—convinced of their divine mandate, the various intrepid explorers accompanied by their foolish wives . . . How many died and how many begged to return home even if it meant losing their liberty! They may have had reason to be afraid, but she did not! But had she not also read a novel about the kidnapping of a young white woman and the terrible police conduct in Guinea?

She did not know whether to laugh or cry.

Clarence reviewed her surroundings and felt a prick of uneasiness when moving away from the river. She tried to picture the map of the city that she had studied umpteen times on the plane as she set off to go west, to the busy Avenida de la Independencia . . .

She had barely gone a couple of meters when a car's horn made her jump.

"Would you like me to take you somewhere?"

She located a young man with glasses in a blue 1980s Volga.

Just what she needed!

Without answering, she quickened her step.

The man sped up and added, "Miss, I'm a taxi driver." Clarence, wary, gave him a sideways look. "In Malabo, the taxis don't have a specific color or special plate."

Clarence gave him a weak smile. This was something that she had learned in the airport that same day. The singing and slightly melodious tone inspired confidence in her. She stopped, guessing him to be about thirty. His hair was very short, and he had a big forehead and a large nose and jaw. He seemed to have an honest smile.

She felt so tired and disoriented that she finally nodded.

A few minutes after getting into the taxi, Clarence was relaxed and feeling very lucky. The driver, whose name was Tomás, turned out to be a schoolteacher who drove the taxi in his free time. The fact that she herself was in education led to an interesting conversation.

Automatically, she began to mentally list the characteristics, hardly noticeable because he spoke Spanish very well, of the stuttering way Tomás spoke. Not an article was left out, nor did he confuse his tenses, pronouns, or prepositions, as she had read in some articles. At most, he pronounced *rr* the same as *r*, the *d* like a weak *r*, softened the *ll* a little, mixed the *s* and the *z*, and showed a tendency to put the emphasis on the final syllable.

Her nerves had certainly let her down, but the linguistic analysis soothed her.

She took another deep breath.

"And what do you think of Malabo?" Tomás asked.

"I haven't been able to see much, as I only arrived today," she admitted as she thought, *Dirty, full of cables, and I got lost.*

Tomás looked at her through the mirror.

"I'm sure you find it very different from your home. Visitors are surprised that a country as rich in oil as Guinea can look so poor. The new upper-class district of Pequeña España is near the shanty district of Yaundé." He shrugged. "We are used to these contrasts. If you like, I could give you a quick tour."

As if reading her mind, Tomás showed her some of the beautiful sites that she had seen in photos: the Town Hall Plaza, with its pretty gardens; the horseshoe-shaped bay; the Plaza de la Independencia, with its red-colored Palacio del Pueblo with its numerous arch windows; the Palacio de la Presidencia high above the old port . . . Neither the few black-and-white images from the colonial period that Clarence had seen nor the current color photos on her computer did justice to what she was seeing by night.

With her mouth open and her heart beating rapidly, Clarence transported herself to another time and imagined her father and her uncle, in white suits, walking along these same places, decades ago, waving to the people they knew, blacks and whites. She remembered she had read somewhere that life expectancy in Guinea was around fifty, and the image blurred. The people who could have lived with Kilian and Jacobo had to be all dead. The historic buildings now belonged to other eyes.

Her taxi driver finally got to the Avenida de la Independencia, full of civic buildings and restaurants, turned down Avenida de la Libertad, and then stopped the car; he got out and quickly opened the door for her. She paid him and added a generous tip in dollars.

"This is a good place," said Tomás. "On the same street there are three restaurants and a small shopping center." He hesitated. "Will you allow me to give you some advice? It's better not to go out at night. A white woman, alone? It's unusual."

Clarence shivered, remembering her disastrous walk.

"Don't worry, Tomás." She found it strange that they were being formal with each other, but he had started it, and she did not want to appear bad mannered. "And thank you. Tomorrow I have to go to the Sampaka plantation. Could you take me?"

"Tomorrow . . ." Tomás thought for a few seconds. "Yes. Tomorrow is Saturday, and I don't have school. I would be delighted to take you."

He paused, then let his curiosity get the better of him. "Do you know anyone in Sampaka?"

"The manager. My father knows him. I've a meeting with him," she answered with a half-truth.

In fact, Clarence had sent an e-mail to a certain F. Garuz, asking if he could show her round the plantation for her studies, to which he had readily agreed. The surname coincided with the manager of the plantation in her father's time and, as regards the "F.," she had concluded that it would be too much coincidence that it could correspond to a . . .

"With Mr. Garuz?" asked Tomás.

"Don't tell me you know him . . ."

"This is a small island, miss. Here we all know one another!"

She looked at him in amazement. "Ah, of course. Then would ten o'clock be all right?"

"I'll be here. Oh . . . who should I ask for?"

Clarence realized that she had not told him her name. "My name is Clarence."

"Clarence! Like the city!"

"Like the city."

After what she had read about Guinea, she supposed that in the following days, she would hear that comment more than once. She stretched out her hand.

"Thanks again and until tomorrow, Tomás."

Back in her room, Clarence collapsed onto the bed, completely exhausted. She could never have imagined such an intense first day. Luckily, she had plenty of time to rest before her trip to Sampaka, she thought with relief.

At ten on the dot, Tomás stopped the car at the door of the hotel. As on the previous day, he was wearing khaki shorts, a white shirt, and sandals. Clarence, who at the last minute had decided to change from a long summer skirt into trousers and a jacket, waited for him with a frustrated look.

It was pouring rain.

"It looks like you won't be able to tour the plantation today," said Tomás. "We're in wet season. Water and more water. Luckily, today, I don't think there'll be any tornadoes."

Clarence could not see anything, as the windows were spattered with heavy raindrops. She let herself be driven blind down the paved road. After about ten minutes, the car stopped at a tollbooth, where two bored guards, armed to the teeth, asked for the woman's papers. Fortunately, the check went smoothly, as the guards knew Tomás.

Immediately after the young man announced that he had just taken the turnoff that led to what had been the iconic plantation, Clarence's heart jumped, and she pressed her nose against the window.

"If it continues to rain like this," Tomás predicted, "we won't escape the *poto-poto*."

"And what's that?" she asked, without taking her eyes off the blurred landscape.

"The mud. I hope you don't have to stay in Sampaka for too long, or we won't be able to get back."

Just then, Clarence made out the white paint on the trunks of some enormous royal palm trees rising up into the sky like sacred guardians, immutable against the heavenly shower.

"Stop the car, Tomás, please," she asked in a shaky voice. "It will only be for a second."

She opened the window and let the same rain wet her face. Being in the place where Antón, Jacobo, and Kilian had been for years brought on a tormenting mix of joy and sadness. Clarence thought of the men in her family. To see with her own eyes what they had built decades ago filled her with a curious sense of nostalgia.

How could she feel this way for a place she had never been? How was it possible that she could be filled with such a deep yearning for the memory of a loss she had yet to suffer?

This is what Kilian and Jacobo must have felt when their eyes filled with tears on remembering their young years in Guinea. A slight tightness of the chest and throat. A dull pain in the pit of her stomach.

"Are you feeling all right, Clarence?" Tomás asked. "Do you want me to continue?"

"Yes, Tomás." She already knew that she would come back here. She had to see it in the light of a resplendent day. "Let's go into Sampaka."

From then on, the rain did not worry her. Even blindfolded, Clarence would have been able to draw out the car's journey to the yard of red earth where the main house was built, big and square, partially supported by white columns, with a sloped roof and whitewashed walls highlighted by the green-painted wooden shutters, the same as the outside balcony that circled the upper part of the building, and a thick white-columned railing on both sides of the spectacular big steps.

Tomás parked the car in the porch under the balcony and beeped the horn, which could hardly be heard in the storm. However, when they got out of the car, it did not take long for a man around fifty, serious looking, with strong features and bronzed skin, to appear and greet Clarence pleasantly. He was wearing shorts and a blue shirt and had close-cropped gray hair—with a rebellious fringe—a wide face, and slightly sunken eyes.

"Welcome to Sampaka . . . Clarence, is that right? My name is Fernando Garuz."

Clarence froze when she heard his name. Well, yes. *F* for Fernando! Was Julia referring to this Fernando? Was it that simple? Impossible!

"You're younger than I'd thought you'd be." She smiled without stopping to look around at everything she could in amazement.

"So, did you imagine it like this?"

"More or less. What surprises me most is the color. The four photos I saw were in black-and-white. And it's very empty . . ."

"In this weather, nothing can be done. I'm afraid I won't be able to show you around the plantation or the new nurseries. The most I can do is show you the buildings around the yard. You are going to be here for a few days, aren't you? We can choose a more suitable time to tour the outside areas. Today, if you'd like, we can have coffee and chat."

"I'll wait for you here," said Tomás.

"That won't be necessary." Fernando gave him some money. "I have to go to the city at midday. I'll bring her." He turned to the woman. "If that's all right?"

"If you wouldn't mind . . ." She took out a notepad and pen from her bag and asked Tomás to write his telephone number. "I'll call you from the hotel if I need you again."

The young man left, and Clarence followed Fernando to a small room with colonial furniture, where he made her the best coffee she had tasted in her whole life. They sat down in some rattan armchairs near a window, and he asked her more about her relationship to Sampaka. She answered quickly while analyzing his features and gestures, trying to find some trace that could link him to the men in her family. But nothing. They were not alike at all. Unless . . . maybe Julia had meant to say that this Fernando could help her in her search.

Clarence decided to start at the beginning.

"Are you possibly a relation of Lorenzo Garuz? At home, his name was sometimes mentioned."

"Actually, I am." Fernando smiled. She noticed that the gap in his upper incisors gave him a youthful air. "He was my father. He died last year."

"Oh, I am sorry."

"Thank you. He was very old . . ."

"And how is it you're still here? Have you always lived in Guinea?"

"No, no. I was born in Santa Isabel." Clarence pursed her lips. Julia had said to look for a Fernando born in Sampaka. "I spent my childhood between Guinea and Spain. Later, I was away for many years, until I finally settled here at the end of the '80s."

"In Sampaka?"

"At first, in another company in the city."

"And how did you end up on the plantation? Was it not bought by the government after independence?"

"The plantation was left in the hands of someone who could be trusted. He did his best for the few years that the plantations continued, even if it was nothing like your father's time. But they did something. You have to take into account it was the only means of getting foreign exchange for the country's survival. After the liberty coup of '79 did away with Macías Nguema, the old owners, among them my father, who had the majority of the shares, lost the property, and the government granted it to a high-ranking military officer."

"And then, how did you manage to get it back?"

"When the officer died, at the beginning of the '90s, I was already working on an agricultural development project, financed by the European Union and Spanish cooperation programs, to rejuvenate the cocoa plantations and to try and bring in new crops like pepper and nutmeg. The heirs of the officer agreed to sell the plantation." He proudly added, "I managed to get back what belonged to my family from the beginning of the last century and return to the place of my childhood."

Fernando offered Clarence another coffee, and she accepted.

"I suppose they named you Fernando after the island."

"I think that in all Spanish families who had some connection to Guinea, there is a Fernando."

Clarence cringed. That made things even more complicated.

"In yours too?" he asked, misinterpreting her expression.

"Eh? Ah, no, no. Only women at home," she said, smiling. "And no Fernanda . . ." She stopped and decided to be careful. "Out of curiosity, did any of the archives from the 1950s survive?"

"There are some things. Before leaving, my father stored the workers' files in a bookcase. When I came back, the office was a mess, but they had not burned anything, which was unusual. They must have realized that there was nothing dangerous."

"And your father, did he ever come back?"

Fernando shrugged. "Yes, of course. He couldn't go for very long without stepping foot on his island. He missed it constantly. I kept my promise of burying his remains under a ceiba. Do you know, until he died, my father dreamed of returning the plantation to its old glory?" He looked out the window, with a nostalgic gaze. "In this land, there is something infectious. I still believe the cocoa from Sampaka could return to mass production."

Clarence sighed. "Fernando, now that I'm here . . . would it be too much to ask if I could have a look at the archives? It's something stupid, but I'd like to see if there is anything on my grandfather or my father."

"It's no trouble at all." He stood up. "But know that the papers were returned to the cabinet in no particular order." He picked up an umbrella from the corner and walked toward the door. "Come on, the old office is just across the way."

He opened the umbrella and, like a gentleman, held it over Clarence as they crossed the yard to the one-story white building with the single sloped roof and a small porch.

They entered a large room with a big table in front of a window that looked like a picture of a lush, wet landscape. On her right, a cabinet with lattice doors filled half the wall. Fernando began opening the doors, and Clarence sighed. The shelves were overflowing with bundles of papers dumped everywhere. It might take hours to sift through.

"See? Here is the chaotic history of Sampaka. What years did you say your father was here?"

"My grandfather came in the 1920s. My father, at the end of the '40s. And my uncle, in the early '50s."

Clarence picked a random sheet. It was a handwritten chart with a list of names on the left and fingerprints on the right, dated 1946. She put it back in its place and picked up another one that was the same, but from three years later.

"Let me see." Fernando came over. "Yes, these are the weekly food-ration lists. Well, just with a simple glance, a lot of the papers can be disregarded." He looked at his watch. "I don't have to go back to Malabo until three. If you want, you can stay here till then. I hope you don't mind if I leave you to it."

"Of course." Clarence was delighted to be left alone, so she could calmly look for something about the children born a few years before herself, just as Julia had told her. "And in exchange I'll leave it a little tidier. I'm good at paperwork."

"Very good then. If you need anything, look for me in this yard or"—he went to the doorstep and pointed to the wall outside—"ring this bell, okay?"

Clarence nodded. At last she was alone and prepared to make good use of her time. She began by taking out armfuls of papers from the bookcase and putting them on the table. She took her notebook from her bag and wrote on several sheets the titles of her listing criteria:

workers' lists and contracts, allocation of houses to families, food-ration lists, accounts, bills, material orders, employee files, medical certificates, and unimportant items. Next, she started to divide the papers into different piles.

An hour later, she opened a folder full of files, with faded and unclear photos of young men stapled to work contracts, wage dockets, and medical certificates. She went through them one by one until she identified first her grandfather and, just after that, her father and her uncle. She gasped in excitement. The mere fact of imagining any one of the three signing their name on the dates stated brought out that same strange nostalgia, but topped with a touch of pride. She spent a few minutes running her fingers over the photos. Had they been that young and handsome? And that brave! How, if not, would they have dared go off to Africa from the mountains of the Pyrenees?

The folder held almost fifty files of other men like them. In her notebook, she wrote down the names of those who worked on the plantation in the 1950s and 1960s. She would ask Kilian and Jacobo if they remembered Gregorio, Marcial, Mateo, Santiago . . .

Before continuing, Clarence spent a good while carefully reading the information about the men in her family. What surprised her most was part of her father's medical file. She learned that he had been very sick with malaria.

She frowned.

Jacobo and Kilian told them how careful they always were to regularly take their quinine tablets and Resochín to avoid coming down with malaria. If you ever forgot to take them, it was easy to get a high temperature and the shivers, but from what they said, it felt like a bad dose of the flu. From that to being hospitalized various weeks. She decided to ask her father about it when she returned to Pasolobino.

She looked at her watch. One o'clock! At this rate, she would never finish. She reckoned she had sorted about sixty percent of the material. She stretched her limbs, rubbed her eyes, and yawned. She suspected that she would not find anything about the other matter, the birth of Fernando. In the laborers' contracts, the head of the family and his family were put down, without specifying anything else, neither names nor number of children. On some of the medical files, the birth of a child was listed and whether it had been a male or a female child, but the name of the newborn did not appear. She assumed they were native births. As far as she knew, at that time the only white couple on Sampaka was Julia and Manuel. She was beginning to get discouraged. Nevertheless, she decided to continue with the task a while longer. If someone like her, some descendant of her father's companions, decided to visit the plantation, at least the papers would be tidy.

Engrossed as she was, murmuring the headings beside which she was placing the corresponding documents, Clarence did not realize that someone had entered until she heard a few steps just behind her. She jumped and turned around with her heart racing.

She stayed fixed to the spot, her mouth open.

Before her was a giant with skin as black as night, observing her with a mixture of curiosity, surprise, and disdain. She was tall, but she had to look up to see that the well-muscled body ended in a completely shaved head with drops of water trickling down it.

"You frightened me," she said, diverting her gaze to the door. She bit her lip, a little nervous.

"I'm looking for Fernando," he said in a deep voice.

Oh. So am I, she thought. She let out a little laugh.

"As you can see, he's not here. Maybe in the building opposite."

The man nodded and looked thoughtful. "Have you been hired as a secretary?" He nodded toward the table.

"No, no. I came to visit and . . . well . . ." She looked at her watch again. Fernando would not be long in coming. "I was looking for documents from when my father worked here."

The man raised an eyebrow. "You are the daughter of a colonist."

His tone was neutral, but she took the sentence as an insult.

"Plantation employee," she corrected. "It's not the same."

"Yeah."

An awkward silence followed. The man would not stop looking at her, and she did not know whether to continue her work or go look for Fernando. She chose the latter option.

"If you would excuse me, I have to go to the other building."

She passed beside the man and crossed the yard very quickly. The torrential rain had eased, but it was still coming down. There was nobody on the ground floor of the house. She went toward the porch where Tomás had parked. Apart from a 4x4 that she had not seen before, it was empty. Where were the hundreds of workers? This was a ghost plantation. The best thing to do was go back to the office. But . . . if the big man was still there? She let out a snort. She was acting ridiculous. Was she really so skittish?

She turned with the intention of going back to her papers and saw that a not-very-tall man with completely white hair was coming toward her, waving his hands and speaking in a language she did not understand. The man scrutinized her, went back a few centimeters, and came closer again, murmuring strange words and shaking his head.

"I'm sorry, but I don't understand what you are saying," said Clarence nervously, her heart beating rapidly.

She began to walk toward the red earth of the yard. The man followed, lifting his arthritis-deformed hands to the heavens and then directing them toward her as if he wanted to grab her. She got the feeling that he was scolding her.

"Leave me alone, please, I'm going now. Fernando Garuz is waiting for me in the office, do you see?" She pointed to the small building. "Yes, over there."

She quickened her step and entered the room, looking behind to make sure that the strange man was not following her.

Then she ran into a granite wall wearing jeans and a white shirt.

"Are you blind?" A strong pair of hands gripped her arms and moved her away. She felt something damp dripping on her face. "Your nose is bleeding."

Clarence brought her hand to her face and realized it was true. She went over to her bag to look for some tissues. So the giant was still there.

"I thought you would have gone by now," she said as she tore off a piece of the tissue to plug her nose and stop the trickle of blood.

"I'm not in a hurry."

"Well, I am. I have to gather all this up before Fernando gets here."

The man sat down quietly in front of the desk. The chair creaked under his weight. Clarence began to move the mountains of ordered papers to the bookcase under his attentive supervision. His intense gaze made her nervous. And to top it all, he had not even offered to help her.

"Sorry for the delay, Clarence." She gave a start. Fernando strode through the door and then greeted the other man. "I thought with this weather, you'd come another day. Have you been here long?"

Clarence came over to pick up the last pile of papers.

"Gosh, what happened to you?" Fernando asked.

"Nothing, I ran into a door."

Fernando went with her over to the cabinet and had a look inside.

"What a difference! I see you have used the time well . . . Did you find anything interesting?"

"Very little I did not know already. I'm surprised there's nothing about the children born on the plantation. Only the names of the mothers who gave birth in the hospital are listed. I had an idea that there were a lot of children in Sampaka, weren't there?"

"Yes, there were." Fernando pointed to the man in the corner. "You were one of them, no?"

Clarence's interest piqued. She reckoned he was about forty, which would put him in the period she was interested in . . .

Fernando went on, "But I couldn't tell you if there were records or not. Maybe in the school, though there is nothing left of it. What do you think, Iniko?"

Iniko, she repeated to herself. *What a strange name.*

"There were a lot of us," he answered, without much enthusiasm. "Though I spent more time in the village with my mother's family than on the plantation. As regards records, the Bubis were normally born in their villages and the Nigerians in the family barracks. Only when there were problems were the mothers brought to the plantation hospital. The whites went to the hospital in the city."

"Why are you interested, Clarence?" Fernando asked.

"Well . . ." She looked for a plausible lie. "In my research, there is a section on the names of the children born in the colonial period . . ."

"What children?" Iniko interrupted her scathingly. "Our parents gave us a name, and in school they made us change it for another."

Which complicates things further, thought Clarence.

"Ah." Fernando clicked his tongue. "This one is a . . . thorny subject."

"Yes." Clarence nodded so as not to raise suspicions. "Well, as I said, I haven't seen anything here that I didn't know already." *Well, only that my father was very sick.*

"I wasn't able to finish tidying everything. If you'd allow me to come back another day, I promise to do it."

"You have to come back. You haven't seen anything!" Fernando turned to the other man. "Are you going to Malabo now?"

The man nodded.

"You could take Clarence back to the city." He said it as a statement rather than a question. "This . . . I'm sorry, Clarence, but a small problem has come up. The generator room has flooded, and I can't leave for the moment." He took a key out of his pocket. "If you would excuse us, I'll only keep Iniko for a minute."

Clarence got her bag while Fernando opened a cabinet. She noticed that Iniko had his eyes, cold as icebergs, still fixed on her. He was probably as pleased as she was at having to spend time alone together. She pursed her lips and left, not looking forward to the ride all the way back to Malabo with him. She assumed that the 4x4 she had seen was Iniko's, but she did not even think of crossing the yard to it for fear of meeting up with the other crazed man. Instead, she waited close to the door.

She heard them talking about accounts. There was a moment when they seemed to be arguing, because Iniko's voice rose, but Fernando quieted him. Soon, they both came out. Fernando insisted that Clarence return to Sampaka as many times as she wished during her stay on the island, handed her a piece of paper with his telephone number, and made her promise to call him for anything she might need.

Before she knew it, Iniko had already crossed the yard. Clarence had to run to catch up with him at the white Land Rover. He got in, started it, and turned around. *Is he not going to give me a lift?* She saw that Iniko stretched to open the window on the passenger's side.

"What are you waiting for?" he asked.

When she got into the car, she saw that her trousers were completely spattered with red drops. She tried to shake them off with her hand, but only succeeded in creating a fine film of dust.

The uncomfortable silence lasted several kilometers. Clarence looked out the window. It had stopped raining, but some low mists covered the brush and thickets along the road. The vehicle motored on at a fair speed to the main road. In a short while, she was able to make out the first buildings of the city in front of her. Beside her, Iniko looked at his watch.

"Where are you staying?"

She told him the name of the hotel, and he nodded.

"I have to go to the airport. If you would like me to take you to your hotel, you'll have to wait. If not, I can leave you around here."

Clarence frowned. She had no intention of walking the streets alone again. "Fine."

"And what does that mean?"

"I'd prefer to go with you to the airport," she responded, irritated. "I only hope that you don't tell me later that you are going to catch a flight."

Iniko almost smiled at her. "Relax. I'm going to collect someone. I'm late."

He turned left to take the ring road that led to the airport, and in a few minutes, Clarence began to recognize the route. When they got to the small parking lot dotted with enormous trees with large white-collared crows resting on them, she made out a young man waving in the crowd. She noticed he was very well dressed, in a pair of light-colored branded jeans and a white shirt. He picked up his bag and walked toward them. Iniko got out of the car, and both men greeted each other affectionately with hugs and slaps on the back. They looked to the car. Clarence assumed they were talking about her. She wondered whether to get out, but decided to wait.

The two of them soon got into the Land Rover.

"Shall I sit in the back?" Clarence asked Iniko in a low voice.

"No, please," said the other man from behind her. "Iniko has told me you are Spanish and that you met each other in Sampaka."

His immediate familiarity put her at ease.

". . . And that your name is Clarence, like the city."

She nodded. She would never be just Clarence again. Here she was *Clarence like the city.*

He held out his hand. "My name is Laha."

"Pleased to meet you, Laha."

"And what are you doing in Malabo? Let me guess! You are an NGO aid worker."

"No."

"No?" He was surprised. He rested his elbows on the back of the front seats, between Clarence and Iniko, and closed his eyes. "Let me see . . . Sent by the United Nations?"

"No." Clarence liked Laha more and more. He was nice, on top of being hugely attractive, and his Spanish was perfect, although he had a slight North American accent.

"Businesswoman? Engineer? Iniko! Help me!"

"Researcher," said Iniko in a neutral voice. "I assume from the university."

Well, he has a good memory anyway, thought Clarence.

"And what do you research?" Laha asked.

"I'm a linguistics lecturer. I came here to gather information for a project on the Spanish spoken in Guinea."

"How interesting! And? How do we speak?"

Clarence laughed. "I arrived yesterday! I haven't had time for anything yet . . . And you, what do you do? Have you come for vacation?"

"Yes and no. I'm an engineer, and the company has sent me to review the assembly of a liquefaction train that is going to be built in the plant." He saw Clarence widen her eyes. "Do you know what I'm talking about?"

She shook her head.

"Look"—he pointed out the window to his left—"somewhere over there is a labyrinth of pipes that make up the petrochemical complex Punta Europa. Here we have a lot of oil and gas, but it is managed by foreign companies like mine, and it's all exported. With the new facilities, we can liquefy the gas here. The next thing will be to build a refinery . . ."

Iniko gave a snort, followed by some African words, and Laha frowned.

"Ah well, there are a lot of projects up and running."

"And of course, you have to come regularly," Clarence intervened. "Where do you live normally?"

"In California. But I was born here."

"Wow!" Laha kept surprising her.

"I studied at Berkeley, and I was hired by a multinational. In one of life's coincidences, my company bought the rights of an oil company in Guinea and offered me the chance to get involved in the expansion of the facilities, precisely because I know this island. That way I get to see my family, don't I, Iniko?" He gave him a slap on the back.

"You're family?" Clarence asked. These two men looked nothing alike.

"Didn't Iniko tell you that he was going to collect his brother from the airport?"

"No, he didn't. In fact, he told me absolutely nothing."

Laha yawned. "And what are your plans? Have you been given a tour of the city?"

"Not yet. On Monday, I'll go to the university." She wanted Laha to propose some plan, but she did not want to sound either desperate or bored. On top of that, he had just arrived after a long trip. "Today, I'll use my time to do some touring of my own."

"We have a family meeting," Iniko said, making clear that she was not included.

"I don't think I'll last long," said Laha, stifling another yawn.

What a pity, thought Clarence, a little frustrated. She looked out the window and recognized the street her hotel was on.

Iniko stopped the car at the door but made no movement to get out. Laha did, however.

"Clarence . . . would you like me to go with you to the university on Monday?" he offered. "I have friends in the mechanical engineering department. I normally go and see them."

She thought for a few seconds. "How about ten o'clock at the door of the cathedral? Or would you prefer if I met you here?"

"At the cathedral would be fine. Thanks a lot."

"Until Monday then."

Laha put out his hand to say good-bye, and Clarence held out hers, grateful and happy to have met him. Then she realized she had not said good-bye to Iniko. At the end of the day, he had done her the favor of giving her a lift. She bent down to see inside the Land Rover, where he sat looking straight ahead. Clarence held back a courteous smile.

She had never met anyone so unfriendly in her whole life.

After eating and taking a siesta, Clarence felt brave enough to go to the cathedral, an impressive building in a neo-Gothic style whose facade was flanked by two forty-meter towers. She noticed that everyone was looking at her again. She felt uncomfortable, and for the first time, she was sorry for not having convinced Daniela or one of her friends to come with her.

She found refuge for a good while inside the cathedral—the only place where she felt relaxed and safe—captivated by the pale-yellow columns, high and thin, perched on black marble bases that held up the main nave's vaulted ceiling. She approached the altar and spent some time contemplating the sculpture of a black Virgin with her right hand resting on her left shoulder. Behind her she could make out the carved head of a small child. The evening light, seeping through the stained-glass windows, lit up the face, slightly inclined toward the floor. She felt that the black Virgin had a very sad expression. Why had she been carved like that, so mournful? Clarence wondered. She shook her head. Maybe it was just her imagination.

She decided to return to the hotel, where she lay on her bed, her eyes fixed on the ceiling. What would she do until Monday?

She turned on the television but did not get any signal. She called reception, but the girl told her, with broken pronunciation full of *s*'s, that the channel was off the air. According to her, they sometimes forgot to refill the fuel tank of the electricity generator that fed the radio and television transmitters located on top of Basilé Mountain.

A whole new country, and Clarence had nothing to do?

Truthfully, she was irritated. Not only was she afraid to go out on her own, but her visit to Sampaka had not been as fruitful as she would have liked. On the one hand, she had not been able to see anything due to the rain, and on the other, Julia's clues now seemed more impossible than ever.

She would have to wait until she met Laha to wheedle information out of him about his childhood. Thankfully, he was not like Iniko, who was about as easy to talk to as finding snow in Bioko. If Iniko had been born or lived on Sampaka, it was logical to think that Laha had as well. *At least that's something,* she thought.

She reflected a few more minutes about what to do and finally picked up the phone to call Tomás.

She had noted down three places to visit on Bioko. She was already familiar with Sampaka. Why not use the following day to see the second?

"I don't like this place at all, miss," said Tomás, creasing his brow while casting nervous looks at Malabo's old cemetery, located in the Ela Nguema district. "I'll wait for you outside."

"Tomás, don't be so formal with me. Okay? We're the same age."

"As you wish, but I have no intention of going in."

"Fine, but don't even think about leaving."

As soon as she got to the gate, Clarence was sorry she had decided to visit the cemetery. She did not like the idea of wandering alone through a place that felt so sinister. She asked Tomás with a look, her last attempt to get him to go with her, but he shook his head. She placed her hand on the rusty railings and stopped.

"Can I help you with something?" asked a deep masculine voice.

She got such a fright that she turned to leave, but then the voice continued, "You can come in. The gate is open."

Clarence stopped and saw a small, friendly old man with hair completely white and almost no teeth.

"I am the caretaker of the cemetery," he said. "Can I help you with anything?"

She walked toward him with the small bunch of orchids that she had bought at a street stall and explained that her grandfather had been buried there in the 1950s. She wanted to visit the grave if it still existed.

"From the date," the man said, "it would have to be in the old section. If you like, I can take you there. Not a lot of people visit."

Not even in the abandoned villages of her home had Clarence seen a cemetery so badly kept. Some of the graves were hidden in the weeds, and others had sunk. It seemed it was true that the natives did not like to visit the graves of their dead. Her guide explained, with the ease of delivery that comes with age, that due to the country's high mortality rate, it was common to dig one grave on top of another, which led to some very disagreeable situations. Neither the perfectly ordered gravestones nor the inscriptions that Clarence was used to could be seen anywhere. It looked like a jungle, even though, according to the man, it was now much better looked after than before. A couple of years ago, he said, you could not even come in without running the risk of being eaten by a boa.

The old part of the cemetery, however, turned out to be more reassuring. Perhaps because the graves were easier to make out, surrounded by railings rusted by age. Or maybe because the graves were at the feet of some enormous and beautiful trees whose bark reminded her of elephant skin. From their size, they looked to be over a hundred years old, and although some seemed dried out, none had lost their majesty.

"What beautiful ceibas!" exclaimed Clarence.

"It's a sacred tree," the old man began to explain. "Neither hurricanes nor lightning can conquer them. Nobody touches the ceibas. To cut them down is a sin. And ceibas do not forgive. If your grandfather is buried here, his grave will be as intact as they are."

A shiver went down Clarence's spine. One part of her still wanted to run, but something held her back. There was a special peacefulness calming her fears.

She began reading the names on the crosses and gravestones. She went over to one in particular that seemed hidden between the folds of two intertwined ceibas. It was also guarded by a smaller tree that she could not identify.

She looked up and read out loud, "Antón of Rabaltué. Pasolobino 1898 to Sampaka 1955."

Clarence's heart skipped a beat, and tears fell.

How strange to see the name of her village in a place like this! As if there were not thousands of kilometers separating the beginning and the end of her grandfather's life!

She wiped away the tears and bent down to remove an almost completely withered bunch of flowers that someone had placed against the stone cross, and added her own.

But how . . .

Someone continued to bring flowers for Antón!

She frowned.

"Do you know who visited this grave?" The cemetery caretaker shook his head.

"No, miss. The few who come don't need me. Only the foreigners like you ask for my help . . . And none have visited this grave. I would remember that, yes, that I would remember."

"And those few who do come, natives from what you're saying, are they men or women?"

"I wouldn't be able to say. I'm sorry I can't help you."

"Thank you anyway."

He guided her back again to the entrance, where she gave him a small tip and he shook her hand repeatedly in thanks.

Tomás noticed her reddened eyes and said, "This island doesn't suit you, Clarence. Wherever you go, you cry."

"I'm overly sentimental, Tomás. I can't help it."

"Do you want to go and have a beer on a terrace overlooking the sea? It works for me when I'm sad."

"Good idea, Tomás. I'm very lucky to have met you. You're very kind."

"It's because I'm Bubi," he said with pure conviction.

On Monday morning, Clarence went to her appointment with Laha a little early. As on the previous day, the weather was still fresh and sunny. As the hours went by, the unbearable heat would probably prevent her from doing anything except sleeping or drinking on a terrace.

She had already been warned that she could not take photos or film in the country—and that it was advisable to be discreet in her comments and her attitude in public—but at this time of day, everything was very quiet, so she took out a small digital camera and began taking shots of the cathedral. She started with the main facade in front of a round white marble fountain, with a number of figures that held a small ceiba on their shoulders. Then, she walked down a side alleyway. At that moment, her enthusiasm made her careless, and suddenly, she found herself being approached by two police officers who gruffly asked for her papers.

She grew nervous when she saw that neither her passport nor all the other papers she showed them seemed to satisfy them. The pitch of her voice rose. Did she look like a spy? They took her fear for arrogance. When one grabbed hold of her arm, Laha came out of nowhere, intervened, and very politely offered to clear up the situation.

Laha spoke quickly, but firmly. He explained who she was and what she was doing there. He reached in his pocket and, as subtly as possible, took out some money, slipping it into a handshake with one officer. "You don't want the rector of the university to find out how we treat his guests, do you?"

Before Clarence could open her mouth to express her shock and thanks, Laha gently but firmly pushed her in the direction of a car.

The police looked to be satisfied, even giving a friendly wave to her savior, who at that moment seemed to the most attractive and marvelous man in the world. That morning he had put on a light-colored suit. He probably dressed like that to go to work.

"Thank you very much, Laha," she said. "I was under a little stress."

"I'm sorry, Clarence. It's what I detest about my country. Well, that and more, but anyway, you'll have time to find out yourself . . ."

"Don't you have to be at work?" she asked.

"That's where I'm coming from. The good thing about American engineers is that nobody tells us what to do." He laughed. "At least not me. The majority prefer to stay in their bungalows in *Pleasantville*. That's what we call the fairy-tale district with its air-conditioning, supermarkets, and creature comforts. They live away from everything. Although I know more than one who has been deported from here for criticizing the regime. So it's better not to take risks. You know what they say, what the eye doesn't see . . ."

Laha accompanied his words with infectious laughter. She studied his profile. There was something in his proportioned features that seemed familiar. She had the vague sensation of having seen it before. Probably his natural friendliness made her feel as if she had known him all her life.

"By the way," he continued, "the day before yesterday, I wanted to ask you something, and in the end, I didn't. Did you know that Malabo was once called Clarence? Isn't it a strange name for a Spaniard?"

"Yes, I know," she answered, shaking her head in resignation. "For years I thought it was the name of some heroine from an English novel. Later I discovered that the island had been given that name when it was declared an English colony, in honor of King George, Duke of Clarence."

She briefly explained to him that several men from her family had lived here during the colonial period. After meeting Iniko, she gathered that not everyone had fond memories of the colonization. And she was very aware that she knew only stories from the white side, which made her cautious when talking about Spain. Yet Laha did not seem to mind that a descendant of those colonists showed interest in the past.

"That's why you went to Sampaka!" he exclaimed. "Iniko told me that you were looking for old documents, from when your father worked there. A lot of water has flowed under the bridge since then! I imagine that you see things very differently from what you have been told."

"Well, yes, quite differently." She nodded. "For the moment, I haven't seen any pith helmets or machetes or sacks of cocoa."

Laha laughed and Clarence smiled.

"I don't know if you're aware," he said, "that Malabo was called *Ripotò*, or "place of foreigners," in Bubi. Just as well your father chose one and not the other! If your father gave you the name of this place, it's because he really felt something toward it."

"I'm going to tell you something, Laha. Everyone I've met who lived on this island admits to still dreaming of her." She paused before continuing. "And then their eyes fill with tears."

Laha nodded as if he understood from the bottom of his heart what she meant. "And they weren't even born here . . ." He interrupted her with a sad look.

Something that she had read about the whites came to mind, something that nobody talked about. Those who had been born on the island felt that it was a part of them, and yet they had been forced to leave what they considered the country of their childhood. But it was unlikely that Laha was referring to them.

"Imagine how those who are living in exile feel!" Laha interrupted her again after a short sigh. "Well, here we are. I hope you find what you are looking for, but don't get your hopes up. In countries with huge shortages, education is at the bottom of the list."

She nodded, pensively. They walked in silence toward the white-walled buildings with arches under red roofs finished off with narrow green eaves that made up the university area, full of bright grassed areas dotted with palm trees and bordered with red-earth paths. When they got to the door of the main building, Clarence said, "Tell me something, Laha. I can guess the answer, but to be sure. You and your brother, are you Bubi or Fang?"

"We're Bubis. Just as well you asked me and not Iniko!" Laha laughed. "He would have answered you in an offended tone, 'Isn't it obvious?'"

Over the next few days, Laha was the perfect host. In the mornings, each worked on what he or she had to do. While he reviewed the oil installations, Clarence looked for old documents on the history of Guinea—not only in the university library but also in others in the city, especially the Spanish-Guinean Cultural Center and the Spanish College in the Ela Nguema district—with the faint hope of finding something useful on the period that interested her, be it censuses, photos, or testimonies. In the afternoons, Laha took her around to see different corners of the city, and they finished up by having a relaxed chat in one or another terrace on the seafront. At night, he wanted to take her to restaurants with local food and cooking, but after two days it was clear to Laha that Clarence tended to lean more toward the fish and seafood of Club Nautico and Italian food from Pizza Place than toward the enormous snails in many establishments.

Yes, Clarence was really enjoying a true vacation, but she was also conscious that the days were quickly passing by and she had not advanced one bit in her research.

She did not know where to go looking either.

She remembered that Fernando Garuz had told her that he would soon be going on a trip and figured she had better go back to Sampaka. With a little bit of luck, she might bump into Iniko and ask him about his childhood, as he had not bothered to join any of her afternoons with Laha. She had not gotten much information out of Laha because he barely remembered the plantation. He was six years younger than his brother, and his first memories were of school in Santa Isabel and his house in the city. Clarence had come to the conclusion that the first years of life for both brothers had been very different, but she still had not dared go into it any further. Only once had she asked Laha about Iniko, casually, and he had told her that he worked as an agent for several cocoa companies, which meant he had to travel a lot around the island. That was how she happened to meet him in Sampaka: Iniko did the accounts there and was in charge of paying the Bubi farmers.

On Thursday night, Clarence decided not to postpone it any longer. However, when she called Fernando from her hotel room, he was sorry to tell her that he had had to change his plans and was leaving for Spain the following day on urgent family business. He did not know if he would be back before she left Bioko. But regardless of that, he said, she had his permission to visit the plantation as often as she wished, and he had left orders that she be shown around all the facilities. She thanked him and wished him a pleasant trip.

Clarence snapped closed the notebook where she had jotted down Fernando's number, and the piece of paper that was the reason for her visit to Bioko flew into the air. She bent down to pick it up, and her eyes fixed on a sentence:

. . . *I will resort to Ureca friends again* . . .

She sighed. She had not even dared to book a trip to Ureca.

Needless to say, she thought, she would never earn a living as a private detective.

The following day, Laha called to tell her that his mother had invited them to dinner that very night at her house. Them and Iniko.

Clarence quickly forgot her disappointments of the last few hours. She only hoped that Laha and Iniko's mother, like all older people, liked to talk about her memories, especially those about the Sampaka plantation. According to her calculations of Iniko's age, his and Laha's mother's life there would go back to the 1960s. Maybe she had even known her father. A little bug of urgent expectation went round in her stomach all day.

She had not finished deciding what to wear. She wanted to be well dressed but informal. She knew nothing about Laha's mother, and she did not want to look dressed too casually or too smartly. She opted for comfort with a pair of beige jeans and a white shirt with gemstones and a neckline she knew suited her. She hesitated on whether to leave her hair loose or gathered in a plait and chose the second option, more suitable for dinner with the mother of some friends. That is, if she could consider Iniko a friend.

The home of Laha and Iniko's mother was a modest low-rise building in a housing estate that appeared to be from the 1960s in the Los Angeles district. She noticed that it was modern, but needed updating. However, the house's interior, with colonial-style furniture, was welcoming. Everything was very clean and tidy and decorated with African objects and pictures, simply and tastefully. When Clarence met Laha's mother, she understood where that simplicity and taste came from.

They were still greeting each other when a door closed and a man entered like a hurricane into the room. Iniko kissed his mother, slapped his brother on the back, and, to the young woman's surprise, opened his mouth and said in a deep voice, "Hello, Clarence."

9

Hard Times

Clarence inspected the woman closely. She was truly beautiful and very slim, and she had the most expressive light-colored eyes. She was wearing a long tunic over a pair of trousers, both turquoise blue, with matching embroidery on the cuffs of the sleeves and the bottoms of the trousers. A silk scarf of the same color covered her hair, which Clarence guessed was slightly tinged with gray. With her hair gathered, her eyes stood out with an unsettling intensity.

Her name was Bisila, in honor of Mother Bisila, patroness of the island of Bioko, cultural and spiritual reference of the Bubi culture. Clarence realized then that the sculpture of the sad Virgin in the cathedral showed Bisila, who, for the Bubis, represented the native and creator mother of life whose honor they continued to celebrate, but now more discreetly, as—according to what she had been told—in recent years, the festival had been banned in Guinea by the ethnic majority, the Fang.

The dinner that Bisila prepared was a traditional feast, made with palm oil, yam, malanga, vegetable *bóka'ò*—a slightly spicy mix of vegetables and fish—and antelope. It was delicious. Clarence felt like a very special guest thanks to Laha and his mother.

Of course, Iniko was the only one put out by her presence.

Clarence was sitting across from the brothers. At first glance, the most notable difference was their physical statures. Iniko was older than Laha, but his body retained the muscly build of a young man. She tried to find some feature common to both but soon gave up, defeated. Iniko had his head shaved, and Laha had long, thick streaks of curly hair. Iniko's skin was much darker than his brother's, who beside him looked like a mulatto. Iniko's eyes were big like his mother's, although black and slightly almond shaped; Laha's were dark green and got hidden behind tiny wrinkles when he laughed, something that happened quite frequently.

She concluded that the only tic they had in common was rubbing an eyebrow with their index finger when mulling over something. She looked at Bisila. How could a woman have two children so unlike each other? She would not have been at all surprised if one of the two were adopted.

As far as their temperaments, Laha was elegant, friendly, and talkative. It was evident that his stay in the United States had infected him with the mannerisms typical of North Americans. Iniko, on the contrary, was abrupt and quiet, verging on sullen. He would not even bother to answer the questions she asked about the people from Bioko and their customs. Clarence tried on various occasions to get him to participate in the conversation, asking about his work and his life, but his answers were short and dry, even scornful.

Bisila noticed her frustrated attempts, and using the excuse of getting up to go to the kitchen for coffee, she said something in Bubi to her son. From that moment on, Iniko pretended to show some interest.

"Could I ask you something, Bisila?"

The woman turned her head toward Clarence and smiled.

"I understand that you and your children lived in Sampaka. Could you tell me exactly when?"

Bisila blinked, and Clarence hastened to clarify.

"I'd like to know if you coincided with my father. He worked on the plantation between the '50s and '60s, more or less."

"The truth is the blacks didn't mix much with the whites. They must have told you that there were hundreds of people on the plantation. It was like a big village."

"But there weren't that many whites." Clarence frowned. "I assumed everyone knew them, or at least knew who they were."

"Actually," said Bisila a little tensely, "I used to spend more time in my village than on the plantation."

Laha and Iniko exchanged a quick and knowing look. Both of them knew that their mother did not like to talk about her time in Sampaka. They were not surprised that she had deflected Clarence's questions politely.

"Do you know, Mom," Laha interrupted, "that Clarence lives in the North of Spain?"

"Well," the young woman qualified, "the North of Spain is very large, and my valley is as small as this island."

"It snows and it's very cold, isn't it?" Laha added.

"I couldn't live in a cold place," Iniko said, playing with a small shell hanging from a leather band knotted round his neck.

"You couldn't live anywhere else except Bioko," Laha retorted, amused.

"I understand." Clarence shrugged. "Sometimes I complain about the climate, but I couldn't stand being away from my home for too long. It's a curious love-hate relationship."

Iniko raised his huge eyes to her, and she blushed.

"And what's the name of your village?" asked Bisila, who had gotten up to serve more coffee.

"Oh, it's very small," Clarence answered, "although many people know it now because there is a ski resort there. It's called Pasolobino."

Everyone startled as the coffee cup bounced off the table and smashed onto the floor. Bisila reacted quickly, apologizing, and went to the kitchen to get something to clean up. Everyone else tried to brush off the situation.

"The truth is that the name is frightening," Laha joked.

"They say all names mean something." Iniko looked at Clarence, and his eyes at last seemed to smile. "In this case it's easy. Pasolobino, path of the wolves."

She arched her left eyebrow.

"Well, you don't look like you could frighten anyone." It was the first time he had been informal with her.

"That's because you don't know me," she answered, boldly holding his gaze.

"If there is a ski resort," Laha interjected, "it must be a rich place, correct?"

"Now it is," Clarence answered. "A few years ago, the valley was close to being completely depopulated. There was no work, only cold and cows. Now everything has changed. Many people from outside have come to live there, others have returned, and services have improved."

Laha turned to his brother.

"See, Iniko? Progress isn't so bad."

Iniko spent a few moments stirring his coffee with the spoon. "That is something you would have to ask the natives," he said.

"And who am I then?" Clarence felt offended.

"For Iniko, you are like me," said Laha sarcastically. "You belong to the enemy-of-the-land group."

"That is a ridiculous oversimplification," she protested, with flushed cheeks. "It's very easy to jump to conclusions if you don't ask. You don't know anything about me!"

"I know enough," Iniko defended himself.

"That's what you think!" she retorted. "The fact that my father was a colonist doesn't mean I have to walk around asking for forgiveness—" She stopped dead. For an instant, she wondered if one day she would have to take that back before a biological brother.

Iniko made a face, looked at Laha, and whistled.

"Well, I have to admit that she does have a strong character."

He said it in a conciliatory fashion, but it annoyed Clarence. She leaned back in the chair with no intention of continuing the discussion. Fortunately, Bisila returned from the kitchen with a brush and a dustpan. She looked very tired. Laha moved to help, but his mother would not let him. They remained silent while Bisila gathered the bits of the cup until she asked, in a trembling voice, "What was your father's name?"

Clarence sat up in the chair and rested her arms on the table. "Jacobo. His name is Jacobo. He's still alive." Bisila's renewed interest rekindled Clarence's hopes. Her father's name was not that common. Was it her imagination or was Bisila in a state of shock? She waited a few seconds before asking, "Does it sound familiar?"

Bisila shook her head and brusquely finished cleaning. "I'm sorry."

"He came here with my uncle, my uncle Kilian. It's a very unusual name. I don't think you could forget it easily." Bisila stood still. "My uncle is still alive . . ."

"I'm sorry," Bisila repeated in a subdued voice. "No, I don't remember them."

She went to the kitchen murmuring, "My memory is getting worse and worse."

Laha frowned.

A brief silence ensued, until Iniko rose to serve some glasses of sugarcane spirit.

Clarence bit her lip, deep in thought. Everything that had to do with Sampaka always finished in a dead end. If someone like Bisila said that she did not remember her father, the only thing left to do was to put an ad in the national newspaper. She remembered her visit to the cemetery and decided to use her last shot. She waited until Bisila returned to tell them about the strange sensation she had when reading the name of Pasolobino written on a gravestone in Africa.

"I'd like to know," she wondered aloud, "who takes the time to bring flowers to my grandfather . . ."

Bisila kept her head down and her hands crossed on her lap. It was evident that her mood had changed.

"Well." Clarence looked at her watch. "Thank you very much for the dinner, Bisila. And for your hospitality. I hope to see you again before going back to Spain."

Bisila made a small gesture with her head, but said nothing.

Laha understood that Clarence was saying her good-byes, but he had other ideas.

"What type of music do you like?" he asked, getting to his feet. Clarence was surprised at the unexpected question, but finally understood that he was suggesting going out. "Are you up for it, Iniko? I was thinking of taking her to our favorite hangout."

His brother clicked his tongue, possibly annoyed at Laha for inviting her.

"He'd probably get embarrassed if a foreigner gave him dance lessons," she said scathingly, looking at Laha.

Iniko pursed his lips, put his hands on the table, and slowly got up.

"We'll see who is giving the lessons," he said with a mocking glint in his eye.

After saying good-bye to Bisila, they took Iniko's Land Rover and went to a club called Bantú, like the hotel, where they could listen to soukous, *bikutsí*, and Antillean salsa, or *antillesa*, as they called it. Just after entering the club, several people waved to the brothers.

"Look who it is! Tomás!" exclaimed Clarence on recognizing her taxi driver, who got up to shake hands. "Don't tell me you know one another!"

"And who doesn't know Iniko on the island?" he joked, pushing his glasses up every other second. The place was hot, and he was sweating a lot.

They all sat down together, and after the introductions, the group of men and women, drinks in hand, shared laughs and cigarettes. Some of their names were simple, like that of a pretty girl with her hair done up in tiny braids called Melania, who insisted that Iniko sit beside her. But it was difficult to memorize the names of the other two women— Rihéka, small and round, and Börihí, tall and muscled like an athlete, with very short hair—and of the other man in the group, a young man named Köpé.

At first, Clarence felt inhibited, although the company of the brothers gave her a sense of security. Every now and then, one or the other got up to dance, but she preferred to remain sitting down close to Laha, who admitted he was not a good dancer, and close to the drinks—which did nothing to alleviate the heat—moving her feet timidly to the repetitive and lively beat of the music. She watched the other dancers on the floor and asked herself how in hell they could move as they did. It was crazy.

She gave most of her attention to Iniko, who, to her amazement, was shaking every kilo of his muscles in front of Melania with the same grace as if he were made of feathers. His shoulders, slightly hunched, and his hips swung, following the rhythm as if it flowed through the tips of his fingers and toes. Now and again, he closed his eyes and smiled. The music changed. Melania returned to the table, but he stayed out on the floor.

Clarence could not take her eyes off him as Iniko turned and hit her with a defiant stare. He raised his hand and signaled her to come up onto the dance floor. She waved at him to reject his offer. It was obvious that her comments in Bisila's house were without foundation. Iniko shrugged and continued dancing more suggestively than ever. Clarence suddenly regretted not accepting the challenge. She finished her drink in one gulp and strode over to him.

Iniko smiled and copied her rigid and brusque European moves until she turned to leave. He grabbed her by the wrist and leaned down.

"Don't you want to learn? I'm an expert."

Iniko brought Clarence close, put his arm around her, and signaled for her to let him lead, to relax and loosen up, and to let her mind go blank. Wherever she looked, the mirrors that surrounded her began to reflect the exciting image of a woman surrendering to the invisible strings of a man who radiated heat.

Clarence closed her eyes and tried to forget everything, her fears, her worries, Pasolobino and Sampaka, the reason for her trip, her past, and her future. The only thought she allowed herself was the one that repeated to her over and over again—that her body had been screaming for the closeness of a man like this for ages.

The music stopped. Clarence opened her eyes and found Iniko's face just a few centimeters from hers. For the first time since their meeting in Sampaka, he seemed to be looking at her with curiosity. Maybe, like her, he felt a little disoriented by their dance.

"Happy with your student?" she finally asked.

"Not bad," he replied. "But it's a little early to make an assessment."

I wouldn't mind repeating the exam one bit, she thought.

"It has been years since I last felt so tired!" Clarence protested, and the rest laughed.

She had just finished dinner with her new friends in a restaurant with colored oilcloths on the tables and tiled walls that offered a curious mix of Spanish, Italian, and American food. Every afternoon, one plan or another came up that went on till the early hours.

Clarence wondered how they could stand this pace and continue working. The attractive but difficult Melania worked as the concierge in the Cultural Institute of French Expression; the small Rihéka had a Bubi arts stall in the Malabo market; the friendly Köpé was in charge of maintenance at the power facilities; and the athletic Börihí, who had just left, worked in the offices of a construction company.

"The only one with a bit of common sense is Börihí," she added. "The rest of you will end up being fired. You first, Laha. Don't you work with dangerous materials?"

She thought about continuing the joke when Melania pointed to something outside. Everyone turned to look.

Several dark cars signaled the beginning of a large official cavalcade escorted by police on motorbikes. As it passed, numerous people thronged the streets to have a peek. The majority were natives, although one or two Westerners could also be spotted. On the other side of the street, a white woman began to take photos. When the cavalcade had passed, another dark car stopped in front of the woman, and two men forcibly took her camera, then pushed her against the car and searched her. From the restaurant, they saw the woman shouting and crying.

"But what are they doing?" Clarence jumped to her feet.

Iniko took her arm and made her sit down.

"Are you crazy? Please just don't say a word!" he hissed. Melania put her arm around his shoulder and stroked him.

Clarence angrily pressed her lips together and looked at Laha.

"No, Clarence," he said, shaking his head. "Today nothing can be done."

"But . . . !"

"You have heard Iniko." His tone was hard this time. "It would be best to shut up."

Clarence saw with horror how the men handcuffed the woman and put her into the car and sped away.

"And what happens to her now?" she asked in a whisper.

No one answered.

"How about leaving now?" Rihéka asked, with worry reflected on her round face.

"Better not. It would be too obvious," suggested Köpé quietly. "At the back, on the right, behind me, there are . . . spectators. Don't look. Just talk normally."

"Do they look like *antorchones?*" asked Rihéka.

"And what's that?" Clarence asked.

"Young spies controlled by the party," explained Tomás.

"I don't think so," said Köpé, "but just in case . . ."

Tomás began to tell a stupid joke, and the others let out forced laughs. Clarence took the opportunity to glance at the strange couple at the back table. The woman was a plump old woman with a big, flaccid chest and completely white hair. She had on too much makeup and was dripping in jewels. In front of her, and with his back to Clarence, sat a thin and bony mulatto much younger than she.

"The woman hasn't stopped looking at us," she said.

"I'm not surprised," said Melania, irritated. "A bit more and we would all have been arrested because of you."

"But why?" Clarence protested.

Of all the group, Melania was the one she liked the least. She never missed the chance to have a go at Clarence. Iniko had been friendly of late, but when Melania was around and pestered him with loving gestures, he became brooding again. She looked at Laha, and he gave her a slight nod.

"You have to be careful, Clarence," said Laha in a friendly voice. "Here things don't work like they do in Spain or the United States."

"Anyone can accuse you of being against the regime," Tomás agreed in a low voice. "Anyone . . ."

Clarence took a quick breath. For a minute she had forgotten what country she was in.

"I'm very sorry," she apologized.

Köpé got up to ask for another round of the popular 33 beer. When he sat down again, he commented, "I think we can relax. Don't you know who the woman is?"

Tomás and Iniko both sneaked glances and smiled. "Ah, yes, the very one."

"Do you know her?" Clarence wanted to know.

"Who doesn't know Mamá Sade?" Tomás rolled his eyes.

"No!" Laha half shut his eyes. "She's gotten much older since the last time I saw her."

"I thought she didn't leave her house anymore," commented Melania.

"And I thought she was dead!" Rihéka laughed.

Clarence was dying with curiosity.

"For us, Mamá Sade is like a ceiba," Laha began to explain. "She's always been there, at least from the colonial times of our childhood. Legend says that she began work as a . . . well, with her body. She was so beautiful that everybody fought over her. She made a lot of money and invested it in one club and then another until there was no successful nightspot in the city that was not managed by her."

He took a sip of his beer, and Tomás added, "And she continued making money under Macías. A mystery. They said only she knew how to please the tastes of the important men. And she hired the best girls . . ."

"And the man who is with her?" Clarence asked.

"Her son," Köpé answered. "He now runs the business."

"He looks mulatto." Clarence lifted the bottle of beer to her lips without taking her eyes off the couple.

"He is." Rihéka leaned forward and adopted a confidential tone. "The story goes that she fell in love with a white man who worked on the plantations. He got her pregnant and left her." Clarence went red in the face and began to cough. Rihéka gave her some pats on the back. "After that, she didn't want any more children."

"I would have had dozens," Melania commented vengefully. "That only child must have been a daily reminder of his cowardly father."

Clarence's heart began beating rapidly. She almost wanted to walk over to the table to see the face of Mamá Sade's child. Idiotic! And what would she do? Innocently ask him if his name was Fernando? Rihéka was right. Her story was probably that of many other women. Beside her, she noticed that Laha had strangled his bottle of beer with his hands. He had a frown on his face. He was the only one of the group whose skin was not completely black.

Laha got up and said he had to relieve himself. Clarence turned again to look at the table at the back.

"And if you think that she's not dangerous, why is she continuing to look at us?"

"She seems to be looking at you," said Iniko with a teasing smile. "Maybe she'll ask you to work for her. Mamá Sade has always had a good eye . . ."

Clarence blushed. "Ha!" she answered, tilting her head. "I'll take that as a compliment."

Everyone laughed except Melania, who made a face.

"And do you know the son's name, by any chance?" Clarence immediately regretted asking the question out loud.

"And what does it matter to you what his name is?" Melania wanted to know, gluing her body to that of Iniko. "Ah well! That's right! Now he's running the business!" More laughing ensued, and Melania went on. "A white woman would give him prestige, although it appears to me that the white women aren't as hot-blooded as us blacks."

Clarence struck her down with a look. Tomás, Köpé, and Iniko hid their smiles behind their bottles as Rihéka told Melania to hush.

Iniko decided to redirect the conversation. "Clarence is interested in the names of the children born in the colonial period," he said, leaning back in his chair and allowing his right arm to pass around the back of Melania's body. "It's for her studies. She publishes research papers."

Clarence looked at him in surprise. It seemed that Iniko had been paying more attention to her than she thought. Melania shrugged and moved closer to the man.

Clarence was surprised by a touch of envy. *A little more and you'll be sitting on him.*

"Well, in that we will be able to help you," said Tomás. "Now you can take out that notebook that you bring everywhere."

Tomás began to go over the names of all the people he knew, from their family members to neighbors and friends. The others copied him. Clarence used this brief respite to analyze why she was irritated. Was it possible that she felt . . . jealous? Of Melania? Over this strong man who was reserved and mistrustful? It was ridiculous. But why did she not stop giving them looks to see if Iniko responded to Melania's attentions? To her relief, he did not. Iniko did not seem to be one of those men who expressed his feelings openly, but it was clear that if he did not move away from Melania, it was because he was happy to be beside her. Melania was very pretty, had personality, was Bubi, and lived in Bioko. The perfect combination. Clarence held back a sigh.

"When you publish your research," Köpé said, handing her the notebook, "you'll have to send us a copy."

Clarence took a glance at the lists. In a couple of minutes, they had written down over a hundred names. She felt a little guilty for tricking them. She was not used to lying, and since she had arrived in Guinea she had not done anything else. She would never write that article. She was only interested in finding this Fernando.

Laha came in and stood beside the table.

"Should we go somewhere else now?" he suggested. "How about our favorite club?"

"But you said you don't like dancing." Clarence laughed as they got up.

She noticed that Mamá Sade and her son were walking toward them. She straggled behind in order to get a good look at the couple. Compared to his hefty mother, the man was thin and bony. She could finally see his face. Individually, his features were nice. He had dark almond-shaped eyes, a thin nose and lips, and a dimpled chin. But altogether, his expression was cold and slightly disagreeable. She felt a shudder.

"Is there a problem, white woman?" The man stared at her. "Don't you like what you see?"

"No, sorry, I . . ." Someone took her arm, and Iniko said, "Shall we go, Clarence?"

"You, Bubi! Tell your girlfriend to learn some manners," the thin man said with disdain. Iniko tensed. "I don't like people to look at me like that."

Beside him, Mamá Sade began to say in a bossy voice, "Don't waste your time . . ." She looked up at Clarence, frowned, and let out a harsh, throaty sound. She pushed her son to one side and moved in front of her. Despite her age, she was still a tall woman. She raised a wrinkled hand toward the young woman's face and, without touching it, went over her features, from her forehead to her chin. Clarence took a step backward, and Iniko pulled her toward the door.

"Wait!" growled Mamá Sade from a toothless mouth. "I'm not going to hurt you!"

Clarence stopped.

Mamá Sade inspected her again, muttering incomprehensible phrases. She alternated between nodding and laughing insanely. When she was satisfied, she shook her head.

"And so?" asked Clarence, irritated, but also intrigued by the situation.

"You reminded me of someone."

"Yes? Who?" Suddenly, she regretted having asked the question with such interest. Could it be possible that the only person who remembered her father was an ex-prostitute who looked like a witch?

"Of someone I knew a long time ago. Someone from your country. You're Spanish, aren't you?" Clarence nodded. "Descendant of colonists?" Clarence again nodded, but this time vaguely. "Where are you from? From the north or the south?"

"From Madrid," she lied.

She was sorry for not having left the restaurant in time. She did not want to even imagine that a connection existed between this couple and her. She began to feel very hot, suffocatingly hot. She tightly held on to Iniko's arm.

"You must have mistaken me for someone else. I'm sorry, but we're in a hurry. They are waiting for us."

Her son took her arm with a peeved look.

"One more question!" the woman almost shouted. "What's your father's name?"

"My father died many years ago."

"What was his name? Tell me!"

"Alberto," lied Clarence once again. Her sight was becoming blurred. She was on the point of having a panic attack. "His name was Alberto!"

The woman twisted her lips. She looked at her for a few seconds more and finally bowed her head, retaining her dignified and proud bearing while waving her hand in the air in search of her son's arm.

Clarence breathed a sigh of relief. She rested against the table. There was still some beer left in her bottle. She took a long swig. It was warm, but she did not care. Her mouth was so dry.

Iniko looked at her with a frown, his arms folded across his chest.

"Where have the rest gone?" she asked.

"They've gone on ahead."

"Thanks for waiting for me."

"I'm glad I did."

Neither of them moved.

"Let me see if I understand," Iniko finally said as he stroked an eyebrow. "You're not from Pasolobino. Your father's name is not Jacobo, and in addition, he's dead. Who are you? An *antorchona*?" He gave a little smile. *The bravest spy in the world. As soon as she discovers something she doesn't like, she has a panic attack.*

"You were the ones who insisted that I be careful."

They left the restaurant. The moon was shining like a lighthouse amid wisps of clouds.

"Do you know, Iniko? Here the moon is nice, but in my mountains, it's something else."

"Ah! So Pasolobino does exist. Now I feel better . . ."

Clarence slapped his arm. It seemed that Iniko did have a sense of humor. What a discovery.

"And why did you wait instead of Laha?" She would have preferred to ask, *How is it that Melania let you out of her sight?*

"I'd like to suggest something to you."

What would she say to him?

Time was running out, and Clarence was down to her last bullet: Ureca.

How could she refuse an opportunity like that?

And more so now, when she had abandoned nearly everything else. She had lied to those in the university, saying that her fieldwork recording oral interviews for their later analysis had her very busy. With regard to her progress in solving the family mystery, it had been reduced to casual and innocent conversations, using the recorder as an excuse, with mulattos slightly older than herself whom she interviewed until they revealed that their name was not Fernando or that their scant childhood memories of the colonial period did not have anything at all to do with Sampaka.

On various occasions, she had bumped into men who refused to answer any questions for a *white woman*.

Her eyes scanned the sea's tranquil water. She was sitting with Laha on the terrace of the Hotel Bahía, from whose white tables and chairs they could see a huge ship anchored not far away. Laha had collected her from her hotel a little earlier that day. It would be a while yet before Iniko arrived.

What would she say to him?

"It seems," said Laha in a casual manner as he stirred his coffee with his spoon, "that my brother likes you. And that's not an easy feat."

Clarence could not avoid blushing.

"It's strange that, being brothers, you live such different lives . . ."

"I always say that Iniko was born too soon. The six years between us was crucial in the island's history. He had to put up with a law that forced everyone over the age of fifteen to work on the state plantations. All the Nigerian workers had been expelled from the island."

Laha suddenly stopped, confused by how attentively she was listening.

"I suppose Iniko has already told you all this."

In fact, Iniko had told her a lot about the recent history of Guinea. After independence was achieved in 1968, the country suffered the worst eleven years of its history at the hands of Macías, a cruel dictator. There was no press of any type; all things Spanish were renamed; schools and hospitals were closed; cocoa production was ended; Catholicism was banned. The repressions, accusations, detentions, and deaths affected everybody—Bubis, Nigerians, Fang, Ndowé from both Corisco and the two Elobey islands, Ámbös from Annobón, and Krios—for any reason at all.

Clarence only a few days ago had learned that Iniko was a widower and had two children who were ten and fourteen and lived with their maternal grandparents. She finally said, "Iniko talks a lot about everything, but little about himself."

Laha nodded and took a sip of coffee. He remained quiet for a few seconds.

"How were your parents able to pay for your studies in the United States?"

Laha shrugged. "My mother has always been a resourceful woman, both in her work and in managing to get scholarships and grants. With Iniko staying here, the two of them were able to help me a lot in allowing me to continue my studies, because I was good at it."

"And your father?" she dared to ask. "What happened to him?"

Laha let out something like a snort. "You should really say *your fathers*. Iniko's father died when he was a child. I never knew mine. My mother has never talked to me about him."

Clarence felt ashamed for having asked. "I'm sorry" was the only thing she could say.

Laha waved his hand. "Don't worry. It's not that strange here."

She decided to continue with another, less offensive, question. "And what scrapes did Iniko get into when he was young?"

"When he was young . . . And not so young, as well!" Laha sat into his chair, looked around him, and lowered his voice. "Have you heard of Black Beach or Blay Beach?"

Clarence shook her head, intrigued.

"It's one of Africa's most famous prisons. It's here, in Malabo. It's known for its mistreatment of prisoners. Iniko was there."

She opened her mouth. She could not believe it. "And why was he put in prison?"

"For being Bubi."

"But . . . how is that possible?"

"Since Guinea got its independence in 1968, the people in power mainly have come from the Fang race. Five years ago there were troubling incidents in the city of Luba, which you must know as San Carlos. A group of armed and masked men killed four workers, and the authorities accused a group that supported the island's independence and self-determination of being responsible. As a result, there was wide-scale repression of the Bubi community by the army. Real atrocities were committed." Laha paused.

"I . . ." Clarence swallowed. "I don't remember having read anything at home."

Laha took another sip of coffee and shook his head. "They detained hundreds of people, among them my brother. I was lucky, I was in California. My mother made me promise not to put a foot on Bioko until things had quieted down."

"And what happened to Iniko?" she asked in a barely audible voice.

"He spent two years in Black Beach. He never talks about it, but I know he was tortured. They later sent him with others to the Evinayong prison, in Mbini, on the continent, which you would know as Río Muni, where he was made to do forced labor. One of the people with my brother was eighty-one years old . . . can you imagine?" Laha took a deep breath. "Remember that the two parts of Guinea, the island and the continental part, are separated by over three hundred nautical miles. It's not only a geographic separation, but also a cultural one. The Bubis are foreigners in Muni. They were sent there to separate them from their families and make their incarceration more painful."

"But," she softy interrupted, "what were they accused of?"

"Of anything. Of treason, terrorism, unlawful possession of explosives, arms smuggling, attempts against national security, coups, secession . . . Surreal, isn't it? Fortunately, two years ago, several prisoners were pardoned, among them Iniko. It was a conditional release, but at last he was able to get out of that hellhole. So did Melania. They met there."

Clarence was stunned. These things happened in the twenty-first century? She took for granted the democratic state that her forefathers had fought for not so long ago—it was very difficult to comprehend everything Laha had told her. She now understood the nervousness of the group when that foreigner was arrested.

Poor Iniko!

Then, she remembered the suggestion that Iniko had made to her, and she felt an uneasy throb in her chest. She had felt tempted to accept the offer, but after what Laha had just told her, she was not so sure.

That night it was difficult for Clarence to sleep.

In the end, she had accepted Iniko's offer. She would travel around the island with him. She would get to know villages that, just by their names, evoked stories and anecdotes of Jacobo and Kilian. Two or three days. Her journey was coming to an end, he argued, and she had not been out of Malabo. The trip included a visit to a special place named Ureca and a quick stop in Sampaka. He had promised that she would not forget this trip, that Bioko was a beautiful island, and that with him she would get to see places unknown to many.

And if they were stopped at a checkpoint?

Iniko was a well-known cocoa company agent, in charge of paying the Bubi farmers. Also, he knew the island like the back of his hand.

Nobody, except Laha, would know where they were. If something happened to her, it would take days for her to be missed in Spain.

On the other hand, how fortunate that Iniko had to make the trip! This would force her to exhaust all remaining possibilities relating to her family. She felt a renewed excitement. How could she have given up her search so soon?

The answer was simple. Each time she reproached herself for cowardly abandoning the search for answers, images of Mamá Sade and her son appeared. Maybe it was not such a good idea to rake up the past. Maybe there were things better left unfound. All families had secrets. Life went on . . .

She sighed deeply.

Go around the island with Iniko . . .

This crush was ridiculous. She felt as if she were fifteen!

Well, well, she thought, *the timid Clarence is going to the jungle with a hunk of a man who has been in prison and who probably has a girlfriend.*

Iniko.

A man who was intelligent, sensitive, committed, a good talker, and attentive.

A couple of days with him. Alone.

She was in the lobby of the hotel at seven o'clock, surprised to find out that Bisila would be traveling with them on the first part of the trip. To a certain degree, Clarence was relieved not to be completely alone with

Iniko. Her dreams at night were one thing; the reality was altogether another.

Clarence went over to Bisila and gave her two affectionate kisses. She silently approved of her dress, pleated below the bust and made from the same orange material as the scarf that covered her in the African style of headdress.

They got into Iniko's white Land Rover, and he explained to her that although the two main roads on the island, which went to Luba in the east and toward Riaba in the west, were perfectly surfaced, the rest of Bioko was connected by secondary roads strewn with roadworks every few kilometers, delays, potholes, temporary detours on dusty tracks, and dirt roads difficult to travel on without a suitable vehicle. In particular, the southern part was the most isolated because of the natural characteristics of the terrain, making access difficult in the rainy season.

And they were in the rainy season. The day dawned fairly cloudy. Some light mists rode around the summit of the majestic Basilé Peak, at whose feet Malabo was situated. Clarence had been lucky recently, with hot days unusual for the month of May. This morning the sky threatened rain.

She looked out the window of the car and silently prayed not to see a tornado.

Iniko put her mind at ease.

"We'll be going to well-known places. This island can be driven across quickly. Most of the time, we will be in villages where we can shelter if it rains."

"Fine. And what is our first destination?" she asked, assuming that it would be Sampaka.

"I thought about driving clockwise. We will start in Rebola."

"Ah! As it is so close to Malabo, I thought our first stop would be Sampaka."

"Well, if you don't mind, we'll leave the plantation until the end of the trip." Iniko turned around slightly. "My mother doesn't like going to Sampaka."

Clarence turned to Bisila, who, sitting beside her in the backseat, watched her in silence. She did not know if it was her imagination or if the woman was actually studying her movements, wanting to find some familiar gesture. In the light of day, she looked even more beautiful. Bisila smiled at her timidly.

"Of course I don't mind," said Clarence with a smile.

As they distanced themselves from the city, the rising mountain peak brought on memories of her Pasolobino valley. Except in Bioko, the vegetation was much greener.

"Basilé Mountain is impressive," she murmured, turning to Bisila.

She nodded. "It's the highest peak on the island," she explained. "From the summit, you can see the whole island on a clear day. It's actually an old volcano, now extinct. The last recorded eruption was in 1923."

"It must be stunning to see a volcano erupting," commented Clarence, lost in thought. "I imagine it like an outpouring of passion. For a period it remains dormant, contained, hidden from the outside. The only one who knows how alive it is inside . . ." She realized how serious she had become and laughed. "I'm not surprised that volcanic land is so fertile. Well, that's what they say, isn't it?"

Iniko looked at her in the mirror with an intensity that made her blush.

"I like that," he said. "I think it fits our way of life very well."

"Don't be upset," she replied with irony, "but I thought your people were known for being quiet and peaceful."

"Until we explode." Iniko gave her a wry smile.

Bisila cleared her throat. "Did you know that the peak has five names?" she asked.

"I know two, Basilé and Santa Isabel. My father and my uncle always referred to it as Santa Isabel. And the other three?"

"In Bubi it's called *Öwassa*," answered Bisila. "The Nigerians called it *Big Pico*. And the British called it *Clarence Peak*."

"Well, well!" exclaimed Iniko sarcastically. "The Clarence volcano! Don't be upset, but I think you are a quiet and peaceful woman."

The three of them burst out laughing. Even Bisila seemed more relaxed. They continued chatting until they got to Rebola, a town on a small hill at the feet of a beautiful Catholic church. Iniko went to visit some people, and the two women strolled along the streets until they got to the upper part of town, where they had a wonderful view of Malabo Bay. It was the first time Clarence had been alone with Bisila.

"I find it strange that churches like those in my village are in a place full of spirits," mused Clarence.

Bisila explained why the Catholic religion had become so deeply rooted. Clarence listened, surprised by the similarities between the Bubi story of creation and the one she had learned as a child.

"There isn't that much difference," added Bisila, "between our *Mmò* and the Holy Spirit, between our *bahulá abé* and the evil spirits and demons, between our *bahulá* and the pure spirits and angels, or between Bisila and the Virgin Mary."

"But admittedly, you are known for being much more superstitious than we are. Everywhere there are amulets, animal bones, shells, and feathers . . ."

Bisila looked at her with an amused expression. "And what do you say of your relics—saints' bones, holy cards, and medals?"

Clarence did not know how to counter this argument, so she decided to ask why the Bubis so honored the souls of the dead. Bisila explained that the world consisted not only of the material but also included the ethereal, or spirit, region. The pure spirits, or *bahulá*, were in charge of the world's physical laws. But the human souls were in charge of the *baribò*, or the souls of the various family heads that made up the Bubi people. When she saw Clarence frowning, she explained.

"I'll give you an example. God created my soul, but he ceded or sold it to the *morimò*, or the soul of one of my ancestors, who has protected it and will protect it all my life in exchange for me honoring him as is due. And I, as any heir of my family or line, make an effort to give homage to both my protector spirit and those of the rest of my family so they can safeguard our prosperity, both on earth and when I've gone from it."

"You mean when you have . . . died."

"You say it as if it were something terrible," said Bisila, raising her eyebrows.

"Because it is."

"Not for me. When we leave here, the soul goes to a much better world. Precisely to prevent the soul of a dead body losing its way, wandering in torment, and becoming an evil spirit, it's necessary to have funerals of mourning and adoration to our ancestors."

Clarence could understand respect for their ancestors, but believing in spirits seemed a little childish.

"So," she said carefully, "you believe it's possible that here and now, there are one or more wandering spirits, trying to find their way."

"If their families haven't honored them well," responded Bisila with conviction, "yes, of course."

Clarence gazed over the red roofs of the small houses and paused at the spectacular view of the sea fading on the horizon. A light breeze began to rustle the palm trees. Beside her, Bisila rubbed her forearms.

Suddenly, something ran toward them and stopped a few paces away. Clarence let out a scream and clung on to Bisila, who showed no signs of fear.

"What is it?" she asked.

Bisila chuckled. "It's only a lizard, Clarence. Don't be frightened."

"You mean an alligator or colored crocodile," said Clarence, looking at the enormous green, red, and yellow animal.

"It'll leave soon."

But the reptile did not leave. It looked at them inquisitively, moving its short and wrinkled neck from side to side until it shot toward her. She stayed as still as she possibly could, willing to give it a kick when she got the chance, but the lizard did not seem aggressive. It halted a few centimeters from her, and as if possessed by a fit of madness, it started to go around in circles trying to bite its tail. It spent a good while at this until it managed to do so. Then it stopped, looked at the women, let its tail go, went around Clarence a couple of times, and disappeared.

Clarence was perplexed. She turned to Bisila and saw that she had covered her mouth with her hand.

"It's a message," she said in a deep voice. "Something is going to happen. And soon."

A shiver ran down Clarence's spine.

"Ready to continue!" exclaimed Iniko behind them.

He looked at her and asked with a worried face, "Have you seen a ghost?"

"Poor Clarence!" explained Bisila. "We were talking about religion. I think I might have frightened her a bit with so many spirits and dead souls."

"Thank God it's midday!" joked the young woman. "If we had talked about this at night, I would have died of fright."

Iniko turned and stood in front of Clarence. Bisila continued walking toward the car.

"I think I have the cure for your fears," he said.

He brought his hands up to his neck and undid the leather cord from which a small shell hung. Carefully, he moved her hair away from her neck and knotted the cord.

Clarence could feel Iniko's hands on her skin. She shivered once again, but this time with pleasure.

She turned to look into his eyes. "Thank you," she said. "But . . . who will protect you now?"

"We have two options," he whispered. "I can buy another one, or I can stay close to you so that the same amulet can protect us both."

Clarence bowed her head.

At that moment, she felt how the real Bioko and the imagined Fernando Po began to meld together in her heart.

10

The Guardian of the Island

"What's our next destination?" Clarence asked while she pored over the simple map.

"Are you afraid of getting lost?" Iniko gave her a mocking look.

Bisila noticed that the young woman blushed. "I have family in Baney," said Iniko's mother. "From time to time, I stay with them for a couple of days."

Her last visit had been just two weeks ago. Iniko found it strange that his mother had asked him to take her again. Bisila bit her bottom lip. If Iniko knew the real reasons. She heard her son speak and Clarence giggle. She was a cheerful young woman; she would have inherited that from her father.

From Jacobo.

How long had it been since she had thought about him? More than thirty years. She had managed to erase him from her mind completely until Clarence mentioned his name the night of the dinner. From that moment, she recognized him in his daughter's movements, in her features, in her eyes . . . Bisila had been angry with the spirits for having woken up memories that she thought were buried. But after mulling things over, she began to understand.

The spirits were being very cunning. From the start, she knew that sooner or later, everything would make sense, that the earthly suffering would find eternal relief. The signs that the moment was approaching were obvious. Clarence was in Bioko, and a lizard had danced in front of her.

The cycle would soon close.

"We're nearly there," Iniko announced.

Clarence looked out the window. The dense vegetation had made way for unpaved streets with small one- and two-story houses at either side, similar to the outskirts of Malabo. Iniko drove toward the high part of the village, and they passed in front of a run-down red church with a very high bell tower, a large cross on the moldy facade, and two arcades over a wide set of steps. He had to beep the horn several times to warn the numerous children who were playing in the streets that a car wanted to pass.

Clarence thought they were all very good-looking, especially the girls, with their light-colored dresses and their hair tied up in immaculate little buns and braids. When the car stopped in front of the houses, several children crowded round to greet them. Bisila went straight into the building, and the other two stayed with the small ones. Clarence regretted having nothing in her bag to give them. She looked for her purse and decided to give them some change. She had only handed out three or four coins, which the fortunate ones received with grateful smiles, when Iniko asked in a temper, "What are you doing?"

"Giving them some change."

"Just like a typical paternalistic tourist."

"I loved it when I was young," she whispered, irritated. "Look at their faces! Do you really think I'm doing something wrong?"

"In Baney, there are two thousand people," he said mockingly. "If these little ones spread the news, you'll be left with nothing."

Iniko went into the house. Clarence remained outside a few seconds longer, upset. She was not used to such criticism. The amulet had not lasted long! She decided to forget about it and followed the man inside.

When they saw that Bisila had arrived with a European, Bisila's sisters, Amanda and Jovita, also with their hair covered under pretty scarves, turned an informal family party into a real feast. Clarence did not know how, but some seventeen people—Bisila's sisters and their husbands, their sons, their daughters, the wives and husbands of their children, and their grandchildren—took their seats around a rectangular table covered by a printed floral oilcloth that was being covered with dishes of chicken with yucca, bream with avocado sauce, and the *bóka'ó* of vegetables that she had tried in Bisila's house. Clarence found the stews very tasty, but what she liked most was the dessert: the crunchy coconut biscuits and the ginger and pineapple drink.

With the hubbub around the table, they did not even notice that a tropical storm passed over with the same speed as it had arrived.

Clarence went out to smoke a cigarette on the veranda. Iniko had not said a word to her during the whole meal. *His loss,* she thought. She was upset that an innocent act caused him to draw a conclusion more in keeping with their first meeting in Sampaka. It looked like their relationship veered between attraction and repulsion. One minute they would be joking like teenagers, the next attacking each other—him especially, treating her as an outsider. She was afraid that the argument would end the trip and that Iniko would decide to go back to Malabo.

She concentrated her attention on the extraordinary view of the stretch of sea that separated the island from the continent. The skies cleared for an hour and showed the distant and majestic Mount Cameroon crowned by cloud. Bit by bit, the mists closed in on the summit.

"Beautiful, isn't it?" Bisila came over to the railing that Clarence was leaning on.

"This is . . ." Clarence looked for a word that would do honor to what she had just seen. "Exceptional. I'm not surprised my father fell in love with this island."

Bisila pressed her lips together.

"I suppose he would tell you many stories of his life here," she murmured, without taking her eyes from the horizon.

Clarence studied her profile. There was something about Bisila that attracted her. Her disturbingly clear eyes and her firm lips reflected intelligence, strength, and determination, although she appeared to be a physically fragile and delicate woman. Laha and Iniko said she was responsible, hardworking, and cheerful, but she transmitted sadness and vulnerability.

"I'm afraid parents never tell us everything," she said.

Bisila gave her a sideways glance. Clarence remembered Mamá Sade. She guessed she was a little older than Iniko's mother. How different her reaction would have been had Bisila remembered her father!

"Do you know what happened to me the other day?" she asked. "I don't know if Iniko has already told you." Bisila gave her a perplexed look and Clarence felt brave enough to continue. "In a restaurant, I was set upon by someone called Mamá Sade. She was certain I reminded her of someone, a man she knew a long time ago." She forced a tense smile. "It was daft, but for one minute, I thought she could have known my father." She paused, but Bisila's face did not show any surprise.

"Mamá Sade has dealt with many people in her life."

"Then you also know who she is."

Bisila nodded. "And why does it worry you so much that she might have known your father?"

"Well . . ." Clarence hesitated, but a voice inside her head pushed her to be sincere. *Why do you not say out loud once and for all your reason for visiting the island?* She opened her mouth, but Iniko interrupted them.

"Ah! Here you are! Clarence, we're going now," he said without looking at her. "I'd like to get to Ureca before dark."

The two women followed him to the entrance. Amanda and Jovita insisted that they accept some food wrapped in packets and a bag of the coconut biscuits that Clarence had liked so much. The children surrounded them again. The white woman had been the day's, and probably the year's, novelty.

At the last second, Clarence noticed that Bisila's gaze was fixed on the simple necklace that Iniko had tied around her neck. She could not be sure if the sight of the small shell awoke some special memory in her. Bisila's eyes clouded over in tears, and before they rolled down her cheeks, she gave Clarence a big good-bye hug, as if they were never going to see each other again.

Once inside the car, Clarence did not stop thinking about Bisila. She was sorry she had not been brave enough to ask her more about her life. Most Equatorial Guineans her age had been educated only in those tasks deemed suitable for women: the home, the kitchen, growing the crops, and maternity. As an alternative, some had stalls in the market. From what she had been told by Rihéka, Melania, and Börihí, things had not changed much, despite the country's constitution, which—in theory—gave women equal rights.

Bisila had managed to be an independent woman who began her studies in the colonial period. Clarence did not know how much a woman earned in those times but supposed it was not much. And what's more, hers was the only salary in the family. How had Bisila managed to raise her two children without the help of a man?

"What are you thinking about that has you so quiet?" Iniko broke his silence.

The white lines on the narrow tarmac road weaved through the green weeds.

"I was thinking about your mother," Clarence answered. "I'd like to know more about her. She seems a very special woman."

"And what would you like to know?" he asked in a conciliatory way that Clarence accepted as an apology.

"Well, why is it she doesn't live in Baney with her family? How did she settle in Malabo? How was she able to study? How many times did she marry? Who was your father? And Laha's father? What was life like for you in Sampaka?"

"Okay, okay!" he chuckled. "That's far too many questions!"

"I'm sorry. You asked." She was afraid she had gone too far, but Iniko did not seem to mind.

"My mother," he began to say, "worked in the hospital on the Sampaka plantation as a nurse's assistant. She married someone who worked there, and they had me. My father died in an accident, and we moved to Malabo. At some point, she had an affair with a man, and Laha was born. She has never wanted to talk about it, and we didn't push the subject. From my time in Sampaka, I have the odd memory of school and the Nigerian barracks where a neighbor looked after me. Then I spent many years with my grandmother in the village. I liked it more than the plantation because there I felt free . . ."

For a moment, the letters that mentioned a nurse who had looked after her grandfather Antón on his deathbed came to Clarence's mind. Just then, she imagined the hands that had held a damp cloth on his forehead belonged to a woman with Bisila's face.

Could it be?

Iniko drove looking straight ahead, with his head cupped in his hand and his elbow out the open window.

"And what happened afterward?" asked Clarence.

"After what?"

"How did Bisila avoid having to leave the country like so many others after Guinea gained its independence from Spain in '68? Didn't they expel many Bubis and Nigerians?"

"Well, she did not pose any political threat. If anything, she was necessary, since her abilities in the field of medicine were the same or better than any doctor's."

He fell silent in anger. Clarence put a hand on his thigh to comfort him, and Iniko put his right hand on top of hers while holding the steering wheel with his left.

They left behind Riaba, called Concepción during the colonial period, and drove toward the south of the island.

"What does *Iniko* mean?" Clarence asked. "Don't you have another name? I thought that everyone here had a Spanish name and a Guinean one."

"Something like Iniko Luis?"

She giggled. "Yes, something like that."

"Well, I only have this name. It's actually Nigerian. The priest in school told us that God wouldn't recognize our names and we would go straight to hell. He didn't frighten me, and I only answered when he called me by my real name. In the end, he gave up."

"And does it mean anything?"

"'Born in hard times.'"

"Very appropriate . . . for the period you were born in, with the change from a colony to independence and all that, for everything you've gone through . . ."

"If I hadn't been named Iniko, the same things would have happened to me, I suppose. A name doesn't hold that much power."

"Yes, but it makes you special."

"Well, we make a good combination. Clarence, the city and the volcano"—his voice became soft and warm—"together with Iniko, a man born in hard times. What can we hope for from all this?"

Clarence felt her cheeks burning. She had to take advantage of this magical moment before it was ruined and grab on to that fine thread that an invisible spider had spun around both of them before it disappeared.

"Yes," she replied, trying to make her voice sound suggestive. "What can we expect from a volcano and a Bubi warrior?"

Fire, pure fire, she thought.

It seemed to her that the surrounding jungle, thick and dense, had suddenly fallen silent, as if someone were watching them. Once again she remembered, with relief, that on the island, unlike the continent, there were no dangerous animals like elephants or lions, only monkeys. Still, the calm made her suspicious. It would soon be dark. As if he had read her mind, Iniko said, "It's not far to Ureca now."

A new excitement grew inside her. Would someone there remember her father?

The Land Rover took a narrow, unpaved road, and Clarence had the feeling that all signs of civilization were disappearing. The 4x4 drove with difficulty over unposted dirt tracks. After a few kilometers, they made out a simple barrier that blocked the traffic.

"It's a police checkpoint," announced Iniko, a little tense. "Don't say anything, okay? They know me. It will only take a minute."

Clarence nodded.

As they approached, she saw that the barrier was made up of a barrel at either side of the road and a bamboo trunk resting on top of them. Iniko stopped the car, got out, and said hello to the guards. The uniformed men gave the vehicle the once-over and asked Iniko a few things with serious expressions. Clarence had the feeling that something was not right. Iniko shook his head, and one of the men raised a finger threateningly. Clarence decided to disobey Iniko's warning, took out her papers and some money from her purse, and got out of the car.

"Good evening," she said politely with a timid smile. "Is there something wrong?"

Iniko pursed his lips and gave her a look of reproach.

One of the police officers, a thick-set man with an unfriendly face, went over to her and, after looking her up and down with a disagreeable scowl, took her papers. He studied them with a deliberate lack of haste.

Then he walked over to the other officer, showed them to him, came back to Clarence, and returned them with a grunt. A few seconds went by, but neither of them made any movement to raise the barrier. Clarence, remembering how Laha had rescued her from those police in front of the cathedral, stretched out her hand with the notes and quickly reached toward the officer before he could notice her nervousness. He opened his hand, quickly calculated the amount that she had given him, and, to Clarence's relief, seemed satisfied. He signaled to the other, and they let them go through.

Once inside the vehicle, Iniko, more relaxed, said, "Could you tell me who taught you the customs of the country?"

Clarence shrugged. "Laha." She gave him a satisfied smile. "As you can see, I am a quick learner."

Iniko shook his head. "That Laha! They gave him the right name."

"Oh, really?"

"Laha is the Bubi god of music and good emotions. Translated it would be something like 'someone with a good heart.'"

"It's a beautiful name."

"Much better than his other one. His full name is Fernando Laha."

"Stop the car!"

Iniko stopped dead. Clarence opened the door, got out like a shot, and leaned against the car. She raised her hands to her face and rubbed her temples. Laha was called Fernando!

She went over all the clues: Julia's advice to search for a Fernando older than she and born in Sampaka, the little she knew of the life of Bisila, the coincidence that she had lived on the plantation, the cup of coffee smashing to the floor on hearing the word *Pasolobino*, the flowers in the cemetery . . . Could it be? Laha was mulatto, and he was also called Fernando! And if . . . ? And if . . . ?

Iniko put a hand on her shoulder, and she jumped.

"Are you feeling all right?"

"Yes, Iniko, sorry, I . . ." She took a deep breath. "I got a bit dizzy. It must have been the heat, and the tension of the police checkpoint."

Iniko nodded.

It was hot, but Clarence rubbed her forearms as if she were cold. She peeked at Iniko, who looked at her with a furrowed brow. And if she told him her suspicions? She shook her head and closed her eyes. What would she achieve by telling him that there was a small possibility that they shared a brother? Was she going to waste some promising days based on a hasty conclusion held together by a thread? How long had it been since she had allowed herself a bit of excitement? Would it not make more sense to wait until Ureca?

She opened her eyes, and there was Iniko, standing with his legs slightly apart, his arms folded across his rock-hard chest, and his enormous half-closed eyes looking at her patiently.

"I'm feeling better, Iniko," she sighed. "We can continue, if you like."

The last part of the journey turned into a constant battle between the 4x4's powerful engine and the vegetation that had reclaimed the track.

"And this remote and inaccessible place is part of your work route?" Clarence asked, her stomach slightly queasy because of the potholes.

"I don't come here very often," he admitted. "More for pleasure than for work."

"And when was the last time you were here?"

She pretended not to be jealous, but a cheeky question did go round in her head: *Has he made the same journey with Melania?*

"I can't remember." He smiled. "Actually, it's a place I would like you to see. Accept it as a present."

He stopped the vehicle in a small clearing from where some houses could be seen.

"Now we have to walk a bit to go down to Moraka Beach, but it's worth the effort."

The way to the sea first followed a gently sloping cocoa plantation, and later they walked along a path through a forest closed over by enormous trees whose roots extended along the surface and tripped up Clarence. After a short while, they heard the roll of the waves, and a large gap opened in the canopy to reveal an indescribable panorama.

At their feet, a cliff fell away for almost a hundred meters. She swayed, seeing that Iniko was taking a narrow, steep, and winding path, practically hanging off the precipice. Though frightened, she followed him. She slipped on the stones and the tree trunks that sometimes acted as steps, making Iniko laugh and throwing into doubt her skills as a mountain woman. When they got to the bottom, Clarence turned and looked up, not sure she would be able to climb back up.

If she ever wanted to go back.

She opened her mouth, dumbstruck. The effort had indeed been worth it. All the possible images of paradise she had in her head materialized in that very instant.

Before her eyes was the most gorgeous sight she had ever seen in her life. It was a long, wide beach of black sand and clear water. Close to the end of the path, an enormous waterfall cascaded down, creating a crystalline pool. It was the mouth of the Eola River, its death turned into pure beauty.

Entering the sea, an outcrop of rocks rested on the sand, placidly lapped by the waves. Where there was no beach, the blue of the sea and the green of the jungle shared each other's frontiers.

"What do you think?" Iniko asked, happy to see her expression.

"My father, in spite of not being poetic, always claimed to have had the good fortune of knowing two earthly paradises: our valley and this island. And it's true. This is paradise!"

Iniko took off his boots and motioned her to do the same. Then he took her by the hand, and they began walking along the beach.

"Each November or December, thousands of giant sea turtles end their migration across the Atlantic Ocean here. The majority were born on this beautiful beach and come back to lay their eggs. They come out of the water to the dry sand, where they lay the eggs and bury them. Some return to the sea. Others die from exhaustion. Others are caught by the hunters who wait in hiding, even though they are a protected species and in danger of extinction. They turn them over with the shell on the ground. They can't right themselves, and they stay like that until they have died." He moved his arm over her shoulders and squeezed her against him. "When I think of the turtles coming out of the water and dragging themselves to the shore, Clarence, I think of those from my country who left and couldn't return, of those who came back and were mistreated, and of those who, at all costs, try and succeed in keeping their descendants on the black beach."

Clarence did not know what to say.

They walked barefoot along the sand for a long time and then paused before a huge rock covered in moss and birds, which rose up thirty meters into the air. A small cascade seemed to flow from its top.

"This is the guardian of the island," explained Iniko. "Its purpose is to watch over the town of Ureca."

He put his hand in his trousers pocket and took out some seeds mixed with petals and placed them at the feet of the rock while murmuring some words.

"What are you doing?"

"I'm leaving it an offering."

"You could have told me. I've brought nothing."

Iniko rummaged with his hand and took out a pinch of seeds. "Enough."

Clarence leaned down and placed the small gift. She asked for help not only in the search that had brought her to Bioko, but also going forward in life. She smiled. It was a lot to ask for such a small present.

"Wouldn't you like to know what I asked for?" she teased.

Iniko smiled. "I suppose the same as me. That they germinate well."

She agreed. He took her arm and silently guided her back to the start of the beach.

They arrived at the edge of the pool under the Eola River waterfall. Without undressing, Iniko got into the water with his arms open wide and his hands toward the sky. Clarence was entranced, contemplating how the drops from the waterfall, actors in a natural journey that was at the same time circular and eternal, splashed against his skin. Then Iniko turned and signaled her to do the same.

Clarence got into the water and allowed Iniko to circle her waist with his enormous arms. Very slowly, he drew her to his body until the embrace was complete and his head nuzzled in her hair. Her heart began beating out of control. Clarence could feel him breathing close to her ear, causing her to feel a delightful tingle. She heard him inhale her scent while softly resting his lips on her damp skin, sliding them down from her neck to her shoulder and again to her earlobe.

She remained with her eyes closed to appreciate the full intensity of his caresses. At that moment, nothing existed except for her body, stuck to Iniko's, in the middle of this beach. Never before had she been able to carry out such a fantasy. He wanted to taste her bit by bit, as if she were the last sweet morsel on earth. He rubbed gently against her, passing the tips of his fingers along her arms, which hugged his broad back. He slid his full lips over her cheeks, he looked at her for a few moments . . . and began again, with a slowness that did nothing but awaken her desire for him even more.

Iniko began to unbutton her blouse very gently, still looking at her. Clarence felt her breathing accelerate and her skin tingle at the touch of his hands. He embraced her in his strong arms, and his lips busied themselves on her neck before daring to slide down to her breasts that hardened from the heat and moistness of his mouth.

She could not remember the last time a man had tasted her with such passion.

With the same steady rhythm, Iniko put his full lips on hers and kissed her while holding his arms around her waist. Clarence needed air and opened her lips slightly, allowing him to bite them before his tongue took control of her mouth.

They were so close that despite the noise of the waterfall, she could make out the rapid beat of his heart. She slid her hands along Iniko's strong arms and broad back to his waist to caress the skin under the damp shirt stuck to his muscles.

Iniko moved apart a few centimeters and took off his shirt. Clarence reached out with her fingertips; he was a warrior, several scars furrowed his skin. She made no comment, putting her hands over the wounds and caressing them. She then brought her lips to them.

In the same way as he had enjoyed her bosom, she wanted to taste his chest, while strong fingers fondled her neck and played with her hair until managing to release the plait that held it. Then Iniko placed his hands on either side of her face to hold her tightly, lift her toward him, and kiss her again, this time with more intensity. Clarence felt a wave of excitement and responded with a desire deep within her.

Iniko kissed her lips, her forehead, her ear, her neck . . . In a whisper, he suggested that they lie on the sand. Their breathing began to adjust to the rumbling of the waves that lapped the shore.

Clarence could not stop caressing him. Her hands wanted only to read each fold of his skin for when she would not have him with her, in Pasolobino. There, it was always cold. There would not be any sand. Nor two naked bodies beside the sea. This moment with Iniko would become one of the most beautiful memories of her life. On remembering it, she would smile and rememorize the tingles of desire that made her arch her back to receive him with all his force. Maybe she would find someone to share the rest of her life with, she thought in a brief lapse into lucidity, but it would hardly surpass this strange connection. No promises. No regrets. A connection born from a mysterious affinity in spite of the cultural and geographic distances. Each time she would hear the word *Africa*, in her mind she would outline Iniko's handsome face and sad smile.

And from the way he had taken her, she could see that Iniko felt the same.

Both of them would always know that someplace in the world, there existed someone whose scent had invaded their senses, a body whose sweat had drenched their thirsty skin, a body whose taste had sated their needs.

When they took the road back to the village, Clarence turned to look at the horizon from the upper part of the cliff. The sea in all its splendor, and the full moon, framed by palm leaves, creating thousands of silver reflections on the water's surface.

She seemed to have been in that place for an eternity. She felt comfortable, quiet, and relaxed. However, an unexpected feeling of loneliness overcame her. She did not know exactly what it was, but she began to have the worrying feeling that Iniko wanted to take over her body and her soul. *Don't forget these names, or these places. Don't forget me. Go back to your country and remember the imprint that I have left on you.* Under that waterfall, she had thought she had seen in his eyes a confused expression of desire and faint touches of resentment. *Don't you forget that for a few days, I took you for mine.*

"You're very quiet, Clarence," Iniko interrupted. "The climb has left you out of breath? Is Pasolobino very flat?"

"I can't believe I have been in such a place!" she exclaimed so he would not notice her confusion.

Iniko stretched out his hand and stroked her hair. "From now on," he murmured, "each time I hear your country's name, it's possible I'll feel something different. I will think of you, Clarence."

Clarence closed her eyes. "The same will happen to me when I hear talk of this piece of Africa. Which, by the way, happens very often in my house." She sighed before taking the way back. "In fact, I think I'm condemned not to forget you."

They went back to the car, took the bags out of the trunk, and entered the village of Ureca, made up of bamboo-roofed houses covered in palm leaves and surrounded by a green hedge, but built on stilts to protect them from the rain.

There were around thirty houses built along an earthen avenue bordered by trees and staked trunks from which hung monkey and antelope skulls and snake skeletons to ward away the evil spirits. If Jacobo and Kilian were there, they would probably feel they had gone back in time. It was nothing like either the capital or the northern part of the island.

At one end of the avenue, a larger building with no walls could be seen. At a certain distance, several people recognized Iniko and waved to him.

"What is that?" Clarence asked.

"It's the village house. It is the most important place for us. It is used for meetings, to explain stories, to discuss day-to-day problems, and to sort out disputes. Everything I know about my people, I heard it here. By the way"—he signaled to the crowd coming over to greet them—"from now on, you also form part of the oral tradition of all the places we have visited."

"Ah, really?" Clarence looked at him, intrigued. "For being white?"

"The whites don't surprise us as much as you think. You'll go down in history as Iniko's girlfriend. Even if you leave in a few hours!" He smiled wryly. "There is nothing you can do now."

He turned around and walked toward a group of neighbors. They greeted each other very warmly and exchanged a few words, and a woman pointed to one of the houses.

"Come, Clarence," said Iniko. "We'll leave our things in our *hotel*."

Clarence raised her eyebrows, amused. On entering the house, she whistled in surprise.

The floor of the simple house was of beaten earth, and there was hardly any furniture, but the room could not have been more romantic and welcoming. In the center, there was a circle of stones with wood prepared to light a fire. Close to the rudimentary fire, there was a large bamboo cot raised off the floor like a bed. On a small table, someone had prepared a bowl of fruit that looked very appetizing.

"We will sleep here," Iniko explained while he left the bags on the floor. "Now we have to accept the invitation of the chief. It's time for dinner."

Clarence felt butterflies in her stomach. She was going to meet the inhabitants of the village? What better occasion to ask about her father's supposed friends?

Nervous and expectant, she followed Iniko to the village house, which was filling up with people.

The chief was called Dimas. He was small and sturdy, with curly gray hair. Two deep wrinkles marked his cheeks. From the way he greeted Iniko, with the same affection as the majority of the men, Clarence was able to judge that her friend was very well liked.

They sat on the ground in a wide circle. Clarence and Iniko were seated in a place of honor near Dimas. Some of the men gave curious looks to Iniko's companion, and several children sat around them. It was inevitable that Clarence would be the center of attention that night. During the feast, consisting of fish, fried banana, yucca, and roasted bread-tree fruit, she answered many questions about life in Spain. The men remained comfortably seated, and the women came and went with bowls of food and drink—especially drink—trying to avoid the children who swarmed between the white woman and the dishes. When the inevitable subjects of snow and skiing came up, Clarence became infected by everyone else's laughs.

Her eyes were filled with tears and her throat burned from the palm wine. "How do you make it so strong?" she wanted to know.

Beside the chief, a man so thin that you could see all his bones, who went by Gabriel and who seemed to be around the same age as Dimas, answered.

"We make it in the traditional way. We climb up the palm trees, helped by liana arcs and thin ropes. We cut the stems of the male flowers"—he gestured by moving his hand horizontally—"and we gather the liquid in a gourd or a container. Then we leave the liquid to settle for several days to let it ferment"—he stretched his hands with the palms facing the ground—"very, very slowly. Yes. It has to settle to gain strength."

"Like the Bubis," Iniko pointed out, and everyone laughed and nodded.

They finished their meal, and the chief took on a serious pose. Everyone became quiet, and Dimas began to narrate, in Spanish, the history of his people, which they had certainly heard hundreds of times before, thought Clarence, but nobody showed any signs of impatience. On the contrary, they often nodded as Dimas described how the Bubis had first arrived on the island, thousands of years before; the wars between the various tribes over the best land; the list of kings and their great deeds; Ureca's fortunate location, which made it difficult to find at the time of slaving; the arrival of the first colonists and the conflicts with them; and life under the Spanish.

Dimas's voice took on a grave tone when naming the kings.

"Mölambo, Löriíte, Löpóa, Möadyabitá, Sëpaókó, Möókata, A Löbari, Óriítyé . . ."

Clarence closed her eyes to listen to the history of the Bubi nation. Her mind traveled back to the time of slavery and the conflicts between Bubis and Spaniards that took place before the Bubis were completely pacified.

"The colonists removed the king," murmured Iniko, "but we retained our national symbol. I knew Francisco Malabo Beösá. He was like our spiritual father. He was born in 1896 and died a couple of years ago, at the age of one hundred and five."

"I can't believe it!" exclaimed Clarence in a low voice. "He shattered the life expectancy—"

"Listen," Iniko interrupted. "The part I like most is coming now, when he tells of the deeds of Esáasi Eweera."

Dimas told the tale of King Moka's deputy, who was proclaimed king in Riaba before Malabo. He described Esáasi Eweera as a strong, brave, and determined young man, who detested the colonists and attacked with fury the peoples who came from outside to take over the arable land, and those Bubis who showed sympathy toward the whites. In the end, he and his men were captured by the colonial forces and sent to the prison in Black Beach along with his wives. They were brutally raped by the colonial guards in the presence of their husband and king, who went on hunger strike.

A silence fell when Dimas told of the end of Esáasi Eweera, who, according to the colonists, was converted, baptized, and buried with the name Pablo Sas-Ebuera. According to the Bubis, he was murdered by the colonists and buried on the high grounds of Moka, sitting up, in accordance with the Bubi customs for the burial of a king.

Dimas finished the story and began to talk of his own life. After a while, Iniko whispered, "Now comes the part when Dimas admits how well he lived under your people."

Indeed, the chief nostalgically went over his adolescence in Santa Isabel; how comfortably he lived in the city in a small house along with his wife and children; the money he earned as a foreman of *batas*—or workers—on a cocoa plantation called Constancia, which even allowed him a small car; and how lucky his children were to have been able to go to school. Clarence saw out of the corner of her eye how Iniko kept his eyes fixed on some point on the ground, his hands clenched.

Dimas paused to drink from his bowl, and Clarence spoke up. "And this plantation, Constancia . . . was it close to Sampaka?"

"Oh, yes, very close. I didn't go very often, but I knew people who worked there. There was a doctor"—Dimas half closed his eyes—"called Manuel. A very good man. He helped me once. Later I was able to return the favor. I wonder what happened to him."

Clarence's heart skipped a beat. A doctor called Manuel? From Dimas's age, she reckoned that the dates could fit. What favor would that have been? Was he referring to the money installments? To this out-of-the-way village? It did not make sense . . .

"Do you know if this Manuel was married to a woman called Julia?"

Dimas opened his eyes in surprise. "Yes, that was the woman's name. She was Emilio's daughter . . ." His voice weakened. "Is it possible you know them?"

"Manuel died not so long ago. I know Julia very well." She tried not to appear too eager. "They were here with my father, Jacobo, and my uncle Kilian." She observed the face of the man and noticed no change. "I don't know if you remember them . . ."

Dimas shook his head while mumbling some words. "Their names sound familiar," he answered, "but their faces have been erased from my memory. I might have known them, but after so many years . . ."

Clarence decided to push a little further. She had to know if there existed the remotest possibility that Dimas was one of those friends in Ureca whom her father supposedly sent money through. But to whom? Why?

"And you say that Manuel helped you and that you later returned the favor . . ."

Dimas rubbed between his eyebrows as if trying to forget. "They were hard times for everyone, blacks and whites—"

"The whites imprisoned your brother," Iniko said abruptly. "And they sent him to Black Beach. And they tortured him."

Dimas nodded at first and then shook his head. "The whites didn't kill him. Macías killed him. He made sure of liquidating all those who were economically stable. Those who were spared, he ruined. Like me. But it's not the same."

"The whites placed Macías in power," insisted an obstinate Iniko.

"But they also gave you independence," pointed out Clarence quickly. "Wasn't that what you wanted, that my country leave you in peace?"

"Nobody gave me my independence," he replied in an offended voice. "I am Bubi. The inhabitants of this island, the first ones, the natives, before any ship had the damned luck to bump into the island, were the Bubis. Here there weren't any Portuguese, English, Spanish, or Fang. But when it was in Spain's interest and they had no choice but to give independence to Guinea because the UN insisted on it, they did it in the most glorious way they could think of. Handing it over to a paranoid Fang with the brilliant pretext that we would be one single nation. As if it was possible to unite night and day!"

He passed his gaze over those present and raised his voice.

"This island and the continental part of Mbini are—well, were until very recently—two completely different worlds with different ethnic races. My Bubi traditions are different from Fang traditions." He turned to Clarence, and she saw that his eyes were glowing. "Earlier you were told how we Bubis make our palm wine. We go up the tree and extract the liquid. Do you know how the Fang do it?"

He did not wait for her to answer.

"They cut the tree . . . Yes, Clarence, those from your country made us accept a fictitious, unitary, and unbreakable state, knowing that it couldn't work. And what happened then? Have you listened to Dimas? He, at least, was lucky enough to seek refuge here."

The older men nodded. Clarence pursed her lips. Whenever the conversation was diverted to political matters, his attitude toward her changed completely. And what was worse, she mightn't have another chance to ask Dimas without raising suspicions.

"Iniko, you're right," Gabriel intervened in a soft voice, "but you are talking with your heart. The old times won't come back. Before it was the cocoa, now it is the oil."

"Blasted natural sources," said Iniko. "If only this island was a desert! I'm sure nobody would want it then."

Clarence frowned and took another sip of wine. How could she tell him he was wrong, that these resources could mean progress for a nation? She still had memories from her childhood in struggling Pasolobino. The roads were not paved, power and water cuts were frequent, the cables hung from the walls, some of the houses looked as if they had been abandoned, and, of course, there was a lack of medical services. She still remembered the killing of pigs, the milking of cows, the traps for the thrushes, the hunts for mountain goats, the cleaning of the sheds, the collecting of hay for the livestock, the dirt of the streets used by animals, and the muddy tracks.

When she was ten—not that long ago—any European from France northward or any American who saw photos of her village would think they were living in the Middle Ages. In less than forty years, Spain had turned itself around to the extent that places as isolated as Pasolobino had become small tourist paradises. Maybe this tiny part of Africa also needed time to balance its extremes.

"I don't agree with you, Iniko," she began to say. "Where I live, thanks to the skiing, life has improved for a lot of people—"

"Please!" he interrupted her angrily. "Don't compare! Here there is money, corrupt politicians, and millions of people living in precarious conditions."

Clarence shot him a stern look and bit her tongue. A rising murmur confirmed that they were commenting on the words spoken up to that point. Iniko held her look, frowned, and sought refuge by pretending to look for something in the rucksack that was beside him. Clarence drank in silence. The liquor was drilling a hole in her stomach, but she managed to contain the urge she had to get up and leave.

A few minutes later, Dimas raised his hand, and the gathering fell quiet.

"I see you bring papers, Iniko. Any news?"

"Yes. The government is preparing a new land law. I have brought you a draft application for you to register them in your names."

"For what?" asked an albino man with bright eyes.

Clarence looked at him with curiosity. She found it strange that the man had the same features as the others, but that his skin was completely white. A unique fusion between black and white, she thought.

"The forest belongs to no one, but man belongs to the forest. We don't need papers to know what is ours."

Several men agreed.

"You talk like a Fang." Iniko rose a finger in the air. "They are going to destroy the centuries-old property rights of many families."

"For centuries, our word has been accepted concerning the ownership of the land we occupy," said Dimas. "The word is sacred."

"The word doesn't work anymore, Dimas. Now you have to have your papers in order. The new law continues to follow African law, which rejects the private ownership of land and favors its use, but at least it includes a clause on traditional familial property inheritance. They say that no one can bother you on the lands that you have been habitually occupying for agriculture and housing. It's a start. If my grandfather had presented plans to manage the plantation when the Spanish left, it's possible he could have kept it. But he didn't do it. The Spaniards couldn't transfer the property rights because they didn't own the land, but they could have transferred the right of concession so that others could have continued to operate it. I want your children to receive this right of concession of the land. So that others don't come and take it away."

There was a murmuring. Clarence saw that the majority of those present nodded. In the distance, songs could be heard.

"Thank you, Iniko. We will study what you have said, and we will talk the next time you come. Now we will enjoy the dancing. We have spent a long time talking, and we don't want our guest to get bored."

Clarence was pleased that the chief had brought the meeting to a close. The palm wine was going to her head, and she felt sleepy. The day had been long and intense. Iniko's various teachings and his capricious moods had left her a little confused and upset. On the one hand, she felt privileged after having visited such marvelous and remote places in the company of a man she so desired. But on the other, she regretted that Iniko was not able to separate the true Clarence from her nationality. Would he do the same if she were Australian? She wondered.

Iniko gave her a slight poke and motioned to her to look in front of her. Clarence lifted her head. With her vision somewhat blurred, she looked at a group of women performing a simple dance. They were dressed in raffia skirts and adorned with shell collars and wrist and ankle straps with amulets hanging from them. Their breasts were bare, their faces painted with white marks, and their hair gathered in tiny braids. Some of them carried wooden bells that made a deep sound, similar to the voices chorusing the song. Others beat the ground with sticks and feet in a simple but intense dance. After a while, Clarence found herself murmuring some of the verses. She did not understand what they were saying, but she did not mind. In spite of the drink and the tiredness, the message was clear and pure. Everyone formed part of the same community, the same earth, the same history. Everyone shared the same life cycle from the beginning of time. The ancestral spectacle reduced temporal distance from the infinite to this very moment, which had happened before and would happen again.

When the dance finished, Clarence felt at peace, comforted, and relaxed. Beside her, Iniko gulped the last drops of his drink. Clarence watched him. How to tell him that there were more things that united them than he thought? She felt she had more in common with him— the same language, the same Catholic tradition, the same childhood

songs—than with a Dutchman. How to end his resentment? How to
tell him that rancor was not good, that it ended up affecting those who
were not at fault? How to make him understand that when you can no
longer fight for a lost cause, the best option was to find a balance? That
sometimes years had to go by before troubled waters could find calm?

Iniko slowly stretched, showing off his enormous span, put out a
hand toward her, and, with a captivating smile, leaned over in search
of her eyes.

"I could stay here for weeks. Wouldn't you like to bathe in the
waterfall every morning?"

She tingled. It seemed that the charming Iniko had returned. "It's
very tempting, yes, but I have my small paradises in Pasolobino as well.
Also, what about the rest of the island, San Carlos or Luba as it is now
called, and its giant crater, the marvelous white sandy beach in Alena,
from where the fishermen go to the Loros Islands? What about Batete
and its church constructed entirely of wood? Don't you want to show
me all that? How could you ask me to give up half of the best vacation
of my life?"

"I'll make it up to you now, and I will owe it to you if you ever
come back to Bioko."

She gave him an impish smile. "Okay," she agreed, hoping he
would get the double meaning of her reply. "In any case, I don't believe
anything can beat Moraka Beach."

"Wait and see!"

Clarence half closed her eyes while a shiver of pleasure ran down
her spine.

"I'm referring, of course, to the fact that you will finally travel
around the whole of Sampaka." He noticed that she blushed and
paused. "What did you think? That I'd also ask you to give up your visit
to the place where we met?" He got to his feet and put out his hand to
help her up. "Do you know, Clarence? It would have been impossible
for you to have met anyone else other than Laha and me upon your

arrival. The spirits wanted it so. And I don't know how to fight against the will of the spirits. They must have some reason."

She remembered having asked herself why she felt attracted to Iniko and not to Laha. Possibly the spirits had some reason for that as well.

It began to rain outside.

"Remember the day I bumped into you?" It had happened barely three weeks ago, but to Clarence, it seemed like ages.

"When I took you for a newly arrived secretary?" asked Iniko.

Clarence laughed. "Yes! I have to admit you scared me a bit."

"I hope you're over it."

"Not completely. When I met you in Sampaka, and then in your mother's house, you seemed gruff and distant."

He turned to her in surprise.

"Yes," she insisted. "I even thought you didn't like me. Don't you remember? At the dinner, your mother said something to you in Bubi and you changed." Iniko nodded. "What did she say?"

"A cliché. She told me not to judge you until I knew you."

"Well, it was very good advice. Look at how things have changed. If King Eweera were ruling now, you'd be under threat for consorting with a white woman."

He burst out laughing. "If King Eweera were ruling, you would be under threat for trying to control a Bubi."

Iniko stopped the 4x4 in front of the rusted gate with remains of red paint on it, over which a name, soldered on, could be seen— Sa_pak_—which had lost two of its letters.

"Since you are so smart, and are so interested in names, do you know what Sampaka means?"

Clarence thought for a couple of seconds. The plantation was set up beside the village that used to be called Zaragoza.

"I presume it's the original name of the village."

317

Iniko smiled with a look of superiority. "Sampaka is the contraction of the name of one of the first freed slaves who disembarked in Port Clarence when the island was occupied by the English. The name of this freed slave, Samuel Parker, became Sam Parker, then Sampaka."

Clarence turned toward him. "And how do you know this?"

Iniko shrugged. "They must have told me in school when I was young. Or I must have heard it when I was working as a laborer. I can't remember. Well, shall we go in?"

"One more question. I'm curious to know if you ever feel nostalgic about the years you spent on the plantation."

Iniko thought for a few seconds. "I was happy here as a child, but when I was forced to come back, the work was hard and boring. Maybe I feel a mixture of indifference and familiarity."

She directed her gaze toward the majestic palm trees whose feet were painted white up to a height of about two meters. Each palm was barely a meter apart from the next. They formed two parallel rows, which were separated by a dirt avenue and seemed to meet at a point in the distance. The entrance closed in on itself, swallowing up the traveler.

She said, "Fate wanted my family to come and work in Sampaka instead of other plantations like Timbabé, Bombe, Bahó, Tuplapla, or Sipopo. These were beautiful sounds that evoked images of distant lands in my mind when I was growing up. Today, since it's not raining and I can see it properly, I feel as if I can finally enter into the enchanted castle of my childhood stories."

"I don't know what you hope to find, Clarence, but in this case, the reality is at best . . . poor . . . to say the least."

"See those palm trees?" Clarence pointed ahead of her. "The men of my family replanted some of them. That makes me proud and comforts me. My father and my uncle grow old and bent, but the palm trees are still here, strong and straight up to the sky." She shook her head. "To you it seems insignificant, but to me, it means a lot. One day they will all disappear, and there will be nobody to tell the generations to come about palm trees in the snow."

She pictured the family tree in her house and felt the same deep tingling that she felt the day she discovered the mysterious note between the letters and decided to call Julia.

"I will. One day I will tell them all I know." *And will you also tell them what you suspect, but have yet to find out?* she thought fleetingly.

Iniko started the car, and they entered the plantation, which was full of life: men dressed in tracksuit bottoms and T-shirts, pushing wheelbarrows; small vans raising dust; a tractor transporting firewood; a woman with a basket on her head; one or another abandoned container. Then, the yard. On the right, two white storehouses or sheds with red roofs. On the left, a unit built with a white-columned veranda. The main building. The small archives building. Piles of cut firewood here and there. Bare-chested men slowly moving from one place to another. Clarence felt deeply emotional once again.

They parked under the veranda beside several jeeps, and Iniko led her over to the nearest cocoa trees. Clarence saw some men picking cocoa with a long pole that had a sharp flat metal hook at its end, which allowed the men to separate the ripe pods from the green ones and to make them fall without touching the others.

"Look, Iniko! My uncle brought two things back from Fernando Po: a hook and a machete that he still uses to prune and cut the thin firewood."

The cocoa trees seemed lower than she had imagined. Some men were walking with baskets on their backs; they collected the orange-colored pods from the ground using machetes and put them into the basket. They were wearing high Wellington boots. There were a lot of weeds all around. Other men carried the pods in wheelbarrows and moved them to a pile around which six or seven men were splitting them. They held pods in one hand and opened them with two or three gentle strikes of a machete, which was also used to extract the beans from inside. Almost all of them were young men. Their clothes were dirty. It was certain they spent many hours like that, opening pods and chatting.

There was a sparkle in Clarence's eyes. Jacobo and Kilian talked to her from afar: *"When the cocoa had to be dried in the dryers, even if it was four or five in the morning, I didn't miss it once in all the years that I was there."*

She would tell her father and her uncle that cocoa was still being produced, and in the same way that they remembered. The cocoa dryers, although old and neglected, were intact. Time seemed to have stood still in that place: the same machinery, the same structure supporting the roofs, the same wood-burning furnaces. Everything worked in the same way and used the same techniques as in the middle of the twentieth century. There were not five hundred workers, nor the order or cleanliness that Kilian and Jacobo used to boast about, but it worked. It had been real and still wanted to be so.

Neither they nor others like them were there now, but the cocoa was.

Iniko was surprised by her interest in something that for him was nothing more than heavy work. They went around each and every corner of the main yard and the surrounding land, with Iniko giving her a detailed explanation of all the activities. After several hours, they crossed a small bridge with no rail and took the path back toward the vehicle. They arrived at the white-columned veranda, took the bags out of the car, and sat on the steps of the old employees' house. Clarence was exhausted and sweaty, but happy.

A man in his sixties came over. Iniko recognized him, and they talked for a while. The man, who looked familiar to Clarence, would not stop staring at her. Then she realized it was the crazy man who had followed her, making windmills with his arms, on her first visit to Sampaka. She found it strange to see him so calm.

Suddenly, her curiosity increased as she thought she heard the words *Clarence, Pasolobino . . .* and *Kilian!*

"Clarence!" Iniko exclaimed, motioning her over. "You're not going to believe this!"

Her heart began to beat quickly.

"I'd like you to meet Simón. He is the oldest man on the plantation. He has been here for over fifty years. He can't work anymore, but they allow him to come and go on the plantation as he pleases, gather firewood, and give orders to the young tenderfoots."

Simón looked at her with incredulity. He had fine incisions scarring his forehead and cheeks. He must be one of the few scarified ones left; he was the first one she had seen, and its effect was a bit frightening. But beside Iniko, she was not afraid.

The man decided to talk to her directly, but he spoke in Bubi. Iniko whispered something in her ear.

"He's known Spanish since he was a child, but one day decided not to speak it anymore. He has never broken his promise. Don't worry, I'll translate for you."

Another person who keeps his promises, she thought, remembering Bisila's refusal to return to Sampaka.

Iniko stood to one side of Simón and began translating his first sentences.

"I have been watching you all the time," said Iniko. "You remind me a lot of someone I knew well. Now I'm sure. You're a relation of Kilian . . . maybe his daughter?"

"I'm not his daughter." On seeing the disappointment in his face, Clarence hurriedly explained, "I'm his niece, daughter of his brother, Jacobo. Tell me, did you know them well? What do you remember of them?"

"He says that for years he was Massa Kilian's boy. Kilian was a good man. He treated him very well. He also knew Massa Jacobo, but didn't speak much with him. He wants to know if it still snows as much in Pasolobino—your uncle always spoke of the snow—and if they are still alive and how old they are now, and if Massa Kilian married."

"The two of them are still alive." Clarence's voice began to tremble in emotion. "They are over seventy and are both healthy. Our family still lives in Pasolobino. The two of them married, and each had one daughter. My name is Clarence. Kilian's daughter is named Daniela."

The name Daniela surprised him. He was quiet for a few moments.

"Daniela . . . ," he murmured, after thinking for a couple of seconds.

He looked at Iniko. He looked at Clarence. Besides the incisions, his face was also furrowed with wrinkles. Even so, it could clearly be seen that he was frowning. He looked at Iniko again and asked him something.

"He wants to know how we met." Iniko laughed, put a hand on Simón's shoulder, and answered his question warmly. "I told him that we ran into each other here a few days ago, and that we later met up with Laha several times in the city."

Simón gave a small grunt and fixed his eyes on Clarence.

"Yes, Simón. She also knows Laha," said Iniko. "Yes. It was a coincidence."

"Why do you say that?" Clarence wanted to know. There was something in his face. She turned to Iniko. "I thought you didn't believe in coincidence, that everything was the work of the spirits."

Simón rapidly intervened. Iniko took over translating again. Simón's words made sense, but his voice told her that the conversation was diverting down another path.

"Simón says that he was a good friend of my grandfather. And the two of them were friends of your uncle and your grandfather."

"Then he also knew my grandfather?" Clarence asked. Her heart skipped a beat when she remembered the flowers on the grave.

Simón answered and signaled to Iniko with his finger.

"He says he did, but his image has been erased from his mind because he died so long ago. Simón was very young then and had only been working for Massa Kilian for two years. It seems my grandfather knew him very well."

"Your grandfather?" asked Clarence. It was difficult to imagine that he would be alive, but . . . the last Bubi king died at the age of 105! "And he . . . ?"

"My grandfather died many years ago." Iniko nodded.

"And what was your grandfather's name?"

"Ösé. For you, José. He lived all his life here, in Sampaka—well, between the plantation and the village he came from, which no longer exists. It was called Bissappoo. In 1975, Macías ordered it to be burned. According to him, the village had been involved in subversion."

"Bissappoo . . . ," she repeated under her breath.

"A beautiful name, don't you think?" Iniko asked.

"Very nice, yes, like all of them around here," she admitted, but that was not the only thing that had her intrigued. "Then, José was Bisila's father . . ."

"Yes, of course. I never met my father's parents."

Now something else joined her to Iniko. Her grandfather and his had been friends, if that was possible during a period where the divisions between blacks and whites were stark.

"The things they could tell us if they were alive, couldn't they?" Iniko was thinking the same as she was. "If Simón says they were friends, it's because they were friends. Simón always tells the truth."

Then why did he look at her with the expression of someone who knew something and did not want to say it?

"Are you going to stay long in Bioko?" asked Simón through Iniko.

"I have to leave the day after tomorrow." Clarence suddenly became very sad.

"Simón says to say hello to Massa Kilian from him. And to tell him that life hasn't treated him too badly after all. He will be pleased to know that."

"I'll do that, Simón, I'll do that."

Simón nodded and, as if he had forgotten something, hurriedly made a comment.

"And say hello to your father as well," translated Iniko.

"Thank you."

Simón shook Iniko's hand, said something else to him in Bubi, then turned and left.

"And what did he say to you now?" Clarence asked.

"That he recognized you from your eyes. That you have the same eyes as the men in your family. They are not a common color. From a distance they look green, but if you come closer, they're gray." He came so close to her face that she could feel his breath. "I think he's right. I hadn't noticed it!"

Iniko took her hand, and they began to walk toward the veranda, where the 4x4 was parked.

"Ah! And he asked me to tell you something, a little odd, by the way . . ."

Clarence paused and looked at him impatiently.

"He asked me to tell you that if the eyes don't provide the answer, you must look for an *elëbó*."

"And what's that?"

"A Bubi bell used in rituals and dances, like you saw in Ureca, remember? It's rectangular, made of wood, and has several clappers."

"Yes. And why did he say that? What does it mean?"

"I haven't a clue. But he said that one day you might understand it. That's the way Simón is. He says something. If you understand it, good, and if you don't, good as well."

Clarence stopped and turned. She could see Simón's figure some meters away, watching them.

"Wait a second, Iniko."

She walked over to Simón. She looked him straight in the eyes. "Please, just make a gesture with your head. I need to know something. Bisila and my father knew each other?"

Simón pursed his lips, and the corners of his mouth curved downward in obstinacy.

"Only yes or no," she pleaded. "Did Jacobo and Bisila know each other?"

The man grunted and moved his chin toward his chest in one swift gesture. Clarence took a deep breath. Had that been a yes?

"Were they friends? Maybe . . ."

Simón raised a hand in the air to get her to keep quiet. He said some words in a bitter tone and left.

Clarence bit her lip. Her heart was beating wildly. Jacobo and Bisila knew each other.

She felt an arm weave through her own.

"Shall we go?" Iniko asked.

They started walking again, and after a few seconds, Clarence stopped again.

"Iniko . . . why do you think your mother never wanted to come back to Sampaka?"

Iniko shrugged. "I suppose that everyone has memories they don't want to relive," he answered. "As Dimas said, those were very hard times."

Clarence nodded, deep in thought. She began to imagine a confused and impossible story based on jigsaw pieces that only partly fitted. She would have to read all the letters that were at home!

A sudden urgency to return to Pasolobino and bombard her father with questions came over her, but when they got to Malabo, evening had fallen and this feeling had turned into one of disquiet.

She would have given anything to go back to the beach at Moraka and the little house in Ureca.

"Do you want to stay with me in the hotel tonight?" she asked Iniko. She did not want to be alone.

No . . . It was not that exactly.

She did not want to be *without him*.

11

The Return of Clarence

"Why are you staring at me?" Laha half shut his eyes while taking a sip of his beer and licking his lips. "Is it because you don't want to forget my face?"

Clarence lowered her eyes, a little embarrassed, and he patted her on the arm.

"I promise to find any excuse for the company to send me to Madrid. How long is it from Madrid to Pasolobino?" He looked at his watch. "Iniko is taking a long time. Where could he have gone?"

"To Baney," she answered in a subdued voice. "To collect Bisila." She was not feeling very talkative that night.

"Ah!" Laha laughed. "You know more than me then!"

They were sitting on a terrace beside Malabo's old port. It was a beautiful night, the most beautiful of all in her time there.

It was as if the heavens had conspired to offer her a good-bye she could not forget.

She looked at Tomás. She would also miss him. Rihéka, Köpé, and Börihí had left a while ago, and Melania had not come to the simple going-away party that had been prepared for Clarence, even though she was already back from Luba. Nobody made any comment about the girl's absence, an absence that Clarence appreciated because she would not have been able to look her in the face after her trip with Iniko, knowing that it would be Melania who would enjoy him once she left the island.

"I'm very sorry, but I have to go now," said Tomás, getting up to go over to Clarence. "If you ever come back, you know." He coughed and cleaned his glasses with the corner of his T-shirt. ". . . Call me and I'll bring you wherever you want to go."

"Even to the cemetery?" she joked.

"Even there. But I'll wait at the gate!"

The two of them smiled. Tomás took one of Clarence's hands, shook it in his, and put it on his heart as the Bubis would.

Clarence stayed standing until he was out of sight. She had to make a real effort not to burst into tears. She sat down and took a large sip of her drink.

"I hate good-byes," she said.

"Well, the good-byes of today are nothing like before," commented Laha, trying to cheer her up. "The Internet has gotten rid of a lot of tears."

"It's not the same," she argued, thinking of Iniko. Laha was used to traveling the world and to making use of technology; not so for his brother. She very much doubted that she would see Iniko again, unless she came back to Bioko.

"Something is better than nothing." Laha pushed back a lock of his curly hair.

Clarence looked at him with certain envy. Laha exuded a contagious optimism. If only she could spend more days with him! Well . . . with him and his family. She did not know how to explain it, but she had the feeling that she had been very close to discovering something. She had hardly had any time to think about Simón's words and the fact that

Laha, like so many others, was also called Fernando. Neither Iniko's impetuosity nor her disappointing advances nor even her aversion toward Mamá Sade's son had made her forget the initial reason for her visit. And if this was her last chance to ask Laha in person about his childhood . . . She decided to tell him about her meetings with Simón, leaving out the discovery that Bisila knew her father.

"Simón," he said, puzzled. "His name sounds familiar, but I don't know him. The truth is I know very little about Sampaka. When I was small, my grandfather used to take me there, but I've been there only a couple of times with Iniko since then. I already told you that my first memories were of school, here, in the city."

"I thought since you were born there."

"No. I was born in Bissappoo. My mother had gone there to spend a few days with her family in the village, and I got the urge to arrive early."

Clarence froze. She had assumed that both brothers had been born in Sampaka.

"Oh . . ."

Laha squinted. "It seems as if you're disappointed . . ."

"No. It's just that I learned more about this place than I ever imagined I would, but I would have liked to have learned more about life in Sampaka when my father was there. It seems that the only one who remembers my family is Simón. And your mother," she added, a touch reproachfully, "doesn't like to remember her life there."

"I don't know why she doesn't, Clarence, but I'm sure that if she remembered your father, she would have said it."

Clarence shook her head. She had seen too many films. And in any case, if there was a grain of truth in any of it, the only way to continue would be, in addition to torturing her father with questions, for Laha to follow through on his suggestion and visit her in Spain. In Bioko, she could not do any more now.

"A last 33?" suggested Laha, getting to his feet.

"Yes, please."

The bad thing about good-byes is that you begin to miss things as trivial as a beer before you leave, she thought.

At that moment, Iniko arrived and sat down beside her. He had a plastic bag in his hand.

"Sorry I'm late," he said with a wink. "There was no way of getting out of that house. Here. My mother told me to give you this."

Clarence opened the bag and took out a round hat of cloth and cork.

"A pith helmet?" she asked, giving the object a puzzled look. It seemed worn and had a tear on the rigid hoop.

"She said that you'd like it because it once belonged to someone like you." He put his hands up. "Don't ask me, because I don't understand either. She also repeated several times to give her best regards to where you are going, that someone will accept them."

"Is it a Bubi good-bye tradition or something like that?"

"I'm not sure. My mother is often a mystery even to me."

Clarence put the helmet away. Soon after, Laha arrived with two beers.

"You don't want one?" Clarence asked.

"I'm going now. Tomorrow I've to get up very early." She noticed the lie in his voice and was grateful for his understanding. It was clear to Laha that on that final night, Iniko and Clarence did not need anyone else.

Clarence got up to give him a big hug, and her eyes filled with tears once again; because of that, her last image of Fernando Laha, walking along the run-down promenade, where decades before the sacks of cocoa from Sampaka departed for the rest of the world, was blurred.

The plane arrived in Madrid on time. A taxi took her to the train station. Three hours later, Clarence arrived in Zaragoza, stunned by the rapid change in scenery. In a few months, it would be even more drastic, with the introduction of the first high-speed train. She had left her car in the garage of the apartment she was renting in the city. She was tired, but in a good two hours, she could be in her village. She decided against it. She could not adjust so quickly, going from Iniko's arms and the exuberant foliage of the island to the abrupt mountains of the valley in just a few hours. For an instant, she was jealous of the long boat journeys of the last century. The long days at sea inevitably gave the soul time to mend. It was possible to prepare for the next stage on life's journey.

So Clarence spent the night in Zaragoza. She needed to be alone, even if just for a few hours. Maybe things would look different in the morning.

Lying on the bed in her apartment, her skin free of the stickiness that had accompanied her in the last few weeks, she could not get to sleep. Iniko was still beside her, on top of her, under her.

Why had she felt attracted to him and not to Laha? Would not a relationship with someone whose life was more similar have been easier? Laha was intelligent and well mannered. He was used to traveling and dealing with different people . . .

But no, she had to set her eyes on Iniko! She smiled. Probably the spirits that permeated each centimeter of the island had something to do with it. Or maybe it was just chance that had joined twin souls together. There was one point of total convergence between Iniko and her: he would never live in a place other than Bioko, and she could never live far from Pasolobino, even if the intensity of the last few days would be remembered for the rest of her life. Her eyes filled with tears. The freely accepted chains that tied them to their respective worlds could not be broken either by love or passion.

Maybe if Iniko and she were younger, the moment of their parting at the airport, fused in a deep and silent hug, would have been more dramatic. Or maybe if both of them had been forced to separate due to circumstances beyond their control, bitterness would pursue them for the rest of their lives. However, a reasoned love, a permitted passion, and an agreed separation had forged another type of very different drama: that of resignation, even crueler, if possible, she thought as she wiped away the tears with a tissue, because it lets you go through life not letting anything really affect you.

How she would miss that man! Iniko possessed the power of the waves of the beach of Riaba, the majesty of the tongues of foam of the waterfalls of Ilachi that fell hundreds of meters down the vertical walls of the Moka forest, the energy of the cascade in Ureca, and the ardor of a tropical storm over the plumes of the palm trees. Above all, she would miss the unyielding solidity of that guardian of the island, faithful Bubi heir of the high priest, *abba mööte*, at whose feet she had placed a small offering in exchange for an enormous wish.

She was still very young. It was certain that many seeds would germinate through her life, with or without the help of the gods. But would she be brave enough when the time came to gather the fruit, or would she let the harvest spoil?

All these recurring thoughts accompanied Clarence until, the following day, she parked the car in the outside yard of the House of Rabaltué.

The first one to come out to greet her was her cousin. Daniela gave her a big hug and asked, "So, Clarence? Was everything as you expected? Were our parents right?"

"Believe it or not, Daniela," Clarence answered, "there was a lot of life outside Sampaka and the parties in Santa Isabel."

When she went into the house, the familiarity mingled with the unsettling certainty that the possible existence of a brother could only be answered in Pasolobino. She longed for the island just then.

"God knows what you've been eating the last few weeks!" Carmen did nothing but refill her daughter's plate.

"Did you eat turtle?" Daniela wanted to know. "And snake?"

"Snake meat," Jacobo butted in, "was very tasty and tender. The turtle soup, a feast. Wasn't it, Kilian?"

"Almost as good as monkey stew," Kilian teased.

"Clarence!" Daniela opened her big brown eyes. "Tell the truth."

"I mainly ate fish. And I loved the *pepe-sup*."

Jacobo and Kilian laughed.

"I see you remember the spicy fish soup!" They nodded. "And a lot of fruit—papaya, pineapple, banana . . ."

"Ah, the fried banana of Guinea!" exclaimed Jacobo. "That really was delicious! In Sampaka, we had a cook from Cameroon who prepared the best bananas."

Clarence nodded. That night, everyone was happy and expectant, peppering her with silly questions. Finally, Kilian adopted a serious tone to ask her how she found everything. She told them the more entertaining anecdotes and about the tourist sites that she had visited, and she summarized the curious aspects she had learned about the Bubi culture. The marvelous journey to the east of the island was whittled down to the names of the villages she had visited with—she lied—two lecturers from Malabo University.

She left her visits to Sampaka for the end. She described how the plantation now looked and how it still continued to produce cocoa. Suddenly, she realized that it had become very silent around her. Daniela and Carmen were attentively listening. Jacobo was playing with a piece of bread and clearing his throat. And Kilian had his eyes fixed on his plate.

Clarence understood that her story had already transported them to another place, so she decided to tell what for her was one of the highlights.

"Do you know what struck me most during my time in Bioko? There is still someone who puts flowers on Grandfather Antón's grave."

Carmen and Daniela gasped.

Jacobo froze.

Kilian raised his eyes and fixed them on his niece to make certain she was not lying.

"Have you any idea who it could be?"

Both of them shook their heads, but both were frowning.

"I thought it might be Simón . . ." She shook her head. "But I don't think so, not him."

"Who is Simón?" her mother asked.

"Uncle Kilian, in Sampaka, I met an old man who told me he had been your boy while you were there."

Kilian's eyes misted up. "Simón . . . ," he whispered.

"What a coincidence!" exclaimed Jacobo, in a forced cheerful voice. "Simón is still alive and still in Sampaka! But how did you meet up with him?"

"Actually, it was he who recognized me," she explained. "He said I looked a lot like both of you."

She remembered that Mamá Sade also thought her face looked familiar, but Clarence did not say anything. *Not yet,* she thought. *Later.*

"Well, and we were introduced by a man who knew him, as he had worked on the plantation. His name was . . . His name is Iniko." His name came out almost in a whisper. He had become a character in her story. He was not flesh and bones.

Jacobo and Kilian exchanged a quick and meaningful look.

"Iniko . . . What a very strange name!" Daniela commented. "Very nice, I like it, but strange."

"The name is Nigerian," Clarence explained. "His father worked in Sampaka during the period you were there. His name was Mosi."

Kilian rested his elbow on the table and supported his head in one of his enormous hands. Jacobo crossed both hands over his face to hide the sign of surprise that was forming on his mouth. Both of them were very tense.

"Doesn't it ring a bell?" Clarence asked.

"On the plantation there were more than five hundred workers!" bellowed her father. "You don't expect us to remember all of them!"

She fell silent, but quickly recovered.

"I know there were a lot of you," she defended herself in a loud voice. "But Gregorio, Marcial, Mateo, Santiago . . . ? I suppose you remember them!"

"Mind your tone, Daughter!" Jacobo wagged his finger in the air. "Of course we remember them. They were employees like us." He paused and gave her an odd look. "How did you get their names?"

"I got to see the plantation files. I found both your files and Granddad's. They're still there, with the medical histories. And, Dad . . . I didn't know you were hospitalized for several weeks. It must have been serious, but it didn't say what."

Carmen turned to her husband. "I didn't know that, Jacobo. Why did you never tell me?"

"Please! I didn't even remember it!" He took the bottle of wine to pour himself a glass, and his hand trembled. He looked at Kilian for help.

"It would be that time when you had a serious dose of malaria. The fever wouldn't come down, and you had us all worried." Kilian smiled at Clarence. "Every other week someone came down with it. I'm surprised they had made a note of something so common."

Clarence looked at the other women. Was she the only one who thought they were lying? It seemed so. Carmen got up to serve dessert as Daniela changed the subject.

"Where are the presents you brought us?" she asked in a tinkling voice. "You did bring us presents, didn't you?"

"Eh, of course I did!" Clarence had not finished her initial attack, and she was still left with the most difficult part.

"One more thing before I go look for them . . ." She hesitated. "Simón wasn't the only one to recognize me."

Kilian raised an eyebrow.

"In a restaurant, a woman with her mulatto son came over to me . . ." She had hesitated over the word *mulatto*. "She was convinced that I reminded her of someone from her youth. Everyone there called her Mamá Sade . . ."

"Sade . . . ," Daniela repeated. "Are all the names in Guinea that pretty? It sounds like the name of a beautiful princess."

"Well, there's nothing left of that." Clarence made a face. "She was, well, *is* an old toothless woman who looks like a witch."

The men looked at her impassively. Several seconds went by. Nothing. They did not even twitch. Would not a quizzical look have been more logical?

"I imagined she mistook me for someone else, but she insisted on knowing my father's name."

Kilian cleared his throat.

"And what did you say?"

"I told her he was dead."

"Thanks a lot," Jacobo commented in a forced cheerfulness that made Carmen and Daniela laugh. "And why did you do that?"

"Because I didn't like that woman at all. They told me she had been a prostitute in the colonial period before becoming a successful businesswoman in that profession. And that"—she coughed—"she had fallen in love with a white man who she became pregnant by and"—she coughed again—"he abandoned her. That was the reason she didn't want any more children."

"What a scoundrel!" Carmen pursed her lips. "Though, if you say she was a prostitute . . . I can only imagine the type of men she would have hung around with."

Clarence finished off her glass of wine. "Mom, I imagine many of her customers were the white employees from the plantations." She paused on seeing the warning look from her father.

"Right, Clarence. That's enough."

Clarence nodded.

"And those presents, dear?"

On the way to her room, she cursed her bad luck under her breath. There was no way of her getting any further in that, not even the slightest bit. She could have sworn that neither Jacobo nor Kilian was telling the whole truth. Carmen and Daniela had not seemed to have found anything odd, but Clarence was sure the brothers were hiding something. How was she to discover anything if nobody gave her answers?

Okay, the name Sade seemingly meant nothing to them. *Let's see what happens with Bisila's name.* Clarence was certain they would not remember Bisila, just like she could not remember them. What bad memories everyone seemed to have all of a sudden! She picked up several bags from her bedroom and returned resolutely to the dining room.

After everyone had opened the packages and commented on the carved wooden animals, the mahogany walking sticks, the ebony figurines, the ivory amulets, the necklaces of shells and gemstones, the leather bracelets, and the beautiful and colorful party dress she had chosen for Daniela, Clarence opened the bag that Iniko had given her from Bisila and took out the pith helmet.

"A final gift!" she announced, putting the cloth-and-cork helmet on her head. "Iniko's mother gave me this. One day she invited me to dinner at her house. There was Iniko, his brother, Laha, well, Fernando Laha, and her. Her name is Bisila, a charming woman. She worked in Sampaka as a nurse during your time."

She paused. Nothing. Not even a comment.

"Ah! And she asked me to send her best wishes to the person I gave the helmet to. It could belong to either of you! It's almost an antique."

She took off the helmet and gave it to Daniela, who put it on, took it off, looked at it curiously, and passed it to Carmen, who did the same.

Kilian did not take his eyes off the helmet. He had his lips tightly closed, and his breathing seemed forced. Carmen passed it on to Jacobo.

It looked to Clarence as if her father's hands were trembling as he quickly passed it on to his brother. Was it her imagination, or did Kilian close his eyes as if in pain? Unlike Jacobo, he spent time stroking the helmet with extreme delicacy. His fingers went over the tear in the rigid hoop time and time again. All of a sudden, he got up and whispered, "Sorry. It's very late and I'm very tired. I'm going to bed." He looked at his niece for several seconds with a sad expression. "Thank you, Clarence."

He left the dining room with a slow, ponderous step. Clarence felt he had aged in a matter of seconds. She never thought of the men of the house as people who were entering their twilight years. Kilian's shoulders and legs were heavy. His strength had disappeared.

Everyone else remained in silence. Clarence hung her head. Her curiosity was hurting everyone else's feelings. Her mother put out her arm and took her hand.

"Don't worry, Clarence," she said sweetly. "He'll be fine. Tonight you've spurred a lot of memories." She turned to her husband. "You spent many years in Guinea, and it was a long time ago. It's only normal to be nostalgic."

"This always happens." Daniela sighed. "In the end, it's better not to bring it up."

Jacobo shook his head. "And you, Clarence?" he asked wearily. "Has Africa gotten into you?"

Clarence turned beet red.

The unusually cold spring gave way to summer. The valley of Pasolobino filled with tourists who had fled the heat of the lowlands. At the end of August, the last summer festival was held in honor of the patron saint, which, in times past, had been the celebration of the harvest and a farewell to the good weather until the following year.

Clarence stuck her nose out the window. A band appeared around the corner and stopped in front of the door. The noise of the trumpets and drums echoed in the street, festooned with small flags hanging from the front of the houses. The poor things had to face the buffeting of the wind and the children who jumped up to try and take them. After the musicians, many children and young people danced with their hands in the air, shouting with joy. Two girls went over to the door with a big basket, and Daniela put in various sweets and desserts for the villagers to eat after the mass. The band finished the number, and Daniela offered them a glass of tasty wine from the special cask in the House of Rabaltué's cellar.

Clarence smiled. Daniela always said that the village festivals were as distasteful as that wine, which spent too much time in the barrel, but then she was the first one to help out and applaud. The music began to fade in the distance as the band moved toward a new destination. Daniela ran up the stairs. When she met Clarence, there was a twinkle in her eye.

"What are you waiting for? Get dressed! The procession will soon be starting."

As tradition demanded, every year, several men carried the saint on their shoulders through the streets of the village, followed by a parade of villagers decked out in the typical dress of the valley. Once the procession was over, the statue of the saint remained in the square while the neighbors dedicated a dance to the saint, and then it was returned to the church until the following year. The traditional costume consisted of so many petticoats, skirts, sashes, and ties that Clarence needed nearly an hour to put it on. And then there was the complicated chignon, the pins, the neck and head scarves, the jewelry . . . For the first time in her life, she could not be bothered.

"And you, Daniela," she asked as every year, "what are you waiting for?"

"Me? I'm not one for these sort of things. But I love to see you dressed up." She shrugged while smiling. "By the way, who is your partner this year in the dance?"

"I'll find someone."

Clarence closed her eyes and imagined Iniko beside her, dressed in tight dark trousers, a white shirt with the cuffs folded to the elbow, a sash around his waist, a waistcoat, and a scarf around his head. *How would the onlookers react?* she thought wryly. His enormous body would stand out in the circle of couples, jumping and turning to the sound of the castanets adorned with colored ribbons. She bit her bottom lip and remembered the night in the disco in Malabo. Since him, she found fault in all other men. None of them had his captivating magnetism. Not one.

"I could always ask one of our unmarried cousins . . ."

"Girl, it sounds dreadful, but some of them aren't half bad. We might have to go back to the old customs. Do you know if you still need a papal bull to marry a cousin?"

"What nonsense you are talking!" Clarence smiled. "Come on, let's go!"

"Wait a minute . . ." Daniela put the last touches to the hairstyle. "Have you noticed you've got a few gray hairs? They say they appear with worry."

I'm not surprised, thought Clarence.

The weeks passed, and still she made no progress. Jacobo and Kilian avoided the subject of Guinea, and she did not have the courage to be direct. Julia had arrived in Pasolobino a month ago for the holidays, and they had met only on a couple of occasions. When Clarence mentioned the trip, putting emphasis on certain people—Sade, Bisila, Laha, and Iniko—if her friend knew something, she had managed to keep a straight face. Since then Clarence had had the feeling that the woman was avoiding her.

On more than one occasion, she had been tempted to go up to her father and share her suspicions. But she needed definitive proof to disclose a family secret of this magnitude. And each time she was more and more frustrated: Julia's clue had led to a dead end, not much could be gotten from the reactions of Jacobo and Kilian, and no matter how many times she tried, she could not decipher the meaning of Simón's vague comments. He had told her to look for a Bubi bell if the eyes did not give her an answer. What a riddle . . . So she had decided to wait for the heavens to send her a sign.

"You're being very quiet, Clarence." Daniela's voice broke into her thoughts. "I asked you if you were worried about anything."

"Sorry. Lately I've had too much free time. When I go back to work, I'll be okay."

"Dad has also been a little down. Have you noticed it?"

Clarence nodded. Kilian spent the days walking the fields and paths close to the house or in his room. After dinner, he went right to bed. In fact, he did not even talk at the table.

"Our parents are getting old, Daniela."

"Yes. It's a stage in life where two things happen: either you become bitter, or you switch off. The first is the case with your father, the second with mine." Daniela sighed deeply, then gestured to Clarence's costume. "It's turned out perfectly."

After the procession and the dance, they enjoyed a large meal in the House of Rabaltué with all the uncles, aunts, and cousins from around the valley. The talk after lunch went on and on due to the wine: well-worn anecdotes, stories about the village and the valley, and comments about the previous generations and the neighbors. Clarence enjoyed this annual routine with a certain wistfulness. It seemed like a village house in miniature. In this way she had learned all she knew about her past.

Toward the end of the afternoon, the guests finally got up from the table to attend a concert of regional songs and dances. Before the traditional group of guitars, lutes, and flutes, a singer began in a deep voice, plucking at Clarence's very heartstrings with the beautiful theme. Clarence bowed her head and closed her lips tightly to prevent her eyes from filling with tears. The man repeated the verse once more: "The plants grow green again when the month of May arrives. What no longer revives is the love that dies. It's the love that dies, when the month of May arrives."

She was capable of waiting to solve the family mystery, but Clarence could not stop thinking about Iniko. Almost three months had gone by since she had gotten back from Bioko. They had not written. What would she have told him? They had not called. What would she have said? She knew he was well through Laha, who sent her an e-mail once a week. That was all.

"What's wrong, Clarence?" Daniela put a hand on her arm. "And don't say 'nothing,' because I don't believe you. You've been distracted and sad the whole day. In fact, ever since you came back from Africa."

She looked directly at Clarence.

"Did you leave someone there?"

Clarence refused to tell her about the possible existence of a brother for the same reason she did not talk to Jacobo. She was not completely sure. She racked her brain for a vague enough answer. She opted to just let her continue to believe that she had had a romance in distant parts. And in this, she was not lying.

"You are not far wrong, but I don't really want to talk about it."

"Fine," Daniela relented. "But will you see each other again?"

"Hopefully."

Daniela frowned, but did not press any further. She patted Clarence's arm and then concentrated on the last piece, which the audience applauded before dispersing.

The cousins went to the bar to order two glasses of punch and bumped into Julia on the way. While Daniela was saying hello to some acquaintances, Clarence decided to use those moments alone with her. Since she had returned from Guinea, Julia was always in a rush, which Clarence found very suspicious. Had Julia regretted putting Clarence on the—fairly useless—trail of a possible lost relation? To avoid her escaping again, she decided to get straight to the point.

"Julia, I'd like to know if this Fernando, older than me, could have been born in some other place like, for example, Bissappoo."

On hearing the name, Julia immediately looked up at her. She wanted to correct her reaction, but realized that it was too late, and she blushed. Clarence felt a renewed hope.

"I . . ." Julia rubbed her forehead, wavering. "It's possible that . . ." She paused. "What difference would it make?"

What do you mean, what difference would it make? Clarence thought, wanting to shout it out. *That would change everything!*

"Simón led me to believe that Jacobo knew Bisila," she insisted. "Is it true?"

"I'm not telling you anything more, no matter what you say." Julia's voice was unequivocal. "Talk to your father."

"Here's your drink, Clarence." Daniela arrived on her uncle's arm, and Clarence suppressed a curse. "Did you know that your father lasted the whole performance? And you know how little he likes these things!"

Julia turned.

"How are you, Julia?" asked Jacobo. Both hesitated, then finally decided on two pecks on the cheek. "It's been ages since I last saw you."

"Yes, a long time. Ridiculous, when you consider how small a place this is."

"Yes." Jacobo cleared his throat. "Are you staying long?"

"I'm going back to Madrid next week."

"We'll also be going to Barmón soon."

"Don't you stay here now you're retired?"

"We come and go, as always. The habit . . ." Jacobo's eyes dropped, and he cleared his throat again. "You're looking very well, Julia. I see time has stood still for you."

She blushed. For an instant, she imagined if it was Jacobo and not Kilian who had been widowed like herself. Would anything remain of the sparks that flew between them when they were young? She stared at his inflated stomach and raised her eyes to the lines furrowed on his face.

"Thank you very much, Jacobo," she said in a neutral tone. "And for you too."

Daniela broke the brief silence. "Hello, Dad," she said as Kilian came over to the group. "Do you want us to go home now? You look tired."

"We'll go now." He looked at Julia. "How are you?"

"Not as well as you." Julia waved to a person leaning on a car at the bottom of the slope. "One minute, I'm coming!" she shouted. "I'm sorry, but I have to go."

"I'll walk with you to the car," Kilian offered.

He held out his arm so she would not slip on the slope, and they began to move away.

"I'd like to ask you something." Kilian requested as he paused and looked into her eyes. Despite the wrinkles, Julia was still an attractive woman. "Has Clarence told you about her trip to Guinea?"

"Yes. In great detail."

She waited. His prominent facial features had softened over the years, and he had one or two dark marks on his cheeks and forehead, but his bearing, his voice, and his green eyes were the same as when he was on Fernando Po. She remembered the long conversations that they used to have when they were young and how lucky she felt to consider him a good friend. She thought she knew him well, but she had later been very disappointed. How could he have lived with *that* all his life? She would not have been so shocked if it were Jacobo, but him? Yes, it was a shock.

"I burst into tears remembering." Her tone got harder. "I suppose it was the same for both of you."

Kilian nodded. "Do you remember, Julia, how irritated Manuel used to get at the laborers and the Bubis with their beliefs in the spirits?"

She nodded as a nostalgic smile appeared on her face.

"After so many years on the island, I became a little affected by it. I don't know how to explain it, but I have the feeling that one day everything will fall into place."

Julia pursed her lips. After a few seconds, she said, "I don't really understand what you mean, but I hope it's soon, Kilian. We're closer to the grave than anywhere else."

"I can assure you I've no intention of dying . . ." He saw that she gave him a look of disbelief, and he changed to a forced joking tone. "Until the moment arrives. Until then, promise me that you'll keep out of this."

"As if I hadn't done that all these years?" she retorted. She looked at her friend who, beside the car, pointed at her watch. "Sorry, but I have to go."

"One more thing, Julia. You once told me that sometimes things are as we would wish them to be. You told me to worm out the reason why I didn't want to go back to Pasolobino after my father's death. We made a deal. I would explain my reasons to you and you would tell me a secret, which you then avoided telling me."

Julia's eyes began to moisten. Was it possible that he remembered that conversation in such detail? How could she have told him, recently married as she was, that she still had feelings for Jacobo?

"I still don't agree with you, Julia. Most of the time, things are not the way we would like them to be."

Julia blinked hard to stop the tears from falling down her cheeks. She lowered her head and held on to the man's arm.

"When I said that, I was very young, Kilian. If only I could relive those years with the experience I have now . . ." She sighed deeply and walked away.

When Kilian came back to the square, everyone except his niece had gone home.

"Everything all right, Uncle?" Clarence asked. "I thought you were arguing."

"With Julia? That's impossible. You must have misinterpreted."

Something I've become an expert at, she thought.

Kilian held on to the young woman's arm to begin the walk back to the house while the colored flags fluttered above their heads.

Except for the burden of the memory of Iniko, which weighed on her heart, the hunch that Julia's doubt had opened a new line in her investigation, Kilian's downcast demeanor, and Jacobo's continuous foul mood, to Clarence the summer festival of 2003 felt the same as always.

She did not know then that the following year, one member of the family would be missing.

The insistent autumn wind from the north stripped the trees of their leaves with unusual aggression.

Carmen and Jacobo migrated down to Barmón and, unlike other years, spaced out their visits to the village more and more. Daniela had more work than normal in the health center and also enrolled in an online children's medicine course that kept her busy every afternoon. And Clarence, who, like the leaves on the trees, did not exactly find herself at the calmest moment in her life, immersed herself in preparations for a couple of research articles, her classes, and her doctoral courses, which would all be happening after Christmas.

On a gray November day, she received an e-mail from Laha letting her know he would be visiting his company's facilities in Madrid in the middle of December. Clarence let out a shout of joy and quickly answered, inviting him to spend the Christmas holidays in Pasolobino with her family. To her pleasure, Laha accepted delightedly.

Until the last minute, she dithered over revealing Laha's identity, but finally opted to tell her family that she had invited a *special* friend— she put a lot of emphasis on the word—an engineer she had met in Guinea, to spend the holidays in Pasolobino. If this was the sign she had been waiting for, she did not want to miss Jacobo's and Kilian's reactions.

Her mother was delighted with the idea—finally—of having a *special* friend of Clarence's enjoying her stews. Her father complained from the other end of the phone that he would have to put up with a stranger during the family Christmas holidays and suggested spending the holiday period in the flat in Barmón for the first time. Daniela became very curious to know exact details about the man who was probably the cause of her cousin's love problems. And Kilian came out of his daydreams to look at her with an indescribable expression in his eyes and said nothing, absolutely nothing. But after years of not smoking, he stretched out his hand to Clarence's packet of cigarettes, took one, leaned over one of the four Advent candles that Carmen had placed in the center of the table with a green pine wreath, and lit it.

And Clarence, she felt enormously happy—although nervous— with the possibility of having the brother of her unforgettable Iniko near her.

Or should she start thinking of Laha as her brother?

12

Báixo la Néu

In the Snow

The journey by train and coach from Madrid to Pasolobino was not comfortable, but at least it allowed him to get a sweeping view of the country that had so influenced his own.

Laha was really looking forward to seeing Clarence and her beautiful village, but he was especially anxious to spend a few days with a Spanish family. Without knowing it, his new friend had awoken surprising feelings of curiosity in him, which could even be described as slightly morbid. He would now have the chance to imagine how his life would have been if his white father had taken care of him. Why would it be so outlandish to assume that his father was Spanish and that somewhere, there lived people he shared blood with?

The fact that Laha was one of the many did not mean that he had taken the absence of a father figure well. Iniko, at least, could name his. Laha could not. When he was a boy, any lie would have consoled him. How many times had he dreamed that his father was an explorer devoured by a lion after a terrible fight or a man who had to leave on a secret mission? As he grew up and began to understand the reality, his questions became direct and incisive. He had tried to get his grandfather to tell him where he came from, but he only told him to ask his mother, who was inflexible and repeated to him hundreds of times that he was just Bisila's son.

He remembered having searched his mother's house, looking for some memory or clue. His fragile reward had been the fragment of a blurred photo of a white man leaning on a truck, along with the sparse images of Bisila's childhood. She never found out that he had removed this photo from the rest just long enough to make a copy that, since then, he always kept in his wallet. It was foolish, but for a long time, he had treated this faceless man as his father.

With the passing of time, Laha had managed to accept that his mother's story was no different from those of Mamá Sade and so many others and that his father had abandoned them without a guilty conscience. He was not the first nor the last, which was no consolation, but this made his interest in finding out who he was disappear. What was the point in looking for someone who did not care about his own child? Laha had forgotten about him and had happily gone on with his life.

. . . until Clarence appeared.

He looked at his watch. He had been on the bus for two hours, and it had just then taken a turn away from the lowlands toward the mountains. From fields covered in furrows, where the vines shrank in the cold, he passed almost without warning to a halfway zone of rolling hills, a reservoir, and towns and villages each time smaller in size. Little by little, the architecture changed. Instead of apartment blocks, he saw brick houses of no more than three or four stories, some old, some newer, and others with the crane ready to intervene. He got the impression that all those places had been transforming for years: they showed the cheerful aspect of all the small places that for centuries have been yearning for the arrival of civilization, with all its consequences.

However, when the bus began to travel along the last part of the route, Laha's heart shrank. The road became so narrow that he had the sensation that there was not enough space between the precipice over the river and the mountain to his right. For forty minutes, the bus fought against the sharp bends gouged from the rock of the narrow canyon before breaking into a new landscape.

What the hell had sent men from here to a place as different as Equatorial Guinea? Had it just been out of necessity or also because of a faint sensation of claustrophobia?

The valley in which Pasolobino was located was surrounded by enormous mountains whose foothills were covered in fields and forests with rocky crests. The small villages spread around the slopes and hillsides painted two pictures: the dark houses of stone, with steeply sloped roofs and robust chimneys, mixed with fresh new houses.

When it seemed as if there were no more mountains, the bus stopped in a town called Cerbeán. Laha finally arrived at his destination on Christmas Eve, on an afternoon when it snowed as much as it ever could. While the previous day had been calm and peaceful, flakes as big as hazelnuts now fell.

A woman wrapped up in an anorak, with a woolen hat, gloves, scarf, and a pair of high thick rubber-soled boots, waved her arm to get his attention. The only visible part of her body was her unmistakable smile. Laha felt a special joy on seeing his friend. He was certain he was going to have an unforgettable holiday.

Clarence thought that Laha looked wonderful. He wore a dark woolen coat, a scarf, and a brown pair of leather ankle boots that gave him the appearance of a city gent. They gave each other a friendly hug, which Clarence held a little longer, imagining Laha's arms were his brother's.

No, she said to herself. *Iniko was bigger.*

"You don't know how happy I am to see you." Clarence stepped away and gave him another smile. "I hope you don't mind the snow!"

"On Bioko, it doesn't stop raining for six months of the year." Laha chuckled. "I think I can put up with a little snow!"

Clarence drove along the path opened up by the snowplow on the steep, narrow, and winding road. During the drive to the House of Rabaltué, they brought each other up to date.

"How is your brother?" she asked offhand. She felt incapable of saying his name.

"Iniko goes on with his daily routine, his work, his children, his meetings . . . ," Laha responded. "When you left, he started brooding again. You know he's not very talkative."

He was very talkative with me, she thought. *And he laughed a lot.*

"He sends you his best regards."

As they approached, Clarence began to get nervous. She had told her family about Laha, but they did not know that he was the special guest for the Christmas holidays. How would they react?

"We're almost there," she announced in a high-pitched voice. "Get ready not to move from the dinner table until tomorrow afternoon! And I'll give you some basic advice. Hesitating when my mother offers you more food is the same as saying yes."

Inside the House of Rabaltué, Carmen opened and shut the oven door, waiting for that small sign that would tell her that the roast was perfect. Clarence had finally invited a friend to spend Christmas with them; Carmen had the firm intention of, after giving him a thorough going-over, making a good impression, starting with her culinary skills.

Kilian had been restless all day. He first blamed this restlessness on the unsettling calm that he felt, like just before a big snowstorm or a tornado. But this afternoon, he felt something different, something more intense and difficult to explain, as if a silent gust of wind were going right through him. He shivered.

He looked at Jacobo, who was showing unusual interest in the king's Christmas speech on the television. He still had not dared talk to him alone about the news and presents that Clarence had brought from Guinea, but Kilian knew that the memories had to be preoccupying his brother as much as him. They had spent so many years acting as if nothing had really happened. Neither of them wanted to risk breaking their pact of silence. But Jacobo must have realized that Clarence was suspicious. How much did she know? Could Bisila have told her something?

Jacobo turned, and his eyes met Kilian's. He frowned. Why was Kilian being so odd? Was it not his daughter who had chosen the holidays to introduce them to a special friend? Carmen was very excited, hoping the invitation meant that the relationship was serious. Jacobo had mixed feelings about the news. He did not feel like making a good impression on a stranger who might or might not end up being part of the family. It made him feel older than he already was, and he did not like that one bit. Ah well, it was the law of life. He was happy for his daughter, whom he loved more than anything else in the world. He promised himself to try and behave around the lad.

"Family!" The door opened and Clarence entered. "We're here!

"I'd like you to meet Fernando Laha. Everyone knows him as Laha, pronounced in low pitch and with the *h* sounding as an *x* . . ." She stepped to one side, swallowed hard, nervous, and concentrated on everyone's reaction, especially those of her father and uncle.

Everyone stopped what they were doing to welcome this tall and attractive man. He greeted them with a beaming smile and, in spite of being in a strange house, oozed confidence.

Carmen twisted her lips in a silent whistle of surprise. Jacobo jumped out of his seat, as if he had seen a ghost. Kilian remained still, looking at Laha very closely, and tears welled up in his eyes. Daniela dropped the box of golden stars that she had been decorating the tablecloth with. They scattered and turned the floor into a fleeting celestial mosaic as she hurried to gather them up, blushing at her clumsiness.

Carmen was the first to greet him. Laha handed her a box of chocolates.

"There is a shop in Madrid," he said in a confidential tone, "called Cacao Sampaka. It's got nothing to do with the plantation, but I've been told that they have the best chocolates in the world. I thought it would be a good opportunity to see if it's true."

Carmen thanked him while out of the corner of her eye, she saw her husband's face go paler and paler.

Jacobo tried to control himself. Fernando Laha? One of Bisila's children? This was the person his daughter had fallen in love with? It was not possible. In God's name! If Carmen knew! He cursed the bad luck that had put his daughter in contact with the only people on the whole island she shouldn't have met. Could Laha know what had happened with his mother? Kilian and he had managed to bury it. Then how was it possible that he noticed an expectant glow in his brother's eyes? Unless Kilian knew of the existence of this lad . . . and he had not said anything? Jacobo remembered the scrap of a letter that he had read many years ago, when he had been looking for a deed in the sitting room. He had not given it much thought then, but now it took on a whole new meaning. Clarence and Laha together? Jacobo shook his head. He did not yet know how, but he would make sure that his daughter did not get too involved with this man.

Laha went over to say hello, and Jacobo coldly shook his hand. Carmen went over to her daughter.

"He's very handsome, Clarence," she whispered, "but you should have warned us. Have you seen your father's face?"

Clarence did not answer, carefully watching Kilian and Laha. Her uncle took his hand affectionately between his enormous hands for several seconds, as if he wanted to make sure he was real, and did not stop looking into his eyes. So many years wondering what he looked like, and now he had the answer in front of him! Everything was starting to fit into place. He heard Jacobo mumbling under his breath.

Kilian let Laha's hand go and went over to his brother while Clarence introduced Daniela, who seemed to dither on the best way to greet the young man. She finally put out her hand, which Laha went to shake just when she got on tiptoes to give him two kisses. The scene ended in laughter.

Carmen interrupted to announce that the dinner would be ready in a few minutes. Clarence showed Laha to the guest room so he could unpack his bags. Soon after, when he entered the dining room, Clarence had just placed the box of chocolates in the center of the table beautifully decorated by Daniela. For the first time in that house, the name of Sampaka would be with them throughout the evening.

Everyone agreed that Carmen had prepared an unforgettable meal. The first course was Christmas soup, with tapioca and broth cooked for hours over a low heat, followed by eggs stuffed with foie gras on a bed of fine slivers of the best Spanish Jabugo ham accompanied by prawns and tender broad beans; for the third course, she surprised them with the finest roast lamb and sliced roasted potatoes they had had in years; and for dessert, she managed to get the island of beaten egg white to perfectly float on a lake of homemade custard.

With full stomachs and good wine coursing through their veins, the family had gotten over the initial slight tension of the introductions.

"Clarence told us many things about her trip to Guinea," said Kilian, reclining in his chair.

This movement indicated that the conversation was about to veer into more serious matters.

"We"—he gestured toward his brother—"were very pleased to get firsthand information after so many years. Nevertheless, given that you're here, I'd like you to tell us how things are going."

Kilian had made a big impression on Laha. He must be over seventy years old, but his energy had not left him. He gesticulated passionately when giving his opinions, and his smile was always frank. Jacobo resembled his brother physically, but there was something in his look that was off-putting. It was not exactly the speck, like a small thick spiderweb, in his left eye; it was that he did not look straight at Laha. He also kept out of the conversation, as if it did not interest him in the slightest.

Daniela and Clarence watched their fathers, confused. Something did not fit. It was Kilian who led with the stories. And Jacobo was grumpier than ever. Maybe they had both had too much wine.

"Actually," said Laha, "I don't know what to add to Clarence's report. I assume she told you that life isn't easy there. The country's lacking in infrastructure, good jobs, labor laws, progress in justice, in the administration, in sanitary conditions . . ."

As a nurse, Daniela was interested in the state of public health. In fact, she was becoming interested in everything Laha said and did. She began to understand why Clarence had suffered this man's absence in silence. But how could she have hidden this secret from her? If Daniela had fallen in love with someone like that, she would have announced it to the four corners. Was her cousin's love unrequited? She had not stopped looking at them since they arrived. Clarence treated him with exquisite deference, even a mutual understanding, and glanced from Laha to Jacobo continuously, as if she were waiting to see what impression the young man made on her father. Jacobo, for his part, did not look too pleased with his daughter's companion. Was it because of the color of his skin? *Poor Uncle Jacobo,* she thought. Surely such a thing had never occurred to him! Daniela bit her bottom lip. She was going too quickly. She saw Laha and Clarence very happy together, but she had yet to see any gesture that meant anything more than a good friendship. Or that's what she wanted to believe.

Laha criticized the lack of resources and qualified personnel not only in the larger-population medical centers, but also in the rural areas. The infant mortality rate had remained very high. Daniela listened, hanging on his every word. Laha was wearing a white shirt and had put on a tie. He had curly hair, with rebellious locks that fell over his forehead. His head tilted back when he laughed, and his eyes gleamed.

Daniela did not want Laha to stop talking to her. She felt a pang of guilt, but Clarence did not seem to mind Daniela hogging his attention.

"But how could a small country with so much oil still live with such conditions?"

Laha shrugged. "Bad management. If the production was properly programmed and controlled, the country would have one of the highest per capita incomes on the African continent."

"Clarence told us that most of it is due to the rivalry between Fang and Bubi," Carmen chimed in, her cheeks red from the wine.

Laha sighed. "I don't agree. You see, Carmen, I have many Fang friends who understand the unease of the Bubi population. But the Bubis aren't the only ones who are marginalized. There are many Fang not among the privileged members of the power circles. The race conflict is often used as an excuse. If a Bubi is detained or murdered, the family paints all Fang with the same brush. That is how race hatred is perpetuated. A hatred that is very convenient for the regime."

Kilian got up to refill the glasses. Suppressing a smile, Jacobo asked, "And what's this that Clarence was telling us, that there are still some asking for the island's independence?" He rubbed the scar on his left hand. "They weren't happy enough when they broke from Spain . . . now they want independence for the island itself?"

Clarence shot him a hard look, but Laha did not seem upset.

"There are also independence groups here, yes? On Bioko, the independence movement can't even get recognition as a political party.

Even though they defend nonviolence and the right to freely debate ideas and opinions, as in any democracy."

A small silence followed, broken by Daniela. Clarence was surprised at how talkative she was.

"I suppose it'll be a question of time. Things don't change overnight. Clarence told us that she saw many things being built and that the university was not as bad as she had thought it would be . . . That's a good sign, isn't it?"

Laha turned to her. Daniela looked very young, definitely younger than Clarence. She was wearing a black dress with straps and had her shoulders covered with a woolen sweater. She had gathered up her light-brown hair in a small bun above her neck. Her skin was very white, almost porcelain, and she had expressive eyes that he had been staring at all night. Daniela blinked, looking away toward the table, then focused on the box of chocolates and spent a few seconds choosing her favorite. Laha noticed that she left it there, slowly taking her hand away so that nobody would notice that she had just gotten nervous.

"Yes, Daniela." Laha continued to look at her. "You're completely right. It has to start somewhere. Maybe, one day—"

"Listen!" interrupted Carmen, in a lilting voice. "Tonight is Christmas Eve! You have plenty of days to solve Guinea's problems, but now we are going to talk about more cheerful things. Laha, would you like more custard?"

Laha hesitated while rubbing his eyebrow, and Clarence burst out laughing.

The same scene repeated itself the following day, only the menu and the conversation were different. Everyone had gotten up late, except Carmen, who once more deployed all her talents and surprised everybody with a marvelous Christmas meal with an enormous turkey stuffed with nuts. The skies had granted them a brief respite before snowing again, and almost half a meter accumulated on the roofs and the streets, making it difficult to get out for a walk. Clarence, Daniela, and Laha helped in the kitchen and laid the table. Jacobo and Kilian turned up, listened to the conversation between the women and the guest, and disappeared. The house was so big that there were many places to hide with memories.

Carmen asked Laha about Christmas at home. Laha asked which home, African or American. Carmen said she could imagine the American one from the films, so she was more interested in his African one. Laha began to laugh, and Daniela sneaked a glance at him.

Despite her constant worry about Laha's identity, Clarence felt happy. She liked this time of year, with the fire always burning, the white landscape, the lights decorating the streets, the children hiding under their caps, and the kitchen full of dishes, pots, and pans filled with one thing or another.

The kitchen was very big, and even so, Daniela and Laha always seemed to pick the same time to go for the door, bumping into each other and apologizing.

Laha told Carmen that Christmas in Pasolobino was the real Christmas. In Guinea, it was the dry season, and people most liked cooling down in the shower—those who had a shower—or in the rivers and in the sea. There were Christmas lights in the cities that sometimes went out because of power cuts, but the villages remained dark. It seemed strange to see decorations and hear carols in such heat, but you did see and hear them. The children were not bombarded with advertisements for toys, as no one gave or got presents. Finally, people drank to celebrate the holidays; he did not know if quite as much as in the House of Rabaltué—the women laughed—as alcohol was cheap and people drank in the streets in short sleeves.

Laha had brought presents for everyone and asked when it would be a good time to give them out. Carmen smiled. The more she got to know this young man, the more she liked him. She would not mind having him as a son-in-law. Daniela wondered what he could have brought her. She was left with no choice but to wait until dessert to find out.

When the family exchanged gifts, the women received perfume, rings, and new purses. Jacobo got a sweater. Kilian, a leather wallet. Then it was Laha's turn to give out his presents. He had brought Carmen three books, one on the customs and traditions of home, an anthology of Guinean literature, and a small recipe book. For Jacobo, some films that a Spanish director had taken on Fernando Po between 1940 and 1950 and that Laha had gotten in Madrid. For Clarence, music from Guinean bands that had recorded albums in Spain. And for Daniela, sitting beside him, a gorgeous shawl that he delicately placed on her shoulders. Daniela did not take it off all afternoon, not even when clearing the table, because Laha had touched it.

Last, Laha handed over a small packet to Kilian, sitting at the head of the table. Before it was opened, he said, "I ran out of ideas. I asked my mother for advice and . . . I hope you like it!"

Kilian unwrapped the packet and took out a small wooden object in the shape of a rectangular bell from which hung not one but several clappers.

"It's an . . . ," Laha began to explain.

". . . *elëbó*," Kilian finished the sentence in a hoarse voice. "It's a traditional bell used to ward away the evil spirits."

Everyone raised their eyebrows. Clarence rested her chin in her hand. What had Simón said in Sampaka about the instrument? He said that if the eyes did not give her the answer, she should go and find an *elëbó*. Where should she look for it? First the pith helmet, and now that bell . . . Why had Bisila suggested to Laha to buy Kilian precisely that present? As far as she knew, Simón and Bisila were not in contact.

"Thank you very much," her uncle added, pale. "I appreciate it more than you can possibly imagine."

Daniela picked up the object and looked at it closely.

"Where have I seen this before?" she asked, frowning. "It reminds me of . . ."

"Daniela, Daughter," Kilian brusquely interrupted. "Where are those excellent chocolates we ate last night?"

Daniela got up, forgetting her question.

"Lately," Carmen said, "this house has been getting some very unusual presents."

Laha tilted his head slightly.

"She's talking about a pith helmet that your mother asked Iniko to give me," explained Clarence.

"A helmet?" Laha gave her a puzzled look. He did not remember ever having seen that in his life. He turned to Kilian. "Where could she have kept it? When I was seven or eight, Macías ordered all houses searched to destroy any object associated with the Spanish colonial period."

Kilian blinked. "Something similar happened here. With the Francoist law on confidential documents, it was forbidden to speak about or give out information on Equatorial Guinea until the end of the 1970s. It was like a dream, as if it had never existed. It was impossible to know anything about the nightmare going on."

"Was it that bad, Laha?" asked Carmen sweetly.

"Fortunately, I was a child," Laha responded. "But yes, it was terrible. There were the repressions, accusations, detentions, and the deaths of hundreds of people. I could give you specific examples of how crazy the man was."

Daniela sat down beside him.

"Macías couldn't stand the idea that anyone was better qualified than he, so he attacked those who overshadowed him intellectually. Possession of the *Geography and History of Equatorial Guinea* textbook from the Sacred Heart fathers was punishable by death. In its place, he imposed a compulsory textbook that insulted Spain, even as he sought out economic aid. Pamphlets appeared saying he was a murderer, and all typewriters were confiscated. He ordered all books burned. He ordered all scholarship students in Spain to return, and when they did, some of them were murdered. Use of the word *intellectual* was forbidden. He organized the invasion of the island by the continental Fang Guineans. They were young and uneducated, coming from the deepest part of Guinea, and he supplied them with arms. He shut down the press. He forbade both Catholicism and the visits to our Great Morimò in the Moka Valley." Laha rubbed his eyes. "Well, what do you expect from a man who publicly praised Hitler?"

Everyone fell silent.

Daniela poured more wine into Laha's glass.

"But, Laha," Jacobo began to say, "wasn't Macías democratically elected?"

"He was always on the television," mused Kilian. "He was very popular because he knew how to take in the people by using liberation talk. He promised to return to the blacks what belonged to the blacks."

Laha cleared his throat. "The Spanish trusted the wrong person when leaving the island in his hands. He had learned the pruning technique very well . . ."

"And how long did that horror last?" asked Daniela, who looked at him with eyes open in indignation.

"Eleven years," Laha answered. "From 1968 to 1979."

"The year I was born," murmured Daniela.

Laha quickly did the math in his head. Daniela was younger than he had thought.

"Do you know, Daniela, that the terror he awoke among the natives was so bad that no Guinean soldier dared join his firing squad? They had to use Moroccan soldiers to shoot him." He moved closer and lowered his voice. "The legend also says that he murdered the ex-lovers of one of his women and that, when they were going to shoot him, he placed his outstretched arms behind him, palms facing toward the ground, prepared to fly . . ."

Daniela gave a start, and Laha smiled impishly.

Clarence remembered very well where conversations about the spirits could lead to, and she raised her hand to her neck to stroke the necklace that Iniko had given her.

"Well, everyone," she cheerfully said. "Laha has yet to open his presents."

She handed him a woolen hat with matching gloves and then a copy of a recently edited book titled *Guinea in Pasolobinese*.

"It's a book written by someone from our valley," Clarence explained, "about the people from here who lived for years in Guinea during the colonial period. Sure, it only gives one side of the story, the white side, but well, it could be interesting to know the context . . ." She began to think that maybe it had not been such a good idea to give him the book. "And there are photos of Kilian and Jacobo in it!"

Laha helped her. "Of course I find it interesting, Clarence!" he said, with a smile. "You can't deny what happened."

He opened the book and began to turn the pages, closely looking at the photographs. In them, he saw white men dressed in white cotton and linen clothes, with their inseparable pith helmets and, in many cases, holding a rifle. He also saw black men in worn clothes working on the plantations. When the black men were posing for the photographer, they were often sitting at the feet of the white men, and it was not uncommon to see a white man's hand resting on the head of a black. *As if he were a dog,* Laha thought in disgust. There were also photos of men holding up large boa skins. He tried to rack his brain for early childhood memories, but he did not find anything he saw in the photos. Either he had not been born, or he had been very young when the last photos had been taken. Maybe Iniko would recognize some of those shots.

Kilian and Jacobo also made comments about the emblematic buildings in colonial Santa Isabel, like the Casa Mallo, on the old Avenida Alfonso XIII, and the cars of that period and the names of the ships: *Plus Ultra, Dómine, Ciudad de Cádiz, Fernando Poo, Ciudad de Sevilla* . . . Kilian took a breath on hearing this last name. How many times had he thought that the life of that ship had run parallel to his own! The luxurious and elegant flagship of Trasmediterránea, after traveling half the world, was partially scrapped in the middle of the 1970s. Then it was refitted, and one day it was found drifting near the port of Palma, in danger of breaking in two. Later, it suffered two big fires and had to be fitted out once again . . . But despite everything, after seventy-six years in existence, it was still out there.

When there were no more photos to comment on, Kilian shook his head and sighed. "How times have changed! It doesn't feel as if so many years have gone by since we were in Fernando Po."

Jacobo nodded. "And from what Clarence and Laha say, it doesn't seem to have changed for the better."

Laha arched an eyebrow. "What do you mean?" he asked.

Jacobo took a sip of coffee, cleaned his lips with a napkin, put his hands on the table, and looked seriously at Laha.

"In our time, around fifty thousand tons of cocoa used to leave the island, and from Sampaka alone, six hundred thousand kilos, thanks to us. And now, how much?" He looked at his brother. "Three thousand five hundred kilos? Everyone knows that since we left, the country hasn't gotten its head above water." He spoke to Laha directly. "You live worse now than forty years ago. Is that true or not?"

"Jacobo," Laha answered in a level tone, "Guinea is a newly independent country that is trying to improve after centuries of oppression."

"What do you mean, oppression?" Jacobo leaned forward. "Didn't we bring you our knowledge and culture? You should be thankful that we took you out of the jungle . . ."

"Dad!" exclaimed Clarence, furious, as Carmen put an arm on her husband's thigh to quiet him.

"Two things, Jacobo." Laha sat back in his chair, his voice no longer calm. "One, we assimilated your culture because we had no choice. And two, unlike other Spanish colonizations, the conquistadors of Guinea only got involved enough to mix their blood with the conquered. That's how inferior they considered us to be!"

Kilian observed both of them silently.

Jacobo opened his mouth to counter him, but Laha raised his hands. "Don't give me lectures on colonization, Jacobo. The color of my skin makes it obvious that my father was white. It could be either of you!"

An uncomfortable silence ensued.

Clarence hung her head, and her eyes filled with tears. If there was any remote possibility that Laha was her half brother, he could not have had a worse meeting with his biological father. Jacobo's attitude was unforgivable. Why couldn't he be like Kilian?

Daniela rested her arm on Laha's shoulder. Laha turned and looked at her sadly. His soul was wounded, and it was not something he normally talked about.

"It's a difficult subject," said Daniela in a warm voice. "Even now, although we don't realize it, we are all being colonized, in subtle ways, by networks woven by economic, political, cultural interests . . . It's a different time."

That was Daniela, thought Clarence. She never got agitated. She always tried to express herself in the same tone of voice, sweet, quiet, rational.

"I'm sorry for getting worked up," said Laha, looking at Carmen, who waved her hand and smiled. She was more than used to heated discussions.

Daniela took the spoon out of her cup, clinked it against the edge a few times to get the last drops of coffee off the metal, took a sip, and frowned. "For me, colonization is like the rape of a woman. And if the woman resists, the rapist has the cheek to say that the woman was not serious, that deep down she was enjoying it, and he was doing it for her own good."

Everyone froze. Daniela hung her head, a little embarrassed by her frankness.

Clarence got up and began to clear the plates from the table. Jacobo brusquely asked for another coffee. Kilian tapped his fingers on the table. Carmen began to flick through the recipe book that Laha had given her, and she asked him a couple of questions.

"Good," Kilian said at last. "It's Christmas. Let's drop the hard topics." He turned to Laha. "Tell us, how did someone from Bioko end up in California?"

"I think it was my grandfather's fault," he said thoughtfully, cupping his chin in his right hand. "He was insistent that his descendants focus on their studies. He always said the same thing, over and over. My brother, Iniko, used to get very annoyed. He took his own meaning out of it." He wagged his index finger in the air as he mimicked the voice of an old man. "'The most intelligent thing that I've ever heard a white man say, a good friend of mine, is that the biggest difference between a Bubi and a white man is that a Bubi lets the cocoa tree grow wild, but the white man prunes it to get more out of it.'"

Kilian choked on a piece of nougat.

The twenty-sixth of December dawned to a clear sky and a bright sun that blinded when reflected off the snow. After two days shut up in the house with nothing else to do but eat, Laha, Clarence, and Daniela were finally able to go to the ski slopes.

The girls had been able to get a ski suit for Laha, who felt ridiculous and clumsy in the rigid boots. Daniela gave him the basic instructions on how to walk on frozen snow and made sure she was close to him in case he fell. Beside him, she looked smaller. When they had managed to get the skis on him, Laha did not stop looking at her, terrified and holding on to her shoulders while she held on to his waist.

Clarence watched them, amused.

They made a good couple.

Her cousin was concentrated on giving the proper instructions. Laha tried to have confidence in her, but his brain went one way and his body the other.

After suffering through the first few runs, Laha decided he needed a coffee. Daniela went with him while Clarence took the chance to go down some of the pistes from higher up the mountain. She got onto the ski lift, almost grateful for the chance to be alone with the snowscape. As she went up the mountain, she noticed how the silence absorbed the voices and laughs of the skiers and calmed her mood. The brilliant white slope below her, the reflection of the nearby summits, the increasing cold on her cheeks, and the slight rocking of the lift gave her a sense of sluggishness, of vertigo, of unreality.

During these moments of drowsiness, her mind filled with fragments of conversation and images like the pieces of a jigsaw puzzle. She found it hard to believe that Jacobo would have fallen in love with Bisila and then abandoned her with a small child. If it were true, her uncle Kilian must have been complicit. How could they have kept such an enormous secret? Was the moment of truth finally approaching? Was that why she was so nervous?

The only way to free the tightness in her chest was to ski down the hardest slope at top speed, pushing her body to the limit, while the other two, completely oblivious to her suspicions, relaxed in the cafeteria.

Laha felt happy talking to Daniela. He liked being with her. He liked how she held her cup with both hands to warm herself and how she blew on the white coffee to cool it down. As Daniela talked, her expressive eyes went from the coffee to him, to those at the table beside them, to those taking off their skis at the door of the cafeteria, and to what was happening at the bar. Laha deduced that it was not nervousness, but an ability to observe and analyze. How different she was from her cousin, he thought. Apart from being shorter and slimmer, Daniela seemed much more easygoing and rational than Clarence. She shared Carmen's impulse to make those around her feel well—which he especially appreciated. Maybe for that reason he had not felt like a stranger for one moment since his arrival in Pasolobino. What was happening to him? He had just met her!

"You're very quiet," Daniela commented. "Has your first time skiing left you that wrecked?"

"It seems that it is not my forte!" Laha answered sadly. "And frankly"—he lowered his voice—"I don't really understand what all the fuss is about. The boots are so tight that the blood can't reach my feet!"

"Don't exaggerate!" Daniela gave a big laugh, and her face lit up.

"Would you like another coffee?" he asked, getting to his feet.

"Do you think you'll be able to walk to the bar?"

Laha made as if he were concentrating on the difficult task of slowly putting one foot in front of the other, and Daniela, amused, followed him with her eyes. She felt very comfortable with Laha, *too* comfortable. She bit her lip. It was Clarence who should be with Laha rather than she. Then why had she left them alone? Her cousin had her confused. She and Laha behaved like two good friends, maybe especially close friends, but they had not held each other's hand, nor looked with passion at each other. And if Clarence was in love with Laha and his feelings were not the same as hers? It was difficult for her to believe that someone like him would have accepted the invitation to share a few days with her family. It was also possible that he did not know and that Clarence was waiting for the right moment . . . Whatever way you looked at it, the situation got more complicated. It was the first time in Daniela's life that her knees felt like rubber, thousands of butterflies fluttered in her stomach, and a constant hot flush was on her cheeks. Not good.

Laha brushed against her shoulder when he leaned down to leave the cup in front of her. He sat down, stirred the coffee with the spoon to dissolve the sugar, and asked her directly, "Do you like living in Pasolobino, Daniela?"

"Yes, of course." A slight hesitation had preceded her answer. "Here I have my work and my family. And as you can see, it is a beautiful spot." If Laha did not stop staring at her, she would end up blushing. "And you, where do you feel you're from?"

"I don't know how to put it." Laha sat back and rested his chin in one of his hands. "I really do suffer an identity crisis. I'm Bubi, Equatorial Guinean, African, a bit Spanish, European by an unknown father, and an adopted American."

Daniela was sorry that this confession had brought on a thin veil of sadness.

"Maybe in your heart you feel one option stands out above the rest," she said.

He looked outside and recovered his cheerful attitude. "Look, Daniela." He tilted his head slightly. "How is a black man meant to feel surrounded by so much white?" He stretched out his hand to point toward the snow. "Well, gray."

"You're not gray!" exclaimed Daniela, raising her voice.

"Who isn't gray?" asked a red-faced Clarence, sitting down beside her cousin.

They looked at the clock and realized that they had been talking for over an hour. For the first time in her life, Daniela lamented the presence of her cousin.

Since neither of them answered, Clarence said, "Well, Laha. Are you prepared to make a second go of it?"

Laha gave a pained expression and put out his arm to take Daniela's hand. "No, please!" he begged her. "Don't let her torture me anymore."

Daniela squeezed his fingers in hers. Laha had large, thin hands. You could see that they had not seen much physical work.

"Don't you worry," she said, looking directly into his eyes. "I'll look after you."

Clarence arched her left eyebrow.

Well, well, thought Clarence as she walked toward the exit. *Is it my imagination, or are my darling cousin's eyes gleaming each time they meet Laha's? What mischievous spirits! Perhaps they have reserved Laha for Daniela?*

Suddenly, something unexpected happened.

Laha, walking clumsily in his boots, did not judge the height of the step between the building and the snow correctly. He slipped and had time only to grab on to Clarence, who, on turning to help him, fell on her back to the floor.

Laha collapsed on top of her.

With all the sunlight of that radiant day concentrated in one shaft of light on the eyes of her friend, his face a few centimeters from hers, Clarence's stomach jumped. She no longer had any doubts . . .

What had Simón said on the Sampaka plantation?

He had recognized her from her eyes, the same as the men in her family, which from a distance appeared green, but up close were gray . . .

In that same instant, Clarence recognized in Laha's eyes her own, and Kilian's, and Jacobo's. Up to that very moment, she could have sworn they were green. But at this distance, she could clearly make out the dark little lines of the iris that made them a deep gray. Laha had inherited the family eyes!

She felt like crying with relief, happiness, and fear for what she had finally discovered.

And now that she knew it was Laha—and not another—whom she had gone to find on Bioko, in some part of her heart, she let surface her shame as the daughter of someone who had abandoned his own child and denied him the right to his space, beside hers, on the house's family tree.

13

Boms de Llum

Wells of Light

"Are you sure you don't want to come?" Daniela zipped up her anorak.

"My head still hurts a bit," Clarence answered, resting her book on her lap.

Laha looked at her, distraught. "You don't know how sorry I am about the fall."

Daniela frowned. She hoped it was just the bumps and bruises making Clarence reluctant to join their drive, but she doubted it. When Clarence and Laha were on the ground, their faces so close together, Daniela had felt a sudden twinge of jealousy. Laha and Clarence had held each other's gaze for much longer than necessary. And her cousin still seemed dazed.

There were voices and laughing coming from the kitchen. Clarence rolled her eyes.

"I'd go out the back door."

"I'm surprised they took so long . . . ," Daniela remarked.

Laha opened his mouth to ask what they meant, but Daniela made a gesture for him to hush. They could clearly hear the neighbors interrogating Carmen about Laha.

Daniela pulled Laha's arm. "We'd better go," she whispered. "Don't make a sound. Bye, Clarence."

Laha swallowed a laugh and, on tiptoe, followed Daniela. Clarence tried in vain to focus on her book again, but the neighbors' nosy questions continued. How would the neighbors of Pasolobino have reacted if her father had brought his African son home decades ago? And now . . . what would happen when they found out he *was* another member of the family?

Fernando Laha of the House of Rabaltué.

Clarence sighed.

She felt incapable of looking him in the eye for fear that he would guess her torment. She felt incapable of explaining something that was still perhaps nothing more than a coincidence. How was she going to ask her father? If it was not true, she would both insult Jacobo and wound Laha with false hopes. And if it was true, she could not imagine how she was going to get confirmation.

And to top it all, those two, Laha and Daniela, seemed to be getting on like a house on fire. She remembered Daniela's joke about the papal bull that was needed in times past to marry a cousin . . .

Her heart gave a start.

What was she thinking? Daniela was the first person she should have shared her suspicions with! She should know! Her silence was allowing the blossoming of . . .

She closed her eyes, and her mind wandered to a beach passionately bathed in cyan waters. A man and a woman lay on the sand, enjoying each other's bodies, oblivious to the hundreds of turtles who veered around them. In the distance, the songs of the birds and the chattering of the colored parrots could be heard, insistently repeating that what was an intensely clear blue was not the sea, but the sky, that what was white was a blanket of snow covering the meadows, that the turtles were not turtles but enormous rocks, and that the bodies that desired caresses were not those of Clarence and Iniko, but others.

The sun trail got its name from the dozen villages that had been built over the centuries on the highest part of the mountain's southern slope, which was bathed in sun from the first rays of dawn to the last at dusk. The houses of each village had been laid out in tiers so that all could enjoy the king of light, a precious gift in such a cold place.

The narrow, battered road started at the valley's main road, twisted round the slope until it reached the first village, cut a straight scar along the mountain, and wound back down to the last bend, the tightest one of all, tossing travelers back onto the main road again.

During the journey, it was possible to feel as though time had stood still. Laha marveled at the Romanesque churches, the emblazoned gates, the houses with arched entryways and porticoes with crosses carved in stone. He found it incredible that, a few kilometers away, the tourist maelstrom was in full flow.

"I didn't think so many people lived in these villages," Laha commented.

"Many of the houses are second homes refurbished by the descendants of the original owners," Daniela explained. "I call them the prodigal sons."

"And why's that?"

"Because when they visit, they insist on finding out about recent changes, then hold meetings to suggest ideas or protest what's been done. As the days pass and the end of the holidays get closer, their energies weaken until they file back toward the city. And so on until the next holidays."

Laha remained thoughtful. Daniela's words had had an impact on him.

"I'm one of them as well," he murmured with a heavy heart.

Whenever he got to Bioko, the first thing he did was talk to his brother about the latest events. Then he would leave for California and his comfortable life. From far away, he sometimes had the feeling that Iniko judged him for not staying to help build their country.

Daniela stopped her Renault Mégane in a small square almost completely surrounded by pretty little houses with doors and timbers stained in dark colors. She looked at her watch and saw that there was still a good bit of time before night fell.

"In the upper part, there is a beautiful hermitage." She pointed to a narrow paved alleyway that went up toward the forest and signaled him to follow her. "It's abandoned, but it's worth a visit."

While Laha prowled around the ruins, she contemplated the snowy landscape. After a while, he called to her, like a child who had just discovered treasure.

"I don't believe it!" He took her arm and hurried to the interior of the hermitage. "Look!" He pointed to a stone carved with a date.

Daniela did not understand. "Yes," she confirmed. "Fourteen hundred and seventy-one."

"It's the oldest thing that I've touched in my life!" Daniela did not seem very impressed, so he added, "This is the year that the Portuguese Fernão do Po discovered the island of Bioko. Do you see? As a mason carved his stone, a sailor discovered an island! And now you and I are here, more than five hundred years later, joined by destiny! If that man had not discovered the island, we wouldn't be here at this moment!"

"What a way of summarizing history!" Daniela exclaimed, flattered to know that Laha felt euphoric in her company. "You've only left out saying that destiny has brought us together."

Laha came closer. He held out his hand toward her and moved away a copper-colored lock that partially hid her face. Daniela jumped due to his unexpected touch.

"And why not?" he said hoarsely.

At dusk on a calm, clear, and cold winter's day, inside an ancient hermitage, awash in an intense ray of sunlight that filtered through a chink in the wall, Laha leaned toward Daniela and kissed her.

All of her senses, which up to a few seconds before had been frozen by the snow, woke, startled, as his lips settled on hers, gently at first and then harder. She concentrated all her attention on those warm lips, full of sweetness. She parted her mouth so he could taste her, and their tongues brushed against each other with the promise of a deeper encounter, so their breaths could fuse in a single ardent mist.

She raised her arms to circle Laha's neck. The kiss lasted until the ray of sunlight faded and then disappeared. Laha moved away a few centimeters and gazed into her eyes.

"I'm happy," he said with faltering breath, "that I was unable to stop myself."

She moistened her lips and blinked, still shaken by his intensity, and gently pushed him back so he could rest against the altar stone.

"I'm also happy," she said, pressing her body against his and gripping the lapels of his coat. "I'm sorry about only one thing."

Laha arched his eyebrows.

"I'm sorry," she continued, giving him a sensual look, "we are not closer to a hotel room . . ."

Laha smiled, relieved. "Let's find one," he suggested, holding her more tightly in his arms. Daniela fit into them perfectly. He felt like an impatient twenty-year-old. *Why haven't I met her before?*

"I can't do that!" she exclaimed. "Tomorrow the whole valley would know . . ."

"We haven't done anything yet, and you're already ashamed of me?" he asked, loosening his hug and feigning annoyance.

"Don't be silly!" Daniela threw her arms around his neck. "For the moment, we'll have to settle for this."

Laha tightened his arms around her again and began to nibble her neck.

"With this?" he murmured.

"Yes."

Laha got his hands under Daniela's layers of clothes and delicately caressed her back.

"And this?"

"Yes, and that as well."

Daniela slid her fingers through Laha's hair and put her head back to allow more space for his lips along her neck, her throat, her cheeks, and her temples before returning to her lips. After a few delightful minutes, she sighed in resignation.

"How about calling home and telling them not to wait on us for dinner?" she suggested. She wanted to make the most of their time alone, though she felt a little guilty when she thought about Clarence. "Where we parked, there is a very good restaurant."

They went back to the square, which opened like a balcony onto the slope of a hill, and stopped to watch the moon rise and glisten on the snow. Daniela moved closer to Laha to feel his heat. It would be a wonderful night. Every second spent with him made her more convinced that she had finally found her place in the world. Laha held her in his arms and breathed deeply. The village was silent, and the lampposts were weak. Beside this woman, solitude and darkness did not exist. He leaned down and kissed her again.

Daniela groggily separated herself. Just then, she heard the sound of a car engine and, instinctively, moved away from Laha. A Volvo parked just beside their car, and someone called her name.

"What a coincidence!" Julia walked over, followed by a friend.

"Julia!" Daniela slowly gave her two kisses. "What are you doing here at this time of year? Don't you normally stay in Madrid?"

Julia shot a quick glance at Laha. "One of my sons decided to spend New Year's Eve here and encouraged us to come."

The woman came over. Her blond hair was so light it looked white.

"Ascensión, this is Kilian's daughter." Ascensión opened her eyes wide, and Julia explained, "Ascensión and I have been friends since Guinea. She married Mateo, one of your father's old friends. He died a few months ago."

"I'm sorry to hear that," Daniela said, and gave her two kisses as well.

"Thank you," said Ascensión, her blue eyes blurred with tears. "Every year Mateo and I talked about coming up to the valley of Pasolobino, but for one reason or another, we never did."

"I convinced her to spend a few days with me, to see if it would cheer her up a bit."

Daniela noticed that Julia kept sneaking looks at Laha. She silently cursed her luck. She did not want anything to break the night's spell.

Laha came over and greeted the women.

"So both of you lived in my country?" he asked with a friendly smile.

Ascensión nodded, pressing her lips together to stop herself from crying. Julia half closed her eyes.

"Laha . . . ," she murmured.

"Yes," said Daniela. The last thing she wanted was another drawn-out conversation about Guinea. "He's spending a few days with us. Clarence met him on her trip."

"Yes, she told me." Julia felt a tightness in her chest. She fidgeted with her gloves. "She met your family, Laha, Iniko and Bisila . . ." She immediately regretted being so explicit.

"Isn't Bisila . . . ," Ascensión began, raising her eyebrow.

". . . an unusual name?" Julia completed the question. "And where is Clarence?"

"She wasn't feeling well."

"Ah."

Julia could not stop looking at Laha. His thick hair, his wide forehead, his firm jaw, his rounded chin, his eyes . . . It was him. As

clear as the snow that covered the fields. Clarence had found him, but
was she sure? She looked at Daniela. The girl's cheeks were reddened,
and she had a special gleam in her big brown eyes. Would she know?

A brief silence ensued.

"And are you here sightseeing?" Daniela asked, just to say something.

"We have a reservation in the restaurant." Julia pointed to the
building behind her and looked at Laha. "I hope you enjoy your stay
in our valley."

Laha gave her a roguish smile and looked at Daniela out of the
corner of his eye. "I can assure you that I will."

Daniela bit her bottom lip to stop from laughing.

They watched the women enter the restaurant. Daniela took the
car keys from her bag.

"But weren't we going to have dinner there as well?" Laha asked.

"It's just that I've thought of a better place," she replied.

With Julia and Ascensión there, she would not be able to even
brush the tips of her fingers against Laha without them noticing. Her
dream restaurant suddenly seemed small and stuffy.

Julia found the perfect excuse to visit the House of Rabaltué the
following day.

"They are organizing a reunion of old friends of Fernando Po in
Madrid at Easter," she announced. "From our group, Manuel and
Mateo will be missing, but it could be very nice. You should come."
She turned to Carmen. "You too, of course."

"Too many memories . . . ," said Jacobo before addressing his
brother. "Would you like to go?"

Kilian shrugged. "We'll see."

"Are their children also invited?" Clarence asked.

"Of course, but you'd get bored, Clarence," said Ascensión. "What
would you do with a load of old codgers reminiscing over their youth?"

"Oh, I love finding out things about my father's past."

Daniela had tuned out from the conversation a while ago. Almost all that afternoon's questions had begun with a *Do you remember* . . . and ended in a deep sigh. Both Ascensión and Julia reached for their hankies on several occasions, while Jacobo and Kilian pursed their lips and slowly bobbed their heads. Daniela wondered how Carmen could put up with anecdote after anecdote of a past she did not share, but there she was, with a pleasant smile fixed on her face. The same as Clarence, who did not miss the smallest detail. Daniela was convinced that if she had a pen in hand, her cousin would be taking notes. Daniela yawned and fixed her eyes on the flames. There was nothing left of the pile of logs that Kilian had prepared, and nobody seemed to be in any rush.

She looked up, and her eyes met Laha's. A pleasurable shiver ran through her, and she decided to take the chance to escape. Would Laha get the message?

"I'm going to go and fetch some wood before the fire goes out," she said, getting to her feet.

"Do you need help?"

She smiled and nodded.

As soon as they entered the small woodshed, Laha's kisses made her forget the boredom of the last couple of hours. For the moment, they would have to make do with those fleeting encounters.

Inside the house, Clarence took mental note of everything. She was just as interested in what they said as in what they did not say. Julia had not stopped glancing from Jacobo to Laha and back again. Perhaps she was comparing them? And now that Laha had gone out, the woman's attention continued to focus on Jacobo, as if there were nobody else in the room. She even thought she had seen her mother frowning on a couple of occasions.

"Ascensión . . ." Clarence decided to steer the conversation. "What was the thing that you most hated leaving behind?"

"Oh dear. Everything. The color, the heat, the freedom . . . I noticed a big change when we came back to Spain." Ascensión smiled for the first time that day. "I remember sometimes, I was just talking normally about how . . . well, how the coloreds lived, and many in our circle of friends looked at me in shock. Afterward, Mateo told me off for being so open."

"They must have thought we had grown up in the jungle." Julia laughed.

"I suppose it was hard"—Clarence coughed—"to say good-bye to so many friends."

Julia peered at Clarence. She was still searching . . . Julia saw Kilian and Jacobo shoot a quick glance at each other. They had yet to reveal Laha's identity. She hoped that Ascensión was careful with her answers. The previous night it had taken Julia a lot of effort to make little of the fact that one of Bisila's sons was staying in Kilian and Jacobo's house. She put it down to coincidence, but she was not sure she had convinced her.

"In fact, our friends were foreigners like ourselves," Ascensión was saying. "Although I have asked myself once or twice what ever became of our cook and her family."

Clarence decided to divert the question to the men in her most innocent voice. "And you? Did either of you miss anyone when you left? Anyone special?"

Kilian took a thin metal poker and stoked the embers. Jacobo looked at Carmen, smiled weakly, and answered, "As Ascensión has said, our real friends were all whites. Well, of course I've sometimes wondered about the *wachimán* Yeremías, or about Simón, who you met, or about one or another of the laborers . . . I suppose you're the same, right, Kilian?"

Kilian made a small movement with his head.

And Bisila, Dad? thought Clarence. *You never thought about her?*

The door opened, and Laha and Daniela entered, each of them carrying several logs. Clarence noticed that her cousin's cheeks were red and her lips slightly swollen.

"It's freezing cold!" exclaimed Daniela in answer to Clarence's scrutinizing gaze. "And the north wind is getting up."

Julia looked at her watch.

"We'd better go. It's quite late."

Carmen politely insisted that they stay a little longer. It was clear that she had not enjoyed the conversation at all.

Kilian, Jacobo, and Clarence accompanied them to the car. Clarence took Julia's arm, and they walked behind the others.

"Tell me one thing, Julia." Julia grew tense. "How do you think my father is looking?"

"How . . . what?" asked Julia in surprise. "Well, I don't know, Clarence . . . How would you be, in such a complicated situation?"

Clarence looked for an answer to Julia's question. How would she feel if she had abandoned a child thousands of kilometers away and, more than thirty years later, she saw herself forced to spend a few days with him under the same roof? Nervous, bad tempered, irritated, restless, and tetchy.

Exactly what Jacobo had been like since Laha had arrived in Pasolobino.

A strong and sudden gust of wind violently pushed them backward. Julia thought of a night when the unleashed force of a tornado drowned out the laments of a tragic event. She remembered Manuel's downcast face when she told him the news and his shock on hearing it, the speed with which Jacobo's act was covered up, the Jacobo she had loved so much . . .

"Get into the car quickly, Julia!" Jacobo came over. "You'll catch pneumonia."

"Fine, I'm coming." Julia, overcome by the memories, clutched Clarence's arm as the girl whispered a final question in her ear.

"How could Dad have done something like that?"

Julia blinked, perplexed. Had Clarence read her mind? She sat in front of the wheel slowly and murmured, "He also suffered."

Julia started the car, and a couple of seconds later, the Volvo was climbing the dirt track to the main road.

Clarence watched the car until it disappeared into the cold night. Should she take Julia's phrase as confirmation of her suspicions? A wave of bitterness trembled in her chest. How could he have suffered as well? She went over Jacobo's life and could not find any evident signs of suffering, unless his bad temper was the result of an unhealed past.

When New Year's Eve was over, Clarence decided that she couldn't wait another day to talk to Daniela. After the long interlude from her return from Bioko to Laha's arrival, everything was going too fast. The signs were more than obvious. Daniela blushed each time her hands accidentally bumped against Laha's, and he smiled like a fool in love. It was impossible that the rest of the family had not noticed it. And that glint in Daniela's eyes . . . It was the first time she had seen it in her cousin.

Clarence looked at her watch. It was almost dinnertime, and there was no one at home. Carmen had managed to convince Kilian, Jacobo, and a few neighbors to go for a hot chocolate. Laha and Daniela had gone shopping. It was impossible to get a minute alone with her cousin. When everyone went to bed, she decided, she would sneak into Daniela's room.

She started to prepare dinner without much enthusiasm. Carmen was a natural at cooking, be it for two or sixteen people. It took Clarence a lot of effort to even think about where to start. She had mastered only basic things like a salad or a Spanish omelet. She sat at the kitchen table and began to peel the potatoes. The house was silent. She heard voices coming from the street. The noise got louder, and she made out Jacobo's strong voice.

"Open the door, Clarence!"

Clarence peeked out the window. Below, Kilian and Jacobo were carrying her mother up in their arms. She ran down to open the heavy door to the entrance and let them in. Carmen's face was a picture of pain. A trickle of blood ran from her forehead down past her temple to her cheek.

"What happened?" Clarence shouted nervously.

"She slipped on a sheet of ice," her father answered, panting. "She never looks where she is going!"

Carmen moaned. They finally sat her down on an armchair in front of the fire. Clarence did not know what to do. She cursed Daniela's absence and went looking for gauze to stanch the cut that was bleeding more and more.

"Where are you sore, Carmen?" Kilian asked.

With her eyes closed, his sister-in-law responded, "Everywhere . . . my head . . . my ankle . . . my arm. Most of all my arm." She tried to move, and her face twisted in pain.

"Where the hell is Daniela?" roared Jacobo.

"She's gone out with Laha," Clarence answered. "I don't think she'll be too long."

"Is there no one else in this house except this Laha?"

"Dad!"

"We should call for a doctor," Kilian said calmly.

They heard laughs, and the back door to the kitchen opened. Daniela, followed by Laha, stopped dead on seeing the situation. She quickly got to work. Moving calmly and assuredly, she cleaned the wound, felt her aunt's body, and gave her diagnosis.

"She has broken her arm. It's not serious. But she will have to be taken to Barmón hospital. I'll make a sling so the journey won't be too painful, but the sooner you go, the better."

Clarence hurriedly packed some things for her and her parents. Laha took Carmen in his arms and carried her to the car. The goodbyes between everyone were quick, although Clarence used her cousin's hug to whisper, "I've something important to tell you. It has to do with Laha."

Daniela frowned. Had she not had enough time to talk to her all these months? Now she had picked the most inopportune moment?

"Are we going now or not?" shouted Jacobo impatiently through the window of his silver Renault Mégane.

Daniela opened the car door to let Clarence in.

"Is it Laha you have been missing all these months?" she asked in a low voice, her heart in her mouth.

"What?" Clarence blinked. It took her a few seconds to realize Daniela's error. She thought she was in love with Laha! "Eh, no, no. It's not that."

Daniela breathed a sigh of relief. "Then everything else can wait."

Daniela prepared a quick dinner for the three of them. Laha asked Kilian some questions about the valley, and he answered with many amusing anecdotes that his daughter had not heard since she was a child. After dinner, they sat down together by the fire, waiting for Clarence's call, which did not come. Kilian's eyes were beginning to droop.

"Go to bed, Dad," Daniela told him. "If there is something important, I'll get you."

Kilian agreed. He gave a good-night kiss to his daughter and patted Laha on the shoulder. "Enjoy the fire."

Daniela smiled, warmed by the flames and the thick embers. She got up and went looking for two glasses, which she filled with *rancio* wine.

"This drink is only served on special occasions," she whispered.

The house was very big, and Kilian's room was in the farthest corner. He could not hear them unless they shouted, but her low voice masked the nervousness she felt knowing that, in less than two minutes, she would be in Laha's arms under the same roof as her father.

"It's stored in a small barrel where a small quantity of the original wine is kept over many decades. Only a few liters are made each year."

"And what's so special about this occasion?" Laha moistened his lips with the liquid, which was intensely sweet and similar to brandy.

"You'll see soon enough."

The telephone rang, and Daniela ran to answer it. A few minutes later, Laha heard steps from the stairs that led to the upper floor. When Daniela came back, the last ash log had just split on the bed of embers licked by flickering tongues of fire.

"Carmen will be in a cast for three weeks, so they will stay in Barmón. Clarence will come up to collect their things."

"I'm sorry I won't be able to say good-bye to your uncle and aunt."

"Well, I hope you'll see them again." She paused. "Would you like to?"

"Yes, because that would mean seeing you again."

Daniela refilled their glasses. She was going to sit down on the armchair beside Laha, but he took her wrist and drew her onto his lap.

Laha took a sip of the wine and looked at Daniela with desire in his eyes. She leaned toward him and drank from his lips. Laha half closed his eyes, and from his throat, a purr of pleasure sounded when he felt the warmth of Daniela's hands on his face, in his hair, on his neck. He rested a hand on one of her hips so he could hold her tighter, put the other under her sweater, and began massaging her stomach, rising slowly until he reached her breasts. Daniela moved away a few centimeters and looked at him expectantly. When he began to slowly caress her breasts, she bit her bottom lip, and her breathing got faster. Laha fixed his eyes on her face. Her porcelain cheeks were tinged an intense pink. Her enormous eyes looked at him with a mixture of desire and anticipation. Under normal circumstances, the young woman's gaze was disconcerting. At that moment, a mysterious force surged from the depths of those two sources of light to draw him in like a defenseless insect. He wanted only to hover eternally around those beams, enjoying the challenge and the temptation before submitting to certain death . . .

A short time later, in the guest bedroom, Daniela studied Laha's bare chest. There was a huge difference between the boys in her past and this fully fledged man. She had known she wanted to spend her life with him, even before sleeping together. Laha moved closer till his body joined hers. No more words were necessary. There were no nerves, nor awkward laughs, nor superfluous pauses, nor confused thoughts. Their hands knew what they wanted to feel. Their lips and their tongues knew well how to sate their desire. It only took one glance into each other's eyes to be sure that one felt the same intimate hunger as the other.

Laha had made a tremendous effort in delaying the moment when he would take her. He wanted to enjoy every second of exploration. It was the supreme celebration of all the senses. He had traveled half the world, had slept with many women, but he had never experienced pleasure like this, with a young woman whom he had just met in a forgotten corner of the coldest mountains he had ever known. If at any stage he had worried that age difference would be an obstacle, he was now certain he had been completely wrong. His body no longer belonged to him. It would no longer be able to feel anything away from her. He was sure of it.

Daniela moved under him, more than ready to welcome him. If he did not enter her soon, she would scream, even if it woke half the village. Laha positioned himself tenderly between her legs and began moving, stroking her hair with his hands. Daniela moaned and arched her back. She needed to feel him in the deepest part of her being, to rock with him, to melt into the complete union, to explode in unison.

Laha, completely out of breath, collapsed on his back, with his heart beating at a dizzying speed. Daniela placed her arm on his chest. Laha wrapped his arms around her.

"This has never happened to me before," he said in a low voice. "It was as if . . ."

She finished his sentence before submerging into a deep sleep, ". . . as if someone were manipulating us at will, wasn't it?"

Clarence returned two days later. The holidays were coming to an end, and her mother's convalescence would coincide with the start of classes, so it would be a while before she returned to Pasolobino. There had been no progress made on the subject of Laha. For one reason or another, it was never the right moment. It was difficult enough for her father to look after his wife in the flat in Barmón without having to hear such an accusation from his daughter. With regard to Daniela, she was not going to wait one minute more: the moment Laha got on the bus, she would tell her everything.

Clarence watched the quiet and affectionate farewell between Laha and Daniela at the stop in Cerbeán, which was nothing like her complicated good-bye from Iniko on Bioko. Did this mean that Daniela and Laha meant to see each other again?

When her turn came, Laha hugged her tightly.

"Dearest Clarence. Thanks for everything! I've had a marvelous holiday!"

Clarence was overcome by a sudden burst of sincerity. "Ah, Laha! A few months ago, you and Bisila and Iniko were strangers. Now, it's like we have known each other all our lives! As if our lives had been intertwined!"

"Do you mean," he whispered jokingly, "that you have the strange feeling that you can't fight the spirits?"

Clarence loosened her hug with a sudden jerk and moved away. Laha planted a quick kiss on Daniela's cheek and got on the bus. Daniela did not stop waving her hand in the air until the vehicle disappeared from sight.

"And now you and I are going for a beer," said Clarence. It came out more as an order than a suggestion. "How long has it been since we've had time alone?"

When Clarence finished recounting her version of the facts—leaving out her special relationship with Iniko—she lowered her eyes and sighed deeply. At a few points during the story, Daniela's eyes had filled with tears, but she never let them roll down her cheeks. She pursed her lips, arched her eyebrows, rested her chin in her hands, peeled off the label from the beer bottle, and shredded it into a thousand pieces, but she did not say a word.

"Even the note I found has more meaning than ever," finished Clarence. "It said that one was working and the other studying hard. It's obvious. The two brothers, Iniko and Laha." She lit a cigarette. Her hands were trembling. "The only thing I don't understand is the relationship between Dimas of Ureca and Manuel in all of this . . . And you? Have you anything to say?"

"And what could I say?" answered Daniela, still in shock. "You yourself have said you don't have conclusive proof, apart from the coincidence in names and other details."

They went over all the dates and information once again, but always came to the same point. It was very probable that Laha and Clarence were brother and sister, but only Jacobo could confirm that.

And even if it is true, thought Daniela, *that wouldn't change how I feel about him in any way.*

A long silence followed.

And I had thought that my cousin was jealous . . . Daniela shook her head.

"And now what?" Clarence asked, finally free of the secret that had tormented her for months.

"I can't believe it." Daniela let out a small, nervous laugh. "Laha could be my . . . cousin!"

Just then, she felt a tightness in her chest.

"What's the matter?" Clarence asked. "You've gone very pale."

"Oh, Clarence . . . What if . . . Are you sure there isn't the slightest possibility that Laha's father could be . . ." She ran out of breath before finishing the question. "My dad?"

Clarence shook her head in certainty.

"Julia practically confirmed Jacobo's paternity to me. Also, could you imagine your father hiding something so serious?"

"He'd have had to really fool me." Daniela took another sip of beer. The tightness in her chest disappeared as quickly as it had come. "Dad is quieter than usual, sure, even gloomy, but he's relaxed. If it were his son, he'd be on edge."

"And the person who seems nervous is my father, yes? Then . . . when will we announce what we know?"

Daniela thought about her answer. "For the moment, we won't say anything at home. Before that, I'd like to talk to Laha."

During the first few months of 2004, as Jacobo helped Carmen recover and Clarence buried her head in work, Daniela made several trips to Madrid, traveling there every three or four weeks. Because she lived in an isolated area, it was easier to use a job refresher course as an excuse. Clarence could not understand how everyone else—especially her uncle Kilian—had not picked up on the change in her cousin. How did they do it with the distances involved? The only thing she could think of was that Laha was making a stopover in Madrid every time he went from California to Bioko and vice versa.

After each weekend away, Daniela arrived home exhausted but radiant. Clarence thought, with envy, that if Laha was half as good a lover as Iniko, Daniela had reason to be happy. Still, she was concerned. So many trips could mean only one thing: that Daniela and Laha had successfully gone beyond the honeymoon phase of the relationship and showed no signs of wearing out. They wanted to learn every detail of each other's pasts, and think about living together for the rest of their lives.

Far from Pasolobino, what Daniela and Laha still did not know was how, where, and when.

The situation was not easy; Bioko, California, and Pasolobino formed a huge geographical triangle. One of the two would have to consider following the other around the world. Either Laha moved to Spain or Daniela would be between California and Bioko. Laha argued that the big advantage of being a nurse was that she could work anywhere. And in Guinea, she would have the opportunity of really making a difference, even if she earned less. Bisila would be a great help in placing her. What a coincidence that the two most important women in his life were nurses!

But Daniela was less worried about her work situation. For one, she had yet to confess to Laha her suspicions about his identity. She was being very selfish, but she was afraid that the news would threaten their closeness. And she had not dared talk to her father.

She had always been so close to Kilian that she was finding it very difficult not to tell him how happy she felt with Laha. She and her father had never lived apart from each other; even in college, she stayed with him on weekends. Jacobo, Carmen, and Clarence were close family, but the relationship between Kilian and Daniela was special, as if they really only had each other. How was she going to tell him that she wanted to fly far away, just when he most needed her?

At the speed her relationship with Laha was going, she would have to choose sooner rather than later. But she found herself fighting with her practical side. A love story with such a different man, a man a few years older than she, and with whom she could share genes, frankly, had never been part of her plans.

And Laha's touch and delightful obsession with nibbling at her breasts was not helping her find the right path.

"You're very quiet, Daniela," said Laha. "Are you feeling okay?"

"I was thinking about my father," she answered, sitting up against the bed's headboard. "I will have to tell him!"

Laha lay on his side beside her as she wrapped her arms around her knees, deep in thought.

"Do you think he'll care about the color of my skin?"

Daniela turned toward him, shocked. "Not for one moment have I ever thought anything like that!"

Laha stroked her foot. "This is something completely new in the House of Rabaltué."

Daniela's eyes blazed in fury. "Well, it's about time someone disrupted the historic peace of my house!" She sighed before continuing. "It's possible that it will give Uncle Jacobo a fit . . . a black in the family!" She winced. A black who could also be his son. "But my father is different. He will respect my decision above all."

"Then what's worrying you?"

Daniela sighed deeply. "Any decision we make to live together means leaving him alone in Pasolobino." She picked up Laha's shirt, put it over her shoulders, and sat on the edge of the bed. "Maybe it's too soon to tell him. We've known each other for only three months."

"It's enough time for me." Laha knelt behind her and hugged her. "There is a popular African proverb that says no matter how early you rise, your destiny will have risen before you."

She leaned back against his chest and closed her eyes.

That night, in the Madrid hotel, she found it nearly impossible to sleep. In her mind, she ran through her childhood, her father, and a mother she recognized only from photos. She also saw Clarence, Carmen, and Jacobo. She thought of her friends, neighbors, colleagues, and of people she greeted every day on her way to work or when out shopping. She thought of how lucky she had been growing up.

Like Clarence, she was a part of the fields scored by streams, tarns, and glacial lakes; of the woods of black pine, ash, walnut, oak, and rowan; and of the meadows dotted with wildflowers in spring, with the smell of freshly cut hay in summer, with the fire colors of autumn, and with the solitude of the snow.

This had been her world.

Clarence would not understand.

She remembered another African proverb that Laha had shared in one of their many conversations about his home.

"The family is like the forest," he had told her. *"If you are outside it, you only see its density. If you are inside, you can see that each tree has its own place."*

Her family would not understand that she was ready to move on. *"Daniela,"* they would say, *"you can't transplant a grown tree, nor a flower in bloom. It will die."*

"Unless you dig out a huge hole," she would answer, *"and allow the roots to take as much soil as possible and water it continuously. Also,"* she would add, *"a person's roots are kept inside. They're the tentacles that extend the length of our nervous system and keep us whole. They go wherever you go, live wherever you live . . ."*

When sleep finally came, Daniela continued to dream.

The meltwaters from the glaciers in her valley formed a large pool that flowed along a plain before falling as a waterfall into an enormous chasm. There, it disappeared completely. As if by magic.

In one of nature's whims, at the foot of Pasolobino's highest peaks, an exceptional karstic phenomenon occurred.

The river was gobbled up and flowed along a subterranean path robbed from the rock. The acidic meltwater was capable of dissolving rock. The subterranean water made new galleries and bends along which the river flowed away from any sunlight. After several kilometers, the river reappeared in other lands, in another valley. It resurfaced in the form of a huge fountain that contributed to the flow of water in another river, which, once joined, fed into the French coast, far from its source.

In her dream, Kilian and Daniela leaned over the huge chasm.

Daniela was happy for the mysterious journey the waters would take before a happy ending.

And oddly enough, in Daniela's dream, Kilian was not sad. On the contrary, he gave her a triumphant smile.

He knew that the same water that entered the dark caves and remained hidden from the outside world, after eroding and dissolving the rock, would find a way to the surface.

In the end, it found a way out.

14

Temps de Espináulos
Time of Thorns

April 2004

As soon as the family left for Madrid to attend the gathering of old friends of Fernando Po, Daniela gave in to her excitement.

She went through every room in the house to make sure everything was perfect. This time, Laha would sleep with her in her beautiful blue room, decorated in antique furniture, all belonging to her great-grandparents, her grandfather Antón's parents. An enormous bed, its size a rarity from that time, took over the room. Daniela could hardly wait to have Laha with her under the feather-filled eiderdown.

She crossed to her father's bedroom, smaller than hers and simply decorated with honey-stained pine furniture. The only decorations in the room were two etchings, one of St. Kilian and the other a sad-faced black image of Our Lady, hanging on the wall opposite the head of the bed. These were the first two things her father saw when he woke up and the last things before he went to sleep.

Her eyes wandered over the room.

On top of the bedside table was Kilian's old wallet.

For his trip to Madrid, Daniela had managed to get her father to try out the wallet that she had given him on Christmas Eve. She herself had hurriedly changed over the documents and the numerous pieces of paper filled with telephone numbers and notes after a lot of insisting, just before he got into the car with Jacobo. Her father was reluctant to hand it over, and she had had to promise that she would take only the money, credit cards, and his ID and that she would keep it in the drawer of his bedside table with the others.

She went over to the table to put it away. As she bent down to open the drawer, which always got stuck, her eyes noticed a piece of paper sticking out from under the bed, half hidden by the rug.

She picked it up and saw that it was a black-and-white photo of a beautiful smiling black woman with a small boy in her arms.

Daniela did not know who they were. She had not seen the photo before. What she did know was that the author of *Guinea in Pasolobinese* had asked the people of the valley who had traveled to Guinea decades ago for material. Maybe this was one of the few photos Kilian found when rooting around in the sitting room cabinet. In fact, several images of the Rabaltué brothers appeared in the book.

Yes, that would be it.

She put it in the drawer and went down to the kitchen to get dinner ready. It would not be long before Laha got there.

In a hotel in the center of Madrid, Jacobo and Kilian did not stop chatting. As well as meeting Marcial and Mercedes, Clarence had also met a wizened old man in a wheelchair named Gregorio, whom her uncle had given a cold greeting to.

The celebration was marred by the recent terrorist attack on four suburban trains in Madrid, which had seen almost two hundred people lose their lives. Even so, most conversations revolved around Guinea. Many commented on the brief headline that had appeared in the press about the setting up in Madrid of a government of Equatorial Guinea in exile, aimed at giving a democratic option to the country by returning to Malabo and preparing open and democratic general elections. Clarence had quite quickly divided the guests into two groups: the outdated colonists, like her father, who defended the theory that Guineans lived better under the colony, and the paternalistic conservatives, like her uncle, who claimed that Spain had a historic debt to the old colony and that something should be done to compensate for the abuses of the past.

She wondered if anyone was there like herself or Fernando Garuz, who thought that the mother country and the ex-colony did not owe each other anything. The best thing would be simply to respect the decisions of the small country. Why not treat it as an equal, as a partner, as an independent and sovereign republic to do business with?

Clarence took a glass and sat down in an armchair until the meal began. She missed Daniela, even if their last conversation had been unsettling. There were very few of their generation there. Daniela had accused her of being jealous that she was spending more time with Laha than Clarence. She remembered choking on her whiskey. If anything, Clarence was simply bitter that distance had not undermined Daniela's and Laha's feelings toward each other. No matter how frustrating it was to admit that she missed Iniko a lot, she was aware that in her case, once the initial passion had passed, her relationship would not have worked.

To convince Daniela she was wrong, Clarence had opened her heart and confessed her own romance with Iniko. Daniela had bombarded her with questions, wanting to compare the two relationships. She was especially interested to know if the cultural differences with Laha could become too much . . . Maybe Daniela had thought about changing Pasolobino for Malabo? Just in case, Clarence recounted all the difficulties she would have to face, one by one, in great detail. She wanted Daniela to think about what she was leaving behind and the problems she would face in adapting to a country like Guinea, assuming that she and Laha decided to settle there, even if only temporarily. How could she be happy under those conditions?

It was very clear to Daniela, even if it seemed to Clarence she was only repeating Laha's words, there was much to do in an emerging state, a country with new infrastructure and big plans for the future. To end, she had roundly stated, "I can't be happy anywhere without Laha."

If things were moving that quickly, thought Clarence, Daniela could not really delay talking to Laha.

She took a large swig from her glass.

Both of them were in Pasolobino, and it was Saturday.

Could she have told him yet?

Spring took much longer in the highest part of the Pyrenees than anywhere else. The first green never arrived in Pasolobino before May. In April, there were no flowers, only fields shorn by the last snows. The only hint of the new season was the sun rising a little earlier and setting a little later.

With Laha, it did not matter to Daniela whether it was cold or warm, whether the flowers began to adorn the meadows or not, or if the birds were livening things up with their trills. But the days and nights seemed so short.

Laha had arrived on Thursday night, and by Saturday, they still had not sated each other. Daniela had not found the right moment to tell him they could be cousins. Neither of them wanted to think of anything other than being together. The following day, Laha would leave, and they did not know when they would see each other again. They had given each other until summer to make definitive decisions on how to approach their future. For the time being, they clung to their intimate moments as if it were the last time they could be together, as if some unexpected twist of destiny could threaten their happiness in each other's arms.

In the days before the return of life to the valley, time had stopped, and the expectant calm was altered only by the beating of their hearts. Daniela's hand traveled over Laha's chest, halting occasionally on his heart, waiting for it to slow. Laha turned his head, and Daniela raised hers to look at him. His forehead was beaded with sweat. Daniela thought he had the most beautiful face she had ever seen, with his special green eyes and caramel skin. Beside him, her skin appeared even whiter. She squeezed against his body as hard as she could and stayed in silence for a few minutes, enjoying the warmth.

"Can you imagine what our lives would have been like a hundred years ago?" Daniela asked in a sleepy voice.

Laha laughed at the unexpected question.

"Well . . . in Bioko, I would get up very early to hunt antelope in the jungle or fish in the sea in my canoe." He freed himself from Daniela's embrace and put his hands behind his head. "Or I would have a job on one of the cocoa plantations . . . In any case, my beautiful wife, Daniela, would stay in the house and look after the vegetable garden and the children."

Daniela lay beside him, bent her elbow, and cupped her head in her hand. "You'd probably have more wives."

"Probably." He grinned slyly.

Daniela gave him an affectionate pinch on the arm.

"In Pasolobino, *I* would do the same. But meanwhile, my darling husband, Laha, as well as hunting and fishing, would be in charge of work in the fields and the animals. He would fix up the house and the sheds, prune trees and get firewood ready for the winter, milk the cows, open up paths in the snow, and would rest for a little while to regain strength and"—she put a lot of emphasis on the final words—*"satisfy his only wife."*

Laha burst out laughing. "This reminds me of a very old Bubi story, from the precolonial period." He cleared his throat and began speaking slowly: "Many years ago, in a village called Bissappoo, lived a young married couple. Everything went fine at first, but as the days passed, the woman cooked and the man did not come to dinner, so she put the food in bowls and stored it in the dryer. When the husband returned, he went to bed without eating. This went on for days and days. Finally, the woman could not take it anymore and went to the wise old men of the village to denounce him. The men counted more than a thousand bowls, but did not make any decision, so the woman decided to go and find her husband. She went to the edge of the village and found him there, in the company of other men. Her husband called to her. She stopped and looked, but did not answer. He called to her again and asked, 'What has he done to you, he who eats and doles out?' The woman answered him, 'Nothing, nothing. I am not the husband. You are the man. The food is in the dryer. It has been there for four days and is dry and with cobwebs. It is now dried out. It is now dried out.'"

Daniela remained silent for a moment. Laha lay on his side to face her. He put his arms around her and drew her toward him.

"I'll never let your food go dry," he whispered in her ear.

"I think I'm happy to be living in this age," she joked. "I don't like the idea of cooking all the time."

Daniela got up on her knees and started to bite and caress all of Laha's body, from his neck to his shoulder blades, down the middle of his back. She signaled him to turn over with a light touch so she could continue, although she now began at his feet and rose to his groin.

Laha began to moan in pleasure and stretched out his hand to stroke Daniela's soft hair, swaying like a fine curtain on his delicate skin.

All of a sudden, he felt her stop.

Laha opened his eyes and raised his head a few centimeters to look at her. Daniela remained still, looking at something very closely.

"What's wrong?" he asked, wanting her to continue.

"This mark here." Daniela spoke in a whisper. "When I saw it before, I thought it was a scar, but now that I'm looking at it closely, it's like a pattern."

Laha laughed. "It's from scarifying, like a tattoo. My mother did it to me when I was very young. It's a Bubi tradition. Many people make deep incisions, especially on the face, but in the colonial period, the tradition was dying out and my mother didn't want to disfigure me." He paused.

"But . . . it's . . . ," sputtered Daniela. "It looks like . . . I saw one . . ."

"Yes, it's an *elëbó*, a small Bubi bell to protect me from the evil spirits. Do you remember? I gave your father one for Christmas."

Daniela had gone pale. Was not that instrument one of the clues that Clarence had told her about? Had not that man Simón told Clarence to look for an *elëbó*? She felt her chest tighten. She looked up. "My father has a tattoo exactly like it on his left armpit. Exactly the same."

Laha was stunned. "Well, after so many years in Bioko, he probably decided to get a scarification—"

"It's the same!" Daniela interrupted him. "Tell me, Laha, why did people get scarified?"

Laha listed the reasons to her aloud. "Let me see . . . As an artistic expression, as a differentiating mark from other races, for therapeutic reasons to get rid of pain . . ."

Daniela shook her head.

". . . to mark a person for some specific behavior, for love . . . The slaves also scarified themselves in one form or another to be able to recognize each other when in exile . . ."

"To recognize themselves . . . ," repeated Daniela in a low voice. She had a terrible premonition. She remembered the piece of photograph she had found on the floor in her father's room. "Wait a minute."

She went out and soon returned with the photograph and gave it to Laha.

"Do you know the woman and child?"

Laha sprung out of the bed. "Where did you get this?"

"So you know them . . ."

"The woman is my mother!" His voice trembled. "And the child she is holding is me."

"Your mother and you," repeated Daniela, hanging her head.

Laha went over to the chair where he had hung his trousers and took his wallet from the pocket. He opened it and took out a piece of a photo of a man leaning against a truck.

Daniela did not have to look at the photo for long to grasp two things. First, the man in the photo was Kilian. And second, the piece fitted like a jigsaw with the one she had.

She wanted to cry.

Laha began getting dressed.

"This can only mean one thing," he said in a strange tone, as if the dream they had been living together had become a nightmare.

When he finished getting dressed, he began walking from one side of the room to the other, possessed by a fury that Daniela had never seen in him before. He kept raising his hands to his head in despair.

Just then he realized that Daniela was watching him in a mixture of confusion and sadness. She was still naked. On seeing her in front of him with no clothes on, a shiver went through his body, and he felt like screaming out.

How could she not understand the seriousness of the situation?

"Daniela, for the love of God!" he pleaded. "Get dressed."

Daniela went over to the wardrobe and took out some clothes. Her whole body was trembling.

"There's something I haven't told you, Laha . . . ," she finally allowed herself to say. "Up to a few minutes ago, Clarence and I suspected that Jacobo was your real father."

Laha came over to her and grabbed her by the arms so hard she let out a yelp.

"The two of you thought we could be related and you hid it from me?" Laha shook her violently. His green eyes had become a harsh gray.

"I wanted to tell you during this visit, but it was never the right moment," she murmured, letting the tears roll down her cheeks. "I was worried about how you would react, of course, but I was convinced that even if we were cousins it wouldn't change anything."

"But don't you realize that you and I are . . . ?" he shouted.

"I don't want to . . . ," she whispered between her teeth. "Don't say it."

Laha was hurting her.

And it was not his strong hands gripping her arms, but the terrible suspicion that what they had discovered was true. She would never be able to forgive her father! He should have warned them . . .

She just wanted to cry, cling to Laha's arms, feel his body next to hers, and wake up from the nightmare.

"You're hurting me, Laha," she managed to say in a weak voice.

Laha felt gutted. He had never reacted so violently before. Daniela's arms were fragile. Daniela was fragile. For a moment, he had given in to his rage.

Daniela did not speak. She just cried without making a sound. He had to calm down.

He felt an urge to sweep her into the enormous bed.

Whose did she say it was? Her great-grandparents, Kilian's grandparents.

His own great-grandparents!

His head hurt. What was he supposed to do now?

Daniela raised her head toward him.

"Look at me, Laha. Please . . ."

Laha did not meet her eyes. He squeezed her in his arms with the despair of someone who was hugging the person they most loved for the last time.

"I have to go, Daniela. I have to go."

He went over to the wardrobe, took out his suitcase, and packed. Neither of them said anything. Outside, after weeks of calm, the north wind began to howl.

Daniela remained sitting in the same position for a long time after she heard the sound of Laha's car disappearing down the rear track. If she had scrubbed her skin with the thorn-filled branches of the hawthorn outside, she could not have felt a deeper pain.

Only when her subconscious had accepted that Laha was so far away that there was not the slightest possibility of him turning around and coming back to her arms, only then did Daniela strip the sheets from the bed while screaming in anger.

She took the sheets, went down to the kitchen, opened a bag, and put them in it.

She would not throw the sheets away.

She would burn them.

She had to burn the threads that had absorbed the sweat of an incestuous passion.

Still, despite the evidence, Daniela still refused to believe that Laha was her brother.

"You're looking beautiful tonight!" It was the first time Clarence had met Julia in the city. Julia was wearing a light chiffon patterned dress and elegant high heels. Nothing like the thick clothes she wore in Pasolobino. Since the party had started, they had not had a minute together.

Julia smiled. That night, she was happy. She accepted a glass from the waiter and took a sip.

"Today is all memories . . ." Her eyes shone. "Manuel would have enjoyed it a lot."

"Even my mother looks to be having a good time," joked Clarence to dispel the woman's sadness about Manuel. "She doesn't have many opportunities to get out to parties like this."

"Yes." Julia sighed. "It's just like the Santa Isabel casino."

The music began to play. Jacobo was the first on the dance floor. Carmen followed his lead with the precision acquired after years of dancing with the same partner.

Julia watched them. She wondered if they had had a happy marriage and felt a pinch of nostalgia for what could have been but never was. If Jacobo had not been so stupid, she would be in Carmen's place now. She took another sip. It was ridiculous to have those thoughts at her age. Jacobo had probably ended up making the right choice. Carmen seemed to be a loving and sensible woman capable of tempering Jacobo's mercurial character. Julia might not have succeeded in that.

"It's been a while since I've seen my parents looking so well," said Clarence. "In that suit, my father looks twenty years younger."

"Your father was very handsome, Clarence," said Julia. "You can't imagine."

Clarence had promised herself not to mention Laha's paternity. She understood that it was a special night, and she did not want to ruin it. Nevertheless, Julia's comment brought an image to mind.

"Knowing Laha, I think I have a fair idea . . ." She noticed that Julia frowned. She added, "I'm not at all surprised that Daniela has fallen in love with him."

"What did you say?" Julia went completely red. Her hand went to her chest as if she could not breathe.

Clarence got a fright.

"What's the matter, Julia? Are you not feeling well?" She looked around her for help, but the woman caught her by the wrist.

"But that's not possible," murmured Julia.

"They're not the only cousins in the world to have fallen in love."

"I need to sit down, please, Clarence."

"Wouldn't it be better if I got a doctor?" She took Julia over to a comfortable chair away from the racket.

"Tell me, Clarence. Do your father and uncle know?"

"I think my mother is the only one who suspects something."

Julia buried her face in her hands and began to sob. "Oh, Clarence . . . You have to know. I thought you were going in the right direction. I'm afraid there has been a terrible mistake." Julia looked at Clarence with her eyes filled with tears. "I should have told you before."

Clarence had a terrible feeling. She looked down at her knuckles, white from clenching her fists.

"Laha's real father is Kilian. Your uncle sent money regularly to take care of him. At first, he did it through my husband and the doctors from the humanitarian organizations. When Manuel stopped traveling to the island, it was Lorenzo Garuz who passed on the money. He gave it to an intermediary so Bisila was not associated with any white man. I should have told you. I'll never forgive myself."

"I was always referring to Dad! The day you were in our house with Ascensión, you told me that Dad had also suffered . . ."

"I was referring to what happened to Mosi! Oh my God!" Julia got up and quickly walked away.

Clarence remained sitting with her face in her hands, crestfallen. Minutes later, she retired to her room, saying that something she had had at dinner had not agreed with her. She called her cousin, both the home phone and the cell, but got no answer.

She lay on her bed and broke down crying with all her might.

Not even the journey from Malabo had felt so long and painful as the journey from Madrid to Pasolobino on Easter Sunday. Clarence had to make a real effort to make sure her parents and uncle did not suspect that she was suffering from more than just indigestion.

While the others unloaded the car, she ran to Daniela's room.

Daniela was sitting in a corner, surrounded by dozens of tissues, with her knees in her chest and her hair tossed over her face. In her right hand, she held a piece of paper. She raised her head to look at Clarence with her beautiful eyes swollen.

She had not found anything to prove it was not true, that it was a mix-up, an inexplicable and damned twist of fate.

"He's gone," Daniela repeated over and over again between sobs.

Clarence sat down beside her and gently put her arm around her shoulders.

"How could he abandon him? What was he thinking?"

Daniela raised the piece of paper she was holding in her hand. She could barely contain her rage when she added, "Laha has the same scarified *elëbó* that Dad has on his left armpit. Do you want to know where Laha has his? My God! I'm embarrassed even to think about it!" She rubbed her temples as thick tears started to roll down her cheeks again. "I don't know if I'll be able to face him . . . No. You'll have to do it. You'll talk to them, Clarence. Today. Right now."

"I'll try."

How was Clarence going to put the question to Jacobo? Would she look into his eyes and say, *"Dad, I know that Laha is Kilian and Bisila's son. Dad, have you noticed that Laha and Daniela have fallen in love? Dad, have you any idea how terrible this is?"*

Daniela shook her head with her eyes closed. She had stopped crying, but she felt exhausted.

"Unforgivable!" she murmured between gritted teeth. "They have *no* excuse, either of them!"

"It was a different time, Daniela," answered Clarence, remembering Mamá Sade's son. "White men with black women. Many children were born from these relationships . . ."

Daniela was not listening to her. "You might think I'm crazy or sick, but you know what, Clarence? I even thought I could continue seeing Laha! No one, apart from ourselves, would have to know the truth. My feelings for him can't change overnight."

Clarence got up and went over to the window. She saw the drops from an intermittent drizzle trembling on the leaves of the nearby ash trees.

If she had not opened the cabinet where the letters were kept, if she had not found the note and asked Julia, if she had not gone to Bioko, none of this would be happening. Life in the mountains of Pasolobino would continue just the same as always. The embers of an old fire would have gone out with the death of the parents, and nobody would have known that somewhere else in the world flowed the same blood that flowed through their own veins.

And no harm would have come of it.

But it was not to be. With her search, without realizing it, she had blown over the dying ashes to reawaken them. Now it would take them a long time to go out again.

The search had come to an end, but the grail contained poisoned wine.

Clarence ran down the stairs, looking for her father, and found him in the garage. She took a deep breath. "Will you come for a walk with me? It's a lovely afternoon."

Jacobo arched his eyebrows, not surprised by the invitation but by the fact that his daughter thought that the afternoon was beautiful, but immediately nodded and agreed. "Fine," he answered. "It'll do me good to stretch my legs after such a long drive."

The furious north wind of the previous night had abated enough to allow them to walk without fear of a tree branch falling, although it did kick up from time to time to bring down some of the squall from the peaks and whip up a fine powder of the remains of the snow that clung to the barren fields.

Clarence held on to her father's arm and began up the path from the rear of the house toward a terrace with a beautiful panoramic view of the valley and the ski slopes.

Clarence mustered all her courage and told him everything.

She was going backward and forward in time as she recounted her tale, in such a way that the names of Antón, Kilian, Jacobo, José, Simón, Bisila, Mosi, Iniko, Laha, Daniela, Sampaka, Pasolobino, and Bissappoo disappeared and reappeared like the underground karst waters of a mysterious river.

At the end of her story, Clarence, nerves on edge, dared to ask the question. "It's true, isn't it, Dad?"

Jacobo breathed with difficulty.

"Please, Dad, I'm begging you. Did it happen like that?"

Jacobo's face was beet red, his jowls trembling. He had listened to Clarence's story without opening his mouth, without breathing, without interrupting her.

Jacobo kept his eyes fixed on his daughter for several seconds and then turned his back on her. His whole body shook. He started going down the slope, and an unexpected gust of wind carried his final words to his daughter.

"Damn it, Clarence! Damn it!"

Two days later, the obstinate silence of Jacobo had spread through the rest of the house.

Carmen went around the rooms with a notebook, writing down the things that needed to be done when the good weather came, from washing the curtains to painting a room, without forgetting the stock in the larder. She did not understand what had happened to her husband. He had been so happy in Madrid.

"It must be this village." She shook her head. "I don't know what it is, but his mood changes here."

Daniela kept herself occupied in her room, desperately hoping that her e-mail or telephone would alert her of a new message that never arrived.

And Clarence's patience was wearing thin. Had Jacobo told Kilian yet?

She decided to look for her uncle in the garden. At that time of year, he began the annual task of clearing the stubble, branches, and leaves to get the soil ready for the summer.

Yes. She would talk to him. Kilian would react differently.

The garden was surrounded by a stone wall as high as a person. Clarence walked along a narrow path flanked by a hedge that ended at the entrance, crowned with an even taller hedge, which Kilian had cut into an arch. Why had she not noticed it before? At that moment, Clarence was certain that the path to the entrance to the garden was a miniature of the royal palm tree path in Sampaka. The arch also reminded her of the ones she had read about that had to be crossed through to enter the villages on the island. She had never thought about it. There was surely an arch similar to that at the entrance to Bissappoo.

Just after walking through the arch, she heard Kilian and Jacobo. It seemed they were having a row. She got a few steps closer and hugged her body against an apple tree.

Kilian was leaning on a rock with his Guinean machete in his right hand. In his left, he was holding a thick branch of ash whose bottom end he was turning into a point with violent slashes of the machete. Jacobo paced near him.

They were arguing in their native language.

Her heart began beating strongly, and she retraced her steps to hide behind some bushes. If she peeked out a little, she could see their profiles.

There were words she did not understand. When both brothers spoke quickly in their mother tongue, it was not easy to follow the conversation. Daniela and Clarence had learned a lot of Pasolobinese from listening to neighbors and family, but in their house, Spanish was spoken because neither of their mothers were from the valley.

Clarence regretted more than ever not having a deep knowledge of the oral language of her forefathers, like Laha and Iniko did. She had no problems reading it; in fact, her doctoral thesis had been on the dialect's grammar, but her pronunciation was not quite as good.

Nevertheless, names were easily understood. They were talking about Laha and Daniela. After a while, she was able to understand the two brothers' conversation more clearly.

"You have to do something, Kilian!"

"And what do you want me to do? If I talk to her, I will have to tell her everything, and I don't think you'd want me to do that."

A blow of the machete.

"You don't need to tell her everything! Only about you and that woman!"

"That's my business."

"Not anymore, Kilian, not now. This isn't right. Daniela and that man . . . You don't even seem to be worried?"

A blow of the machete.

"It was inevitable. I have finally understood that."

"Kilian, you're worrying me. For God's sake! They're brother and sister! How could you lose your head with that black woman?"

A blow of the machete.

A pause.

"Her name was Bisila, Jacobo. Her name *is* Bisila. Do me the favor of referring to her with respect. But what am I saying! You? Respect Bisila?"

A blow of the machete.

"Shut up!"

"A moment ago you wanted me to talk."

"To confirm that you are Laha's father and that's an end to it! Relationship over and we forget about the matter."

"Yes, as we've done for almost forty years . . . I separated from him once, Jacobo, and I have no intention of doing it again. If I know my daughter like I think I do, she won't forget about Laha that easily. And if Laha is anything like his mother, even the slightest bit, he won't let Daniela go free either."

"And you're so relaxed!"

A blow of the machete.

"Yes, I'm glad I've lived to see it. You don't know how happy it makes me!"

Clarence peeked out to see them better.

Kilian put the machete on the ground. He raised his right hand to his left armpit to touch his small scarification, the one Daniela had said was hidden just there.

Was he smiling?

Kilian smiling?

"You're going to make me go mad! Damn you, Kilian! I know you! Your head and your heart can't bless this aberration. Fine, very well. If you don't want to talk to her, I'll do it!"

He turned around and began to walk toward the spot where Clarence was hiding. He would bump into her.

Kilian called out.

"Jacobo. Will you also tell her about Mosi?"

Jacobo stopped dead and turned, furiously, toward his brother.

"That has nothing to do with this."

"You're asking me to remember my past, and you won't even mention yours!"

"Then I'll also have to talk to them about Sade? Maybe she also was right! For all that is holy, Kilian! Why are you set on complicating things? Why can't you understand it's just about making sure that Daniela doesn't suffer?"

"I know what suffering is. What's happening to Daniela is nothing compared to what I went through. You have never suffered in your life, so don't play the victim now."

Despite the distance, Clarence could make out the deep resigned tone in his voice.

"So that's it? You want her to suffer like you? It's your daughter!"

"No, Jacobo. Daniela won't suffer like me."

What was Kilian saying?

Was there something else they did not know?

Suddenly, Clarence felt something running over her feet and let out a scream.

Kilian and Jacobo grew silent and looked up. Clarence had no choice but to come out.

When she approached the men, her face burned in shame for having spied, so she looked at them, first one and then the other, and said in a low voice, "Dad . . . Uncle Kilian . . . I . . . I heard everything. I know everything."

Kilian picked up the machete from the ground, gently cleaned the blade with a cloth, and got up.

He looked his niece straight in the eye. The intensity of his stare had not been vanquished by the wrinkles. He raised his hand and lovingly stroked her cheek.

"My dear Clarence," he said in a firm voice, "I can assure you that you know nothing."

Clarence went cold. "Well, tell me once and for all! I want to know!"

Kilian put his arm around Clarence's shoulders and began to walk toward the entrance to the garden. "I think it's time to have a family meeting," he said seriously. "I have something to tell you all." He stopped to wait for his brother. "The *two* of us have something to tell you."

Jacobo dropped his head and murmured some unintelligible protest.

"What does it matter now, Jacobo?" said Kilian, shaking his head. "We're old. What does anything matter?"

Clarence felt the pressure of Kilian's arm on her shoulder, as if he needed help to stop him from falling.

"I'm afraid, Jacobo, that you don't know everything either."

He put his right hand into his pocket, took out a thin strip of leather with two shells hanging from it, and tied it round his neck.

"I've always had it on me," he murmured. "But it's been twenty-five years since I've worn it. I won't be taking it off again."

Thousands of kilometers away, Laha looked for his mother at home and could not find her.

The previous week had been the worst in his life. He had gone from heaven to hell in a matter of seconds. He could not erase the image of Daniela trembling in his arms.

Even worse.

He could not erase the terrible image of his beloved Daniela brokenhearted, alone and abandoned in the bed they had shared.

Not even in his worst nightmares could he have imagined that his white father would be the father of the woman he most loved in the world. He always suspected that in some part of Spain, his same blood flowed, the blood of the man who had fathered him, a man with a blurred face leaning on a truck.

He had even fantasized about the remote possibility that Kilian or Jacobo could have been his biological father. A fantasy that had been relegated to oblivion when his mind, body, and soul became devoted to Daniela.

But now everything had changed.

The hidden desire to meet his father had become a reality at the cost of his happiness.

And what was worse, the certainty that Daniela and he were brother and sister had not made the burning passion he felt for her fade in any way.

He had had to force himself not to stop the car, turn around, embrace Daniela, and tell her that he did not care, that they were not like brother and sister since they had not grown up together. In some African tribes, relations between siblings with the same father were allowed. Relations between siblings with the same mother were not. He and Daniela had not shared the same breast, and no one had to know they shared a father.

But they would know.

He had spent several days in Madrid, locked up like a caged lion, pacing round and thinking about what to do, hardly eating or drinking at all.

In the end, he had decided to take a flight to Malabo, look for his mother, and take his fury out on her.

His mother was not at home.

He went to the Malabo cemetery.

An old man with a friendly look came out to meet him. "Who are you looking for?"

"I don't know if you can help me." Laha was tired, very tired. "I'm looking for the grave of a man called Antón, Antón of Pasolobino."

The man's eyes opened wide in surprise.

"That grave has gotten a lot of visits lately," he said. "Come with me."

In the old part of the cemetery, the dead rested at the feet of the beautiful ceibas.

Laha recognized his mother's figure leaning over a stone cross. She was putting a small bunch of fresh flowers on the grave.

On hearing steps, Bisila turned around and met her son's recriminating gaze.

"Mom," said Laha. "We have to talk."

"Have you met Kilian?"

"Yes, Mom. I've met *my father*."

Bisila came over to him and stroked his hands, his arms, and his face. She knew exactly what terrible marks love could imprint on the soul.

"Let's take a walk, Laha," she said. "I think there is something you should know."

They began to wander through the trees and the graves.

Laha had met Kilian.

What would he look like now? How much would he have aged? Would the sun still cause copper to glint in his hair? Would he have retained his vigor?

Laha had met Kilian.

He had been able to look at those green-and-gray eyes.

Laha's eyes in front of Kilian's eyes.

Bisila stopped and scrutinized her son's eyes. They transformed into Kilian's, erasing distance and time, to tell her that it was time to admit the truth.

That their souls remained together.

Bisila smiled and told her son, "Laha . . . Kilian is not your father."

15

Bihurúru Bihè
The Winds of Change

1960

Before the tremendous storm broke, when there was less than two hours to get to the capital of Niger, Kilian was pleased with his decision to fly from Madrid to Santa Isabel. Now the journey from Pasolobino to Sampaka took little more than a day. Admittedly, the trip was more expensive, and the four-engine plane had to make frequent landings to refuel, but the time saved was worth it.

However, when the Douglas DC-4 began to be violently buffeted by turbulence, the fifty passengers started screaming. His father's story about the shipwreck that had nearly killed him came to his panic-stricken mind. While waiting for the plane to take off again from Niamey to Nigeria, Kilian, his face still pallid, finally decided that he would gladly accept a Cinzano vermouth or a glass of champagne from the flight attendant. Once in Bata, before getting aboard the substitute to the Dragon Rapide, a small low-winged, two-engine, angular-shaped corrugated sheet-metal junker, which would finally get him to the island, he had no doubt that, in the future, he would return to the tranquility of a ship like the *Ciudad de Sevilla*.

In the improvised airport of Santa Isabel, Simón, instead of José, was waiting for him. He was not at all like the teenager with the round sparkling eyes who had burst into his room on his first day of work on the plantation. After more than a year's absence, Kilian could hardly recognize the well-built, handsome man decorated with fine incisions, crossing the long horizontal wrinkles and adding gravity to his expression.

"Simón!" exclaimed Kilian, taking off his jacket. "I'm pleased to see you again." He pointed toward the scars. "I see you've changed."

"In the end, I decided to get scarified with the marks of my tribe, Massa," responded Simón, effortlessly lifting the heavy luggage. Kilian thought it was time for the young man to get a better job for himself. "Father Rafael doesn't like it one bit . . ."

They got into a light-colored Renault Dauphine, Garuz's latest purchase.

"Why didn't Ösé come?" Kilian asked.

"You arrived at the same time his grandson was being baptized. He asked me to bring you, if you want, straight up to the Obsay yard."

Kilian smiled. The August festivals in Pasolobino had finished two days before. The sounds of the orchestra were still resonating in his brain, and there was already another party on the go. Which grandson would that be? He had lost count, but it was odd that the celebration was on the plantation.

Then he remembered.

José's daughter, the nurse, lived there.

"Is it the baptism of Mosi's child?" he asked.

Simón nodded.

"His first! Mosi is over the moon. They've been married for years, and he was upset that they hadn't had any children yet." Confirmation of his suspicions made Kilian feel strange, similar to how he felt when he imagined the girl in the arms of her huge husband the first time he saw her, the day of her wedding. He imagined that that would be the first of many changes that had occurred during his long holidays, but this one especially vexed him. The child would unite his parents even more. He was overcome by a stab of jealousy.

Images came to mind of the beautiful woman whom he had fantasized about for so many nights. He had felt her fresh breath on his face in that bed when he was sick, after the death of his father; he visualized her figure walking determinedly through the plantation toward the hospital, the pharmacy, the church, or the stores; he remembered the softness of her hands on the skin around his ankle when she removed the chigger.

Kilian sighed. He had barely been back on the island for a couple of minutes but felt as if he had never left. It had taken him weeks to adjust to Pasolobino and recover his place in the House of Rabaltué. He now understood that just as the passing of the centuries had not undermined the strength of the house, he could never renounce the responsibility of his role in it. At the same time, as he faced the same tasks in the same fields as his forefathers and paced the same paths, his soul was comforted by and reconciled with his past and his present. His father was no longer there, but he was, and his house was still alive after five hundred years. Contributing to this certainty was also the infectious strength of Mariana, who took care of everything as if time stood still, as if Antón and Jacobo were to arrive at any moment from Fernando Po, as if Kilian were not going to depart, leaving her with the sole company of a weak Catalina, who spent most of her time in Rabaltué, trying to absorb some of her mother's energy to get over the death of her only child, or simply to survive.

He inhaled deeply, and the smell of the cocoa trees filled his lungs. The man who the talkative Simón was bringing up to date with the latest happenings was not the impressionable and inexperienced young man who missed his home and could not tell the difference between a good cocoa bean and an excellent one. Kilian knew exactly what would happen next. The entrance to the plantation. The royal palm trees. The *wachimán* Yeremías and his hens. The roasted cocoa. The friends. Her.

Would she still be so beautiful?

"So, Massa?" Simón distracted him from his thoughts. "Are you happy to be back?"

Kilian's heart skipped a beat when the vehicle turned into the royal palm tree avenue. The answer was so clearly inscribed on his mind that he felt a little guilty.

"I think so, Simón," he responded dreamily. "I think so."

Kilian wanted to clean himself up before going up to Obsay. Simón had prepared his same room. He hung up his jacket and started to unpack. Minutes later, someone knocked on the door and opened it without waiting for an answer.

"I see the holidays have treated you well!" Jacobo flung himself at his brother and gave him a strong hug. "How are things at home? How are our women?"

Kilian found Jacobo as bright and robust in health as when he had left. He had gained a bit of weight, so his belt now did not fit at his waist.

"They're fine. You'll never guess what I have in the cases. Food and more food!" He raised his eyes, and Jacobo laughed. "Mom thinks we never eat here."

He tapped his brother a few times in the stomach, went over to the mounted wooden washbasin, poured in some water, and prepared to shave.

"And you? Are you still going from one party to another with your friends?"

"I do what I can . . . I'm lucky that Dick and Pao come from Bata fairly often, because Mateo and Marcial are more and more tied down by their girlfriends."

Jacobo sat down, and Kilian started to lather his face.

"How do you think the plantation is looking?"

"The little I saw surprised me. Everything is very tidy and clean. It's obvious you didn't miss me."

"No one is indispensable, Kilian!" joked Jacobo. "Last week we were honored by a visit from the one and only regional governor of Equatorial Guinea. Can you believe it? You should have seen Garuz! They gave us a couple of days' warning, and he had all of us fixing up the plantation day and night. Waldo spent a whole day waxing the Mercedes that the governor was going to use to tour Sampaka."

Kilian smiled.

"His visit coincided with another from some journalists from *La Actualidad Española* who wanted to do an article on our cocoa."

"In all this time, I haven't heard much about the island." Kilian remembered how much he had missed the weekly news from Fernando Po's *Hoja del Lunes*. Apart from a tiny announcement about a book on elephant hunting and the showing of two films, *On the Beaches of Ureca* and *Balele*, in the provincial edition of *La Nueva España* newspaper, only four lines had appeared about the decree from March's ministers council that divided the Guinean territories into two Spanish provinces: Fernando Po and Río Muni.

"I also thought that nobody could be interested in daily events in Guinea, but according to them, the article will help show many Spanish readers how well things are done in the colony."

"Precisely *now* . . . ," said Kilian while looking for a white shirt in the case. "On the plane, I heard a conversation between two men, I think they were civil guards . . ."

"Many of them are coming. Of course, double salary, a six-month tour, and six months of vacation . . . Things can't be going very well in

Spain. The other day, Garuz said that in spite of the new economic plan that was supposed to attract companies from abroad, many Spaniards are emigrating to Europe. Just as well that for the moment, we have a guaranteed salary here!"

"They commented that new times are coming, that the colonies' days are numbered."

Jacobo waved a hand in the air. "The day the colonies disappear, these people are lost. Also, what sense would there be in forming the provinces if they weren't sure that things would continue as is?"

Kilian remembered the argument Julia's father had with Gustavo in the casino and the conversation that New Year's Day in Manuel's house. Now the colonies were more closely linked to Spain, so independence was not necessary. Was that not what Emilio had said his friend Gustavo was afraid of?

"I don't know, Jacobo. The world is changing very quickly." Still echoing in his ears was the noise of the airplane that had flown through the air at over four hundred kilometers an hour. The day before, everything had been stone and slate in the mountains and new apartments being built on the lowlands; a few hours and several airports in different African countries later and he was on the island.

Jacobo nodded. "Who could have told us that there would be black mayors in Bata and Santa Isabel and black representatives in Parliament? And coloreds in the cinemas. Even they feel uncomfortable and out of place. Well, I won't repeat the nonsense that some people are saying, but I admit it seems strange."

"And what are some people saying?" Kilian finished buttoning his shirt and turned toward the mirror.

"Well, they are saying that"—Jacobo lowered his eyes to the floor and hesitated—"that . . . even if they are suddenly now all Spanish, they're still monkeys."

Kilian gave his brother a long and hard look. Jacobo coughed, a little embarrassed. Finally, Kilian took a deep breath and turned around.

"How is everyone else?" he asked, changing the subject.

"Santiago left for good about two months ago . . . He said he was too old for this type of work. And there is a new man with me in Yakató."

"Better he's with you than with Gregorio. And Julia and Manuel?"

"I don't see them much." Jacobo looked down. He had no intention of offering further explanations about the happy family. Julia only had eyes for her little Ismael. "Any other questions?"

"How is the harvest?"

"The dryers are going at full belt. You've just arrived for the worst part!" Yes, until January, life on the plantation would be frenetic, thought Kilian, but he loved that time of the year. Soon the rains would stop and the dry season and its suffocating heat would begin. He felt strong and well prepared. "Although, I do have a piece of good news. The beans are now sifted automatically. You don't have to go from one end to the other with paddles."

"That is good news."

There was silence for a few seconds. Kilian picked up a tie and put it round his neck. Jacobo sat up in his chair.

"Why are you getting so dressed up?" he asked.

"I'm going to Obsay. Today is the baptism of José's grandson."

"And you need to dress up?" He frowned.

Kilian bristled and finished tying the knot.

"A christening is a christening, here and anywhere else. Would you like to come?"

"I have better plans in the city." Jacobo stood and walked toward the door. "By the way, I almost forgot! There is someone there who has missed you a lot. I suppose she's hoping that you have brought her some present from Spain."

"Sade . . ." Kilian sighed. How long since he had thought about her? He would have understood if, during his long holidays, Sade would also have forgotten about him, but his brother's words made it clear that this was not the case.

"She's getting more beautiful every day." Jacobo clicked his tongue. "Luckily you're my brother, because if you weren't . . ."

Kilian shot him a look of warning.

"Don't worry, lad, it's a joke." He winked. "I'm sure that, after so many months of abstinence, you'll take care of her with pleasure. Unless you have met some Spanish girl." He gave Kilian a sideways look, but gave it up for lost. "Anyway, if you've come back, it's because no girl has set her cap on you."

Kilian stayed silent. He would rather let his brother believe what he wanted if it meant ending that conversation. He had not the slightest intention of wasting his time talking to him about his few and insipid romantic flings or speculating about a possible reunion with Sade, which he did not want in the least. At that moment, he had something infinitely more important to do. He opened the jar of brilliantine, took a small amount between his fingers, and combed his hair back. He looked at himself for a final time in the mirror and went out after his brother.

José was happy to see his friend again. Either that or the palm wine led to the continuous hugs he gave Kilian.

The party was in full swing when he arrived in the Obsay yard. There were many people singing and dancing to the beat of the drums. Everyone was dressed in their best clothes: the men in long trousers and white shirts and the women in long dresses and colorful headdresses, although some had chosen to wear a European-type dress to the knee, tailored at the waist. Kilian remembered that they dressed up like that only when they were going to spend the afternoon walking around Santa Isabel, but this time they had preferred to be with Mosi.

José hugged him again and lowered his voice.

"I really have missed you, *white man*."

"I missed you too, Ösé, *mi frend*." Kilian said it in all seriousness, although he could not take the smile off his face. "I always arrive in time for one of your parties!"

"In this life, everything must be celebrated. We're here today, and tomorrow . . . with the spirits!"

"And where was he baptized? Don't tell me that Father Rafael came all the way up here!" Things were certainly changing, but Kilian was sure that the priest had not given up guiding the faithful along the right path, something that did not actually run parallel to their customs and traditions.

"Father Rafael celebrated a very beautiful ceremony in the village of Zaragoza. We have fulfilled our obligations with your church." José winked. "And we didn't take off our shoes until we crossed the main yard."

Kilian let out a loud snort. He looked around. The shouts carried words in Bubi and Pidgin English. He still did not understand Bubi, but he understood the Nigerians' dialect as easily as his own from Pasolobino. Several men raised their glasses to him in welcome. Others, among them Waldo, Nelson, and Ekon, came over and greeted him with slaps on the back. As with Simón, he also found Waldo older. Nelson had put on weight, making his jowls even bigger. And Ekon, who now spoke Spanish almost fluently, sported a gray or two in his curly hair, although his dimples helped him retain his youthful demeanor.

A short, round woman who introduced herself as Lialia, Ekon's wife, went over to her husband and dragged him up to dance, making everyone laugh. Kilian suppressed his surprise when he realized that it was the first time he had seen the woman that Ekon had shared with Umaru. A fleeting thought brought him back to that awful night. What kind of life would Umaru be leading in his homeland? It was not that Kilian cared much; after all, if it were not for José, Umaru would probably have killed him. Still, Kilian's regret made him impossible to forget.

Waldo offered him a small bowl of alcohol, and Kilian took a sip. The liquid burned his insides. The music of the drums and the high-pitched songs of the women resounded in his chest. It really was a true celebration of life. There was no holy water, nor a paschal candle, nor oils to anoint the newborn to free him from original sin and welcome him into the Holy Church. But there was fresh sweat, hot blood, tense muscles, and penetrating sounds with which to honor the majesty of existence.

"As if nothing has changed in hundreds of years . . . ," murmured Kilian, completely captivated.

José heard the comment. "Ah, *mi frend*! Here all days seem as if nothing has changed, but the truth is nothing is the same." He placed his hand on Kilian's shoulder. "And now I have another grandchild, blood of my blood. Is that not a change?"

"Now you are more grandfatherly!"

José laughed heartily.

"By the way, where are the parents? I'd like to congratulate them."

It happened again. She raised her eyes to him, and the world stopped and the songs fell silent.

This time it was for more than an instant. Her big bright eyes did not go through him like two lances. They settled on his, and he understood that she was pleased to see him again.

She was sitting down and holding a beautiful and chubby baby in her arms. Her immaculate wide-strapped white dress highlighted her smooth caramel skin. A few meters away, Mosi toasted and danced with everyone, but out of the corner of his eye, he watched his wife, who was paying a lot of attention to the massa.

Kilian lowered his eyes and gazed at the child.

"Congratulations. He's beautiful," he said. "What's his name?"

"Iniko," she answered. "It means 'born in hard times.'"

Kilian looked up again. "Are these hard times?"

She held his gaze. "They might change now," she answered, her voice trembling.

They looked at each other in silence.

"I'm happy you are back, Kilian," she whispered.

Kilian froze.

He did not even know her name!

She had always been José's daughter. José's daughter, the nurse. The nurse who had looked after Antón before he died. The caring woman who had comforted him in his grief. The face that had appeared in his dreams.

And he did not know her name . . .

He felt himself redden in embarrassment.

"I'm sorry," he began to stutter, "b-but . . . I don't know your name."

She smiled. Her right hand rose to stroke two shells hanging from a leather collar.

I thought you'd never ask me.

"My name is Daniela Bisila."

A boy of about two with blond locks and sky-blue overalls played on the doorstep with a Studebaker Avanti. His chubby little hands expertly opened and closed the doors and hood of the small car with its round headlights.

"You must be Ismael." Kilian bent down to pet his head. "You've grown a lot . . . Is your mommy around?"

The child stared at him, wrinkled his forehead, and began to cry.

"Oh . . . Did I give you a fright?"

"Oba!" Kilian heard Julia's happy voice. "Can you get the boy?"

A small woman with a childish face and hair tied back in a green scarf immediately appeared and looked at him with a surprised face.

Kilian recognized Sade's friend. He frowned. What was she doing there? Oba would not take long in telling her friend that she had seen him.

"Could you tell your mistress that a friend has called to see her?"

"Kilian!" Footsteps approached rapidly, and Julia, dressed in white culottes and a tank top, gave him an affectionate hug. "Heavens above! How long has it been?" She pressed her finger to his chest. "Could you please enjoy your vacations like everyone else, two campaigns and six months in Spain? What's the meaning of disappearing for more than a year? I thought you wouldn't come back at all."

Kilian laughed. "I got back a few days ago," he said, "but they told me you were away."

"From time to time, Manuel takes me on one of his botanical expeditions . . . Come in, we'll have some coffee."

In Oba's arms, Ismael had stopped crying and curiously observed the man.

"You have a very handsome son."

Julia thanked him with a smile and asked Oba to take the boy out for a walk.

"Oba as a nanny?" asked Kilian. "I thought she worked in the shop."

"She does, but she's fallen in love with the baby, and she likes to spend time with him." Julia lowered her voice. "Actually, she looks for any excuse to come to the plantation. It seems the man who holds her heart, Nelson, works here."

"Now I understand why he's in charge of purchasing goods!" Kilian followed Julia to the terrace, left his helmet on a low table, and sat in a wicker chair. "And your parents? Is Emilio still involved in the Neighbors Council?"

"He's got more work than ever. I don't know how he doesn't get bored, all day attending to complaints, making judgments about problematic land boundaries, preparing projects, and designing new infrastructure. At first I thought he did it more for Mom—you know how she likes to be on top of everything that goes on around here—but in the end, I think he's really interested in doing his bit in the development of Santa Isabel." She sighed deeply. "I'll go get the coffee, and we'll catch up."

Kilian busied himself by leafing through a magazine on the table; on the cover appeared a blue photo of the caudillo Francisco Franco in military uniform with his wife and daughter dressed in matching mantillas over conservative dresses, celebrating the first communion of one of his granddaughters. Julia soon returned. Kilian felt comfortable in the company of his friend, who, on the one hand, seemed content in her new role as mother and, on the other, worried about the political news circulating the island. He was going to ask her how Emilio felt about having a native superior, the mayor, when they heard an alarmed woman's voice calling insistently for Manuel. Kilian immediately jumped to his feet, and they both rushed to the front door.

"Bisila!" exclaimed Julia. "What's wrong?"

"I need the doctor. It's urgent." She caught her breath. "They have brought . . . It's . . ."

Kilian had to stop himself from taking her hands. "Calm down, Bisila," he said in a soft voice. "Tell us what happened."

"Father Rafael has brought a badly injured man for Doctor Manuel. He can barely talk. He just repeats he's a friend of your father's."

"Of my father?" said Julia in surprise. "Manuel is in the city, I don't know when he'll be back. Bring me to him."

"I'll go with you," Kilian offered.

Julia gratefully accepted.

They crossed the small yard that separated the house from the hospital as quickly as they could. When they went up the stairs, Father Rafael came out to meet them. Kilian found him aged. He had lost hair and walked with difficulty. His white suit was stained with blood.

"What happened, Father?" Julia asked, alarmed.

"I was coming back from the city when I found the poor man on the side of the road. As best as I could, I got him into the car, intending to go back to the hospital in the city, but the unhappy soul constantly repeated the names of Doctor Manuel from Sampaka and Emilio. He wouldn't let my hand go, that's why I sent Bisila to look for Manuel."

"He's gone to the city. I don't know when he'll be back."

"Oh, child. I don't know if I've done the right thing bringing him here, but he insisted. I've managed to get out of him that his name is Gustavo."

"Gustavo!" exclaimed Julia, upset. "Oh my God!"

Kilian remembered the argument in the casino.

"He was detained a few months ago and taken to Black Beach." Julia turned to the priest. "Thank you, Father. All I ask is you don't say a word to Mr. Garuz. He wouldn't like to know that we are looking after someone from outside the plantation."

"I'm sorry I can't stay any longer. I have mass to celebrate in Zaragoza. If you think it necessary, when the moment comes, send someone to fetch me."

"Yes . . . Another favor, Father. When leaving the plantation, tell Yeremías that he or Waldo should tell Dimas that Gustavo is here. They know how to find him."

Seconds later, they entered the main ward, a large room with a dozen beds laid out in two rows, which was almost empty. They had placed the man in one of the beds at the far end, separated by a thin white curtain that was tied back against the wall. From a few paces away, Kilian and Julia understood the seriousness of the situation. Gustavo's body was a shredded mass of bloodied clothes. Julia covered her mouth with her hand to hold back a sob. Gustavo's face was completely disfigured from the blackened swelling of the bruises. Whoever had done this had the perverse idea of placing his big square glasses, with the lenses broken, back on his nose to give him an even more grotesque appearance.

With her eyes filled with tears, Julia bent down to his ear. "Gustavo, can you hear me? I'm Emilio's daughter."

The man let out a moan.

"Don't worry. We'll look after you here. You'll get better, I promise."
She stood back up and murmured between her teeth, "And Manuel in
the city!"

Bisila came over.

"First we'll take off his clothes to wash and disinfect the wounds . . .
If you wouldn't mind, you could sit beside him and talk to him to keep
him calm."

During the whole process, Julia avoided looking directly at
Gustavo's lacerated body. Kilian noticed that she grew pale. That man
had received the most awful beating. On more than one occasion,
Kilian had to make a serious effort to stop himself from retching. In
front of them, Bisila cleaned the wounds with an exquisite gentleness.
Kilian marveled at her composure. She alternated her ministrations
with expressions in Bubi that appeared to comfort the injured man,
who tried to smile.

"I wish I knew your language," murmured Kilian, leaning toward
her. "You must have said something very special for someone in his
state to smile."

Bisila raised her sparkling eyes toward him. "I told him that he is so
ugly that the spirits won't want him, and when I finish fixing him up,
he'll feel so well that then it will be him who won't want to go."

"Do you think he can be saved?"

"It will take him time to recover, but I don't see any life-threatening
wound."

"Who did this to you, Gustavo?" whispered Julia.

"The ones who turn up like this," Bisila commented, "thrown at the
side of the road like dogs, are normally penal prisoners."

"You couldn't be satisfied with your job as a teacher?" Julia asked,
and Gustavo let out a grunt. "Well, if you survive this, I don't think
you'll want to continue with your liberation crusade."

"How could this have happened to him?" Kilian asked. "He's now
a Spanish citizen."

Bisila snorted, and Kilian looked at her, perplexed.

"How are we meant to understand if those in Spain can't agree about it either?" Julia said. "According to my father, the Spanish government is divided. On the one side, there are the moderates, who, like the foreign minister Castiella, think that we should favor a gradual path toward independence for the provinces. And on the other side, there are those who think like the minister to the presidency, Carrero Blanco, who is in favor of a tough colonial policy and tight control of local indigenous leaders."

"I'm afraid our governor is of the same opinion," Bisila commented ironically.

"Mistress!" Oba's voice resounded from the other end of the ward. "Are you there? I have to go now."

Julia stood up. "I'm sorry. You'll have to continue without me."

Kilian and Bisila remained in silence for several minutes after Julia left. Gustavo was in a deep sleep thanks to the tranquilizers the nurse had given him. For the first time in their lives, Kilian and Bisila were alone, and neither one of them really knew what to say. Gustavo's body was finally clean of blood. The only thing left was to stitch some deep cuts in one leg. Kilian's presence was no longer necessary. But he had not gotten up to go, and she had not suggested it. For a good long while, they enjoyed each other's company in silence, as they had done that day when she extracted the chigger.

"You've done an excellent job," he said finally when she cut the thread of the last suture stitch. "I'm in awe."

"You were also a great help." Bisila stood and stretched her back.

"Anyone would have done the same."

"No," she said firmly. "Not anyone."

Kilian felt a little guilty. To what point had his answer been honest? If instead of Bisila, another person had been in charge of looking after Gustavo, would he have been so helpful? Despite the seriousness of the situation, he had enjoyed each gesture, look, and breath she had made.

"Now we'll let him rest," said Bisila. "Until the doctor comes, I'll watch over him. Come, let's go and wash ourselves." She pointed to his hands. "You can't go back to the dryers like that. You look like a butcher."

Bisila guided him to a small washroom beside the infirmary, where there were two basins. They washed their hands, faces, and necks. When they were finished, she took a towel, dampened a corner, and brought it to his face.

"There are still a couple of spots."

Kilian closed his eyes and squeezed his fists together to resist the temptation of putting his arms around her waist and drawing her to him. He was certain that she wouldn't stop him, because she was taking longer than necessary in removing whatever had been on his face. A small voice inside him reminded him that Bisila was married to another man with whom she had a child. But his attraction to her went beyond all common sense.

"That's it," she said, with her faltering breathing only a few centimeters from his chest. "But you'll have to put on another shirt."

"Bisila! Are you there?"

She gave a start. "Yes, Doctor," she said out loud. "Beside the infirmary."

She took the towel and made as if she were finishing drying her hands while going out to meet Manuel, followed by Kilian.

Manuel approached, accompanied by a sturdy man with very marked features. Two deep wrinkles scored his cheeks.

"Hello, Kilian." Manuel shook his hand. "Julia just told me everything. Thanks very much for helping Bisila."

"I'm happy to have been of help."

"This is Gustavo's brother. His name is Dimas. He works as a foreman on the Constancia plantation, just beside us."

"How is he?" the man asked.

"He's asleep now," answered Bisila. "I think everything will be all right."

Dimas blessed himself.

"Good, let's go and see him," said Manuel.

Kilian waited behind. Bisila turned around and gave him an intense look of good-bye. He made a slight movement with his head and left with his heart beating excitedly.

Bisila approached the dryers, looking for her father, the perfect excuse to see Kilian. The desire to meet him again made her pulse quicken.

It was always like this, for the last . . . how many? Five years?

No, her first sight of Kilian did not go back to her wedding day, when she was fifteen and he had asked her why she looked so sad. The answer was very simple. She did not love Mosi. But Kilian was a white man and, therefore, unattainable. That this white man would lower himself to even congratulate her on her wedding day, and that he could read in her eyes that she was not happy, was more than she could ever have imagined the first few times he had come to her village with José.

From a distance, an adolescent Bisila had observed him so attentively that she had learned all his features and gestures by heart. Kilian was young, tall, and well built. He had dark hair with light-copper streaks, always worn short and combed back, and a pair of expressive green eyes that were often half shut because he smiled so much. His smile was honest and sincere, the same as his eyes. His hands, big and accustomed to hard work, danced in the air each time he told a story, but very often he crossed them under his chin to hold his head up. Then his look became dreamy, and Bisila thought she noticed that Kilian's spirit transported him to his own world, establishing a silent dialogue between his two homes.

Despite her youth, Bisila was fully conscious that she would never know Kilian's world. Probably, they would never even speak to each other. He was a young, handsome white man who had come to Fernando Po to make money and who, one day, would return home to raise his own family. She was a black teenage girl from an African tribe on a small island. Her life was decided for her when she was born. No matter how hard she studied, nothing would save her from marriage and bearing children. With a little bit of luck, she would be able to get work in something that had nothing to do with the land, and that idea partially consoled her. She had managed to maintain her illusion in secret, well hidden under layers of conformity and renouncement.

But that was a long time ago. Things had changed. Thanks to her marriage to Mosi and her work in the hospital, she could live on Sampaka and be close to him. For a long time, the vision of Kilian on the plantation, even if he did not pay her any attention, had been enough for her to get up every morning and go to her work in the hospital and return at night to the bed she shared with an insatiable Mosi. She even had been fortunate enough to hold Kilian's hand after his father died. The memories of that caress and the minutes during which she held his foot when he came looking for her to extract the chigger had accompanied her every night of his vacation at home and had prevented her from sinking into despair at the thought that she might never see him again.

How distant those sad days now seemed! She remembered how during the first weeks of his absence, she had to make a huge effort not to submit to the idea that it had been nothing but a childish dream and that she had to continue with her life and do what was expected of a wife who had been lucky enough to marry a good man. Mosi did not complain about the hours she spent outside the home. He supported her in her work. He wished only that Bisila would give him a son. She had contrived, thanks to her knowledge of traditional medicine, to delay that moment as long as she could. In her heart of hearts, she feared that a son would join her to Mosi forever.

But the months passed, Kilian did not return, and Mosi began to lose hope of becoming a father. Bisila finally decided to let nature take its course, continue with her real life, and relegate her fantasy to her nights of insomnia. Thanks to the spirits, being pregnant with Iniko had acted as a balm for her state of mind, and his birth had given her a peace and happiness that she had believed impossible at her twenty years.

This superficial calm had threatened to become a storm when Kilian appeared at Iniko's christening and learned her name. Since then, several weeks ago, it was rare that they did not bump into each other in the plantation yard.

Bisila was now convinced that it was not just her imagination. Kilian shared in her feelings.

The path from where the Europeans lived to the dryers did not go near the hospital. That could only mean that Kilian changed his normal route to see her. And he had increased the frequency of his visits to the infirmary, always complaining of some pain or other. Bisila had finally figured out that Kilian's injuries were imaginary, an excuse for her to touch him, take his temperature, and look after him and, what both most desired, to listen to each other.

Once again, Bisila silently gave thanks to the spirits for those brief, happy encounters. They filled her days with smiles, accelerated heartbeats, and trembling knees. When she arrived home at night, she had to pretend to be tired after her day at work. That lie, together with the effort of raising a child—who she really only saw at night—managed to keep Mosi away when she got into bed. Then she closed her eyes and slept, counting the minutes left for a new day, when dusk gave the dryers a golden hue as she waited to meet her beloved.

Bisila greeted her father, José, and Simón, but she did not see Kilian and did not ask for him either. She prowled around for a few minutes, pretending to stretch her legs and showing a feigned interest in the quality of the beans before claiming she had to get back to work.

She decided to walk past the main house in a final attempt to meet up with Kilian, and suddenly stopped dead.

Sade was going up the stairs to the employee rooms. She was wearing a tight turquoise chiffon dress with matching high-heeled sandals, and her long hair was tied up in a high ponytail. Two men passing turned to say something, and she smiled flirtatiously while continuing her undulating walk to the upper balcony. Once there, on turning right, she noticed the woman looking at her from below and found her face familiar.

Bisila waited a few seconds, chest tight.

Sade stopped in front of Kilian's room, knocked on the door, waited for him to open it, and went in.

Bisila hung her head and exhaled all the air in her lungs. Her face was burning, and her eyes filled with tears. In an instant, she had gone from euphoria to disappointment. She would have to make do with her fantasies. She began walking briskly to the Obsay yard. What did she expect? She was a married woman and he a single man. He had every right to enjoy himself with a woman. He had been with Sade for years. Why would he not keep seeing her? For a few laughs and a couple of nice conversations with a married nurse? Was it not true she also pleasured her husband?

Night fell before Bisila could get home. At the doors to the barracks, several women lit oil lamps that splashed the shadows with flickering tongues of light. She heard some shouts and recognized Iniko's cries. She quickened her step, her thoughts centered on her baby. When she entered her small house, he was calmer. Mosi smiled at her and handed her over her son. Bisila sat down and cradled him in her arms, whispering words in Bubi to him. Outside, some drums could be heard, and Mosi opened the door. Several neighbors were out on the street with bottles and glasses to liven up the party. There was seldom an afternoon when some short dance was not held at the end of the workday. Any excuse would do: a birthday, a wedding announcement, a pregnancy, a farewell. Lately those meetings led to a political discussion. The Nigerians were worried about the future of Fernando Po, as their work depended on it.

Bisila watched them. Like her, all her neighbors had desires, dreams, and secrets. Ekon came over, raised a glass toward Mosi, who nodded. Lialia, Ekon's wife, waved to Bisila, then came in and sat down for a while beside her.

"Iniko is very well behaved," said Lialia in Spanish with a heavy Nigerian accent as she petted the baby's head with her chubby hand.

"I don't know what I'd do without you. He spends more time with you than with me."

"I don't mind. You have a good job. You also look after us." She leaned toward Bisila. "You look tired . . ."

"Today was a hard day."

"Here, all the days are hard, Bisila."

The music of the drums got louder. They went outside. Mosi put his arm around his wife's shoulders and drew her toward him. Bisila closed her eyes and lost herself in the rhythm of the hollow wood. That day's beats would repeat their rhythm the following day, rebounding against the small gray-walled cement barracks laid out, one after the other, to house families like hers.

That was the world she belonged to. She was not anybody special. Everyone worked to keep their families going. The Nigerians dreamed of returning home one day, and she and Mosi of having a small house in the city. Meanwhile, they patiently occupied their place in the barracks while the children enjoyed their childish pranks in the dusty street they considered their home, as happy as they would be anywhere else.

She opened her eyes. Beside her, Lialia offered her breast to Iniko, who greedily grabbed hold of it. Lialia had four children, the last one Iniko's age, and breasts overflowing with milk. Bisila looked at her with affection. Thanks to Ekon's wife, she had not had to give up her work in the hospital to look after her son, as had every other woman who was now enjoying the party and their men. Mosi leaned down, searching for her lips. Bisila mechanically responded to his kiss while her mind wandered to the room where, probably, Kilian was kissing Sade.

Each in their own place, she thought. Like yesterday, and like each and every other day before. She did not feel jealousy or anxiety or even a deep sadness, rather, the inner certainty that the past and the present would not conquer the future. Time did not exist. A century's wait would be reduced to a second the moment Kilian was completely hers.

She was a reasonable woman and extremely patient. More than that. She had an unquenchable faith in destiny's strange designs.

"What are you doing here?"

"Oba told me you have been back for weeks. Since you didn't come to visit me, I came to you."

Sade strode into Kilian's room with determination. She threw a glance around the simple room, went over to the bed, and sat down. The narrow dress tightened even more against her thighs. She crossed her legs and rocked her foot in the air.

"Aren't you happy to see me?"

Kilian closed the door and leaned against it with his arms folded across his chest.

"You shouldn't be here."

Sade patted the bed, and her voice took on a syrupy tone. "Come on, sit beside me."

"I'm fine here, thanks," Kilian said brusquely.

Sade twisted her lips. She got up and walked toward him. "Relax, Massa." She stopped just a few centimeters from him, raised a hand, and slid a finger along his strong jaw. "We have to make up for lost time."

She planted a soft kiss on his lips, which he received coldly. With the tip of her tongue, she began to draw along the outline of Kilian's mouth, as she had done so many times before.

Kilian closed his eyes and clenched his fists. After such a long time, she knew perfectly well how to excite him. If this continued, he would end up giving in. He had not been with a woman for many months, and Sade was more than tempting. Any other man, including himself in other circumstances, would gladly accept her offer. He would throw her on the bed and absorb all her exuberant heat. But something had changed in him. In his mind and his heart, there was only room for one person. He gently put his hands on Sade's shoulders and moved her away.

"I'm sorry, Sade. No."

She scowled. "Why?"

"It's over."

"You've gotten tired of me." Sade pursed her lips. After a few seconds, she said, "Now I understand. There's someone else."

"No, that's not it."

"You're lying. You're not like your brother. He likes all girls. If you don't want to be with me now, it's because someone, and only one, has stolen your heart. Tell me, do I know her?" Her tone was high-pitched. "What has she got that I haven't?" She shook her head. "Maybe she's Spanish . . . Have you made plans for the wedding yet?" She cackled. "When you get tired of her, you'll come back to me, as they all do."

Kilian became defensive. "As far as I know, I have shared you with other men. I don't owe you anything."

Sade's chin began to tremble, and her breathing became agitated. "Just because I make my living as I do," she said through her teeth, "doesn't mean I don't have feelings. You're like the rest of them!"

Kilian wiped his brow. Large drops of sweat dissolved in his fingers. He had known for a while that this unfortunate scene would happen.

He had thought of offering Sade different excuses, hoping that she, used to dealing with many men, would just accept it. But she was right. Not for one moment had he thought about her feelings. He felt his mouth go dry. He went over to the basin and filled a glass of water. Sade remained close to the door, her head held high. She was beautiful, much more so than Bisila. But she was not Bisila.

During his stay in Pasolobino, Kilian sometimes remembered his encounters with Sade, but he had not missed her. Besides, he now felt he did not need her. A new and exhilarating feeling followed him everywhere. He did not care that Bisila was married to someone else or that being with her was impossible. Life had many twists. And he was prepared to wait as long as necessary. Meanwhile, he would not enjoy the company of any other woman. He could not turn Sade into his Regina as Dámaso had done; he could not have a lover for years to then abandon her.

"The best thing to do is to forget me, Sade," he said. He lit a cigarette and blew out the smoke slowly. "Nothing will make me change my mind."

"We'll see about that," she responded in a threatening tone as she left the room.

The open door framed a starry night. Kilian went out onto the balcony and leaned on the railing.

Below, Sade briskly walked toward a small open-topped SEAT 600 where one of the young waiters from the club was waiting for her. A few steps before reaching the car, she heard a voice.

"Kilian now lets you into his room?" asked Gregorio as he came over to her. "He must have really missed you."

"There's nobody here that interests me," she responded haughtily.

Gregorio stroked his small mustache as he let his eyes wander over the woman's body.

Sade tolerated his scrutiny as an idea crossed her mind. She raised her eyes toward the bedroom balcony and saw that Kilian was still watching.

"And you?" she asked in a forced honeyed tone. "Have you not gotten bored with Regina? I can't believe she tends to all your needs."

Gregorio arched his eyebrow. "And you could?"

Sade bit her bottom lip. "Come visit me, and we'll see."

Gustavo stayed in the hospital for several weeks. It was not until after Christmas that his wounds healed completely.

At the beginning of the new year, and after ten years of total opposition to independence, the Spanish administration surprisingly initiated some actions to promote it. With the intention of treating the Guineans as Spanish and avoiding discriminatory attitudes, the emancipation law that went back to the 1940s was repealed, which meant that, after complying with a series of requirements before the Council for Indigenous People—such as having reached the age of majority, holding some academic certificate, or working for a colonist—the blacks now had the same rights to purchase the same products as the whites, provided the emancipated person had the necessary means.

To the astonishment of Emilio and Generosa, Gustavo was elected to one of the Neighbor Councils of Santa Isabel, one of the 188 seats created in the whole country. Men like him and his brother Dimas began to lead lives similar to that of the Spaniards. They moved into small houses with gardens in front, where they parked their small cars every afternoon after work, and collected their children from school.

"And not only that, Julia," protested Emilio as he bounced Ismael on his knee. "On top of that, they speak to me arrogantly. If their father could see them! Ah! The old Dimas really was a good man."

"Of course . . . ," said his daughter. "He never contradicted you."

"Then each person knew their place, Daughter," intervened Generosa as she cleared the plates from the table. "Not like now. With this obsession they now have of getting rid of our sensible laws, soon they'll allow marriages between whites and blacks, just wait and see."

"I don't see why you find it strange." Julia shrugged. "France and England have opened the way to emancipate their Equatorial and Western African territories. Why would Spain be any different?"

"Because, child, thanks be to God, we have a *caudillo* who has known how to maintain order for a long time both here and in Spain." She sighed loudly. "If he had the same energy as before, I can assure you he wouldn't let himself be dragged along in this."

"Times change, Mom."

"Yes, but I don't know if it's for the better, Julia," added Emilio. He looked at his watch, got up, and set the child on a rug with several cardboard horses. "Anyway, give our good-byes to Manuel. It was unfortunate he had to leave."

"We've had a lot of accidents. The laborers have been fighting. That's what politics does to people."

Generosa bent down to kiss her grandson before saying good-bye to her daughter. Julia followed them outside.

"Don't you have to take Oba with you?"

"That girl!" Emilio rolled his eyes. "Since she has fallen in love with that big ox, the only thing she cares about is going to Sampaka. Lately, she's been very absentminded in the store, forgetting customer orders . . . If she doesn't change, we'll have to look for someone else."

"Yes, as if it was a good time to train another . . . ," commented Generosa, fluffing out her hair with her hands.

Just then, Oba appeared with sparkling eyes and swollen lips.

"A little longer and you'd have walked back," Emilio scoffed.

"I'm sorry, sir."

"Come on, get into the car."

"I'm sorry, sir, but I need to speak to the mistress for a moment." She looked at Julia with imploring eyes.

Julia noticed her father's annoyed look and promised him she would not take long.

Once inside the house, Julia asked her, "What's so important?"

"It's to do with . . ." Oba rubbed her hands nervously. "It's my friend Sade. A few days ago, she admitted to me she was pregnant . . ."

"And . . . ?"

"Well, the father is one of the employees of this plantation, and when he found out, he did not want anything more to do with her. My friend is very sad and worried, and I thought that, well, since you know him, you might be able to help with the situation and—"

"Who is it?" Julia cut her off.

"Massa Kilian."

"But . . ." Julia sat down and rubbed her forehead, surprised.

"They've been friends for a long time."

"Well . . . I thought that"—Julia tried to be as polite as possible—"that your friend had many friends."

"Yes, but she's sure that he's the father. She's very upset, Mistress. I know how much she loved the massa and how worried she is now that he has abandoned her."

"Oba!" Emilio's voice came from outside. "We're going now!"

Julia stood up, grabbed hold of Oba's elbow, and went with her to the door while whispering in her ear, "Not a word to anyone. To anyone, you hear?"

Oba nodded.

"I'll see what I can do."

When everyone had left, Julia picked up Ismael and hugged him as hard as she could. *And what laws exist for these cases?* she thought. None. It was the word of a black woman of doubtful reputation against that of a white man. Sade's word against Kilian's. A fine pickle. Was it that difficult to take steps to stop this from happening? She found it difficult to believe what Oba had told her, but she found it even more difficult to consider the possibility, if it was true, that Kilian had opted for the most cowardly option. The truth was that he would not be the first or the last to do so. You only had to take a trip around the streets of Santa

Isabel to get some idea. And what could she do? At most, talk to Kilian and hope that it was all a lie.

Manuel came into the sitting room, looking tired, and fell onto the sofa beside his wife and child.

"A little free time at last." He bent down and kissed Ismael on the head, and Ismael put out his arms for Manuel to lift him up. He noticed that Julia seemed a little distracted. "Are you okay?"

She thought about whether she should share the news with her husband.

"You know, Julia, on days like today, I wonder what the hell we are doing here. I know they pay me well, but I'm beginning to get tired of the cuts, the quinine, the imaginary illnesses and snakebites . . ."

It was definitely not the best day to bring up Kilian.

"You're exhausted. Once you can get away to the jungle, you'll forget about it."

Manuel smiled. "Kilian was just telling me the same thing!"

Julia bit her bottom lip. So Kilian was at the hospital once again.

Although, she thought, if Sade's claim was true, that chigger would be the least he deserved.

In the infirmary, Bisila finished giving Kilian's toes a very thorough examination.

"You don't have any chiggers, Kilian."

"No? Believe me, it's very itchy."

Bisila gave him a skeptical look. "Then we'll wait a couple of days and see what happens."

"Bisila, I . . ." Kilian leaned toward her. "I wanted to see you. Before, we used to bump into each other everywhere." His voice became a whisper. "Don't you like talking to me anymore? Have I said or done something to upset you?"

Bisila diverted her eyes to the window.

Someone knocked gently on the door and opened it without waiting for an answer. Julia entered and addressed Kilian directly.

"I need to speak with you . . . alone." She turned to Bisila. "Have you finished?"

"Not quite," Kilian responded rapidly. "But if what you have to tell me is so important, we can continue later, if that is all right with you, Bisila?"

Bisila nodded, picked up her implements, stood up, and walked to the small adjacent bathroom. When she had finished washing her hands, she clearly heard the voices of Julia and Kilian through the wall. Was she imagining it, or had they mentioned Sade's name? She listened closer.

"Sade asserts," Julia said, "that you are the father and when you found out about it, you decided to end it with her."

Bisila held her breath.

"In the first place, Julia, I have just learned from you that Sade is pregnant." Kilian's voice was level. "And second, it's impossible I could be the father."

"Yes, I know she's a . . . I mean, you're not the only one . . ." She clicked her tongue, a little uncomfortable. "But she's sure about it."

"And what do you think, Julia? If you have come here so quickly to tell me, it's because you have doubts."

"Kilian, even I know that during all these years, you have only wanted to be with Sade. It's reasonable that . . ."

"You should ask Gregorio. Or didn't you know that she has become his favorite *mininga* in the last few months? Maybe both of them thought that this would make me jealous, but it hasn't worked. Sade has made up this story out of spite." A long silence followed. "Julia, I give you my word that the last time I was with Sade was before I went on vacation to Spain. When I came back, she came to see me one afternoon, and that was when I made it clear to her that . . . well . . . our friendship . . . was over. It's impossible that I was the one to get her

443

pregnant, and I will not put up with any blackmail. Is that clear?" His voice was hard.

"I'm sorry for having doubted you." Julia lowered her voice. "I don't know what to say. If Sade's reasons are what you suspect, I don't think she'll miss the opportunity to defame you."

"No one can say they have seen me with her in the last few months." Kilian paused. "You know me better than anybody, Julia. Were you really able to believe, even for one second, that I would have shirked my responsibilities?"

Even through the wall, Bisila noted a tone of reproach in Kilian's voice. Seconds passed, and Julia did not answer. She heard the door close. She waited a bit longer before returning to the infirmary.

Kilian's face lit up when he saw her. "I was afraid you wouldn't come back."

"You asked me to wait."

Bisila knew now that Kilian had not been with Sade for months, but she did not want to get her hopes up again. The possibility existed that he had exchanged her for another *friend*. Even so, the relief made Bisila as daring as the first nighttime shadows.

"And what do you do after work? You don't have any woman to keep you company?"

"Of course I do," Kilian responded forcefully. Bisila looked at him, surprised by the clear and swift response, and he, with a gleam in his eyes, stared back at her for a long moment before continuing in a hoarse voice, "I'm never alone. Not for one second in the day. For months, you've been the only one in my thoughts."

When Bisila got to the entrance to the dryers, she saw her father, Simón, and Kilian, and a smile lit up her face. The secret shared between the two of them accompanied her at all hours. She held her breath. They would probably have to make do with their intense and fleeting private encounters while offering casual greetings in public for the rest of their lives. Unless the spirits had pity on them and changed the course of things. For the moment, she consoled herself, the day had begun well.

That morning, Simón was impatiently moving across the metal sheets where the cocoa formed an uneven carpet, making sure that everything was working properly.

"What has you so nervous, Simón?" asked Kilian, drying the sweat that was blinding him. It was terribly hot. "The beans won't roast any quicker no matter how many times you go round them."

"I don't want any delays, Massa. I don't want the big massa to force me to be here on Saturday."

"And what's happening on Saturday?"

"My father is going to become the new chief, or *botuku*, for the Bissappoo area." Simón puffed out his chest.

"Wow, congratulations, Simón," said a surprised Kilian. "I have before me the son of a chief."

"Yes, a *real* chief," Simón specified. "And not like yours, who tried to be one without earning it."

José shot a severe glance at Simón. The young man liked Kilian, but he was also a Bubi who sought independence for the island, separate from the continent. He never missed an opportunity to criticize the white colonists. José shared many of his ideas, but was very careful not to offend Kilian.

Kilian had heard stories about how the Bubis were going to name the governor their *abba*, or spiritual leader. The idea had seemed ridiculous to him. In Bubi culture, *abba* was the name given to the spiritual leader of the Moka region who had a sacred influence over the whole island. It was a hereditary title; not just anybody could be named *abba*. For that reason, he had taken it for granted that it was only a malicious rumor. No Bubi would ever think of bestowing the honor of being the supreme spiritual leader on a white man.

"He was a whisker away from becoming it."

Simón was down with them in one leap. His face was red from the heat. He took a brush and began to vigorously sweep the shells that had fallen from the transporter belt.

"I was with my father in several meetings between village chiefs and whites. You already know"—since he had stopped being Kilian's boy, Simón had automatically stopped addressing him so formally—"that my people don't like to be impolite, so they decided to consult the spirits of our ancestors."

"Ah, and what did the spirits say?" Kilian turned, trying not to laugh, and saw Bisila approach.

She was wearing a white skirt and blouse with the sleeves rolled up to her elbows. Normally she left her short fringe loose, but that day, she had her hair done in fine braids, which highlighted her enormous eyes. The sight of her beauty gave him a pleasant shiver.

She held his gaze. They said nothing so as not to raise suspicions among the other men. It was very difficult, but they tried with all their might not to show the slightest sign of their special relationship.

Bisila raised her fingers to her lips to get Kilian to keep quiet while Simón continued his explanation in a loud and clear voice.

"The spirits aren't fools, of that I'm certain, and they spoke through different men to show us that such a thing had more to do with the Spanish interference than with actual homage. Some said that we Bubis wanted to sell the island to Spain. Others suggested to lease the island for forty years and continue with you as long as you looked after us. Others remembered that you hadn't always wanted us, giving as an example the slaughter during the rebellion of 1910." He paused for breath. "And others even defended you, saying there were a lot of good Spaniards, that you hadn't come here to colonize, but to work, and that you had helped us prosper."

"I myself have heard more than one Spaniard criticize this act and call us stupid," José intervened, forcing the young man to shift his eyes away from Bisila and pay attention to the conversation. "They are the whites that want the Bubis to be anti-Spanish and independent, I suppose with the intention of managing the country through their native friends if independence is ever achieved."

Kilian rubbed his forehead, shocked and confused. "I'm Spanish, I don't have any hidden agenda, and I also think it's stupid. So what's it to be?"

"To smooth the situation over and offend neither white or Bubi, it was thought that they could name him simply *motuku* or *botuku*, that's to say chief, a good man, the visible head of a district or area, or person who should be obeyed because of his character. The title would be granted in a ceremony of respect where he would receive typical mementos of Bubi artisanship . . ."

"And also a young virgin . . . ," Bisila added as she came over. "*Tuë a lóvari é.* Good morning, Kilian."

"*Wë á lo è, Bisila,*" answered José with a smile. He could not hide how proud he was of his youngest daughter. "*Ká wimböri lé?* How do you feel today?"

"*Nimböri lèle, potóo.* I am feeling well, thank you."

Kilian loved the sound of the Bubi language, especially on Bisila's lips. He remembered the times she had tried, unsuccessfully, to get him to learn more than just a few words of greeting and farewell in the makeshift classroom the hospital infirmary had been turned into. A very diligent student, Kilian allowed her to take his hand to feel the vibrations in her throat when there was an especially difficult sound, but he immediately forgot all about the classes and began to gently caress her, first the neck, and then her jawbone on his way to her cheeks. She then closed her eyes, raised her chin, and offered him her lips for him to absorb the letters, words, and sentences that he did understand.

Kilian shook his head, feeling a pleasant throbbing in his groin. They were not alone now. He had to control himself.

Bisila continued, with some irony. "Ah, but the deal was that the governor had to keep her intact, just as he received her, and would accept her as his daughter, with all his love and affection."

Simón's face took on an air of triumph. "Between the protests and the letter we sent him asking for it to be canceled, the fact is the governor has said there will be no homage. And now, if you don't mind"—he turned his back on them—"let's not waste any more time and finish this as quickly as possible."

José smiled as Simón got back to work. He turned to his daughter.

"And what brings you here today, Bisila?"

"Are you going up to Bissappoo on Saturday for the crowning of the new chief?"

José nodded while looking out the corner of his eye at Kilian, who listened intently.

"I would also like to attend," added Bisila, "but I don't want to go up on my own."

Alone? Without Mosi? It was now clear to Kilian that he also wanted to go. He felt a stab of guilt in his chest. Bisila was a married woman, and in the last few weeks, both of them had acted as if she were not.

But a few days with her away from Sampaka . . .

"Ösé," he began to say, seeking an invitation, "on Friday, we will finish work on the drying. There is no reason for you not to go with Simón for such a special event."

Kilian waited for José, finally, to say, "Maybe you'd like to attend the chief's naming ceremony?"

"It would be an honor, Ösé," Kilian hurriedly answered, directing a quick, satisfied glance at Bisila, who lowered her head to hide a smile before returning to the hospital.

"*Ö má we è*, Simón. *Ö má we è*, Ösé. *Ö má we è*, Kilian."

"Good-bye, Bisila," answered Kilian, who, to the astonishment of the others, tried to repeat the same words in Bubi. "*Ö má . . . we . . . è, Bisila.*"

Simón burst out laughing.

Kilian quickly went back to work. It was only Wednesday. Still three long days left to finish. He began pacing, making sure that everything was going smoothly.

Simón's impatience had infected him.

When they left the dryers, it was almost nightfall. It had been an exhausting day, in spite of the breath of fresh air that Bisila's unexpected visit had brought.

The men had not mentioned the political situation again, but Kilian had thought about it. While crossing the yard toward their respective rooms, he said to José, "After listening to Simón, I have the feeling that this new period is taking shape on the basis of gossip. We hear rumors rather than facts. Not in the *Ébano*, nor in the *Poto-Poto*, nor in the *Hoja del Lunes de Fernando Po*, not even in *La Guinea Española* or in *ABC* is a word said about all the different movements. They only talk of peace and harmony between whites and blacks."

José shrugged. "It could be that the government doesn't want the whites to be nervous knowing that sooner or later, the colony will come to an end."

"If so, we all should be nervous." Kilian raised his hands in the air and said, "You are as Spanish as me now."

"Ah, really? I'd like to see your neighbors' reaction in Pasolobino if I moved in with you. Do you really think that they'd consider me Spanish? The laws might change rapidly, but people don't, Kilian. Maybe I can go to places reserved for whites, go to the cinema, take the coach, sit beside you in the cathedral, and even bathe in the same swimming pool without fear of arrest, but that doesn't mean that I don't see the looks of disgust . . . My papers say I'm Spanish, Kilian, but my heart knows I'm not."

Kilian stopped and put a hand on his arm.

"I've never heard you talk like this, Ösé. Do you also agree with the ideas of men like Simón and Gustavo?"

José looked at his friend. "There is an old African proverb that says that when two elephants fight, it's the grass that suffers." He waited for Kilian to understand before walking on. "No matter what happens, it will be the grass that suffers. It's always been like that."

16

Ribalá Ré Ríhólè
Marriage for Love

On the way to Bissappoo, Kilian felt privileged to attend the naming of the new Bubi chief. On more than one occasion, José had admitted to feeling sad that the new generations of his tribe were lax about tradition. Thanks to the Spanish influence on education and daily life, the young people did not listen to the words of their elders as before. One day, they would regret not knowing about many of their customs.

The ceremony was special because although Spain had meddled in the life of the tribe by appointing the village chiefs and creating the position of Spanish administrator in the native villages, Bissappoo continued to name its own chief, even if it was just to uphold the symbolic value. It was perhaps one of the few villages that kept its traditions practically intact. And of course, the young man who contributed to this, Simón, was now guiding them with a speed and energy that surprised them all.

Kilian knew the route to Bissappoo by heart. The path through the palm trees. The stream. The cedar forest. The ascent of the slope. He had gone up to the village at least twenty times in the years he had been on Fernando Po. He no longer had to follow José's steps or wait for him to clear the weeds with his machete. He knew for certain that, even in the darkness of the night, he would find his way.

However, on this occasion, he preferred to be in last position, just behind Bisila, admiring the movement of her body.

She was wearing a knee-length, green leaf-patterned dress, which was gathered at the waist and buttoned at the front, and a pair of white sandals. When walking up the steepest parts, Kilian could see how the material stuck to her body, outlining her figure. Bisila noticed his silence and turned her head from time to time to smile at him.

Kilian thought it was an honor to attend the naming ceremony of a Bubi chief, even if Jacobo had criticized him for participating in an event that did nothing but add fuel to the fire of independence sentiments. His brother could not know the real reason for his escape to Bissappoo. What really excited Kilian was the possibility of enjoying Bisila's company for a few hours.

A short distance from Bissappoo, just after crossing the *buhaba*, they made out a large number of people nervously awaiting the arrival of the new chief under the wooden arch guarded by the two sacred trees, which sometimes served as the threshold to the village. That day, it was decked out with every type of amulet. Simón went off in a hurry to change. José began greeting one and all. Everyone was dressed up in the traditional style: the men sported huge straw hats topped with hen feathers; the women wore long strands of glass beads, shells, and snake bones on their arms, legs, and necks. The majority had rubbed themselves with *ntola* ointment, whose strong smell Kilian had become used to.

Bisila used the commotion to explain to Kilian everything that had gone on up to that moment. She moved close enough for their arms to brush against each other but made sure that, in the eyes of everyone else, her posture seemed normal, raising her hand in the air from time to time to point out one thing or another.

"The election and coronation ritual of a new chief," she explained, "follows very strict rules on the burial and mourning of the previous chief, although some things have changed according to the area's elders, like the ancient custom of burning the village of a dead chief."

"Could you imagine burning down Santa Isabel if the mayor died?" he joked.

Bisila laughed and increased the elbow pressure. "Once the date for the ceremony is chosen, a house is built for the new chief and his principal wives to live in for a week—"

"How unusual"—he interrupted again, with a keen look—"and tiring . . ."

". . . after which," she continued, a smile on her lips, "the new *botuku* is placed under the shade of a tree, consecrated to the souls of previous deceased *botuku*. There we invoke the souls, the spirits, the *morimò* or *borimó* of the other world to bless and protect the new chief so that he never tarnishes the memory of those who occupied the seat before him. We also sacrifice a goat, and with its blood, we anoint the chest, shoulders, and back of the new chief. Later, the king has to climb to the top of a palm tree with wooden arcs on his feet and undertake the task of extracting the palm wine and cutting the bunches from where the palm oil comes. And last, we take him to a beach or a river, where we wash his body to purify it and remove all the stains of his previous life. We anoint him with *ntola*, and we dress him before returning to the village in procession, joyfully singing and dancing the *batele*, or ritual dance."

Kilian's voice became a whisper. "I would love for you to name me *botuku* and bathe me in the river, but I'd have problems going up a palm tree, unless you were waiting for me."

Bisila bit her bottom lip. She was finding it very hard not to jump into his arms and let everyone know how happy she felt.

The people began to gather at the chief's new house. Kilian and Bisila stayed behind and watched from a back row. A murmur indicated that the chief was leaving for the public square. Kilian could not make out the face of Simón's father, a small, muscular man with wide shoulders. What he did notice was that his whole body was decorated in white shells called *tyíbö*, which was used as currency by the Bubis in the past. The shells had been strung in bracelets and rings for his arms and legs and as a belt from which a monkey's tail hung.

The new *botuku* walked on a few meters accompanied by the enthusiastic shouts of his neighbors and sat down on a rudimentary stone throne where he was crowned with a headpiece of goat horns and pheasant and parrot feathers. In his right hand was a scepter, a cane with a goat's skull on top and with corded shells hanging. Everyone, Kilian included, made a high-pitched noise to express their excitement.

When Kilian shouted in unison with the crowd, he felt Bisila's soft fingers cradle his own, and he caressed her palm with his thumb, memorizing her creases and savoring the gaps in her fingers.

An old man approached the chief and placed his hands on his head, murmuring a prayer in which he urged him to honor previous chiefs. He finished his sermon with a phrase that Kilian repeated in a low voice after Bisila translated it for him.

"Do not drink any water that is not from the mountains or the rain."

Kilian nodded. For someone who came from a valley surrounded by high peaks, the words had a special meaning. For him there was no purer water than that from melted snow.

Bisila squeezed his hand a little more tightly before letting it go. As best he could, he again focused his attention on the ceremony with his heart beating wildly. A group of men escorted the new king, all dressed as warriors and armed with long wide-bladed serrated spears

and enormous cowhide shields. All were well built and muscular, and
the vast majority bore scarification on different parts of their bodies.
They had dyed their hair—which, for some, fell in tiny braids like
Bisila's—with reddish mud.

She pointed to two of them.

"Look who's there!"

It took a bit for Kilian to make out Simón, one of the ancient
warriors! It was the first time that Kilian had seen African warriors with
his own eyes, as the wars had ended years ago, and they dressed up only
on special occasions.

"Despite his youth," Bisila commented, "Simón is a good keeper of
the customs of our people."

"And who is that beside him?"

"Don't you remember my brother Sóbeúpo?"

"But surely he was just a child the other day! And look at him now.
All grown up."

"Yes, Kilian. Time passes quickly . . ."

Especially when we are together, they both thought.

The ceremony ended, and the festivities began that, according to
Bisila, would last a week. They would do nothing but eat, drink, and
dance one *balele* after another.

"It's a shame we can't stay that long," he complained.

"We should make the best of what we have," she replied.

During the banquet, Kilian and Bisila kept a prudent distance from
each other, although every now and then, they pretended to scan the
scene to steal a look at each other. Beside José, his sons, and other men,
Kilian ate goat meat with yams and *bangásúpu*, or banga sauce, and
drank *topé*, the palm wine, and brandy.

José cajoled Kilian into taking his shoes off and trying to imitate the
men's dance, which was not easy, as he did not have an African or any
other beat in his body. However, he was pleased that the Bubi dances
had a slower tempo than the hectic dances of the Nigerian laborers.

With his eyes closed, he managed to relax his body and feel the syncopated rhythm of the bells guiding his feet. A sudden shiver made him open his eyes, and he turned to meet Bisila's clear gaze, shining in the reflection of the bonfire's flames. Without taking his eyes from her, he danced as well as he could manage, without stiffness. His efforts were rewarded by the approving smile she held on her lips until the dance ended. Though a bit dizzy, he accepted a final bowl of palm wine from José and began to wander around, saluting everyone, just like Bisila, with the aim of getting a few seconds together with her.

He remembered festivals in Pasolobino: the men clambering up a tree trunk placed in the square, the dances to the beat of the castanets decorated with colored ribbons, the band music, the saint's procession . . .

Kilian realized that he had thought about Pasolobino and its inhabitants very little lately. He hardly missed them at all! When did that start? He was sure it began with Bisila.

Even his own mother had reproached him by letter that his notes were getting shorter and shorter, centered only on managing the House of Rabaltué.

Jacobo had commented on it as well, maybe because Mariana had written that she was worried about Kilian, but had not gone into detail because he himself was too busy with work, his friends, and parties. It had been years since they had shared the same pastimes and companions. They had a good deal: each one led his own life and did not meddle in the other's.

Jacobo would never have imagined Kilian falling in love with a black woman. For him, native women were for enjoyment, not love. Even if he found out that his brother was smitten, he would strongly insist that the affair did not have any future. It was just a question of time before they left. Jacobo did not know of any white man who had taken his black mistress to Spain.

Kilian closed his eyes and let the African songs, the smell of the food, and the taste of the palm wine take control of his senses.

There would be other hard days of work and decision making, but at that moment, he was in Africa sharing some days of festivity with good friends.

At that moment, he had Bisila beside him. He needed nothing else.

It was very dark when Kilian retired to the cabin that they had prepared for the only white man at the party, one that continued on with intensity. He had decided to disappear before the drink left him out for the count, and after Bisila, tired, had said good night to all. When she was gone, a terrible feeling of loneliness came over him. He had been tempted to drown his sorrow in *topé*. Fortunately, common sense had come to his rescue. He wanted all his senses, if even the possibility existed that something more than flirting might happen with Bisila.

On crossing the threshold, he felt a sharp pain in his right foot. He looked down and saw that he had cut himself on something. Blood began to flow from the wound. He went in to look for a piece of cloth to cover his foot. The sight of his own blood made him feel dizzy and somewhat light-headed.

The door opened, and to his relief, he saw it was Bisila.

A gasp of admiration escaped his throat.

She had taken off her European clothes and dressed up in shells and glass beads like the other Bubi women. Her body shone from the reddish and ochre oils she had painted herself with. They had to be special, thought Kilian, because they did not smell like the typical *ntola* ointments. She was wearing a colored garment around her body, which stuck to her like a second skin.

Bisila felt the pleasant heat of Kilian's intense gaze, but she saw the wound and knelt down to get a closer look.

"What happened to you?" she asked as she gently took his foot in her hands. "I always end up kneeling before you," she joked.

Kilian smiled. "I stepped on something."

Bisila dampened a piece of cloth in a bowl of water and washed the wound carefully.

"You've got a palm shoot stuck in you."

Kilian opened his eyes, surprised. "You mean to say there is a palm tree growing right in the middle of the door?"

"At our doors, we place *Achatina* shells with holes in them, through which we put palm shoots."

"And why do you do that?"

Bisila answered without lifting her eyes from the bandage she was applying. "To protect us from the devil. When he touches one of those shells with his claws, he immediately retreats."

Kilian put his head back and gave a hearty laugh. "Well, Satan must have very delicate feet."

Bisila tugged the bandage tight. "Careful, Kilian. You shouldn't joke about these things. And it only took a weak shoot to knock you down . . ."

Kilian sat up and looked her straight in the eye. "I didn't mean to laugh. In Pasolobino there are also people who still use goats' feet or birds of prey to ward off the evil spirits and witches."

In silence, Bisila lit the fire in the middle of the house, extended the thick matting on top of the deerskins that were on the floor, and hung the mosquito net round the full length of the improvised bed.

Then, fixing her eyes on Kilian, she allowed the wrap covering her body to slide to the floor, turned around, lay on the matting, and stretched out her arm, inviting Kilian to come to her.

Kilian got up without taking his eyes from Bisila's body.

She looked much more beautiful than he had ever imagined. Motherhood had given her breasts a fullness well hidden by the blouses she normally wore. His heart began beating strongly. He lay down beside her and put out his left arm like a pillow so that Bisila could snuggle up beside him.

Kilian slipped his right hand along her side till he reached her waist, stopping at her hips and returning his hand to her stomach then to her breast. He wanted to make sure that Bisila was really in his arms. Her skin was soft and smooth. Mystifyingly, he felt nervous. He was experienced with women, but Bisila was special.

When she smiled, he forgot everything.

Bisila inhaled the scent of him. She wanted to steep herself with his musk. She felt her heart beat differently, joyful and expectant. They were, at last, alone.

The future did not matter.

Mosi did not matter.

"We are finally together, the cocoa and the snow," said Kilian hoarsely. "You've no idea how many times I've dreamed of this moment."

Bisila raised her head and looked at him with her enormous eyes. "Me too. Let me honor you tonight like a real chief. My body is not virgin, but my heart is. I give myself to you."

Kilian was moved by Bisila's words. He bent down his head and placed his mouth on her full lips.

"Tonight you will be my queen," he murmured. "You will be my *wairibo*, the guardian of my spirit."

Their two bodies fit perfectly together, the predestined outcome after a long wait of stolen looks, words, fleeting kisses, and hopeful caresses. They could finally feel the heat and refreshing dampness of the deepest breath in every pore of their bodies.

Both had been with others, but they had never entrusted their souls to anyone.

Now they did.

A good while later, they could still hear songs, no longer so intense. Kilian assumed that most had gone to bed in order to be rested for the following day's festivities. Soon Bisila would have to return to her cabin to avoid raising suspicions.

Kilian lay on Bisila's lower belly, his head rested between her breasts. She stroked his hair and, every now and then, placed her lips on his forehead. He felt he was in heaven, although he could not get a worrying thought out of his mind.

"It's unfair that we have to hide," he said in a sleepy voice.

"We'll have to be even more careful now," she said, sitting up. "I'm an adulterer."

The word fell like a ton of cocoa sacks on both of them. Bisila belonged to Mosi. And there was no solution to that. If anyone were to find out, Bisila would be severely punished. It was a risk she had decided to take, but she would always be the one to lose.

"In that way, there is not much difference between your country and mine," Kilian admitted. "A man can have several women, but if a woman is unfaithful, only hell awaits her, in every sense."

"When I was small, to frighten us, they told us that women adulterers were hung from a tree with rocks tied to their feet, or that their hands were cut off, or even that they were buried alive with just their head exposed for the vermin to eat them."

Kilian shuddered.

"However, according to Bubi tradition, if a woman is widowed and fulfills the mourning rituals, then she can have all the men she wants, though she can't marry again."

Kilian could not help smiling. "If you were my wife, I wouldn't want to share you with anyone."

Bisila slid her hands over Kilian's chest and rested them on his heart.

"We will have to be very careful," she murmured. "It will be our secret. We can't hope for more. But this is more than I ever dreamed of."

Kilian took her hands in his and brought them to his lips.

"I still hope for more, my sweet *wairíbo*, my guardian," he whispered.

Bisila moaned. The night had engulfed all sounds. She should go. She carefully moved Kilian's head away and picked up her colored dress. She got onto her knees and wrapped it round her. Kilian lay on his side, resting on his elbow. He did not stop looking at her and caressing her thighs. Bisila halted his movements with her hands, leaned down to kiss him once more, and stood up.

Before creeping away, she turned to look at him one last time. "Whatever happens, Kilian, I won't forget this night." A breath of fresh air wafted through the room, carrying her words as she left. "I'll always be with you."

Weeks later, Bisila closed the door to Kilian's room carefully so as not to make any noise; she made certain that her dress was well buttoned and walked along the corridor, lost in thought. She turned left, toward the stairs, and stopped dead. Had she heard a voice?

She withdrew a few steps, pressed her body against the wall, and listened closely.

Nothing. She must have imagined it. The moon's position showed it was later than other nights. On weekdays, all the employees were asleep at this time. She went down the steps, hanging on to the railing to soften the sound of her steps, as if that would be much help if she met anybody. Her heart began beating strongly. She knew it was a risk to go to Kilian's room, but what other option did she have?

Since the naming ceremony, she and Kilian had secretly continued to see each other. He came around to the hospital, pretending to collect medicine, take his blood pressure, or visit a sick laborer just when she was finishing her shift. They made love hastily, barely speaking, in a small storeroom.

But both preferred the nights when, taking advantage of her late shift, Bisila came to Kilian's room in the darkness. And precisely for that reason, she had asked for more night shifts, something Mosi readily accepted because it paid better. Bisila and Kilian could share his bed, talking in whispers, and enjoy themselves with less fear of being discovered.

Bisila got to the bottom of the stairs, then crossed the white-columned porch and walked along the wall, looking to her right and directly ahead to make sure that the main yard was empty. There was not a soul in sight. Suddenly, a door opened and hit her so hard that she staggered. She let out a yelp and raised her hands to her face.

"By all that is holy! But where are you coming from at this time of night, girl?" Lorenzo Garuz could guess the answer. He was not very pleased when the employees allowed their girlfriends to visit, but after so many years, he had learned it was better not to talk about the subject.

"Bisila!" José approached and looked at her face. "Have you hurt yourself? It's my daughter," he explained to Garuz. "She works as a nurse for Doctor Manuel."

The manager peered at her.

"And what are you doing here in the middle of the night?"

Bisila swallowed. Two more men came out of the room, and she recognized Jacobo and Mateo. José's face went from worry to curiosity. Her legs began to shake. She took a deep breath and answered as calmly as possible. "They sent me a message that Simón wasn't well, not even enough to walk to the hospital." She paused and silently thanked the cloud that had covered the moon and left them in almost total darkness. That way they would not see the lie reflected in her eyes.

"Simón?" asked Jacobo. "I saw him at dinnertime. He looked as well as ever."

"He could not stop vomiting. Something must have disagreed with him. But I think he will be all right by tomorrow. These indigestions only last a few hours. If you don't mind, I should get back to work." Bisila gave her father an enchanting smile. "Good night, Dad."

The cloud moved away from the moon, which once again shone on Bisila. Garuz and Mateo were struck by the unusual beauty of José's daughter; Jacobo remembered it was she who had stitched his hand. José continued to frown. Was it his imagination, or did his daughter lately radiate a glowing happiness? Not even after Iniko's birth had he seen her so dazzling . . .

Bisila continued her journey with a quick step. For a few seconds, she had been afraid that Simón would be the next to appear behind Jacobo and Mateo. Fortunately for her, it had not happened. Before going to bed, she would find him and ask him to lie if anyone asked. Simón would do that for her and much more. They had been friends since childhood. She sighed as her spirits revived and the memories of her meeting with Kilian came back to her.

José remained thinking. Had his daughter gone to treat a sick person without her small medical kit?

The following morning, José was the first to see Simón, long before Bisila could get to him.

"How is your stomach?" he asked directly.

"My stomach?" Simón asked in surprise.

José sighed. "If anyone asks, tell them you're over your indigestion thanks to Bisila, right?"

"Can I ask why? You know I would do anything for you and Bisila, but . . ."

José rolled his eyes. What strange reasons moved the spirits? Perhaps they had gone crazy. Was it not enough he was worried about the future of his own family? Why add another worry? Had he not carried out all his obligations? The world was becoming a very complicated place.

"I'm not telling you anything more," he muttered.

One person suspected; that was more than enough.

"I think Ösé knows about us."

Kilian finished his cigarette before putting it out in the ashtray on the small table. Bisila lay on her side, resting on her arm. She looked up and said without the slightest sign of worry, "Has he said anything to you?"

"It's his"—Kilian hesitated—"silence. We don't see or talk to each other as much anymore. But he has neither asked me nor made any comment of disapproval."

Bisila rubbed his chest. "And that worries you?"

Kilian weighed his words. "I'd be very upset if he thought I'd offended him." He stroked his hair and looked at the ceiling. "And you? You're not worried?"

"I think, in other circumstances, he'd be pleased to have you as a son-in-law."

"Maybe it would be a good idea for me to go out with everyone else, I don't know, take a trip down to the casino with Mateo and Marcial . . . If your father knows about us, others could know too, and that puts you in a dangerous position."

"He'd never say anything," Bisila protested.

"But there's also Simón," he interrupted her. "I don't know if we can trust him. Just yesterday, he asked me cheekily what new ailment brought me to the hospital again."

Bisila had a fit of giggles. "And what did you say?"

She sat astride him, bending down to caress him gently with her lips: his eyes and eyelids, his nose, his ears, his bottom lip, his mouth, and his chin, naming them in Bubi.

"Dyokò, mö papú, mö lümbo, lö tó, möë' ë, annö, mbëlü?"

Kilian shivered every time she whispered to him in her mother tongue.

"It wasn't there that hurt," he said mischievously, turning himself to one side so she had to place herself behind him.

Bisila continued with her caresses, sliding her hands along his back, his waist, his bottom, and his legs.

"*Attá, atté, matá, möësò?*"

Kilian lay on his back and drew her toward him.

"No, Bisila," he whispered. "I told him it hurt me here."

He brought his hand to his chest. "*Ë akán'völa.* In my chest."

Bisila gave him a wide grin. "You've said it very well. You're learning!"

Kilian returned the smile and looked at her with gleaming eyes. "Now it's my turn," he said, getting on top of her. "I don't want you to forget the little you know of my language."

He started covering Bisila's body with his lips.

"*Istos son els míos güells, els míos parpiellos, el mío naso, els míos llabios, la mía boca, el mío mentón . . .* These are my eyes, my eyelids, my nose, my lips, my mouth, my chin . . ." He slid around behind her and caressed her back, her waist, her thighs, and her legs. "*La mía esquena, la mía cintura, el mío cul, las mías camas . . .*" He moved his hand upward and stopped on her breast. "*Iste ye el mío pit.*"

Bisila took his hand in hers.

"What a strange combination!" she said pensively. Bubi and Pasolobinese.

Kilian began to nibble her ear. "And what's wrong with that?" he whispered as he slid his hand toward the inside of her thighs.

Bisila pressed herself against his body as hard as she could. Kilian could feel the heat of her skin and the humidity that invited him to enter her.

"*Wë mòná mö vé,*" said Bisila slowly, turning to lie on her back. "I think in your language it means something like, yes . . . *un . . . bordegot . . . borche!*"

She pronounced the words slowly to make certain that Kilian understood. Kilian stopped, surprised. She learned much more quickly than he.

"You've said it," he said. "I'm a bad boy! But not half as bad as I could be . . ."

He sat up, and they enjoyed each other once more.

Later, when both of them had recovered their breath, Kilian sighed and commented, "I wish we didn't have to hide . . ."

Bisila gave a timid smile. "Kilian . . . in other circumstances, would you take me as your wife?"

He looked at her intensely. His voice was hard. "What I really want is to walk with you, arm in arm in broad daylight, go dancing in Santa Isabel, and have our own house, where we would wait for the day when marriages between Spaniards and Guineans were allowed . . ."

Bisila blinked, swallowed, and dared ask, "And you wouldn't mind what they would say about you?"

"The opinion of the whites here doesn't worry me much, including my brother's, who, by the way, is fed up with sleeping with black women. And the rest of my family is so far away that no matter what they said, I couldn't hear them." He hugged her tightly in his arms. "We belong to two different worlds, Bisila, but if you weren't married, I can assure you everything would be different. It's not my fault that the laws and customs are what they are." He paused. "And would it matter to you what your family said?"

Bisila released herself from Kilian's arms. She sat down so he could rest his head in her lap and stroked his hair. "I would have it easier. I wouldn't stop seeing my people. I would be with you in my own place. And my father would give his delighted consent to see me marry a man he respects, for love."

She slid her small hands across his cheeks. Kilian listened with closed eyes.

"Kilian, if I weren't married, your situation would be difficult. You would be choosing between two worlds, and sacrificing a lot."

Kilian was dumbstruck.

Bisila always found the hidden parts of his heart. The fact that Kilian would live his days for Bisila did not mean that the ties that held him to the House of Rabaltué could dissolve like the threads of a cobweb. He knew perfectly well that he was tethered to his past, in the same way his father, Antón, had been and many more before him. For that reason, on his deathbed, Antón had asked him to take charge of the centuries-old house, which was nothing but a millstone inherited generation after generation: a millstone whose weight was not so easy to renounce.

His brother, Jacobo, was lucky not to worry about anything. He worked and sent money home, yes, but sooner or later, he would return to Spain. He did not even consider settling in another place other than his own country.

However, for Kilian, the House of Rabaltué was a burden.

Bisila knew this. She knew it better than anyone. She understood that the ties that held him to his world were stronger than chains; they could slacken, but also become taut and squeeze harder. Maybe that was why Bisila had never asked him for anything. She was fully conscious of each one's place in the world.

But he was as afraid as she was of the day when the whites would have to leave the island. For months they had lived in romantic oblivion, especially to the movements toward independence, a word that neither of them wanted to say out loud. Sure, it was inevitable that nearly all conversations at that time had a political bent. And it was difficult to ignore the voices, growing louder: *"We'll kick out the whites. We'll expel them all."*

It might be the work of the spirits. Maybe it was written that their paths would end up crossing only to continue on their way. In the deepest recesses of their souls, both wanted those same spirits to stop time, so that nothing would happen, that nothing would change, that they would not be forced to decide.

Kilian took Bisila's hands in his and kissed them.

"How do you say 'beautiful woman' in Bubi?"

"*Muarána muèmuè,*" she answered with a smile.

"*Muarána . . . muèmuè,*" he repeated in a hushed voice. "I promise I'll never forget it."

Jacobo cocked the 9 mm Star pistol, extended his arms, squinted his eyes, and fired. The bullet whizzed through the air and went through the target a few centimeters from the bull's-eye.

"A few more weeks, and you'll be as good as me," said Gregorio, mopping the sweat with a handkerchief. "Who wants to try next?"

The others shook their hands and said no. Gregorio shrugged, prepared the pistol, positioned himself in front of the line, and fired. The bullet tore through the center of the target. He grunted in satisfaction, put on the safety catch, and hung the gun from his belt before sitting down with everyone else.

The afternoon sun beat down on the shooting club, just below the gardens of Punta Fernanda. Sampaka's Spanish workers were finishing some beers. It had been a while since they had all been together. For one reason or another, there was always somebody missing. That afternoon, Mateo had invited his companions for a few rounds, like the old times, to celebrate his birthday before going to dinner at the house of his fiancée's parents. Jacobo had suggested the shooting club, where he had been spending more time. Once he got used to the noise of the shots, he began to enjoy the marvelous view of the sea. It was also very close to Plaza de España, where Ascensión, Mercedes, and Julia could join them later.

"So what's this? Have you now decided to learn to shoot a pistol, Jacobo?" Kilian asked. "Mountain goats are still hunted with a shotgun, yes?"

"What do you mean, goats?" exclaimed Marcial. "But weren't you becoming an expert elephant hunter?"

Everyone laughed. They all had heard of Jacobo's one and only excursion in Cameroon. He had repeated it so many times that it seemed he had hunted not one, but dozens of elephants.

"Actually, Dick taught Pao and me how to improve our shooting skills, just in case."

"Is he afraid?" asked Kilian. He thought of the Englishman's sun-blotched face and his grim blue eyes. "I thought your friend was not afraid of anything or anyone. The other, the Portuguese, seems more timid, but Dick, certainly not."

"If you spent more time with them, you'd like them better," Jacobo protested.

Kilian put his hands up in a sign of peace.

"You lot should also be practicing." Gregorio pointed at them with his bottle. "In these times, it's better to be prepared."

Marcial shrugged. "The day things turn ugly here, I'll collect my things and go."

"Same here." Mateo took a big swig of his drink. "But I don't think I'll have to run as fast as the new recruit . . ."

The comment brought on a chorus of laughs. Jacobo's young companion had not lasted even one campaign on the plantation. One night, some men had decided to pick on him in Anita Guau for being white. Nothing happened in the end, thanks to the timely intervention of some employees from another plantation, but the following morning, he asked for his pay and left without giving any explanation. Garuz was not happy losing someone who had already been trained. It was more and more difficult to find Spaniards willing to travel to Fernando Po, so Jacobo had to take on double the work.

"You lot could leave without looking back," Manuel butted in. "But not so for people like my in-laws, who have their business here. They'd have to abandon the shop."

"But what are you saying?" Kilian did not want to hear a word about leaving the island. "There's cocoa here for a good while. Everything is working the same as before."

"What world are you living in?" Jacobo reproached. "Did you not listen to the minister saying that it's the time for big changes?"

His brother rolled his eyes.

"Who would have thought, huh, Kilian?" Gregorio shook his head. "In the end, you are the one who has really taken to the island. Sade is probably right. You know what she's saying, don't you?"

Kilian became tense. He began to regret coming out. His nights in the casino with Mateo and Marcial were fine, but he still could not stand Gregorio.

"And what is she saying?" asked Jacobo. "Why am I the last to hear?"

"Probably because you spend more time with Pao and Dick than with us," said Marcial. "Are the clubs in Bata better than the ones here?"

Jacobo turned to Gregorio. "So what is it?"

"She says that your brother abandoned her for someone else, just as . . ." Seeing Jacobo's confused expression, he continued. "Sade had a child by your brother. Well, that's what she says, of course," he added hurriedly. "And it is certainly mulatto."

Jacobo opened his mouth, dumbstruck. A long silence followed. "But . . . how?" He frowned. "Kilian?"

His brother had not flinched.

"One moment." Jacobo looked at everybody. "And you all knew? Manuel?"

"I never believed it for an instant, Jacobo," he said. "Gregorio, isn't it true that Kilian stopped seeing Sade long before she got involved with you?"

Jacobo breathed easier. It was one thing to enjoy the girls, another entirely to leave them with child.

"Gregorio, maybe we should be congratulating you on becoming a father," said Kilian in a calm voice. "Weren't you the one who always criticized the owners of the plantations for being *miningueros* and having mulatto children around? Now you've become one of them."

"I'm not the only one to have slept with her."

"Yes, but I'd bet anything you'd like to be the one who hit the target."

Gregorio gave him a threatening look.

"I don't like it one bit that she's going round slandering my brother," Jacobo interrupted. "I hope she isn't thinking of going to the authorities."

"And if she did?" Gregorio lit a cigarette. "No one would pay much attention to her."

"That's a relief, isn't it, Gregorio?" Kilian stood up. He had had enough socializing for the day. Fortunately, in a few hours, he would be with Bisila. "Well, I'm off."

Mateo patted him on the arm.

"You're getting more like your father every day! From work to home and from home to work."

Kilian said nothing. His eyes happened to meet Manuel's, and Manuel rapidly looked away. The doctor believed he knew the reason for Kilian's frequent visits to the hospital. He was not blind. Kilian was always attended to by the same nurse.

"You know what Julia says?" Manuel said finally, minutes after Kilian had left. "That if we took a trip around the city orphanage, we'd hang our heads in shame."

Sade picked up her pace along the dusty path that led to the native maternity hospital in Santa Isabel, where she had given birth to her son three months before. The building was made up of one two-story wing beside a four-gabled turret joined onto another building with an upper balcony. She approached the entrance steps and paused. She raised her eyes to the starry sky and took a deep breath. No sound could be heard as nature enjoyed its final minutes of calm before dawn.

The baby slept quietly in her arms. She covered his little body with a thin white cloth, stroked his cheeks, bent down, and left him at the door. She remained for a few seconds, watching him, then turned around and left.

When she got to her house, near the club, she prepared a *crontiti* infusion and sat down beside the window of the small sitting room. She told herself once again that she had done the right thing in freeing herself of the child. In some corner of her heart, she felt a pang of remorse and sighed deeply. None of her entreaties to the island's government administrations nor those to the Sampaka plantation's manager had had any effect. The most she got was a hurried investigation, after which it had been concluded, thanks to the firm declarations of Kilian's friends, that there was not the slightest chance Kilian was the father. They had also warned her that if she persisted in her accusations, the law would come down on her for slander. At what moment had her pride convinced her that since she was now a Spanish citizen, some possibility existed that someone would force Kilian to assume responsibility? Was that not what they did in Spain? During her months of pregnancy, she had even fantasized about a life together to bring up the child she had just abandoned.

After the investigation, it did not make any sense to admit who the real father was. Everything had gone wrong. She had lost Kilian and had brought a baby into the world.

She brusquely dried a traitorous tear. Never again would she allow her feelings to interfere, although, thanks to her pregnancy, a promising future had opened up for her. She had a lot to think about now.

Over the past few months, Anita had agreed to allow her to help in the management of the club. As the days went by, the woman, now old, had noticed the girl's ability to, among other things, attract clients, give advice to the new girls, and design the band's playlist so that customers never felt like leaving the club. Sade had also redecorated. Anita wanted to live the last years of her life quietly. She had discovered in Sade the ideal person to inherit the business.

For Sade, the numbers added up, if and only if she could free herself of the one obstacle that would hinder her ambitions. All her energy needed to be focused on running the business, and, if possible, expanding it. The orphanage would surely look after the baby well, she thought, making sure he got an education. She only had to look at the difference between the children who grew up neglected by the other mothers in the club and those brought up in the Spanish center. If everything worked out, she would even be able to get the boy back in the future . . . After all, she was not a bad mother. She had only led a bad life.

Only she, and she alone, could change her circumstances.

"Why can't you do me this small favor?"

Generosa did not yield at her daughter's insistence. "I don't understand why you're interested after so long. What does it matter what that woman did?"

"Oba told me that whenever she can, her friend goes round to the orphanage to see him. The child should now be over a year old. I'd just like to know what name they gave him. You never know, maybe one day his real father would like to know . . ."

"The whole thing was so unpleasant, it's best forgotten about." Generosa raised her hands to hush her daughter. "Also, it's none of your business."

Ismael stretched from the small crib to the bookshelf; he wobbled, fell back, and started to bawl. His little shouts mixed with others that came from the street. Generosa took him in her arms and peeked out the window.

"They're at it again."

"What's going on?" Julia asked.

"Your father and Gustavo."

"I'll go."

When Julia got downstairs, she met up with Oba, who had also gone out to have a look from the door of the shop.

"How did this start, Oba?"

The girl pointed to the group, and Julia recognized Gustavo and his brother, Dimas.

"They came into the shop to buy alcohol to celebrate Christmas, and your father wouldn't serve them without a police permit. They said that they could now buy the same products as whites, and your father agreed, but not alcohol, because Christmas was still days away, and if they drank, they wouldn't go to work. Your father kicked them out, and they went to get Gustavo, as the representative of the Neighbors Council."

A dozen men surrounded Emilio, who, out of control, shouted, "We are equal for what interests you, right? Well, if we are equal, why won't I be able to vote? I have the same right as you! The same? I have more right than some of you! I've lived here longer than many of you coming from the continent, claiming that this is your land! And now only Guineans with Spanish nationality can vote. To give up that nationality! We've all gone crazy!"

Julia sighed. A referendum had been announced to vote on a self-governing Guinea. Things were moving quickly. If the forecasts were right, in less than six years, the old colony would go from a Spanish province to having a self-governing regime before independence was granted. The United Nations had lobbied for definitive independence to be granted to countries under colonial control. Spain would have no choice but to comply. Julia shook her head. She had lived on the island for years, but the situation was confusing. Up to a short time ago, the colonial forces had detained pro-independence figures like Gustavo and anyone else who fought against the Spanish regime, even sending them to Black Beach. Now independence was a certainty. Who could understand it?

And what was more, though the change should satisfy the natives, there were clashes about how to achieve it. It was becoming routine to encounter heated arguments everywhere. On the one side were the independence gradualists, in favor of accepting self-government organized and imposed by and from Spain prior to independence, as they appreciated the many ties that joined the two countries after so many years of colonial government. On the other side were the independence radicals, the majority Fang from the African continent, much greater in number, who wanted automatic and joint independence of both the continental part and the island. The second group criticized the first for accepting the Spanish regime, and the first group criticized the second for hastily pushing self-government.

To complicate things further, many Bubis like Gustavo wanted a separate independence for the island of Fernando Po. Their main complaint was that the budgetary distribution was not proportional to each province's actual contribution. In fact, the greater part of the budget income came from the island, but an obvious trend was seen where all the improvements and investments were for Río Muni, the continental province. And finally, there were those who agreed with Emilio, vehemently defending that the natives would be better off continuing as a Spanish province. Julia was convinced that someone like Dimas, who had worked so hard to have a privileged life, would be among that group, but he would never admit to it in order to avoid a head-on confrontation with his brother.

Emilio continued to explain his reasoning in a cantankerous tone. "I promise you one thing, Gustavo! From my post on the Neighbors Council, I intend to keep working until I achieve a vote for men like me. I'm not going quietly!"

"You'd blindly vote no so that you could keep your privileges," Gustavo attacked.

"But you would also vote no to self-government!" Emilio threw his hands in the air.

"Your no would be a sign of loyalty to Spain. My no would attest to my wish for an independence separate from Río Muni. If the whites vote, there would be more confusion."

In a flash, the group of people around them grew considerably. The initial murmurs became irate shouts both in favor and against Gustavo's words.

"Well, I'll be voting yes!" shouted a tall young man with a shaved head and a wiry body. "And that's what we should all do, to make them leave us alone once and for all . . ."

"You must be Fang, right?" replied another, smaller man. "You talk like a Fang . . ."

"Well, I'm Bubi and I'll also be voting yes," intervened a third, his arm bandaged.

"Then you're not a true Bubi!" Gustavo reproached him loudly. "No Bubi would ever allow those from the continent to take our wealth!"

"Better than remaining slaves to the whites," the offended party retorted.

"You don't know what you are saying!" Gustavo leaned over him threateningly. "They have brainwashed you!"

"We Fang are now to blame for everything!" the tall young man scoffed. "They have also exploited us. How much timber and coffee have they taken from the continent with our sweat?" He shouted, "You Bubis want to keep supporting those in power!"

"We Bubis have been fighting for decades, suffering reprisals for speaking out," Gustavo interrupted. "Do you want to know how many letters the tribal chiefs and villages have sent to the colonial authorities, to Spain, and to the UN? And what have we got in return? Exile, persecution, and jail." He opened his shirt to show him his scars. "Do you really think that I want to support the ones who did this to me?"

"You're crazy," the young Fang replied. "Spain will never accept the existence of two states. We have to join forces." There was a murmur of approval. "That's what the whites want, to see us fight among ourselves."

Dimas grabbed his brother by the arm when he saw him clench his fists. Emilio let out a sarcastic cackle.

"It's what I told you, Dimas," he said. "This has turned into a chicken coop."

A chicken coop with too many cocks, thought Julia.

"So this is how you intend to take over your own destiny?" Emilio continued.

"Leave it, Dad," Julia intervened. "Get into the house." She turned to Gustavo. "Do as you must, Gustavo, but leave my father in peace. Leave us all in peace."

"That's what you lot have to do!" shouted the young Fang. "Get out! Go home to your country for good!"

Many shouted in agreement. Emilio gritted his teeth. Julia noticed her father's breathing becoming agitated. She pulled his arm with all her might to drag him toward the store. Oba opened the door, and they entered.

A few seconds later, a stone hit the glass facade of the business so hard it smashed into smithereens with the force of an unexpected hailstorm. Nobody moved, neither inside nor outside the shop. Finally, Emilio took a few steps forward over the broken glass and looked at the men beginning to disperse.

"You'll remember us!" he roared. "Remember this! You'll never again live so well!" He stared at Dimas, who stared back at him before sorrowfully shaking his head as he left.

Julia stood beside her father. Large tears of frustration rolled down her cheeks.

Gustavo looked Julia in the eye and murmured a weak "I'm sorry" before leaving.

Oba appeared with a brush and began sweeping up the bits of glass. Julia went with her father to the store to get him to sit down. She offered him a glass of water and made sure he had calmed down fully before going to help Oba.

"And you, Oba, which side are you on?" she asked after a while.

"I can't vote, Mistress," she answered. "Only men will vote, and only the heads of family."

"Yes. But if you could, what would you do? Be honest, please."

"My family is Fang. Many of my ancestors were taken from their land and forced to work on the island's plantations. In my family, it's still remembered how the whites hunted the men and trapped them like animals." Oba raised her chin proudly. "Don't be offended, Mistress, but I would vote yes."

Julia directed her gaze toward the back, where Emilio sat, totally dejected, with slumped shoulders and his hands resting on his thighs. How long had her parents lived on Fernando Po? A lifetime full of dreams and hard work . . . Where would they go? Definitely not to Pasolobino. After Santa Isabel, they would suffocate in a place so anchored to the past. They could set themselves up with her and Manuel in Madrid and start over. No, not at their age. They would simply be able to enjoy Ismael and their future grandchildren between sighs of nostalgia for their lost island.

Yes, Dad, she thought, her eyes filled with tears. *This is over.*

Nelson carried a gin and tonic and a bottle of Pepsi, trying with difficulty to move his large body through the crowd. Never before had Anita Guau been so full. The Nigerian band played one piece after another without a break, filling the dance floor with couples enjoying the fusion of Yoruba and Latin rhythms. The new owner had changed the interior of the place: high stools at the bar, some dark-red fake-leather sofas under globe lamps, smoked mirrors on the walls, and a curved Wurlitzer in the corner. The customers, both old and new, came for the promise of an unforgettable night.

Oba greeted him from one of the tables at the back. Her small hand, her wrist decorated with several colored bracelets, waved in the air. Nelson swelled with joy. He felt as if he had not seen her in months, though he had been separated from her for only a few minutes. Beside her, Ekon and Lialia, hand in hand, followed the beat of the music with their shoulders. Nelson put the drinks on the table and sat down.

"There were so many people at the bar that it took forever to get served," he explained. When Oba was there, they spoke in Spanish, because she had not learned Pichi.

"From what I can see, all the Nigerians are here tonight," commented Ekon. "It's as if we had planned it."

"The occasion calls for it, doesn't it?" said Nelson. That very week, a new four-year labor agreement had been signed between Nigeria and Guinea. In spite of the uncertain political climate, work for the Nigerians had finally been guaranteed.

"So this is where you men come to spend your salary . . . ," Lialia commented, sliding her gleaming eyes around the room.

"You know I don't come often," Ekon protested. "I've too many children to feed."

"And I stopped coming as soon as I met Oba," Nelson agreed. She smiled. "Even if you don't believe it, many marriages have begun here."

"And what are you two waiting for?" Lialia teased.

"We're saving up to open a small business, aren't we, Nelson?"

"We've got plans, yes, but they'll have to wait. We're still young."

"We know Oba is young," said Ekon, "but you're beginning to get on in years."

Nelson bellowed in laughter. He knocked back the gin and tonic in one gulp and cursed his lack of foresight in not having ordered more. He would have to go back through the crowd. Oba offered him her soft drink, and he thanked her with a kiss.

"Look!" The girl pointed in front of her. "Isn't that one of the massas from your plantation? What's he doing?" Oba stood up quickly. "Sade!"

She ran over, followed by the others. A slew of shouting men crowded before her. With great effort, Oba forced her way to the front. A white man was waving a gun at Sade.

"What happened?" Oba asked the man beside her.

"The white asked her for something and she refused. He grabbed her by the wrist and twisted her arm. When several men got up to help her, he took out the pistol."

"The first one who comes close, I'll blow his head off!" the man shouted, using Sade like a shield. His eyes glowed with fear and drunkenness.

"That's enough, Massa Gregor!" Nelson stepped out. "You'd better put the gun down."

"Nelson!" Gregorio cackled. "Have you ever seen such a thing? Since when has it been difficult to choose a woman here?"

"I'm the one who chooses," said Sade furiously. "And I decided to get rid of you a long time ago." She looked at the gathered spectators. "Is it that difficult for you to realize that you're not going to decide for us anymore? This is the true face of the whites. If you do what you're told, they tell you everything is fine. If you stand up to them, they take out the *melongo* switch, the whip, the gun."

Gregorio held on to her even tighter, and she cried out in pain. Several men took a step forward.

"There are a lot of us and only one of you," Nelson said calmly. "You can shoot, of course, but when you run out of bullets, we'll come for you. Do you see any whites here? No. I don't think you've picked the best night to come to the club."

Large drops of sweat covered Gregorio's forehead. The situation was looking fairly grim. Nelson, used to managing dozens of laborers in his brigade, noticed that slight moment of weakness and continued speaking in a firm voice.

"I'll make a deal with you. You give me your weapon, and we'll let you leave."

There was a murmur of protest. Tempers were so high that the smallest spark could lead to a lynching. Gregorio hesitated.

"Today is a day for celebrating," Ekon intervened. "Many of us have brought our wives here to dance. No one wants this to end badly. Nelson and I will take you back to Sampaka."

Nelson agreed. The crowd parted to show their support.

"You give me your word, Nelson?" Gregorio asked in desperation.

The foreman smiled. That a man like him would risk his life on the word of a black was ironic. Fear truly changed people.

"Have you not realized yet that I'm a man of my word, Massa Gregor?" he asked.

Gregorio lowered his eyes and gave in. He let Sade go, tilted the pistol toward the ground, and calmly waited for Nelson to collect it.

"Ekon, stay with the women until I come back."

Nelson took the man by the elbow and guided him quickly to the door.

Bit by bit, the party resumed. Sade agreed to have a drink with Oba and her friends.

"He deserved a good hiding," murmured Sade.

"Nelson did the right thing, Sade," said Lialia firmly. "It's best not to escalate matters. No matter how much they talk about equality, in the end, it's us who would get punished."

Ekon brought more drinks. The band played a catchy tune, and Lialia took her husband by the hand to dance. When they were left alone, Oba asked, "What did he want?"

Sade shrugged arrogantly. "Every man who has been with me has wanted to have another turn." She grimaced and took a sip of her drink.

All except one.

And because of him, all her life, she would have to bear the secret that the real father of her child was someone as disagreeable as Massa Gregor.

In December 1963, the referendum on self-government was accepted by the majority, though the vote was seventy percent in favor in Río Muni and seventy percent against on the island of Fernando Po. Just as Gustavo had suggested, everyone interpreted the result according to their own interest, either as a sign of the island's loyalty to Spain or its desire to become independent separate from Río Muni.

Spain granted self-government for the old provinces by decree. From that moment, the pro-independence Guineans began to be appointed by the Spanish authorities to the top posts in the administration and the recently formed autonomous government, including that of first president and vice president, given to an individual named Macías. All those appointed declared their loyalty to Spain. Many of those who had been persecuted for being pro-independence now began to earn good salaries.

"Such is life, Julia," Kilian commented. "I am still collecting cocoa, and Gustavo is a minister in the autonomous government. Who would have imagined it? I still remember the argument he had with your father in this very place—how long ago was it?"

Julia, wearing a light sleeveless dress, placed her hands over her swollen abdomen. It was a glorious afternoon. A pleasant breeze cooled down the day's intense heat. As on every Sunday, they were meeting up with the rest of the group, but the others were late. Each time it was becoming more difficult to get Manuel to take his head out of his research, and even more so after the good reviews he had received for his first book on the island's plant species. Ascensión and Mercedes were each busy with preparations for their weddings to Mateo and Marcial, which they had decided to hold together in the Santa Isabel cathedral. Given that the brides had been born and raised on the island, the decision had been an easy one. It would be a simple wedding so that the grooms' sides would not seem so small, and although there were still months to go before the day, they wanted to have everything ready in good time, especially the dresses. For their part, the grooms were working as hard as they could during the week, including holidays, to make up for their honeymoons.

Kilian had continued to socialize in order not to raise suspicions about his relationship with Bisila. He alternated between meetings with her and with the people in his circle. His life, he thought sadly, would continue to be divided between two worlds—the mountains and the island, white and black—neither of which he fully belonged to. What he most wished for at that moment was to have Bisila in Julia's place, quietly lying in the hammock, enjoying a tranquil Sunday afternoon. He imagined her hands on her stomach, swollen with the fruit of the union between them. Was that too much to ask for?

The shouts of the young people in the swimming pool reached the terrace. Someone put a Chuck Berry song on the record player, and enthusiastic hoots joined the frenetic sound of rock and roll.

"Don't say it, Kilian."

"Don't say what?"

"That we're getting old."

"What! You must be talking about yourself."

Kilian awkwardly tried to twist to the music's beat, and Julia laughed. The young, sensitive novice from his first years on the island had become a happy, satisfied, and confident man. If she had not known better, she would say that he seemed to be in love, with that permanent smile and dreamy look. Julia knew those symptoms perfectly, although it had been years since she settled into a peaceful affection.

"Hello, hello!" a voice said. "I bring you a small bag full of snow!"

Kilian gave a start. "Jacobo! We weren't expecting you until next week."

"There was a mistake with the airplane ticket, and I had to book an earlier flight."

The brothers hugged fondly. They had not seen each other for six months. Unlike Kilian, who had a good reason not to leave, Jacobo had been going to Spain after each campaign to enjoy his vacation. Each time it became more and more difficult to return, he said, as if he had the feeling that his time in Africa was coming to an end.

Jacobo pointed to Julia's bump. "Manuel told me. Congratulations once again."

"And how were the holidays?" Kilian asked. "You're looking good."

Jacobo smiled and looked him up and down. "You're not looking too bad yourself. Is it my imagination . . . or are you happy?" He squinted. "How come you never get tired of the island?"

Kilian felt himself going red and sat down. "Did everything work out with the car?"

Jacobo had bought a beautiful black Volkswagen in Guinea and taken it to Spain. His eyes lit up in excitement.

"I had no problem reregistering it. And the trip to Pasolobino . . . The whole road to myself! You should have seen the faces of the neighbors when I parked in the square and beeped the horn!" Kilian could imagine Jacobo's smug face at being the center of attention. "It was the biggest story for months. Everyone asked where the TEG on the number plate was from, and I had to explain to them a million times that it meant the car was from the Spanish territories in the Gulf of Guinea . . . You should have seen the amount I spent on petrol taking everyone here, there, and everywhere—"

"I suppose you had to take more than one lady here, there, and everywhere as well," Kilian interrupted, amused.

"All the women of marriageable age fought for the chance."

Julia rolled her eyes. The world changed, but Jacobo did not.

"Well, I'd prefer to know if anyone in particular repeated the trip," joked Kilian. He could not imagine his brother going out with the same woman more than twice.

Jacobo cleared his throat. "Her name is Carmen. I met her at a dance. She's not from Pasolobino."

Julia looked up in surprise. Someone had, in fact, managed to win his heart? She hated to admit it, but she felt a fleeting stab of jealousy.

Kilian went over to Jacobo and patted him on the back. "Dear brother," he teased. "It sounds like your wild and crazy nights are at an end."

Now it was Jacobo who blushed. "Well, we're still getting to know each other." He shrugged. "And I'm now here and she's over there . . ."

Julia sighed. That Carmen, she thought, would have her work cut out making him into a family man.

Kilian glanced toward the horizon. This woman meant more to Jacobo than he let on. His time in Guinea really was coming to a close. Suddenly, Kilian felt a pang of regret. His brother had many defects, true, but he had never hidden anything. He, however, had been hiding his love for Bisila for months. If it could not be announced to the four corners, it could at least be shared with someone who would never betray him. But something inside him told him to wait. In spite of the bonds that joined them, he doubted that his brother would understand. He would think he had gone crazy, which was exactly how he felt: in a daze.

Julia offered to go and get another round of drinks. When they were left alone, Jacobo's face darkened.

"Is there something wrong at home?" Kilian asked, alarmed.

"It's Catalina. She's very sick."

Kilian felt a knot tightening in his stomach.

Jacobo cleared his throat. "I . . . well, I've said my good-byes to her. I've brought you a letter from Mom asking you to go home now to be with them."

"But it is the busiest time of the year!" Kilian protested weakly. He regretted the words the minute he had said them. His heart did not want to accept a reason to be away from Bisila, but his sister was his sister. She had not had an easy life, with a sickly body and a mind weakened by the death of her only child. He had not seen her or his mother for over three years. He could not abandon them. Bisila would understand.

Jacobo lit a cigarette. "It wouldn't be a bad idea to take a trip home, Kilian. Things are changing. There are rumors of a ski resort on the heights of Pasolobino. Do you know what that would mean?" Jacobo's eyes began to gleam. "The land would be worth a lot of money. It's worth nothing at the moment. We could change our lives, work in the construction industry or in the ski resort, even set up a business! Our godforsaken village would become a tourist destination."

Kilian listened attentively.

"Some investors with experience in this business have already visited the area. They say that the snow is the white gold of the future . . ."

Kilian felt stunned. His sister was dying. He would have to separate from Bisila. A deep pain ran through him, and yet here was his brother discussing the future.

The future was what most worried Kilian. He did not want to think of it. All he wanted was for nothing to change, for the world to be reduced to an embrace with Bisila.

"Kilian . . . ," Jacobo said.

"I was thinking . . . that I'll have to go home."

Home.

It had been ages since he had thought of Pasolobino as his home.

"Soon we will all leave here for good, Kilian." Jacobo shook his head with a mixture of resignation and relief. "The future is no longer in Guinea."

Julia came back with the drinks. Jacobo turned to greet an acquaintance.

"Do you know, Julia?" Kilian said. "You're right. We're getting old."

A few weeks later, Bisila sent Simón to bring Kilian to the hospital. Once there, she took out a piece of paper and showed him a drawing of a small rectangular bell with several clappers.

"It's an *elëbó*," she explained. "It's for warding off evil spirits. I would like Simón to tattoo it on you to protect you on the journey. Maybe on your left armpit?"

Kilian loved Bisila's present, something he could always carry with him. On the armpit, close to his heart, he could stroke it whenever he wanted to.

"It will hurt a bit," Simón warned. "The drawing is small, but complicated. Close your eyes and take a deep breath."

"I think I'll be able to take it," said Kilian.

Kilian did not close his eyes or stop looking at Bisila throughout the whole process. The last time he had gone back to Pasolobino, Bisila had had a son by Mosi. He wanted her to be sure that he would not take so long in coming back this time. He barely blinked when Simón drew out the design with a scalpel, or when he put burning pieces of palm on the wound to burn the skin. He did not even bite his lip to withstand the pain. Bisila's enormous eyes transmitted strength and calm.

When Simón finished, he gathered his things. He smiled faintly and said, "Now, Massa Kilian, you're a little more Bubi."

Bisila leaned over him, dabbed his wound with an ointment, whispering almost imperceptibly, "My Bubi warrior."

That night, Kilian wandered around the room, not knowing what to do. Bisila had not turned up. He looked at his watch. They would not even be able to say good-bye to each other! He finally lay on his bed, downhearted, and a slight drowsiness overcame him.

A little later, a dead knock made him jump up. He sensed Bisila, who silently sneaked in, closed the door, and locked it. He cried out in joy. A few steps from the bed, she motioned for him to stay quiet and close his eyes.

Bisila removed her thin overcoat and pleated skirt and blouse and took out some things from a small basket. Finally, she told him he could look.

Kilian opened his eyes and gasped in surprise.

Bisila was dressed from head to toe with *tyíbö* cords covering her naked flesh. The cords, full of small shells, opened over her breasts and hips, hugging her curves. On her head she wore a wide-brimmed hat with peacock feathers. A wooden pin went through both sides of the hat, holding it in place on her head.

Bisila motioned to Kilian to get up and to come toward her.

In complete silence, she slowly undressed him.

When he was naked, she poured water into a bowl and took out some colored powders that she mixed with water to get a reddish paste, which she spread over Kilian's body, beginning with his feet and legs. She gently rubbed it on his thighs and bottom, then his back, and finally his chest.

Kilian remembered that day in the village, when he wished aloud that she and she alone would name him *botuku*, anointing him with *ntola* in a river of pure water. He wanted to circle her in his arms, but she shook her head to stop him and continued the pleasurable torture of painting his stomach and chest. She then washed her hands and took other blue and yellow powders, mixed them with water, and with the resultant paste gently drew lines on his face, as if she wanted to memorize the distance from the nose to each ear, and from his hairline to his chin.

When finished, Bisila washed and dried her hands and took Kilian's in hers.

"I have dressed like a Bubi bride, according to the ancient tradition," she said in a voice filled with emotion. "And I have painted you as a warrior."

488

Kilian was pleased to finally hear the sound of her voice, but said nothing.

"You know that we have two types of marriage," she continued. "One is called *rèötö*, or marriage to buy a woman's virginity. It is the real marriage in law and is what joins me to Mosi. The other is called *ribalá ré ríhólè*, or marriage for love. It is not recognized in law, but it is between ourselves." She raised her eyes toward Kilian and continued with a trembling voice, "We don't have anyone to act as priest, but I suppose it doesn't matter."

Kilian raised her hands and squeezed them hard.

"I must talk first," she went on. "And I must tell you, and you're not to laugh, that I won't forget my duty to cultivate my husband's fields and make the palm oil and promise to be faithful to you, at least in my heart."

Bisila closed her eyes to repeat the promises to herself.

"Now it's my turn," said Kilian in a hoarse voice. "What do I have to say?"

"You have to promise not to abandon this wife"—Bisila opened her eyes—"in spite of the many more you may have."

Kilian smiled. "I promise that I will not abandon this wife, at least in my heart, come what may."

They sealed their vows with a long, warm kiss.

"And now, what happens before going to the marriage bed?" Kilian asked with a special glint in his eyes.

Bisila tilted her head back and laughed aloud. "Well, we would say 'amen,' and someone would ring the *elëbó* and sing . . ."

"I'm already carrying the *elëbó* with me," said Kilian, raising his hand to his left armpit and placing it gently on his tattoo. "Forever. We'll always be together, Bisila. This is my true promise to you, my *muaréna muèmuè*."

17

Ë Ripúrii Ré Ëbbé
The Seed of Evil

1965

Time went by very slowly for Bisila. The days and weeks passed, and Kilian did not return. Neither of them could get news of the other. Exchanging letters would have been too risky.

Thousands of kilometers away, Kilian did write, but the letters were never sent. He read them back to himself as if she could read his thoughts. His body wandered the rooms of the house, but his heart and mind were far away. Without her, life in Pasolobino was familiar but empty.

Almost every day, Bisila approached the main building of the plantation where the foreigners lived. She got as far as the outside stairs, placed her hand on the banister, put her foot on the first step of the stairs, and fought back the impulse to run up to Kilian's room to see if he had already returned. Her heart beat quickly, and her knees went weak. She listened closely to the voices of the Europeans, trying to make out Kilian's deep voice.

That is how another year started and another cocoa harvest ended.

On the island, the weather was excessively hot; only a weak breeze managed to alleviate the stifling air. In the Pyrenees, the weather was excessively cold; the north wind dragged the snow from one place to another as if it were grains of sand on a frozen desert.

On the Sampaka plantation on Fernando Po, the workers began preparing the ground for planting, gathering firewood for the dryers, mending the roads and tracks, and beginning pruning.

In Pasolobino, the walls of the house were closing in on Kilian. It snowed and snowed, and when it stopped snowing, the wind began to howl. It was impossible to go out to the fields. It was impossible to do anything. The hours beside the fire listening to his mother's sighs seemed endless as he endured Catalina's last days, comforting a brother-in-law he hardly knew, and repeating over and over again the same conversations with the neighbors about the riches that the future ski resort would bring to the valley.

He needed to move, to get out. But he could not even spend time mending the house, not when his sister was agonizing; it was not right. She herself had expressed her wish to die in the house she had been born in, so he had to show her respect through his silence.

With his eyes fixed on the flames of the fire, Kilian fought against the slow ticking of the clock by thinking of Bisila. She would die if she had to put up with week after week of cold and snow. Her body was made for heat.

How could he think of a life without her flame?

Catalina was buried in the middle of the terrible frost at the end of February. The cold sped up the first mass in Pasolobino that Kilian had not heard in Latin and the later burial.

The speed at which everything happened—from when they closed the coffin until the shovels gave the last taps on the dampened soil—reawakened a sense of urgency in Kilian. He wanted to go back to Fernando Po, but he had to stay with his mother in her grieving.

How much longer would he have to wait?

At the end of April, the rains arrived on the island.

Bisila was tired. She had spent many hours in the hospital. At that time of year, the number of accidents and machete cuts went up. Work on the plantation was more dangerous than in the dryers, and the rain helped increase the number of pulmonary illnesses. She needed to clear her mind and decided to take a walk.

There was no use fooling herself: her steps always led her in the same direction. She approached the whitewashed main building once again. It was very late on Saturday night, and the yard was empty. She did not want to get her hopes up, but she lost nothing in trying. It had been five months since she had seen him, since she had heard his voice, since she had felt his hands on her skin. She had asked her father nonchalantly if he had any news of Kilian through Jacobo, and that was how she found out about the death of his sister and his intention of staying longer in Pasolobino. How much longer would she have to wait? She was afraid the longer it took him to come back, the greater the chance of him learning to live without the island and without her.

Sometimes she had the horrible feeling that it had all been just a dream. She knew she was not the first nor the last native to fall in love with a foreigner.

Yet Kilian had promised. He had told her they would always be together. She could only trust what he had said. He was now her true husband. Not Mosi, with whom it was getting harder every time to fulfill her role as wife. Mosi was a body she lay with every night; Kilian was the owner of her heart and her soul.

She leaned on the wall and closed her eyes, imagining the instant when the door of his modest room would open and Kilian would come out, with his wide beige linen trousers and his white shirt. He would take a deep breath, light a cigarette, lean on the railing, and meet her eyes below. She would smile, as if to say there she was, waiting as she had promised, his black wife, his Bubi wife; the woman he had chosen above all, in spite of the color of her skin and her customs, traditions, and beliefs. They would always be Kilian of Pasolobino and Bisila of Bissappoo.

The noise of an engine brought her back to the night and the drizzle. The outside lamps flickered before going out. Darkness took over the yard.

She covered her head with a scarf and began her walk back to the hospital, making use of the transient lights of the pickup. She was not easily frightened, but at that time of night, the big yard seemed so empty and dark. She preferred to stick close to the buildings.

The pickup almost knocked her down.

It passed beside her at great speed, raising a dirt cloud that blinded her momentarily and made her cough. The vehicle stopped beside the porch under the bedrooms of the employees. Some men's voices and laughs echoed in the dark. Bisila sensed that the laughs were coming her way.

A bad feeling ran through her body, and she decided to change direction. She would go to the laborers' barracks through the dryers, located to the left of the main building.

A voice resonated like thunder just behind her.

"Well, well! What have we here?"

Bisila quickened her pace, but a figure out of the shadows cut off her path.

Her heart beat quickly.

"Not so fast, darky!" said a man with a strong English accent, catching her by the shoulders.

493

Bisila struggled with him. "Let me pass!" She tried to sound firm. "I'm a nurse in the hospital, and they are waiting for me!"

She freed herself and began to walk quickly away. No one would come to her rescue if it came to it. Suddenly, a strong hand grabbed her arm and forced her to turn around and face a tall man who reeked of alcohol.

"You're not going anywhere," muttered the Englishman in a slurred voice. "A woman shouldn't be out walking alone at this time of night"— his lips curled in a nasty smile—"unless she is looking for something or someone."

Bisila tried to free herself, but the man twisted her arm into her back, got behind her, and began walking toward his friend. Bisila screamed, but the man covered her mouth with his free hand and whispered threateningly, "You'd best be quiet."

She tried to bite his hand, but he reacted quickly and squeezed his hand harder against her mouth while telling his friend,

"Eh! You'll never guess what I found?"

The other man approached, also stinking of alcohol. He stretched out a bony hand and took off the scarf covering Bisila's head.

"It looks like we still have some celebrating to do!" he said in an accent that Bisila did not recognize. He laughed. "I'm ready for more."

He brought his hawkish nose forward and began to lewdly look over her face and body.

"I can't see you properly." He stroked her cheeks, bosom, and hips. "Hmmm . . . Better than I expected!"

Bisila twisted, terrorized, but the man holding her clasped her so tightly she was afraid he would break her arm. Tears rolled down her cheeks.

"Put the handkerchief in her mouth, Pao," ordered the Englishman. "And get Jacobo out of the car."

Bisila clung to a small thread of hope: Jacobo would recognize her and let her go!

Pao opened the door of the pickup and, after much insisting, managed to get the man inside to lurch out. Jacobo was barely able to stand. The Englishman shouted, "Hey, Jacobo! Wake up! The party isn't over! Do you know where we can enjoy this beauty?"

"What about the dryers?" Pao asked hungrily.

Jacobo was having trouble thinking straight. The effects of the alcohol and iboga root had distorted his surroundings. Only once or twice before had he ventured to try the strong drug used by the natives to reduce their need for water and food in extreme work conditions. In small quantities, the bark or root of the thin-leaved bush with orange-colored fruit the size of olives had stimulating, euphoric, and aphrodisiacal properties. A large dose caused hallucinations. The quantity taken by Jacobo that night had sent him into delirium.

"There is a small room . . . where they . . . store . . . just here . . ." He turned and pointed out a small door in the porch. "The empty sacks . . . here . . . yes." He went over to the door and rested against it. "It's . . . comfortable," he added, laughing.

The Englishman pushed Bisila violently.

"Come on! Move!"

Bisila tried to catch Jacobo's eyes with a pleading look. The Englishman pushed her, and she resisted with all her strength, trying to get Jacobo to look at her. When he did, Bisila saw in horror that his glassy eyes did not recognize her. He was drugged. A sob escaped from her chest, and she began to cry.

The Englishman laid her on a pile of empty esparto sacks, then leaped on top of her, ripped her dress, and held her arms. The man was so strong that one hand was enough to hold her hands above her head. With his free hand, he ran along her body with the speedy clumsiness of someone who wanted only to satisfy his instincts. No matter how much she moved, she could not get away from his stinking breath, and he left a stream of spittle on her neck and bosom.

Bisila wanted to die.

She twisted and turned as hard as she could, like a live snake thrown into the fire. She tried to scream, but the handkerchief made her retch. She sobbed, moaning and kicking until a fist hit her in the face and she nearly lost consciousness. In the darkness, she saw the man's face and felt a hand between her thighs and something hard penetrating her. Then another face, another breath, other hands, another body, one lunge after another, more penetration, and then a silence, a pause, some laughs, some voices, and another body and another face.

". . . acobo . . . ," Bisila burbled.

Jacobo stopped on hearing his name. She raised her head and tried to scream.

Again the laughs.

"Ah, Jacobo! It seems she likes you!"

"That's what happens. You have to keep pushing, convince them what is good for them."

"At the start they resist, but later—"

Jacobo was still, stunned by the pair of clear eyes trying to reach him. What were they asking for? What did they want him to do?

"Come on, finish up!"

More laughs.

A weak glimmer of hope conquered by the senses, Jacobo slowly rubbing himself against Bisila's skin, gasping in her ear, quickening his pace, releasing himself into the body his brother adored, humiliating the soul that belonged to Kilian, tamely resting on her breast . . .

A prolonged moan of despair.

Some arms pulling at him.

"It's over. Let's go. And you, blackie, not a word!"

The Englishman tossed her some notes.

"Buy yourself a new dress!"

And then, silence.

An eternity of silence till consciousness fully returned.

A beaten and raped black woman. An ordinary black woman abused by an ordinary white man. All black women humiliated by all white men.

A short while ago, she was Bisila of Bissappoo, Kilian of Pasolobino's wife.

When she opened her eyes, she was a heap of rubbish on top of empty sacks.

Simón heard a scream but did not pay any attention to it. On Saturday nights in the servants' quarters, located just beside the white employees' bedrooms, it was common to hear screams and laughing until the early hours.

He turned around to get back to sleep. Nothing. He was unable to sleep. A few deep breaths and one or another snore told him his companions slept soundly. He decided to open the door to let some fresh air in and lay down again. Some men were going up the stairs amid trips and laughs. He made out Jacobo's voice and those of his friends. They were really plastered. He was not surprised. Jacobo got that drunk only when he went out with the Englishman and the Portuguese.

The men went by the open door. Simón began to feel worried. He got up, put on a pair of trousers, took a lantern, and went down the stairs. Nothing could be seen or heard. He lit the lantern and retraced his steps. He saw the pickup badly parked under the porch and the sack room door ajar. He peeked in and heard a groan. "Is there someone there?"

He got another groan in reply.

"Who's that?"

"I need help," whispered Bisila.

As if shot from a gun, Simón got down on his knees beside her. The light from the lantern revealed that his friend was injured. She had blood on her face and body and lay motionless. In one hand she held a damp handkerchief.

"What happened to you?" he asked, alarmed, in Bubi. "What have they done to you?"

"I need to go to the hospital," she answered in a wooden voice.

Simón helped her get to her feet. Bisila fixed her clothes with difficulty with her injured arm. He started to become enraged.

"I know the men responsible!" he murmured between his teeth. "They'll pay for what they've done!"

Bisila leaned on Simón's arm and nudged him to start walking. She needed to get out of that damned place.

"No, Simón." She gently clasped her friend's arm. "What has happened stays here." She closed the door, and they went out into the yard. "Promise me you'll say nothing."

Simón pointed to her bloodied eye.

"How are you going to hide that?" he protested. "How are you going to explain your arm to Mosi?"

"I'm not worried about my body, Simón," answered a crestfallen Bisila.

He could only feel rage. "And what'll happen when Kilian finds out?"

Bisila stopped dead. "Kilian must never find out about this. Do you hear me, Simón? Never!"

Simón nodded slightly to show he had agreed, and they continued walking.

Kilian won't find out, he thought, *but they will pay for what they have done.*

When they got to the hospital, Bisila gave him instructions on how to reset her dislocated shoulder. She put a gag between her teeth and closed her eyes, waiting for Simón's blow. She let out a shriek and fainted. When she recovered, she dressed the wounds from the blows and bandaged up her arm in a sling.

Afterward, Simón took her home. Bisila waited until she was sure that everything was completely quiet. Fortunately, Mosi and Iniko were asleep. They were used to her hours. They would not see the cuts and bruises until the following day.

Simón went back to his room in the main building, still trembling with rage.

What had happened that night was nothing that had not happened before. It was one of the ways the whites imposed their power. No black woman, even if insulted and threatened, would dare report a white man. It would be her word against his, and any court would rule that she had asked for it.

In bed, Simón clenched his fists. According to the law, they were now as Spanish as those in Madrid. It was all a lie! Whites were whites and blacks were blacks, even if they were now allowed to go into cinemas and bars. The impending independence would not change anything: others would come, and they would continue to exploit the island before the helpless eyes of those who once cared for it. That was the Bubis' destiny.

He decided to tell Mosi everything.

Bisila had made him promise not to say anything to Kilian and he would not—at least, not for the moment.

But Mosi would know what to do.

On Monday morning, Simón looked for Mosi in the southern area of the plantation. His men advanced in rows of ten, slashing with their machetes to clear ground for planting from the jungle. He soon made out the foreman, as his head stuck out above the others. He waved for him to come over. They moved away so no one could eavesdrop.

"Bisila was attacked. Three white men. I found her."

Mosi cursed and leaned against a tree. The expression on his face became harder. "Do you know who they were?" he asked.

Simón nodded. "There were three of them. I know who they are."

"Tell me their names and where I can find them. I'll take care of everything else."

"Two of them don't live here. They'll leave today. Massa Dick and Massa Pao. I heard them say that they'd be back in two or three weeks."

"And the third?"

Simón swallowed. "The third is a massa on the plantation."

Mosi gritted his teeth and waited for the name. "The third is Massa Jacobo."

Mosi stood up straight, picked up his machete, and ran his thick finger along its blade.

"*Tenki, mi fren,*" he said slowly. "I'll look for you if I need you."

He continued his work as if Simón had not told him anything important.

Simón returned to the plantation yard and was surprised to hear a laugh he knew well coming from the parked trucks.

Kilian had returned!

He raised his eyes to the heavens and noticed a slight change in the air.

The tornadoes would soon be upon them.

Kilian got up early, put on a loose pair of linen trousers and a white cotton shirt, and went out to the balcony. The weather was fresh. The rains of the last few days had left the air so humid that stoves were needed to heat the rooms. He decided to go in and put on a long-sleeved shirt and a jacket. He came back out onto the passageway, took a deep breath, lit a cigarette, leaned on the railing of the balcony, and cast his eyes toward the royal palm tree entrance.

At any other time, Kilian would have found the morning silence comforting. Lately, however, silence seemed set on taking over his life.

Simón was distant and evasive. José was hiding something from him. And Bisila . . .

Bisila was avoiding him.

Just after arriving, he had gone to the hospital to see her. After months of wanting her in his arms, he had been sure that they would end up in the small storeroom. Instead, he had met a thinner, sadder Bisila with her arm bandaged and part of her face swollen. Even so, she walked between the men in their sickbeds in her normal pleasant fashion, a pleasantness that became cold when she turned to him to explain that a truck had knocked her down.

Kilian had not believed a word of it. He even thought that Mosi might have mistreated her, but she denied it. Then . . . why the change in attitude?

If she only knew how much he missed her!

He had hoped Bisila would appear some night in his room, but she had not.

Leaning on the passageway railing, Kilian sighed deeply. Something inside told him that she would not come to his room ever again. Something horrible must have happened for her not to want to see him. He closed his eyes and remembered their wedding.

I promise to be faithful to you, she had told him, *at least in my heart.*

How could Mosi have found out about her infidelity when Kilian was in Spain?

No. Something did not fit.

The sirens marking the beginning of the workday broke the silence. Kilian hated that this terrible noise had replaced the drums. The hustle and bustle in the yard reminded him that he had to hurry up if he wanted to get breakfast before work.

Some minutes later, Jacobo came to breakfast, walking slowly and with his eyes half-closed. He was not feeling well.

"It must be because of the weekend in Santa Isabel," said Kilian.

Jacobo shook his head. "I was to meet up with Dick and Pao, but they didn't show. After the last night with them, I swore I wouldn't drink again."

"And what did you do *without* them?" Kilian asked sarcastically.

"I went to see a couple of girlfriends I'd been neglecting . . . They took me to the cinema." Jacobo shrugged. "A very quiet weekend! I can't make out why I feel as if I'd been run over by a train." He put his hand on his forehead. "I think I have a temperature."

Kilian poured him a cup of coffee. "Have something. It'll make you feel better."

"I'm not hungry."

That was something new.

Kilian got up and said, "Come on, I'll go with you to the hospital."

With a bit of luck, Bisila will be there, he thought.

Kilian was convinced that Jacobo had malaria. His brother was always forgetting to take the quinine tablets, and some nights, especially if he had gone out, he forgot to close the mosquito net properly around his bed. The tiredness and muscular pains, the shivers and the temperature, the headache and the sore throat, and the loss of appetite were all clear symptoms of the illness. He would be in the hospital for a couple of weeks, which would give Kilian the perfect excuse to see Bisila every day, to watch her until he found out what had happened.

"Syphilis?" Kilian opened his eyes wide. "But . . . how's that possible?"

Manuel raised an eyebrow. "I can think of one or two ways of catching it," he said with irony. "He'll be with us for three weeks. Then he'll have to take medication for a few months. I'm sure he'll be more careful from now on."

He snapped his file shut and went off.

Kilian stood for a good while without daring to go into the room. He ran his fingers through his hair, sighed, and went in.

Jacobo was asleep. Kilian sat in a chair. The scene brought back distant memories of his father. How many hours had he spent sitting in a chair with Antón! An eternity had passed!

He laughed to himself, remembering the sight of the Bissappoo witch doctor placing the amulets on his father's body. If it were not for his friendship with José, he would never have thought of the idea. He remembered how furious Jacobo had gotten. Maybe he should send for the witch doctor again to treat his brother, he thought mischievously.

Someone knocked at the door, and a sweet voice asked for permission to enter. Kilian jumped to his feet as Bisila came in. She looked at him in surprise, turned her gaze to the bed, and made out Jacobo. When she recognized him, she gave a whimper and dropped the small tray in her hand.

Kilian went over and gathered up the things she had scattered on the floor. Then he gently shut the door and went to her.

Bisila's breathing was agitated. She could not speak.

Kilian hugged her and began to stroke her hair.

"What's wrong, Bisila?" he whispered. "What's tormenting my *muarána muèmuè?*"

Bisila's body trembled in his arms.

Making a slight gesture in Jacobo's direction, she asked, "What's wrong with your brother?"

Kilian separated from her just enough to look at her face.

"Nothing he doesn't deserve," he said. "He has syphilis."

Bisila clamped her lips together, and her chin began to tremble. Her eyes filled with tears.

"Syphilis!" she repeated in a voice laced with hate. *"Na d'a pa'o budá."*

"What did you say?"

Bisila did not answer. She began to sob and ran out of the room. Kilian leaned on the open door. There was hate in Bisila's look, but also sadness.

Just then, he heard a big commotion as men called for the doctor. He left the room and went to the entrance hall.

Manuel was on his knees, examining the body of a badly wounded man lying on a makeshift stretcher. Kilian noticed his friend shaking his head and curling his lips in worry. A group of men prevented Kilian from seeing who he was treating, although it seemed to be a white man.

He looked at the faces of those around him and recognized one of the men from Mosi's brigade. He went over and asked him what had happened. The man was very upset and answered in a mixture of Pichi and Spanish. Another man interrupted, and then another. Kilian finally understood their story.

Mosi's brigade had begun clearing the forest, like every day. They were walking in columns of around ten people, opening the way with their machetes, when one of them shouted he had found something. Suspended from a tree, rocking gently in the breeze, hung the naked, beaten bodies of two white men with their hands tied together. Several stones had been hung from their feet. One of the men was already dead when they took him down. The other was still breathing.

Kilian cleared the way and knelt beside Manuel. The wounded man had cuts and bruises all over and deep wounds on his wrists and ankles, and he breathed with difficulty. Kilian stared at his face. He had the eyes of a savage beast.

Kilian recognized the Englishman, and the blood froze in his veins.

"Do you know this man?" Manuel asked.

"It's Dick, one of my brother's friends. He lived in Douala, but moved to Bata a while ago. I thought you knew him as well."

"That's why he looked familiar. Wasn't he always with that . . . ?" Manuel had a suspicion. He stood up and gave orders that he be taken to the operating room, although the expression revealed that little could be done. The men moved aside to allow them to pass.

They immediately brought in the dead body of the other white man. They had covered his face with a shirt.

Kilian lifted a corner of the material.

"It's Pao." He brought his hand up to his chin and rubbed it nervously. "Who could have done this?"

The men around them began to talk in hushed tones. Kilian only managed to get the odd word: "whites," "spirits," "revenge . . ."

Manuel took him by the arm and spoke in a low voice, "It's a bad time for this to happen, Kilian. Things are starting to turn ugly for us Europeans. If this spreads, more than one will leave the country. Don't you feel the fear? Now the natives will use this to say it's the work of the spirits—"

"I don't understand," Kilian interrupted. "What have the spirits got to do with this?"

"Two white men appear, murdered in the ancient manner. They'll begin to say that the spirits don't want the whites here. There are rough seas ahead!"

Kilian stayed silent. He looked at Pao's body again. "They told my brother that they'd come to spend the weekend, but they didn't. He thought it was odd."

"Tell your brother to tread carefully."

"Why do you say that? Do we also have to be careful?"

Manuel shrugged and, raising his hands, exclaimed, "Yes, I suppose!"

He went to the operating room but not before telling a couple of men to place the dead body in the mortuary until the plantation management decided what to do.

The men moved aside to let Pao's lifeless body through. Kilian followed with his eyes. After a few meters, the men carrying the body stopped.

Kilian saw how Bisila lifted up a corner of the shirt that covered Pao's face and let it fall again. Bisila clasped her hands together, squeezed them hard against her bosom, and closed her eyes. She did not notice that Kilian was watching her closely.

Beside him, he listened to two nurses murmuring something in Bubi. He turned and asked, "What does something like '*Na á'a pa'o buáá*' mean?"

One of them looked at him in surprise. "It means 'I hope he dies.'"

Kilian frowned.

One man was dead, the second was sure to die, and Bisila wanted the death of a third.

Kilian found José and Simón in the stores. The news had spread like wildfire through the plantation.

"And what do you two think?" Kilian got straight to the point. "Was it the work of the living or the dead?"

José said nothing. It was obvious that Kilian was in a temper.

Simón stood in front of him.

"And what do you think, Massa?" he said. "Do you think it was us, the peace-loving Bubis? Or maybe a Fang on the island on vacation? Or the Nigerians celebrating black magic? I bet it never crossed your mind that it could be other whites who killed them."

José motioned to him to be quiet. Kilian gave him a hard stare.

"The whites," he muttered, "don't tie their victims to trees or hang rocks from their feet."

"Of course not," replied Simón. "They have other ways . . ."

Kilian exploded. "Simón! Is there something you want to tell me?" His eyes flared, and his fists were clenched.

"And you"—he looked at José—"what are you hiding? I thought we were friends!" He started to pace up and down, waving his arms. "This is driving me crazy! Something happened here. I know it's got something to do with Dick, Pao . . ." He paused. "And my brother!"

José looked furtively at Simón, who turned away.

Kilian went over to them. "What did they do, José? Who wants revenge?" He caught hold of Simón's arm and forced him around. "What the hell did my brother do? Do you want to hang him from a tree as well?"

José opened his mouth and shut it again.

"We won't tell you anything," said José.

"If you two won't tell me," grumbled Kilian, "who will?" He looked to the sky, defeated, and asked, "Bisila?"

Simón cleared his throat. "Yes," he said, barely audible.

Kilian felt his strength leave him.

He remembered Bisila's arm and the wounds on her face and suddenly felt like throwing up.

Bisila wanted his brother dead!

What had they done? He leaned against the wall to stop himself falling.

It could not be true! Not his brother!

He remembered that his brother was ill with syphilis, and he retched.

He would kill him. He would kill him with his bare hands!

José came over and put an arm on his shoulder. Kilian moved away. He took a deep breath and tried to pull himself together, feeling only hate inside.

"I have two questions, José, and I expect you to answer both," he warned. "Does Mosi know?"

"I told him," Simón responded.

"And the second," continued Kilian. "Will he come for Jacobo?"

José nodded. "Let Mosi do what he has to do," he said sadly. "This is none of your business."

Kilian clenched and unclenched his fists. "Don't tell me what I have to do, José!" he shouted.

"If you stop him," Simón interrupted, "Mosi will learn about your relationship with her, and you will both end up hanging from a tree."

Kilian, broken, leaned against the wall again.

"In these matters," said José, "white man's law has no place. I've accepted and understood your relationship with Bisila, but she could be accused of adultery. If you really love her, you'll stay out of this. Everything will soon return to normal."

Kilian wiped his forehead before standing up straight. "After this, nothing will ever be the same," he said softly.

He started toward the main building.

He needed to think.

Kilian did not go to see his brother for two weeks. He did not much care if the other thought it odd or if he suffered after finding out about the death of his friends. All his thoughts revolved exclusively around his desire to do him harm . . . and the fear of Mosi's vengeance. He was sure that, for the moment, Jacobo was safe. The giant would not dare do anything while he was in the hospital.

How could his brother have done such an unforgivable thing?

He struck his machete in rage at the trunk of a cocoa tree. The blows fell on the ripe reddish fruit, destroying them, and leaving the beans open to the elements. He stopped dead in his tracks, got his breath back, and shook his head in regret.

Why had he not told Jacobo before that Bisila had been his wife for a long time? If he had known, he would have never laid a finger on her. Even for someone like him, there were limits that should not be crossed.

The only possibility left was that Jacobo had not recognized Bisila . . . Kilian's stomach turned. Any punishment seemed too light to make up for the damage that those three had caused.

He thought of the bodies of Dick and Pao. He visualized the terrible hours of agony that they would have suffered until the relief of death. A sharp pain settled in his chest. Would he remain with his arms folded, knowing that Mosi would come for Jacobo? For all that was holy, of course not! They had spent their whole lives together. They shared the same blood of the forebearers of the House of Rabaltué.

Kilian had no other option. He had to talk to him. Nothing could excuse his brother's actions, but he had to save his life. Despite everything, he was his brother.

And then what? Would they go to the authorities and explain everything? They would arrest Mosi, and he would be punished for the murders. He remembered José's and Simón's words of warning. The Africans had their own way of sorting things out. If Kilian informed on Mosi, they would come for him. An eye for an eye, a tooth for a tooth.

Don't get involved, Kilian, he thought. *You only want to get Bisila back. Drown yourself in her eyes until time stands still again and it is only the two of you.*

He leaned back against the tree and rubbed his forehead in anguish. He had no other choice. He had to warn Jacobo. What his brother did with that information mattered as much to him as the cocoa beans that lay crushed at his feet.

When Kilian entered the room, Jacobo was sitting up against the headboard, finishing his lunch. When he saw his brother, he quickly left the tray on the bedside table and sat on the edge of the bed.

"Kilian," he exclaimed happily. "The hours in the hospital seem like forever." He got up. "Why didn't you come before? I suppose Garuz has enough problems with one of us out of action."

Kilian looked at Jacobo and tried to keep his temper. From his cheerful attitude, he guessed that his brother knew nothing about the deaths of Dick and Pao. Manuel had probably not wanted to frighten him in his condition.

Jacobo went to give him a hug, but Kilian took a step back.

"Hey! It's not contagious!" He hung his head, ashamed. "These days I've been thinking about what Father Rafael said. The longer we went without a woman, the better off we'd be health- and pocket-wise."

Kilian took a deep breath, and said flatly, "Sit down."

"Oh! I'm fine! I've been on my back all day. I want to get up and move a bit."

"I told you to sit down," said Kilian between his teeth.

Jacobo went back to the edge of the bed. "What's the matter?"

Kilian answered with another question: "Have you heard about Dick and Pao?"

"Did they get the same thing?"

"They turned up murdered a few days ago. Hanging from a tree. They had been tortured."

Jacobo let out a shout but did not say anything. Kilian studied his reaction. After a while, Jacobo, his voice trembling, asked, "But . . . how is that possible? Why?"

"I was hoping you would be able to tell me that."

"I don't understand, Kilian. I don't know anything. I told you they were meant to come and see me, and they didn't." He opened his eyes, frightened. "Killed! But who . . . ? Do you think they were killed for being white?"

"No." Kilian moved a few steps closer. "It's for something they did on their last trip to the island. For something *you* did."

"I've done nothing!" Jacobo got defensive. "I have never got mixed up in their problems. Could you tell me what's gotten into you? That day we went to the city and drank like fish. I don't even know how I got to bed. Maybe I overdid the iboga, but that's it."

"You didn't party with any *girlfriend* back here on the plantation?" Kilian chewed his words.

In Jacobo's mind, blurred images appeared of a dark place, some voices, some laughs, a body under him, a voice babbling his name, a pair of bright eyes. He coughed, nervous. He did not understand why Kilian was putting him through this. He got to his feet and stood in front of his brother.

"And what do you care how I finished the night?" he asked arrogantly.

"Bloody bastard!" Kilian sprung at him and began hitting him as hard as he could, aiming his fists at his face and chest. "You raped her! The three of you! One after another!"

Jacobo tried to defend himself, but his brother had caught him unawares, and he was only able to dodge the occasional blow. He covered his face with his hands and let himself fall back on the bed, frightened and shocked.

Kilian swore aloud and stopped as blood trickled from his brother's face. "Do you know who she was?"

"I was so drugged it wouldn't have mattered."

Kilian leaped at him again, but this time Jacobo jumped up and tried to catch his eye.

"I don't go around raping women. I'd swear it was one of Dick's friends."

Kilian gritted his teeth. "It was Bisila. José's daughter."

Jacobo opened his mouth. He blinked several times and tried to speak, but the words got stuck in his throat. His brother narrowed his eyes and, in a cutting voice Jacobo had never heard before, added, "You raped my wife."

Jacobo felt his knees giving way. He sat down again on the bed and hung his head.

His wife. Since when? He felt a sharp pain in his chest. When had they become so distant? Now the scene began to make sense. Kilian's disproportionate reaction proved how important she was to him. What had he done?

Kilian went over to the chair beside the window, let himself fall into it, and buried his face in his hands. After a long silence, he sat up and murmured, "Mosi will come for you. He knows. He'll kill you." He got to his feet and went over to the door. He rested his hand on the knob and said, "For the moment, you are safe here."

He left and slammed the door.

In the adjoining room, Manuel sat down, placed his elbows on the table, and held his head in his hands. Someone knocked at the door and came in without waiting for an answer.

"Can I come in?" Father Rafael frowned. "Are you all right?"

"Please sit down. Don't worry, I'm fine," he lied. The argument he had heard between the two brothers had frozen the blood in his veins. "A lot has happened in the last few days."

"People are very upset." Slightly limping, the priest came over to the chair, sat down, and folded his chubby hands over his abundant stomach. Small nodules circled his finger joints, which looked swollen, rigid, and somewhat bent. "Just now I bumped into Kilian in the corridor. He didn't even say hello to me. That lad . . ." He shook his head. "Do you know how long it's been since he's been to mass? Ah! How different from his father! I hope he's not mixing in bad company. I've heard a rumor, I don't know if you have too."

"He's worried about his brother," Manuel defended Kilian firmly. He normally enjoyed his conversations with the priest, whom he considered an intelligent man hardened by his years on African soil. However, his eagerness to guide everyone along the right path was sometimes uncomfortable. "And more so after the murder of Jacobo's friends."

"Ah, yes. I also heard rumors that they won't be the last ones."

Manuel raised his eyebrows.

"But I don't know whether to believe everything they say . . . Garuz is still in a state. How can this have happened in Sampaka?"

He noticed the latest issue of the Claretian magazine on the desk. "Have you read about the Congo? They murdered another twenty missionaries. That's over a hundred killed since independence. And many are still missing."

"That's not going to happen here, Father. It's impossible. You have been on the island longer than me, but you know the island natives are peaceful."

"As quiet as an illness," said Father Rafael, crossing his arms. "You don't realize you have it till it hurts."

"Have you had your injection today?" The priest came often to the hospital, looking for relief for the arthritis in his hands and knees.

"Not yet. The nurse with the hands of an angel, Bisila, was not there. They told me she would be back soon, so I came to see you while I waited."

"I know you're not going to listen, but I think you're taking too much cortisone. In fact, it was Bisila who showed me some very effective remedies prepared from Namibian devil's claw . . ."

Father Rafael shook his head forcefully. "Never. You think I'm going to trust a plant named *devil's claw*? I wonder what side effects it has! I'd rather put up with the pain."

"As you wish." Manuel shrugged. "But you should know your arthritis is not going to get better. Maybe you should think about moving to a dryer climate."

"And what would I do without my children in Guinea? What would they do without me? If it is God's will, I'll be here until the end of my days, come what may."

Manuel diverted his gaze toward the window, drenched by the last rays of the evening sunlight. He thought the priest's words coincided with those of many of his patients. For the priest, it was God's will; for the others, the will of the spirits. Manuel did not agree with any of them. It was the will of men that made the world go crazy.

"You and me, Manuel"—Manuel listened to the priest—"we owe it to our patients. You wouldn't abandon a wounded man in the middle of an operation? Then . . ."

"Why are you telling me all this, Father?"

"I'll be frank with you, son. I've spoken to Julia, and she told me that you'd like to leave. She doesn't want to."

Manuel took off his glasses and rubbed his eyes. "Sooner or later, she'll agree it's the best thing for our children. Don't take it the wrong way, Father, but I have two children I can save. If you could bring everybody, don't tell me you wouldn't do it. I have seen many sick people in my life, Father, and I can assure you that the sorrows of the soul are nothing compared to physical pain."

"Ah, Manuel! Blessed are you! If you say that, it's because nobody has really done you any harm." Father Rafael got up. "Let me not delay you any further. I'll come around again some other time."

Alone once again, Manuel thought of his words. Maybe the sorrows of the soul were much worse than physical pain. Bisila's arm was healing, and the bruises were disappearing. But there was no medicine, neither native nor foreign, that could mend her grief.

Bisila entered the hospital as Kilian bumped into her. She could see the fire in his eyes and felt an iron grip on her heart. For a few seconds, he held her arms, calming down.

Bisila drew away slowly, but he did not release her.

"Bisila," he murmured.

The words choked in his throat. He wanted to tell her that he missed her, that he loved her, that he was sorry for her suffering, that she should let him share her pain, and that he would always be by her side. But he did not know how to begin.

"I know everything. I'm sorry."

He wanted to hold her tightly in his arms. He wanted to take her from there, go up to Bissappoo, and shut themselves up in the house where he had been her king and she his queen, in that place where they had loved each other.

Bisila cautiously drew away.

"Kilian . . ." It had been ages since she had said his name out loud. Her voice was sweet. He needed sweetness after the bitter discussion with his brother, after the anguish of the last few weeks and the last few months. "I need time."

We don't have any, Bisila, he thought. *Time passes very quickly when we are together. We'll run out of it, and then we'll be sorry.*

But he agreed.

"I want you to tell me one thing, Bisila." He inhaled deeply. The question was not easy. "When is Jacobo getting out of the hospital?"

Bisila turned away, clenching her jaw. She despised that man, just as she had the other two. When she saw their lifeless bodies, she felt no remorse. The hurt would not be erased with their deaths. No. It would stay with her, between them, all their lives.

She knew that Kilian wanted to protect his brother. Protect him from Mosi. But Mosi would not be stopped. Of that she was sure. Jacobo would also pay for what he had done. Kilian should not ask her anything to do with Jacobo.

"I have to know," he insisted.

Bisila fixed her eyes on his and saw him sway between his loyalty to her and to his brother. For her there was no possible justification that could erase Jacobo's sweating face over hers. But he wanted her to understand that in spite of everything, he was still his brother. He was asking her to help him save his life. He was asking her to name the time and place when Mosi's vengeance, and of course her own, would be enacted. What would she do in his position? Would she save her brother? Or would she allow hate to blind her?

"Saturday afternoon," she said in a hard voice. "You could have asked the doctor."

"Does Mosi know?"

Bisila lowered her eyes and began walking toward the door. Kilian quickly put his hand on the knob to stop her.

"You taught me something," he mumbled, "and I believed you. You told me that even when a bad man escapes punishment of this world, he will not escape punishment in the next. Let the *baribò* deal with him."

Bisila closed her eyes and whispered, "Mosi knows. He will come for him. At dusk."

It would take Kilian years to erase the memory of Mosi's enormous body crushing him against the ground, the feeling of asphyxia and shock. Throughout his life, he would often wake up in the middle of the night startled by the sound of a gunshot.

On Saturday, the spirits conspired so that Kilian would not arrive in time to collect his brother. The blasted truck broke down in the most distant part of the plantation. Kilian shouted at Waldo to hurry up, to fix it no matter what. Waldo became nervous with the massa's shouting. At last, he got the engine running, but they had wasted a lot of time, and the vehicle could not go any faster. Sitting beside him, Mateo did not understand the rush.

On the horizon, the darkening speck told them that soon the world would become quiet, an intense calm would precede the noise of thunder, the roar of the wind, and the breaking of trees.

The downpour unleashed as Kilian approached the hospital.

Everything was water.

He put on his helmet and jumped from the truck. Behind the liquid curtain, Jacobo was holding a pistol, threatening Mosi. Why had Mosi come to the very entrance to the hospital? Or had he planned to follow Jacobo and the unexpected storm had given him the perfect opportunity? On the steps, a desperate Manuel shouted at Mosi, trying to get him to stop. The wind and the water swallowed his words.

Mosi was not afraid. He moved closer to Jacobo, wielding a machete in his hand. Jacobo shouted at him to stop, that he would not hesitate to shoot, but Mosi was not listening. Followed by a stunned Mateo, Kilian ran toward them like a madman, bawling at Mosi not to go any farther.

Jacobo's arm tensed. Mosi took another step. Kilian threw himself at him, and a shot was heard.

The bullet grazed Kilian's head and embedded itself in Mosi's chest.

Everything happened at once: Kilian in the air, the bullet close to his head, Mosi's blood mixing with the rain, Kilian on the ground, and the giant falling on top of him.

Steps approached.

Someone got Mosi off him, helped him up.

The doctor. Nurses.

Jacobo trying to explain to a mute Manuel.

"He tried to attack me," he said over and over again. "You saw it."

Mateo shaking his head. "It's obvious that the whites aren't wanted here anymore."

And Jacobo: "We'll all end up sleeping with a gun under our pillows. Thanks be to God nothing happened to you, Kilian."

And Mateo: "I'd never have thought Mosi would do something like this!"

Bisila knelt beside Mosi's body.

All was water and silence.

"Run, Bisila. Go and tell your son his father is dead."

People and more people.

Water and more water.

Kilian needed something to lean on.

And Jacobo: "He tried to attack me. You saw it, Kilian. I had no choice. It was in self-defense."

"Who did you pay, Jacobo, who did you pay to get you the pistol?"

"Why did you jump on top of him? Did you want to save him?"

Bisila picking up his hat from the ground, stroking it with her soft hands.

And Jacobo's voice: "Best let Manuel have a look at you. I'll sort all this out with the police."

"Go, Jacobo. They'll come for you."

"What are you talking about?"

"Get off my island."

18

Bëköttò

Days of Sorrow

1965–1971

Lorenzo Garuz personally sped up the paperwork so that Jacobo could terminate his contract with the Sampaka plantation and return to Spain. The latest happenings needed to be forgotten about as quickly as possible. Jacobo shot someone who had already killed two Europeans. Case closed. For his own safety, it was best that he left immediately, without a farewell party or dinner: only a few pats on the back from his upset friends and two light pecks from Julia, who showed him support and understanding—something he missed from Kilian and Manuel— by clasping his hands for a few wordless seconds.

Kilian did not go to the airport with his brother. He did not go to Mosi's funeral. José had convinced him it was better like that. None of the fellow workers or neighbors of Bisila's husband would understand. Now Kilian was just another white.

Since Mosi's death, it had not stopped raining. The wind blew in their corner of the island stronger than Kilian ever remembered. He had not seen Bisila for twenty days. He had asked José, but he had refused to reveal her whereabouts, and to approach the barracks would have been unwise. The workdays felt unbearably long on the plantation as the men prepared for the coming harvest. The tornadoes brought to mind his father's words: *"Life is like a tornado. Peace, fury, and peace again."*

As time passed, he started to better understand many of the things Antón had told him. At thirty-six, Kilian had enjoyed little peace and much fury. Only Bisila had been able to offer him moments of calm. And he needed more. When would they see each other again?

At last, one night, someone opened the door of his room after he had gone to bed. He sat up, frightened, but an unmistakable voice hastened to calm him, "You still leave the door unlocked."

"Bisila." Kilian sprang up and ran to her.

Bisila's head was covered in a scarf. Her eyes shone in the darkness. Kilian wanted to hold her in his arms and breathe her in, whisper in her ear the torrent of emotions that were overwhelming him, kiss her face and body, make her understand that nothing had changed . . .

Instead, he stood still, waiting for a sign to let him know that she wanted the same.

"I have to talk to you," she said gently.

She raised her hands to her head and took off her scarf. Kilian gasped in shock when he saw that her head was shaved.

"Your hair, Bisila! What happened?"

She took his hand in hers, took him over to the edge of the bed, and sat down beside him. She began to stroke it, and then she brought it to her lips and kissed it. At that moment, he felt hope course through him.

The moonlight filtered through the room. Even with no hair, Bisila was more beautiful than ever. The hardness in her eyes had disappeared, and her lips had lost the bitter grimace of their latest meetings and formed a timid smile.

"I'm so sorry," he began to say. The words came streaming out, tripping over each other. "I shouldn't have gone. All I want is for everything to be as it used to . . . Mosi is dead . . . Now you are free to be with me—"

Bisila put her hand on his lips and said, "I said that that was possible only if the woman carried out the mourning ritual fully. I've never given up my beliefs. What I feel for you has temporarily taken me from what I once was, but something inside me is asking me to go away and think about what has happened, what I want, and who I really am."

Kilian frowned. "Do you need time to admit that in your heart, I'm your real husband?"

Bisila gave a sad smile. "Before the eyes of the divine and the human, Mosi was my husband. As far as my people are concerned, the mourning period is necessary. But there's something else." Her eyes filled with tears, and her voice trembled. "The memories of that night are always there, in my mind. I can't get rid of them. And their words, Kilian . . . They not only seized my body, but also my soul. They made me feel as insignificant as a worm. I have to recover. Otherwise, I won't be free to love you. I don't want to compare you to them, Kilian, with the whites who have abused us for so long. That's why I have to distance myself from you."

Kilian got to his feet and paced the room. The attack suffered by Bisila hurt him deeply, but the dread he felt now was worse.

"Tomorrow I'll go to Bissappoo. I'll be alone for another twenty days in a cabin on the outskirts . . . ," she added.

"Almost another month!" exclaimed Kilian.

Bisila bit her bottom lip. "Then I will lodge in a house beside my mother's, where Iniko will stay. Mosi didn't have any family, so nobody will come looking for my son, which is a relief. I will paint my body in a clay paste, and I will decorate my knees, arms, wrists, and waist with esparto bands. No one will be able to see me dressed in widow's weeds for a couple of days. Then I'll be able to go out and walk wherever I wish, but neither will I come down to Sampaka nor will you come up to see me during the mourning period." She finished. "That's everything."

"And how long will you be like that? How long will *we* be like that?"

Bisila murmured something.

"A year," she whispered as she got to her feet.

Kilian froze. "Don't ask so much of me," he whispered in desperation. "What am I going to do here?" He looked for her eyes. "Aren't you afraid our time is running out?"

She met his gaze with firm determination.

"You can't stop me from coming to see you in Bissappoo . . ."

"If you come . . . ," Bisila warned him, "I'll never return! You have to promise me!"

"I can't promise you that, Bisila," answered Kilian obstinately. His hands caressed the skin on her head, her neck, and her shoulders and descended down her back to the curve of her hips. His voice became soft again, almost pitiful. "Having you so close and not being able to be with you . . ."

"I've told you once, and I'll say it again. I'll always be by your side"—Bisila raised a hand to stroke his cheek and kissed him so tenderly that Kilian shivered—"even if you can't see me."

At that moment, Kilian could not know that the period between May 1965 and April 1966 would not be the most unbearable time in his life, although it seemed so to him. Once more he sought refuge in the routine of work and was pleased that the year's harvest was the most abundant seen in Sampaka in decades. Sleep and work: those were his tasks. Fortunately, the newlyweds, Mateo and Marcial, were occupied with their new lives in the city and left the plantation as soon as their day's work was done, and Julia was looking after her two sons, Ismael and Francisco, full-time. Kilian no longer had to look for excuses to abandon his social life completely. He could count the minutes until Bisila's mourning period—and his own—came to an end, totally removed from the events changing history around him.

Harvesttime came on top of the pruning tasks. José and Kilian walked along the wide cocoa-tree rows, supervising the laborers' work. In each row, the trees were planted the same distance from each other. They rose identically, like fertile goblets, with well-balanced crowns and new shoots, stumps, and intertwined branches. Not far from them, they heard the voice of Simón, who laughed and joined in songs with the Nigerians in his brigade.

Kilian walked on, deep in thought.

The world-renowned Sampaka cocoa came from the daily work of hundreds of workers who spent their days cutting weeds, regulating the shade of the nurse trees, replacing the diseased trees, curing accidental cuts, grafting different varieties of cocoa, and harvesting every fortnight when the trees bore fruit.

And they could always be heard singing.

Some men had spent years without seeing their wives, their children, their relations. They worked from dawn till dusk. They got up, went to the fields, ate, continued their work, had dinner, sang, and talked until they went to their barracks—all the same, in ordered rows like the cocoa trees—certain that a new day would swallow them up in its routine. The only thing they hoped for out of life was to get paid well so they could send money to their home country and give their families a better life.

And they still continued singing.

Day after day. Month after month. Season after season.

It had been eleven months and one week since he had seen Bisila.

Not once had he felt the urge to sing.

"You're very quiet," said José. "What are you thinking about?"

Kilian tapped the ground a few times with his machete. "You know, Ösé? I've been here for many years, and I've never felt like a stranger. I've done the same as the rest of you. Work, eat, have fun, love, suffer . . ." He thought of his father's death and Bisila's absence. "Ösé, I think the biggest difference between a Bubi like you and a white man like me is that a Bubi allows the cocoa tree to grow freely, but the white man prunes the tree to get the most out of it."

José nodded. As it grew, the cocoa tree produced a large quantity of shoots that had to be cut so as not to suck the sap. As the years passed, the trees began to deform. For that reason, pruning started when the tree was young. If too many branches were cut, the tree exhausted itself. If not enough dead, diseased, or badly formed branches were cut and enough suckers and the remains of last year's crop removed, the sun would not be able to get to the trunk, and the tree could rot until it died.

After a while, José said, "There are now blacks who prune like whites and blacks who want the cocoa tree to grow at its own pace. There are also whites who continue pruning and whites who abandon their plantations. Tell me, Kilian, which one are you?"

Kilian considered the question. "I'm a man from the mountains, Ösé"—he shrugged, looking him straight in the eye—"who has spent thirteen years among tropical tornadoes." He shook his head in resignation. "For that reason, I know only one thing is certain. You cannot leash nature. Cocoa trees are pruned, but the trees continue to generate new shoots and disorderly branches in such quantity that there aren't enough machetes to deal with them. The same as the waters of the rivers and gullies, Ösé. The storms increase their flow, and they burst their banks."

"There is a Spanish saying that the waters always return to their original course," responded José.

Kilian smiled briefly. "Tell me, *mi frend*, do you know a saying that could explain how those waters felt while they were free?"

Ösé remained thoughtful. Then he answered, "Wasn't it a big white chief who said, 'Liberty, when it begins to take root, is a plant of rapid growth'?"

The workday was coming to an end when the nightmares made a sleeping Waldo, lying on a pile of empty sacks, moan.

Nobody mistreats Öwassa. The forest is forbidden to those who are not from here. It's only ours. The great spirit of Öbassa thanks you, mysterious man of the forest, who . . .

"Wake up, Waldo!" The lad shot up, startled by Kilian's shout. "I don't know what has happened to you and Simón lately, but during the day, you seem sorrowful." Someone cleared their throat behind him, and he turned. "Ah, I was just talking about you. Don't tell me that you were also taking a nap . . ."

Simón gave him an enigmatic smile.

"Well, you'll have to tell your girlfriends to let you rest a bit," Kilian continued, "if you want to get paid. Work comes first."

Simón sighed. "She's back," he said flatly. "She's returned to work in the hospital."

He added slyly, "I hope you don't fall ill again . . ."

Kilian bolted in the direction of the main yard. *Will she want to see me?* he asked himself. *Will she have thought about me as I have thought about her? Why didn't she tell me herself that she was back?*

Bisila was not in the hospital. Impatience consumed him. He began to circle the main entrance, wondering where he could find her.

He decided to ask in the upper part, near the Obsay yard limits. If Bisila had taken up her job again as plantation nurse, Garuz would probably have given her a house there. He took off with a determined step, holding back the impulse to run. The sweat began to bead on his forehead. He felt anxious and happy to see her again. A year!

When he got to the first barracks, some music drifted over to him. It was impossible not to be affected by the rhythm of the drums. They were dancing a *balele*. He was soon able to make out a large group of children dressed up in green and red dancing to the beat of the drums, in groups, individually, or with their mothers. They looked happy in their celebration. Kilian had managed to understand and share with the Africans their idea that any reason was good enough to dance.

He stopped just a few meters away from the party and allowed himself to become infused with the children's happiness. One of them, about five or six, stared at him with a smile on his face, and Kilian recognized Iniko under the green hat. For a second, he saw Mosi in his features, and he returned the smile with sadness. Iniko looked at him attentively while moving a pendant that hung from his neck with his hand. The boy turned and ran in the direction of a woman carrying a load in her arms and began to obstinately pull at her skirt until she looked in the direction he was pointing to.

Bisila's eyes met Kilian's, and the hearts of both somersaulted in their chests.

The drums repeated the same rhythm over and over again. Bisila's eyes filled with tears as soon as she saw Kilian, tall and muscular, with his shirt rolled up above his elbows, with his well-cut, dark, copper-highlighted hair, his skin bronzed by the sun and some small wrinkles framing the green of his eyes.

Kilian stood still.

There was Bisila, wrapped in a turquoise-blue tunic that could not hide the new fullness of her features. A matching scarf covered her head and showed off the deep expressiveness of her enormous eyes.

He could not stop staring at her eyes.

He began to walk toward her slowly and then saw that she was carrying a baby, only a few months old, in her arms. When he was beside her, Bisila spoke to him softly, "I want you to meet my son."

She removed the white cloth covering the child, and Kilian could see that he was a lighter color than the other children, like coffee with a dash of milk.

"His name is Fernando Laha." Kilian felt a knot in his stomach. "He was born in January, but you can see he has the features and eyes"—her voice broke—"of the men of the House of Rabaltué."

Kilian gazed at the baby in shock. "He could have been mine, Bisila," he murmured.

"He could have been yours, Kilian," she repeated sadly.

Kilian asked her to let him hold the child in his arms. It was the first time he had held a baby, and he was clumsy. He remembered the snakeskin hanging in the square in Bissappoo so that all the newborn children could touch it with their hands.

"Have you taken him to touch the *boukaroko*'s tail?" he asked.

The little Fernando Laha woke up and looked at the man oddly, but he gurgled and made a face that Kilian interpreted as a smile.

"I won't tell Jacobo," he said, amazed. "It will be our secret."

The baby raised its eyes to Bisila.

"His future brothers and sisters won't notice the difference."

Bisila hung her head.

"He won't have any more brothers and sisters," she whispered.

Kilian looked at her, perplexed.

"I was very ill, Kilian," she explained. "I can't have more children."

Kilian did not want to know any more, not at that moment. He was with her, and in his arms, he held a descendant of his father, Antón, and all the other names that appeared on the house's genealogical tree since the first Kilian centuries before.

Nothing else mattered.

"Fernando will be our child, Bisila," he said. "And I like the name you chose for him. It's from there and here, yours and mine. Tell me, what does *Laha* stand for?"

"It means 'someone with a good heart.' Like you."

The baby grabbed hold of Kilian's finger with his small hand, and Kilian smiled, filled with joy.

Bisila felt greatly relieved. At that moment, she knew she would never love a man like she loved Kilian.

She had honored tradition and was now a widow free to do what she wished with her life. But above all, she had come back from the depths strengthened both in her beliefs and in her love for him.

Iniko timidly came over to them, continuing to move his feet to the rhythm of the music. His hand still clasped the pendant round his neck.

"What are you hiding in your hand, son?" asked Kilian.

Bisila touched the head covered in the green hat. "It's a sign of punishment. Father Rafael put it on him for talking in Bubi instead of in Spanish. I'll take him up to my mother again. He's happy in Bissappoo."

Iniko began to pull naggingly at his mother's dress while rubbing an eyebrow.

"Yes, I'm coming," she said. "Today is the beginning of *ëmëtöla* . . ."

They celebrated the transition from *ömögera* to *ëmëtöla*, the subtle change from spring's beginning to its fullness. For the Bubis, *ömögera* meant the beginning, the start, the morning, vitality, and movement, and *ëmëtöla* represented permanence, strength, perseverance, stability, and preservation. The red and the green. The fire and the earth.

"It's time to begin preparing the next harvest," said Kilian. "The crops are growing nonstop. It will be a good one." He returned the baby to his mother's arms. "Meanwhile," he added with uncertainty, "we'll have a little more time . . . for ourselves." Just then, Kilian felt some pats on his thigh. He looked down and found Ismael trying to get his attention. The child asked him if he had also come there to dance and explained to him, with a hurried chatter, that he had come up with his mother, with his brother, and with Oba and that since he was now grown up, they had let him play a drum. Kilian looked up and saw a red-faced Julia looking for the little one.

Julia stopped to say hello to Bisila, without taking her eyes off the baby in her arms. Kilian saw her frown. Bisila and Iniko continued on, followed by Ismael.

"Once Ismael hears the drums, it's impossible to hold him back," said Julia. "I didn't know that Bisila had another child. Have you seen the color of its skin?"

"Yes, Julia," said Kilian, looking at her straight in the eye. "This one is definitely mine."

"Kilian!" Bisila protested, trying to catch her breath. "If I were snow, would I have melted in your hands yet?"

Kilian's burning fingers explored her still-perspiring body and traveled across every centimeter of her skin over and over again, trying to recover the time lost.

"Not yet." Kilian wove his fingers in hers and flattened her with his weight. "You don't know how much I've missed you!"

"You've told me a thousand times!" Bisila delicately pushed him. She could hardly breathe.

Kilian lay down and leaned on his elbow to look at her, tracing her face.

"I was afraid you wouldn't want anything to do with me," he confessed.

Bisila closed her eyes. "I had a lot of time to think of *me*."

Kilian frowned. It tormented him to think of her suffering, trying to join fragments in her mind and soul, in a small village surrounded by forest, fulfilling the rites of mourning for a husband she had not loved, while a forced new life grew inside her. And it was all Jacobo's fault. Kilian clicked his tongue and shook his head to rid the next thought. Jacobo was also the cause of Bisila's freedom. How ironic: violence had led to happiness. If Jacobo had not killed Mosi, they would still be forced to meet in secret.

How had she been able to overcome it all?

Bisila loved him with an energy and a force unknown to him.

When Kilian sank into her, time after time, he felt as if he were a ship and she a whirlpool in the sea that swallowed him up and spat him out to swallow him again.

The assertiveness and strength of passion with which she gave herself to him transformed their intimate moments.

As if each time were the last.

"Are you annoyed?" Bisila asked.

"Why?"

"Because you wanted to hear I did nothing else but think about you . . ."

"Did you think of me or not?"

"Every second."

"That's good."

Bisila leaned on her elbow to face him and began to caress his face, his neck, his shoulder. She moved closer to hug him and continued to stroke his hair, his nape, and his back while whispering words that he did not understand, but which made him moan.

When Bisila wanted to drive him wild, she spoke in Bubi.

"I want you to understand what I'm saying, Kilian."

"I understand you perfectly . . ."

"I'm saying that you are so far inside me there is nothing I can do to get you out."

"And I don't intend to come out. I always want to be inside you."

"Ah, lads . . ." Lorenzo Garuz rubbed his bushy eyebrows. His eyes had never seemed so sunken. "And what will I do now without you?"

Mateo and Marcial exchanged guilty looks.

"I . . . I'm really very sorry . . ." Marcial's hands clung to the pith helmet on his knees.

"And so am I," Mateo butted in. "But I hope you understand. We've been here a long time and—"

"Yes, yes." A scowling Garuz raised his hand in the air.

He did not want to hear their reasons. He himself had sent his wife and children back to Spain, and he himself had moments of weakness when he wanted to throw in the towel and get the first transport back to the peninsula. He would not be the first manager to abandon his plantation to the mercy of the weeds and a handful of natives. His sense of responsibility, however, always managed to win out. He was not just any manager: he was the majority shareholder of Sampaka, the biggest, most beautiful, most productive, and best-run plantation on the whole island. Mateo and Marcial would happily accept any mediocre job in Spain. The new generations lacked the fortitude, the courage, the pride, and even the impetuousness of those who had built the colony. Garuz had managed not only to maintain, but to grow the property inherited from that forebearer of his who had left in search of his fortune more than half a century ago. He could not leave it in other hands.

"And don't you ever think about leaving?" asked Mateo, as if he had read his mind.

"Until the constitution is approved and powers are handed over, Spain won't abandon us." He sighed loudly. "And I don't see why I can't keep producing cocoa, unless, of course, I end up with no workers."

Someone knocked at the door, and Garuz gave him permission to enter. Mateo and Marcial sighed in relief.

The *wachimán* Yeremías poked his head in.

"Excuse me, Massa," he said. "May I come in?"

"Of course. What's the matter?"

Yeremías entered, took off his old hat, and held it in his hands, with his eyes glued to the floor.

"A policeman has come and says he has to talk to you urgently."

Garuz frowned. "You haven't forgotten to take them the usual eggs and bottles?"

"No, Massa, I haven't forgotten. But this one isn't from Zaragoza. He comes from the city and is wearing a very . . . official uniform."

"I'll be with him in a minute." Garuz, puzzled, opened a drawer and took out two envelopes for his employees. "These are for you. A small reward for the fine work you've done over the years. Use it wisely. You both now have families to think about."

He waited for both of them to take a look at what was in the envelope and raise their eyebrows, very pleased. Then he stood up and came over to them.

"Of one thing you can be sure, you won't earn the same salary over there."

Mateo and Marcial accepted the bonus with sincere thanks.

"Everything is already organized," said Marcial. "We're traveling by ship with all our things."

"Nothing in comparison to the two bags we arrived with . . . ," added Mateo.

A silence followed.

"All right." Garuz put out his hand to say good-bye. "If, one day, you change your mind, you know where to find me."

"Who knows?" Mateo opened the door. "We might meet up in Madrid—"

Before he could finish, a man barged into the office. He was quite tall and strong, and his face was marked by smallpox. He wore a gray Spanish police uniform, with brass buttons on the jacket and a red band sewn onto the sleeves, lapels, and cap.

"My name is Maximiano Ekobo," he introduced himself. "I am the new chief of police in Santa Isabel. Which one of you is Lorenzo Garuz?"

Garuz made a gesture for the others to leave and offered his hand to greet the policeman. "What can I do for you?"

Maximiano sat down. "I'm looking for some young men who are sabotaging work on the new television facilities. During the day, laborers build the access way to Big Pico for the material needed for the building, the tower, and the powerhouse. At night, someone destroys what has been done during the day. Tools disappear, reference signs are removed, and the machinery is tampered with."

"I don't know what that has to do with me."

"A few weeks ago, we detained one of these men. They are nothing more than Bubis who want to destroy the gift given to us by Spain. The man has confessed that the ringleader is a Simón"—he paused to observe the manager's reaction—"who works on this plantation."

Garuz crossed his hands behind his back and began to pace. He had just handed final paychecks to two very hardworking men. Only three Spaniards were left on the plantation: Gregorio, Kilian, and himself. José, Simón, Waldo, and Nelson made up the rest of the small team. He did not like it one bit that Simón was involved in subversive activities. In other circumstances, he himself would have gone to the police, but at that moment, he could not allow himself the luxury of losing another employee. He saw no alternative but to lie, and chose his words carefully. Now, more than ever before, it was in his interest to get on well with the new authorities.

"Listen, Maximiano." He looked him straight in the eye. "I give you my word as a gentleman that I am totally opposed to any act of violence and even more so those committed against goods and property valuable for this country. But I'm afraid you have made your journey in vain. The Simón you are referring to had a serious accident. He has been recovering for over two months. He fell from the roof of one of the storehouses and broke both legs. However, if I hear anything that might shed light on your investigation, be in no doubt that I'll get in touch with you."

He remained totally composed, certain that his words had been convincing. He knew what these new and impertinent chiefs were made of, men like Maximiano who thought they were superior, even to whites like himself. You had to be extremely respectful, but also firm and determined.

Maximiano nodded, got up, and went to the door. "That's all for the moment." He left without saying good-bye.

Garuz breathed in relief and went out looking for Simón, whom he had to warn as quickly as possible. The young man would have no other choice but to pretend he had a limp, at least in front of any official uniform. And it was not in any way in his interest to be in that Maximiano's bad books.

"No one talks about us Spaniards who are here! It's not considered for one minute that we can form part of the future nation! But everyone else has their portion. The Bubi separatists, the neocolonial Bubis, the unitarian nationalists, the pro-independence radicals, and those who want gradual independence . . ."

"You forgot about the Nigerians, Kilian." Manuel folded the *Ébano* newspaper and started to flick through *ABC*. "With the civil war in their country between Islamic Hausa and Catholic Ibos, more are arriving here every day. I'm not surprised that Nelson and Ekon are happy that their brothers have come, but there is less and less work available here."

Kilian swigged down his gin and tonic and signaled to the waiter for another round.

"If there is really going to be independence, why have they set up a Spanish National Television transmitter on the Santa Isabel peak?"

"They have done it against the will of the spirits of the forest . . . ," Simón intervened, with a mischievous glint in his eye. He was comfortably sitting in an armchair, triumphantly enjoying his drink in a whites' bar.

"This television thing is a mystery." He raised his eyes toward the box that was placed in a corner of the room. "Remember the first program we saw in this very room three months ago? *Spain, Mother of*

Nations or something like that." His tone became ironic again. "What I remember are the words of your head over there." He sat up in his seat and imitated in a high-pitched voice: "'You know that Spain has never been a colonizer, rather a civilizer and creator of nations . . .'"

Kilian and Manuel smiled.

"And now it turns out," he continued, "that the whites talk about our independence as if it was the greatest success in your country's mission of civilization. I don't like that one bit, no, sir. As far as I know, my people were just fine before you came."

"But you weren't very civilized," the doctor joked, looking over his glasses and returning to his reading. "Now you even have a constitution approved by the majority."

"Not on the island, remember?" Simón interrupted. "The yes won by very few votes."

"It doesn't matter," said Kilian. "The fact is, even the news is now broadcast in Fang, Bubi, and Spanish so that the three points of view can be seen. But the money is still coming here from Spain. It's as if they were investing at a rate of knots to show us that self-determination has its risks." He moved his glass dangerously in the air. "How is it possible, then, to be so certain that independence will come in a matter of weeks? How do you go from complete dependence to independence? Is everything suddenly dismantled and that's it? If we all go, who will heal you, defend you, and educate you?" Simón started to speak, but Kilian waved his hand. "I'm afraid that the administration of the country will fall into the hands of people who, at best, can barely read and write, even if they now drive around in luxury cars to give their speeches. That's not enough to run a country."

Kilian looked at José, who did not take his eyes off the television. Above all, he loved the football match broadcasts.

"You've nothing to say, Ösé?"

José cleared his throat, joined his hands on his lap, and said, "With the help of my spirits, I intend to stay as far away as possible from damned politics." He moved his head in the direction of the television. "Difficult times are coming, and even more so for the Bubis. Macías is Fang."

On the box was the image of a slim man, impeccably dressed in a suit and tie, passionately speaking through a microphone. He had narrow and slightly separated eyes. The four of them stayed quiet to listen to what the vice president of the autonomous government had to say, a former colonial civil servant, son of a famous witch doctor from Río Muni, who had begun in politics as mayor of his village on the continent.

He promised a minimum wage, retirement pensions and grants, loans to fishermen and farmers, and benefits for civil servants; he repeated his motto was unity, peace, and prosperity. He finished his speech with the phrase "What Macías promises, Macías delivers."

"He is strong and charismatic and has conviction," Manuel commented, "but frankly, he seems unstable. Sometimes, he talks of Spain as if it were an intimate friend, and others, he opposes any Spanish initiative. On Bata radio a month ago, he himself asked for a no vote on the constitution, and now look at him, in full election mode."

They stayed silent for a few minutes. Kilian looked around him. Apart from a group of eight to ten whites gulping down their gin and tonics, most of the people in the bar were natives. Kilian stared at the whites. They were sitting around a round table with metal and leather briefcases at their feet. They wore short-sleeved shirts and flared trousers. One of them, a young man in his twenties with a round face, short beard, and bright eyes, raised his glass in salute to Kilian, who reacted in kind. He must be a recent arrival, since his skin was not sunburned, and while he drank, he did not stop looking around him with the amazement, curiosity, and fear of someone who had just landed on Fernando Po. *How has he ended up here at this time?* Kilian asked himself. He sighed, took a sip of his drink, and turned to José and Simón.

"Do you know who you'll be giving your vote to next week?"

"Oh yes," Simón answered in a low voice, leaning forward. "And I can assure you I won't be giving it to the *cock!*"

José laughed. "Macías's motto is 'Everyone for the cock,'" he explained, also lowering his voice. "And I won't be voting for him either."

Manuel folded the newspaper and put it down on the table. "But many others will," he said. "The current president of the autonomous government, Bonifacio Ondó, is campaigning for Spain. Nobody knows Atanasio Ndongo. And Edmundo Bosió's Bubi Union will get votes only on the island. It's obvious, Macías is seen as the devoted and convinced defender of his Guinean brothers and their interests. He's being very well advised by that lawyer, García-Trevijano. He'll be president. And the autumn of 1968 will go down in history."

The four fell quiet.

After a while, Simón broke the silence. "Massa Kilian, don't get annoyed, right?" Kilian raised his eyebrows expectantly. "Sometimes it seems to me that you're against us getting our freedom . . ."

Kilian meditated on Simón's words. "I'm not saying that I don't want you to get independence," he said finally. "It's just that I don't want to leave, Simón."

The noise of chairs being violently dragged along the floor interrupted them. They turned their attention to the whites. The bright-eyed young man was standing beside the bar with a drink in one of his hands and the other extended to signal to his friends not to move. The man apologized to another patron standing in front of him in an aggressive manner.

"I've said I was sorry."

"I'm sure you don't blow cigarette smoke in the faces of your white friends," responded the other drunkenly. "Does it upset you that we now come to your bars?"

"What upsets me is that you don't know how to accept an apology," said the young man, keeping his calm. He quietly walked back to his table.

The man at the bar paid for his drink and made to leave but, before doing so, announced, "Not one of you will leave here alive. We'll slit your throats. All of you."

An unpleasant silence followed, broken by Manuel whispering, "You'll see, Kilian. Julia doesn't pay me any attention either, but in the end, we'll have to hightail it. All of us." He shot a look of certainty at him. "Even you."

"Are you sure that this is for the best?" Julia asked, her eyes filled with tears. "Dad, Mom . . . we still have time to change our minds."

Generosa tidied her hair in front of the mirror on the sideboard in the dining room, beside the elephant tusk. The reflection was very different from that of decades ago, when Emilio and she founded the store and set up house on the floor above. She remembered the tears she had shed leaving her only child with her grandparents until they could give her the kind of life they wished for, and the many happy moments the three of them had had in Santa Isabel. The years had flown by, removing the shine from her dark hair and adding deep lines around her eyes. She sighed.

"Now at least we can leave with something, not much, but more than what we would have when they kick us out."

"But . . . ," Julia protested, "if it was so obvious that this was going to happen, why did a Portuguese want to buy the shop?"

"João knows as much as I do."

Emilio finished sorting out some papers on the table, where there were also four or five 1968 issues of *ABC*, with large photos on the front pages of the latest happenings in Guinea. He stood up and walked with a stoop toward the window.

"Nobody is forcing him to buy the business. I think he's brave. If only we had had the guts not to recognize the new republic, as Portugal has done."

He looked at his watch and then out the window impatiently. He wanted João to get there quickly so they could complete the unpleasant task. A mountain man had his pride. He cleared his throat before adding, "Also, he has a load of children here with a native woman. More than enough reason to stay . . ."

Julia thought of Kilian. Would he not have to leave as well? And leave Bisila's child to such uncertainty? It was more than obvious how much Kilian adored the little one. He could not abandon him.

"Why don't you believe the new president?" Julia hung on to his arm. "Hasn't he been supported by Spain? Since the twelfth of October . . ."

"Don't remind me of that date!" Emilio squeezed his daughter's hand. "All those crazed young men turned the city into hell. That was the beginning of the end, yes, when they smashed all the windows of the businesses and houses, and they knocked down the statue of General Barrera, in front of Fraga Iribarne, no less . . . What a way to celebrate the transfer of power!"

"It was their first day of freedom, Dad. But since then, all of Macías's speeches have been full of praise for Spain. He has promised to continue the Francoist policies of the last thirty years and encourages Spanish businessmen to continue investing in Guinea—"

"Yes, I'll tell you what I'd give that little cock," interrupted Generosa in a biting and tone. "Let's see what happens when he stops getting money. Let's see how he meets his election promises."

Emilio puffed, let go of his daughter's arm, and began to pace the room.

"I'm an old dog, Julia. We're doing the right thing. If we sign today, we'll stay for as long as it takes to gather our things together and ship them. Afterward"—he raised his eyes to heaven—"God knows."

Julia bit her lip to control the rage brought on by her father's resignation. She looked at the clock. She was in no hurry. Manuel had stayed with the children so she could try and persuade her parents to change their minds. But she did not feel capable of witnessing it. She felt a pang of remorse. If Emilio and Manuel were right, she would be putting her children in serious danger. Maybe she should stop being so stubborn and think of them. If anything happened, she would never forgive herself. She decided to reconsider her stance about leaving the city, but she did not want to be present when the contract was signed.

"Sorry, but I can't wait any longer. I have to go for the children. In any case, I don't think I can make you change your minds."

She picked up her bag and her car keys. She went over to her mother to say good-bye and was surprised how calm she appeared, although deep down she was devastated.

"I'll walk you to the street," said Emilio. "Let's see if he finally makes a damned appearance."

Downstairs, the door of the store opened, and Dimas came out.

"If it isn't Emilio! What's this I've been told about you selling your business to a Portuguese?"

"In the end, you got what you wanted. We're leaving."

"Isn't that a bit dramatic?"

"Ask your brother. Haven't they promoted him again?"

Dimas smiled in pride. "Yes, sir. They have appointed him vice president of the supreme court."

Julia gasped. She had heard that the new president, Macías, had included members of the different tribal groups and parties, even defeated candidates, both in the government and the administration. But Gustavo's post was really important.

"I hope it lasts," said Emilio bitterly.

"Dad . . . ," Julia butted in.

"And why wouldn't it last?"

Emilio shook his head. "Don't get your hopes up, Dimas. I also had everything, and now I have to leave it behind. Let's hope I'm wrong and you won't have to go back to the village where you were born. What's it called? Ah, yes, Ureca." Someone called his name, and he turned. "Here is João, at last." He kissed his daughter. "Fine, well, let's finish this once and for all."

"To weed, José." Garuz rubbed his tired eyes. The seven foremen with whom Sampaka continued to work were relaxing after the meal. "Macías has said that he will send all the whites to pull up weeds."

Kilian reread the last paragraph of the letter he had just received from his mother, worried by the news she received through some neighbors who worked on other plantations:

> *Why haven't you come home? I don't understand your stubbornness to stay there in those circumstances. I don't know anymore what is true and what isn't. Some say that the Spaniards sleep with guns under their pillows or are afraid to sleep in their own houses; others say it's not that serious . . . If it's because of the money, don't worry about it. You can't do any more. Your father would be proud of the work you've done so that the House of Rabaltué, your only home, could shine as it does now. Guinea has taken my beloved Antón, I wouldn't like it to take one of my sons as well. It's time we were together. We have already given and taken all that is possible from Fernando Po.*
>
> *A hug from your mother, who loves you.*

He left the letter on the table. He remembered how anxious he had been reading her first letters exactly sixteen years ago, when he was a young man wanting to know the world but still missed home. He now read of Jacobo's expectations for the changes that were beginning to take place in Pasolobino. Everything seemed so strange, so distant to him. As if the letter were addressed to someone else. His place was now beside his new family. He had to work to give them a future.

He cursed under his breath. If things were different, they could have dreamed about buying a house in Santa Isabel. Perhaps it was not what he had planned for his life years ago, but bit by bit, his destiny had been guiding him in that direction, and he did not want to change course.

"What has made Macías so annoyed?" José asked.

"Everything," said Garuz, in a bad mood. "He gets upset about everything. He sees ghosts everywhere. Two weeks ago, he protested that there were still too many Spanish flags flying and ordered them lowered. The Spanish consul refused, and Macías insisted that the Spanish ambassador leave the country. Since then there has been nothing but violence, aggression, and looting of Spanish colonists and their properties. Soon they'll find Sampaka."

Simón finished serving another round of coffee, and everybody, except Waldo and Nelson, had one.

"The planes and ships are leaving full of people," he said. "Maybe you should all leave as well."

"The Spanish troops and the Civil Guard are still here. I've no intention of leaving."

"Slow down, Kilian," Gregorio commented. "Macías has accused the Civil Guard of murder and the National Guard of planning a coup d'état with the Spanish loggers."

Kilian shrugged. "You can leave if you want. Those left here are enough to get the harvest in."

Garuz smiled. Who would have thought that the lad had the guts?

"I've no intention of giving up my salary," said Gregorio. "But when the time comes, I'll leave. I'm not tied here like you."

Garuz frowned.

Before Gregorio could add another unpleasant comment, Kilian, looking straight at Garuz, hastily butted in.

"I'm married by the Bubi rites to Bisila, one of José's daughters, with whom I have a child called Fernando Laha. I don't hide it. I thought you also knew about it."

Everyone waited for the manager's reaction in silence.

Garuz poured himself another coffee. Why had he not heard this? It was true that he had never paid much attention to gossip. It was always about the same thing—affairs, flings, unwanted children—but he found the news about Kilian surprising. So that was the real reason he did not want to leave? He felt a stab of disappointment. What he had taken for courage was nothing more than a whim that would end like all of them, in nothing. Even so, he had to admit that the proud way in which Kilian had brought him up to date on his situation left little doubt about the importance of the relationship.

"I've no intention of leaving them," added Kilian, on seeing how Garuz had been struck dumb.

Garuz recovered his firm tone. "Sooner or later, Macías will realize that he needs us. Where else will he find such income? Anyway, it wouldn't do us any harm to take precautions." He pointed to Simón, Waldo, José, and Nelson. "You four are not to leave the plantation."

"But this has nothing to do with the Nigerians," Nelson protested, thinking of Oba.

"Not yet it doesn't." Garuz pointed to Kilian and Gregorio. "And you . . ."

The sounds of a car horn beeping, accompanied by shouts, interrupted the conversation. Everyone rushed out of the dining room and saw Emilio, shouting furiously with half his body out the window of the car. Beside him, Father Rafael, whom he had collected in Zaragoza village, put his hands to his head.

"Calm down, Emilio!" said Garuz. "What's the matter?"

"I have to warn my daughter! Lorenzo, Kilian, Gregorio. Come to Manuel's house!"

The tires of the Vauxhall raised dust as Emilio pulled up to the doctor's house.

Minutes later, in the sitting room, he told them what had happened.

"There has been an attempted coup. Macías has accused Spain, and the person behind it, Atanasio Ndongo, has been murdered. Bonifacio Ondó and other politicians not in Macías's camp have been detained and jailed. Gustavo as well. Military vehicles have been on the streets all night. We are now in a state of emergency. We should have left a few days ago on the *Ciudad de Pamplona*, with the last ones! Julia, Manuel, take the most important things, money, jewels, and passports, and forget the rest."

"But Spain——" began Julia.

Her father cut her short. "Julia, Spain won't interfere in Guinea's affairs now. I'm going to the city to arrange passage. We'll stay together until we get a ship or a plane, whichever leaves first, today or tomorrow . . . And you"—he turned to the others—"should do the same."

Manuel turned to Garuz in consternation. What would the people left on the plantation do without a doctor?

"Do what you have to do," responded Garuz. "I'm staying."

"Me as well," said Kilian. He would not leave until they came after him.

"And me . . ." Gregorio hesitated. "I'll also stay for the moment."

Emilio shrugged. "And you, Father Rafael?"

"I'm staying, son. My place is here."

"It's up to you, but when the Civil Guard leaves, you'll be here at your own risk." He shook hands with those who had decided to stay, one by one, with pursed lips and a furrowed brow. "Kilian, if I were your father, I'd drag you out of here."

Three hours later, Waldo and Kilian finished loading the dark Mercedes that Garuz had offered to take Manuel's family to the city. The small boys, Ismael and Francisco, played in the dirt, oblivious to the sadness that engulfed their parents. Julia kept going in and out of the house with reddened eyes, and Manuel said his final good-byes to the hospital where he had worked for the past sixteen years.

Kilian lit a cigarette. A child came running over and joined in playing with Julia's children, as he had on so many other occasions. Kilian smiled and looked around for the child's mother. Bisila approached, accompanied by Simón.

"I will miss them," she said.

"Yes, and so will I," Kilian added.

Julia came out with her handbag. She gave a last glance inside her house, closed the door, and bowed her head for a few minutes, sobbing. Finally, she took out a tissue from her bag, straightened up, and turned to walk toward the car.

"Where is Manuel?" she asked in a trembling voice.

"Inside the hospital," Kilian replied.

"Could you go and fetch him? I want this over as quickly as possible."

"Yes, of course."

Kilian found Manuel in the small office where he studied and classified his plants.

"I've hardly been able to take anything," he said out loud as Kilian entered.

"Maybe you can come back someday . . ."

"Yes, maybe."

"I'll miss you, Manuel."

The doctor shook his head. "And I you." He hesitated, preparing to tell Kilian what he had wanted to say for a long time. "Kilian . . . I know what Jacobo did to Bisila." His friend leaned against the desk. "I even have doubts about who Fernando's real father is, but it's obvious you are acting as if . . . I have children too, Kilian. I wouldn't leave them either. But be careful, right?"

Kilian nodded. "Does Julia know?"

"She has always put Jacobo on a pedestal. Why correct her?"

"You are a gentleman. You always have been."

Manuel smiled weakly, gave a look around the room, and put his hand on the doorknob. "Do you remember when we met in Ambos Mundos?"

Kilian nodded.

"It seems centuries ago."

They went outside, where Julia was silently watching the children beside Bisila. Manuel said good-bye to everyone, hugged Kilian hard, put the children into the car, and went to the front, his eyes filled with tears.

"Come on, Waldo. Be our driver one last time."

Julia came over to Kilian and crumpled in his arms. "Oh, Kilian, that child looks more like you every day. Look after him, Kilian, don't abandon him . . . What will happen to you all?" Kilian stroked her hair, his heart in his mouth. Julia stood up and brought the tissue to her nose. "Good-bye, Kilian. Send us news."

Waldo started the car and drove through Sampaka's main yard, heading toward the royal palm tree entrance. Julia closed her eyes and let herself be overcome by listlessness, blurring the journey to the city: a downcast Oba in front of her parents' house; the Factoría Ribagorza, where a young Julia had waited for a good-looking Jacobo to open the door with youthful exuberance and brighten up her day; and the casino, where she had spoken to Manuel for the first time, not knowing that they would end up joined together for life.

Years later, she would hazily remember the ship they finally embarked on in Bata. It was Generosa who told her about the Marines Special Forces Unit ship, which was repatriating the last members of the Civil Guard; a group of missionaries from Fernando Po; the last member of a scientific expedition who, years before, had found and sent to the Barcelona Zoo an albino gorilla they named Copito de Nieve; several plantation managers and owners; cockatoos, parrots, monkeys, and other species the crew brought aboard as souvenirs for their families; the last Spanish flag from those parts; and three generations of the same family. Ironically, the ship's name was the *Aragón*, the same name as the region of Pasolobino, the place that had given them life.

"See? I told you so." Simón pointed toward the sea from the balustrade. "The sacks are still there. They didn't load one of them. The whole harvest will be ruined, if it isn't already."

Garuz could not believe what his own eyes were telling him. Hundreds of esparto sacks, with the Sampaka logo and filled to the brim, were piled up on the small cement jetty of Santa Isabel dock.

"They're crazy," said Kilian, devastated. "It's worth a fortune!"

"Is that how they are going to take care of everything we have fought years for?" Garuz felt a bout of rage building in his insides. "The harvest of a whole year's work rotting because of an incompetent government!" He saw two police officers leaving the guards' hut and made to go down the slope of the fevers. "I'm going to sort this out right now. If necessary I'll talk to the president himself!"

Kilian grabbed his arm. "Wait! I don't think that's a good idea."

"Do you think I'm afraid of those two?" Garuz brusquely freed himself.

"If you go down there in a temper, you'll give them a good excuse to arrest you. We should go back to the plantation. When things have calmed down, you can decide what to do."

Just then, a car stopped, and several men got out and walked toward the slope. Garuz recognized one of them and went over.

"Maximiano. Fancy bumping into you! I'm happy to have caught you. I've just found out that the plantation's harvest hasn't been shipped. I'd like to know why not."

"You'd like *me* to give you an explanation?"

"I cannot allow my business to go down the drain."

Maximiano slowly licked his bottom lip. "Are you questioning our president?"

"What?" Something in the cold stare of the police chief made Garuz realize that it was best to change his tune. "Of course not. Nothing further from it. If you will excuse me . . ." He signaled to the other two. "Good afternoon. Kilian, Simón . . . let's go."

They began to walk toward the car. A voice stopped them.

"Simón! It seems you've recovered very quickly from your limp."

Simón got into the car quickly. Garuz turned around, and his eyes caught those of Maximiano, who raised his index finger in the air in an accusing gesture.

When he got into the car, Garuz collapsed into his seat, cursing under his breath. Kilian understood that he had been left with no option but to swallow his pride and quickly leave his cocoa to rot. *What will happen now?*

Few men went to work. The labor contract with Nigeria had been canceled, but that was not the problem, as there were more than enough workers; you only had to look at them wandering around the place, disoriented, not knowing very well what to do or where to go. In fact, it was as if the whole world had been infected by the despondency of their superiors.

Deep down, Kilian still hoped for a cheerful voice to announce that relations between both countries had never been better and that although the government of the new Guinea was now independent, daily life and work continued as usual. But the reality was very different. The few sources of communication, such as Radio Santa Isabel, Radio Madrid, and the

Ébano newspaper, reported widespread disenchantment and threats against the whites. The hoped-for aid never arrived. There was no money, and it was difficult to adjust to the newly established civil order; the population did not notice any change in their low standard of living. For those who refused to leave, it was difficult not to remember Macías's words. *"Slavery is finished,"* he used to repeat. *"Let no one help the whites, no black should be afraid of whites . . . We are not poor, Guinea is rich, we are over an oil pocket . . . Now I'll put the whites in prison if they go against the government . . ."*

They drove back to the plantation along dirty, rubbish-filled, and bloodstained streets. As the car drove along, they felt the mistrust of many passersby.

Garuz asked Simón to go faster. "I don't know, Kilian," he murmured, deep in thought. "I don't know if we are taking a great risk. Even the television people have now left . . ."

Simón braked sharply. A small woman walked along the roadside, carrying a large bundle of clothes on her head. Simón turned to Kilian, pleaded with his eyes for him to intercede with Garuz to pick up the woman.

Kilian got out of the car. "Oba . . . What are you doing here all alone?"

"I'm going to live with Nelson. There is no work in the store, Massa. I hope the big massa won't mind."

"Come on, we'll take you."

Oba and Kilian got into the car. She was surprised to recognize Garuz sitting beside the driver. Garuz did not turn around. He did not open his mouth either. He could not care less what the girl did or did not do, although . . . He straightened himself up in his seat. If women were the reason why men like Kilian and Nelson had stayed with him, he found it as good a reason as any. Also, there was no lack of laborers' houses on Sampaka.

From summer onward, the tension decreased and the mood calmed down. In October 1969, new bilateral agreements were signed, and Spain guaranteed a multimillion-dollar loan to Guinea. Taking advantage of the return of some colonists to their properties, and after several meetings with them, Garuz decided to attend a gala dinner in the casino.

After the manager insisted it would be a good idea to rub elbows with the upper echelons of the country's administration, Kilian and Gregorio were left with no choice but to accompany him. Kilian had reluctantly agreed. He did not want to go at all, but he would do anything as long as it meant he would be able to stay longer. He reminded Waldo to have several dozen eggs and some bottles of brandy ready to avoid problems at the checkpoints and borrowed a dark suit and a bow tie from Garuz.

Entering the casino, Kilian noticed to his amazement that only two things had changed in the main room. First, most guests were natives, and second, military uniforms almost outnumbered dress suits. Otherwise, the band played on, and the many waiters ensured that everyone was looked after perfectly.

Garuz, escorted by Gregorio and Kilian, greeted many of those present with exaggerated friendliness, especially those introduced as the director general for security, a sturdy man with a severe look, and the secretary of defense, serious and pensive, wearing a major's uniform. Kilian held out his hand and felt a shiver, not a smile to be seen.

The sound of laughter came from the door leading to the outside terrace, where the bandstand was. Garuz looked in that direction and smiled in relief to see a group of Europeans enjoying the party. Kilian had the feeling he had seen them before, but he could not remember where. Garuz greeted them, exchanged a few words with two men, and then went off with them to a small room.

"Hello," said a voice by his side. "If you have come with Garuz, I suppose you must be one of his employees." He put out his hand. "I'm

Miguel. I work in television." He gestured toward the others. "We all work in television. Some in broadcasting and others in the studios."

Kilian looked at the bright-eyed young man with a short beard and remembered the night a drunk man had accused Miguel of blowing cigarette smoke in his face.

"I'm Kilian. Yes, I work in Sampaka. I thought all of you from the television were gone." Out of the corner of his eye, he saw Gregorio beginning to chat with two of the young men from the group. Kilian judged he was trying to show off with stories of his colonial experience.

"They had to hightail it out of here after the March coup, but afterward, they sent us back. And we're still here . . . for the moment."

"How are things in Spain? Have they got any idea about what is going on in Guinea?"

"Well, trust me when I say," replied Miguel, "that apart from family and friends, nobody has any idea about anything. The press only praises Spain's good work. But really, no one on the street talks about it."

"Yeah . . ." Although Kilian could have guessed the answer, it still did not make it less disheartening. "How do you know Garuz?"

"Garuz and almost all the businessmen are chasing after us to get us to write checks so that they can give us Guinean pesetas in return. We spend them, and they are happy. They are afraid the new currency has no value. So you know, if you have money . . ."

Kilian felt a camaraderie with the man. It had been ages since Kilian had spoken to anyone outside Sampaka.

"Thanks," he answered, "but my salary goes into a Spanish bank. I only keep a bit for day-to-day expenses." He lit a cigarette. "And what do you do here exactly?"

"I'm in charge of maintaining the network, up there, on the mountain. On my days off, I come down to the casino to play tennis. Look at that man over there." He pointed to a very tall, well-built man a short distance away. "He's the consul from Cameroon. He's always looking for me to play with him." He laughed. "Probably because he always beats me. Well, and you? How long have you been here? Me, not very long, but you have the look of someone who must be a real expert on Fernando Po, am I right?"

Kilian smiled sadly. Yes, he had a special knowledge of the island and its peoples, but if Miguel knew what he had gone through, his words would not be tinged with envy.

For a long while, they talked amicably about their lives and the political situation. Miguel was blunt: in the street, he always felt unsafe, so he limited himself to going to work and enjoying the facilities in the casino, where he insisted Kilian should go to pass the time and ease the loneliness of the plantation.

"I'm not alone," explained Kilian. "I have a wife and children."

The people close to him found his situation completely normal, but saying it aloud to someone new gave him a pleasant feeling.

"They are still here?" Miguel raised his eyebrows, surprised. "The majority of the colonists still here have sent their families home."

"Well . . . she is, in fact, Guinean. Bubi."

"And what will you do if things turn ugly for you?"

"I don't know." Kilian sighed. "It's complicated."

"Oh . . ."

A waiter approached to tell them they would be serving dinner in a few minutes. Garuz joined the group again, and together they went toward the dining room.

"Do you know, Kilian," said Miguel as soon as he had sat down beside him at one of the round tables, "the first time I came here, I didn't know what to do with so much cutlery. In Spain I don't get the chance to move in such sophisticated circles."

"I understand you perfectly!" Kilian laughed heartily.

Suddenly, the smile froze on his lips, and he looked at Gregorio, who had sat down three or four seats away from him. The other was as surprised as he.

A spectacular woman dressed in a fine white crepe dress on the arm of a man with a pockmarked face entered the dining room toward one of the tables close to them. She crossed the space between the entrance and Kilian and Gregorio's table, swinging her hips and cackling as if what her partner was saying were the funniest thing in the world.

"Will you look at Maximiano," Garuz commented, recognizing the head of police.

Kilian lowered his gaze when Sade shot them an arrogant look filled with hate. Later, when she sat in her seat at the table with the heads of national security, including the major they had met when they arrived, she did not stop flirting and murmuring in Maximiano's ear, who looked at them, frowning on a couple of occasions.

"So you know them?" he asked his partner.

"The one with the dark hair with copper highlights abandoned me for another after leaving me pregnant." Sade paused. "And the other, the one with the mustache, wanted to take me by threating me with a pistol."

Maximiano launched a murderous look at the whites' table.

"I don't know what you've done to my uncle," said a young man sitting beside Kilian, "but I'm happy not to be in your shoes."

"Your uncle?" Miguel asked, surprised, leaning across Kilian.

"Didn't I tell you I had family in high places?"

"Excuse me, Kilian. This is Baltasar, a television cameraman. He studied in Madrid and lives and works there. And this is Kilian"—he winked and smiled faintly—"one of the few colonists who hasn't left yet."

Kilian did not like being called a colonist, but he understood that Miguel had not said it maliciously. Kilian shook Baltasar's hand.

"So you are Fang . . . ," he commented finally.

Baltasar raised his eyebrow. "Does it bother you?"

"No, not for the moment."

Kilian was sorry he had said that. The truth was he had just met the young man, and he had made a good impression on him. Baltasar looked at him quizzically, opened his mouth, but changed his mind. Then Miguel said, "Kilian's wife is Bubi . . ."

"And . . . ?" Baltasar raised the palms of his hands. "Ah, I see now. Yes, an understandable simplification. Bubis are good, Fangs are bad, is that it?"

Kilian said nothing.

Baltasar clicked his tongue and poured himself a glass of wine in front of the glaring disapproval of the waiter behind him. Baltasar lowered his voice. "Let me tell you something, Kilian. Spain has awoken the capricious, resentful, and vengeful monster, not me. At first Macías seemed fine to them, and when they realized their mistake, they tried to overthrow him in a coup d'état, just when he was at the height of his power. And now, if they could, they would kill him. Do you know what Mr. President fears most? Death. Do you know that he punished one of his government delegates for coughing? He accused him of trying to pass a virus to the head of state. And what have the civil servants learned? They take long vacations until they are completely cured." He laughed. "This is surreal! Macías does whatever it takes to keep death away. He will bribe, applaud betrayal, support his loyal followers, and kill on the spot anyone he thinks, suspects, or feels is against him. So, my friend, as long as Spain refuses to accept part of the blame in his election as president, it won't be free of sin in the degeneracy that will follow until one of his lackeys turns on him."

"You shouldn't be telling us these things, Baltasar," whispered Miguel. "You're putting yourself at risk."

"I'll be going soon, thankfully. I leave politics to my relations." He picked up the menu that was on the tablecloth. "Let's see what dishes they'll surprise us with today."

Kilian was pleased with the change in subject and joined in on the jokes about the elaborate menu, consisting of poultry soup, poached eggs *gran duque*, lobster with tartar sauce, cold sea bass Parisian, English-style roast chicken, and tropical fruit salad. Bit by bit, he relaxed, and even had to admit that he was enjoying the buzz brought upon by Miguel's and Baltasar's company and conversation. He was especially curious about Baltasar, who had studied in Spain and had then gotten a full-time position through public examination in the television industry and who had no intention of moving from where he now lived.

"Miguel has told me that in Spain, nobody talks about Guinea anymore."

"I suppose," said Baltasar, "it's in the interest of the politicians over there that whatever happened here is forgotten as soon as possible." His tone became sarcastic again. "An exercise in democracy. The dictator Franco promoted a referendum and elections in Guinea, something unthinkable in his own state."

Kilian frowned. At no point had it occurred to him to see the last few months from that perspective. He felt a little ashamed. He had become so involved in life on the island that he had not paid attention to what was happening in his own country. He had never thought about the fact that Spain was a dictatorship. His life revolved around work and everything else. He would have been incapable of explaining to anybody how the dictatorship was seen or publicized in his small Spanish colony.

"What's your life like in the capital?" Kilian asked.

"I've spent so many years away that Madrid has become my home."

"And you haven't had any problems?"

"Well, apart from the fact I stand out among so many whites"— he laughed—"none. But many Guineans arriving in Spain seeking freedom find that the motherland has become the wicked stepmother. Spanish passports are no longer being renewed for native Guineans, so they become stateless. It didn't happen to me because I'm married to a Spaniard." Baltasar shrugged.

Kilian could not hide his surprise. For a few seconds, a new hope dawned in his heart. He would talk to Bisila and convince her to go with him. They could start a new life somewhere else. If others had done it, why not them?

Just at that moment, the waiters finished clearing the plates and offered the guests whiskey and soda. The band opened its session out on the stand with a James Brown number, and people began to leave their seats to go outside to the terrace. Gregorio got up and said something to Garuz. Kilian heard him answer, "I don't know if it's wise to go alone."

"Where are you going?" asked one of the television men.

"Off to see what's open out there."

"Can we come with you?" another asked. "We'd like to get to know a bit more of the city by night . . ."

Gregorio shrugged and began heading off, followed by the other two.

"Those two don't miss a trick," said Miguel, smiling.

"They should be careful," warned Baltasar, indicating the table where his uncle and the rest of the heads of national security were. "They don't like our women to go off with whites as before."

Gregorio left Anita's alone. His companions had left earlier. He walked a little unsteadily to his car. There was not a soul in sight. He opened the door, but before he could get into the car, a hand with an iron grip held him by the shoulder. In seconds, other hands forcefully grabbed him, put a sack over his head, then shoved him into a car that left at top speed to some unknown destination.

The car stopped. They got him out roughly and made him walk a few steps. He heard the metallic and squeaky sound of an iron gate being opened. In total silence, they jerked the sack off his head. It took him a few seconds to determine where he was. The five or six men broke out laughing when they saw his expression.

He was in front of an open grave beside several tombs. He began to break out in a cold sweat. They had brought him to the cemetery! The urine began to flow down the insides of his thighs.

"See this hole, Massa Gregor?"

They knew his name. The darkness prevented him from seeing their faces. He saw only eyes filled with bloodlust. And what would it matter if he recognized any of them or not?

"Look, we have dug it for you. Yes, just for you."

"Do you think it will be big enough?"

"Why don't we check?"

Laughter.

The first blow was in the back. The second, level with his kidneys. Then, punches all over. Finally, a push that sent him into the grave, then some threatening voices. "This is just a warning, white man. You won't know when, but we'll be back for you."

Again, the squeaking sound of the gate.

A good while passed before Gregorio could drag himself out of the grave, groaning from the pain of the blows, to cross the cemetery in silence with his spirits broken, and to get his bearings. When he reached his car, a few meters from the club, the cuts on his face had stopped bleeding, but he had already made a decision.

When he got to Sampaka, he woke up Garuz and asked for his wages.

As dawn broke, Waldo took him to the airport and Gregorio disappeared off Fernando Po without saying a single good-bye.

Miguel and Baltasar gathered up the material and stored it in the metal cases.

"Thanks for coming with us to film the cocoa production process, Kilian," said Miguel. "It was very enlightening."

"If you had only seen it a couple of years ago . . . Now it's pitiful to look at. With the few of us who are left here, we can't even keep the weeds under control. And the production isn't even a tenth of what it used to be." A few drops of rain began to fall from the sky, and the three quickly got into the vehicle.

The shortest and safest route to the block of flats where the television crew were staying passed through the residential district where the house of Julia's parents had been. The couple of times that Kilian had passed in front of the Factoría Ribagorza, he had felt his heart twinge, hoping that the door would open and Emilio or his daughter would come out.

Without any warning, the street became filled with youths running in different directions. Kilian had a bad feeling. Without slowing down, he drove on, and a few meters from Emilio's old store, he stopped.

"Oh my God! What are they doing?"

Dozens of youths were destroying the shop. Some broke the windows with thick wooden bars. Others went inside to come out with their arms full of goods. Suddenly, they saw them pushing out a white man, probably the new owner, João the Portuguese, who, with his hands together, pleaded with them not to do anything to him. Ignoring his pleas, they began to give him a brutal beating. His blood spattered the ground. Without a second thought, Kilian shot out of the car and ran toward them, shouting and waving his arms.

"Stop! Stop at once!"

He immediately realized his mistake. A tall boy with a shaved head turned and smiled at him. "Here comes another! Get him!"

With his heart beating wildly, Kilian remembered his lessons from the plantation.

"Leave that man alone at once!" he shouted firmly.

"And why should we, white man?" The young man with the shaved head approached him, swaggering in arrogance. "Because you say so?"

In a second, Kilian saw himself surrounded by several men, most of whom could not be older than twenty. He felt his confidence desert him.

"No white gives us orders," said another.

The sticks rose in the air. Kilian crossed his arms over his face. He waited, but nothing happened. Then he heard a familiar voice say in a friendly tone, "If I were you, I wouldn't do that." Baltasar had placed himself between him and the circle of boys. "I am the nephew of the head of police, Maximiano, and this man is a friend of his."

Without turning, he said to Kilian, "Go back to the car. I want to talk to these lads so they can explain to me why they are so angry." He asked them a question in Fang, and the others blabbered out a litany of responses.

Kilian got into the car. His legs were still shaking. Miguel was hunched in the backseat.

Kilian said nothing. He looked through the window into the sitting room of the house and felt a knot in the pit of his stomach. A woman with a baby in her arms squeezed a child of about five or six against her waist. He thought he heard her cries. Would they see their father and husband alive again?

Baltasar returned to the car accompanied by the shaven-headed youth. Baltasar said good-bye to him and got in. The youth leaned down to catch Kilian's eye. "Next time you won't be so lucky."

Kilian started the engine and began to drive off. "Thank you, Baltasar," he said. "You've saved my life."

He waved his hand in the air and said nothing.

"Would you mind telling me what was going on?" Miguel asked after a while.

"A group of Portuguese mercenaries tried to invade Guinea Conakry. Macías gave his youth sections free rein to protest against the Portuguese."

Miguel grunted. "This afternoon I'm going up to the television station on the summit, and I don't intend on coming down for a week."

"It's not a bad idea, given the current mood . . . ," mused Baltasar.

Kilian took a sideways look at him. *What in hell is happening to this blasted country?*

"Why don't we leave?" Kilian repeated.

"Go where?"

They had been through this before.

"To Spain. Together. You're my wife. I'll take you with me."

"My place is here."

"Your place is with me." Kilian got up, sat on the edge of the bed, and hung his head. "Everyone is leaving," he said.

Bisila sat beside him. "The children of a white and a black are Guinean, not Spanish. They wouldn't let them leave."

A silence.

"I don't belong in Pasolobino. I would always be the black woman that Kilian of Rabaltué brought back from the colony."

Kilian protested, "You would be my wife! They would get used to you!"

"But I don't want anyone to have to get used to me."

"We could also live in Madrid, or in Barcelona. I would get a job in any factory."

"You're a man of the land, of the mountain, of the plantation. In a city, you would be unhappy. As the years passed, you would blame me for your sadness, and our love would end."

"Then I will stay. I still feel safe on the plantation."

Bisila got up and went over to the table with a small mirror resting on it. On the mirror, Kilian had stuck the only photo of them both together. She smiled, remembering the day when Simón came to show them his new camera: *"Let's see, Bisila. You put yourself here . . . Like that . . . Fernando come to your mother. Here and still. And now smile . . . Kilian, now you, here, yes, that's good. You can lean on the truck if you want."*

Life was full of ironies; as soon as they became free to love each other, the persecution of the whites had begun.

"Yes, on the plantation, you're safe," she repeated without taking her eyes off the photo. "But . . . for how long?"

"Where are they going?" Kilian, puzzled, followed Garuz to the middle of the main yard. A group of laborers carrying large bundles with their few belongings had gathered there. Their wives and children were with them. He saw Bisila holding on to Lialia's arm, and Oba with one of Ekon's children in her arms.

"Where are you going?" Garuz repeated.

"We're also leaving, Massa," Nelson answered in a deep voice. "News has come that we can go back home. There's very little for us here."

"But . . . the war?" Kilian asked.

"It's over. They are going to pardon those who were defeated. Well, that's what they say. And they have sent ships for us."

"We don't want the same to happen to us as happened to the Portuguese," Ekon intervened. "The president here only wants Guineans."

Kilian hung his head. They were also leaving. His last companions. And the harvest? Who would collect the fruit ripening on the trees?

Garuz swore and went to his office.

Bisila stood beside Kilian. Nelson put out his hand to say good-bye to his boss, but Kilian shook his head.

"I'll take you in the truck. It's a long walk for the children."

"I don't think it . . ."

"I couldn't care less if it's risky or not. I'll go with you."

"I'll go as well," said Bisila.

An hour later, the group of Nigerians began descending the slope of the fevers, hesitant. Hundreds of people were piled up on the small jetty as the Guinean authorities asked for their identification documents one by one, before allowing them on the narrow gangway.

Kilian and Bisila leaned on the balustrade of the upper balcony with other curious onlookers. Fortunately, he was not the only white there, thought Kilian. He saw Miguel and Baltasar in the distance. Every few seconds, Bisila raised her hand and waved to Lialia and her children. Kilian admired her ability to put on a cheerful smile when he knew how sad she was to lose her best friend. Ekon and Lialia's children, whom Bisila had cured of little cuts and illnesses since they were small, also waved until it was their turn to board.

Nelson and Ekon showed their papers; Lialia did the same. When it was her turn, Oba showed them her passport, and the policeman frowned. He talked to his partner for a few seconds and finally said, "You're Guinean. You cannot leave."

Oba felt the earth swallow her up.

"But I'm going with my husband."

Nelson moved back a few steps. The passengers behind Oba began to shout in protest. "What's going on?"

The officer looked up at the colossus with the round face.

"What's it to you?"

"This woman is my wife."

"Let's see papers."

Nelson and Oba felt a sudden panic. They had planned to get married, but for one reason or another, they had kept putting it off.

"Where is the marriage certificate?"

"We've lost it," Nelson answered rapidly, hoping with all his heart that the police would accept his lie and let Oba through.

"Well, then she's not going." He grabbed her by the arm and removed her from the line with such force that Oba fell to the ground. The impatient shouts increased, now mixed with indignation at the man's rough treatment of Oba.

"Oba!" Nelson pushed the two police and hunkered down beside her. From the boat, the desperate voices of Ekon, Lialia, and Nelson's family could be heard, confused that they were taking so long to get on board. The ship's horn sounded, warning that it would soon be departing. Those left on land began to push forward, and they knocked down the police officers. From the ground, one of them took out his weapon and began to fire indiscriminately. The other followed suit, and several people fell to the ground. The cries of impatience became howls of pain and panic. Those who were able to get on board got to the gangway. Others, stunned, tried to help their wounded relatives.

From above, Kilian and Bisila watched the scene in shock. When the gunfire stopped, the ship began to slowly move away on the waters, unaware of the bewilderment of the people who leaned over the deck's railings in a vain attempt to find out what had happened to their friends or relations. On the jetty, several bodies lay on the ground, men and women raising their hands to their heads in grief. Bisila tightly held Kilian's hand and stifled a scream when she recognized Oba.

Sitting down, with Nelson's bloody face in her lap, Oba moved backward and forward, rocking him. Not a sound came from her throat. She opened and closed her mouth as her small hands stroked her man's hair, soaked in his blood.

"What a surprise, Kilian!" exclaimed a biting voice. "Still here?"

Kilian grimaced. He still had suspicions that Sade and her friends were behind Gregorio's beating. As had been made clear in the casino, she enjoyed the friendship of high-ranking people. He took Bisila by the hand.

"We'd better leave," he said.

Sade squinted. Why did that woman look so familiar? Where had she seen her before? Those big, bright eyes . . . Then she remembered that day in the hospital. There she was, holding his hand . . . And later, the same day Kilian split up with her, she had seen her close to his quarters. So this was the one who had robbed her of Kilian's favor? She licked her bottom lip.

She did not know how, but someday she would get her revenge on her as well.

The three men drained some brandy *saltos* after dinner. European food had become scarce, but the vegetable plots still grew in abundance, and the hens, left abandoned to their wiles after Yeremías's mysterious disappearance, continued to lay eggs.

"He must have gone to his village," said Garuz. "One less."

"Where was he from?" Kilian asked.

"Ureca," Father Rafael answered. "He's gone with Dimas, who comes and goes from the village to Santa Isabel to help his friends escape. This time he didn't even wait for the farce trial Macías has arranged for those in last year's attempted coup. The majority have already been killed. And of the others, like his brother Gustavo, nothing is known."

Suddenly, the light over the dining room table went out. Instinctively, they looked out the window and only saw darkness.

"Blasted generators . . ." Garuz looked for some matches in his pocket.

"I'll go and see what's wrong." Kilian took a lantern from a side table.

He went out, skirted the building, and opened the door of the small generator room.

A blow to his back left him breathless. He could not even shout. Before he realized what was going on, more blows, punches, and kicks rained down on each centimeter of his body until he collapsed and lost consciousness.

In the dining room, Garuz and Father Rafael began to get worried. When they got to the small room, Kilian was lying on the ground in a pool of blood.

"Kilian, everything's already been organized," announced José. "Next week you're taking a plane home to Spain. You'll be traveling with Garuz and Father Rafael. The last of the last. If you don't go, Simón and I will drag you there."

He sighed.

"Say something, Kilian. Don't look at me like that. I'm doing it for you. I'm doing it for Antón. I promised your father. I promised him I'd look after you!"

"Bisila . . ."

"Bisila, come! Come with me!"

"I can't, Kilian, and you know that."

"I can't leave either."

"If you don't go, they'll kill you."

"And if I go, I'll also die."

"No, you won't. See? The spirits have answered your dilemma. You must go and live your life, take your place in the House of Rabaltué."

"How can you talk to me about spirits? Is this what they want? Is this what God wants? For us to separate? What will happen to Iniko and Fernando? What will happen to you?"

"Don't worry about me. Nurses always have work, even more in times of conflict. Nothing will happen to me, you'll see."

"How will I know? How will I get news of you?"

"You'll know, Kilian. You'll feel it. We will be far away, but close. I will always be by your side."

How was Kilian to remember what he could never forget yet remain continuously present, even when surrounded in haze, sometimes crystal clear, sometimes blurred?

Waldo's handshake.

Simón's tears and his whispered promise never again to speak his friend's native language.

Lorenzo Garuz's heavyhearted words leaving José in charge of the plantation.

The silent tears of Father Rafael.

The texture of Fernando Laha's hair.

The desperation with which he made love to Bisila on the last night. Her essence. The taste of her skin. The sparkle of her clear eyes.

The tropical rain. The lightning. The shell collar on his chest.

His guardian, his *wairibo*, his love, his *mötémá*, his sweet company in uncertainty, in fear, in moments of weakness, in joy and in sadness, until death do us . . .

The warm, thick, lazy, and cruel tenderness of the last kiss.

The sobs.

The royal palm trees, resolutely reaching the sky, undaunted by the pain left at their feet.

The weak handshake from Ösé. The last touch of his fingertips. The long, deep, and emotional hug. His promise to put flowers on his father's grave.

The DC-8 over the green island that had invaded his very being and now became a faint mark on the horizon until it disappeared.

Garuz, Miguel, and Baltasar beside him.

His father's words, spoken thousands of years before: *"I don't know how or when . . . but the day will come when this small island will take control of you, and you'll never want to leave . . . I don't know anyone who has left here without shedding tears of grief."*

The brief journey that made him yearn for the tranquil scything of a ship.

The landing in Madrid.

His good-bye to Garuz, after he gave his wife a hug: "Cheer up, at least we're alive."

Baltasar's words: "One day we'll return, no problem."

Miguel's words: "Do you know the first thing my television bosses told me when I got off the plane? Not a word about this to the press."

The train to Zaragoza. The coach to Pasolobino.

The eleven years of darkness.

The silence.

The tenuous ray of light when his daughter was born, a few months after his fiftieth birthday.

Daniela.

Like her.

19

Official Secrets

1971–1980

"If you ever get out of here, Waldo," said Gustavo, leaning against the cold wall of his cell, "promise me that you'll look for my brother, Dimas, from Ureca and tell him about me."

Waldo agreed with closed eyes and made himself another promise.

He would get out of that place.

Suddenly, they heard a commotion of shouts, insults, blows, and footsteps. Seconds later, the lock on the iron door squeaked, the door opened, and two hefty guards dragged a naked body onto the earthen floor, as if it were a sack of potatoes.

"Here's a new cellmate for you!" shouted one of the guards as he threw an empty tin after him. "Teach him the rules!" He howled with laughter.

Gustavo and Waldo waited until the footsteps had receded and then knelt down by the badly wounded man. How many times had they been here before? More than a dozen since that day when first Gustavo and Waldo some time later had crossed through the iron gate. Both had gone through the same routine. They were taken to the warden's office, whipped until they lost consciousness, and then locked up in a cement box, the height and width of a man, laid out in rows in one of the sheds. A small skylight, protected by bars, allowed for the disturbing sounds of the night and the communication with other prisoners, provided they had not gone through the interrogation room yet. If they had, the only sounds that would reverberate around the walls of Black Beach Prison were ones of inhuman shrieks, shouts of desperation and suffering, and the occasional guttural snore.

The man tried to move.

"Stay still," said Gustavo. "It's better that you lie on your chest and stomach."

His back and legs were full of open wounds, and skin and bits of flesh were missing. It was obvious that the sergeant major of the prison had let his dog loose. It would take three or four days before the man could change position. When he was able, they would take him to whip the sore-covered body again. And like that until he died, or they got tired, or they decided to send him to clear weeds, like Gustavo and Waldo. For the wardens, the prisoners had no soul. If they were to read the inscriptions on the wall, thought Gustavo, where the prisoners had written their last anguished thoughts in their own blood, the wardens would know what they had done with their souls.

For a good while, Gustavo and Waldo talked to the new arrival without getting any reply. They knew from experience that words of comfort did a lot of good. They explained to him where they were, the meal routine, and the cleaning out with the tin where he would have to do his deeds. They told him his body would become used to the blows and that there was a possibility of surviving—like them, who had been imprisoned a long time and were still alive—or getting out, by whatever stroke of luck.

When he noticed the man's breathing relaxed, Waldo asked, "What's your name?"

"Maximiano . . . Why are you here?"

"The same reason as everyone else."

Gustavo preferred not to give any more explanations. Since Macías had created a one-party regime, a never-ending and cruel hunt had begun, and an indiscriminate purge of both the opposition and all those who could try and become president of the republic through their ability or influence. From one day to the next, anyone could become a subversive or an enemy of the people. In the case of Gustavo, who had been a member of a political movement, the reasons for his arrest were obvious; not so with Waldo, whose outspoken comments in the presence of a former colonial guard, dressed in plainclothes and converted into a Macías spy, had been enough to imprison him. In many other cases, a system of informing took over, even among members of the same family, in order to get a promotion or settle an old score. Thanks to the comings and goings of prisoners, Waldo and Gustavo had been receiving news from the outside about the paranoia of the president of the republic.

"And you? What are you in for?"

"Someone accused me of complaining about my salary."

"Oh, very serious," Gustavo joked bitterly.

The civil servants never knew when they were going to get paid or exactly how much. When it suited Macías, he took out some of the nation's money, which he kept in a bathroom in his house, and made government employees attend a mass meeting to give them whatever amount he fancied as fruit of the benevolence of the "untiring worker at the service of the people."

"We know one who was imprisoned for criticizing the quality of Chinese rice . . . Isn't that right, Waldo?"

"And what happened to him?" Maximiano asked, a hint of desperation in his voice.

"They took him from our cell," Gustavo lied.

Waldo leaned against the wall. It had been weeks since he had shed tears of pain and rage like Maximiano. Only one idea allowed him to put up with the beatings and whippings.

He did not know how yet, but one day he would find the chance to escape.

"Let's see, Laha. Who expelled the imperialist and colonizing Spaniards from Equatorial Guinea?

"His Excellency, Macías Nguema Biyogo Ñegue Ndong!"

"Very good. And who defeated the Spanish imperialist plot of March 5, 1969?"

"His Excellency, the Grand Master of Popular Teaching Art and Traditional Culture, the Untiring Worker at the Service of the People!"

"And who has built Malabo's magnificent new buildings?"

Laha remembered reading a board with the name of a construction company.

"The Transmetal Company," he replied without hesitation.

The teacher gave him a smack with his cane. Laha yelped and rubbed his shoulder.

"No. His Excellency built them. Be careful, Laha. In a few days, he will visit us in person and will ask you these same questions."

The following week, Laha and his classmates, perfectly dressed for the occasion, stood waiting for the door of the classroom to open and the object of their reverent praise to visit them. Outside, the line of elegant cars that made up the presidential cavalcade could be seen. The minutes passed, and nobody came to the classroom. Suddenly, they heard shouts and voices. The teacher was the first to go over and look out the window. Several bodyguards were forcefully taking away the school principal and three of his colleagues. One of the bodyguards waved a photo of the president, like the ones that hung in every classroom, so that all those who were looking out the windows could see. Someone had drawn a noose around Macías's neck.

The teacher sat down at his desk and continued the class in a trembling voice. Laha and his classmates felt disappointed at not being able to meet the country's "one miracle."

A few minutes later, Laha looked out the window and saw someone he recognized. He jumped to his feet and called the teacher. They went back to pushing their noses against the glass. Another teacher who taught older children was giving instructions to four or five boys, one of whom was Iniko. Laha's teacher left the room. A short while later, he joined the group in the yard. Laha did not understand what was happening, but the adults were making nervous gestures as they talked to the boys, who, after nodding several times, disappeared. Laha placed his hand against the windowpane. Where could his brother be going?

The teacher came back to the classroom and went directly to Laha. He leaned down and whispered, "Tell your mother that Iniko has gone to Bissappoo. It's best that he stays there for a while."

"Hey, you! What are you doing there?"

Waldo, overwhelmed by Madrid's high buildings and the hundreds of cars that drove along the widest avenues he had ever seen, came out of his hiding place and stood in front of the police officer with his eyes fixed on the ground.

"I only wanted to sleep a little."

"Oh! Your Spanish is very good. Where are you from?"

"Equatorial Guinea," he repeated for the umpteenth time since arriving in Spain.

"Show me your papers."

Waldo took out a small laminated card he had found near the dock in Bata and handed it to him, confident that the man would not notice the difference between his face and that of the photograph.

"This is no longer valid. We have been told by the General Headquarters of Security to take away the identity cards from those Guineans who have one."

"I've nothing else."

Waldo rubbed his upper arms. He was cold, and he had not eaten in days. His eyes filled with tears. All his efforts had been in vain. He still had not recovered from the exhausting journey that had begun the day a two-and-a-half-meter-long boa caused confusion in the reed beds at the airport and started an argument between the guards to see who would kill it and take it as a present to the warden of Black Beach so he could eat it. Waldo had dragged himself along like a snake, crawling without breathing to get away from the horror, for hundreds of meters until his skin bled. Hours later he had continued his escape from the island in a canoe to the continent and later, the terrifying nights in the jungle, the dangerous crossing to Cameroon, the odyssey as a stowaway in a merchant ship to the Canaries and from there in another one to Cádiz.

He had worked there for a few days on the dock to get enough money to pay for the bus fare to Madrid, a bus on which he had had to put up with suspicious looks from those who avoided sitting beside the shabbily dressed black man who spoke Spanish. He thought things would be easier, that when he told them they had once all been Spanish, they would open their arms to him.

"I've nothing else," he repeated bleakly.

The police officer raised his cap with one hand and scratched his head.

"Well, we don't want vagrants or beggars. I'll have to take you to the station."

Waldo looked at him in surprise. Had he taken such a terrible risk to end up in the same situation? He felt tempted to run away, but his strength was beginning to fail him.

"There you will at least get something to eat and clean clothes," continued the officer. "Later we'll see what will happen to you."

Waldo resignedly agreed. The officer put him into his car. During the short journey, Waldo shut his eyes and sank into a light sleep until they got to the basement of a gray multistory building where the station was located. There, in the waiting room, he was told to wait.

After what seemed like forever, the officer returned with another.

"You're in luck," he said. "My colleague here has told me he knows someone who looks after people like you. We'll take you to him."

The other added, "We'll walk. Father Rafael's parish isn't very far."

Waldo felt his hopes renewed. Could it be possible that it was the Father Rafael from Sampaka? When he saw the priest's bulky frame, his limp, and his bushy gray beard, Waldo gave thanks to God.

It was not until after long minutes of sobbing and blubbering that, sitting on one of the church benches, he could narrate the calvary suffered by the priest's abandoned children.

That same day, Father Rafael called Manuel and told him of Waldo and the terrible news he brought from Guinea. Manuel sent an urgent telegram to Kilian, telling him to get in contact.

"I know how I can help Bisila," he wrote.

The path leading up to Bissappoo had been cut open with machetes and trampled by many pairs of boots. José had a bad feeling. When he got to the *buhaba*, out of breath, his suspicions were confirmed. It was then, more than ever, he regretted that his hunched body had lost its agility. He had not gotten to the village in time to warn them that they were looking for his son Sóbeúpo, something he had just learned from Simón. A penetrating smell of smoke came from the other side of the entrance arch. He approached carefully and saw the flames. Bissappoo was burning among the anguished cries of its neighbors,

huddled together and threatened by the guards' guns. José brought his
hands to his head, now covered completely by gray hair.

Something stuck in his ribs.

"You, old man. Walk."

They put him with the rest. The first one he recognized was Iniko.
But he was still too young! He motioned to them all to keep quiet. A
quick look round showed him that according to the mass recruitment
plan to substitute the Nigerians on the plantations, men of working
age included old men, sick people, and children. José located the
commanding officer and approached him to show him the document
he always carried in his pocket.

"I'm in charge of the Sampaka plantation."

The officer read the document and returned it to him in a
condescending manner.

José frowned. He took some banknotes out of his pocket and gave
them to the officer.

"Sorry, I forgot the other papers."

The man smiled. "That's better."

Once again, José silently thanked Kilian for his help. If he could
only tell him how essential the money he was sending for him and his
family really was!

"I came up to look for workers for the plantation," José lied. "I
need a dozen."

"You can take five. The rest are going somewhere else."

"Why are you burning the village? Isn't it enough to take the men
away?"

"They didn't want to tell us where a conspirator was hiding."

"So you didn't find him?"

"No."

José breathed a sigh of relief. They would not find his son Sóbeúpo
so easily if he had hidden in the forest. With a broken heart, he saw
how the flames devoured his house. The women gathered together what

they could in bundles and said tearful good-byes to their men. Some of them came over to José.

"And where do we go now?" they asked him.

"Go to Rebola. They'll help you there."

"And the men? What will they do with them? When will we see them again?"

"I'll try and find out which plantation they're being sent to. They need workers. They'll be fed. Nothing will happen to them." Not even he believed what he was saying. "Someday, all this will end."

He pointed to Iniko and four nephews around the same age and motioned them to come with him. They walked over to the officer.

"I'm taking these."

"Very young. You're not stupid."

"They're strong, sure, but they've no experience. It will take me a while to train them."

"Don't forget the two daily hours of military training."

The six of them gave a last look at what remained of Bissappoo and walked away not knowing if they would ever again see the men who, disconsolate, waited between rifle barrels for the moment of their last good-bye to their mothers, wives, and daughters.

The radio began its usual daily broadcast with a litany of the positions held by Macías. That was followed by the playing of the first songs praising his person. Bisila turned the thing off.

"Don't you like the music?" the doctor asked with a friendly smile.

"I'm trying to concentrate."

Edmundo smiled.

Bisila was fed up with many things. There had never been such a shortage of everything, even basics like sugar, salt, milk, and soap. There was no electricity, water, roads, or transport. To top it off, a few days ago, some police officers had searched her home when Laha was in school. They were looking to destroy any reminder of the colonial period, and they had been informed that she, specifically, had been very friendly with the Spaniards. She had hidden the pith helmet in a gap in the wall, which she later closed up. She still remembered the officer's look when she foolishly asked, "Isn't it a lot of work to go around to all the houses on Fernando Po?"

"It's no longer called Fernando Po but Macías Nguema Biyogo Ñegue Ndong Island." The man leaned over. "Or is it because you miss your Spanish friends?"

Bisila had been forced to resort to bribery once again, risking giving them the excuse to return another day and ask where she had got the money from. And that was how things went on, alternating between fear and uncertainty, surviving thanks to her guardian angel.

"Are you coming in?" asked Edmundo. "It's expected to be a difficult delivery."

Edmundo was an excellent doctor and work colleague. Since she had started work in Santa Isabel Hospital—well, Bisila corrected herself, Malabo Hospital—her life had improved. Edmundo was a prestigious doctor, and thanks to his influences, he could always get food on the black market.

They went into the delivery room. A woman lay on the bed with her eyes slightly glazed. A nurse came over and whispered, "She refuses to help. She says she doesn't care whether she or the baby dies, that we can get it out whatever way we want, but she has no intention of pushing."

Bisila frowned.

"Why wouldn't a mother want her baby?" Edmundo asked.

"It seems she was raped by a gang of the President's Youth Wing," explained the nurse in a low voice.

Bisila approached the woman and got her attention. "What's your name?" she asked.

"Wéseppa."

"Is it true that you don't want your baby, now that it's about to be born?"

The woman's dark eyes filled with tears.

Bisila took her hand, leaned down, and whispered in her ear. Only someone like her, who had gone through the same situation, could understand.

"We have to hurry," said Edmundo from the foot of the bed.

Bisila looked at him and nodded. "Wéseppa will help us," she said.

The delivery was difficult, but after two hours, Bisila placed a beautiful girl on the woman's bosom.

"What are you going to call her?"

"I hadn't thought about it," answered Wéseppa, stroking one of the baby's tiny hands.

Bisila remembered a pretty name from Bubi mythology. "What do you think of Börihí?" she suggested.

The woman agreed.

Suddenly, the door opened, and two police officers entered.

"We're in a hospital!" the doctor cried, indignant. "You can't come in here like this!"

"We're looking for Bisila."

"Me?" she said, startled. "Why?"

"Aren't you the sister of Sóbeúpo from Bissappoo?"

Bisila's heart skipped a beat. The newborn baby began to cry.

"Yes."

"Tell us where the conspirator is." He turned to the bed, where a terrified Wéseppa was rocking her daughter. "Make it stop!"

The woman brought the baby to her breast.

"I don't know where he is," answered Bisila.

The officer grabbed her arm. "You come with us."

Bisila stayed silent. She was thankful that Iniko, who was at a difficult age, was in Sampaka with his grandfather Ösé. But what would happen to Laha? Who would collect him from school that afternoon?

Edmundo hastily intervened. "Release her immediately!"

The other policeman came over. "Would you like to come with us as well?"

"I am Edmundo Nsué. I know the president personally. Bisila is essential in this hospital. If necessary, I'll talk to the president myself."

The two police looked at each other. Bisila released herself and moved away.

The men did not move.

"Very well," said Edmundo, taking off his white coat. "I'll go with you to see our president, great master, and one miracle. He will know how to resolve this. And he will do it well, as he always does."

The officers were surprised by the doctor's determination. One of them made a sign to the other to go to the door. "We'll check what you've said," he said threateningly before leaving.

Bisila sighed and fell into a chair. "Thank you, Edmundo. Is what you said true?"

The doctor nodded. "Yes. Relax. You're safe. I haven't met a bigger hypochondriac than Macías, and your plant remedies work on him. I've tried them out."

Bisila smiled. In any other circumstance, Edmundo could have been a good life partner. It was obvious he wanted something more with her. She could not reject his advances openly. She would not be the first to be accused of conspiring against the regime because of the spite of a rejected suitor.

She got to her feet and walked toward the window. The afternoon sun tried to force its way through the mist. In a few hours, night would come and, with it, the memories. She brought a hand to her lips, missing Kilian's kisses. Years had passed since his departure, and she could still remember his smell, his taste, and the sound of his voice. She sometimes dreamed of him, and the images were so clear she hated waking up. What would Kilian be doing at that moment? Would he be missing her as much as she missed him?

579

"Give me the baby." Carmen took Daniela from Kilian's arms. "We're going home, Clarence. It's starting to get cold."

"We're going as well," said Jacobo.

The last rays of autumn sunlight filtered through the windows of the enormous hotel by the river. Kilian and Jacobo followed Carmen, although more slowly. Soon, they lost sight of her.

"How everything has changed, hasn't it?" Jacobo commented.

Kilian nodded. The old path that led to the fields farthest away from the village had been turned into a wide road with blocks of apartments on either side. His mind wandered to another place where the forest and traditions had succumbed, first to foreign colonization, and then to chaos. He thought often of those people whom he had not seen in a decade and whom he had not heard anything about since Waldo's news.

Jacobo cleared his throat. He did not really know how to broach the subject. In the last few years, much had happened. The negotiations over the transfer of lands to the ski resort were taking longer than expected. Jacobo could not attend the meetings, because they made his blood boil. Both brothers felt insulted by the condescension of the ski resort company executives, who were trying to get the neighbors' lands at a ridiculous price, promising that, in exchange, they would get building plots at some stage in the future.

They talked to them as if they were some ignorant oafs, as if they had never left that enclosed valley and did not know how the outside world operated.

"Remember, Jacobo," Kilian had asked him, "how the Bubis' land was obtained? In the end, we will have to be thankful to them for the lesson."

What they never talked about in the meetings was the profits the building speculators would make for land whose price was artificially inflated the very moment it no longer belonged to the inhabitants of Pasolobino.

Jacobo looked at his brother. How had he managed to keep going after everything that had happened? When Kilian had finally managed to settle in Spain, he had lost his wife. Jacobo remembered the day that Pilar, a quiet, sensible, and cautious woman, had arrived in the house to look after Mariana in her last months of life. Who would have said that little by little, she would open a place for herself in his brother's heart and lead him to the altar? It was true that Kilian had not hesitated to marry her when he found out that she was pregnant. But it was also true that thanks to her, his brother had managed to calm the unease he had brought back with him from Africa. Pilar had been a brief parenthesis of peace in Kilian's life. Now the unrest had returned and Jacobo had a slight inkling why.

"I suppose you've read the press recently . . ."

Kilian nodded. "It's been years since we heard anything, and now nothing but terrible things are coming out."

"They're not all terrible. They say that the one in charge now wants to have good relations with Spain."

"Let's see how long they last." Kilian was not so interested in the latest political developments as in the descriptions of journalists who had been in Malabo after the so-called Liberty Coup of August 1979, at the hands of the new president, Teodoro Obiang, when the doors of the houses opened and the streets filled with people who, stunned, began hugging one another in happiness.

All the journalists described the country that Macías had left behind as catastrophic. Malabo was in ruins, submerged in neglect and devoured by the forest and corruption. Could people really believe that the nightmare was over? Would they be freed of forced labor? Would the pillaging of their crops come to an end? Thanks to the news on the trial in which Macías was condemned and executed, Kilian had read spine-chilling articles that confirmed the barbarism that had reigned in Guinea. The country had turned into a concentration camp. The regions were devastated due to the flight of their inhabitants, because of the genocide carried out by that lunatic, and because of the epidemic of diseases brought on by the lack of food and sanitation. Guinea had been on the edge of complete oblivion. And he had abandoned his Bisila with two children there? How many times had he been disgusted with himself!

If it had not been for Manuel's help, he would have gone crazy. Every so often, he sent his friend a check, and Manuel gave the money to the doctors who went there on humanitarian missions. Only money. No letters. Not even one line that could be used to accuse her of anything. They both knew that they were alive thanks to the chain of doctors. That small gesture had been his nighttime consolation, as it confirmed the permanent feeling in his chest, intimate, secret, mysterious, hidden, that she was alive, that her heart was beating.

"Don't think about it too much," said Jacobo. "I'm happy that things are going better for them, but that is all behind us now, isn't it?"

He rubbed his blemished eye, an indelible reminder of the beating once given to him by his brother. He knew that Kilian had never forgiven him, and he would not forget what he had done.

Kilian remained in silence. For him, nothing was behind him.

Every second of his life, he refused to accept that his forced earthly separation was the end.

20

The End or the Beginning

2004 . . .

"And Mom?" Daniela asked, her brow wrinkled in confusion and relief. "What was her role in this story?"

Since Kilian had relived what he had locked in his heart for over thirty years, the trickle of questions had not ceased. It had not been enough to realize that Laha was Jacobo's biological son, Clarence's half brother, and Daniela's cousin. No. The truth demanded more explanations.

Kilian sighed. He had never said and she had never asked, but Pilar had been certain that his heart belonged to another. The only thing she asked him to do, the very day they got married, was to take off the African collar he wore.

"Your mother and I had many good times together, and she gave me you," he answered at last. "God willed it that she die soon afterward."

He did not tell her that he had suspected that the spirits had taken her early so his soul could be completely faithful to Bisila.

"Uncle Kilian," interrupted Clarence, "didn't you ever think of going back to Guinea?"

"I hadn't the courage."

Kilian paced around the sitting room. He stopped in front of the window and contemplated the vivid June landscape. It was very complicated for him to explain. As time passed, he tended to remember all he had given up or lost, rather than what had been gained.

No doubt. He had been a coward. And what was ten times worse, he had finally become comfortable in his valley. He remembered everything he had been reading in the press about the happenings in Equatorial Guinea's recent history and its relations with Spain. How had they gone from a close union to a painful reminder? Some said that the decision not to send a military unit to protect Obiang just after he overthrew Macías—which had allowed the Moroccan Guard to come on the scene—had been the main reason for the subsequent failure of Spanish interests, marked by the absence of a clear and decisive foreign policy and a fear of being labeled neocolonialist. Spain had not responded quickly enough to the request to support the ekuele, the Guinean currency, nor to the request to cover the Guinean budget for five years, which would have guaranteed it preferential treatment in future negotiations, nor to the country's need to create a legal and economic climate that would lend security to possible investors.

The most widely heard argument was that the Spanish had never got round to seriously considering a modern plan for cooperation like the French. France spent millions, while Spain spent hardly anything. Manuel had told him that many of the old owners like Garuz had complained that the millions paid in cooperation salaries would have been better employed if they had been given to people with experience in Guinea, like them, to recover some properties with which they could have generated employment and economic activity. In a nutshell, all the news showed the incompatibilities of a complex situation that had, on one side, all the contradictions of the Guinean authorities—many of whom were the same people as under Macías, and who did not take long in returning to their old habits—and, on the other, the lack of coordination of the Spanish administration in taking on a task of such magnitude without any previous experience.

Afterward, both the Spanish government and the opposition began to ignore the subject, in part because they were tied up in other issues such as Tejero's failed coup d'état, Basque terrorism, NATO, and the European Economic Community and, in part, because it was the easy option. And later, when the oil appeared, it was already too late. Other countries had sliced up the pie.

Like Spain, Kilian had not been decisive enough. An idea—incorrect, as events had proved since Clarence's visit to Bioko—had occupied his mind and his heart for many years: it was impossible for Bisila to have continued loving him after he had abandoned her.

"And now?" persisted Daniela. "Why don't you come with me? Laha and I will be on Bioko for a few weeks before going to California. I'm going to meet her, Dad."

Clarence studied her uncle's face. She saw how he pursed his lips, trying to hold back the emotion. It was difficult to imagine what thoughts were going through his head.

"Thanks, Daniela, but no."

"Wouldn't you like to see her again?" It was not clear to Clarence whether Daniela's question was born out of curiosity or out of fear of the jealousy the supposed usurper of her mother's heart, who would now become her mother-in-law, caused in her.

Kilian hung his head. *See her again . . . yes, as I remember her, with her light dresses, her dark-caramel skin, her enormous clear eyes, and her infectious laugh. If only I could be the young muscular man with the white shirt . . .* "I think both of us would like to remember each other as we were, not as we are."

"I don't understand."

"How can this Technicolor world understand the days of black-and-white that are now past? I want to remember Bisila just as I have kept her in my mind. In our hearts, the embers of that fire are still glowing, but we now don't have firewood to make it burn again . . . It's better like this, Daniela." *It's better like this. Maybe there exists a place far away from this changing and impatient world where we will be able to meet again. What did she call it? It wasn't the world of the dead, no. It was the world of the* unliving. *This I believe.*

"What does it matter that you are both old? Do you really think she won't see photos? I intend to bring her a full album on Pasolobino!"

"I don't want you to show her photos I'm in, and I don't want to see any of her. Promise me that, Daniela. Don't show either of us how we have changed. Why ruin the dreams of two old people? Isn't it enough that you talk about me?" *Tell her that I have never forgotten her! Not one day of my life has gone by that I haven't thought of her! Tell her she has always been my* muarána muèmuè . . . *She will understand.*

Daniela went over to her father and hugged him. A new future had opened up for her: a future with Laha. While still holding him in her arms, Daniela began to miss her father, thanks to whose past her own life was beginning at the same age as when he had embarked on his way to a distant African island, full of palms and cocoa trees, where the pods of black cocoa ripened in the sun, leaving behind the stone-and-slate houses huddled against each other under the thick blanket of pristine snow.

"Now, now, Daughter, that's it." Kilian, touched by Daniela's show of affection, got up with his eyes glistening. "I'll leave you here. I'm tired."

The cousins remained in silence for a few minutes. Finally, Clarence said, "I'm going to miss you a lot, Daniela. It will never be the same again."

Daniela drummed her fingers on the table, deep in thought. She understood how Clarence felt. Both she and Laha had been shocked on learning the real identity of Laha's biological father, who, in addition, had killed Iniko's father. No matter that it had been in self-defense; it did not make it any easier. But in spite of this, both she and Laha had been able to appreciate better than anyone the meaning of the word *relief.*

Clarence's situation was more complicated. On the one hand, and partly because she had already suspected it for a while, she was delighted that ties greater than friendship joined her forever to Laha, through whom Iniko had also turned from just being a vacation fling to being her brother's brother. She would know about him and he about her even if they were following their own paths. On the other hand, however, she was finding it difficult to accept her father's role in the whole story. She had not spoken to him.

"Clarence . . ." Daniela took a deep breath. "Don't you think it's time you talked to your dad? Sooner or later, you'll have to."

"And what would I say to him? I still can't understand how Kilian could hide Laha's existence from us. I think it was shameful, but at least he suffered the punishment of being separated from Bisila. But Dad"—her eyes filled with tears—"Dad raped and killed and got away with it. I don't know how Mom can stay with him. What he did is unspeakable. How much does the past weigh on people? For Mom, it seems, not much. Do you know what she said to me the other day on the phone? That they were old, that it had happened before they got married, and why wouldn't thirty years of marriage forgive the unforgivable act of a drunken night." She wiped away the tears. "It's terrible, Daniela. I don't know my parents."

Daniela came over and hugged her.

"Jacobo didn't get away with it, Clarence. The African blood that will flow through the veins of his grandchildren will remind him of what he did for as long as he lives. And now that he has found out about the existence of an unwanted son, he's afraid of losing his only daughter."

"He hasn't even wanted to talk to him . . . to his own son . . ."

Clarence bit her lip hard to control her sobs. She closed her eyes and thought about everything that had happened since she found that piece of paper in the cabinet. Learning the truth had now joined them, those from the island and those from the mountain, together forever for the rest of their lives, with bonds impossible to break. But as a result of this union, the characters from these stories would begin disappearing one by one in one way or another before her eyes, and nothing would ever be the same. She did not know whether it would be better or worse, but it would definitely be different.

So near, and yet, so far, she thought. Or was it the other way round? Her heart wanted, in spite of the good-byes, for it to be the other way around. So far, and yet, so near.

Etúlá, Formosa, Fernando Po, Macías Island, and Bioko.

Ripotò, Port Clarence, Santa Isabel, and Malabo.

Pasolobino.

So far and so near.

In the following years, the House of Rabaltué was filled with words shouted in English, Spanish, Bubi, one or two in Pasolobinese— Clarence made sure of that, trying to ensure that her nephew and niece knew something of the language of their forebearers—and even in Pidgin English. Samuel and his baby sister, Enoá, Laha and Daniela's children, took everything in, like sponges. Clarence was certain that if they spent more time in Guinea than in California, they would end up learning French, Portuguese, Fang, Annobonese, Balengue, Ibo, and Ndowé. What a land, that Bioko, that little Tower of Babel! Clarence noticed Samuel's big dark eyes and remembered those of Iniko, to whom she had once said that having two languages was like having two souls. Now Samuel and Enoá had millions of words to combine in different languages, and she only hoped they knew how to construct beautiful phrases with them.

Clarence enjoyed enormously the short visits of Daniela, Laha, and the children, during which the lonely house was filled with fresh air. For a few days, the walls reverberated to the echoes of past conversations, now bolstered by the voices of the new generation. Daniela pulled Clarence's leg for still not having found a suitable man. Clarence slid her gaze over the toys scattered on the floor and smiled because when the children were there, it seemed that the house was being hit by a tornado that only Granddad Kilian enjoyed, since Carmen and Jacobo did not leave Barmón anymore.

Jacobo, selflessly cared for by Carmen, had gone through the aggressive stages of Alzheimer's and was now in an almost-vegetative state. To Clarence, her father's illness seemed a tragicomic twist of destiny. He had lost his memory, the past over whose consequences the cousins still had differing positions, both at a political and personal level.

Whenever Daniela got to Pasolobino, she spoke excitedly of the large number of improvements she noticed in Bioko, from the good fortune of the casino, which had finally been refurbished, to political, social, economic, and judicial reforms, without omitting the advances in the country's democracy and human rights. Daniela passionately listed the public campaigns to combat child labor and discrimination and violence against women and against people from other races and religions; the efforts to make people aware of the importance of education, health, and children's rights; the fight against AIDS; the improvement in access to new technologies; the increase in skills training . . .

Clarence was surprised because what her cousin told her did not coincide with the information she had read on the Internet. She criticized her for sounding like the minister for foreign affairs who admitted that Spain would continue to support the dictatorship in spite of the fact that part of the Spanish people and society were against it.

"And you, Clarence? What would your position be? Guinea needs international aid, but giving it means dealing with the dictator. It's a quandary, isn't it? Well, look, to me the answer is clear. Moral principles are difficult to maintain in situations of poverty and need. The more you invest there, the more jobs are created and the easier progress becomes. Everything else goes smoothly after that."

"I don't know . . . And wouldn't it be easier to overthrow the blasted regime once and for all and free the country of tyranny?"

"Do you really think a coup from the outside would be organized for humanitarian reasons? If there wasn't any oil, do you think there would be that much interest? There is life there, Clarence. There are political parties who are looking for change from within, participating in the institutions and waiting for the hoped-for change to arrive one day. They have resisted so much . . . I think it's now time for the criticism to stop and that people accept that the Equatorial Guineans want to make their own future without outside interference."

Clarence wanted to believe what she said. Maybe things had changed from when she had learned about Bioko's history from Iniko's lips . . .

The last journey that Daniela, Laha, and the children made to Pasolobino was different from the previous ones. There was neither joy nor jokes nor heated discussions. Clarence had called her cousin to give her the sad news that Kilian had been hospitalized. The prognosis was not reassuring.

They hid the seriousness of the situation from him, but one afternoon, just after going into his room, Clarence got the impression that Kilian was more than aware that the end was near. He conveyed a feeling of peace and tranquility.

Kilian had his head tilted toward the window, his gaze lost in some point in the sky. Daniela stayed sitting by his side, holding his hand as she had done for the last three weeks. Laha was close to both of them. Clarence leaned on the door, partly hidden so they would not see her tears. She admired the composure of Daniela, who had not shed a tear in front of her dying father in all the time she had spent with him. Rather, she made sure to appear happy—and she really looked it—so that her father would not notice the suffering she was going through.

Kilian spoke without taking his eyes from the sky, that day being especially bright and clear. Where was the rain that had always framed the saddest moments in his life?

"Daniela, Daughter, I would like you to answer a question for me. I can say I'm at peace and happy . . ." He paused. "But I want to know if I've been a good father."

Clarence felt a sharp pain in her chest. It was impossible, since Jacobo had lost all his cognitive and physical faculties, but if her own father could ask her the same question in similar circumstances, she would be struck dumb. What would she say?

"The best, Dad," answered Daniela while covering his face in kisses. "The best."

Kilian closed his eyes, pleased with the answer. At least part of his waning life, after having separated from Bisila, had had meaning.

Heavy tears rolled down Clarence's cheeks. She would now never have the chance to answer that question for her own father, and she then deeply regretted not having let Jacobo know, when he was still able to understand her, that if those who had suffered directly from his actions had partially forgiven him—as it was impossible to forget what he had done—and had managed to cast from their hearts their initial feelings of outrage, resentment, and shame, she had no reason not to do so. Too late, she thought, she realized she had inflicted the worst punishment possible on Jacobo; she had made him suffer the rejection of his own daughter.

Kilian opened his eyes and turned his head.

"Your mother," he began, "told me that she would like us to be buried beside each other, and I'm not going to go against her." Daniela gave a barely noticeable nod. She pressed her lips together hard to hold back her emotion. "But I'd like you to do something . . . I'd like you and Laha to do something for me. When you go back to Fernando Po, take a bag with two handfuls of soil from my garden and spread one on Sampaka's royal palm tree avenue and the other on Grandfather Antón's grave in the Santa Isabel cemetery."

Laha noticed that Daniela was finding it very difficult to keep her composure. He went over to her and put a hand on her shoulder. Kilian gave him a weak smile. It had been inevitable that Bisila's and his paths would cross again. It had only been a question of time for the spirits to allow them some peace. He was completely sure that Bisila, like him, was happy to have lived long enough to see their children together.

Kilian rubbed his fingers over the small shells on the well-worn leather collar. "Help me, Daniela. Undo the knot."

Daniela did so. Kilian held the collar in the palm of his hand for a good while, closed his fist, and stretched out his arm to his daughter.

"Take this to Bisila and tell her that where I'm going, I won't need it. Also tell her that I hope it protects her as it has protected me." He shrugged and looked again at the blue sky. "That's all. Now I'd like to sleep . . ."

That's what he wanted: to finally rest in a small island carpeted by cocoa trees with bright leaves and pods, where the days and the nights were the same length and no shade of green was missing, and where he had helped cultivate the food of the gods; to cross the ribbon of coves and bays before climbing the slope of the fevers and note the smell of the small, delicate white flowers of the *egombegombes*; to hear the laughs, the jokes, and the songs from the throats of the Nigerians and vibrate to the rhythm of their drums; to brighten his view with the color of the *clotes* on the streets of a charming city laid out at the feet of the misty mountains of Santa Isabel; to bathe himself in the sweet odor and sticky warmth; to walk under the paradise's green nave of palm trees, cedars, ceibas, and ferns where the small birds, monkeys, and colored lizards played; to feel the force of the wind and the rain of a tropical storm on his skin and then let himself be caressed by a warm breeze infused with the scent of roasted cocoa.

Oh, how he wished to be on that island and feel Bisila's clear gaze!

Kilian lost consciousness that same night. He was delirious for two days and, in his terrible agony, spoke words that Daniela and Clarence could not understand; Laha would not translate them. From time to time, the dying man spoke Bisila's name, and all signs of suffering left him; he even seemed to brighten before shrinking back. This went on until he gave his last breath and peace returned to his body.

A week after the funeral, Laha had to leave for work, and Daniela stayed with the children to tidy up and sort out Kilian's clothes and effects. The cousins did not allow tears to flow so as not to further upset Samuel and Enoá, who did not understand why their grandfather was not in the House of Rabaltué, where he had always been. As an explanation, they told him that their granddad had transformed into a butterfly and flown up to heaven.

One afternoon, when they had finished putting Kilian's things in boxes, Clarence saw Daniela putting away the collar with the cowrie and *Achatina* shells and thought it strange. Her cousin answered, "I owe my mother a little justice. If I take it to Bisila, I'm accepting that my father was unfaithful to my mother in his heart. And I don't want to look at the past anymore. Laha and I have a present and a future to enjoy. There is so much to do! Enough with the nostalgia that has impregnated the walls of this house. I mean this for you as well, Clarence . . ."

She sat on the bed with the collar in her hands and cried. Clarence said nothing. She let her get it all out, freeing herself of the loneliness that comes when the older generation dies.

After a while, Daniela dried away the tears and gave her the collar. "Here," she said in a mixture of resignation and decisiveness. "Do whatever you want. I neither want nor wish to understand it."

Then Clarence remembered how Iniko put the collar, which she still had, around her neck to keep away the evil spirits that surrounded them. She did not find it in the least strange how different the stories of the people in that house had been, as if some higher force had decided to pair them up in the most suitable manner as events unfolded.

Kilian and Bisila had loved each other beyond distance and time, and even though they had not heard from each other in decades, they had maintained an intimate and secret conversation. In contrast, Iniko and she had loved each other at one specific moment in their lives and had separated by mutual agreement, conscious that neither of them was going to give up their life for the other.

However, Daniela and Laha were the ones who had suffered most from a past that had marked their relationship from the beginning and from which they had to unshackle themselves to find their true place, to be free.

Clarence sighed. Daniela was right to say that she was too nostalgic. She lived more in the memories, her own and others', than in her own present. She took so seriously the task of perpetuating the traditions that she was becoming another stone in that sturdy house. But what was she to do? In a couple of days, there would be no one left there. After centuries, the task would fall on her of closing the doors on a House of Rabaltué that would become, like so many others, just a summer home. There she would leave the voices of dozens of lives whose owners were listed on the genealogical tree in the hall, a silent witness of those who had left and would never return. That was it. Life.

She looked into her hands at Bisila and Kilian's collar and knew exactly what she would do with it. She would prepare a package with two handfuls of earth from the garden and send it to Iniko, along with the collar, so he would give it to Bisila together with Kilian's final words. Since she had given up her idea of moving her grandfather's remains to Pasolobino, at least she would make sure the soil of his home valley would be with him. She was certain that Iniko would know how to tell Bisila what had happened with the same thoughtfulness and love as she would. To other people, all that respect for one's forebearers might seem stupid, but she knew that Iniko would understand. And she had no doubt that there was nobody better than Bisila to fulfill the last wishes of her uncle just as he had expressed.

A small girl with braided hair appeared in the room, hugging her teddy bear. Daniela picked Enoá up in her arms and took her back to bed.

Clarence thought of her nephew and niece, and her heart brightened.

Daniela could not have chosen two more appropriate names. *Enod* meant "sea," and *Samuel* referred to that Sam Parker whose name in Pichi had given Sampaka its name. The day would arrive when everything that had happened there would be forgotten, but the names of her nephew and niece would sum up the past and the future. The sea and the tunnel of royal palms. The symbols of the resurrection and victory over time itself.

Clarence's heart became glad when she thought about the children, but she also felt a stab of jealousy. They would be lucky enough not to think it strange to be black and white, islanders and from the mountains. She would tell them their story of the Bubis and the genealogical ancestors of Pasolobino; she would relate the love story of their grandparents, and they would listen to it with no anguish. They already belonged to another generation, a generation that would see it as normal, even anecdotal, that a small part of the Pyrenees was forever joined to an African island.

Yet for her, it would always be the story of a few people whose great feat had been to change the immovable pages of the book of a centuries-old stone house that now faced the future with the same quivering determination as that of a fragile butterfly.

I told you, Kilian, I did, right at the beginning. You were afraid the snow on the palms would melt, evaporate, and disappear forever. You were afraid the palms would not root in the snow.

Rise up now! Use your wings and gaze upon your house from the heights of the mountain! Look how life clings on! The river of existence that runs across the garden in the House of Rabaltué is now finally fed by small streams of various origins.

I told you, Kilian, I did.

You knew you would never again see each other, but now . . .

Use the impetus of the north wind and fly toward the valley! Cross the plains and stop at the cliffs! Get on the back of the harmattan and glide toward the island!

You are no longer lost at sea. You are no longer a ship aground. No bell toll can make you lose your bearings.

You see?

Bisila smiles.

She will soon come to you. You will be together again in a place with no time, no haste, no limits, far from fury and close to peace, where you will only drink rainwater.

And now that you have been reborn in the arms of the *baribò*, you will finally be able to understand what Bisila always wanted you to know:

That the footprints of the people who walked together never, never fade away.

AUTHOR'S NOTE

The romantic plot that brings together and divides the characters of this novel, both the inhabitants of Bioko and those of Pasolobino, is pure fiction. However, the story of those men and women from the Pyrenees who spent years of their lives on the island is inspired by real events. Some of them were my father, Francisco Gabás Pallás, and my grandfather Francisco Gabás Farré from Casa Mata in Cerler; my grandmother Rosario Pallás Ventura from Casa Llorgodo in Cerler; and my father's first cousin Ismael Lamora Pallás from Casa Caseta in Ramastué. Thanks to their memories, both spoken and written, I knew from a very young age of the existence of the island of Fernando Po and so many other things about that part of Africa that is the same size as the county of my roots.

The story of dozens of people from the Benasque Valley, in the county of Ribagorza, part of the province of Huesca, who, from the end of the nineteenth century, decided to go and work in Equatorial Guinea was compiled by José Manuel Brunet, José Luis Cosculluela, and José María Mur in an essential and interesting book entitled *Guinea en patués: De los bueyes del valle de Benasque al cacao de la isla de Fernando*

Poo, published in 2007, soon after my father passed away. I would especially like to thank José María Mur, who rescued from oblivion experiences only known to a few of us, for allowing me to be present when recording those people whose memories and anecdotes permeate my novel, and who—without realizing it—gave me the final push to finish giving shape to an idea I had had in mind for years, an idea where other things became predominant: the curiosity to know the things they had not told us and to discover the *other* version, that is to say, the version of the natives from there who, in my opinion, were not or have not always been represented either in stories or in travel novels with the respect and dignity they deserve.

The place where my father was born, Cerler, is a small, beautiful, cold, and sunny village located 1,540 meters above sea level. It is part of the Benasque municipality, which can boast of being surrounded by high and beautiful mountains. Our valley has a long history, even if it is now known for being a ski resort. I decided to baptize the birthplace of some of the Spanish characters in the novel with the name Pasolobino for two reasons: to be objective, I needed to distance myself from the place where I have lived much of my life; and Pasolobino could well be a setting like so many others from which hundreds of Spaniards left to spend decades in Guinea. (In the 1940s, there were around a thousand Spaniards on Fernando Po. When the country gained its independence, it was estimated that there were around eight thousand in the whole colony.) In the same way, the village of Bissappoo is fictional, although its description would match many others of the place at the time the novel is set in. It is true that in 1975, Macías ordered a village to be burned because he believed its inhabitants were involved in subversive activities.

All historical events, along with the novel's setting, have been rigorously checked. Nevertheless, I know that the most erudite readers on the topic of Guinea will be able to forgive some slight changes (such as the Nigerians leaving, which I brought forward in time in the novel) or subtleties (such as Anita Guau's refurbishment) for literary reasons.

I am also conscious that the action is confined to the island of Fernando Po and not all of Guinea. The cultural differences between the insular and continental part, much bigger in size, made it impossible to give a deeper analysis of other points of view that have been dealt with only tangentially. My original idea, which I have kept to at all times, was to establish the comparison between the two small paradises my father always alluded to: the island and his home valley.

To familiarize myself on the contextual political and social history of Equatorial Guinea, I spent an extended period reading the maximum possible amount of material published on the region. Detailed below are those books, articles, and authors that have had an influence on the writing of this novel.

1. For the geography, history, economy, and politics of Equatorial Guinea, I generally used the following texts: *Aproximación a la historia de Guinea Ecuatorial* by Justo Bolekia Boleká (2003); *El laberinto Guineano* by Emiliano Buale Borikó (1989); *Macías, víctima o verdugo* by Agustín Nze Nfumu (2004), a revealing tale on the atrocities of the Macías dictatorship; *Fernando el africano* by Fernando García Gimeno (2004), an essential, moving, and detailed account of his twenty years in Guinea until shortly before independence; *Fernando Poo: Una aventura colonial Española en el África Occidental 1 (1778—1900)* by Dolores García Cantús (2004); *De la trata de negros al cultivo de cacao: Evolución del modelo colonial español in Guinea Ecuatorial de 1778 a 1914* by Juan José Díaz Matarranz (2005); *Apuntes sobre el estado de la costa occidental de África y principalmente de las posesiones españolas en el Golfo de Guinea* by Joaquin J. Navarro, naval lieutenant,

secretary of the government of Fernando Po and its dependencies (this document was written in 1859 at the request of Queen Isabel II in order to get trustworthy information on the possessions in the Gulf); and *Cronología de Guinea Ecuatorial: De la preindependencia (1948) al jucio contra Macías (1979)* by Xavier Lacosta, a clear, interesting, and complete work that allowed me to order the dates correctly of the events narrated in the book.

Articles from the magazine *La Guinea Española*, edited by the Claretian Fund, from 1904 until 1969, whose issues can be read at www.raimonland.net. In fact, the magazine that Kilian was reading on his first trip by sea in 1953 is real, and the article he mentions on the Bubi linguistics was written by Father Amador del Molino of the Claretian mission, who researched the history of Guinea for years. I also found very useful the illustrations of the African botanist and chair of natural sciences Emilio Guinea, author of the books *En el país de los pámues* (1947) and *En el país de los bubis* (1949), and the documentary *Memoria Negra* by Xavier Montanyà (2007).

Of all the articles read in the last ten years, I would like to mention "La dictadura de las tinieblas" by Juan Jesús Aznárez (2008); "Guinea Ecuatorial: De colonia a estado con derecho" and "Guinea Ecuatorial: Vídeos y bibliografía" by Miguel Ángel Morales Solís (2009); the essay "Guinea Ecuatorial" by Max Liniger-Goumaz and Gerhard Seiber for the *New Enciclopedia de África* (2008); "Guinea Ecuatorial Española en el contexto de la Segunda Guerra Mundial" by José U. Martínez Carreras (1985); "Guinea Ecuatorial: La ocasión perdida" by Juan M. Calvo (1989); articles published in *La Gaceta de Guinea Ecuatorial* that can be seen at www.lagacetadeguinea.com; and articles in *Historia 16* and the online newspaper libraries such as those of *ABC* and *Diario del AltoAragón* (formerly *Nueva España*), not only in searching for news about Guinea from the beginning of the twentieth century, but also for news about Spain.

Of all the encyclopedias, websites, magazines, forums, blogs, and travel reviews to be found on numerous webpages, I found the following invaluable: www.raimonland.net, a marvelous meeting point, a place for news, and a historical review by and for all those who lived in Guinea or those who want to know more about the country; www.asodegue. org, the webpage of the *Asociación para la Solidaridad Democrática con Guinea Ecuatorial*, where political and economic news along with various articles on Equatorial Guinea can be found; www.revistapueblos. org, website of the *Pueblos* magazine, with numerous articles on African subjects; www.guinea-ecuatorial.org, official webpage of the government in exile of Equatorial Guinea; www.guinea-ecuatorial.net, where a wide collection of information on Guinea can be found; the *Fundación España-Guinea Ecuatorial*; the magazine of the association of Equatorial Guinean women living in Barcelona, *E'Waiso Ipola*; and the *Malabo.SA.* magazine.

Last, in order to explain the sections given over to the growing of cocoa, I used different manuals and, more specifically, the article "Un buen cacao que se llama Sampaka," which appeared in 1957 in the special issue *Nuestra Guinea* of *La Actualidad Española* magazine, where my father appears in nearly all the photos.

2. For the Bubi history, culture, religion, and traditions, I found especially useful the book *Los bubis en Fernando Poo* by Father Antonio Aymemí, who lived on the island as a Claretian Fathers Catholic missionary from 1894 until his death in 1941. It was published in 1942 as a collection of a series of articles that he wrote for the *La Guinea Española* magazine. As copies of the book are not to be found, I have used Colleen Truelsen's 2003 translation in English, titled *The History and Culture of an Endangered African Tribe*, for the setting of the fictional village of Bissappoo. As the 2003 edition explains, the second

generation of Bubis in exile have found their way from Spain to the United States, and that is why I decided for my novel that Fernando Laha would work in California, a place I know well. Truelsen recognizes that without knowing Spanish, it is very difficult to find information on the cultural history of the Bubis.

Other texts consulted were the following: *A través de la magia bubi: Por las selvas de Guinea* by José Manuel Novoa (1991); *Los bubis, ritos y creencias* by Father Amador Martín del Molino (1989), a Claretian missionary who lived with the Bubis for twenty-four years; the aforementioned magazine *La Guinea Española*, published by the Claretian Fund; and the official webpage of the Movement for Self-Determination for Bioko Island, where information appears on the history of the Bubis.

Finally, the previously mentioned books *Aproximación a la historia de Guinea Ecuatorial* by Justo Bolekia Boleká (2003) and *El Laberinto Guineano* by Emiliano Buale Borikó (1989) were especially useful in helping me focus on the political aspects directly related to the island of Fernando Po and the Bubis.

3. Given that the character of Clarence is a university linguistics lecturer and is interested in African-Hispanic, Equatorial Guinean, and Spanish literature and the literary output from Equatorial Guinea, I will mention the following documents and authors that have also helped me: *La formación de identidad en la novela hispano-africano: 1950—1990* by Jorge Salvo (2003), lecturer in Spanish at the University of South Carolina and also author of several articles related to this subject; *Literatura emergente en español: Literatura de Guinea Ecuatorial* by Shosténe Onomo-Abena and Joseph Désiré Otabela Mewolo (2004); "La literature Africana de expression castellana: La creación literaria en Guinea Ecuatorial" by Mbaré

Ngom (1993), from Morgan State University in Maryland; and "La creación semántica y léxica en el español de Guinea Ecuatorial," the doctoral thesis of Issacar Nguen Djo Tiogang (2007). I also consulted various articles by the following authors: Mariano L. de Castro Antolín, chair of geography and history in Valladolid and author of works on the history of Equatorial Guinea and the relationship between Guinea and Spain; Humberto Riochí, spokesperson for the Movement for Self-Determination for Bioko Island (MIAB) in 2009; Michael Ugarte, lecturer in Spanish literature in the University of Missouri; Juan Tomás Ávila Laurel, writer, editor-in-chief of Malabo's *El Patio* magazine, and guest speaker in several North American universities; Carlos González Echegaray, renowned Spanish Afrophile; and Germán de Granda, who has worked on the languages of Equatorial Guinea.

Specifically on the Spanish spoken in Equatorial Guinea, it's worth mentioning the articles by Sosthéne Onomo-Abena and Aminou Mohamadou from the Yaounde I University (Cameroon). Mohamadou has an article on *spaguifrenglish*, as a language made up of marks from the different languages it lives with: Spanish, Guinean—from the large ethnic groups of Fang, Bubi, Annobonese, Benga, Ndowé—French, and English. And of course, I must mention John M. Lipski, chair in linguistics at the University of Pennsylvania and specialist in dialectology, contact languages, Creole languages, and African elements in Spanish and Portuguese. His magnificent article "The Spanish of Equatorial Guinea: Research on la Hispanidad's Best-Kept Secret" is what Clarence would probably have read when starting her linguistic research in Guinea, had she ever carried it out.

With regard to the literary production related to Equatorial Guinea—from the precolonial period, characterized by its oral nature; from the colonial, represented by descriptions of the exotic; and from the postcolonial, both from the unhappy memory period and the beginnings of native literary creation, of collections of stories and legends and of new narrative works and essays—and so that the reader might have some idea of its importance, I would recommend the very interesting paper by Justo Bolekia Boleká, which appears in the 2005 *Central Virtual Cervantes Annuary*, and the works of Mbaré Ngom Fayé and Donato Ndongo-Biyogo. Ndongo-Biyogo, the Guinean journalist, historian, essayist, author of the novels *Las tinieblas de tu memoria negra* and *Los poderes de la tempestad*, and expert on Spanish modern literature in Equatorial Guinean, published in 1984 the indispensable *Antología de la literatura de Guinea Ecuatorial*, an anthology of the authors and their narrative, poetic, and drama works.

In a different section from the works produced by the native Equatorial Guineans are the works written by Spaniards after their stay in Guinea. I know there are some more—I have yet to read *El corazón de los pájaros* by Elsa López (2001) and see the film *Lejos de África* by Cecilia Bartolomé (1996)—but these are the ones that I have read and have helped me in the setting of my novel: *En el país de los bubis* by José Más (written in 1919 and reedited in 2010); *Manto verde bajo el sol* by V. López Izquierdo (1973); *El Valle de los bubis* by Maria Paz Díaz (1998); *La casa de la palabra* by José A. López Hidalgo (1994); *Al sur de Santa Isabel* by Carles Decors (2002); the hard and unsettling *Guinea* by Fernando Gamboa (2008); *Una historia Africana* by Javier Reverte (2009); *La aventura de Muni (Tras las huellas de Iradier: La historia blanca de Guinea Ecuatorial)* by Miguel Gutiérrez Garitano (2010); and the aforementioned *Fernando el africano* by Fernando García Gimeno (2004).

My novel adds, therefore, to the long list of books about Equatorial Guinea, something that pleases me deeply. Clarence and Iniko coincide in that they form part of a long chain that includes both their forebearers and those yet to come. In the same way, this novel forms part of a long chain of written and yet-to-be-written words about the history of Equatorial Guinea. Not only that, I hope that the reader can get to know or recognize a culture and a different historical, political, and social context that is both close and distant, and I also hope that the Equatorial Guinean reader gets to know something about those who went to their country, the reasons why they went, my valley and its customs, and the changes we have lived through.

ACKNOWLEDGMENTS

To Justo Bolekia Boleká, Equatorial Guinean intellectual of Bubi extraction; chair of French language in the University of Salamanca; author of numerous articles, books of essays, and linguistic and sociolinguistic publications; expert in Bubi language, culture, and anthroponomy; poet; politician; and historian, for granting me the privilege of his revision of a novel such as this, where there is a little bit of everything he is an expert in. I owe the corrections of the Bubi and Pidgin English dialogues and expressions to him (for the expressions in Pidgin English, I had used the dictionary my father and grandfather took with them, a 1919 edition, the same one that Kilian reads on his first trip by sea). I must also thank him for his clarifications on Bubi traditions and culture, as well as for his revision of the historical and political aspects. And I would like to especially mention his kindness in allowing me to use the Bubi story entitled "Wewèöbuaaröö" that Fernando Laha relates to Daniela and that is published in his collection of Bubi stories. But most of all, I must thank him for his gracious words in showing me his gratitude for allowing him to enjoy this continuous journey from Pasolobino to Bioko.

To Ismael Lamora and Mari Pe Solana, who lived for many years in Fernando Po, and to José Antolín, who worked for Spanish National Television on the island just after independence, for all their anecdotes and memories of that period.

To Luis Acevedo for bringing Sampaka closer to my mountains and for persevering in his efforts on the plantation.

To José María Mur for infecting me with his desire to learn about the past, for helping me in my research, and for bringing me fresh news of his trip to Guinea, news also brought to me by Brother Josean Villalabeitia.

To Maruja de San Lucas for helping me out on fashion and menu issues from past decades.

To Fernando García Gimeno for being the best guardian of the details and descriptions of some years that would have been forgotten without him and for kindly answering all my questions.

To Ana Corell, Pedro Aguaviva, and Felisa Ferraz for their judicious and useful comments on the first draft.

To Ramón Badía Vidal for his first impressions of the novel, his professionalism, and his understanding.

To Cristina Pons for her wise, accurate, opportune, and indispensable advice, without which this novel would not have reached a successful port. But most of all, for helping me to fearlessly ascend the slope of the fevers.

And finally, to my editor, Raquel Gisbert, for believing in this project and for offering me the exceptional and exciting possibility of allowing my novel to see the light of day. Thanks to her, I can very specially dedicate it—as a humble tribute—to those from here who lived there and to their descendants and to those from there who had to live with those from here and to their descendants.

I hope we can all understand one another a little better.

Anciles, September 2011

ABOUT THE AUTHOR

Luz Gabás was born in 1968 in the city of Monzón, Spain. After spending a year in San Luis Obispo in California, she studied in Zaragoza, Spain, where she graduated with a degree in English literature. She later became a professor at the university. For years she has combined her academic work with translation projects, writing articles and literary and linguistic research and participating in cultural, theatrical, and cinematic projects. She moved to the beautiful town of Anciles in 2007 and lives next to the Benasque villa, where she now spends most of her time writing. Her debut novel, *Palm Trees in the Snow*, was a bestseller upon publication in Spain and was adapted into a major motion picture.

ABOUT THE TRANSLATOR

Noel Hughes was born in 1967 in Dublin, Ireland. After a degree in history and economics from University College Dublin, he spent many years in the business world before deciding to move to Spain in 2006 and concentrate on English teaching and translation projects.